PENGUIN  CLASSI

THE WOMEN'S WA

ALEXANDRE DUMAS was born in 1802 at Villers-Cotterêts. His father, the illegitimate son of a marquis, was a general in the Revolutionary armies, and died when Dumas was only four. Dumas was brought up in straitened circumstances and received very little education. He joined the household of the future king, Louis-Philippe, and began reading voraciously. Later he entered the *cénacle* of Charles Nodier and started writing. In 1829 the production of his play, *Henri III et sa cour*, heralded twenty years of successful playwriting. In 1839 he turned his attention to writing historical novels, often using collaborators such as Auguste Maquet to suggest plots or historical background. His most successful novels are *The Count of Monte Cristo*, which appeared during 1844–5, and *The Three Musketeers*, published in 1844. Other novels deal with the wars of religion and the Revolution. Dumas wrote many of these for the newspapers, often in daily instalments, marshalling his formidable energies to produce ever more in order to pay off his debts. In addition, he wrote travel books, children's stories and his *Mémoires*, which describe most amusingly his early life, his entry into Parisian literary circles and the 1830 Revolution. He died in 1870.

ROBIN BUSS is a writer and translator who contributes regularly to *The Times Educational Supplement*, *The Times Literary Supplement* and other papers. He studied at the University of Paris, where he took a degree and a doctorate in French literature. He is part-author of the article 'French Literature' in *Encyclopaedia Britannica* and has published critical studies of works by Vigny and Cocteau, and three books on European cinema, *The French through Their Films* (1988), *Italian Films* (1989) and *French Film Noir* (1994). He is also part-author of a biography, in French, of King Edward VII (with Jean-Pierre Navailles, published by Payot, Paris, 1999). He has translated a number of other volumes for Penguin, including *The Count of Monte Cristo*, Jean Paul Sartre's *Modern Times*, Zola's *L'Assommoir*, *Au Bonheur des Dames* and *Thérèse Raquin*, and Albert Camus's *The Plague*.

ALEXANDRE DUMAS

The Women's War

*Translated with an Introduction and Notes
by* ROBIN BUSS

PENGUIN BOOKS

PENGUIN CLASSICS

Published by the Penguin Group

Penguin Books Ltd, 80 Strand, London WC2R ORL, England

Penguin Group (USA) Inc., 375 Hudson Street, New York, New York 10014, USA

Penguin Group (Canada), 90 Eglinton Avenue East, Suite 700, Toronto, Ontario, Canada M4P 2Y3
(a division of Pearson Penguin Canada Inc.)

Penguin Ireland, 25 St Stephen's Green, Dublin 2, Ireland
(a division of Penguin Books Ltd)

Penguin Group (Australia), 250 Camberwell Road,
Camberwell, Victoria 3124, Australia (a division of Pearson Australia Group Pty Ltd)

Penguin Books India Pvt Ltd, 11 Community Centre,
Panchsheel Park, New Delhi – 110 017, India

Penguin Group (NZ), cnr Airborne and Rosedale Roads, Albany,
Auckland 1310, New Zealand (a division of Pearson New Zealand Ltd)

Penguin Books (South Africa) (Pty) Ltd, 24 Sturdee Avenue,
Rosebank, Johannesburg 2196, South Africa

Penguin Books Ltd, Registered Offices: 80 Strand, London WC2R ORL, England

www.penguin.com

First published 1844
Published in Penguin Classics 2006

1

Translation and Notes copyright © Robin Buss, 2006
All rights reserved

The moral right of the translator has been asserted

Set in 10.25/12.25pt PostScript Adobe Sabon
Typeset by Rowland Phototypesetting Ltd, Bury St Edmunds, Suffolk
Printed in Great Britain by Clays Ltd, St Ives plc

ISBN-13: 978-0-140-44977-8
ISBN-10: 0-140-44977-9

Contents

Chronology

1802 Alexandre Dumas is born at Villers-Cotterêts, the third child of Thomas-Alexandre Dumas. His father, the illegitimate son of a marquis and a slave girl of San Domingo, had been a general in the Republican, then in the Napoleonic armies.

1806 General Dumas dies. Alexandre and his mother, Elisabeth Labouret, are left virtually penniless.

1822 Dumas takes a post as a clerk.

1823 Granted a sinecure on the staff of the Duke d'Orléans. Meets the actor Françoise Joseph Talma and starts to mix in artistic and literary circles, writing sketches for the popular theatre.

1824 Dumas's son, Alexandre, future author of *La Dame aux camélias*, is born as the result of an affair with a seamstress, Catherine Lebay.

1829 Dumas's historical drama, *Henri III et sa cour*, is produced at the Comédie-Française. It is an immediate success, marking Dumas out as a leading figure in the Romantic movement.

1830 Victor Hugo's drama *Hernani* becomes the focus of the struggle between the Romantics and the traditionalists in literature. In July, the Bourbon monarchy is overthrown and replaced by a new regime under the Orléanist King Louis-Philippe. Dumas actively supports the insurrection.

1831 Dumas's melodrama *Antony*, with its archetypal Romantic hero, triumphs at the Théâtre de la Porte-Saint-Martin.

1832 Dumas makes a journey to Switzerland which will form the basis of his first travel book, published the following year.

1835 Travels extensively in Italy.

1836 Triumph of Dumas's play *Kean*, based on the personality of the English actor whom he had seen performing in Shakespeare in 1828.

1839 *Mademoiselle de Belle-Isle*, Dumas's greatest success in the theatre, is staged.

1840 Dumas marries Ida Ferrier. Travels down the Rhine with Gérard de Nerval; they collaborate on the drama *Léo Burckart*. Nerval introduces Dumas to Auguste Maquet, who will become his collaborator on many subsequent works.

1844 *The Three Musketeers* begins to appear in serial form in March, the first episodes of *The Count of Monte Cristo* in August. Dumas starts to build his Château de Monte-Cristo at Saint-Germain-en-Laye. Separates from Ida Ferrier. Publishes *The Women's War*.

1845 *Twenty Years After*, the first sequel to *The Three Musketeers*, appears at the beginning of the year. In February Dumas wins a libel action against the author of a book accusing him of plagiarism. Publishes *La Reine Margot*.

1846 Travels in Spain and North Africa. Publishes *La Dame de Monsoreau*, *Les Deux Diane* and *Joseph Balsamo*.

1847 Dumas's theatre, the Théâtre Historique, opens. It will show several adaptations of his novels, including *The Three Musketeers* and *La Reine Margot*. Serialization of *The Vicomte de Bragelonne*, the final episode of the *The Three Musketeers*.

1848 A revolution in February brings in the Second Republic. Dumas stands unsuccessfully for Parliament and supports Louis-Napoléon, nephew of Napoleon I, who becomes President of the Republic.

1849 Publishes *The Queen's Necklace*. In May travels to Holland to attend the coronation of King William III.

1850 *The Black Tulip* is published. Dumas, declared bankrupt, sells the Château de Monte-Cristo and the Théâtre Historique.

1851 In December Louis-Napoléon seizes power in a *coup* *d'état*, effectively abolishing the Republic. Victor Hugo, joined by Dumas, goes into exile in Belgium.

1852 Second Empire proclaimed. Dumas publishes his memoirs.

1853 In November returns to Paris and founds a newspaper, *Le Mousquetaire*. Publishes *Ange Pitou*.

1858 Founds the literary weekly *Le Monte-Cristo*. Sets out on a nine-month journey to Russia.

1860 Meets Garibaldi and actively supports the Italian struggle against Austria. Founds *L'Independente*, a periodical in Italian and French. Garibaldi is godfather to Dumas's daughter by Emilie Cordier.

1861–70 Continues to travel throughout Europe. Writes six plays, thirteen novels, several shorter fictions, a historical work on the Bourbons in Naples and a good deal of journalism. Has a last love affair, with an American, Adah Menken.

1870 Dumas dies on 5 December.

Introduction

Alexandre Dumas was an impressively prolific and varied writer. He wrote poetry, plays, novels, historical works, travel books, memoirs and even a couple of books on cookery, as well as huge amounts of journalism (some of it in the periodical *Le Monte-Cristo*, which he also edited), political writings and pamphlets. A leading figure in the Romantic movement, through his work as a playwright during the 1830s, he pioneered the form of the *feuilleton* (serial fiction published in the newspapers). In the following decade, he concentrated on fiction, writing over thirty novels and many shorter narratives in what seems an impossibly brief period of time. Today, over 130 years after his death, several of these works remain best-sellers in France and in translation throughout the world: *The Three Musketeers* (1844, and its sequels); *The Count of Monte Cristo* (1844–5); *The Black Tulip* (1850) and *La Reine Margot* (1845). But these books represent only a fraction of Dumas's incredible output and, despite the enduring popularity of his work, he remains a continent of which most of us know only a corner. There is a huge amount there waiting to be rediscovered – and a lot that is well worth discovering.

The Women's War (*La Guerre des femmes*) is one of those books. It last appeared in English (in a reprint of a nineteenth-century translation) during the 1920s,[1] and had even been out of print in French for many years before it was republished in 2003. When this new French edition appeared, it was an immediate success. The weekly magazine *Télérama*[2] called the novel 'a great Dumas', the daily *La Marseillaise*[3] hailed it as 'a great, forgotten Dumas', and the newpaper *Le Figaro*'s literary

supplement[4] made *La Guerre des femmes* its 'book of the week'
and devoted an article of several columns to this 'forgotten
novel' – the words 'forgotten' and 'great' echoed through the
French press, and readers hurried out to buy it.[5] The publisher,
Phébus, set about remedying similar literary oversights and in
2004 brought out another of Dumas's neglected historical
novels, *Sylvandire*. In France, gradually, the Dumas continent
is being opened up.

The wonderful thing about this recent revival of interest is
that it allows one to read the 'new' works with a real sense of
discovery. Because of their very popularity, the plots of *The
Three Musketeers* and *The Count of Monte Cristo* are known
to many people before they even open the books, either from
hearsay or from adaptations in other media: *The Count of
Monte Cristo*, for example, is one of the most frequently
adapted novels in the history of cinema and many people know
the outlines of the story of Edmond Dantès, his unjust imprisonment and his re-emergence as the vengeful count. By contrast,
very few readers who pick up this book will know anything
about the story, which is based on an actual incident during
the period of civil unrest in sixteenth-century France known as
the Fronde. For that reason, it would be unfair in this introduction to give away details of the plot, so I have decided to discuss
only the broader historical background and the characters of
the novel here. But because it is instructive to see how Dumas
and his collaborator, Auguste Maquet, made use of the raw
material of history, and because the facts on which the novel is
based are interesting in themselves, I am including as an appendix some historical material: four extracts from seventeenth-
century memoirs and one from a nineteenth-century history
of the period that would have been available to Dumas. This
present introduction should be helpful in explaining what was
going on politically and socially at the time of *The Women's
War* and why the different factions in France were in conflict.

Some admirers of Dumas find it hard to accept the fact that he
used collaborators (of whom Auguste Maquet was the most
important), but he never denied that he had assistants, just as

a Renaissance painter would not dispute that he used appren-
tices to fill in details of a picture. Dumas was no great stickler
for historical accuracy, either; he saw the events and characters
of history as a springboard for his imagination, not as a field
for minute exploration, so Maquet and others would be entrusted with a lot of the spadework: obtaining historical background material, verifying facts and writing some chapters
(though there is still uncertainty about how much was done by
assistants and how much by Dumas himself). Almost at one
and the same time, the Dumas factory would be devising and
writing novels on very different historical periods: the sixteenth-
century wars of religion (*La Reine Margot*), the seventeenth
century (*The Three Musketeers*) and the nineteenth-century
empire and Restoration (*The Count of Monte Cristo*). It may
be that Dumas came across accounts of the episode around
which *The Women's War* was based, while doing research for
his history of Louis XIV and his times (which also led to the
Three Musketeers trilogy), and marked it for separate use. The
novel first appeared in serial form in 1844, a few months after
The Three Musketeers.

Dumas had a particular liking for the seventeenth century,
and the idea of a novel set at the time of the so-called Women's
War, as a means to stay in the period and to cash in on the
success of his trilogy, would have been attractive to him. It was
a period of drama, intrigue and civil unrest. The troubles of the
Fronde were the outcome of the political situation in France
following the death, in 1643, of King Louis XIII. His son and
heir was only five years old, and Louis XIII's widow, Queen
Anne of Austria, daughter of King Philip III of Spain, was
unpopular in France, not least because her country of adoption
was at war with her country of origin: they were to remain in
conflict until 1659. The queen had also attracted hostility
because of her long estrangement from her late husband, giving
rise to doubts about the paternity of their child – though it
seems that these doubts were unjustified: historians have proved
that a series of remarkable coincidences, including a thunder-
storm, brought the couple together in the same bed at the very
time when the future Louis XIV was conceived.[6]

No less unpopular was the country's chief minister, Cardinal Mazarin. Like Anne, he was a foreigner: born Giulio Mazzarini, he had come to France from Italy as papal envoy in 1634, before being appointed an assistant to Cardinal Richelieu, and rapidly gaining in power and influence thanks to Richelieu's support. After the death of Louis XIII, Anne and Mazarin were made members of a regency council, which was empowered to govern the country until her son was old enough to rule. The late king's younger brother. Gaston d'Orléans, who until the birth of Louis XIV in 1638 had been heir to the throne, was also a member of the council, as was the late king's cousin, the Duke d'Enghien, later Prince de Condé. The presence on this council of a disappointed heir and a powerful prince almost guaranteed discord.

Popular dislike of what was seen as rule by the two foreigners, Anne and Mazarin, may have been an underlying cause of the unrest, but the most important one was the ambition of a group of powerful nobles around Gaston d'Orléans, who had been long preparing to succeed his sick brother and confidently expected to do so because of the estrangement of Louis XIII and Anne. Even before the king's death, there had been opposition to the ruthless rule of Richelieu and the concentration of power in an absolute monarchy. This unrest had culminated in the conspiracy of the Marquis de Cinq-Mars, a young favourite of the king and Richelieu who quarrelled with the cardinal and decided to form a conspiracy against him, in collaboration with France's enemy Spain: the discovery of letters from the Spanish king promising to support Cinq-Mars proved the conspiracy and the marquis was beheaded in 1642. But the deaths in the following year, within a few months of each other, of both Richelieu and the king, left a serious power vacuum in the country.

The situation began to deteriorate in the late 1640s with growing conflict between the regency and the Paris *parlement*. The *parlements* were in essence judiciary bodies, composed of local magistrates, which acted as a higher court in Paris and in most important towns in the provinces. However, as well as their legal function, they also had administrative powers; and, even though they could be overruled by the king and were not in any way democratically elected, they considered themselves to represent the popular will. Given the precariousness of the situation in the country, a conflict between the Paris *parlement* and the regency was bound to be a source of serious instability.

Mazarin's arrest of the leading members of the Paris *parlement* in 1648 led to riots: slingshots hurled at the windows of Mazarin's supporters resulted in the anti-Mazarin movement being christened the Fronde – *fronde* meaning 'a sling'. In January 1649, following the peace of Westphalia, the Prince de Condé's army returned from the war against Spain, and took the side of the Parisian mob against Mazarin. For a while, it looked as though there might be an accommodation between the Frondeurs and Mazarin, but relations broke down again when Mazarin felt that he was strong enough to confront his opponents. In January 1650 he carried out a sudden coup against the Frondeurs, having the three princes, Condé, Conti and Longueville unexpectedly arrested. This move against the great Condé, responsible for French victories at Rocroi and elsewhere, was especially shocking. With her husband under arrest, the Princess de Condé became the leader of the insurrection. Opposing her, as it were at the head of the royalist side, was the Queen Regent, Anne of Austria. The stage was set for the Women's War.

On the face of it, the queen's side was by far the stronger, since she had the government and Mazarin behind her. But support for the Frondeurs was potentially strong in the south-west, especially around what was then France's second city, Bordeaux. The feelings of the people in the region had been aggravated by food shortages (this was an agriculturally poor region), and the *parlement* in Bordeaux had fallen out with the Governor of the province of Guyenne, the Duke d'Epernon. However, conciliatory moves during 1649 by both d'Epernon and Mazarin had apparently warded off the threat of rebellion, until the imprisonment of the princes. It remained to be seen how the Bordeaux *parlement* would react. The Princess de Condé and her followers were being kept under virtual house arrest at Chantilly, but if Bordeaux was sympathetic to their cause and if they could somehow make their way there, the region would provide an invaluable base for rebellion against Mazarin. This, in essence, is the situation when Dumas's novel opens.

In fact, the reader does not need to have more than the vaguest idea of the historical context: the best way to start reading *The Women's War* is to go with the flow and simply to laugh at the list of combatants – king, queen, clergy, noblemen and their mistresses – without worrying too much who is who – when, in Book I, Chapter II, Cauvignac remarks to the Duke d'Epernon:

> 'At the moment, Monsieur de Mazarin is fighting for the queen, you are fighting for the king, the coadjutor is fighting for Monsieur de Beaufort, Monsieur de Beaufort is fighting for Madame de Montbazon, Monsieur de La Rochefoucauld is fighting for Madame de Longueville, the Duke d'Orléans is fighting for Mademoiselle Soyon, the parliament is fighting for the people ... and, finally, they have imprisoned Monsieur de Condé who was fighting for France.'

And yet, at the same time, as one gets deeper into the story, the desire grows to know about the history behind it. How far is Dumas sticking to the facts? Where did he get his material? Were the characters that he depicts historical or invented? Were they really as he depicts them? It is because he invites us to ask such questions that Dumas has been said to have taught history to the people, and the translator and editor of his work may have a responsibility to answer some of the questions or to suggest how they can be answered – hence the cluster of notes generated by Cauvignac's cynically humorous analysis of the forces on all sides in the Fronde.

Despite that, the history is secondary. Dumas had no doubt about what he was doing: he was writing a romance. But, like the background to the novel, the majority of the characters are taken from history or inspired by historical reality. In the Women's War, the opposing forces were conveniently balanced. On the royalist side there was the queen and her young son, King Louis XIV; on the side of the Fronde, the princess and her young son, the Duke d'Enghien. The royalist forces also include the politician Mazarin and the soldier Marshal de La Meilleraie, while among the Frondeurs we have the princess's councillor, Pierre Lenet, and the Duke de La Rochefoucauld, one of the military leaders of the rebellion. Other historical characters play secondary roles, and one quite minor figure, the Baron de Canolles, becomes the hero of the story.

To this historical background, Dumas pins his imaginary characters, the most prominent of whom are the two heroines of the novel: the humbly born Nanon de Lartigues, who has made her way in the world as mistress of the ageing Duke d'Epernon, and the aristocratic Claire, Viscountess de Cambes, lady-in-waiting to the Princess de Condé. These two, on opposite sides in the civil war, are also rivals for the love of Canolles. And then, among the important fictional characters, we have Nanon's brother, the mercenary Cauvignac, who happily changes sides according to the interests of the moment. Cauvignac's optimism and cynical attitude to the conflict take us back to the happy-go-lucky world of Dumas's musketeers.

Finally, there is a secondary cast of both real and invented characters who closely resemble figures from theatrical comedy: the Duke d'Epernon, Nanon's protector, is given the role of the foolish old man in love with a much younger woman (a stock figure in stage comedy). Madame de Tourville, one of the princess's ladies-in-waiting and advisers, believes herself to be a brilliant military strategist, and is constantly proposing unworkable or inappropriate plans of action; she is a kind of *précieuse ridicule*, a bluestocking who makes herself ludicrous by her pretensions. Claire de Cambes's servant, Pompée, is a veteran of earlier wars who boasts of his prowess (another stock figure in comedy since classical times), until he is confronted with actual danger, when bravado gives way to common sense and he takes to his heels. More unusual is the innkeeper, Biscarros, who runs a small country inn, but exhibits a chef's pride in his cooking; Dumas, a considerable gourmet, may even have based him on an acquaintance.

One character, who is in fact historical, is fictionalized to such an extent that Dumas reinvents him: Pierre Lenet, about whom relatively little is known. His family had been in the service of the house of Condé for many years, and Lenet became an adviser to the Princess de Condé; he is remembered chiefly because he wrote a long, wordy memoir of the events in which he took part – readable only because of its authenticity as a first-hand account. Dumas transforms this rather dull character into someone far more interesting: a clever politician who will, despite his political skills, become one of the moral pillars of the narrative.

The years leading up to the time when Dumas wrote his historical novels, the period of the Restoration and the July Monarchy, from 1815 to 1848, saw a new delight in history and historical writing. Writers and scholars in the previous century had taken an antiquarian interest in sources, digging up old memoirs and histories, and republishing them in collections such as the *Recueil des historiens des Gaules et de la France*, which was produced by the Benedictines of Saint-Maur between 1738 and 1752; others in that period felt a philosophical desire to comprehend the general movement of human history: the reasons for the rise and fall of empires, for example, or the whole course of human development through time, which was often seen as mirroring the progress of an individual from childhood towards maturity. But the upheavals of the Revolution and the Napoleonic Empire (the period of Dumas's childhood) disturbed the notion of a smooth evolution towards enlightenment, while giving historians an urgent desire to understand the workings of cause and effect. So the increase in the number of writings on history during the period after the fall of Napoleon had to do partly with a desire to understand the past and to make sense of the changes that the country had gone through in the previous thirty years, but there was also a broader interest in historical events for their own sake, and (as Claude-Bernard Petitot, editor of a collection of memoirs on the history of France published in 1824,[7] remarks) no earlier period in French history had been so productive of historical memoirs as the seventeenth century, and in particular the period of the Fronde.

The new tendency in historical writing was towards smaller narratives: history as a succession of meaningful events, regardless of how these fitted into the broader pattern of human development. This was consistent, too, with the rise during the nineteenth century of nationalist feeling: rather than universal histories, writers and their public were interested in narratives shaped by particular localities and customs – and nothing catered to this better than the historical novels of Sir Walter Scott. In his romantic tales, set against authentic historical backgrounds and mixing real and imaginary characters, Scott found a winning formula for historical fiction. From the moment of the translation of his novel *Quentin Durward* into French in 1823 Scott's work was immensely popular across the Channel. And *Quentin Durward*, being set in France at the time of Louis XI, was particularly successful among French readers.

Scott's first French imitator was Alfred de Vigny, with a novel describing events from the seventeenth century. *Cinq-Mars* (1826) is the story of the conspiracy of the nobility against Cardinal Richelieu, led by the tragic figure of the young Marquis de Cinq-Mars (the conspiracy is mentioned by Dumas in *The Women's War*). This novel was followed, among others, by Victor Hugo's *Notre-Dame de Paris* (1831), a fifteenth-century tale in which the cathedral becomes one of the chief protagonists. What is unusual about both these novels is that they set out not only to tell a good story, or even to recount historical events, but to use fiction as a means to explore the workings of human society in its historical context. Vigny, for example, sees Cinq-Mars's conspiracy as a tragic failure of the nobility in its struggle for power with the monarchy, leading eventually to the absolutism of Louis XIV. Hugo goes even further in interpretation of events, using the form of the novel for a sweeping account of historical change during a period when, as he sees it, the cathedral, with its stories in stone, was giving way to the printed word as a means of what we would now call 'mass communication'. From the nineteenth century Hugo looks back to the Middle Ages, then often considered as a period of barbarism, with what is almost nostalgia for an age when the great cathedrals, with their carvings and stained glass windows, could be understood as vast encyclopedias of human knowledge.[8]

Dumas had no grand aim of this kind. He looked at the past less as a great edifice to be restored, than as a treasure house for plundering. The incident on which he bases *The Women's War* is a good example of the kind of jewel that he hoped to uncover. But, nonetheless, as the saga of the three musketeers shows, he is capable of projected nostalgia: history is about time, time means change and change, however desirable overall, implies loss. When he and Maquet decided that they could do with another novel to cash in on the success of *The Three Musketeers* and its sequels, they were conscious of the moral dividing line that was perceived to exist between the reign of Louis XIII and that of his son, Louis XIV. The earlier period was seen as one of daring deeds and devotion to noble causes (such as the Cinq-Mars conspiracy), marked by passionate intrigue and intriguing, often illicit romance (for example, the affair between Queen Anne of Austria and the Duke of Buckingham). For Dumas, it represented a time governed by a spirit of adventure and freedom that he adored. The reign of Louis XIV, by contrast, was considered to be sober and marked by the influence of the austere doctrines of political absolutism and religious Jansenism. The latter was a movement within the Catholic Church, but one that, with its belief in predestination, had a good deal in common with puritanical Calvinism. One of those known to have been influenced by Jansenism was the Duke de La Rochefoucauld, who plays a significant role in *The Women's War*.

La Rochefoucauld was the author of memoirs of the period of the Fronde, but his name is remembered today for a series of reflections on human nature and society, the *Maxims* (1665). These take the form of pithy observations, such as: 'People prefer to speak ill about themselves than not to speak about themselves at all'; or 'Society more often rewards the appearance of merit than merit itself'; or 'When our crimes are known only to us, they are soon forgotten.' They betray a deeply disenchanted outlook on human motivation, a cynicism that accords with the Jansenist belief that most human beings are wicked and that virtue can only be attained by a few – and then only through God's grace. La Rochefoucauld is one of the villains of *The Women's War*, where Dumas depicts him as a man without human feeling or sympathy.

As a character in the novel, La Rochefoucauld's first appearance is carefully prepared: we meet his name several times before he finally rides in, and when he does appear, we see him from the point of view of Claire, Viscountess de Cambes, as:

> a horseman of modest height and dressed in an affectedly simple way ... looking at her with bright little eyes, sunk like those of a fox. With his thick black hair, his slender, shifting lips, his bilious pallor and his woeful brow, the man aroused a feeling of melancholy in daylight, but after dark, he could well have inspired terror. (Book II, Chapter XI)

Before the novel ends, the viscountess will have had the opportunity to compare the character of La Rochefoucauld with that of Lenet, much to the advantage of the latter; we, as readers, are invited to adopt her point of view on these two powerful men.

Is *The Women's War* a feminist novel? Though women play the leading roles, the answer, at least in the modern sense of the term, has to be no. It is the circumstances of the time that lead Anne of Austria and the princess to become so prominent in the affairs of state, and neither woman (as Dumas depicts them) is truly equal to the task. At one point, Dumas says explicitly: 'It is one of the eternal ambitions of that half of the human race which is destined to seduce, that it aspires to exercise the rights of the half that is destined to command' (Book III, Chapter XVIII). He could hardly make his feelings on that score more clear; and the character that he gives to both Anne of Austria and the Princess de Condé shows what, in his view, happens when women try to perform outside what he sees as their natural sphere. Both women come across as capricious, vain, unwilling to take advice and unnaturally hard-hearted. Neither of them, incidentally, seems to bear much relation to the historical personalities of the queen and the princess (as we shall later see, in the princess's case, from the source materials in the Appendix).

On the other hand, it would be wrong to dismiss this as merely another nineteenth-century attack on women who aspire to achieve something other than to seduce. The two main female characters in the book, Claire de Cambes and Nanon de Lartigues, are both depicted as more than just the playthings of men. Both are competent and resourceful. Nanon, the brunette, has risen from humble beginnings to become the rich and influential mistress of a very powerful man. She has attracted some of the popular hatred directed against him, but has helped him to escape from attack and even protected him against the fury of the mob. Her spirit and good humour make her one of the most attractive characters in the novel.

Her rival, the fair-haired Claire de Cambes, is quite different in personality and background, but equally resourceful and almost as courageous when pressed. She does not mind riding around the countryside, with only her timorous old servant for company, and dressed in men's clothes. This is not by any means the typical heroine of nineteenth-century fiction – even though, as the representative of beauty and intelligence, as opposed to Nanon's sensuality and generosity, she is the more constrained by convention.

Above all, what comes across at every point of the narrative, is Dumas's affectionate respect for the two women he has created. He may feel that it is inappropriate for women to meddle in affairs of state or war, but that does not mean that he has any less regard for the qualities of women as individuals. On the contrary: the people that Dumas despises most – whether in affairs of state, in love or in war – are the cold, unfeeling politicians: Mazarin and La Rochefoucauld. They are the empty beings who manipulate others and are themselves manipulated in this game of move and counter-move. By contrast, as the critic Pierre Marcabru said in his review of *The Women's War*, there is nothing cold or unfeeling about Nanon and Claire: they are 'free women who, without neglecting their interests, go to the extremes of their passions, whether these are political or amorous'.[9]

Indeed, only one other character in the book seems to enjoy the same freedom as these two women: this is not Canolles, the ostensible hero, but Cauvignac, Nanon's deplorable brother, who has no principles or loyalties, but switches sides whenever it appears to be to his advantage, relying on sheer effrontery to get him out of every scrape. There is no way, we think, that Dumas can approve of this outrageous character – and yet there is no way that he can have failed to enjoy him. This is a novel full of those scenes of humour and sheer enjoyment that are the hallmark of Dumas's work, intrigues, disguises, mistaken identities, trickery and hoaxes, with battles and chases, trial and imprisonment . . .

Yet, despite his amorality, there are two reasons for seeing Cauvignac, not Canolles, as the story's hero. The first is that he is the one character who, in the course of the narrative, shows that he is capable of change. Indeed, he comes to embody one of its messages, which is about the power of redemption. The other reason why Cauvignac is the key to the meaning of the novel, is that he better than anyone else expresses the futility of war. Certainly, the wars of the Fronde were particularly devoid of sense, being the outcome essentially of struggles for power between a few leading figures in the state – palace intrigue played out on a national stage. But Cauvignac, switching lightly from one side to the other, ends as the eternal adventurer, setting off for a colonial war with the remark that:

'There is a war in Africa. Monsieur de Beaufort is off to fight the infidel, so I can go with him. To tell you the truth, it's not as though I don't think the infidels are a thousand times more in the right than the faithful, but what of it? That's a matter for kings, not for us. You can get killed over there, which is all that matters to me.' ('Brother and Sister')

There can be no doubt that Cauvignac is the masculine hero of this women's war and the character closest to Dumas's heart.

On 30 November 2002, the remains of Alexandre Dumas were transferred to the Pantheon in Paris where they now lie beside those of his friend and rival, Victor Hugo. The year for this transfer was chosen because it was the bicentenary of Dumas's birth and the Dumas Society (*Société des Amis d'Alexandre Dumas*) had long been pressing for this honour for a writer whom they felt had been unjustly neglected by the country to which he had given so much.

This was not the first posthumous move for Dumas. He died near Dieppe, in Normandy, in 1870 and, because of the Franco-Prussian war, could not be buried at his home town of Villers-Cotterêts until 1872. His progress from there to the Pantheon was a triumphal one.

Addressing the coffin when it arrived in front of the Pantheon, President Chirac recalled the fact that Dumas was the grandson of a Haitian slave and deplored the racism that he had suffered; a wrong was being righted by his move to the temple which is the resting place of France's great men and women. He also quoted a remark by the nineteenth-century historian Jules Michelet, who told Dumas: 'You have taught more history to the people than all historians put together.' Most of us, he said, first read Dumas when we were young; he was the 'yeast' that got our imaginations working.

He died, according to his son, Alexandre Dumas *fils*, wondering if his work would survive, so he would have been gratified by this posthumous homage. He would not have been surprised, either, to learn that *The Three Musketeers* and *The Count of Monte Cristo* remain the most popular of his novels, or that they have been successful in adaptations for other media; he and Maquet adapted most of their work for the stage (including *The Women's War*), and he would surely have loved the cinema. We, who are familiar with that medium, may often be surprised by how cinematic Dumas's writing is. He came to the novel as a dramatist and obviously often thinks in terms of scenes, visualizing the action as he describes it, so we can easily imagine *The Women's War* on the screen, ideally with all the benefits of wide-screen technology and technicolour, from the opening scenes at the inn, through the great hunt at Chantilly, to the viscountess's night ride, the battles and the rest ... With its dramatic confrontations, its colourful costumes and locations, its clearly delineated characters, intrigues and disguises, this is a novel that was waiting for the cinema to happen. Meanwhile, a 'forgotten' part of the Dumas continent is waiting for us to explore and enjoy.

Robin Buss

NOTES

1. See the Note on the Text.
2. 2 July 2003.
3. 3 August 2003.
4. *Le Figaro littéraire*, 7 August 2003.
5. Reaction to the novel has not always been so complimentary. A. Craig Bell, in his biography (*Alexandre Dumas*, London: Cassell, 1950), calls it 'poor stuff' and attributes it mainly to Maquet, apparently on internal evidence alone, saying that the slow opening is not typical of Dumas. Against that, one could argue that *The Count of Monte Cristo* also opens quite slowly, introducing all the characters in the early chapters, just as *The Women's War* brings its main protagonists together in or around Biscarros's inn. The style, the humour and the characterization are all typical of Dumas.
6. See, for example, the discussion in Philippe Erlanger's *Louis XIV*, trans. Stephen Cox (London: Phoenix, 2003), pp. 7–9.
7. C.-B. Petitot, *Collection des mémoires relatifs à l'histoire de France* (Paris: Foucault, 1824), vol. XXXV.
8. All of which is lost, of course, when the novel is translated as *The Hunchback of Notre-Dame* or adapted as a romance about a bellringer and a gypsy girl.
9. *Le Figaro*, 7 August 2003.

Further Reading

Hemmings, F. W. J., *The King of Romance* (London: Hamish Hamilton, 1979)

Maurois, André, *Three Musketeers. A Study of the Dumas Family*, translated by Gerard Hopkins (London: Jonathan Cape, 1957)

Schopp, Claude, *Alexandre Dumas. Genius of Life*, translated by A. J. Koch (New York: Franklin Watts, 1988)

Stowe, Richard, *Alexandre Dumas, père* (Boston: Twayne, 1976)

A Note on the Text

In making this translation, I have referred to both the 1848 Calman-Levy text of Dumas's novel, which includes some chapter headings and the two epilogues, and (for comparison) the first edition in book form, published in Brussels in 1845 (which omits the epilogue and has a slightly different division into chapters). For the sake of consistency, in this translation, I have retained only the titles of the four books and the two epilogues, giving all the chapters numbers and omitting the occasional chapter titles where these were included in earlier editions.

La Guerre des femmes (*The Women's War*) was first published in serial form in the newspaper *La Patrie* in 1844. In the following year, it appeared in book form, in four volumes, in Brussels (Meline: Cans et compagnie). This was followed by an eight-volume French edition (Paris: de Potter, 1845), divided into four sections: 'Nanon de Lartigues', 'Madame de Condé', 'Viscountess de Cambes' and 'The Abbey of Pessac', the last volume also containing the epilogues. This was republished by Calman-Levy (Paris, 1848) in two volumes, then in one volume in the same publisher's 'Musée littéraire'. Dumas and Maquet did a version for the theatre which was staged in 1849.

The first English translation appeared in 1857 as *Nanon; or Women's War* (London: Simms and Macintyre). This was followed by two more translations under the title *Nanon*: one published by Clarke (London, 1860) and a much abridged version, published by Routledge (London, 1867). It was quite normal for nineteenth-century English translations of Dumas's novels to cut the text quite considerably, omitting not only material that might offend Victorian ladies, but also passages of description that were felt to hold up the narrative. The last nineteenth-century translation was *The War of Women* (two vols., London: Dent, 1895; reprinted in 1906 and 1927). This translation, with two illustrations of scenes from the novel, is complete and quite readable, but slightly quaint in its language. Another translation appeared under the title *Nanon* in 1904 (London: Methuen). After more than a century, the novel needed to be retranslated if it is to come alive for the modern reader.

In this translation, considering that *The Women's War* is meant first and foremost as an entertainment, I have tended to 'over-translate' rather than 'under-translate'. In particular, I use English equivalents for titles of nobility, so that the Princesse de Condé becomes 'Princess de Condé', the Duc de la Meilleraie, 'Duke de la Meilleraie', and so on. I have also used the English word 'parliament' for any of the *parlements* (though, as I explain in the Introduction and in an endnote, they do not at all imply the same kind of institution); and I have translated the name of Biscarros's inn. I hope that purists will forgive me for the 'naturalizations'.

I am grateful to my friend, Dr Jean-Pierre Navailles, for his help in clarifying several small points in the text, and to Louisa Sladen, whose meticulous copy-editing saved me from more errors, infelicities and ambiguities than I care to remember. I would also like to thank my editor at Penguin, Laura Barber, who was enthusiastic about this project from the start and so ensured that a lesser-known Dumas novel has joined its more famous fellows among the Penguin Classics.

R.B.

THE WOMEN'S WAR

BOOK I
NANON DE LARTIGUES

I

A short distance from Libourne, that joyous town reflected
in the swift waters of the Dordogne, between Fronsac and
Saint-Michel-la-Rivière, there was in former times a pretty
village of white walls and red roofs, half buried in fronds of
sycamore, lime and beech. The road from Libourne to Saint-
André-de-Cubzac ran through the midst of its symmetrical rows
of houses and offered the only view that they had. Behind one
of these rows of houses, and roughly a hundred paces from it,
wound the river, its width and powerful current starting at this
point to announce the nearness of the sea.

Then the civil war came here. First of all, it uprooted the
trees, then it depopulated the houses, which, being exposed to
all its furious whims and not able, like their inhabitants, to run
away, gradually collapsed into the lawns, protesting in their
own way against the barbarism of internecine strife, and bit
by bit the earth, which seems to have been created as a tomb
for all that ever was, spread over the corpses of these once so
merry and pleasant dwellings. Finally, grass grew over this
artificial ground, and today the traveller who follows the solitary road would never imagine, as he looks at one of those
great flocks that you find everywhere in the south of France
grazing on these uneven hillocks, that the shepherd and his
sheep tread on the graveyard where a village lies.

But at the time of which we speak, namely around the month
of May in the year 1650, this same village extended on both
sides of the road, which nourished it like a great artery with

the most delightful wealth of life and vegetation. The stranger who passed through it in those days would have been gladdened by the sight of the peasants harnessing or unharnessing the teams from their ploughs, the boatmen drawing their nets to the bank shimmering with the white and pink fish of the Dordogne and the blacksmiths smiting hard on their anvils, their hammers throwing off in all directions a spray of sparks that lit up the forge with every blow.

However, what would have charmed him most, especially if his journey had given him the proverbial appetite attributed to travellers on the highway, would have been a long, low house some five hundred yards beyond the village, consisting only of a ground floor and first floor, from the chimneys of which emerged certain exhalations and from the windows certain agreeable odours that indicated more clearly even than the gilded calf's head painted on a sheet of red metal, creaking where it hung from an iron rod fastened into the entablature on the first floor, that he had reached at last one of those hospitable establishments whose owners, at a price, undertake to refresh the hungry visitor.

Why, you ask, was this hostelry of the Golden Calf situated five hundred yards outside the village, instead of occupying its natural place amid the charming houses ranged on either side of the main road?

The first reason is that the innkeeper, despite being buried in this obscure hamlet, was a master of his art when it came to cooking. And, had he chosen at the start a spot in the middle or at the far end of one of the two long rows of houses that made up the village, he risked being mistaken for one of those cheap eating houses that he was obliged to accept as his fellows in the restaurant trade, but which he could not bring himself to consider as his equals; while, on the contrary, by setting himself apart, he attracted the attention of connoisseurs, who, when they had tasted his cooking just once, would tell each other: 'When you go from Libourne to Saint-André-de-Cubzac – or from Saint-André-de-Cubzac to Libourne – do not fail to stop and lunch, dine or sup at the inn of the Golden Calf, five hundred yards beyond the little village of Matifou.'

So these connoisseurs would stop, leave well pleased and send along other connoisseurs, with the result that the clever innkeeper gradually made a fortune for himself, though this, remarkably, did not prevent him from maintaining the same high gastronomic standards at his table – which only goes to prove, as we said earlier, that Master Biscarros was a true artist.

On one of those lovely May evenings when Nature, already reawakened in the south, starts to wake in the north, thicker tufts of smoke and more delicious scents than usual were wafting from the chimneys and through the windows of the inn of the Golden Calf, while on the threshold of his premises, Biscarros himself, dressed in white according to the universal and timeless custom of sacrificial priests, was plucking with his own noble hands some partridge and quail intended for one of those fine dinners that he knew so well how to compose, and which he was in the habit of supervising down to the last detail, purely out of love for his art.

Daylight was fading, and the waters of the Dordogne were starting to whiten beneath the blackness of the foliage on its banks. The river at this point, in one of those meanders that bestrew its course, turned away from the road to lie about one quarter of a league away[1] and passed beneath the little fort of Vayres. Something calm and melancholy spread across the countryside with the evening breeze. The ploughmen were returning with their horses unharnessed, and the fishermen with their streaming nets. The sounds of the village were hushed, and when the last hammer blow had sounded, marking the end of the day's labour, the first song of the nightingale was heard from some bushes nearby.

With the first notes that emerged from the throat of the feathered musician, Master Biscarros also began to sing, no doubt to accompany it. Thanks to this harmonic competition and the attention he was paying to his work, the innkeeper did not observe a little troop of horsemen appearing at the far end of the village of Matifou and proceeding towards his inn. But an exclamation from a first-floor window and the brusque, noisy closing of the same made the worthy innkeeper look up, and it was then that he saw the rider at the head of the troop coming directly towards him.

'Directly' is not quite the word, and we hasten to correct ourselves: the man stopped every twenty paces, cast an enquiring glance to right and left, scanning the paths, trees and bushes with his eyes and holding a carbine on his knee to be ready for either attack or defence, while now and then signalling to his companions, who were copying his every movement, to start walking. At which he would once more risk advancing a few steps, and the whole manoeuvre began again.

Biscarros was watching this rider, whose unusual behaviour so utterly absorbed him that all this time he forgot to remove the bunch of feathers that he was holding between thumb and index finger from the body of the bird.

'It's a nobleman looking for my house,' said Biscarros. 'This worthy gentleman is doubtless short-sighted – and yet my Golden Calf has been freshly repainted and the sign projects out a long way. Come now, let's show ourselves.'

He went and stood in the middle of the road, where he continued to pluck his partridge with expansive, majestic gestures.

This movement produced the result that he had been waiting for: no sooner did the horseman notice him than he rode directly towards him, greeting him courteously.

'Excuse me, Master Biscarros,' he said. 'I don't suppose you have seen a troop of men-at-arms hereabouts, who are friends of mine and must be looking for me? Men-at-arms? I may exaggerate. Swordsmen is more like it, in brief, armed men, what? Yes, that's it! You haven't seen a troop of armed men?'

Biscarros, greatly flattered at being greeted with his own name, returned the greeting affably. He had not noticed that a single glance at his inn had allowed the stranger to read Biscarros's name and title, just as he had identified the owner from his bearing.

'As for armed men, sir,' Biscarros answered, after thinking for a moment, 'I have seen only a gentleman and his attendant, who arrived here an hour or so ago.'

'Ah, ha!' said the stranger, stroking his chin – manly, though almost entirely beardless. 'Ah, ha! There is a gentleman and his attendant in your hostelry. And both of them are armed, you say?'

'Yes, sir. Do you wish me to tell the gentleman that you would like to speak to him?'

'Now, is that entirely proper?' said the stranger. 'To bother a person one does not know in this way may be to exhibit an excess of familiarity, especially if the other is a person of quality. No, no, Biscarros, just describe him to me, pray, or better still, point him out without him seeing me.'

'It would be hard to point him out, sir, since he appears to be hiding himself, because he shut his window as soon as you and your companions appeared on the road. It's easier to describe him to you: he's a little gentleman, young, fair-haired and delicate, barely sixteen years old, who seems to have just enough strength to carry the little dress sword hanging from his belt.'

The stranger furrowed his brow at the shadow of a memory.

'Very well,' he said. 'I can see what you mean: a blond, effeminate young master on a Barbary horse, followed by an old servant as stiff as a pole. That's not the one I'm looking for.'

'Ah, so that's not the person the gentleman is after,' said Biscarros.

'No.'

'Well, while the gentleman is waiting for the person he *is* after, who is bound to pass this way, he might as well come into my inn and refresh himself, along with his companions.'

'No, thank you. All that's left is for me to thank you and ask you the time.'

'There's six o'clock sounding on the village clock, Monsieur. Can you hear its great voice?'

'Indeed. And one more favour, Monsieur Biscarros?'

'Certainly.'

'Pray, can you tell me how I might procure a boat and a boatman?'

'To cross the stream?'

'No, to go for a trip down the river.'

'Nothing could be simpler. The fisherman who supplies my fish ... But do you like fish, Monsieur?' Biscarros asked, in a kind of parenthesis, returning to his idea of getting the stranger to take something at the inn.

'It's a dull food,' the traveller replied. 'However, when it is passably well seasoned, I don't refuse it.'

'I always have excellent fish, Monsieur.'

'I congratulate you on it, Master Biscarros, but let's return to the person who supplies it for you.'

'Of course. Well, at this time he has probably finished his day's work and will be taking his dinner. You can see his boat from here, tied up to those willows near the elm tree over there. As for his house, it is hidden by that other clump of willows. You'll surely find him at his table.'

'Thank you, Master Biscarros, thank you,' said the stranger, and, signalling to his companions to follow him, he quickly headed for the trees and knocked on the door of the hut in question. It was opened by the fisherman's wife, and, as Biscarros had said, the fisherman himself was at his table.

'Take your oars and follow me,' said the horseman. 'You can earn a crown.'[2]

The fisherman leapt up with a haste that indicated how poorly the innkeeper at the Golden Calf reimbursed him for his wares.

'Does the gentleman want to go down to Vayres?' he asked.

'I just want you to row me to the middle of the river and stay there with me for a few minutes.'

The fisherman's eyes bulged at the idea of this odd whim, but since there was a crown to be earned, and because he could see the outline of the other riders twenty yards behind the one who had knocked on his door, he did not argue, considering that any lack of goodwill on his part might lead to the use of force and that in the struggle he would lose his promised reward. So he hastened to let the stranger know that he himself, his boat and his oars, were at his service.

The little band of men headed directly towards the river and, while the stranger was proceeding to the waterside, it halted at the top of the embankment, spreading out so that it had covered all directions, no doubt from fear of being surprised. From where the men were placed, they could keep a watch on the flat ground behind them and protect the boat and those embarking in it at the foot of the embankment.

At this the stranger, a tall young man with fair hair, pale complexion and nervous manner, though thin and intelligent-looking, despite the dark rim around his blue eyes and the expression of vulgar cynicism hovering on his lips – this stranger, we say, carefully inspected his pistols, slung his carbine on his shoulder, tried a long rapier a few times in its sheath and stared hard at the opposite bank, a wide meadow with a path cutting across it from the river's edge, running in a straight line to the little town of Isson, where one could see the brown church steeple and the white smoke in the golden mists of evening.

Still on the far side, about an eighth of a league away on the right, stood the little fort of Vayres.

'Well, then!' the stranger, who was starting to grow impatient, said to his companions at the lookout. 'Is he coming, can you see him at last, to the right or the left, behind us or in front?'

'I think I can see a black group on the Isson road,' one of the men said, 'but I'm not sure yet, because the sun's in my eyes. Hold on! Yes, yes, that's right: one, two, three, four, five men, a trimmed hat and a blue cloak. It's the messenger we've been waiting for, with an escort for greater security.'

'He has every right,' the stranger said phlegmatically. 'Come and get my horse, Ferguzon.'

The man to whom this order had been addressed – in a voice that was part friendly and part commanding – hastened to obey and ran down the embankment. Meanwhile, the stranger dismounted and, as the other came up to him, threw the reins across his arm and prepared to get into the boat.

'Listen, Cauvignac,' said Ferguzon, putting a hand on his arm. 'No rash valour now. If our man makes the slightest suspicious gesture, start by putting a bullet through his head. You see he's bringing a whole troop with him, the sly dog.'

'Yes, but they are fewer than we are. And, quite apart from

our greater courage, we have the advantage of numbers, so there is nothing to fear. Ah! You can just see their heads.'

'What about that!' said Ferguzon. 'What can they do? They won't be able to find a boat. Well, I never! There is one, as if by magic.'

'It belongs to my cousin, the ferryman of Isson,' said the fisherman, who appeared to be very interested in the preparations, though terrified that a naval battle was about to take place between his boat and his cousin's.

'Good, the blue cloak is going aboard,' said Ferguzon. 'Alone, strictly as required by the treaty.'

'We mustn't keep them waiting,' the stranger remarked, and, jumping into the boat himself, he signalled to the fisherman to take up his place.

'Be careful, Roland,' Ferguzon went on, repeating his appeal for caution. 'The river is wide, so don't get too close to the opposite bank and attract a burst of musket fire that we couldn't return. As far as possible, keep on this side of the demarcation line.'

The man whom Ferguzon had just called 'Roland', and before that 'Cauvignac' – and who responded to both names, no doubt because one was his given name, and the other his family name or *nom de guerre* – nodded his head.

'Don't worry, I was just thinking about that. It's all very well for those who have nothing to lose to take risks, but in this matter I have too much to win to risk idiotically losing it all. So if there is any rash move here, it will not be from me. Row on, Boatman.'

The fisherman untied his boat and stuck his long boat-hook into the grass. The boat began to move away from the bank just as the Isson ferryman's rowing boat was leaving the opposite shore.

In the middle of the stream there was a little pier of three posts, with a white flag on top, serving to warn the long barges that sailed down the Dordogne that there was a dangerous outcrop of rocks at this point. When the water was low one could even see the tips of these rocks, black and smooth beneath the current; however, at this moment, the Dordogne was full and only the small flag and a slight boiling of the water revealed the presence of the reef.

The two boatmen no doubt realized that the parley could take place at this point, so they directed their skiffs towards it. The Isson ferryman was the first to reach the spot and, on his passenger's orders, tied his boat to one of the rings on the pier.

At that moment, the fisherman, who had set off from the opposite bank, turned round to his traveller for instructions and was not a little surprised to see only a masked man, wrapped in a cloak, sharing the boat with him. This only increased the anxiety that he had felt from the start, and he was only able to manage a stammer as he requested his instructions from this odd personage.

'Tie up the boat at that piece of wood,' said Cauvignac, pointing towards it. 'As close as you can to the other gentleman's boat.'

His hand pointed away from the post, towards the gentleman who had been brought there by the Isson ferryman.

The rower obeyed and the boats, brought side by side by the current, allowed the two plenipotentiaries to begin the following conference.

II

'What! You are masked, Monsieur,' the new arrival said with a mixture of surprise and scorn. He was a fat man of around fifty-five, with grimly staring eyes like those of a bird of prey. He had a grey moustache and small beard, and, though he was not himself masked, he had hidden as much as possible of his hair and face under a wide-brimmed hat, and his clothes and body behind a blue cloak with long folds.

Cauvignac, taking a closer look at the man who had just spoken to him, could not refrain from giving an involuntary start of surprise.

'Well, Monsieur,' said the other. 'What's wrong?'

'Nothing, I almost lost my balance. But I believe you did me the honour to address me. May I enquire what you said?'

'I was asking why you are masked.'

'It's a frank question,' the young man said. 'And I shall reply with equal candour. I am masked to prevent you seeing my face.'

'Do I know you then?'

'I think not, but having seen me once you might recognize me later, and that, at least in my opinion, would be quite unnecessary.'

'Well, I think you are at least as open as I am.'

'Yes, when my candour cannot harm me.'

'And does this candour go so far as to reveal the secrets of others?'

'Why not, if the revelation can do me some good.'

'It is a strange part that you are playing here.'

'Heavens! One does what one can, Monsieur. I have been by turns lawyer, doctor, soldier and partisan. You can see that I am not short of a profession.'

'And what are you now?'

'I am your humble servant,' the young man said, bowing with a pretence of respect.

'Do you have the letter we mentioned?'

'Do you have the letter of attestation[3] requested?'

'Here it is.'

'Do you want us to exchange?'

'One moment, Monsieur,' said the stranger in the blue cloak. 'Your conversation pleases me, and I am loath to deprive myself of the pleasure so soon.'

'Why, Monsieur, it is entirely at your disposal, as I am myself,' Cauvignac replied. 'Let's talk a while then, if it pleases you.'

'Would you like me to come into your boat, or would you rather get into mine, so that we can keep our boatmen away from us in the one that is left free?'

'No need, Monsieur. I suppose you speak some foreign language?'

'I do speak Spanish.'

'So do I. We'll speak in Spanish then, if that language suits you.'

'Perfectly!' the other man said, from then on using the agreed language. 'What made you reveal to the Duke d'Epernon the infidelity of the lady in question?'

'I wanted to perform a service to the noble lord and gain his approval.'

'Do you have any grudge against Mademoiselle de Lartigues?'

'Me? Not at all. I must even confess that I owe her some favours and should be most displeased if any misfortune were to befall her.'

'So is your enemy Baron de Canolles?'

'I have never met him and know him only by reputation, and, I must say, he has that of being a gallant knight and courageous gentleman.'

'So you are not acting out of hatred for anyone?'

'Pah! If I had a grudge against the Baron de Canolles, I should entreat him to blow out his brains or cut his throat with me, knowing that he is too gallant a fellow ever to refuse a duel.'

'So I should trust what you have told me?'

'I really think that is your best course.'

'Very well, do you have the letter proving the infidelity of Mademoiselle de Lartigues?'

'Here it is! With all due respect, this is the second time I have shown it to you.'

Without coming closer, the old nobleman cast a look full of sadness on the fine paper and the writing that could be seen through it. Slowly, the young man unfolded the letter.

'I suppose you recognize the writing?'

'I do.'

'Then give me the letter of attestation, and you shall have the letter.'

'In a moment. But might I ask you a question?'

'Go on,' said the young man, calmly folding the letter and returning it to his pocket.

'How did you obtain this missive?'

'I am happy to tell you.'

'Well . . . ?'

'You must surely know that the Duke d'Epernon's[4] somewhat spendthrift government caused him a great deal of trouble in Guyenne?'[5]

'Yes, carry on.'

'And you are not unaware that the horribly tight-fisted government of Monsieur de Mazarin brought him a lot of trouble in the capital?'[6]

'What do Monsieur de Mazarin and Monsieur d'Epernon have to do with this?'

'I'll tell you. Out of these two opposite forms of government came a state of affairs that is very much like a general war in which everyone takes sides. At the moment, Monsieur de Mazarin is fighting for the queen, you are fighting for the king, the coadjutor[7] is fighting for Monsieur de Beaufort,[8] Monsieur de Beaufort is fighting for Madame de Montbazon, Monsieur de La Rochefoucauld is fighting for Madame de Longueville,[9] the Duke d'Orléans[10] is fighting for Mademoiselle Soyon, the Parliament[11] is fighting for the people . . . and, finally, they have imprisoned Monsieur de Condé, who was fighting for France.[12] Now, since I have little to gain by fighting for the queen, the king, the coadjutor, Monsieur de Beaufort, Madame de Montbazon, Madame de Longueville, Mademoiselle Soyon, for the people or for France, I had an idea, which was not to take any side but to follow whichever one attracted me at any given moment. So for me it is all a question of opportunity. What do you say of my idea?'

'It's ingenious.'

'So I have mustered an army. You can see it assembled on the bank of the Dordogne.'

'Good heavens! Five men!'

'One more than you have yourself, so it would be most misplaced of you to despise them.'

'And very ill-dressed,' the old man went on. He was in a bad mood and so inclined to disparage.

'It is true,' the other man agreed, 'that they are somewhat similar to the companions of Falstaff. Let that be: Falstaff is an English gentleman of my acquaintance. But this evening they will be freshly clothed, and if you should meet them tomorrow, you will see that they are in fact fine young lads.'

'Let's talk about you. I'm not bothered about your men.'

'Very well, then. While I was fighting on my own behalf, we met the tax collector for the district who was going around from village to village, filling His Majesty's purse. As long as he had a single tax left to collect, we escorted him loyally, and, I must tell you, as I watched his money bags getting fatter and fatter, I did have a yen to join the king's side. But the devilish complexity of it all, a momentary annoyance with Monsieur de Mazarin and the complaints that we heard from all sides against the Duke d'Epernon, brought us back to our senses. We considered that there were good things, and many of them, to be said for the princes' cause,[13] and we embraced it eagerly. The tax collector ended his round in that little house that you see over there, standing on its own among the poplars and the sycamores.'

'Nanon's house,' the nobleman said. 'Yes, I can see it.'

'We waited for him to come out, followed him as we had been doing for five days, crossed the Dordogne with him a little below Saint-Michel and when we were in the middle of the river, I informed him of our political conversion and asked him, as politely as I was able, to hand over the money he was carrying. Would you believe, Monsieur, that he refused? So my companions searched him, and since he was shouting in a way that might have roused the neighbourhood, my lieutenant, a lad of considerable resource – he is the one you can see over there, with the red cloak, holding my horse by the bridle – considered that the water, since it interrupts currents of air might, by the same token, interrupt sound waves. This is a principle of physics that I understood, being a doctor, and I applauded his deduction. So, after enunciating the proposition, he bent the recalcitrant tax collector's head towards the river and held it a foot beneath the water, no more. And the tax collector did, indeed, cease to shout; or rather, one should perhaps say that we did not hear him shout. So we were able to take all the money he had, in the name of the princes, and

the correspondence with which he had been entrusted. I
gave the money to my soldiers, who as you most judiciously
remarked are in need of new equipment, and I kept the papers,
including this one. It appears that the brave tax collector was
serving as go-between for Mademoiselle de Lartigues.'

'As you say,' the old nobleman muttered. 'Unless I am
mistaken, he was one of Nanon's slaves. And what became of
the wretch?'

'Believe me, we did well to give him a ducking, this wretch,
as you call him! Had we not taken that precaution, he would
have roused the whole county. Just imagine, when we did pull
him out of the river, though he had been there no more than a
bare quarter of an hour, he was dead of apoplexy.'

'So you threw him back, I suppose?'

'As you say.'

'But if the messenger was drowned . . . ?'

'I didn't say that he was drowned.'

'Let's not quibble about words. If the messenger is dead . . .'

'Ah, now we're talking. He's quite dead.'

'Then Monsieur de Canolles will not have received the
message and will not come to the meeting.'

'One moment! I am fighting the powers that be, not individuals. Monsieur de Canolles received a duplicate of the
letter giving him the rendez-vous. However, considering that
the original manuscript might have some value, I kept it.'

'What will he think when he does not recognize the handwriting?'

'That the person who is making the assignation used the help
of a strange hand, for reasons of security.'

The stranger looked at Cauvignac with a certain admiration,
inspired by the combination of so much impudence with such
presence of mind. He was interested to see if there might not
be a way of unsettling this bold gambler.

'But what about the government? What about the investigation?' he said. 'Haven't you thought of those?'

'Investigation!' the young man repeated, with a laugh. 'Oh,
yes. Monsieur d'Epernon has nothing better to do than an
investigation. And didn't I tell you that what I did was in order

to obtain his favour? He would be very ungrateful if he did not accord it to me.'

'So, in that case, I am not quite sure,' the old nobleman remarked, 'since on your own admission you have embraced the princes' side, why you got the odd idea of wanting to be of service to Monsieur d'Epernon.'

'Nothing could be simpler. Examining the papers taken from the tax collector convinced me of the king's good intentions. His Majesty is entirely justified in my opinion, and the Duke d'Epernon is right a thousand times against his subjects. So this is the good cause, and I opted for it.'

'Here is a bandit whom I shall have hanged should he ever fall into my hands!' the old man muttered, tugging at the bristles on his moustache.

'You were saying . . . ?' asked Cauvignac, blinking under his mask.

'Nothing. Now, one more question: what will you do with the letter of attestation you have demanded?'

'Devil take me if I know! I asked for a letter of attestation because it is the most convenient, most portable and most flexible thing. I shall probably keep it for some extreme emergency, though it is possible that I shall throw it away on the first whim that enters my head. I may present it to you myself before the end of the week, or it may only return to you in three or four months with a dozen endorsements, like a bill of exchange. In any case, don't worry, I shall not misuse it to do anything that will make either of us blush. We are men of quality, after all.'

'You are a man of quality?'

'Yes, Monsieur, of the best.'

'Then I'll have him broken on the wheel,'[14] the stranger muttered to himself. 'That's what his letter of attestation will bring him.'

'Have you made up your mind to let me have the paper?' Cauvignac asked.

'I have no alternative,' said the nobleman.

'Let's be quite clear: I'm not obliging you to anything. I'm offering an exchange. You keep your paper, I'll keep mine.'

'The letter?'

'The letter of attestation?' He held out the letter in one hand, while cocking a pistol in the other.

'Put up your pistol,' the stranger said, opening his coat. 'I've got pistols of my own and ready cocked. Fair play on both sides. Here is your letter of attestation.'

The exchange of papers took place fairly and squarely, and each side examined the one that he had just been given closely, in silence and at leisure.

'Now, Monsieur,' said Cauvignac. 'Which way are you going?'

'I have to cross to the right bank of the river.'

'And I to the left bank,' Cauvignac replied.

'What are we to do? My men are on the side where you are going, and yours on the side where I am going.'

'Why, nothing could be easier. Send me my men in your boat, and I shall send you yours in mine.'

'You have a quick wit and a sharp one.'

'I should have been a general.'

'You are one.'

'Why, so I am,' said the young man. 'I'd forgotten.'

The stranger signalled to the ferryman to untie his boat and row him across to the bank opposite the one from which he had come, towards a clump of trees which extended as far as the road.

The young man, who may have been expecting some treachery, half rose so that he could watch him as he went, his hand still on the trigger of his pistol, ready to fire it at the slightest suspicious movement, but the stranger did not even deign to notice the mistrust directed at him and, turning his back on the younger man with what was either real or pretended indifference, began to read the letter, and was soon entirely absorbed in it.

'Remember the time,' said Cauvignac. 'This evening, at eight.'

The stranger did not reply and even seemed not to have heard.

'Well, well,' said Cauvignac softly to himself, stroking the butt of his pistol. 'Just think: if I wanted, I could open the way for a successor to the Governor of Guyenne and stop the civil war.[15] But with the Duke d'Epernon dead, what use would my letter of attestation be? And if the civil war were to end, how should I make a living? Quite honestly, there are times when I think I'm going mad! Long live the Duke d'Epernon and the civil war!'

'Come on, Boatman, take your oars, and let's head for the other bank. We mustn't keep this worthy lord waiting for his escort.'

A moment later, Cauvignac landed on the left bank of the Dordogne, just as the old nobleman was sending him Ferguzon and his five bandits in the boat of the Isson ferryman. He did not want to behave any less properly than the other man, so he once more ordered his boatman to take the stranger's four men in his boat and ferry them across to the other bank. In midstream, the two boats passed and saluted one another politely, then each arrived at the place where it was expected. After that, the old nobleman and his escort plunged into the thicket that stretched from the river bank to the highway, and Cauvignac, at the head of his army, took the path leading to Isson.

III

Half an hour after the scene that we have just described, the same window at Biscarros's inn that had closed so abruptly, now reopened cautiously and a young man of between sixteen and eighteen, after looking attentively to right and left, leant on his elbow on the sill of this window. He was dressed in black, with sleeves puffed around the cuff, according to the fashion of that time, while a shirt of fine embroidered cambric emerged proudly from his jerkin and fell in folds across his knee-breeches, which were puffed out with ribbons. His hand, small, elegant and chubby – a truly aristocratic hand – was impatiently crumpling a pair of suede gloves embroidered on the seams, while a pearl-grey felt hat, bending at one end under the curved weight of a magnificent blue feather, shielded his long hair, shimmering with gold, which splendidly framed an oval face, pale in colour, with pink lips and black eyebrows. It must be said, though, that this elegant ensemble, which should have made him one of the most charming young cavaliers imaginable, was slightly overshadowed at the moment by an ill-tempered look, caused no doubt by waiting in vain, because the young man was peering into the distance along a road already starting to disappear into the gloom of evening.

In his impatience, he was tapping his left hand with his gloves. At the noise, the innkeeper, who was completing the task of plucking his partridge, looked up and said, taking off his cap: 'What time will you take supper, sir? We are only awaiting your word before serving you.'

'You know very well that I shall not be supping alone, and that I am waiting for a friend,' he replied. 'When you see him arrive, then you can serve us.'

'Ah, Monsieur,' Biscarros replied, 'I have no wish to criticize your friend, who is surely free to come or not as he pleases, but it is a very bad habit to keep people waiting.'

'It's not one of his habits, though, and I'm surprised by the delay.'

'And I am more than surprised, Monsieur, I am distressed by it: the roast will burn.'

'Take it off the spit.'

'Then it will be cold.'

'So put on another in its place.'

'It won't be done in time.'

'In that case, my friend, do as you will,' said the young man, unable despite his annoyance to repress a smile at the innkeeper's despair. 'I must leave it all up to your supreme wisdom.'

'There is no wisdom,' the innkeeper replied, 'not even the wisdom of Solomon, that can make a reheated dinner fit to eat.'

At this maxim which, some twenty years later, Boileau would put in verse,[16] Master Biscarros returned to his inn, sadly shaking his head.

At that, the young man, as though to calm his impatience, went back into the room, his boots clattering for a moment on the floor; then, thinking that he heard the sound of horses' hooves in the distance, quickly went back to the window, exclaiming: 'At last! Here he is! Thank heaven!'

The young man did indeed see the head of a rider appear behind the clump of trees in which the nightingale was singing – though, doubtless because his mind was so much taken up with other matters, had paid no attention to its melodious notes – but to his great astonishment, he waited in vain for the rider to come out on to the road; the new arrival turned right and entered the bushes, where his hat soon vanished from view, a clear sign than he had dismounted. A moment after this, the young man saw the leaves parted cautiously and, between them, a grey paletot,[17] and the flash of one of the last rays of the setting sun on the barrel of a musket.

The young man remained at his window, deep in thought. Clearly, this rider hidden in the bushes was not the friend for whom he had been waiting, and the look of impatience that had furrowed his expressive features gave way to one of curiosity.

Very soon, a second hat appeared in the bend of the road, and the young man stepped back out of sight.

The same grey coat, the same manoeuvre with the horse and the same shining musket; the second man said a few words to the first that our observer could not hear because of the distance, and, no doubt in response to the information provided by his companion, he made his way into the copse opposite the clump of trees, dismounted, hid behind a rock and waited.

From his high vantage point, the young man could see the felt hat above the rock and beside it a glistening point of light: this was the end of the musket barrel.

A vague feeling of terror crossed the mind of the young gentleman, who was moving further and further out of sight as he watched the scene.

'Now, now,' he wondered. 'Can they be after me and the thousand louis[18] that I am carrying? Surely not, because if Richon does arrive and I am able to set off this evening, I shall be going to Libourne and not to Saint-André-de-Cubzac, so

I shall not be going towards where these fellows are waiting. If only my old Pompée were here, I'd ask him. But, if I'm not mistaken ... yes, by Jove! Two more men are coming. Huh! This looks to me very much like an ambush.'

And he took a further step backwards.

At that moment, two other riders appeared at the same high point in the road, but this time only one was wearing a grey jacket; the other, riding a powerful black steed and wrapped in a great cloak, had a hat trimmed with braid and decorated with a white feather, and under his cloak, where it was lifted by the evening breeze, you could see rich embroidery winding across an orange-red jerkin.

It was as though the day had lingered to illuminate this scene, because the last rays of the sun, bursting through one of those banks of black cloud that sometimes spread along the horizon in such a picturesque manner, suddenly cast the light of a thousand rubies on the windows of a pretty house standing some hundred yards from the river – a house that, otherwise, the young man would not have noticed, since it was hidden among the branches of some densely planted trees. This burst of light let him see first of all that the faces of the spies were turning alternately towards the entrance of the village and the little house with the shining windows; secondly, that the grey paletots seemed to have the greatest respect for the white feather, doffing their caps to it whenever they spoke; and finally that one of the illuminated windows was open, and a woman appeared on the balcony, leant out for a moment, as though she, too, were waiting for somebody, then shrank quickly back inside, no doubt afraid of being seen.

As she went back inside, the sun was dipping beneath the mountain, and as it did so the ground floor of the house seemed to be sinking into darkness, the light gradually leaving the windows, climbing the slate roof and finally disappearing, after having played for one final moment over a bunch of golden arrows that served as a weathervane.

Any thinking person had here a number of signs on the basis of which one might establish, if not certainties, at least some probabilities.

It is probable that the men were watching the little, solitary house, on the balcony of which the woman had momentarily made her appearance. It was also probable that this woman and those men were waiting for one and the same person, but with very different intentions. Meanwhile, it was also probable that the person for whom they were waiting was to come through the village and consequently pass in front of the inn which was situated halfway between the village and the clump of trees, just as the clump of trees was situated halfway between the inn and the house. Finally, it was likely that the rider with the white feather was the leader of the mounted men with the grey cloaks and that, by his keenness as he rose in his stirrups to see further, this leader was jealous and certainly interested on his own account in keeping watch.

Just as the young man had mentally reached the last in this chain of arguments, the door of his room opened, and Biscarros came in.

'My dear chap,' said the young man, for whom the inn-keeper's entrance was most convenient, not giving Biscarros time to explain why he had come (which the young man guessed, in any case). 'Come here and tell me, if the question is not indiscreet, who is the owner of that little house you can see over there, like a white dot among the poplars and the sycamores?'

The innkeeper looked in the direction the young man was pointing and scratched his forehead.

'Why, sometimes this one, at others that,' he said, with what he tried to make into a scornful smile. 'It could be yours, if you had some reason to seek solitude, either because you wanted to hide there yourself, or because you wanted to hide someone else.'

The young man blushed. 'But who is living there now?' he asked.

'A young lady who claims to be a widow, to whom the shades of her first, and perhaps also of her second husband return for the occasional visit. However, there is one remarkable thing, which is that the two ghosts must have an agreement among themselves, because they never return at the same time.'

'And for how long,' the young man asked with a smile, 'has the lovely widow inhabited this lonely house, so convenient for apparitions?'

'For about two months. But she keeps herself to herself, and no one in those two months, I think, can boast of having seen her, because she rarely comes out, and when she does, she wears a veil. A little maid, who is a quite delightful girl, comes here every morning to order the meals of the day from me. They are sent over, and she takes the dishes in the hall, settles the bill generously and immediately shuts the door in the waiter's face. This evening, now, there is a feast, and it is for her that I was preparing the quails and partridges which you saw me plucking.'

'And with whom is she sharing her dinner?'

'Presumably with one of the two shades I told you about.'

'Have you occasionally seen these two shades?'

'Yes, but only as they went past, in the evening when the sun had set or in the morning before it had risen.'

'I am certain, nonetheless, that you must have noticed them, my dear Master Biscarros, because one can tell by talking to you that you are an observer. Now, tell me, what have you noticed particularly in the appearance of these two shades?'

'One is that of a man aged between sixty and sixty-five, and it looks to me like that of the first husband, because it comes like a shade convinced of the primacy of its rights. The other belongs to a young man of between twenty-six and twenty-eight, and I have to say this one is more shy and looks just like a tormented soul. This is why I would swear that it belongs to the second husband.'

'And what time have you been ordered to serve supper this evening?'

'At eight.'

'It is half past seven,' the young man says, taking a very pretty watch, that he had already glanced at several times, out of his fob pocket. 'Which means you have no time to lose.'

'Oh, don't you worry, it will be ready. But I came up here to talk to you about your own supper and to tell you that I have just begun it again from scratch. So please, would you now try to ensure, since your friend has managed to arrive so late, that he doesn't come until an hour from now.'

'Listen, my good fellow,' the young gentleman said, with the air of a man for whom this serious matter of a meal served at the correct time was only a secondary consideration, 'don't bother yourself about our supper, even when the person whom I am expecting arrives, because we have to talk. If the supper is not ready, we shall talk before dining, and if it is ready, we shall talk afterwards.'

'Indeed, sir,' the innkeeper said, 'you are a most accommodating gentleman, and since you are prepared to leave yourself in my hands, you will be pleased, don't worry.'

At this, Master Biscarros bowed deeply, before leaving. The young man replied with a slight nod.

'Now, I understand everything,' the young man said to himself, resuming his place at the window, with some curiosity. 'The lady is waiting for someone coming from Libourne, and the men in the shrubbery intend to attack the visitor before he has time to knock on the door.'

At the same time, and as though to justify our sharp-witted observer's prediction, there was the beat of a horse's hooves coming from his left. Swift as lightning, the young man's eyes swept the undergrowth to see the response of the ambushers. Although nightfall was making it hard to distinguish objects in the darkness, he thought that he could make out some of them pushing aside the branches and others raising themselves to look over the top of the rocks, both groups apparently preparing for a move that had every appearance of aggression. Meanwhile, three times he heard a dry click, like the sound of a musket being cocked, his heart leaping at each one. He quickly turned towards Libourne in an attempt to see the person who was threatened by this deadly noise and saw a handsome young man trotting along on a fine, strapping horse, his head held high, with a triumphant manner and one hand resting on his hip, his short cloak lined in white satin elegantly open to reveal his right shoulder. From a distance, the figure seemed debonair, full of gentle poetry and joyous pride. As he drew closer, one noticed the fine features, high colour, burning eye and mouth half-open from its habit of smiling, with exquisite white teeth beneath a delicate black moustache. The triumphant twirling of a switch of holly and a little whistle such as those affected by the dandies of the time, made fashionable by Monsieur Gaston d'Orléans,[19] completed the picture, making the new arrival a 'parfit gentil knight' according to the laws of good taste in force at the time in the French court, which was already starting to set the fashion for all the courts of Europe.

Fifty yards behind him, riding a mount whose pace he adjusted to that of his master's, was a very showy, very arrogant-looking lackey whose place among domestic servants seemed no less distinguished than that of his master among the gentry.

The handsome young man at the window of the inn was probably still too young to stand idly by and witness the kind of scene that was unfolding here, so could not repress a shudder when he thought that these two fine specimens, who were approaching so light-heartedly and so full of self-assurance, were in all likelihood about to be mown down when they reached the waiting ambush. He appeared to fight a brief inner battle between the shyness natural to his age and a feeling of love for his fellow men. In the end, it was this generous feeling that won the day, and, as the rider was about to pass in front of the door of the inn without even turning his head, the young man gave way to a sudden impulse and irresistible determination and leant forward, calling out to the handsome traveller: 'Hey, Monsieur! Stop, I beg you! I have something important to tell you.'

At this voice and these words, the horseman looked up and, seeing the young man at the window, halted his mount with a hand movement that would have done credit to the finest riding instructor.

'Don't stop your horse, Monsieur,' the young man went on, 'but on the contrary ride over towards me calmly, as though you knew me.'

The traveller hesitated for an instant, but seeing that the young man addressing him was a well-presented, good-looking person of gentle birth, he took off his hat and came over with a smile.

'I have done as you said, Monsieur,' he remarked. 'Now, how can I serve you?'

'Come a little closer still,' the stranger at the window went on, 'because what I have to tell you cannot be said in a loud voice. And put your hat back on, because people must believe that we have known each other for a long time and that I am the person you are coming to see in this inn.'

'But, Monsieur, I don't understand . . .' said the traveller.

'You will very soon. Meanwhile, put your hat on. Good, now come closer, closer . . . Give me your hand! That's right! Delighted to see you! Now, do not go beyond this inn, or you are lost.'

'What's the matter? What you say is most alarming,' the traveller remarked, with a smile.

'The matter is that you are going to that little house where the light is burning, are you not?'

The rider sat up.

'. . . But on the way to that house, there, where the road bends, in that dark thicket, there are four men waiting in ambush for you.'

'So!' said the rider, staring hard at the pale young man. 'So, really! Are you sure of this?'

'I saw them coming one after the other, dismounting and hiding, some behind the trees and some behind the rocks. And then, when you emerged from the village just now, I heard them cocking their muskets.'

'Well, now!' said the rider, who was himself starting to feel alarmed.

'Yes, Monsieur, it is as I said,' the young man in the grey hat continued. 'If it was a little lighter, you might be able to see them and recognize them.'

'Oh, I don't need to recognize them,' said the traveller. 'I'm perfectly aware of who they are. But who told you that I was going to that house and that I am the person for whom this ambush was laid?'

'I guessed . . .'

'You are a delightful Oedipus,[20] thank you. So, they want to shoot me . . . And how many of them are there to carry out this mission?'

'Four, one of them apparently the leader.'

'This leader is older than the rest, isn't he?'

'Yes, as far as I can judge from here.'

'Stooping?'

'Round-shouldered, with white feather, embroidered jerkin, brown cloak – a man of few gestures, but a commanding manner.'

'Precisely. It's the Duke d'Epernon.'

'The Duke d'Epernon!'[21] the young man exclaimed.

'Ah, now I'm telling you my business,' said the traveller, with a laugh. 'That's the way I am, but no matter. You're doing me a great enough service for me not to be over nice about such matters. And what were the men with him wearing?'

'Grey cloaks.'

'Exactly, those are his stave bearers.'

'Who have today become musket bearers.'

'By my honour, I am most obliged to you. Now, do you know what you should do, my young sir?'

'No, but please tell me, and if what I should do can be of service to you, I have already agreed to it.'

'Do you have any weapons?'

'Yes, I have my sword.'

'And do you have a servant with you?'

'Of course, but not here. I sent him to meet someone I am expecting.'

'Well, you should give me a hand.'

'To do what?'

'To attack those wretches and make them and their leader plead for mercy.'

'Are you mad, Monsieur?' the young man exclaimed, in a tone that suggested he was far from inclined to join such an adventure.

'Of course, I apologize,' said the traveller. 'I was forgetting that the affair does not at all concern you.' Then, turning towards his servant, who seeing his master stop had done the same, while keeping his distance, 'Castorin,' he said. 'Come here.'

At the same time he felt the holsters on his saddle, as though making sure that his pistols were in good order.

'Monsieur, no!' the young man cried, reaching out as though to restrain him. 'In heaven's name, don't risk your life in such a venture. Why not come into the inn, to avoid arousing any suspicion in the person waiting for you. Remember, a woman's honour is at stake.'

'You are right,' said the horseman. 'Though in this particular case it is not precisely a matter of honour, but of fortune. Castorin, my friend,' he went on, addressing the servant who had ridden up to him. 'We shall not go any further for the time being.'

'What!' Castorin exclaimed, almost as disappointed as his master. 'What is Monsieur saying exactly?'

'I am saying that Mademoiselle Francinette will be denied the pleasure of seeing you this evening, since we are spending the night at the inn of the Golden Calf. So, go inside, order some supper for me and have a bed made up.'

Since the horseman must have noticed that Castorin was preparing to reply, he accompanied these last words with a nod that showed he would have no further discussion. So Castorin vanished through the main door, with his tail between his legs, not daring to hazard a single word.

The traveller briefly looked after Castorin, then with a moment's reflection, seemed to make up his mind, dismounted and followed his servant through the main gate, throwing him the reins of his horse, and in two bounds he was in the young man's room. The other, seeing his door suddenly flung open, gave a start of surprise and fear, which the new arrival could not see in the darkness.

'So, now,' said the traveller, merrily walking over to the young man and heartily shaking a hand that had not been offered to him. 'It's a fact: I owe you my life.'

'Monsieur, you are exaggerating the service I have done you,' said the young man, stepping back.

'No, let's not be modest: it's as I said. I know the duke, he's

a savage devil. As for you, you are a model of perspicacity
and a phoenix of Christian kindness. But tell me, since you're
such a good fellow and so compassionate, did you oblige us so
far as to tell them in the house?'

'What house is that?'

'Why, the one where I was going! The house where I'm
expected.'

'No,' said the young man. 'I didn't think of that, I confess,
and even if I had, I should not have had the means to do it.
I have been here for barely two hours myself, and I don't know
anyone in that house.'

'Damnation!' said the traveller, with an anxious frown. 'Poor
Nanon! I hope nothing happens to her.'

'Nanon! Nanon de Lartigues!' the young man cried in
astonishment.

'Well, I never! You really are a sorcerer!' said the traveller.
'You see men in ambush on the road, and you guess whom they
hope to ambush. I tell you a Christian name, and you guess the
family name. Explain this to me at once, or I shall denounce
you and have you burned at the stake by the parliament of
Bordeaux.'[22]

'Now this time you have to agree,' the young man said, 'that
it did not take much to find you out. Once you had named the
Duke d'Epernon as your rival, it was obvious that, when you
mentioned a Nanon, it must be that same Nanon de Lartigues,
who, they say, is so beautiful, so rich and so witty that the duke
is enchanted by her, and she governs in his stead, with the result
that throughout Guyenne she is almost as hated as he is . . .
And you are going to this woman?' the young man said,
reproachfully.

'Yes, I am. I admit it. And since I have named her, I shall not
retract. In any case, Nanon is misunderstood and slandered.
She is a charming girl, entirely faithful to her word, whenever
it pleases her to keep it, and utterly devoted to those she loves,
while she loves them. I was to have dined with her this evening,
but the duke has knocked over the pot. Should you like it if
I were to present you to her tomorrow? After all, heaven knows,
the duke must go back to Agen some time or other.'

'Thank you,' the young man said dryly. 'I only know Mademoiselle de Lartigues by name and have no wish to know her otherwise.'

'You're wrong there, I promise you. Nanon is a young woman who is worth knowing in every conceivable way.'

The young man raised an eyebrow.

'Oh, forgive me,' said the traveller, in astonishment. 'I thought that at your age . . .'

'Of course, my age is one at which people normally accept such a proposal,' the young man went on, seeing that his sense of propriety had not gone down well. 'And I should accept it gladly were I not merely passing through here and obliged to continue on my journey tonight.'

'My goodness! At least you won't leave without letting me know the name of the noble knight who so gallantly saved my life.'

The young man appeared to hesitate a moment before replying: 'I am the Viscount de Cambes.'

'Ah, ha!' the other man said. 'I've heard speak of a charming Viscountess de Cambes who owns a large estate all around Bordeaux and who is a friend of the princess.'[23]

'She is a relative of mine,' the young man said quickly.

'Well, then, I congratulate you, Viscount, because she is said to be amazing. I hope that if chance should favour me in this respect, you will introduce me to her. I am the Baron de Canolles, captain in Navailles, at present on leave of absence, which the Duke d'Epernon was good enough to grant me on the recommendation of Mademoiselle de Lartigues.'

'Baron de Canolles!' the viscount exclaimed, looking at the other with all the curiosity aroused by a man whose name was celebrated at the time for his love affairs.

'Do you know me?' asked Canolles.

'Only by reputation.'

'And ill repute, I have no doubt. Too bad! Everyone follows his own bent, and I like an exciting life.'

'Monsieur, you are perfectly free to live however you wish,' said the viscount. 'But would you allow me to make one observation?'

'And what may that be?'

'Only that we have here a woman who is terribly compromised because of you and on whom the duke will take revenge for his disappointment where you are concerned.'

'Damnation! Do you think so?'

'Of course. Even though she is a ... loose ... woman, Mademoiselle de Lartigues is a woman for all that, and one who has been compromised by you. So it is your duty to ensure her safety.'

'You are quite right, my young Nestor,[24] and the delight of your conversation was making me forget my duties as a gentleman. We must have been betrayed, and in all probability the duke knows everything. It is true that had Nanon been warned, she is clever, and I should rely on her to beg the duke's pardon. Now, then, let's see: do you know about war, young man?'

'Not yet,' the viscount replied, smiling. 'But I think that I shall be learning about it where I am going.'

'Well, here is a first lesson. You know that in wartime, when force is ineffectual, one must use guile. So help me to do so.'

'I ask nothing better. Just tell me how.'

'The inn has two doors.'

'I don't know anything about that.'

'I do: one door leads out to the main road and the other to the fields. I shall go out through the latter, make a half circle and knock at Nanon's house, which also has a door at the back.'

'Yes, and then let yourself be discovered in her house!' said the viscount. 'A fine tactician you are, I must say.'

'Be discovered?' said Canolles.

'Of course. The duke, when he gets tired of waiting and does not see you come out of here, will go back to the house.'

'Perhaps, but all I shall do is to go in and out.'

'Once you are inside ... you won't come out.'

'Young man,' said Canolles, 'you most definitely are a magician.'

'You will be discovered and killed in front of her, that's all.'

'Pooh!' said Canolles. 'There are wardrobes.'

'Oh!' said the viscount. And this *Oh!* was said in such a way, in such a meaningful tone of voice, suggesting so many unspoken reproaches, so much outraged modesty and such tactful delicacy, that Canolles stopped short and, despite the darkness, stared hard at the young person in front of him leaning against the window sill.

The viscount felt the full weight of this stare and carried on in a more bantering tone: 'Actually, Baron, you are right. Go on, but hide yourself well, so that you are not discovered.'

'No, no, I was wrong, and you are right,' said Canolles. 'But how can I let her know?'

'I would have thought that a letter . . .'

'Who will deliver it?'

'I thought I saw a servant with you. In these circumstances, a lackey only risks a beating, while a gentleman is at risk of his life.'

'Decidedly, I must be out of my mind,' said Canolles. 'Castorin will do the job perfectly – and all the more so since I suspect the rascal of having some secret contacts inside the house.'

'So you see, everything can be arranged here,' said the viscount.

'Yes. Do you have some ink, paper and pens?'

'No,' said the viscount, 'but there are some downstairs.'

'Excuse me,' said Canolles. 'I really do not know what is wrong with me this evening, I am saying one stupid thing after another. No matter! Thank you, Viscount, for your good advice which I shall follow immediately.'

And Canolles, still staring at the young man, whom he had been studying very closely for the last few moments, crossed to the door and went down the staircase, while the viscount, uneasy, almost anxious, was muttering: 'How he looked at me! Can he have recognized me?'

Meanwhile, Canolles had reached the ground floor and, after looking with deep distress at the quails, partridge and delicacies that Biscarros was personally loading into the wicker tray on the head of his assistant chef – delicacies that another than himself might perhaps enjoy, even though they were certainly intended for him – Canolles asked for the room that should have been prepared for him by Castorin, had ink, pens and paper brought there to him, and wrote the following letter to Nanon:

Dear lady,

If Nature has endowed you with the ability to see in the dark, you will be able to observe the Duke d'Epernon some hundred yards from your door in a clump of bushes, where he is waiting to have me shot and subsequently to compromise you most horribly. However, I have no desire either to lose my life or for you to lose your peace of mind. So stay where you are and in peace. As for me, I am going to make use of the leave of absence that you had me obtain the other day so that I might take advantage of my freedom to come and see you. Where I am going, I know not, or even if I am going somewhere. However that may be, remember your fugitive when the storm is past. They will tell you at the Golden Calf what road I took. I hope that you will appreciate the sacrifice I am making. But your interests are dearer to me than my own pleasure. I say my pleasure, because I should have had some enjoyment in thrashing Monsieur d'Epernon and his henchmen in their disguise. So, dear lady, believe me to be your most devoted and, above all, most faithful servant . . .

Canolles signed this letter, bubbling with Gascon bravado, knowing the effect it would have on the Gascon, Nanon. Then, calling his servant, he said: 'Come here, Castorin, and tell me candidly how things stand between you and Mademoiselle Francinette.'

'But, Monsieur,' Castorin replied, quite amazed at the question. 'I don't know if I should . . .'

'Calm down, booby, I have no designs on her, and you do not have the honour to be my rival. All that I'm asking is for some simple information.'

'Ah, well, in that case it's different. Mademoiselle Francinette has been intelligent enough to appreciate my qualities.'

'So you are well in there, are you, you dog? Excellent. Then you can take this letter and go through the meadow.'

'I know the way, Monsieur,' Castorin said smugly.

'Right. Then go and knock on the back door. You also know the door in question, I suppose?'

'Indeed, I do.'

'Better and better. So go by that way, knock on that door and give this letter to Mademoiselle Francinette.'

'In that case, Monsieur,' said Castorin, in delight, 'I can . . .'

'You can leave at once, you have ten minutes to go there and back. This letter must be given to Mademoiselle Nanon de Lartigues without delay.'

'But, Monsieur,' said Castorin, sensing some impending disaster, 'what if they do not open the door to me?'

'You will be an idiot, because you must have some special way of knocking so that a suitor is not left out in the cold. If not, I am a very unfortunate man for having such a good-for-nothing as you in my employ.'

'I do have one, Monsieur,' said Castorin, with a mighty swagger. 'First I give two equally spaced knocks, then a third . . .'

'I'm not asking you to tell me how you knock – it doesn't matter as long as they open to you. Go on, and if anyone surprises you, eat the paper, or else I shall cut off your ears when you get back, unless it has already been done for me.'

Castorin was off in a flash. But when he reached the bottom of the stairs, he stopped and, contrary to every instruction, slipped the letter into the top of his boot; then, going out through the door into the yard and taking a long way round, breaking through the bushes like a fox and leaping the ditches like a greyhound, he reached the door and knocked on it in the way that he had tried to explain to his master, to such effect that it opened at once.

Ten minutes later, Castorin was back without any mishap and announced to his master that the letter had been placed in the lovely hands of Mademoiselle Nanon.

Canolles had spent the intervening ten minutes opening his portmanteau, getting out his dressing gown and having his table set up. He listened with visible satisfaction to Castorin's report and went to look at the kitchen, giving his orders for the night out loud and yawning excessively, like a man who is impatiently waiting until he can go to bed. The aim of this pantomime was, in case the Duke d'Epernon should be having him watched, to let him know that the baron's intention had always been to go no further than the inn, to which he had come, as a simple and harmless traveller, to seek his supper and a bed for the night. And this plan did indeed have the effect that the baron had intended, because a kind of peasant, who was drinking in a dark corner of the room, called the waiter, paid his bill, got up and left discreetly, while humming a little tune. Canolles followed him to the door and saw him walk towards the clump of trees. Ten minutes later, he heard the sound of several horses riding away: the ambush had been lifted.

So the baron went back inside, and with his mind at rest where Nanon was concerned, had no thought except to spend the evening in the most entertaining manner possible. For this reason he ordered Castorin to prepare some cards and dice and, once this was done, to go and ask the Viscount de Cambes if he would do him the honour of receiving him.

Castorin obeyed and, at the entrance to the room, found an elderly groom with grey hair, who was holding the door half open and replied in a very surly manner when he presented his compliments.

'Impossible just now, the viscount is busy.'

'Very well,' said Canolles. 'I shall wait.'

And since he could hear a lot of noise coming from the direction of the kitchen, he went to pass the time and see what was going on in that important part of the house.

It was the poor scullery boy, coming back more dead than alive. At the bend in the road he had been stopped by four men, who had questioned him about the purpose of his nocturnal walk and who, learning that he was going to take supper to the woman in the isolated house, had divested him of his chef's hat, his white jacket and his apron. The youngest of the four men had then put on the badges of his profession, balanced the basket on his head and continued, in the young cook's stead,

towards the little house. Ten minutes later he had returned and
spoken in an undertone to the man who seemed to be the leader
of the troop. Then he gave the boy back his jacket, hat and
apron, planted the basket on his head and gave him a kick up
the backside to send him in the right direction. The poor devil
asked nothing better than to continue on his way. He set off at
a run and arrived almost dead with fright in the doorway of
the inn, where they had come to retrieve him.

This adventure was quite incomprehensible to everyone
except Canolles, but since he had no reason to explain it, he
left the innkeeper, waiters, servants, cook and scullery boy to
make their own conjectures, and, while they were hunting
around as best they could, he went up to the viscount's room,
where, assuming that the first enquiry that he had made through
Castorin had removed the need for any further request of the
same kind, he opened the door and walked straight in.

A well-lit table with two places set was standing in the middle
of the room and waiting only for the dishes of food to complete
it. Canolles observed these two places and drew a happy conclusion from them.

The viscount, however, on seeing him, leapt so abruptly to
his feet that it was easy to see that he had been surprised by his
visitor and that it was not for himself, as Canolles had at first
assumed, that the second place was intended. This suspicion
was confirmed by the first words that the viscount addressed
to him.

'Might I ask, Baron,' the young man said, coming over and
greeting him stiffly, 'to what new circumstance I owe the honour
of your visit?'

'To a very natural one,' Canolles replied, somewhat miffed
by this discourteous reception. 'Hunger overcame me, and I
thought that it might have affected you as well. You are alone,
I am alone, and I wanted to have the honour of suggesting that
you dine with me.'

The viscount looked at Canolles with evident mistrust and
seemed to be at a loss to reply.

'On my honour!' Canolles exclaimed with a laugh. 'Anyone
would think you were afraid of me ... Are you a Knight of

Malta, by any chance? Are you destined for the Church or has your respectable family brought you up with a horror of the Canolles? Come, now, you won't be damned for an hour spent together with me on different sides of a table.'

'I can't possibly come to your room, Baron.'

'Well, then, don't. And as I've come to yours . . .'

'Still less possible, I'm afraid. I am expecting someone.'

This time it was Canolles's turn to be thrown off balance.

'Oh! You're expecting someone?'

'Yes.'

'My goodness,' said Canolles, after a moment's silence. 'I swear, I would almost rather that you had let me continue on my way and take the risk of whatever might happen than to spoil the favour that you did me, and for which I thought I had not thanked you enough, by this repugnance that you are showing towards me.'

The young man blushed and came over to Canolles.

'Please forgive me, Monsieur,' he said, his voice trembling. 'I realize how rude I have been. If it were not a matter of serious business, of family business that I have to discuss with the person for whom I am waiting, it would be both an honour and a pleasure for me to invite you to join us, although . . .'

'Enough!' said Canolles. 'Whatever you say, I have decided that I shall not get angry with you.'

'Although,' the young man continued, 'our acquaintance is one of those unexpected matters of chance, one of those accidental meetings, those brief encounters . . .'

'Why should that be?' asked Canolles. 'On the contrary, this is how a long and sincere friendship starts: one has only to see the hand of Providence in what you attribute to chance.'

'Monsieur,' the viscount answered with a laugh, 'Providence has decided that I should leave in two hours and that in all probability I shall be taking the opposite direction to yours. So please accept my regret at not being able to respond as I should wish to this offer of friendship, which you have so warmly made and which I appreciate at its true worth.'

'My word,' said Canolles, 'you certainly are an unusual lad and to begin with your generous impulse gave me a quite different idea of your character. But after all let it be as you wish: I have no right to make any demands on you, since I am the one who is obligated to you, and you have done far more for me than I had any reason to expect from a stranger. So, I shall go back and take supper alone, though I have to admit, Viscount, that I don't like it. I'm not used to monologues.'

And, in reality, despite what Canolles had said and his expressed determination to leave, he did not do so. Something kept him rooted to the spot, something of which he was almost unaware. He felt overwhelmingly attracted to the viscount. But the young man picked up a torch and, taking it to Canolles, said with a charming smile and offering his hand: 'Monsieur, however things may be and however short our acquaintance, please believe that I am delighted to have been of some service to you.'

Canolles heard only the compliment. He grasped the hand that the viscount offered him, but which, instead of replying to his friendly, masculine pressure, shrank back, warm and trembling. Then, realizing that, though it had been wrapped up in a flattering phrase, the young man's dismissal of him was nonetheless a dismissal, he withdrew, disappointed and, above all, thoughtful.

At the door he met the toothless grin of the old valet, who took the torch from the viscount's hands, conducted Canolles with much ceremony back to his apartment and straightaway went back to his master who was waiting at the top of the stairs.

'What is he doing?' the viscount whispered.

'I think he has decided to sup alone,' Pompée replied.

'So he will not come back up?'

'I hope not.'

'Order the horses, Pompée – we shall save that much time at least. But what's that noise?' the viscount added, listening attentively.

'It sounds like the voice of Monsieur Richon.'

'And that of Monsieur de Canolles.'

'I think they are arguing.'

'No, quite the contrary, they know one another – listen . . .'

'As long as Richon keeps quiet about everything.'

'Oh, don't worry about that. He is a very cautious man.'

'Hush!'

The two listeners stopped talking and they heard Canolles shouting. 'Two places, Master Biscarros! Two places! Monsieur Richon is going to sup with me.'

'No, no,' said Richon. 'Please, I can't.'

'Why on earth not? Do you want to dine alone, like the young gentleman?'

'What gentleman?'

'The one upstairs.'

'What is his name?'

'The Viscount de Cambes.'

'Do you know the viscount, then?'

'Huh! He saved my life.'

'He did?'

'Yes, he did.'

'How was that?'

'Take supper with me, and I'll tell you about it while we are eating.'

'I can't. I'm due to sup with him.'

'Yes, he said he was waiting for someone.'

'That was me and as I am late, Baron, you will be good enough to let me go.'

'No, I won't! I forbid it!' Canolles exclaimed. 'I've got it into my head that I am going to have company for dinner, so you will eat with me and I with you. Biscarros! Two places!'

But while Canolles was turning round to see if the order was being carried out, Richon set off rapidly up the staircase. When he reached the top stair, his hand met another, small hand, which led him into the Viscount de Cambes's room. The door was shut behind him, and, to make assurance doubly sure, the two locks ensured that it would not be opened.

'Well, I never,' Canolles muttered, looking in vain for the vanished Richon, then sitting down alone at the table. 'I really don't know what they have against me in this accursed country. One lot of them are chasing after me to kill me, while the others are fleeing from me as though I had the plague. Confound it!

I'm losing my appetite. I can feel a sadness coming over me, and I might well get as drunk as a coachman this evening ... Hey, there, Castorin, come here and let me beat you!

'They're locking themselves in up there as though they were hatching a conspiracy. Oh! What a numbskull I am! Of course, they are conspiring! That's it: it explains everything. Now, on whose behalf are they conspiring? For the coadjutor? For the princes? For the Parliament? For the king? For the queen? For Monsieur de Mazarin? Dammit, let them conspire against whoever they wish, I couldn't care less. My appetite has returned.

'Castorin, order my supper and pour me some wine. I forgive you.'

Philosophically, Canolles got to work on the first supper that had been prepared for the Viscount de Cambes, and which, having no further provisions, Master Biscarros was obliged to serve up to him reheated.

IV

While the Baron de Canolles was searching in vain for someone to dine with him and, exhausted by his fruitless endeavours, was finally resigning himself to supping alone, let us see what was going on at Nanon's.

Nanon, whatever may have been written and said about her by her enemies – and most of the historians who have written about her must be counted in that number – was at this time a charming creature of between twenty-five and twenty-six years old, small in height and dark-skinned, but with a supple, gracious manner, bright, fresh colouring and deep, dark eyes whose limpid corneas sparkled, like those of cats, with fire and light. Despite being superficially light-hearted and apparently cheerful, Nanon was far from being carried away by all the whims and frivolity that usually weave such baroque embellishments into the richly gilded pattern that makes up the life of a fashionable young woman. On the contrary, the most serious meditations, matured and long weighed in her mischievous head,

acquired an appearance that was at once full of charm and
lucidity when they emerged in the vibrant tones of her voice,
with its strong Gascon accent. No one would have guessed at
the tireless persistence, the concealed tenacity and the states-
manlike understanding that lay behind this pink mask, with its
fine, smiling features, and this look, full of voluptuous promise
and sparkling with passion. Yet these were Nanon's qualities –
or her defects, depending on whether one chooses to look at
the head or the reverse of the medal: this was the calculating
mind and the ambitious heart beneath the outer covering of a
most elegant body.

Nanon came from Agen.[25] This petite bourgeoise, daughter
of a country lawyer, had been raised in station by the Duke
d'Epernon, son of that inseparable friend of Henri IV,[26] who
was in the king's carriage at the moment when Ravaillac's knife
struck him and who was the object of suspicions that extended
even to Catherine de' Médicis.[27] The Duke d'Epernon himself
had been appointed Governor of Guyenne, where his arrogance, his haughty manners and his oppressive rule had made
him generally loathed; he had courted Nanon, only triumphing
in his suit with great difficulty and against a defence that had
been conducted with the skills of a great tactician, who wishes
to make her conqueror feel the full cost of his victory. As the
price of her already lost reputation, Nanon had deprived the
duke of his power and his freedom. Six months into her affair
with the Governor of Guyenne, it was she who in reality governed that lovely province, repaying with interest the wrongs
and insults that she had received to all those who had previously
wronged her or slighted her. Queen by chance, she became a
tyrant by design, anticipating with her fine understanding that
she would have to compensate by exploitation for the probable
brevity of her reign.

For that reason, she seized everything: wealth, influence and
honours. She became rich, appointed officials, received visits
from Mazarin[28] and the leading nobles at court. Showing admirable skill in deploying all the assets that she possessed, she
combined them into a whole that was to the advantage of his
name and profitable to her purse. Every service that Nanon did

was assessed at its own value. A rank in the army or an office in the judiciary each had their price: Nanon arranged for the rank or the job to be granted and was paid for them in coin of the realm or by a splendid, regal present. In this way, while relinquishing a fraction of her power to someone's benefit, she recovered the fraction in a different form, granting the authority, while keeping the money that is its sinew.

This explains the length of her reign, because however much they may hate, men are reluctant to overthrow an enemy who will be left with a consolation. What vengeance craves is total ruin and utter prostration. A nation is loath to drive away a tyrant who will take its gold and quit it with a laugh. Nanon de Lartigues was a millionaire twice over!

In this way, she lived with some kind of security on the volcano that was constantly rocking everything around her. She had felt popular anger rising like a tide, its waves swelling and beating against the power of Monsieur d'Epernon, who, driven out of Bordeaux in a moment of rage, had towed Nanon with him as the ship tows its bumboat. Nanon bent to the wind, ready to rise again when the storm was over; she took Monsieur de Mazarin as her model and at a distance adopted the policies of the clever and pragmatic Italian like an obedient pupil. The cardinal noticed this woman, who was rising in society and becoming rich by the same means that had made him a prime minister and the owner of fifty million in gold. He admired the little Gascon girl; more than that, he let her be. Later we may learn why.

In spite of all this, and though there were some who claimed to be better informed and who said that she was in direct correspondence with Mazarin, there was little gossip about the political intrigues of the lovely Nanon. Canolles himself – who, being young, good-looking and rich, could not understand the need for intrigue – did not know what to believe on the matter. As for her amorous intrigues, either because Nanon had put these aside for the time being, having more serious matters to worry about, or because Monsieur d'Epernon's love for her resounded so loudly that it drowned out the murmurs made by any lesser affairs she might have, even her enemies kept

relatively quiet on his score, so that Canolles had some reason
to believe (which flattered his personal and native pride) that
Nanon had been invincible until he arrived on the scene.
Whether indeed Canolles had enjoyed the first loving impulse
of a heart until then touched only by ambition, or whether
prudence had inspired absolute discretion in his predecessors,
Nanon as a mistress must have been a charming woman. And
Nanon, when provoked, would be a fearful enemy.

Nanon and Canolles had met in the most natural way.
Canolles, a lieutenant in the regiment of Navailles, wished to
become a captain and for this he had to write to Monsieur
d'Epernon, Colonel-in-Chief of Infantry. Nanon, it was, who
read the letter and replied in her usual manner, expecting to
have some business to deal with and giving Canolles a business
appointment. Canolles chose a magnificent ring among the
family jewels, a ring worth some five hundred pistoles[29] (it was
still cheaper than buying a company of soldiers), and went to
his appointment. But this time the victorious Canolles, supported by the fine array of gifts that fate had bestowed on him,
routed Mademoiselle de Lartigues's calculating business sense.
It was the first time that he had seen Nanon, and the first time
that Nanon saw him: they were both young, handsome and
quick-witted. The interview consisted of mutual compliments;
the matter in hand was not mentioned (and yet it was resolved).
On the following day, Canolles received his captain's licence,
and when the precious ring passed from his finger to that of
Nanon, it was no longer as the price of ambition satisfied, but
as a token of requited love.

V

As for explaining how Nanon came to reside near the village
of Matifou, history can do that. As we said, the Duke d'Epernon
had attracted hatred in Guyenne. Nanon had been done the
honour of being considered his evil genius and was abhorred.
An uprising drove them from Bordeaux, and they retreated to

Agen, but in Agen, the riot resumed. One day, the gilded coach in which Nanon was going to meet the duke was overturned while crossing a bridge. Nanon, somehow or other, found herself in the river, and it was Canolles who fished her out. One night, Nanon's town house was engulfed in flames, and it was Canolles who just managed to get to her bedroom and save her from the fire. Nanon decided that, if they tried for a third time to kill her, the people of Agen might succeed. Even though Canolles stayed as close to her as he could, it would have been a miracle if he could always be there just when she needed to be saved from danger. She took advantage of the duke's absence, while he was making a visit to his province, and of the presence of an escort of twelve hundred men, in which the regiment of Navailles had its share, to leave town at the same time as Canolles. As she did so, she taunted the populace through the window of her coach – a coach that they would gladly have torn to pieces, had they dared.

So the duke and Nanon chose (or, rather, Canolles secretly chose for them) the little village where it was decided that Nanon would live, while a house was prepared for her in Libourne. Canolles took some leave, allegedly to go and arrange family matters at home, but in reality so that he could leave his regiment, which had returned to Agen, and not go too far away from Matifou, where his tutelary presence was more urgently needed than ever. Events were indeed starting to take a disturbingly serious turn. The princes of Condé, Conti and Longueville,[30] having been arrested the previous 17 January and imprisoned in Vincennes, provided the five or six rival factions that existed in France at the time with an excellent excuse for a civil war. The Duke d'Epernon's unpopularity, of which the court was fully aware, continued to grow – though reason should have given hope that it could grow no further. A catastrophe that all parties desired (since, given the strange situation in the country, they no longer knew themselves where they stood) was becoming imminent. Nanon, like those birds that sense the approach of a storm, vanished from the horizon and went back into her leafy nest to await the outcome of events in anonymity and obscurity.

She gave out that she was a widow looking for peace and quiet. One may recall that this is how Master Biscarros described her.

So Monsieur d'Epernon had come to visit the charming recluse to tell her that he was leaving for a week on duty, and no sooner had he left than Nanon sent a note via the tax collector, one of her protégés, to Canolles, who, thanks to his own leave of absence, had been waiting nearby. However, as we have seen, this original short note had disappeared from the messenger's hands and, beneath Cauvignac's pen, had become a copy of an invitation. The unsuspecting beau was hastening to respond to this invitation, when the Viscount de Cambes had stopped him four hundred yards from his goal.

The rest, we know.

Nanon was therefore waiting for Canolles as a woman in love waits, that is to say, taking her watch out of her pocket ten times a minute, constantly going over to the casement, listening for every sound and watching the magnificent red sun setting behind the mountain as it made way for the first shades of night. First of all, there was a knock on the front door, and she sent Francinette to answer. But it was only the scullery boy bringing the dinner (the guest for which was still awaited). Nanon stared into the antechamber and saw Master Biscarros's fake messenger, while he in turn was staring into the bedroom, where there was a small table with two places laid on it. Nanon instructed Francinette to keep the food hot, sadly closed the door and went back to her window, which, as far as one could see through the gathering darkness, showed her an empty road.

A second knock, and one delivered in a special manner, sounded on the little door at the back, and Nanon exclaimed: 'He's here!' But, fearing that it might again not be him, she stopped, frozen in her tracks. A moment later the door opened, and Mademoiselle Francinette appeared, with a look of consternation, silently holding the letter. The young woman saw it and leapt forward, took it from the chambermaid's hand, quickly opened it and read it anxiously.

The letter had the effect on Nanon of a lightning bolt. She

loved Canolles very deeply, but ambition was for her an emotion almost equal to love, and if she lost the Duke d'Epernon
she would not only lose all her fortune to come, but perhaps
even the fortune that she had already acquired. However, being
a resourceful woman, she extinguished the candle, which might
cast her shadow, and ran over to the window. Just in time: four
men were walking towards the house and were a mere twenty
yards from it. The man in the cloak was at their head, and in
this figure in the cloak Nanon quite clearly recognized the
duke. At that moment, Mademoiselle Francinette came in,
holding a candle. Nanon looked in despair at the table, with its
two place settings, at the two chairs, at the two pillows, glaring
in insolent whiteness against the crimson background of the
damask curtains, and finally at her alluring nightgown, which
was so much in keeping with all these preparations. 'I'm lost!'
she thought.

But almost immediately this subtle mind recovered its wits,
and a smile crossed her lips. Swift as lightning, she snatched
the simple crystal glass intended for Canolles and threw it out
casually into the garden, then took the golden goblet bearing
the duke's arms out of a case and placed his silver-gilt knife
and fork next to the plate. After that, chilled with fear, but with
a hastily composed smile, she ran down the steps and reached
the door just as a deep, solemn knock sounded on it.

Francinette was about to open up, but Nanon seized her arm,
pushed her aside and, with that swift glance that so perfectly
expresses the thought in a woman surprised, said: 'It's the duke
that I'm expecting, not Monsieur de Canolles. Serve us.'

Then she drew back the bolts herself, and, throwing her arms
round the neck of the man with the white plume, who was
preparing to show her his most furious expression, she exclaimed: 'Oh! My dream was right! Come, my dear Duke, the
table is laid and we can dine together.'

D'Epernon was struck dumb, but since a woman's embrace
is always pleasant to endure, he let himself be hugged. But then,
remembering the damning evidence that he had, he said: 'One
moment, Mademoiselle, there is something that must be settled
between us, if you would.'

Signalling to his henchmen, who stepped back respectfully, though without going away altogether, he stepped gravely and stiffly into the house, alone.

'What is it, my dear Duke?' Nanon asked, with such a fine show of merriment that one might have believed it to be natural. 'Did you forget something here the last time you came? Is that why you are looking around everywhere?'

'Yes,' said the duke. 'I forgot to tell you that I was not one of those old loons, a greybeard of the kind that Monsieur Cyrano de Bergerac[31] puts in his comedies, and having forgotten to tell you, I have returned in person to prove it to you.'

'I don't understand, Monseigneur,' said Nanon, in the calmest and most open manner. 'Please explain what you mean.'

The duke's eyes rested on the two chairs, then turned to the two places at the table, and from them turned to the two pillows. Here, they stayed longer and a flush of anger rose to his face.

Nanon was expecting all this and awaited the outcome of the inspection with a smile that revealed her pearly-white teeth. However, this smile seemed quite like a grimace, and those whitest of teeth would have been chattering were it not that anxiety kept them pressed against one another.

The duke once more turned his furious gaze on her.

'I am still awaiting your lordship's pleasure,' Nanon said, with a gracious curtsey.

'My lordship's pleasure,' he replied, 'is for you to explain to me the meaning of this supper.'

'As I already told you, I had a dream, which told me that although you had left me yesterday, you would return today. And my dreams are never wrong. So I had this supper prepared for you.'

The duke made a grimace, which he intended to appear as an ironic smile.

'And those two pillows?' he asked.

'Does his lordship intend to go back and sleep in Libourne? In that case, my dream was wrong, because it told me that he would be staying.'

The duke gave a second grimace that was still more significant than the first.

'And what about this charming negligee, Madame, and these exquisite perfumes?'

'It is one of the negligees I am accustomed to wear when I am expecting your lordship. These perfumes come from the sachets of Spanish leather that I put in my cupboards, and which his lordship himself told me often that he liked above all other scents, since it was the one that the queen preferred.'

'So you were expecting me?' the duke said, with an ironic chuckle.

'Now, now, my lord!' Nanon said, raising an eyebrow in her turn. 'Heaven forgive me, I believe you want to look in the cupboards. Could you be jealous, by any chance?' And she burst out laughing.

The duke assumed a lordly air.

'I, jealous! Most surely not! Thank God, I am not such an ass. Of course, as I am old and rich, I know that I am liable to be deceived. But at least, I want to prove to those by whom I am deceived that I have not been fooled.'

'And how can you prove that?' Nanon said. 'I am curious to know.'

'Oh, it won't be hard. I just have to show them this piece of paper.' The duke took a letter out of his pocket. 'I have no illusion,' he said. 'At my age, one does not dream, even when awake. But I do get letters. Read this one; it is interesting.'

Trembling, Nanon took the letter that the duke held out to her and shuddered when she saw the handwriting – though the shudder was so slight as to be imperceptible. She read:

Monseigneur the Duke d'Epernon is advised that this evening a man who for nearly six months has enjoyed the intimacy of Mademoiselle Nanon de Lartigues will go to her house, staying to supper and to sleep.

Since we do not wish to leave any doubt in the mind of Monseigneur the Duke d'Epernon, we advise him that this fortunate rival is called the Baron de Canolles.

Nanon went pale. The blow had struck home.

'Oh, Roland, Roland!' she murmured. 'I thought I had seen the last of you.'

'Is my information correct?' asked the duke in triumph.

'Hardly,' Nanon replied. 'And if your political intelligence is no better than your amorous intelligence, I am sorry for you.'

'You are sorry for me?'

'Indeed, since this Monsieur de Canolles, to whom you accord the undeserved honour of believing him to be your rival, is not here; and moreover you can wait if you wish and see whether he comes.'

'He has been here.'

'Here!' Nanon exclaimed. 'That is not true.'

This time there was a note of absolute truth in the accused woman's voice.

'What I mean is that he came to within four hundred yards of here and stopped, fortunately for him, at the inn of the Golden Calf.'

Nanon realized that the duke knew far less than she had at first imagined. She shrugged her shoulders; then another idea, coming no doubt from the letter, which she was still turning over and over in her hands, began to spring up in her mind.

'Is it possible,' she asked, 'that a man of genius and one of the most subtle politicians in the kingdom should allow himself to be taken in by an anonymous letter?'

'Well, then, anonymous or not, how do you explain this letter?'

'Oh, it's not hard to explain: this is another plot by our friends in Agen. Monsieur de Canolles asked you if, for family reasons, you would grant him leave of absence, which you did. They knew that he was coming this way and constructed this ridiculous accusation around his journey.'

Nanon observed that the duke's face, instead of relaxing, darkened even more.

'This would be a good explanation,' he said, 'if the famous letter that you attribute to your friends did not have a particular postscript which you, in your confusion, have overlooked.'

A mortal shudder ran through the whole of the young woman's body. She felt that if chance did not come to her aid, she could not sustain the contest.

'A postscript!' she repeated.

'Yes, read it,' said the duke. 'You have the letter in your hands.'

Nanon tried to smile, but felt herself that her drawn features would not lend themselves any longer to such an expression of calm. So she merely read the letter, in the most confident tone that she could muster.

'"I have in my hands the letter from Mademoiselle de Lartigues to Monsieur de Canolles, in which she fixes the rendezvous that I mentioned for this evening. I shall exchange this letter for a letter of attestation that the duke will make available through a single man in a boat on the Dordogne, opposite the village of Saint-Michel-la-Rivière, at six o'clock this evening."

'And you were rash enough . . . ?' said Nanon.

'Anything that you write is so precious to me, dear lady, that it did not occur to me that I could pay too much for a letter in your hand.'

'Entrusting such a secret to the indiscretion of a third party! Oh, my lord Duke!'

'Madame, this is the kind of confidence that one receives in person and that is how I received it. The man on the Dordogne was myself.'

'So you have my letter?'

'Here it is.'

Nanon quickly tried to remember what was in the letter, but she could not, and she began to feel confused. For this reason, she was forced to take her own letter and reread it. It contained a mere three lines. Nanon glanced over them eagerly and realized, with unspeakable joy, that the letter did not compromise her entirely.

'Read it aloud,' said the duke. 'I am like you, I have forgotten what was in this letter.'

Nanon at last found the smile that she had tried in vain to call up a few moments earlier, and, in response to the duke's invitation, read the following:

'"I shall sup at eight. Are you free? I am. In that case, be on time, my dear Canolles, and have no fear for our secret."'

'I think that is clear enough!' the duke exclaimed, pale with fury.

This will absolve me, Nanon thought.

'Come, come,' said the duke. 'So you have a secret with Monsieur de Canolles!'

VI

Nanon realized that a second's hesitation would destroy her. In any case, she had had time to elaborate the plan that the anonymous letter had suggested to her.

'Well, yes,' she said staring hard at the duke. 'I have a secret with this gentleman.'

'You admit it!' the Duke d'Epernon exclaimed.

'I must, since one can hide nothing from you.'

'Oh!' the duke shouted.

'Yes, I was expecting Monsieur de Canolles,' Nanon continued calmly.

'You were expecting him?'

'Yes, I was.'

'You dare to admit it?'

'Most openly! Now, do you know who Monsieur de Canolles is?'

'He's a bumptious idiot, whom I shall punish soundly for his impudence.'

'He is a brave and noble gentleman, whom you will continue to favour with your goodwill.'

'I swear by God that I shall do nothing of the sort, damn it!'

'Don't swear anything, Duke, at least not until I have spoken,' Nanon answered, smiling.

'Speak then, but hurry up.'

'Have you not noticed – you, who can see into the deepest recesses of the heart,' Nanon continued, 'how much I favoured

Monsieur de Canolles, how I appealed to you on his behalf, the captain's commission that I obtained for him, that allocation of funds for a journey to Britanny with Monsieur de La Meilleraie and this recent leave of absence ... in a word, my constant eagerness to oblige him?'

'Madame! Madame!' said the duke. 'You have gone too far!'

'For heaven's sake, Duke, wait until I have finished.'

'Why do I need to wait any longer? What more can you have to tell me?'

'That I have the most tender affection for Monsieur de Canolles.'

'As I know well enough, by God!'

'That I am devoted to him, body and soul.'

'Madame, this is too much....'

'That I should serve him to death and do so because ...'

'Because he is your lover, as anyone could guess.'

'Because ...' Nanon continued, grasping the trembling duke's hand with a dramatic gesture. 'Because he is my brother!'

The Duke d'Epernon's arm fell to his side.

'Your brother!' he said.

Nanon gave a nod, together with a smile of triumph.

Then, after a while, the duke exclaimed: 'This demands some explanation.'

'Which I shall give you,' said Nanon. 'When did my father die?'

'Why ...' said the duke, calculating. 'Some eight months ago.'

'And when did you sign the captain's commission for Monsieur de Canolles?'

'Around the same time,' said the duke.

'A fortnight later,' said Nanon.

'Perhaps ... a fortnight later.'

'I regret having to reveal the shame of another woman,' Nanon went on. 'And to divulge this secret, which is our secret, you understand ... But your strange jealousy has driven me to it, and your cruel manner gives me no alternative. I shall follow your example, my lord Duke, and lack generosity.'

'Go on, go on,' said the duke, who was already beginning
to be ensnared by the contrivances of the lovely Gascon's
imagination.

'Well, my father was a lawyer who enjoyed a certain reputation. Twenty-five years ago, he was still young, and he was
still quite handsome. Before getting married, he fell in love with
Monsieur de Canolles's mother, whose hand had been refused
him, because she was of noble birth and he was a commoner.
Love, as often happens, took it upon itself to put right the
mistake of Nature, and while Monsieur de Canolles was away
on a journey . . . Well, do you understand now?'

'Yes, but why did it take you so long to develop this friendship for Monsieur de Canolles?'

'Because it was only after my father's death that I discovered
the bond between us. The secret was contained in a letter that
the baron himself handed to me, calling me his sister.'

'And where is this letter?' the duke asked.

'Have you forgotten the fire that destroyed all my possessions? My most precious jewels and my most private papers!'

'That's true,' said the duke.

'Twenty times I wanted to tell you this story, being quite sure
that you would do everything for the man whom I know,
secretly, as my brother. But he always prevented me, begging
me to spare the reputation of his mother, who is still alive. I
respected his feelings because I could understand them.'

'Really!' said the duke, quite touched. 'Poor Canolles!'

'And yet,' Nanon went on, 'he was rejecting a fortune.'

'He is a sensitive and considerate soul,' said the duke. 'This
scrupulous behaviour is to his credit.'

'But I went further: I swore that this secret would never be
revealed to anyone in this world. But your suspicions forced
it out of me. Wretch that I am! I forgot my oath! Oh, wretch!
I have betrayed my brother's secret!'

And Nanon dissolved into tears.

The duke fell on his knees and kissed her pretty hands, which
she allowed him to take, with an air of exhaustion, while her
eyes, raised to the heavens, seemed to be begging God to forgive
her disloyalty.

'You say "Wretch that I am!"' said the duke. 'You should say "Good fortune for all!" I want this dear Canolles to make up for lost time. I do not know him, but I should like to. You must introduce me, and I shall love him like my own son!'

'You should say "like a brother",' said Nanon, with a smile. Then, thinking of something else, she exclaimed: 'Monstrous traitors!', screwing up the letter and pretending to throw it on the fire, while in fact putting it carefully into her pocket with the idea of eventually discovering the author.

'I've just thought,' said the duke. 'Why is the boy not coming? Why should I wait to see him here? I will go at once and have him brought from the inn of the Golden Calf.'

'Oh, yes!' said Nanon. 'So that he can find out that I can hide nothing from you and that, despite my oath, I have told you everything.'

'I shall be tactful.'

'My lord Duke, now it is my turn to pick a bone with you,' Nanon said, with the smile that demons give to the angels.

'Why is that, my dearest?'

'Because there was a time when you were more eager to enjoy an evening alone with me. Come, have supper with me, and tomorrow there will be time to send for Canolles.'

Between now and tomorrow, Nanon thought, I shall find the opportunity to warn him.

'Very well,' said the duke. 'Let's eat.' And, still retaining a small suspicion, added under his breath: 'I shall not leave her between now and tomorrow, and if she finds a way to contact him, she's a witch.'

'So, now,' said Nanon, putting her arm on the duke's shoulder, 'might I be allowed to ask a favour of my friend for my brother?'

'What?' said d'Epernon. 'Anything you wish . . . Money?'

'Oh, no,' said Nanon. 'He doesn't need money. He it was that gave me the magnificent ring you noticed, which belongs to his mother.'

'A promotion, then?'

'Yes, yes! A promotion. We'll make him a colonel, won't we?'

'Blast it! A colonel! You're pushing a bit hard, my dear,' said the duke. 'He has to have given some service to the cause of His Majesty before he can become a colonel.'

'He is ready to perform whatever services are required of him.'

'Ah, now,' said the duke, looking at Nanon out of the corner of his eye. 'Yes, I might well have a confidential mission for the court . . .'

'A mission for the court!' Nanon exclaimed.

'Yes,' said the old courtier. 'But it would mean you being separated.'

Nanon saw that this last hint of suspicion had to be abolished.

'Oh, don't worry about that, my dear Duke. What does separation matter, as long as it is of advantage to him! If I were to stay close to him, I should serve him ill – you are jealous of him – but from afar, you would extend your powerful hand over him. Exile him, send him abroad, if it is for his good, and don't worry about me. As long as I still have the love of my dear Duke, what more can I need to be happy?'

'Very well, it's done,' said the duke. 'Tomorrow morning I shall send for him and give him his instructions. And now, as you said,' the duke went on, casting a much more tender glance at the two chairs, the two place settings and the two pillows, 'now let us dine, my loveliest.'

Each of them sat down at the table, with a smiling face – so much so, indeed, that even Francinette, used as she was, in her role as confidential chambermaid, to the manners of the duke and the character of his mistress, thought that Nanon's mind was perfectly at ease and the duke's completely reassured.

VII

The rider whom Canolles had greeted by the name of Richon had gone up to the first floor of the inn of the Golden Calf and was taking supper with the viscount. He was the person for whom the viscount had been waiting so impatiently, when chance had made him a witness to the hostile preparations of Monsieur d'Epernon and put him in the way of doing the Baron de Canolles the signal favour that we have described.

He had left Paris a week earlier and Bordeaux that same day, so he was bringing recent news of the somewhat complicated affairs that, from Paris to Bordeaux, were at that time being woven into such disturbing webs. While Richon was speaking – about the imprisonment of the princes, which was the affair of the moment, and about the parliament of Bordeaux, which was the authority in the locality, or about Monsieur de Mazarin, who was the king of the hour – the young viscount was silently observing the bronzed, masculine face, the piercing, self-assured eyes and the sharp white teeth visible beneath his long black moustache, all of which marked Richon out as the typical officer of fortune.

'So,' the viscount said after a while, 'the princess is now in Chantilly.'

As we know, this is how the two duchesses of Condé were designated, while the mother was also called the 'dowager'.

'Yes,' Richon replied. 'She is expecting you there at the earliest possible moment.'

'And what is her situation there?'

'One of veritable exile. She and her mother-in-law are kept under the closest watch, since it is suspected at court that they will not restrict themselves to petitioning Parliament and are plotting something more effective to help the princes. Unfortunately, as ever, money . . . And, on the subject of money, have you received what was owing to you? I was specifically told to ask you that question.'

'It was only with great difficulty,' said the viscount, 'that I managed to obtain some twenty thousand livres, which I have here in gold, that's all.'

'That's all! My word, that's ripe, Viscount: one can see that you are a millionaire – talking so casually about such a sum, and at such a moment! Twenty thousand livres! We shall be less rich than Monsieur de Mazarin, but we shall be richer than the king.'

'So, do you think, Richon, that this modest offering will be acceptable to the princess?'

'She will accept it gratefully. You're bringing the price of an army.'

'And you think we'll need it?'

'What? An army? Certainly, and we are engaged in mustering one. Monsieur de La Rochefoucauld[32] has enrolled four hundred gentlemen, on the pretext of their attendance at his father's funeral. The Duke de Bouillon is going to leave for Guyenne with a similar number or even more. Monsieur de Turenne promises to press on as far as Paris in order to surprise Vincennes and seize the princes in a surprise attack; he will have thirty thousand men – the whole of his army in the north, which he is poaching from the service of the king. Oh, everything's underway, don't worry,' Richon continued. 'I don't know if we'll do a great job, but we'll certainly draw attention to ourselves.'

'And you haven't come across the Duke d'Epernon?' the young man interrupted, his eyes shining with joy at this list of forces that promised the success of the party to which he belonged.

'The Duke d'Epernon?' the soldier of fortune asked, with a puzzled expression. 'Where might I have met him? I don't come from Agen, but from Bordeaux.'

'You might have encountered him a few yards from here,' the viscount went on, with a smile.

'Of course! That's right: doesn't the lovely Nanon de Lartigues live somewhere hereabouts?'

'A mere two musket shots from this very inn.'

'Well, now! That explains the presence of the Baron de Canolles at the inn of the Golden Calf.'

'You know him?'

'Who? The baron? Yes … I might even venture to say that I am his friend, were it not that Monsieur de Canolles comes from a fine noble family, and I am merely a poor commoner.'

'Commoners like you, Richon, are worth princes in our present situation. By the way, you may know that I saved your friend the Baron de Canolles from a beating and perhaps something worse …'

'Yes, he did say something about that to me, but I did not fully take it in: I was in a hurry to come up and see you. Are you sure that he did not recognize who you are?'

'One has difficulty recognizing a person one has never seen.'

'Then I should have said "guess".'

'Now you mention it,' said the viscount, 'he did look closely at me.'

Richon smiled.

'I can believe that. It's not every day that one meets a gentleman of your kind.'

'He seems a merry sort of blade to me,' said the viscount, after a moment's silence.

'Merry and good, a charming spirit and a generous heart. A Gascon, as you know, is never run-of-the-mill: either he's outstanding, or he's nothing. This one is a fine fellow. In love as in war, he's both a stylish gallant and a brave captain. I'm sorry that he is against us. In fact, since chance put you in contact with him, you should have taken advantage of the situation to win him over to our side.'

A blush passed as swiftly as a meteor across the viscount's pale cheeks.

'Well, too bad,' said Richon, with that sad and philosophical resignation that one sometimes meets with in men who have seen a lot of the world. 'Are we ourselves so serious and so reasonable, we who are bearing aloft the flame of civil war in our rash hands like a church candle? Is the coadjutor such a serious man, when he can calm Paris with a word, or rouse it? Is Monsieur de Beaufort a serious man, when he wields such influence in the capital that he is called "King of Les Halles"? Is Madame de Chevreuse a serious woman, when she can make or break a minister at will? And Madame de Longueville, even though she reigned for three months in the Hôtel de Ville – is she serious? Or what about the Princess de Condé, who only yesterday cared for nothing except dresses, jewels and diamonds: is she serious? And finally is the Duke d'Enghien an entirely serious faction leader, when he is still playing with his dolls and in the charge of women, and who may put on his first pair of knee-breeches only to turn all France upside down? And last of all am I myself – if you will permit me to mention my name after so many illustrious ones – am I such a grave personage, the son of a miller in Angoulême, former servant to Monsieur de La Rochefoucauld, to whom one day, in place of a brush and a cloak, he gave a sword, which I bravely slung at my side, reinventing myself as a soldier? Yet here is the son of the Angoulême miller, former valet to Monsieur de La Rochefoucauld, who finds himself a captain. Here he is, mustering a company, assembling four or five hundred men with whose lives he will juggle, as though God had given him the right to do so . . . Here he is, marching on the path of glory, perhaps to be colonel or the governor of a fortress – who knows? Here he is, who may perhaps for ten minutes, or an hour, or even a day, hold the destiny of a kingdom in his hands. You see? It's all very much like a dream, yet it is one that I shall take for reality until the day when some great catastrophe wakes me . . .'

'And on that day, woe betide whoever does wake you, Richon,' said the viscount, 'because you will be a hero . . .'

'A hero or a traitor, depending on whether we are the stronger or the weaker. Under the other cardinal,[33] I should have looked twice, because I should have been risking my neck.'

'Come now, Richon. You're not going to try to persuade me that such considerations weigh with a man like yourself, who is spoken of as one of the bravest soldiers in the army!'

'Well, maybe,' said Richon, with a movement of the shoulders that it is impossible to describe. 'I was brave enough when King Louis XIII, with his pale face, his blue riband and his eye shining like a carbuncle, cried in his strident voice, while chewing his moustache: "The king is watching you; forward, gentlemen!" But when I have to see this same blue riband, no longer behind me, but in front of me, and on the chest of the son, as I can still see it on that of his father, and when I have to shout to my men: "Fire on the King of France!", then on that day, Viscount,' Richon continued, shaking his head, 'I'm afraid I might funk it and not shoot straight . . .'

'What side of the bed did you get out of today, my dear Richon, to be seeing everything in the blackest colours?' the young man asked. 'Civil war is sad, I know, but there are times when it is necessary.'

'Yes, like the plague, like yellow fever, like the black death, like pestilences of every colour. Do you really believe that it is necessary, for example, Viscount, that I who this evening was so pleased to shake hands with that fine fellow Canolles should have to stick my sword in his belly tomorrow, because I am the servant of the Princess de Condé, who doesn't care a fig for me, and he is the servant of Monsieur de Mazarin, for whom he doesn't care a fig? Nonetheless, that's how it will be.'

The viscount shuddered in horror.

'Unless, of course, I am mistaken,' Richon continued, 'and he is the one who drills a hole in my chest somehow or other. Oh, you people don't understand war! You think of it in terms of a sea or an intrigue, and plunge into it as into your natural element. Why, I was saying only the other day to Her Highness, "From where you are, the artillery fire that kills us looks to you like mere fireworks", and she agreed with me.'

'Truly, Richon,' said the viscount, 'you alarm me, and if I was not sure of having you there to protect me, I should not dare set out on the road. But with you escorting me, I fear nothing,' said the young man, holding out his small hand to the irregular soldier.

'Escorting you?' said Richon. 'Ah, yes! That's right. And that reminds me: you will have to do without my escort, Viscount; the deal's off.'

'But weren't you supposed to go back to Chantilly with me?'

'True, I was supposed to go back, in one event, which is that I was not needed here. But as I told you, my importance has increased to the extent that I have a definite order from the princess not to leave the area of the fort, on which apparently someone has designs.'

The viscount gave an exclamation of terror.

'I am to leave like this, without you!' he cried. 'To leave with that worthy Pompée, who is a hundred times more of a coward than even I am, and cross half of France alone or almost alone ... Oh, no! I'm not going, I swear! I'd die of fright before I got there.'

'Oh, my dear Viscount,' Richon retorted, bursting into laughter. 'Have you forgotten the sword hanging at your side?'

'Laugh if you like, but I'm not going! The princess promised me that you would come with me, and it was only on that condition that I agreed.'

'As you wish, Viscount,' said Richon, with feigned gravity. 'Even so, they are counting on you in Chantilly – and, beware: princes are quick to lose patience, especially when it is money that they are waiting for.'

'And to make matters worse,' said the viscount, 'I have to leave at night.'

'So much the better,' said Richon, laughing. 'No one will see that you are afraid, and you will meet greater cowards than yourself and make them run away.'

'Do you think so?' asked the viscount, not greatly reassured, despite this promise.

'In any case, there's a way to solve everything. You're afraid for the money, aren't you? Well, leave the money with me, and I'll send it with three or four reliable men. Though, believe me, the best way to ensure that it arrives is to take it yourself.'

'You're right, I'll go, Richon. And since I have to be a thorough hero, I'll keep the money. From what you tell me, I think Her Highness needs the money more than she needs me, so perhaps I should not be welcome if I were to turn up without it.'

'I told you when I came in that you looked like a hero. In any case, the King's soldiers are everywhere, and we are not yet at war; however, don't put too much faith in that and tell Pompée to prime his pistols.'

'Are you saying that to reassure me?'

'Of course. If you know the danger, you can't be taken by surprise. So off you go,' Richon went on, getting up. 'It's going to be a fine night, and before daybreak you could be in Monlieu.'

'But won't our baron see me leave?'

'Huh! At the moment he's doing what we've just done, that is, he's having supper, and if his supper was anything like ours, he'll be too keen on his food to get up from the table without good reason. In any case, I'll go down and make sure of it.'

'Then make my excuses for my impoliteness to him. I wouldn't like him to seek a quarrel with me, if he should one day meet me in a less forgiving mood than he was today. Apart from which, he must be a bit of a stickler for form, your baron!'

'You've said it, and he would be the man to follow you to the ends of the earth just to cross swords with you. But don't worry, I'll pass on your respects.'

'Yes, but do wait until I've left.'

'I certainly shall.'

'And don't you have some message for Her Highness?'

'I do indeed. Thank you, I was forgetting the most important thing.'

'Have you written her a letter?'

'No, there are just two words that she needs to know.'

'What are they?'

'*Bordeaux – yes.*'

'Will she know what that means?'

'Definitely. And with those two words, she can leave with her mind at rest. Tell her that I guarantee everything.'

'Come on, Pompée,' the viscount said to the old servant, who, at that moment, was poking his head round the door, which he had just half opened. 'Come on, my friend, we have to go.'

'Oh, no! To go?' said Pompée. 'Does the viscount realize? There's going to be a frightful storm.'

'What are you talking about, Pompée?' Richon retorted. 'There's not a cloud in the sky.'

'But we might lose our way in the dark.'

'That would be hard, since you have only to follow the highway. And in any case, the moonlight is quite splendid.'

'Moonlight! Moonlight!' Pompée muttered. 'You realize it's not for my own sake that I'm saying this, Monsieur Richon.'

'Of course,' Richon said. 'An old soldier . . .'

'When you've fought the Spaniards and been wounded at the Battle of Corbie . . .'[34] Pompée said, puffing himself up with pride.

'You don't fear a thing, huh? Well, that's excellent, because the viscount is not at all easy in his mind, I can tell you.'

'Oh! Oh! Are you worried?' Pompée asked, the colour draining from his face.

'Not when I'm with you, my brave Pompée,' the young man said. 'I know you, and I know you would sacrifice your life before anyone could harm me.'

'Of course, of course,' Pompée replied. 'But if you're too scared, we should wait until tomorrow.'

'Impossible, my dear Pompée. Put this gold on the pillion of your saddle, and I'll be with you in a moment.'

'This is a lot of money to risk going out with at night,' said Pompée, weighing the satchel.

'There's no danger – or so Richon assures me. Come now, are the pistols in their holsters, the sword in its sheath and the musket on its rest?'

'You are forgetting,' said the old servant, drawing himself up to his full height, 'that when you have been a soldier all your life, you don't let yourself be caught out. Yes, Viscount, everything is at the ready.'

'There you are!' said Richon. 'How could you be afraid with such a companion? So, bon voyage, Viscount.'

'Thank you for your good wishes, but it's a long road ahead,' the viscount replied, still with a hint of anxiety that Pompée's martial bearing could not dispel.

'Pooh!' said Richon. 'Every road has a beginning and an end. My respects to the princess. Tell her that I am with her and Monsieur de La Rochefoucauld until death. And don't forget the two words I told you: *Bordeaux – yes*. Now I'm going back to Monsieur de Canolles.'

'Tell me, Richon,' said the viscount, taking him by the arm, as he was putting his foot on the first stair. 'If this Canolles is as worthy a captain and as fine a gentleman as you say, why not make some attempt to lure him over to our side? He could join us either at Chantilly or during the journey. As I already know him a little, I could introduce him.'

Richon looked at the viscount with such a peculiar smile that the other, no doubt reading on the soldier's face what was going on in his mind, hastened to say: 'On second thoughts, Richon, forget that I said anything and do whatever you see fit. Farewell.'

He shook his hand and hastily retreated into the room, either because he was afraid that Richon would see the flush of red that covered his face, or for fear of being overheard by Canolles, whose louds outbursts of laughter could be heard on the first floor.

The soldier left to go downstairs, followed by Pompée, carrying the case in a deliberately casual manner, so that no one would suspect what it contained. Then, after a few minutes, the viscount looked around to make sure that he had not forgotten anything, snuffed out the candles and went downstairs in his turn, risking a cautious glance through the brightly lit gap in a door on the ground floor. Then, wrapping himself in the thick cloak that Pompée offered him, he put a foot in the servant's hand, sprung lightly on to his horse, upbraided the old soldier with a smile over his slowness and vanished into the night.

Just as Richon entered Canolles's room – with the idea of keeping him amused while the little viscount was preparing to depart – a shout of joy from the baron, rocking back in his chair, showed that he held no grudges.

On the table, between the two transparent objects that had once been full bottles, stood a flask, plump and proud of its rotundity, bound with reeds, between which the light of four candles threw sparks of topaz and ruby: it was a flagon of one of those old wines of Collioure,[35] the honeyed spice of which delights an already warmed palate. Fine dried figs, almonds, biscuits, sharp-tasting cheeses and candied grapes revealed the innkeeper's self-interested scheme, the scientific precision of which was demonstrated by two empty bottles and one half-full: undoubtedly, whoever touched this persuasive dessert would be sure, however sober he might be, to consume a great deal of liquid.

Canolles did not pride himself on his abstemiousness: he was no anchorite. Perhaps too, as a Huguenot (he was of a Protestant family and more or less professed the religion of his ancestors), Canolles did not believe in the canonization of those pious hermits who got to heaven by drinking water and eating roots.[36] So, however sad, or even however much in love he was, he was never unmoved by the scent of a good dinner or the sight of those bottles, with their peculiar shape, their red, yellow or green stoppers, which, beneath the faithful cork, preserve the finest lifeblood of Gascony, Champagne or Burgundy. In this particular instance, Canolles had therefore given in to what charmed the eye, and from the eye to the sense of smell, and from the scent to the taste – and since out of the five senses, with which he was endowed by the good mother of us all whom we name Nature, three were completely satisfied, the other two decided to be patient and to await their turn in a state of the most beatific resignation.

This was the moment at which Richon entered and found Canolles leaning back in his chair.

'I say!' he exclaimed. 'You've come just at the right time, my dear Richon. I needed someone to whom I could extol the virtues of Master Biscarros, and I was about to be reduced to singing his praises to that good-for-nothing Castorin, who doesn't know the first thing about drinking, and whom I have never managed to teach how to eat. Now, then, look at that dresser, dear boy, and cast your eyes on this table, at which I invite you to sit down. Is he not a true artist, the innkeeper at the Golden Calf, a man whom I should like to recommend to my friend the Duke d'Epernon? Listen to the menu and judge for yourself, Richon, as a connoisseur: a bisque, an hors-d'oeuvre of marinated oysters, anchovies, some pigs' trotters, a capon with olives in a bottle of Medoc (the remains of which we have here), a partridge with truffles, some caramelized peas, a jelly of wild cherries, and all washed down with a bottle of Chambertin here present. In addition to those, there is this dessert and bottle of Collioure which are doing their best to keep their end up, and which will go down like the others, especially if we attack on two fronts. Devil take it, I'm in a damned good mood and Biscarros is a great master of his art. Sit down there, Richon. You've had supper? So what? So have I, but that doesn't matter: we'll start again.'

'Thank you, Baron,' said Richon with a laugh. 'But I'm not hungry any more.'

'I accept the possibility: one may not be hungry, but one is always thirsty, so try some of this Collioure.'

Richon held out a glass.

'So you've had supper, have you?' said Canolles. 'With that silly little viscount of yours! Oh, I beg your pardon, Richon . . . No, not at all, I'm wrong . . . a charming fellow, on the contrary, thanks to whom I can enjoy the best things in life, instead of giving up the ghost through the three or four holes that the Duke d'Epernon was expecting to make in my skin. So, I'm very grateful to the pretty viscount, that delightful Ganymede.[37] Ah, Richon! You do indeed seem to me to be what is said of you: that is, the true servant of Monsieur de Condé.'

'Come, come, Baron!' Richon said, roaring with laughter. 'Don't suggest such things, or I'll die laughing.'

'Die laughing! You? Come, come, my good man. *Igne tantum perituri, Quia estis, Landerini.* You know the song, I suppose? It's one of your patron's carols, composed on the German river Rhenus one day, when he was reassuring one of his companions, who was afraid of drowning.[38] What a devil you are, Richon! No matter, but I can't stand your little gentleman: that way he has of taking an interest in the first handsome fellow who rides by!'

And Canolles threw himself back on his chair, with a roar of laughter, his moustache curling in a paroxysm of hilarity that Richon could not avoid sharing.

'So, then,' said Canolles. 'Seriously, my dear Richon: you're a conspirator, aren't you?'

Richon went on laughing, but his laughter was more constrained.

'Do you know, I had a good mind to have you arrested, you and your little gentleman? By heaven, it would have been amusing and quite easy. I had the strong men of my good friend d'Epernon right here. Huh! Richon in the guardhouse and the little gentleman as well! *Landerini!*'

At that moment, they heard the sound of two horses galloping away.

'Ah, ha!' Canolles said, listening to the sound. 'What's that, Richon? Do you know?'

'I think I can guess.'

'So tell me.'

'It's the little gentleman leaving us . . .'

'Without saying goodbye to me!' Canolles exclaimed. 'He is quite definitely a bumpkin.'

'No, my dear Baron, just a man in a hurry.'

Canolles raised an eyebrow.

'What peculiar manners!' he said. 'Where was the boy brought up? Richon, my friend, I must warn you that he does you no credit. That's not the way that gentlemen behave. *Corbleu!* I do believe that if I had him here, I'd box his ears. Devil take his old father, who was too stingy no doubt to provide him with a tutor!'

'Don't upset yourself, Baron,' said Richon with a laugh. 'The viscount is not as ill-bred as you think, because as he left he instructed me to convey his apologies to you and told me to say lots and lots of flattering things to you.'

'Good, good!' said Canolles. 'An empty gesture, though, but one that makes a great impertinence into a small slight, that's all. Darn it! I'm in a savage mood. Pick a fight with me, Richon! Don't you want to? Wait . . . *Sarpejeu!* Richon, my friend, you're an ugly devil.'

Richon started to laugh.

'In that mood, Baron, you could well win a hundred pistoles from me if we play at cards this evening. You know: unlucky in love, lucky at cards.'

Richon was well acquainted with Canolles and knew what he was doing when he suggested this outlet for the baron's bad temper.

'Why, yes, by Jove! Cards! Yes, cards! You're right, my friend, you've said just the right thing. Richon, I think you're a fine fellow. Richon, you're as handsome as Adonis, and I forgive Monsieur de Cambes. Castorin, bring us the cards!'

Castorin hurried back, accompanied by Biscarros, and the two of them set up a table, at which the friends started to play. Castorin, who had been dreaming for ten years about a martingale for trente-et-quarante,[39] and Biscarros, who was looking hungrily at the money, stayed standing at either end of the table watching them. In less than an hour, despite what he had predicted, Richon was winning eighty pistoles from his friend, so Canolles, who had no money on him, told Castorin to go and fetch some from his suitcase.

'No need,' said Richon, hearing this. 'I don't have time to give you your revenge.'

'What! You don't have time?' said Canolles.

'No, it is eleven o'clock, and at midnight I must be at my post.'

'Come on, you can't be serious?'

'Baron,' said Richon, 'you are a military man so you surely know that orders are orders.'

'So why didn't you go before you had won my money?' Canolles asked, half amused and half cross.

'Could you by any chance be reproaching me for coming to see you?' asked Richon.

'Heaven forbid! But, listen: I haven't the slightest desire to sleep, and I'm terribly bored here. Suppose I offered to come with you, Richon?'

'I should refuse the honour, Baron. Business of the sort that I am charged with must be conducted without witnesses.'

'Very well, then. Which direction are you going?'

'I was about to ask you to refrain from asking me that.'

'And which way did the viscount go?'

'I must answer that I know nothing about that.'

Canolles looked at Richon to make sure that there was not a trace of irony in these rude responses, but the Governor of Vayres,[40] with his kind eyes and his open smile, while they may not have lessened Canolles's impatience, at least disarmed his curiosity.

'Come, now,' said Canolles, 'you're stuffed with mystery this evening, my dear Richon. But that's your business! I should have been very annoyed, myself, if someone had been following me three hours ago – although, when it comes down to it, the person following me would have been as disappointed as I was. So let's have a last glass of this Collioure and farewell.'

At this, Canolles refilled the glasses, and Richon, after clinking his glass against the baron's and having drunk his health, went, without the other trying to find out which way he was going. But left alone among the half-burned candles, the empty bottles and the scattered cards, the baron felt one of those melancholies that can only be understood when one experiences them, because his merriment earlier in the evening had been the outcome of a disappointment that he had been trying, not altogether successfully, to forget.

So he went wearily towards his bedroom, casting a glance full of anger and regret through the windows in the corridor at the little isolated house, one window of which was lit up by a reddish glow and crossed from time to time by shadows, showing that Mademoiselle de Lartigues was spending a less lonely evening than he was.

On the first step of the staircase, the toe of Canolles's boot touched something: he leant down and picked up one of the viscount's little pearl-grey gloves, which he had let fall in his hurry to get away from Master Biscarros's inn, presumably considering it not valuable enough to waste time in looking for it.

Whatever Canolles might have imagined, in a moment of misanthropy that was quite excusable in a frustrated lover, there was no more satisfaction to be found in the little isolated house than in the inn of the Golden Calf.

Nanon spent the night in a state of disquiet and agitation, imagining a thousand ways to warn Canolles; she had employed all the wit and guile that exist in the head of a well-managed woman to get herself out of her present perilous situation. All that was needed was to evade the duke's vigilance for a minute to speak to Francinette or two minutes to write a line to Canolles on a scrap of paper.

But it was as though the duke, guessing what was going on in her mind and reading her anxiety through the happy mask that she put on, had sworn to himself not to allow her the moment of freedom that she needed so much.

Nanon had a migraine, but Monsieur d'Epernon would not

allow her to get up and find her smelling salts, going instead to get them himself.

Nanon pricked herself with a pin, suddenly causing a ruby to appear on the end of her pearly white finger, and so wanted to go to her work-basket and fetch a piece of that famous rose taffeta that was starting to become so popular at the time. Monsieur d'Epernon, tireless in his attentions, cut off the piece of red taffeta with infuriating skill and double-locked the work-basket.

So Nanon pretended to fall fast asleep, and almost at once the duke began to snore. Consequently, Nanon opened her eyes and by the night light in its alabaster on the bedside table, tried to take the duke's own notebook out of his jerkin, which was within reach, close beside the bed; but, just as she was holding the pencil and had torn off a sheet of paper, the duke opened one eye.

'What are you doing, my dearest?' he said.

'I was looking to see if there was a calendar with your note-book,' she answered.

'Why did you want one?' he asked.

'To see the date of your birthday.'

'My name is Louis, so my birthday is on 25 August, as you know, so you have lots of time to get ready for it, my lovely.' And he took the notebook from her hand and put it back in the pocket.

At least this last manoeuvre had gained Nanon a pencil and some paper. She put both of them under her pillow and cleverly tipped over her night light, hoping that she would manage to write in the dark. But the duke immediately rang for Francinette and called loudly for lights, pretending that he could not sleep if he couldn't see. Francinette ran up before Nanon had written half her sentence, and the duke, fearing a repeat of the recent accident, ordered Francinette to put two candles on the mantel-piece. This time it was Nanon who declared that she could not sleep in the light and, feverish with impatience, turned her face to the wall, waiting for daylight with an anxiety that can easily be understood.

This dread day eventually shone on the tips of the poplars, and the light of the two candles paled. The Duke d'Epernon, who made a point of sticking to the habits of military life, was up with the first ray of sunlight shining through the shutters, dressed by himself, so as not to leave his little Nanon for a single moment, put on a dressing gown and rang to find out if there was any news.

Francinette replied to the question by bringing the duke a packet of dispatches that Courtauvaux, his favourite groom, had brought overnight. The duke began to unseal them and read them with one eye, while the other eye, to which he tried to give the most loving expression he could, did not leave Nanon.

If she could, Nanon would have chopped the duke in pieces.

'Do you know what you should do, my dearest?' the duke asked after reading some of his dispatches.

'No, my lord,' Nanon replied. 'But if your lordship would be good enough to give his orders, I shall comply with them.'

'You ought to send for your brother,' said the duke. 'I have just received a letter from Bordeaux with the information that I was expecting, and he could start at once, so that on his return I should have an excuse for giving him the promotion that you want.'

The duke's face expressed the most unalloyed benevolence.

'Come, now,' Nanon said to herself. 'Take heart! There is a chance that Canolles will read something in my eyes or understand a hint.'

Then, aloud, she said: 'You send for him, my dear Duke' – guessing that if she undertook to do it herself, the duke would not let her.

D'Epernon called Francinette and sent her off to the inn of the Golden Calf with no message except this: 'Tell Baron de Canolles that Mademoiselle de Lartigues is expecting him for lunch.'

Nanon glanced at Francinette but, eloquent though the glance was, Francinette could not read in it: 'Tell the Baron de Canolles that I am his sister.'

Francinette set off, realizing that there was something fishy going on and that the fish could well turn out to be a snake.

Meanwhile, Nanon got up and stood behind the duke, so that she could immediately warn Canolles to be on his guard, and she got to work preparing a cunning speech which would, from the first words, inform the baron of all that he needed to know to avoid playing any false notes in the family trio that was about to be performed.

Out of the corner of her eye, she could see the whole road as far as the bend at which Monsieur d'Epernon had hidden with his men.

'Ah!' said the duke suddenly. 'Here's Francinette coming back.' And he stared at Nanon, who was obliged to look away from the road and respond to the duke. Her heart was beating fit to burst. She had only managed to see Francinette, while the person she wanted to see was Canolles, to discover some reassuring sign on his face.

Someone was coming up the stairs. The duke prepared a smile that was both noble and friendly. Nanon fought back the blushes that were rising to her cheeks and prepared for battle.

Francinette lightly knocked on the door.

'Come in!' the duke said.

Nanon honed the famous speech with which she was to greet Canolles.

The door opened. Francinette was alone. Nanon looked eagerly into the antechamber, but there was no one there, either.

'Madame,' Francinette said with the imperturbable poise of a lady's maid in a comedy. 'Monsieur the Baron de Canolles is no longer at the inn of the Golden Calf.'

The duke opened his eyes wide, then scowled.

Nanon looked heavenwards and breathed again.

'What!' said the duke. 'Is the Baron de Canolles really not at the inn of the Golden Calf?'

'You must surely be mistaken, Francinette,' Nanon added.

'Madame,' Francinette replied. 'I am merely repeating what Monsieur Biscarros himself told me.'

'Dear Canolles,' Nanon murmured under her breath. 'He must have guessed everything. He is as clever and wise as he is brave and handsome.'

'Go and fetch Master Biscarros at once,' said the duke, with the look of a man who has got out of bed on the wrong side.

'Oh, I should imagine that he realized you were here,' said Nanon quickly. 'And he was afraid he might disturb you. He is so shy, poor Canolles!'

'Shy, is he?' said the duke. 'That's not what I've heard, I think.'

'No, Madame,' said Francinette. 'The baron really has left.'

'But, Madame,' said d'Epernon, 'how is it that the baron was afraid of me, since Francinette was only instructed to invite him on your behalf? So you told him that I was here, did you, Francinette? Tell me!'

'I could not tell him, Duke, because he wasn't there.'

Though Francinette's reply came with all the speed of truth and honesty, the duke seemed no less suspicious. Nanon was so happy that she did not have the strength to say a word.

'Do I still have to go back and call Master Biscarros over here?' Francinette asked.

'Yes, more than ever,' said the duke, emphatically. 'Or rather . . . wait a moment. You stay here, your mistress may need you. I will send Courtauvaux.'

Francinette vanished and five minutes later, Courtauvaux was scraping on the door.

'Go and tell the innkeeper at the Golden Calf to come and speak to me,' said the duke. 'And when he comes, let him bring a breakfast. Give him these ten louis, so that he will make it a good one. Off you go.'

Courtauvaux put the money in the pocket of his tailcoat and set off at once to carry out his master's orders. He was a valet who came from a good house and knew his job well enough to teach it to all the Crispins and the Mascarilles of his day.[41] He went to find Biscarros and told him: 'I've managed to persuade his lordship to order your best breakfast. He gave me eight louis, and naturally I am keeping two as my commission, so here are six for you. Come at once.'

Biscarros, trembling with joy, tied a white apron around his waist, pocketed the six louis, shook Courtauvaux by the hand

and set off behind the groom, who led him at the double to the door of the little house.

VIII

This time, Nanon was not worried, Francinette's confidence having completely calmed her. She even felt the strongest desire to chat with Biscarros, so he was shown in as soon as he arrived, apron smartly tucked up in his belt and hat in hand.

'Yesterday,' said Nanon, 'you had staying with you a young gentleman, the Baron de Canolles, didn't you?'

'What's happened to him?' the duke asked.

Biscarros, quite uneasy because the groom and the six louis had made him wary of the great gentleman behind the dressing gown, at first replied evasively:

'But, Monsieur, he has left.'

'Left?' said the duke. 'He has really left?'

'Really.'

'Where did he go?' Nanon asked in her turn.

'That I can't tell you, because in truth I don't know, Madame.'

'You must at least know which road he took?'

'The Paris road.'

'And at what time did he take this road?' asked the duke.

'Around midnight.'

'Did he say nothing?' Nanon asked shyly.

'Nothing. He just left a letter with instructions that it should be given to Mademoiselle Francinette.'

'And why did you not give her the letter, you rascal?' asked the duke. 'Is that how you show your respect for a gentleman's orders?'

'But I did give it to her, Monsieur, I did.'

'Francinette!' the duke yelled.

Francinette, who had been listening, moved in a trice from the antechamber into the bedroom.

'Why did you not give your mistress the letter that Monsieur de Canolles left for her?' the duke asked.

'But, Monseigneur . . .' the chambermaid said, terrified.

'"Monseigneur!"' Biscarros thought, quite overcome, shrinking into the most remote corner of the room. 'Monseigneur! He must be a prince in disguise.'

'I didn't ask her for it,' Nanon said hastily, the colour leaving her face.

'Give it to me,' the duke said, holding out a hand.

Poor Francinette slowly reached out her hand with the letter in it, while looking at her mistress with an expression that meant: 'You can see that it's not my fault; it is that idiot Biscarros who has ruined everything.'

A double flash darted from Nanon's eyes and pierced Biscarros in his corner. The poor fellow was sweating heavily and would have given the six louis in his pocket to be in front of his stove holding the handle of a saucepan.

Meanwhile, the duke took the letter, opened it and started reading. As he was doing so, Nanon, upright, paler and colder than marble, felt that only her heart was alive.

'What does this gibberish mean?' the duke asked.

Those five words told Nanon that the letter did not compromise her.

'Read it out aloud and I may be able to explain,' she said.

'"Dear Nanon,"' the duke read, and after that turned towards the young woman, who, increasingly reassured, bore his look with admirable effrontery.

'"Dear Nanon,"' the duke repeated and continued. '"I am taking advantage of the leave of absence you have given me, and I am going for a gallop along the Paris road for a while to amuse myself. Au revoir, I recommend my fortune to you."'

'Well, I never. He's mad, your Canolles.'

'Mad? Why?' said Nanon.

'Who goes off like that at midnight for no reason?' the duke asked.

'Who, indeed?' said Nanon to herself.

'Come on! Explain this behaviour.'

'Why, nothing could be more simple, Monseigneur,' Nanon said with a charming smile.

'She calls him "Monseigneur" as well!' muttered Biscarros. 'He's definitely a prince.'

'So, tell me.'

'Why! Don't you see what's going on?'

'Not at all.'

'Well, Canolles is twenty-seven. He is young, handsome and carefree. So what do you suppose is his favourite folly? Love! So he must have seen some pretty young traveller riding past Master Biscarros's inn and followed her.'

'In love! Do you think so?' the duke exclaimed, quite naturally smiling at the notion that if Canolles was in love with some passing traveller, he was not in love with Nanon.

'Of course, in love. Isn't that right, Master Biscarros?' said Nanon, delighted at seeing the duke accept her idea. 'Come on, tell us honestly: haven't I guessed correctly?'

Biscarros decided that the moment had come to get back into the young woman's good graces by backing her up, and so, with a smile four inches wide bursting on his lips, he said: 'Indeed, Madame could very well be right.'

Nanon took a step towards the innkeeper, and, shivering despite herself, she asked: 'I am right, am I not?'

'I think so, Madame,' said Biscarros with a shrewd look.

'Do you think so?'

'Yes, one moment ... Yes, now you mention it, I see what was going on ...'

'Ah, then tell us about it, Biscarros,' Nanon continued, starting to feel the first pangs of jealous suspicion. 'Let's see: what lady travellers stopped at your inn last night?'

'Yes, do tell us,' said d'Epernon, stretching his legs and leaning on a chair.

'No lady travellers came,' said Biscarros. Nanon breathed more easily. 'However,' the innkeeper went on, not realizing the effect that his every word had on Nanon's beating heart, 'a little blond gentleman, a pretty fellow, plump, who didn't eat anything, didn't drink and who was afraid to continue on his way at night ... A gentleman who was afraid,' said Biscarros, giving a little nod of the head that was full of meaning. 'You see what I mean?'

'Ha, ha!' said the duke, completely swallowing the bait, with splendid hilarity.

Nanon replied to his laugh with a sort of grunt.

'Carry on,' she said. 'This is charming! And no doubt the little fellow was waiting for Monsieur de Canolles?'

'No, not at all. He was expecting to dine with a tall gentleman with a moustache and was even quite brusque with Monsieur de Canolles, who wanted to take supper with him. But he was not put off by such a small thing, the fine gentleman ... He's an enterprising chap, by all appearances ... And so after the tall man had left and turned right, he sped off after the little one who had gone to the left.'

At this Rabelaisian[42] conclusion, Biscarros noticed the delight on the face of the duke and felt entitled to burst out in a cacophony of laughs so thunderous that they made the window-panes shudder.

The duke, entirely reassured, would have embraced Biscarros had the latter been in the slightest bit a gentleman. As for Nanon, she had gone pale, and her lips were fixed in a convulsive smile: she was hanging on every word that fell from the innkeeper's lips with that consuming passion that drives a jealous lover to drink deeply, right to the dregs, the poison that is killing her.

'But what makes you think,' she asked, 'that this little gentleman was a woman and that Monsieur de Canolles is in love with her and that he is not riding around the countryside out of boredom, on some idle whim?'

'What makes me think so?' Biscarros replied, determined to convince his audience. 'Wait and I'll tell you ...'

'Yes, do tell us, my good friend,' said the duke. 'You really are most entertaining ...'

'His lordship is too kind,' said Biscarros. 'Well, now ...' (The duke was very attentive, while Nanon listened with clenched fists.) 'I didn't suspect a thing. I had simply assumed that the little blond gentleman was a man, when I met Monsieur de Canolles in the middle of the staircase, with a candle in his left hand and in his right one a little glove, which he was looking at and sniffing in a passionate manner . . .'

'Ho, ho!' said the duke, laughing fit to split his sides, now that he was no longer worried for himself.

'A glove!' Nanon repeated, trying to remember if she had not left a small token in her beau's possession. 'A glove like one of these?'

She showed the innkeeper one of her gloves.

'No, no,' said Biscarros. 'A man's glove.'

'A man's glove! Monsieur de Canolles looking at a man's glove . . . passionately sniffing a man's glove! You must be mad!'

'Not at all, because it was one of the little gentleman's gloves, belonging to the pretty blond fellow, who didn't drink, who didn't eat and who was afraid of the dark . . . A tiny little glove, which would hardly have fitted Madame's hand . . . even though Madame certainly has a most pretty hand . . .'

Nanon gave a dull little cry, as though she had been struck by an invisible dart.

'I hope that you are now sufficiently informed, Monseigneur,' she said, making a tremendous effort to control herself. 'And that you know all that you wished to know.'

And, with trembling lips, clenched teeth and staring eyes, she pointed Biscarros to the door – while he, seeing these signs of anger on the young woman's face, was completely nonplussed and stayed on the spot, wide-eyed and open-mouthed.

'Well,' he thought, 'if the gentleman's absence is such a dreadful misfortune, then his return will be most welcome. Let's offer the noble lord some sweet hope, to give him a good appetite.'

Reasoning in this way, Biscarros adopted his most serious expression and stepping forward with the most graceful movement of his right leg, he said: 'After all, the rider left and he may come back at any moment . . .'

The duke smiled at this beginning.

'True,' he said. 'Why shouldn't he come back? Perhaps he already has. Go and see, Monsieur Biscarros, and let me know.'

'What about breakfast?' said Nanon sharply. 'I'm dying of hunger.'

'Quite right,' said the duke. 'Courtauvaux will go. Come

here, Courtauvaux: go to Master Biscarros's inn and see if the
Baron de Canolles has come back. If he is not there, ask about,
enquire, look around ... I want to take breakfast with the
gentleman. Off you go.'

Courtauvaux left, and Biscarros, noticing the embarrassed
silence of the couple, looked as though he were about to make
a new suggestion.

'Can't you see that Madame is signalling to you to leave?'
said Francinette.

'One moment, one moment!' the duke exclaimed. 'What on
earth's going on? You are losing your head too, my dear Nanon
... What about the menu? I'm like you, I could eat a horse ...
Come here, Master Biscarros, add these six louis to the rest:
they're to pay for the amusing story that you have just told us.'

Then he demanded that the historian give way to the cook,
and, we hasten to say, Biscarros was no less outstanding in the
second role than in the first.

Meanwhile, Nanon had reflected and in a flash summed up
the whole situation in which Biscarros's assumption put her.
First of all: was the assumption correct? And then, even if it
should be so, wasn't Canolles pardonable? After all, their failed
meeting was a cruel disappointment for a gallant fellow like
himself. And what an insult the Duke d'Epernon's surveillance
was, not to mention the fact that he, Canolles, was (as it were)
forced to witness his rival's triumph! Nanon was so much in
love that by attributing Canolles's flight to a rush of jealousy,
not only did she excuse him, but also felt sorry for him, almost
applauding the fact that she was so loved by him as to inspire
this little act of revenge. But now, before anything else, the evil
had to be nipped in the bud and the development of this newly
emergent amour had to be cut short.

Here, a dreadful thought entered Nanon's mind and almost
struck the poor woman down. Suppose that Canolles's meeting
with the little gentleman had been prearranged? But, no: she
was going mad. The little gentleman had been waiting for a
man with a moustache and had snubbed Canolles, since Canolles himself might only have realized the unknown traveller's
sex through the chance discovery of the little glove.

No matter! Canolles had to be thwarted in his affair. So, summoning up all her energy, she turned back to the duke, who had just sent Biscarros off loaded with compliments and instructions.

'How dreadful it is,' she said, 'that that silly boy Canolles should be so foolhardy, thus depriving himself of an honour such as the one you were going to bestow on him! Had he been here, his future would have been assured; as it is, he may lose it all by his absence.'

'But suppose we find him . . .'

'Oh, there's no danger of that,' said Nanon. 'If a woman is involved, he won't have returned.'

'What can I do, then, my dearest?' the duke replied. 'Youth is the age of pleasure. He is young, so he's having fun.'

'But I am more sensible than he is,' said Nanon, 'and I really think we should do something to interrupt his ill-timed merriment.'

'Ha! The scolding sister!'

'He may resent it now,' Nanon went on, 'but he will certainly thank me later.'

'Well, do you have some plan? I ask nothing better than to carry it out, if you do have one.'

'I do, indeed.'

'Tell me.'

'You want him to take an important piece of news to the queen, don't you?'

'Yes, but since he has not returned : . .'

'Send someone after him, and as he is on the road to Paris, he can simply carry on in that direction.'

'Goodness! You're right!'

'Let me look after it, and Canolles will receive the order this evening or tomorrow at the latest, I promise you.'

'But whom will you send?'

'Do you need Courtauvaux?'

'Personally, not at all.'

'Then let me have him, and I'll send him with my instructions.'

'What an excellent diplomat! You'll go far, Nanon.'

'Just let me always continue to be taught by such a good master,' said Nanon, 'that's all I wish for.' And she put her arm round the shoulders of the old duke, who shuddered with pleasure. 'What a fine trick to play on our Céladon!'[43] she added.

'It will be delightful in the telling, my dear.'

'In fact, I should love to chase after him myself to see his face when he sees the messenger.'

'Unfortunately – or rather, fortunately – that is not possible, and you will have to stay with me.'

'Yes, but let's lose no time. Duke, you write your order and hand Courtauvaux over to me.'

The duke took a pen and wrote just these two words on a piece of paper: *Bordeaux – No.* After that, he signed it.

Then, on the outside of this laconic dispatch, he wrote the following address: 'To Her Majesty, Queen Anne of Austria, Regent of France.'

Nanon, for her part, was writing two lines that she put in with the paper, after showing them to the duke. Here they are:

My dear Baron,
    As you can see, the attached dispatch is for Her Majesty the Queen. As you value your life, leave at once: the safety of the kingdom is at stake!
Your dear sister,
Nanon

Nanon had hardly finished the letter, when hurried footsteps were heard at the bottom of the staircase, and Courtauvaux, charging up, opened the door with the delighted face of a man bringing news which he knows is eagerly awaited.

'Here is Monsieur de Canolles, whom I met a hundred yards away,' the groom said.

The duke gave an exclamation of surprise and satisfaction, while Nanon went pale and rushed towards the door, muttering: 'Am I then fated not to avoid him!'

At that moment a new figure appeared at the door, magnifi-

cently attired, with his hat in his hand and smiling in the most
gracious manner.

IX

Had a bolt of lightning fallen at Nanon's feet, it would certainly
not have caused her greater surprise than this unexpected
apparition, nor would it probably have elicited a more painful exclamation than that which escaped involuntarily from
her mouth.

'It's him!' she cried.

'Indeed, my dear little sister,' replied an affable and charming
voice. 'But forgive me,' the owner of the voice exclaimed on
seeing the Duke d'Epernon. 'Forgive me! Am I interrupting?'

And he bowed to the ground in front of the Governor of
Guyenne, who acknowledged this with a benevolent gesture.

'Cauvignac!' Nanon muttered, but so softly that the name
was spoken in the heart rather than on the lips.

'Welcome, Monsieur de Canolles,' said the duke, with the
most contented expression in the world. 'Your sister and I have
spoken only of you since yesterday evening, and since yesterday
we have been wanting to see you.'

'Ah! You have been wanting me? Truly?' said Cauvignac,
turning to Nanon with a look that contained an indefinable
expression of irony and suspicion.

'Yes,' said Nanon. 'The duke has been kind enough to wish
you to be presented to him.'

'Only the fear that I might importune you, Monseigneur,'
said Cauvignac, once more bowing, 'has prevented me from
requesting the honour earlier.'

'Indeed, Baron,' said the duke. 'I have been admiring your
tact, but I must also reproach you for it.'

'Reproach me for my tact, Monseigneur? Me? Ha!'

'Yes, because if your good sister had not looked after your
affairs . . .'

'Oh!' Cauvignac exclaimed, with a eloquently reproachful glance at Nanon. 'Oh, so my good sister looked after the affairs . . . of . . .'

'Of her brother,' Nanon said quickly. 'What could be more natural?'

'And today, to what do I owe the pleasure of your company?'

'Yes,' said Cauvignac. 'To what do you owe the pleasure of my company, Monseigneur?'

'Well, of course, to chance, to the simple chance of the fact that you have come back.'

'Ah, ha,' Cauvignac thought. 'It appears that I went away.'

'Yes, you went away, wicked Brother, without telling me, except in two words that only increased my anxiety.'

'What do you expect, my dear Nanon?' said the duke with a smile. 'A man in love must be allowed some licence.'

'Oh, dear! It's getting complicated,' thought Cauvignac. 'Now it appears that I'm in love.'

'Come now,' said Nanon. 'Admit it.'

'I don't deny it,' Cauvignac replied, with a triumphant smile, while trying to find some small parcel of truth in the eyes around him from which he could elaborate a great big lie.

'Yes, all right,' said the duke, 'but let's have breakfast, if you please. You can tell us about your affairs while we are eating, Baron. Francinette, bring a knife and fork for Monsieur de Canolles. You haven't eaten yet, I hope, Captain?'

'No, Monseigneur, and I must tell you that the chill of the morning has sharpened my appetite no end.'

'You mean the chill of the night, you reprobate,' said the duke. 'You've been out and about roistering since last night.'

'Well, I never!' Cauvignac muttered to himself. 'For once the brother-in-law guessed right.'

'Very well, if you like . . . I have to admit it . . . The night air . . .'

'Come on, then,' said the duke, giving Nanon his arm and passing into the dining room, followed by Cauvignac. 'I hope we have something here to defeat your appetite, however healthy it is.'

And, indeed, Biscarros had surpassed himself. There were

not many dishes, but they were delicious and succulent. The yellow wine of Guyenne and the red wine of Burgundy slipped from their bottles like golden pearls and cascades of rubies.

Cauvignac devoured his meal.

'This lad is going to it with a will,' said the duke. 'And you, Nanon, aren't you eating?'

'I am not hungry any longer, Monseigneur.'

'Dear Sister!' said Cauvignac. 'And when I think that it is the pleasure of seeing me that has taken away her appetite! Honestly, I have to reproach her with loving me so much.'

'A grouse's wing, Nanon?' asked the duke.

'For my brother, Monseigneur, for my brother,' said the young woman, seeing Cauvignac's plate emptying with terrifying rapidity and fearing the banter that would follow the disappearance of the food.

Cauvignac held out his plate with an extremely grateful smile. The duke put the bird's wing on it, and Cauvignac put both in front of himself.

'Well, now, Canolles, what are you up to?' asked the duke with a familiarity that seemed to Cauvignac to bode very well. 'I'm not talking about love, you understand . . .'

'Oh, please do talk about it, Monseigneur, please do. Feel quite free,' said the young man, whose tongue was starting to be loosened by successive and equal applications of Médoc and Chambertin, and who, moreover, unlike those who themselves take other people's names, was not afraid of being interrupted by his double.

'He understands the joke very well,' said Nanon.

'So we can put it down to the little gentleman?' the duke asked.

'Yes,' said Nanon. 'The little gentleman you met yesterday evening.'

'Ah, yes . . . on my way,' said Cauvignac.

'And then at Master Biscarros's inn,' said the duke.

'And then at Biscarros's inn,' Cauvignac repeated. 'That's quite correct.'

'Did you really meet him?' Nanon asked

'The little gentleman?'

'Yes. What was he like? Come on! Tell me honestly.'

'Why,' said Cauvignac. 'He was a delightful little fellow, blond, slender, elegant and travelling with a sort of groom.'

'That's it exactly,' said Nanon, biting her lip.

'Are you in love?' asked the duke.

'Who with?'

'With that little, blond, slender, elegant gentleman?'

'Why, Monseigneur!' said Cauvignac, wanting to dispel any misunderstanding. 'What do you mean?'

'Do you still have the little pearl-grey glove against your heart?' the duke went on, with a sly laugh.

'The little pearl-grey glove?'

'Yes, the one you were sniffing and kissing so passionately yesterday evening.'

Cauvignac was completely lost.

'I mean the one that led you to suspect the trick, the me-ta-mor-pho-sis,' the duke went on, stressing each syllable.

Cauvignac understood everything from that one word.

'Oh!' he exclaimed. 'So the gentleman was a woman? Well, well, on my word, I suspected as much.'

'There's no more doubt,' Nanon murmured.

'Give me a drink, Sister,' said Cauvignac. 'I don't know who emptied the bottle over here on my side, but there's nothing left in it.'

'Come, come,' said the duke. 'There's a cure for this love, since it doesn't prevent him from drinking and eating, and the king's cause will not suffer.'

'The king's cause suffer!' cried Cauvignac. 'Never! The king's cause before everything. The king's cause is sacred. To His Majesty's health, sir!'

'So can we count on your devotion, Baron?'

'My devotion to the king?'

'Yes.'

'I should think you can count on it. I'd let myself be cut in pieces for him . . . sometimes.'

'And it's quite simple,' said Nanon, fearing that Cauvignac, in his enthusiasm for Médoc and Chambertin, might forget the character that he was playing and slip back into himself. 'It's quite simple: aren't you a captain in His Majesty's service, thanks to the goodness of my lord Duke?'

'I shall never forget it!' said Cauvignac, in a voice tearful with emotion, putting a hand on his heart.

'We shall do better than that, Baron, in future,' said the duke.

'Thank you, Monseigneur, thank you!'

'And we have already started.'

'Really?'

'Yes, you are too shy, my young friend,' the duke continued. 'When you need protection, you must turn to me – now that there is no further need of disguise, now that you don't need to hide, now that I know that you are Nanon's brother.'

'Monseigneur, from now on I shall come straight to you!' said Cauvignac.

'You promise?'

'I undertake to do so.'

'You would do well. Meanwhile, your sister will explain what it's about: she has a letter to give you on my behalf. Your fortune may be in the message that I am entrusting to you, on her recommendation. Follow the advice of your sister, young man, follow her advice; she has a fine mind, a distinguished wit and a generous heart. Love your sister, Baron, and you will have my goodwill.'

'Monseigneur!' Cauvignac burst out. 'My sister knows how much I love her and that I wish for nothing so much as to see her happy, powerful . . . and rich . . .'

'I like your warmth,' said the duke. 'So stay with Nanon while I go and take care of some rascally fellow. But as it happens, Baron, you may be able to tell me something about the bandit in question.'

'Certainly,' said Cauvignac. 'However, I shall have to know what bandit you mean, my lord, because there are a lot, of every kind, around nowadays.'

'Quite right, but the one I mean is among the most impudent scoundrels I've ever met.'

'Really!' said Cauvignac.

'Just imagine: this wretch, in exchange for the letter that your sister wrote to you yesterday, which he managed to procure

by the basest act of violence, demanded a letter of attestation
from me.'

'Really? A letter of attestation? But what interest was there
for you,' Cauvignac asked, in an innocent kind of way, 'in
having this letter from a sister to her brother?'

'Have you forgotten that I was unaware of the relationship?'

'You're right, I had.'

'And that I was silly enough – forgive me, won't you, Nanon?'
the duke went on, holding out his hand to the young lady,
' – that I was silly enough to be jealous of you?'

'Really? Jealous of me? Ah, my lord, you were very wrong
there.'

'So I wanted to ask you if you had any idea of who he could
be, this man who played the part of traitor to me.'

'No, truly ... But your lordship knows that such actions
do not go unpunished, and one day you will find out who
committed this one.'

'Yes, I certainly shall know it one day,' said the duke, 'and
I have taken measures to ensure that. But I would rather have
known it at once.'

'So,' Cauvignac said, pricking up his ears. 'You have taken
precautions?'

'Yes, indeed I have! And the scoundrel will be very lucky if
his letter of attestation doesn't get him hanged.'

'Really?' said Cauvignac. 'And how will you recognize this
letter of attestation from the other orders you have issued,
Monseigneur?'

'I made a mark on this one.'

'A mark?'

'Yes, a mark that is invisible to everyone, but which I shall
know by means of a chemical process.'

'Well, well, well!' said Cauvignac. 'What you've done is
very ingenious, Monseigneur, but you must beware in case he
suspects the trap.'

'Oh, there's no danger of that. Who's going to tell him?'

'Of course,' said Cauvignac. 'Nanon won't, and I won't . . .'

'Nor shall I,' said the duke.

'Nor will you! So you are quite right, Monseigneur, you will certainly know one day who this man is, and then . . .'

'And then, since I shall have kept my word to him – since I shall have given him what was promised by the letter of attestation – I shall have him hanged.'

'*Amen!*' said Cauvignac.

'And now, since you can give me no information about this rogue . . .'

'No, indeed I can't.'

'Well, then, as I said, I shall leave you with your sister. Nanon, give this boy precise instructions and, above all, let him lose no time.'

'Don't worry, Monseigneur.'

'I'll leave the two of you then.'

The duke made a graceful bow to Nanon and a friendly wave to her brother, before going down the stairs with a promise that he would probably come back during the day.

Nanon accompanied him to the top of the stairs.

'Damnation!' said Cauvignac. 'He did well to warn me, the worthy lord! Well, he's not so much of a ninny as he seems. But what shall I do with his letter of attestation? Why – the same thing that one does with a banknote: I'll discount it.'[44]

'Now, Monsieur,' said Nanon, coming back and closing the door. 'As the duke just said, it's the two of us.'

'Yes, my dear little sister,' Cauvignac replied. 'It's the two of us. Because the only reason I came here was to talk to you. But if we want to chat, we should sit down, so please take a chair.'

He pulled up a chair and gestured to Nanon, to show that it was for her. Nanon sat down with a raised eyebrow that boded no good.

'Firstly,' said Nanon, 'why are you not where you are supposed to be?'

'Now! My dear little sister, this is not very kind. If I was where I am supposed to be, I should not be here, and consequently you would not have the pleasure of seeing me.'

'Didn't you want to take holy orders?'

'No, I certainly didn't. Let's say that some people who are

interested in me, in particular yourself, did have a desire to make me take those vows, but personally I have never had a particularly strong religious vocation.'

'Yet you had an entirely religious education.'

'Yes, my sister, and I do believe that I took advantage of it most religiously.'

'Please, let's have no sacrilege. Don't mock what is holy!'

'I wasn't mocking, my dear little sister, just describing a fact. Here: you sent me to study with the Paulist brethren in Angoulême.'

'Well?'

'Well, I did study. I know Greek like Homer, Latin like Cicero and theology like Jan Hus.[45] So, having nothing more to learn from the worthy brothers, I left them, still in accordance with your intentions, to go to the Carmelites in Rouen and take my vows.'

'You are forgetting that I promised to give you an annual allowance of a hundred pistoles and that I kept my promise. It seems to me that a hundred pistoles should be more than enough for a Carmelite.'

'I don't deny it, dear Sister, but on the excuse that I was not yet myself a Carmelite, it was the monastery that always took the allowance.'

'However that may be, did you not make a vow of poverty in dedicating yourself to the Church?'

'If I did make a vow of poverty, I assure you that I carried it out to the letter. No one has been poorer than I.'

'But how did you get out of the monastery?'

'Ah, now! In the same way that Adam got out of the earthly paradise: knowledge was what damned me. I was too clever.'

'What! You were too clever?'

'Yes. You must realize that among the Carmelites, whose reputation is not that of being any Pico della Mirandolas, Erasmuses and Descartes,[46] I was naturally considered a prodigy of learning. The result was that when the Duke de Longueville come to Rouen to urge the town to declare in favour of the Parliament, I was sent to Monsieur de Longueville to address him, which I did in such elegant and well-chosen words that he showed himself not only very satisfied with my gift of the gab, but even asked if I should like to be his secretary. This was at the very moment when I was about to pronounce my vows.'

'Yes, I remember the occasion. You even, on the pretext of taking your leave of the world, asked me for a hundred pistoles, which I sent to you, to be given into your own hands.'

'And they were the only ones that I ever saw, on my honour!'

'But you were supposed to renounce the world.'

'Yes, that's what I intended, but it was not the intention of Providence, which probably has designs on me. It engineered a different fate for me, through the medium of Monsieur de Longueville. It did not want me to become a monk. So I bowed to the will of that good Providence, and, I must say, I have not repented of doing so.'

'So you are no longer in holy orders?'

'No, at least, not for the time being, dear Sister. I would not venture to tell you that I shall not return there some day, for what man can say on the eve what he will do tomorrow? Hasn't Monsieur de Rancé just founded the Trappist order?[47] Perhaps I shall follow Monsieur de Rancé's example and invent some new religious order. But for the time being I've tasted war, you know, and that's made me profane and impure for a bit. I'll purify myself at the first opportunity.'

'You – a warrior!' Nanon said, with a shrug of the shoulders.

'Why not? Dammit! I'm not saying that I'm any Dunois, Duguesclin, a Bayard or a fearless, blameless knight.[48] No, I am not arrogant enough to say that I have not a few small things to reproach myself with, and I would not, like the illustrious condottiere Sforza, ask what is meant by fear.[49] I am a man, and, as Plautus says: *Homo sum, et nihil humani a me alienum puto*, which means: 'I am a man and nothing human is foreign to me.'[50] So I do feel fear, as a man is entitled to feel it – which does not prevent me from being brave on occasion. I perform quite prettily with the sword and with the pistol, even when I am obliged to do so. But my true leaning, my definite vocation, you see, is for diplomacy. Either I am very much mistaken, my dear Nanon, or I shall become a great figure in the world of politics. Politics is a fine career: look at Monsieur de Mazarin:

if he is not hanged, he will go far. Well, I am like Monsieur de
Mazarin, so one of my fears, even perhaps the greatest of them,
is being hanged. Fortunately, you are there, dear Nanon, and
that gives me a lot of confidence.'

'So you're a warrior.'

'And a courtier when necessary. Oh, I made excellent use of
my stay with Monsieur de Longueville.'

'What did he teach you?'

'What princes are taught: how to make war, how to plot,
how to betray.'

'And where has that got you?'

'To the very top.'

'And you lost this eminent position?'

'Why, Monsieur de Condé has certainly lost his. One does
not control events. My dear sister, I, here before you, governed
Paris!'

'You did?'

'Yes, I did!'

'For how long?'

'For one hour and three-quarters, by the clock.'

'You governed Paris?'

'As an emperor.'

'How did that happen?'

'In the simplest manner. You know that the coadjutor, Monsieur de Gondi, the Abbé de Gondi –'[51]

'Very well!'

'– was absolute master of the city. Well, at that moment I
was with the Duke d'Elbeuf. He is a prince from Lorraine, and
there is no shame in being with Monsieur d'Elbeuf. However,
at that time, d'Elbeuf was the enemy of the coadjutor. So I
staged an uprising in favour of Monsieur d'Elbeuf, in which I
seized . . .'

'Who? The coadjutor?'

'Not at all. I should not have known what to do with him, I
should have found him most awkward. No, I took his mistress,
Mademoiselle de Chevreuse.'

'But that's dreadful!' Nanon exclaimed.

'Yes, isn't it dreadful for a priest to have a mistress? That's just what I thought. My idea was to capture her and take her so far away that he would not see her again. So I told him what I had in mind. But, do you know, that devil of a man has arguments that are irresistible: he offered me a thousand pistoles.'

'Poor woman! Being bargained for like that!'

'What do you mean? On the contrary, she must have been delighted: it proved how much Monsieur de Gondi loved her! It takes a man of the cloth to feel such devotion to a mistress. My belief is that it comes from their being forbidden to have one.'

'So you are rich?'

'Me!' said Cauvignac.

'Of course, thanks to this brigandry.'

'Don't talk about it! Look, Nanon, something dreadful happened to me! Mademoiselle de Chevreuse's chambermaid, whom nobody thought to buy back from me, and who had consequently stayed with me, ran off with the money.'

'At least, I hope, you kept the friendship of those whom you had served by your attack on the coadjutor.'

'Oh, Nanon, anyone can see you know nothing about princes. Monsieur d'Elbeuf made it up with the coadjutor. In the treaty between them, I was sacrificed. As a result, I was obliged to sell my services to Monsieur de Mazarin, but Monsieur de Mazarin is a coward. So much so that, as he was not prepared to make the reward equal to my services, I accepted an offer that was made to me to start another riot in honour of Councillor Broussel, the aim of which was to appoint Chancellor Séguier. But my men, the incompetent oafs, only half bludgeoned him. It was during that scuffle that I faced the greatest danger that has ever threatened me. Monsieur de La Meilleraie shot a pistol at me almost at point-blank range. Fortunately, I ducked. The shot went over my head and the illustrious marshal only killed an old woman.'

'What a tissue of horrors!'

'Not so, my dear sister. These are the realities of civil war.'

'Now I understand how a man who is capable of such things dared to do what you did yesterday.'

'What did I do?' Cauvignac asked with the most innocent look in the world. 'What did I dare to do?'

'You dared openly to pull the wool over the eyes of someone as important as Monsieur d'Epernon! But what I don't understand – and what, I must admit, I should never have dreamt of – is that a brother whom I have showered with my generosity should have coldly devised a plan to ruin his sister.'

'Ruin my sister! Me?'

'Yes, you. I did not need to wait to hear what you have just told me, which proves that you are capable of anything, to recognize the writing on this letter. There! Can you deny that this anonymous letter is in your handwriting?'

Indignantly, Nanon placed in front of her brother the letter of denunciation that the duke had given her the previous evening.

Cauvignac was not the slightest disconcerted as he read it.

'Well, now,' he said. 'What do you have against this letter? Do you by any chance consider it badly expressed? If so, I'm sorry for you, because that would prove that you have no feeling for literature.'

'It's not a question of style, Monsieur, it's the content. Was it or was it not you who wrote this letter?'

'It was undoubtedly me. If I had wanted to deny the fact, I should have disguised my handwriting. But it would have been pointless: I have never intended to hide myself from you. I even wanted you to recognize that the letter came from me.'

'Oh!' Nanon exclaimed, with a horrified gesture. 'You admit it?'

'It's a remaining trace of modesty, dear Sister. Yes, I have to tell you, I was driven by a sort of desire for revenge . . .'

'Revenge!'

'Yes, quite natural.'

'Revenge on me, you wretch! Just think what you are saying . . . What harm have I done you, for you to have the idea of taking revenge on me?'

'What have you done? But, Nanon, put yourself in my position. I leave Paris because I have too many enemies there – that's the misfortune of all politicians – I come back to you, I beg you . . . Don't you remember? You got three letters from me – and don't say that you didn't recognize my handwriting. It was exactly the same as that on the anonymous letter, and those letters were signed. I write you three letters to ask you for a hundred miserable pistoles – a hundred pistoles, from you who have millions! It was a pittance. But, you know, a hundred pistoles is my figure. Well, my sister rejects me. I come to call on her, and my sister has me shown off the premises. Of course, I make enquiries. Perhaps she is in distress, I think; this is the moment to prove to her that her generosity did not fall on stony ground. Perhaps she is not even free. In that case, she may be excused. You see: my heart was seeking excuses for you, and that's when I find out that my sister is free, happy, rich . . . very rich! And that some Baron de Canolles, a stranger, is usurping my privileges and being protected in my place. Well, jealousy turned my head.'

'You should say greed. You sold me to Monsieur d'Epernon, just as you sold Mademoiselle de Chevreuse to the coadjutor. What was it to you, may I ask, if I had a relationship with the Baron de Canolles?'

'To me? Nothing, and I should not even have thought to bother about it, if you had continued your relationship with me.'

'Do you know that if I said a single word to the Duke d'Epernon, if I made a complete confession to him, it would be the end of you?'

'Certainly.'

'You heard just now from his own mouth what he intends to do to the person who took that letter of attestation from him.'

'Don't talk about it. I shuddered to the marrow of my bones at the thought of it, and it took all my self-control not to give myself away.'

'And aren't you still shuddering, since you admit yourself that you feel fear?'

'No, because a straightforward confession would prove that Monsieur de Canolles is not your brother, and in that case the words of your letter, addressed to a stranger, have unfortunate implications. Believe me, it is better to have made an outright confession like the one that you have just made, you ungrateful girl – I don't say "blind", because I know you too well for that. But think how many advantages that I have foreseen will result from this little drama that I have cooked up. At first, it was very awkward for you, and you were scared that Monsieur de Canolles would arrive and, not having been warned, would flounder around quite horribly in the middle of your little family fantasy. But my presence, on the contrary, saved the day. Your brother is no longer a mystery. Monsieur d'Epernon has adopted him and done so like a true gentleman, I have to say. Now the brother no longer needs to hide: he is part of the household. Hence letters, meetings outside and even here indoors, as long as the brother with the black hair and eyes is not so ill-mannered as to look the Duke d'Epernon full in the face. One cloak looks very like another. And when Monsieur d'Epernon sees a cloak coming out of your house, who will be able to tell if it is or is not the brother's? So you are as free as air. The only thing is that, in order to be of service to you, I have rebaptized myself: I'm called Canolles, which is a pest. You should be grateful to me for the sacrifice.'

Nanon, struck dumb, did not know what argument to offer against this verbose flood, pouring out from such incredible insolence. So Cauvignac, taking advantage of the success of his storming attack, went on: 'And, my dear sister, since we have been reunited after such a long absence and you have found your brother again after so many setbacks, you might even admit that from now on you will sleep more soundly thanks to the protection of my love. You can live as peacefully as though the whole of Guyenne adored you – which is not the case, as you know. But it will have to do as we wish. I am setting up home right beside you, Monsieur d'Epernon is having me appointed colonel, and instead of six men, I have two thousand. With those two thousand men, I can perform the twelve labours of Hercules. I am made duke and peer. Madame d'Epernon dies, Monsieur d'Epernon marries you . . .'

'Before all that, two things,' Nanon snapped.

'What things, dear Sister? Carry on, I'm listening.'

'First of all, you will give the letter of attestation back to the duke. You heard the sentence from his own lips. After that, you will leave here at once, or else I shall be hanged, which is nothing to you, except that you will destroy yourself with me. I hope that that argument will make you consider my position.'

'Two replies, dear lady. The letter of attestation is my property, and you cannot prevent me from having myself hanged if that is my wish.'

'God forbid!'

'Thank you. It's not going to happen, don't worry. I told you just now how little I favour that form of death. So I'll keep the letter of attestation, unless you have an urge to buy it from me, in which case we can agree a price.'

'I don't need it. I'm the one who issues such documents.'

'Lucky Nanon!'

'So, are you keeping it?'

'Yes.'

'Even though you know what might happen to you?'

'Don't worry, I know where it's kept. As for retiring, I shall not commit such an error, since I am here thanks to the duke. And, moreover, in your hurry to get rid of me, you are forgetting one thing.'

'Which is?'

'The important mission that the duke mentioned to me, which is to make my fortune.'

Nanon went pale.

'You wretch!' she said. 'You know very well that this mission was not intended for you. You know that to misuse your position would be a crime and one that sooner or later will be punished.'

'So, I'm not going to misuse it – just to use it.'

'In any case, Monsieur de Canolles is named in the commission.'

'So? Aren't I called the Baron de Canolles?'

'Yes, but there they not only know his name, but also his face. Monsieur de Canolles has been to court several times.'

'At last! A good reason – the first you've given me. And so, as you see, I submit to it.'

'You would meet your political enemies there,' said Nanon. 'And it may be that your face, your true one, though under another name, is no less well known there than that of Monsieur de Canolles.'

'Oh, that won't matter if, as the duke said, the mission is meant to do a great service to France. The message will vouchsafe the messenger. A service of that importance implies a pardon, and an amnesty for the past is always the first condition of political conversions. So, believe me, dear Sister, it is not for you to impose your conditions on me, but for me to offer you mine.'

'And what are they, then?'

'Firstly, as I just told you, the first condition of any treaty: a general amnesty.'

'Is that all?'

'Then a settlement of our account.'

'What you're saying is that I owe you something?'

'You owe me the hundred pistoles that I asked for and that you inhumanely refused.'

'Here are two hundred.'

'At last. That's more like you, Nanon.'

'But on one condition.'

'Which is?'

'That you undo the harm you have done.'

'Fair enough. What must I do?'

'You must mount your horse and ride down the Paris road until you meet Monsieur de Canolles.'

'So I have to lose his name?'

'You give it back to him.'

'Saying what?'

'Give him this written order and make sure that he leaves at once to carry it out.'

'Is that all?'

'Absolutely.'

'Does he have to know who I am?'

'Quite the opposite: it essential that he should not know.'

'Oh, Nanon! Are you ashamed of your brother?'

Nanon did not reply. She was thinking. After a moment, she said: 'But how will I know that you carry out my request properly? If anything were sacred for you, I should ask you to swear by it.'

'You can do better than that.'

'How?'

'Promise me another hundred pistoles after the job is done.'

Nanon shrugged her shoulders.

'Agreed,' she said.

'Well, then, listen. I'm not demanding any oath from you: your word is enough for me. So, a hundred pistoles to the person who gives you, on my behalf, a receipt from Monsieur de Canolles.'

'You talk about "the person": don't you expect to come back yourself, then?'

'Who knows? I have business of my own near Paris.'

Nanon could not repress an involuntary movement of delight.

'Ah, now, that's not nice!' Cauvignac said with a laugh. 'But don't worry, Sis, no hard feelings.'

'No hard feelings. Now, be off.'

'I will, immediately. Just the time to drink a stirrup cup.'

Cauvignac poured the remains of the bottle of Chambertin into his glass, waved farewell to his sister with a gesture full of deference and, leaping into the saddle, vanished in a cloud of dust.

X

The moon was starting to rise as the Viscount de Cambes, followed by the faithful Pompée, left Master Biscarros's inn and set off down the Paris road.

After around a quarter of an hour, during which the viscount was entirely taken up with his thoughts, and during the course of which they had covered about a league and a half, he turned to the groom, who was bouncing along gravely on his saddle three yards behind his lord and master.

'Pompée,' the young man asked. 'Do you by any chance have my right glove?'

'Not as far as I know, Monsieur,' said Pompée.

'So what are you doing with your saddlebag?'

'I'm making sure that it is properly attached and tightening the straps so that it doesn't clink. The sound of gold is fatal, Monsieur, and leads to unfortunate encounters, especially by night.'

'Well done, Pompée,' said the viscount. 'I like to see you so attentive and cautious.'

'Those are very natural qualities in an old soldier, Viscount, and perfectly consistent with courage. However, since courage is not the same as foolhardiness, I must admit that I am sorry Monsieur Richon was unable to accompany us, because it is a hard task guarding twenty thousand livres, especially in stormy times such as those we live in.'

'What you say is very sensible, Pompée,' said the viscount. 'I agree with you on every point.'

'I might even be so bold as to say,' Pompée went on, emboldened by the viscount's approval, 'that it is rash to venture out as we are doing. Let's pause for a moment, if you don't mind, while I inspect my musket.'

'How is it, Pompée?'

'The wheel[52] is working well and anyone who tries to stop us will get a nasty surprise. Oh, oh! What can I see over there?'

'Where?'

'In front of us, about a hundred paces, to your right. Look, over there.'

'I can see something white.'

'Oh, dear! White! Some leather jerkin, perhaps. On my honour, I should rather like to make for that hedge to our left. In wartime, it's called entrenching. Let's entrench, Viscount.'

'If those are leather jerkins, Pompée, they are worn by the king's men, and soldiers of the king do not commit robbery on the highway.'

'Don't believe it, Monsieur, don't believe it. On the contrary, one hears constantly of robbers who adopt the uniform of His Majesty to commit a thousand foul deeds, each more accursed than the other, and recently in Bordeaux they broke two of the light horse on the wheel, who . . . I think I can recognize the uniform of the light cavalry, Monsieur.'

'The uniform of the light cavalry is blue, Pompée, and what we can see there is white.'

'Yes, but they often put a smock over their uniform, which is what the wretches did who were broken on the wheel in Bordeaux recently. They are waving urgently, I think. They appear to be threatening: that's their tactic, you see, Monsieur; they set up an ambush like that beside the road and, from a distance, with their guns in their hands, they force the traveller to throw down his purse.'

'But my good Pompée,' said the viscount, who was managing to keep his presence of mind, despite being very scared. 'If they are threatening us from a distance with their guns, you do the same with yours.'

'Yes, but they cannot see me, so my gestures would be useless.'

'If they cannot see you, they cannot threaten you, I should have thought.'

'You really don't understand a single thing about war,' the groom said, in a very bad mood. 'The same thing is going to happen to me as at Corbie.'

'Let's hope not, Pompée, because if I remember rightly it was at Corbie that you were wounded, wasn't it?'

'Yes, and a dreadful wound it was. I was with Monsieur de Cambes, a reckless fellow. We were patrolling at night to reconnoitre the site of the coming battle. We saw some leather uniforms. I told him not to take any unnecessary risks, but he insisted and marched directly towards them. I turned my back as a sign of annoyance. At that moment, an accursed musket ball . . . Viscount, let's be careful.'

'Let's be careful, Pompée, that's all I ask. But they don't seem to me to be moving very much.'

'They are sniffing out their prey. Let's wait.'

Fortunately for them, the travellers did not wait for long. After a short while, the moon came out from behind a black cloud, the edges of which it lit with silver, and splendidly lit up, at about fifty yards from the pair, were two or three shirts drying behind a hedge, with their arms extended.

These were the leather jerkins that had recalled Pompée's fatal patrol in Corbie.

The viscount burst out laughing and spurred on his horse. Pompée followed, shouting: 'Lucky I didn't do what I originally intended! I was going to fire in that direction, and I'd have looked like Don Quixote.[53] You see, Viscount, how useful it is to have gained caution and experience in war!'

There is always a moment of quiet after such excitements. After they had ridden past the shirts, the travellers covered two leagues quite calmly. The weather was glorious, and the shadows fell wide and black as ebony from the tips of the trees in a wood running along one side of the road.

'I definitely don't like a full moon,' said Pompée. 'When you can be seen from a distance, you are likely to be taken by surprise. I've always heard it said by soldiers that when two men are hunting one another, the moon only ever favours one of them. We are fully lit up, Viscount, which is unwise.'

'Well, then, Pompée, let's get into the shade.'

'Yes, but suppose there were men lying in ambush on the edge of this wood: we should be literally heading straight for the lion's . . . When you are campaigning, you never approach a wood until you have had it reconnoitred.'

'Unfortunately,' the viscount said, 'we don't have any scouts. Isn't that what they call men who reconnoitre the woods, Pompée?'

'True, true,' the groom muttered. 'Blast that Richon! Why didn't he come? We could have sent him on ahead, while we stayed behind, making the body of the army.'

'So, Pompée, what have we decided? Do we stay in the moonlight or go into the shade?'

'Let's head for the shade, Monsieur. As far as I can tell, that's the wisest course.'

'To the shade, then.'

'You're afraid, aren't you, Viscount?'

'Not at all, my dear Pompée, I swear.'

'You would be wrong to worry, because I'm here and looking out for you. If I was alone, you understand, I wouldn't worry too much. An old soldier doesn't fear God or the devil. But as a companion you are as difficult to protect as the money I have on my saddle, and the double responsibility frightens me. Ah! Ah! What's that black shadow over there? This time, it is moving.'

'There's no doubt of that,' said the viscount.

'You see what it means to be in the shadows: we can see the enemy, and he doesn't see us. Doesn't it appear to you that that wretch is carrying a musket?'

'Yes, Pompée. But that man is alone, and there are two of us.'

'Viscount, those who walk alone are the most dangerous, because solitude suggests a resolute character. The famous Baron des Adrets[54] always went alone. Ah! Look! I think he's aiming at us. He's going to fire. Get down!'

'No, no, Pompée. He's just changing his musket from one shoulder to the other.'

'So? Let's duck anyway, it's the done thing. We're facing enemy fire.'

'But you can very well see that he is not firing, Pompée.'

'Not firing?' The groom sat upright. 'Good! He must have been scared and our resolute air frightened him. Yes, he's afraid. Let me talk to him and you can talk afterwards, raising your voice.'

The shadow continued to advance.

'Hey there, Friend, who are you?' Pompée called.

The shadow stopped with a clear sign of fear.

'Now, you shout to him,' said Pompée.

'No point,' said the viscount. 'The poor devil is frightened enough already.'

'So! He's frightened, is he?' said Pompée, charging forward with his gun in his hand.

'Spare me, Monsieur!' the man said, falling to his knees. 'Spare me! I'm a poor pedlar who hasn't sold a pocket hand-kerchief in the past week, so I don't have a penny on me.'

What Pompée had imagined was a musket had in fact been the yardstick against which the poor devil measured his goods.

'I must inform you, my friend,' Pompée said – pompously, 'that we are not robbers, but soldiers, travelling by night because we fear nothing. So continue easy on your way. You are free.'

'Here, my friend,' the viscount added in a gentler voice. 'Here is a half pistole for the fear that we caused you. And may God go with you.'

The viscount gave the man half a pistole with his little white hand, and the poor devil set off, thanking heaven for a lucky encounter.

'You were wrong, Viscount, you were very wrong,' said Pompée, after another twenty yards.

'Wrong! Wrong? Why?'

'Giving half a pistole to that man. At night, one should never admit to having money. Did you see? That coward's first cry was to tell us that he did not have a penny on him.'

'That's right,' said the viscount. 'But he was a coward, as you said, while we, as you also said, are soldiers who fear nothing.'

'There is as great a difference between fearing and bewaring, Monsieur, as there is between fear and prudence. And, I repeat, it is not prudent to show a stranger whom one meets on the highway that one has gold.'

'Even if the stranger is alone and unarmed?'

'He may belong to an armed gang. He could be just a spy sent forward to reconnoitre the ground . . . He may return with a bunch of men, and what do you expect two men, however brave, to do against dozens?'

This time, the viscount acknowledged the truth of Pompée's reprimand, or rather, in order to cut short the admonition, seemed to admit his error, and they arrived on the banks of the little river Saye, near Saint-Genès.

There was no bridge, so they had to cross the ford.

At that, Pompée confided to the viscount a learned theory of river crossings, but since a theory is not a bridge, it was no less necessary, once the theory had been expounded, to cross the ford.

Luckily the river was not deep and this fresh incident was further proof for the viscount that seen from afar, especially by night, things are a lot more terrifying than seen close up.

So the viscount was seriously starting to be reassured – and, in any case, daylight would come in around an hour – when, in the middle of the woods around Marsas, the two travellers stopped suddenly: they had heard in the distance, far behind them, but quite distinctly, the sound of several galloping horses.

At the same time, their own horses raised their heads, and one whinnied.

'This time,' Pompée said in a strangled voice, grasping his companion's bridle, 'this time, Viscount, I hope that you will show a little more obedience and let an old soldier's experience decide the situation. I can hear a troop of horsemen. We are being followed. There! You see! It's the gang of that pretended pedlar. I told you so, rash as you are! Come on, no bravura, let's save your life and our money. Flight is often the means to victory. Horatius pretended to flee.'[55]

'Very well, let's flee, Pompée,' said the viscount, trembling all over.

Pompée dug in his spurs, and his mount, an excellent Roman horse, responded to them with an enthusiasm that fired the ardour of the viscount's Barb;[56] and the two of them vied with one another as they thundered along, the rhythmical thud of their shoes striking sparks off the roadway.

The race lasted about half an hour, but far from them gaining ground, it seemed to the two fugitives that their enemies were catching up.

Suddenly, a voice called through the darkness, a voice that, mingling with the whistling of the wind as the two riders cut the air, seemed to carry the mournful threat of spirits of the night. The voice made Pompée's grey hair stand on end.

'They are shouting "Stop!"' he muttered. 'They are shouting "Stop!"'

'Well, then, should we stop?' asked the viscount.

'On the contrary,' Pompée yelled. 'Let's go twice as fast, if possible. Forward! Forward!'

'Yes, yes! Forward! Forward!' the viscount cried, now as terrified as his defender.

'They're catching up,' said Pompée. 'Can you hear them?'

'Alas, I can . . .'

'There are more than thirty of them . . . Listen, they're calling again . . . We're done for!'

'Let's kill the horses, if we must,' said the viscount, more dead than alive.

'Viscount! Viscount! Stop!' cried the voice. 'Stop. Stop, old Pompée!'

'It's someone who knows us, it's someone who knows that we are carrying money to the princess, it's someone who knows that we are conspirators – we'll be broken on the wheel!'

'Stop, stop!' the voices said again.

'They're shouting for someone to stop us,' said Pompée. 'They have people up ahead. We're surrounded.'

'What if we were to ride off that way into the field, and let the ones who are following us go past.'

'It's an idea,' said Pompée. 'Off we go!'

The two riders put pressure on their mounts with knees and reins at the same time, and they turned to the left. The viscount's horse, which had been skilfully broken, leapt the ditch, but the heavier animal that Pompée was riding left it too late, the earth crumbled under its hooves and he fell, taking his master down with him. The poor groom gave a cry of complete despair.

The viscount, already fifty yards into the field, heard this cry of distress and, although himself very scared, turned his horse round and rode back towards his companion.

'Mercy!' Pompée was crying. 'Ransom! I surrender. I belong to the house of Cambes.'

A huge roar of laughter was the only reply to this pathetic designation, and the viscount, riding up at that moment, saw Pompée clasping the victor's stirrup, while the latter, in a voice stifled by laughter, was trying to reassure him.

'The Baron de Canolles!' the viscount exclaimed.

'I am that! *Sarpejeu!* Come now, Viscount, it's not right to make those who are looking for you run like that.'

'The Baron de Canolles!' Pompée repeated, still not sure of his good fortune. 'Monsieur the Baron de Canolles and Monsieur Castorin!'

'That's me, Monsieur Pompée,' said Castorin, standing up in his stirrups to see over the shoulder of his master, who was lying, helpless with laughter, on the pommel of his saddle. 'And what are you doing in this ditch?'

'You can see what,' said Pompée. 'My horse fell just as I was entrenching, thinking you were some enemy, and preparing to make a vigorous defence. Viscount,' he went on, getting up and shaking himself down. 'It's Monsieur de Canolles.'

'What, Monsieur! Are you here?' the viscount muttered, a sort of joy involuntarily creeping into his voice.

'My word, yes, it's me,' Canolles replied, looking at the viscount with a stare that was explained by the discovery of the glove. 'I was becoming terribly bored in that inn. Richon left after winning my money from me, and I learned that you had set off along the Paris road. By good fortune, I had business in the same direction, so I started off intending to join up with you. I did not suspect that I should have to ride my horse into the ground to do so. Curses! What a rider you are, my lad!'

The viscount smiled and stammered a few words.

'Castorin,' Canolles went on, 'why don't you help Monsieur Pompée to remount. You can see that, despite his agility, he can't manage it.'

Castorin dismounted and gave Pompée a hand, so that eventually he was back in the saddle.

'Now,' said the viscount, 'let's be going, if you please.'

'One second,' said Pompée, in a state of some confusion. 'Viscount, I think I'm missing something.'

'I think so, too,' said the viscount. 'You haven't got the bag.'

'Oh, my God!' said Pompée, pretending complete astonishment.

'You wretch!' said the viscount. 'Can you have lost it?'

'It cannot be far away, Monsieur,' said Pompée.

'Could this be it?' Castorin asked, picking up the object in question, though with some difficulty.

'That's it!' said the viscount.

'That's it!' cried Pompée.

'It's not his fault,' said Canolles, wishing to make a friend of the old groom. 'In the fall, the straps must have broken, and the bag fell off.'

'The straps are not broken, Monsieur, but cut,' said Castorin. 'Look!'

'Ah, ha, Monsieur Pompée,' asked Canolles. 'What does this mean?'

'What it means,' the viscount said sternly, 'is that in his fear of being chased by thieves, Pompée skilfully cut the straps so that he would no longer have the responsibility of being treasurer. In military terminology, what's that manoeuvre called, Pompée?'

Pompée wanted to excuse himself for his hunting knife, which he had incautiously taken out, but since he could not give a sufficient explanation, he remained, as far as the viscount was concerned, under the suspicion of having wanted to sacrifice the bag to his own safety.

Canolles was more lenient.

'All right,' he said. 'It happens. But tie the bag on again. Come on, Castorin, help Monsieur Pompée. You were right, Pompée, to be afraid of thieves: this bag is heavy and would be a good catch.'

'Don't joke, Monsieur,' said Pompée, with a shudder. 'At night, all jokes have a double meaning.'

'You're right, Pompée, right as usual. So,' Canolles continued. 'I want to escort you, you and the viscount. Two men as reinforcements will be useful to you.'

'Surely,' said Pompée. 'There's safety in numbers.'

'And you, Viscount, what do you think of my offer?' Canolles asked, seeing that the master appeared less enthusiastic than the groom about the generous offer that he was making.

'I find you as obliging as ever, Baron,' said the viscount. 'And I thank you for it from my heart, but we are not going in the same direction, and I am afraid of taking you out of your way.'

'What!' said Canolles, disappointed, seeing that the struggle at the inn was going to start again on the highway. 'What? We're not going in the same direction? Aren't you going to . . . ?'

'To Chantilly,' Pompée hastened to say, terrified at the idea of continuing the journey with no companion except the viscount.

The latter made a very emphatic and impatient gesture: if it had been daylight, they could have seen the blush of anger rising to his cheeks.

'But Chantilly is right on my way!' Canolles exclaimed, without apparently noticing the furious look that the viscount directed against poor Pompée. 'I'm going to Paris . . . or rather,' he added with a laugh, 'the fact is, Viscount, that I have nothing to do, and I don't know where I'm going. Are you going to Paris? I'll go to Paris. Are you going to Lyon? Then I'll go there. Are you going to Marseille? I've long had an urge to see Provence – I'm going to Marseille. Are you going to Stenay, where His Majesty's army is? Though I was born in the south, I've always had a taste for the north.'

'Monsieur,' the viscount announced, with a note of insistence that he doubtless owed to the irritable mood that Pompée had put him in. 'Do I have to tell you? I am travelling without companions, on private business of the highest importance and for very serious reasons. So forgive me for saying that if you insist, you will force me, to my great regret, to tell you that you are getting in my way.'

Only the memory of the little glove that Canolles kept hidden on his chest between his jerkin and his shirt kept the baron from bursting, being as impetuous and spirited as any Gascon, but he repressed his anger.

'Monsieur,' he continued more seriously, 'I have never heard tell that the highway belongs especially to any one person rather than another. I believe, if I am not mistaken, that it is even called "the king's highway", to indicate that all His Majesty's subjects are equally entitled to use it. So I am on the king's highway, with no intention of getting in your way; I am even here to do you a service because you are young, weak and nearly defenceless. I was not aware that I could be taken for a footpad. But since that is your view, I shall blame my unfortunate features. So excuse my importunity, Viscount. I have the honour to present my compliments. *Bon voyage!*'

And Canolles, after making his horse shy a little, bowed to the viscount and crossed over to the other side of the road, where Castorin followed him, in fact (and Pompée in spirit).

Canolles played out this scene with such grace and good

manners, and with such an attractive gesture, sweeping his broad felt hat across a forehead so pure, shaded with such silken black hair, that the viscount was moved less by his manners than by his noble appearance; Canolles had gone off, as we said, and Castorin followed him, upright and firm on his stirrups. Still on the other side of the road, Pompée was sighing loudly enough to crack the cobbles, so the viscount, who had thought a good deal, also spurred his horse and crossed over to join Canolles who pretended not to see or hear him. The viscount said, in a barely intelligible voice: 'Monsieur de Canolles!'

Canolles shuddered and turned round. A shiver of pleasure ran through him, and it seemed that all the music of the heavenly spheres had come together to provide him with this divine concert.

'Viscount!' he replied.

'Listen, Monsieur,' the other replied in a sweet, smooth voice. 'I am in fact afraid of being rude to a gentleman of your quality. Forgive my timidity: I was brought up by parents who were full of anxieties, born of their affection for me. I repeat, therefore, forgive me, I never meant to offend you and as a proof of our sincere reconciliation, please allow me to ride beside you.'

'What do you mean!' Canolles exclaimed. 'But, yes, a hundred times . . . a thousand times! I'm not someone who holds a grudge, Viscount, and to prove it . . .'

He held out his hand and into it slipped a finely made hand, light and evanescent, like the charming claw of a sparrow.

The rest of the night was spent in madcap chatter from the baron. The viscount listened and occasionally laughed.

The two servants brought up the rear. Pompée was explaining to Castorin how the Battle of Corbie had been lost when it could very well have been won, if only they had not neglected to invite him to the council of war that had taken place in the morning.

'But how did you end your business with the Duke d'Epernon?' the viscount asked Canolles as the first light of dawn was appearing.

'Not hard,' Canolles replied. 'According to what you told me, Viscount, he was the one who had business with me, and not I with him: either he has grown tired of waiting for me and has left, or else he is being stubborn and is still waiting there.'

'But ... Mademoiselle de Lartigues?' the viscount added, with a slight pause.

'Viscount, Mademoiselle de Lartigues cannot be at one and the same time at home with Monsieur d'Epernon and in the Golden Calf with me. We must not expect the impossible of women.'

'That's no answer, Baron. I'm asking how, being in love with Mademoiselle de Lartigues as you are, you were able to part with her.'

Canolles looked at the viscount with eyes that were already too sharp, because daylight had come, and there was no more shadow on the face of the young man than that of his felt hat.

He was greatly tempted to answer with what was in his mind. But Pompée and Castorin, as well as the viscount's serious air, restrained him. In any case, he was prevented by a little uncertainty: 'Suppose I was wrong, and that despite this little glove and little hand, it was a man ... Really! I'd die of shame at my mistake!'

So he held his peace and replied to the viscount's question with one of those smiles that are an answer to everything.

They stopped at Barbezieux to eat and give the horses a rest. This time, Canolles took breakfast with the viscount and over the meal admired that hand whose musk-scented envelope had caused him such a strong emotion. Moreover, the viscount was obliged on coming to the table to take off his hat and reveal hair so smooth, so lovely and so proudly set in such fine skin that only a man who was in love, and so already blind, could still be left in any doubt. But Canolles was too afraid of waking up not to prolong the dream. He found something delightful about the viscount's disguise, which allowed him a host of little familiarities that would have been forbidden by total recognition or a complete confession, so he said not a word to the viscount that might make him suspect that he was incognito no longer.

After breakfast, they set off again and rode until dinner. From time to time, the viscount was no longer able to conceal an exhaustion that gave his face a pearly tint or sent small shudders through his body; Canolles asked him in a friendly manner what it was. At that, Monsieur de Cambes smiled and appeared to be suffering no more; he even suggested increasing their pace, something that Canolles refused to do, saying that they had a long road ahead of them and that it was essential not to overtire the horses.

After dinner, the viscount found it quite hard to get up. Canolles hurried to his aid.

'You need a rest, my young friend,' he said. 'If we carry on like this, it will kill you by the third stage. We shall not ride on tonight, but instead take to our beds. I want you to sleep well, and the best room in the inn is yours, or I'll want to know the reason why!'

The viscount gave Pompée such a terrified look that Canolles could not repress an urge to laugh.

'When we set off on a long journey such as this,' said Pompée, 'we should each have our own tent.'

'Or one tent for two,' said Canolles, in the most casual manner imaginable. 'That would do.'

A shudder ran through the viscount's whole body. The shot had hit its target, and Canolles noticed it. Out of the corner of his eye, he saw the viscount make a sign to Pompée. The latter went over to his master, who whispered a few words to him, and very shortly afterwards, on some pretext or other, Pompée rode on ahead and disappeared.

An hour and a half after this occurrence, the explanation for which Canolles did not even try to discover, the travellers rode into a fair-sized town and saw the groom standing at the door of a decent-looking hostelry.

'Ah!' said Canolles. 'It appears that this is where we shall spend the night, Viscount?'

'Why, yes, if you wish.'

'Why, I wish whatever you do. As I told you, travelling is a pleasure for me, while you, as you told me, are travelling on business. It's just that I am afraid you will not be too comfortable in this shack.'

'Oh, a night doesn't last long,' said the viscount.

They halted and, proving swifter than Canolles, Pompée ran forward and took his master's bridle. In any case, it occurred to Canolles that such an attentive gesture would be ridiculous coming from one man to another.

'Quickly, my room,' said the viscount. 'It is true, you are right, Monsieur de Canolles,' he continued, turning towards his companion. 'I am really very tired.'

'It is here, Monsieur,' said the hostess, indicating a rather large room on the ground floor overlooking the courtyard, but with bars on the windows and situated underneath the loft and granaries of the house.

'So where is mine then?' asked Canolles.

He turned covetous eyes towards a door beside the viscount's: the thin walls would have been a very feeble protection against such burning curiosity as his.

'Yours?' said the hostess. 'Come this way, Monsieur, I'll take you to it.'

Without apparently noticing Canolles's sullen look, she led him to the far end of an exterior corridor, full of doors and separated from the viscount's room by the whole length of the courtyard.

The viscount had been watching this proceeding from the door of his room.

'Now, I'm sure of it,' thought Canolles. 'But I've behaved like a fool. Come, now, making a glum face would be fatal. Let's put on our most gracious manner.' And, going back along the sort of balcony that, as we have said, formed the exterior corridor, he exclaimed: 'Goodnight, my dear viscount! Would you like me to wake you up tomorrow morning? No? Very well, you must wake me at your own time. Goodnight to you.'

'Goodnight, Baron,' said the viscount.

'By the way,' Canolles continued. 'Have you everything you need? You wouldn't like me to lend you Castorin to untie your laces?'

'Thank you, I have Pompée. He will be sleeping next door.'

'Wise precaution. I'll do the same with Castorin. A prudent measure, huh, Pompée? You can never be too sure, in an inn. Goodnight, Viscount.'

The viscount replied with the same wish, and the door closed.

'Very well, very well, Viscount,' Canolles muttered. 'Tomorrow it will be my turn to prepare our quarters, and I shall have my revenge. Well, now, he's closing both curtains and hanging a sheet over the window to prevent anyone even seeing his shadow. Dammit! This little gentleman is a very prudish lad. But not to worry. Until tomorrow . . .'

And Canolles went in, grumbling, and got undressed in a very bad temper. He went to bed sulking and dreamt that Nanon found the viscount's little pearl-grey glove in his pocket.

XI

On the following day, Canolles was in an even jollier mood than the night before, while the Viscount de Cambes relaxed and also gave way to less restrained enjoyment. Even Pompée fooled around while recounting his campaigns to Castorin. The whole morning was spent in pleasant conversation on both sides.

At breakfast, Canolles made his excuses for leaving the viscount, saying that he had a long letter to write to one of his friends, who lived in the region. He also warned that he would have a visit to make to another of his friends, whose house he thought must be situated some three or four leagues from Poitiers, almost beside the main highway. Canolles enquired of this friend, telling the innkeeper his name, and received the reply that he would find the house a little before the village of Jaulnay, where he would recognize it from its two towers.

Then, as Castorin was leaving the little group to deliver the letter, and Canolles himself had to hurry on ahead, the viscount was asked in advance to indicate the place where they would spend the night. The viscount cast an eye on a little map that Pompée was carrying in a case, and suggested the village of Jaulnay. Canolles made no objection and even slyly went so far as to say aloud: 'Pompée, if you are sent on, as you were yesterday, as quartermaster, please try if possible to get me a room close to your master's so that we shall be able to chat to one another.'

The cunning groom exchanged a glance with the viscount and smiled, determined to do nothing of what Canolles was telling him. As for Castorin, who had received his instructions in advance, he came to fetch the letter and was ordered to join them at Jaulnay. There was no question of him mistaking the inn, because Jaulnay possessed only one such establishment, the Great Charles Martel.

They started off. A hundred yards from Poitiers, where they had lunched, Castorin took a right-hand fork. They went on for about two hours more. Finally, Canolles recognized his friend's house from the description he had been given. He showed it to the viscount and took his leave of him, once more inviting Pompée to take care of his lodging, before taking a fork to the left.

The viscount's mind was quite easy: the previous evening had gone off without complications, and the day had passed without the slightest hint of suspicion, so he no longer feared that Canolles might prove in any way an obstacle to his plans, and provided the baron remained a mere travelling companion, kind, merry and witty, he asked nothing better than to complete the journey with him. So, either because the viscount considered the precaution unnecessary, or because he did not wish to separate from his groom and remain alone on the highway, he did not even send Pompée on ahead.

They arrived in the village at night, with the rain coming down in torrents. By good fortune, one room was heated, and the viscount, in a hurry to change his clothes, took it and entrusted Pompée with finding somewhere for Canolles.

'It's done,' said the selfish Pompée, who was himself eager to get to bed. 'The innkeeper's wife has promised to look after it.'

'Very well. And my bag?'

'It's here.'

'My scents?'

'Here they are.'

'Thank you. Where are you sleeping, Pompée?'

'At the end of the corridor.'

'What if I need something?'

'Here's a bell. The innkeeper's wife will come.'

'That all right. This door does close properly, doesn't it?'

'You can see, Monsieur.'

'There are no bolts!'

'No, but there is a lock.'

'Good, I'll shut myself in. There is no other way in?'

'Not as far as I know.'

Pompée took the candle and made an inspection of the room.

'Make sure the shutters are secure.'

'The hooks are fastened.'

'Very well. Off you go, Pompée.'

Pompée left, and the viscount turned the key in the lock.

An hour later, Castorin, who had arrived first at the hotel and was lodged close to Pompée, though Pompée did not know it, came out of his room on tiptoe and opened the door for Canolles.

The latter slipped into the hotel with pounding heart and, leaving Castorin to close the door, got him to point out the viscount's room, then went upstairs.

The viscount was about to get into bed when he heard footsteps in the corridor.

We may have remarked earlier that the viscount was very timid. These footsteps made him tremble, and he listened attentively.

The footsteps stopped in front of his door.

A moment later there was a knock.

'Who's there?' asked such a terrified voice that Canolles would not have recognized its tones, if he had not previously had the opportunity to hear the various modulations of that voice.

'It's me!' said Canolles.

'What! You?' said the voice, changing from fear to terror.

'Yes. What do you know, Viscount? There's no more room in your hotel, not a single room free ... Your idiotic Pompée didn't think of me. And there's no other hotel in the village. But since your room has two beds ...'

The viscount looked, appalled, at the two twin beds next to one another in an alcove, separated only by a table.

'So, you see?' Canolles went on. 'I'm claiming one of them. I beg you, open the door quickly, because I'm dying of cold . . .'

There followed a great sound of confusion from the room, a rustle of clothes and hurried steps.

'Yes, Baron, yes,' said the viscount's voice, still more afraid. 'Yes, I'm coming, I'm coming.'

'And I'm waiting. But for pity's sake, my dear friend, please hurry, if you don't want to find me frozen stiff.'

'I'm sorry, I was asleep, you understand . . .'

'Really! I thought there was a light on.'

'No, you were mistaken.'

The light was put out at once, but Canolles did not remark on this.

'Here I am . . . I can't find the door,' said the viscount.

'I'm not surprised,' said Canolles. 'I can hear your voice from the other end of the room. Come over here . . .'

'I'm looking for the bell to call Pompée.'

'Pompée is at the far end of the corridor; he won't hear you. I tried to wake him up to get something out of him, but – pooh! – it was impossible. He sleeps like the deaf post that he is.'

'Then I'll call the innkeeper's wife.'

'She has given her bed up to a traveller and gone to sleep in the loft. No one is going to come, my good friend. And in any case, why call for people? I don't need anyone.'

'But I . . .'

'All you have to do is open the door. I thank you. I feel my way to my bed, I get into it and that's all. So please open up.'

'But there must be another room,' said the viscount in desperation. 'Even without beds. It's impossible that there is no other room. Let's call someone, let's look.'

'My dear viscount, it has just struck half past ten. You will wake up the whole hotel – they'll think there is a fire in the house. It will be a commotion that keeps us awake all night, which is a shame, because I am dropping with tiredness.'

The last assertion seemed to reassure the viscount a little. Small steps approached the door, and it opened. Canolles went in, shutting it behind him. The viscount, after opening the door, had hurried away from it.

The baron now found himself in a more or less dark room, because the last coals of the fire, which was dying down, did not give enough light. The air was warm and filled with all the scents that indicate the greatest refinement of toilet.

'Ah. Thank you, Viscount,' said Canolles. 'It really is better here than in the corridor.'

'Do you want to sleep, Baron?' the viscount asked.

'Yes, indeed, I do. So just show me my bed, since you know the room. Or else let me relight your candle.'

'No, no, there's no need!' the viscount said quickly. 'Your bed is here, on the left.'

As the viscount's left was the baron's right, the latter went to the right, met a window, tripped over a little table near it and touched the bell on that table, which the viscount had been searching for with such desperation. Just in case, Canolles slipped the bell into his pocket.

'What are you saying?' he exclaimed. 'Come, now, Viscount, are we playing hide-and-seek? You should at least cry beware! But what are you hunting around for in the dark?'

'I'm looking for the bell to call Pompée.'

'But what on earth do you want with Pompée?'

'I want . . . I want him to set up a bed next to mine.'

'For whom?'

'For himself.'

'For himself? What are you talking about, Viscount? Servants in our room! Come, come, you're behaving like a terrified little girl. Fie! We're big enough lads to take care of ourselves. No, just give me a hand and guide me to my bed, because I can't find it . . . or else, let's relight the candle.'

'No, no, no!' the viscount cried.

'Since you don't want to give me your hand, you should a least give me a piece of thread, because I'm in a real labyrinth here.'

He walked forward, arms outstretched, in the direction from which he had heard the voice, but he saw what seemed like a shadow flitting by him and caught a scent wafting past. He closed his arms, but like Virgil's Orpheus, he embraced only air.[57]

'There, there!' said the viscount from the far end of the room. 'You are right next to your bed, Baron.'

'Which of them is mine?'

'It doesn't matter. I shall not be going to bed.'

'What! Not go to bed!' said Canolles, turning round at this unwise remark. 'So what will you do?'

'I'll spend the night on a chair.'

'Now, now!' said Canolles. 'I really will not put up with such childishness. Come on, Viscount!'

Guided by a last ray of light bursting from the hearth, then dying, he glimpsed the viscount pressed into a corner between the window and the chest of drawers, wrapped in his cloak.

The ray of light was no more than a flash, but it was enough to guide the baron and to convince the viscount that he was done for. Canolles walked straight forward with his arms outstretched, and, although the room was once more in darkness, the poor young man realized that this time he would not escape his pursuer.

'Baron! Baron!' the viscount stammered. 'Don't come forward, I beg you. Baron, stay just where you are. Not another step, if you are a gentleman.'

Canolles stopped. The viscount was so close to him that he could hear his heart beat and feel the warmth of his panting breath. At the same time, a delicious, intoxicating scent, made up of all the emanations of youth and beauty, a scent a thousand times sweeter than that of flowers, seemed to enfold him, denying him any possibility of obeying the viscount, even if he had wished to.

Nonetheless, he remained for a moment where he was, with his hands reaching out towards those hands that were trying to repel him in advance, and feeling that he had only to make one more movement to touch this delightful body, whose suppleness he had so many times admired in the past two days.

'Mercy, mercy,' the viscount murmured, in a voice in which

a hint of desire was starting to mingle with terror. 'Mercy!' And the word expired on his lips as Canolles heard the charming body slip down the panelling and fall on its knees.

He took a deep breath. There was something in the imploring voice that told him his adversary was already half overcome.

So he took another step forward, reached out his hands and found those of the young man, clasped in entreaty, as this time, no longer having even the strength to utter a cry, he let out an almost painful sigh.

Suddenly, outside the window, they heard the galloping of a horse and an urgent knocking on the door of the inn. These knocks were followed by cries and other noises. Knocks and calls alternated.

'The Baron de Canolles!' a voice cried.

'Oh, God, thank you, I am saved!' said the viscount.

'Damn the creature!' said Canolles. 'Couldn't he have come tomorrow morning?'

'Baron de Canolles!' cried the voice. 'The Baron de Canolles! I must speak to him this very moment.'

'Now, then, what is it?' the baron asked, taking a step backwards.

'Sir, sir,' Castorin said at the door. 'Someone is asking for you, someone looking for you.'

'But who is it, you vagabond?'

'A courier.'

'From whom?'

'From the Duke d'Epernon.'

'And what does he want with me?'

'On the king's service.'

At this magic word that had to be obeyed, Canolles, cursing all the while, opened the door and went downstairs.

Pompée could be heard snoring.

The courier had come in and was waiting in a low-ceilinged room. Canolles went to find him and read Nanon's letter with the colour draining from his face – because, as the reader has already guessed, the courier was Courtauvaux himself, who, leaving ten hours after Canolles, despite his haste, had only managed to catch him up on the second stage of his journey.

A few questions to Courtauvaux left Canolles in no doubt about the need for haste. He reread the letter and the words 'Your good sister, Nanon' told him what had happened – that is to say, that Mademoiselle de Lartigues had got out of a difficult situation by pretending that he was her brother.

Many times, Canolles had heard Nanon herself speak, in quite unflattering terms, about the brother whose place he had taken. This added not a little to the reluctance with which he obeyed the duke's message.

'Very well,' he said to Courtauvaux, without offering him credit in the hotel and without emptying his purse into his hand, as he would certainly have done on any other occasion. 'Very well, tell your master that you caught me up, and I obeyed at once.'

'And shall I say nothing to Mademoiselle de Lartigues?'

'Yes, do. Tell her that her brother appreciates the feelings that have made her act in this way and is much obliged to her. Castorin, saddle up the horses!'

And, without saying anything more to the messenger, who was quite amazed at this rough reception, Canolles went back upstairs to the viscount, whom he found pale, trembling and once again dressed. Two candles were burning on the mantelpiece.

Canolles gave a look of profound regret at the alcove and, above all, at the two twin beds, one of which bore the signs of a light, brief pressure on it. The young man followed this look with a feeling of modesty that brought a blush to his cheek.

'Be of good cheer, Viscount,' said Canolles. 'You are rid of me for the whole of the rest of your journey. I am leaving on a mission for the king.'

'When?' the viscount asked, in a voice that was still anxious.

'This very instant: I'm going to Mantes, where the court is, apparently.'

'Farewell, Monsieur,' the young man barely managed to say, slumping down into a chair without daring to raise his eyes to his companion.

Canolles took a step towards him.

'Doubtless, I shall not see you again,' he said, with a voice full of emotion.

'Who knows?' the viscount said, trying to smile.

'Promise one thing to a man who will keep the memory of you for ever,' Canolles said, putting a hand on his heart, with a harmony of voice and gesture that left no doubt as to his sincerity.

'What is that?'

'That you will think of him sometimes.'

'I promise.'

'Without . . . anger . . .'

'Yes.'

'And your hand on that promise?' said Canolles.

The viscount held out a hand.

Canolles took the trembling hand with no other intention than to clasp it in his own. But, responding to an irrepressible urge, he pressed it ardently to his lips and fled from the room, muttering: 'Oh, Nanon, Nanon! Can you ever recompense me for what I am losing because of you?'

XII

If we now follow the princesses of the house of Condé to that exile in Chantilly, which Richon described to the viscount as so terrible, this is what we shall see.

Beneath the lovely walks of chestnut trees, sprinkled with a snow of flowers, and on those grassy lawns that extend down to the blue ponds, there is a constant swarm of people walking, laughing, conversing and singing. Here and there, amid the long grass, a few faces of people with books appear surrounded by waves of greenery, in which one can only distinguish the white page that they are eagerly reading, which belongs either to Monsieur de la Calprenède's *Cléopâtre*, or to Monsieur d'Urfé's *L'Astrée* or to Mademoiselle de Scudéry's *Grand Cyrus*.[58] From the depths of the bowers of honeysuckle and clematis, come the sounds of lutes being tuned and the voices of invisible singers. Finally, along the great avenue that leads to the château, from time to time a rider bearing an order flashes by with the speed of a lightning bolt.

Throughout this time, on the terrace, three women, dressed in satin and followed at a distance by silent, respectful lackeys, are walking, gravely making ceremonious gestures, full of majesty. In the middle is a lady of noble bearing, despite her fifty-seven years, authoritatively discursing on the affairs of state. To her right a young woman, stiffly dressed in dark clothes, is listening with raised eyebrow to her companion's learned theory, while finally on the left is another old lady, the stiffest and most strait-laced of all three because she is of less noble lineage, who is speaking, listening and meditating all at once.

The lady in the centre is the Dowager Princess, mother of the victor of Rocroi, Norlingen and Lens, the man whom, since he has been persecuted and this persecution has led him to Vincennes, people have started to call the Great Condé,[59] the name that posterity will retain for him. This lady, on whose features one can still perceive the remains of the beauty that made her the last and perhaps most passionate love of King Henri IV, has just been wounded in her maternal feelings and in her pride as a princess by a *facchino italiano*[60] who was called Mazarini when he was a servant of Cardinal Bentivoglio, and who is now addressed as His Eminence, Cardinal Mazarin, since he became the lover of Anne of Austria and first minister of the kingdom of France.

He it is, who has dared to imprison Condé and to exile the noble prisoner's mother and wife to Chantilly.

The lady on the right is Claire-Clémence de Maillé, Princess de Condé, who, according to an aristocratic custom of the age, is called simply 'Madame the princess', to show that the wife of the head of the Condé family is the first princess of the blood, the princess *par excellence*: she has always been proud, but now that she is being persecuted, her pride has swollen as a result of persecution, and she has become arrogant.

In truth, while she was condemned to play a secondary part as long as her husband was free, his imprisonment has raised her to the status of heroine: she has become more pitiable than a widow, and her son, the Duke d'Enghien, who is coming up to his seventh birthday, is more interesting than an orphan. Eyes are fixed on her, and, were it not for the fear of ridicule, she would dress in mourning. Since Anne of Austria[61] imposed exile on these two weeping women, their shrill cries have changed to muted threats: they will change from victims of oppression to rebels. The princess, a Themistocles in a mobcap, has her Miltiades in skirts[62] and the laurels of Madame de Longueville, temporarily Queen of Paris, prevent her from sleeping.[63]

The duenna on the left is the Marquise de Tourville, who does not dare write novels, but composes in politics. She has not made war in person, like brave Pompée, or like him taken a shot wound at the Battle of Corbie, but her husband, who was a reasonably well-esteemed captain, was wounded at La Rochelle and killed at Fribourg. As a result, having inherited his family fortune, she considered herself at the same time heir to his military genius. Since coming to join the princesses in Chantilly, she has already drawn up three plans of campaign that have successively excited the admiration of the women of the court and which have not been abandoned, but adjourned to the moment when the sword will be drawn and the sheath thrown away. She does not dare to put on her husband's uniform, though she is sometimes tempted to do so, but she keeps his sword hanging in her bedroom above the head of the bed, and from time to time, when she is alone, she takes it out of its sheath in a very martial manner.

So Chantilly, for all its festive air, might as well be nothing more than a vast barracks, and if one were to search hard one would find gunpowder in the cellars and bayonets in the leafy bowers.

The three ladies, in their gloomy walk, are at every turn nearing the main door of the château and seem to be awaiting the arrival of some important messenger. The Dowager Princess has already said several times, shaking her head and sighing: 'We shall fail, my daughter, we shall be humiliated.'

'One must pay a little for a great deal of glory,' said Madame de Tourville, without at all relaxing her stiff posture. 'And there is no victory without a battle!'

'If we do fail, if we are defeated,' said the young princess, 'we shall have our revenge.'

'Madame,' said the Dowager Princess. 'If we fail, it will be God who has defeated the prince. Do you wish to have revenge on God?'

The young princess bowed before her mother-in-law's sublime humility, and the three figures, saluting one another in this way amid a haze of mutual flattery, looked rather like a bishop accompanied by two deacons with censers, using God as the pretext for the homage that they each paid to the others.

'No Monsieur de Turenne, no Monsieur de La Rochefoucauld, no Monsieur de Bouillon!' the dowager muttered. 'Everyone is missing at once.'

'And no money!' added Madame de Tourville.

'Who can we count on, if Claire herself has forgotten us?' asked Madame the princess.

'Who told you that Madame de Cambes has forgotten us, Daughter?'

'She is not coming back.'

'Perhaps she cannot come. The roads, as you know, are guarded by Monsieur de Saint-Aignan[64] and his army.'

'She might at least write.'

'How do you expect her to entrust such an important reply to paper? The rallying of a whole town like Bordeaux to the princes' side. No, that's not what is worrying me.'

'In any case,' Madame de Tourville continued, 'one of the three plans I had the honour to submit to Your Highness had as its essential aim an uprising in Guyenne.'

'Yes, yes, and we shall adopt it if necessary,' replied Madame the princess. 'But I am inclined to share the opinion of my mother, and I am starting to think that Claire has met with some misfortune; otherwise, she would be here already. Perhaps her tenants have let her down; a peasant always seizes the opportunity not to pay his taxes when he can get out of it. And can we tell what the people of Guyenne may or may not have done, for all their promises? Those Gascons!'

'Chatterboxes!' said Madame de Tourville. 'Individually brave, I grant you, but poor soldiers in the mass. Good for shouting: "Long live the prince!" when they are scared of the Spaniards, that's all.'

'However, they loathed Monsieur d'Epernon,' said the Dowager Princess. 'They hanged him in effigy in Agen and promised to hang him in person in Bordeaux if he ever went back there.'

'Had he gone back, they are the ones he would have hanged,' said the princess, contemptuously.

'And all this,' Madame de Tourville went on, 'is the fault of Monsieur Lenet ... Of Monsieur Pierre Lenet,'[65] she said, affectedly. 'That stubborn counsellor, whom you insist on keeping and who is only good for undermining whatever we do. If he had not rejected my second plan, which, as you will remember, had as its aim a surprise capture of the Château de Vayres, the Ile Saint-Georges and the fort at Blaye, we should by now have Bordeaux under seige and eventually the town would have to capitulate.'

'I should prefer, if Their Highnesses are of that mind, that it should come over to us of its own free will,' said a voice behind Madame de Tourville, in a tone that, while respectful, was not without a hint of irony. 'A town that capitulates gives in to force and commits itself to nothing. A town which hands itself over, compromises itself and is obliged to follow those to whom it has given itself right to the end.'

The three ladies turned round and saw Pierre Lenet. While they were on one of their movements towards the main door of the château, towards which their eyes constantly turned, he had emerged from a little door opening directly on to the terrace and had approached them from behind.

What Madame de Tourville had said was true in part. Pierre Lenet, counsellor to the Prince de Condé, was a cold, learned and solemn man, who had been entrusted by the prisoner with the mission of keeping watch on both his friends and his enemies, and it must be said that he had far more trouble in preventing the prince's friends from compromising his cause than in combating the hostile designs of his enemies. But, being as wily and as clever as a lawyer, accustomed to the petty squabbles and ruses of the court, he usually had his way, either by some fortunate piece of countermining or by some unshake-able inertia. Moreover, it was in Chantilly itself that he fought his most cunning battles. Madame de Tourville's vanity, the princess's impatience and the aristocratic inflexibility of the dowager were easily matched by the wit of Mazarin, the pride of Anne of Austria and the vacillations of Parliament.

Lenet, entrusted with correspondance by the princes, had made it a rule not to give news to the princesses until it was necessary to do so and elected himself judge of this necessity – because, since feminine diplomacy does not always proceed through mystification, which is the first principle of masculine diplomacy, several of Lenet's plans had thus been communi-cated by his friends to his enemies.

The two princesses, who, despite the opposition they met with in Lenet, nonetheless recognized his devotion and above all his usefulness, welcomed the counsellor with a friendly gesture, and a hint of a smile even appeared on the lips of the dowager.

'Well, my dear Lenet, you heard,' she said. 'Madame de Tourville was bemoaning her fate, or rather our fate. Ah, my dear Lenet, our affairs! Our affairs!'

'Madame,' Lenet said, 'I do not see things in nearly as black a light as Your Highness. I am expecting a lot from time and the reversals of fortune. You know the proverb: "Everything comes to those who wait."'

'Time! Reversals of fortune! All that's philosophy, Monsieur Lenet, not politics,' the princess exclaimed.

It was Lenet's turn to smile.

'Philosophy is useful in everything, Madame, especially in politics. It teaches us not to become arrogant in success and not to lose patience in failure.'

'No matter,' said Madame de Tourville. 'I'd prefer a piece of good news to all your maxims. Isn't that so, Princess?'

'I admit it is,' said Madame de Condé.

'Your Highness will be happy, then, because you will receive three such dispatches today,' Lenet retorted, as calmly as ever.

'What! Three?'

'Yes, Madame. The first has been seen on the road from

Bordeaux, the second is coming from Stenay and the third from La Rochefoucauld.'

The two princesses gave exclamations of happy surprise. Madame de Tourville bit her lip.

'My dear Pierre,' she said, in a simpering tone, to disguise her spite and to hide the bitterness of what she was about to say under a sugary coating, 'it seems to me that a skilled necromancer like yourself should not stop when things are going so well, but tell us what is in the dispatches after announcing that they are coming.'

'My art, Madame, does not extend as far as you believe,' he said modestly. 'It is limited to being a faithful servant. I announce, but do not guess.'

At that moment, as though Lenet had a familiar demon to serve him, they saw two riders coming through the gates of the château and galloping towards them. At once, a flock of curious people, abandoning the alleyways and the lawn, swooped towards the steps in order to have its share of the news.

The two riders dismounted, and one of them, handing over the bridle of his sweating horse to the other, who seemed to be his lackey, ran rather than walked from one end of the gallery towards the princesses, whom he could see at the other end, making their own way towards him.

'Claire!' the princess exclaimed.

'Yes, Your Highness. Please accept my humble respects.' And, going down on one knee, the young man tried to grasp the princess's hand and kiss it.

'In my arms, dear Viscountess, in my arms!' cried Madame de Condé, lifting her to her feet.

And, after agreeing to be embraced by the princess, with every possible mark of respect, the rider turned towards the Dowager Princess and gave a deep bow.

'Quickly, dear Claire, tell us,' said the dowager.

'Yes, tell us,' Madame de Condé repeated. 'Have you seen Richon?'

'I have, Your Highness, and he gave me a message for you.'

'Is it good or bad?'

'I really don't know. It consists in two words.'

'What are they? Quickly, I'm dying with impatience.'

There were signs of burning anxiety on the faces of the two princesses.

'*Bordeaux – yes*,' said Claire, herself uneasy at the reaction that these two words might produce.

She was soon reassured. The princesses responded to the two words with a cry of triumph that brought Lenet running from the far end of the gallery.

'Lenet, Lenet, come here, quickly!' cried Madame the princess. 'You don't know the news that dear Claire has brought us?'

'But I do, Madame,' said Lenet with a smile. 'I do know, and that's why I was not hurrying.'

'What! Do you know?'

'*Bordeaux – yes*. Isn't that it?'

'Truly, my dear Pierre, you are a wizard!' said the dowager.

'But if you knew, Lenet,' said Madame the princess, reproachfully, 'why did you not relieve us of our anxiety by telling us those two words?'

'Because I wanted to allow the Viscountess de Cambes to gain the reward for her weariness,' Lenet replied, bowing to Claire, who was quite overcome. 'And also because I was afraid of Your Highnesses' outburst of joy on the terrace in view of everyone.'

'You're right – right as ever, my good Pierre,' said Madame the princess. 'Let's keep quiet.'

'Even so, it is to that fine man Richon that we owe this,' said the dowager. 'Aren't you pleased with him, and didn't he arrange things well, eh, my good *compeer* Lenet?'

'Compeer' was the Dowager Princess's pet name for him, a word that she had learned from Henri IV, who often used it.

'Richon is a man of thought and action, Madame,' said Lenet. 'I hope Your Highness realizes that if I had not been as sure of him as I am of myself, I should not have recommended him.'

'What shall we do for him?' asked the princess.

'We'll have to appoint him to some important place,' said the dowager.

'Some important place! Your Highness can't be serious,' said

Madame de Tourville sharply. 'You must be forgetting that Monsieur Richon is not a nobleman.'

'But then neither am I, Madame,' said Lenet. 'But this does not apparently prevent the prince from having some confidence in me. I do surely respect and admire the nobility of France, but there are some circumstances when I would venture to say that a big heart is more valuable than an old coat of arms.'

'And why did he not come to announce this rich news himself, the good Richon?' asked Madame the princess.

'He stayed in Guyenne to muster a certain number of men. He told me that he could already count on nearly three hundred soldiers, but he says that, through lack of time, they will be ill trained for campaigning, and he would prefer to be accorded the command of a stronghold such as Vayres or the Ile Saint-Georges. There, he says, he would be sure of being entirely useful to Their Highnesses.'

'But how can we manage this?' asked the princess. 'We are not well enough in favour at court at the moment to recommend anyone, and anyone whom we did recommend would immediately become suspect.'

'Perhaps, Madame, there might be a way that Monsieur Richon suggested to me himself,' said the viscountess.

'Which is?'

'It appears,' the viscountess continued, blushing, 'that Monsieur d'Epernon is head over heels in love with a certain young lady.'

'Ah, yes! The lovely Nanon,' the princess said, contemptuously. 'We know all about that.'

'Well, it seems that the Duke d'Epernon can refuse this woman nothing and that she grants everything that can be bought from her. Could we not buy a commission for Monsieur Richon?'

'It would be a good investment,' said Lenet.

'Yes, but the treasury is empty, as you very well know, Counsellor,' said Madame de Tourville.

With a smile, Lenet turned towards Madame de Cambes.

'This is the time, Madame, to prove to Their Highnesses that you have thought of everything.'

'What do you mean, Lenet?'

'Madame, he means that I am fortunate enough to be able to offer you a small sum that I have managed with difficulty to extract from my tenants. It's a very modest offering, but I was unable to make more. Twenty thousand livres,' the viscountess continued, lowering her eyes and hesitant, because she was so ashamed to offer such a small amount to the two first ladies of the kingdom after the queen.

'Twenty thousand livres!' exclaimed the two princesses.

'But that's a fortune in times like ours,' continued the dowager.

'Our dear Claire!' cried the princess. 'How can we ever repay her?'

'Your Highness can think about that later.'

'And where is the money?' asked Madame de Tourville.

'In His Highness's chamber, where my groom Pompée was instructed to take it.'

'Lenet,' the princess said. 'Remember that we owe this sum to Madame de Cambes.'

'It is already on our list of liabilities,' said Lenet, taking out his notebook and showing the viscountess's twenty thousand livres at that day's date, in a column the sum total of which would have rather terrified the princesses, if they had taken the trouble to add it up.

'But how did you manage to get through, my dear?' the princess asked. 'We were told here that Monsieur de Saint-Aignan controls the roads and inspects men and goods, just like an official of the customs.'

'Thanks to Pompée's wisdom, Madame, we avoided that danger,' said the viscountess, 'by making a huge detour that cost us a day and a half, but ensured our safe arrival. Otherwise, I should have been with Your Highness the day before yesterday.'

'Don't worry, Madame,' said Lenet. 'No time has yet been lost. We must just make good use of today and tomorrow. Today, as Your Highnesses will recall, we are expecting three messengers. One has now arrived, but the other two are still to come.'

'And can we know the names of these two others?' Madame de Tourville asked, still hoping to catch out the counsellor, against whom she was waging a war that was nonetheless real for being undeclared.

'The first, if my prediction is right, will be Gourville; he is coming on behalf of the Duke de La Rochefoucauld.'[66]

'I think you mean on behalf of the Prince de Marsillac,' said Madame de Tourville.

'The Prince de Marsillac is now the Duke de La Rochefoucauld, Madame.'

'You mean his father is dead?'

'A week ago.'

'Where?'

'At Verteuil.'

'And the second?' the princess asked.

'The second is Blanchefort, the captain of the prince's guard. He is coming from Stenay, on behalf of Monsieur de Turenne.'

'In that case,' said Madame de Tourville, 'I think that to avoid loss of time, we can revert to the first plan that I made, in the probable event of Bordeaux joining us and Turenne and Marsillac being allies . . .'

Lenet smiled in his usual manner.

'Excuse me, Madame,' he said in the politest voice. 'But the plans drawn up by the prince himself are at this moment being carried out and promise complete success.'

'Plans drawn up by the prince!' said Madame de Tourville acidly. 'By the same prince who is in the dungeon at Vincennes and communicates with no one!'

'These are His Highness's orders, written in his own hand at yesterday's date,' said Lenet, taking a letter from the Prince de Condé out of his pocket. 'I received it this morning. We correspond with one another.'

The paper was almost torn from the counsellor's hands by the two princesses, who devoured everything in it with tears of joy.

'Well, I never! Lenet's pockets seem to contain the whole of France!' said the dowager, laughing.

'Not yet, Madame, not yet,' he replied. 'But with God's help

I shall enlarge them enough for that. Now,' he continued, with a significant nod to the viscountess. 'Madame must need a rest after this long journey . . .'

The viscountess appreciated that Lenet wanted to be alone with the two princesses, and, a smile from the dowager confirming this, she made a respectful bow and disappeared.

Madame de Tourville was staying behind, promising herself a fine harvest of mysterious information, but at a barely perceptible sign from the dowager to her daughter-in-law, the two princesses spontaneously performed a noble curtsey, obeying all the rules of etiquette and indicating to Madame de Tourville that they had reached the end of the political discussion in which she had been invited to take part. The lady with the theories perfectly understood what was meant, returned a curtsey even more grave and ceremonious than theirs and withdrew, calling on God to witness the ingratitude of princes.

The two princesses went into their study, and Pierre Lenet followed.

'Now,' said Lenet, after ensuring that the door was well shut. 'If Your Highnesses wish to receive Gourville, he has arrived and is changing his clothes, since he did not dare present himself before you in those he wore for the journey.'

'What news is he bringing?'

'The news that Monsieur de La Rochefoucauld will be here this evening with five hundred officers.'

'Five hundred!' the princess exclaimed. 'But that's a whole army.'

'Which will make our journey harder. I should have preferred just five or six servants to all that paraphernalia; we should have escaped the attention of Monsieur de Saint-Aignan more easily. Now it will be almost impossible to reach the south without being disturbed.'

'All the better if we are!' cried the princess. 'If we are disturbed, we shall fight and win. The spirit of Monsieur de Condé will be marching with us.'

Lenet looked at the Dowager Princess as if seeking her opinion, but Charlotte de Montmorency, brought up at the time of the civil wars under Louis XIII, who had seen so many noble heads bending as they passed the prison gates or falling on the scaffold because they tried to remain upright, drew her hand sadly across a forehead that was heavy with painful memories.

'Yes,' she said. 'That is what we are reduced to: hiding or fighting – dreadful! We were living quietly with the little glory that God has brought to our family and we sought nothing – at least, I hope that none of us had any other intention – apart from staying in the rank where we were born. And now the fortunes of the time are driving us to fight against our master . . .'

'Madame!' the young princess said impetuously. 'I am less afflicted than Your Highness by the necessity to which we are reduced. My husband and my brother are suffering an undeserved captivity. This husband and brother are your sons. Moreover, your daughter is proscribed. This quite certainly justifies anything that we might do.'

'Yes,' said the dowager, in a resigned voice, full of sadness. 'Yes, I can bear this with more patience than you can, Madame, for it appears that it has become our destiny to be outlaws or prisoners. No sooner had I become the wife of your husband's father than I had to leave France, driven out by King Henri IV's love. No sooner did we return than we had to go into Vincennes, pursued by the hatred of Cardinal Richelieu. My son, who is today in prison, came into the world in prison and, after thirty-two years, finds himself back in the room where he was born. Alas, your father-in-law, the prince, was right in his dark prophecies when he was informed of the victory of the Battle of Rocroi, and when he was taken into the hall hung with the standards captured from the Spaniards: "God knows the joy that this action of my son's has given me," he said, turning to me. "But remember, Madame, the more glory accrues to our house, the more misfortune will befall it. If I did not bear the arms of France, which are too fine to give up, I should like to take as my coat of arms a falcon, with the bells that signal his presence and help his recapture, and the motto: *Fama nocet*."[67] We have made too much noise, my daughter, and this is what is damaging us. Don't you agree, Lenet?'

'Madame,' said Lenet, pained by the memories that the princess had just awakened. 'Your Highness is right, but we have gone too far to go back now. Moreover, in the kind of circumstances in which we find ourselves, we must be decisive and have no illusions about our situation. We are only apparently free. The queen is keeping watch on us and Monsieur de Saint-Aignan is constraining us. Very well, we must get out of Chantilly, despite the queen's vigilance and the constraints imposed by Monsieur de Saint-Aignan.'

'Let us leave Chantilly, but let us leave with our heads high!' the princess exclaimed.

'I agree,' said the dowager. 'The Condés are not Spaniards, and they are not traitors. They are not Italians and not plotters. What they do, they do in daylight, with their heads up.'

'Madame,' Lenet said, with conviction in his voice. 'May God be my witness that I should be the first to carry out Your Highness's order, whatever it might be, but to leave Chantilly as you wish, we should have to fight. I am sure you do not intend to be women on the day of battle when you have been men in council. You will march at the head of your followers, and you will be the ones to launch the war cry at your soldiers. But you are forgetting that as well as your own precious lives, another is starting which is no less precious – that of the Duke d'Enghien, your son and grandson. Would you take the risk of burying the present and the future of your family in a single tomb? Do you believe that the father will not become a hostage to Mazarin when daring deeds are undertaken in the name of the son? Have you forgotten the secrets of the dungeons of Vincennes, which were so dreadfully experienced by the Grand Prior de Vendôme, Marshal d'Ornano and Puy-Laurent? Have you forgotten that deadly cell, which Madame de Rambouillet said was worth its weight in arsenic?[68] No, ladies,' Lenet continued, clasping his hands, 'no. You will listen to the advice of your old servant and leave Chantilly in a manner appropriate to women who are under persecution. Remember that your most infallible weapon is weakness. A child deprived of his father, a woman deprived of her husband and a mother deprived of her son must escape in whatever way possible from the trap in which they are held. Wait before you act openly, and speak aloud when you are no longer a surety for those who are stronger than you. While you are captive, your followers will remain silent, when you are free, they will come out into the open, no longer afraid of being dictated the conditions of your ransom. Our plan is agreed with Gourville. We are sure of a good escort, with whom we shall avoid the hazards of the road – because today twenty different parties are in possession of the countryside and live without distinction off their friends and their enemies. Agree. Everything is ready.'

'Leave in secret! Leave like criminals!' cried the young princess. 'What will the prince say when he learns that his mother, his wife and his son have been enduring such shame!'

'I don't know what he will say, but if you succeed, he will owe you his freedom, while if you fail, you will not compromise your resources and, above all, your position, as you would if you were to chance them in battle.'

The dowager thought for a moment, then said with a face full of affectionate sadness: 'Dear Monsieur Lenet, persuade my daughter to go, because I am obliged to stay behind here. I have struggled so far, but I am finally giving way. The pain that is consuming me, and that I am trying in vain to conceal so as not to discourage those around me, will tie me to what may perhaps be my deathbed. But, as you have said, what we must do above all is to save the fortune of the Condés. My daughter and grandson will leave Chantilly, and I hope they will be wise enough to obey your advice – no, I say more than that: your orders. You order us, Lenet, and we shall do as you say.'

'You are pale, Madame!' Lenet exclaimed, supporting the dowager, whom the princess, alarmed by the lack of colour in her face, had already taken in her arms.

'Yes,' the dowager said, in a steadily weakening voice. 'Yes, today's good news has done me more harm than the worries of recent days. I can feel that the fever is devouring me. But we must not show anything: it could damage our cause at such a moment.'

'Madame,' Lenet whispered. 'Your Highness's illness would

be a blessing from heaven if you were not suffering so much. Take to your bed and spread the rumour of this illness. You, Madame,' he went on, turning to the young princess, 'have them call for your doctor, Bourdelot, and since we are going to have to requisition the stables and the equipment, let it be known everywhere that you intend to hunt a deer in the park. In that way, no one will be surprised to see a bustling of men, weapons and horses.'

'You do it, Lenet. But how is it that a man as far-sighted as you has not realized that people might be amazed at this odd hunt, taking place at the very moment when my mother-in-law falls ill?'

'That's all arranged, Madame. Isn't the day after tomorrow the Duke d'Enghien's seventh birthday, and so the day when he leaves the care of women?'

'Yes.'

'Well, we say that the hunt is being given to mark the young prince's first knee-breeches and that Her Highness was so insistent that her illness should not interrupt this solemn occasion that you had to give in to her entreaties.'

'Excellent idea!' the dowager exclaimed with a happy smile, in pride at the first proclamation of her grandson's manhood. 'Yes, it is a good excuse, and you, Lenet, are indeed a good and worthy counsellor.'

'But will the Duke d'Enghien be in a carriage then to follow the hunt?' the princess asked.

'No, on horseback. Oh, don't let your maternal heart feel any anxiety. I have designed a little saddle that his groom, Vialas, will put in front of the pommel of his own and in this way the Duke d'Enghien will be seen. That evening, we can leave safely, because whether he's on foot or on horseback, the duke will be able to go anywhere, while if he were in a carriage, he would be stopped at the first barrier.'

'So when do you think we should leave?'

'The day after tomorrow in the evening, Madame, if Your Highness has no reason to delay this departure.'

'No, on the contrary, let's escape from our prison as soon as possible, Lenet.'

'And once you are out of Chantilly, what will you do?' the dowager asked.

'We shall go through Monsieur de Saint-Aignan's army, finding some way to pull a blindfold over his eyes. We shall join Monsieur de La Rochefoucauld and his escort and arrive in Bordeaux where we are expected. Once in the second city in the kingdom, the capital of the south, we can either negotiate or make war, as Your Highnesses prefer; however, I have the honour to remind you, Madame, that even in Bordeaux we shall not have a hope of holding out for long if we do not have a few strongholds around us that will force the royal troops into a diversion. Two of these sites will be of particular importance: Vayres, which commands the Dordogne and allows supplies to reach the town, and the Ile Saint-Georges, which is considered by the people of Bordeaux themselves as the key to their town. But we can think about that later. For the moment, let us just consider getting out of here.'

'Nothing will be easier, I think,' said the princess. 'We are alone and in charge here, whatever you say, Lenet.'

'Don't count on anything, Madame, before you are in Bordeaux. Nothing is easy against the diabolical mind of Monsieur de Mazarin, and if I waited for us to be alone before telling Your Highnesses of my plan, it was to leave my conscience clear, I assure you, because at this very moment, I fear for the security of the project that my head alone dreamed up and that your ears alone have just heard. Monsieur de Mazarin does not learn news, he guesses it.'

'Well, I defy him to frustrate this,' said the princess. 'But let us help my mother-in-law to go back to her apartment. I shall then immediately spread the story of our hunting party the day after tomorrow. You look after the invitations, Lenet.'

'You can count on me, Madame.'

The dowager returned to her room and got into bed. Bourdelot, the doctor of the Condé family and tutor to the Duke d'Enghien, was called. The news of this unexpected illness at once spread through Chantilly, and in half an hour the groves, the galleries and the lawns were deserted, the guests of the two princesses hastening to the dowager's antechamber.

Lenet spent the whole day writing, and that same evening more than fifty invitations were taken in all directions by the many servants of this royal house.

XIII

The day after next, which was intended to see the accomplishment of Pierre Lenet's plans, was one of the darkest days of spring, that season generally called the finest of the year, yet which is almost always the most disagreeable, particularly in France.

The rain was falling, fine, but dense, across the lawns of Chantilly, cutting through a grey mist that blurred the flowerbeds in the garden and the woods in the park. In the huge courtyards, lined up beside the posts to which they were tethered, fifty horses waited, ready saddled, their ears lowered, their eyes sad, impatiently scraping their hooves on the ground. Packs of hounds on leashes were waiting, grouped twelve by twelve, exhaling noisily amid long yawns and trying, by a joint effort, to pull away the attendant who was holding them, wiping the rain-soaked ears of his favourites.

Here and there, the whippers-in, with their buff uniforms, were walking around with their hands behind their backs and their hunting horns hanging on straps. A few officers, hardened to bad weather by the army camps at Rocroi and Lens, braved the downpour and relieved the tedium of waiting by chatting in groups on the terraces and steps.

Each of them knew that this was a ceremonial occasion and had put on a solemn air to see the Duke d'Engien dressed in his first knee-breeches, hunting his first deer. Every officer in the prince's service and every client of the illustrious family, invited by Lenet's circular letter, had accomplished what he considered a duty by hurrying to Chantilly. Their initial fears for the health of the dowager princess were dispelled by a favourable report from Bourdelot: the princess had been bled and that same morning taken an emetic, the universal panacea at the time.

By ten o'clock, all the personal guests of Madame de Condé had arrived. Each had been introduced on presentation of a letter, and those who happened to have lost this, but were recognized by Lenet, were ushered in by a sign from him to the footman. Together with the family servants, these made a party of eighty or ninety people, most of whom were crowded around the magnificent white horse, which, almost with pride it seemed, in front of its great, French-style saddle, bore a little velvet seat with a back for the young Duke d'Enghien, who would take his place there when his groom, Vialas, had mounted into the main saddle.

Meanwhile, no one was talking about the hunt; they seemed to be expecting some other guests.

At half past ten, three gentlemen, followed by six valets, all armed to the teeth and carrying bags so full that you would imagine they were going on a round tour of Europe, rode into the castle and, seeing posts in the courtyard that appeared to have been set up for that purpose, went to tie up their horses at them.

At once, a man dressed in blue, with a silver baldric, went up with his halberd in his hand to accost the newcomers, who, from their rain-soaked harness and their mud-stained boots, could be seen to be long-distance travellers.

'Where are you from, gentlemen?' asked this kind of door-keeper, crossing his body with his halberd.

'From the north,' said one of the horsemen.

'And where are you going?'

'To the burial.'

'Can you prove it?'

'You can see our crape.'

And indeed, each of the three had a black ribbon tied to his sword.

'Excuse me, gentlemen,' replied the doorman. 'The castle is at your disposal. There is a table laid, a heated gallery and footmen, who await your orders. As for your servants, they will be looked after in the pantry.'

The three honest countrymen, hungry and inquisitive, bowed, dismounted, threw the reins of their horses into the hands of their grooms and, having been shown the direction of the dining room, headed in that direction. A chamberlain was waiting for them at the door and guided them in.

Meanwhile the horses were taken out of the hands of the foreign grooms by those of the house, led to the stables, combed, brushed, rubbed down and put beside a trough full of oats and a rack full of hay.

Hardly had the three gentlemen sat down at table, than six other horsemen, followed by six lackeys, armed and equipped just like those that we described earlier, rode in as they had done, and, like them, seeing the posts, went to tie up their horses to the rings. But the man with the halberd, who had strict instructions, came over and asked them the same questions.

'Where are you from?'

'From Picardy. We are officers in Turenne.'

'Where are you going?'

'To the burial.'

'Can you prove it?'

'You can see our crape.'

Like the previous party, they showed the ribbons hanging from the hilts of their swords.

After them, four others arrived, and the same scene was played out again.

From half past ten to midday, two by two and four by four, or five by five, alone or in groups, magnificently dressed or plainly, but all well mounted, well armed and well equipped, a hundred riders arrived, were questioned by the halberdier in the same manner and replied in the same way as to where they had come from, adding that they were going to the burial and showing their crape.

When finally all had dined and got to know each other, while their servants were taking refreshment and their horses resting, Lenet came into the room where they had gathered and said: 'Gentlemen, the princess thanks you through me for the honour you have done her by stopping here on your way to see the Duke de La Rochefoucauld, who is waiting for you to celebrate the funeral of his father. Consider this house as your own home and please join us for an entertaining hunt, which has been arranged for this afternoon for the Duke d'Enghien, who today takes his first knee-breeches.'

A murmur of flattering approval and thanks greeted this first part of Lenet's speech: being a skilled orator, he had paused in his address at this particular point.

'After the hunt,' he continued, 'you will take supper with the princess, who wishes to thank you herself, and after that you will be free to continue on your way.'

A few of the listeners paid particular attention to the details of this programme, which seemed rather to limit their freedom of choice, but they had no doubt been warned by the Duke de La Rochefoucauld to expect something of the sort, because no one protested. Some went to look at their horses, others turned to their luggage so that they could make themselves worthy to appear before the princess, while still others remained at the table, talking about the news of the day which, given recent events, seemed to have a certain uniformity.

Many of them walked around under the great balcony, on which, once he was prepared, the Duke d'Enghien was due to appear, having been for the last time entrusted to the care of women. The young prince, in his apartment surrounded by nursemaids and his rocking chairs, was unaware of his own importance. He was, however, already full of aristocratic pride and looked impatiently at the rich, yet austere costume in which he was to be dressed for the first time: a coat of black velvet embroidered with unpolished silver thread, which gave his dress the sombre look of mourning, because his mother wanted above all to be considered a widow and had thought of inserting the words 'poor orphan prince' into a speech she had made.

But it was not the prince who was looking most covetously at these magnificent clothes, the mark of his long-awaited coming of age. A couple of yards from him, another child, a few months at most older than he, with rosy cheeks and blond hair, bursting with health, strength and high spirits, was eagerly staring at the splendour surrounding his more fortunate companion. Several times already, unable to contain his curiosity, he had dared go over to the chair on which the fine clothes were set out and had slyly felt the cloth and stroked the embroidery, while the little prince was looking in the other direction. But the Duke d'Enghien did once happen to look back in time to catch him, and Pierrot's hand was removed too slowly.

'Take care!' the little prince said sharply. 'Take care, Pierrot, or you'll spoil my breeches. It's embroidered velvet, you see . . . it loses its bloom when you touch it. I won't let you touch my knee-breeches.'

Pierrot hid the guilty hand behind his back, twisting his shoulders backwards and forwards with that movement of annoyance that is common to all children, whatever their class.

'Don't be angry, Louis,' the princess said to her son, whose face was twisted into a rather ugly snarl. 'If Pierrot touches your clothes again, we'll have him whipped.'

Pierrot changed his pout into something more threatening and said: 'Monseigneur is a prince, but I'm a gardener. And if Monseigneur won't let me touch his clothes, I'll stop him playing with my guinea fowl. Huh! And I'm stronger than Monseigneur, as he well knows . . .'

Hardly had he spoken these rash words than the prince's nursemaid, Pierrot's mother, grasped the unruly infant by the wrist and told him: 'Pierrot, you're forgetting that Monseigneur is your master and the lord of everything in this château and around it, so that means your guinea fowl belong to him.'

'Huh!' said Pierrot. 'And I thought he was my brother.'

'I was his wet nurse, so he's your foster brother . . .'

'So, if he's my brother, we should share things, and if my guinea fowl belong to him, then his clothes belong to me.'

The nursemaid was about to reply by demonstrating the difference between a true brother and a foster brother, but the young prince, who wanted Pierrot present to witness his triumph – because Pierrot was the person whose admiration and envy he chiefly wanted to excite – did not give her time.

'Don't worry, Pierrot,' he said. 'I'm not angry with you, and you'll soon see me on my fine white horse and my pretty little saddle. I'm going out hunting, and I'm the one who'll kill the deer!'

'Oh, yes?' said the disrespectful Pierrot, in the most impertinent tone of irony. 'You'll stay on horseback a long time, I should think! The other day you tried to get up on my donkey, and it threw you off.'

'Yes,' said the young prince with all the majesty that he could summon up and recall from memory. 'But today I'm representing my papa, and I won't fall off . . . Anyway, Vialas will have his arms round me.'

'Come now, come,' said the princess, to cut short this discussion between Pierrot and the Duke d'Enghien. 'Come on, let's get the prince dressed! One o'clock has struck, and all our gentlemen are waiting impatiently. Lenet, get them to sound the start.'

XIV

At the same moment, the sound of the horn echoed outside in the courtyards and rang through all the rooms in the château. So everyone hurried to mount his horse, fresh and rested thanks to the care that had been taken of it. The master with his bloodhounds and the whippers-in with their packs set out first. Then the gentlemen formed a row and the Duke d'Enghien, mounted on his white horse and supported by his groom Vialas, appeared surrounded by ladies-in-waiting, grooms and gentlemen, and followed by his mother, splendidly dressed and riding on a jet-black horse. Near her, on a horse that she handled with elegant charm, was the Viscountess de Cambes, lovely to see in women's clothes, to which she had finally reverted, much to her own delight.

As for Madame de Tourville, people had been looking in vain for her since the previous day. She had disappeared: like Achilles, she had retired to her tent.[69]

This brilliant procession was greeted with cheering on all sides. Some were standing up in their stirrups, pointing out the princess and the Duke d'Enghien, who were unknown to most of these gentlemen since they had never been at court and were unaccustomed to all this royal pomp and ceremony. The child responded with his delightful smile and the princess with gentle majesty: they were the wife and son of the man whom even his enemies called the first captain in Europe. This same first captain was hunted down, persecuted and imprisoned by the very people whom he had saved from the enemy at Lens and defended against the rebels at Saint-Germain. This was more than enough to excite enthusiasm, so the enthusiasm was at its height.

The princess wallowed in all this evidence of her popularity. Then, in response to a few words whispered by Lenet in her ear, she gave the signal for the hunt to start and the party soon passed from the gardens into the park, where all the gates were guarded by soldiers from Condé's regiment. These gates were closed behind the huntsmen, and, as though this precaution was still not enough to prevent unwanted guests, the soldiers remained on sentry duty behind the railings and beside each of them stood a doorkeeper, dressed like the one in the courtyard and armed, like him, with a halberd, with orders not to open up to anyone who could not answer the three questions that were the password.

A moment after the gates were closed, the sound of the horn and the baying of the hounds announced that the fallow deer had been sprung.

Meanwhile, on the other side of the park, opposite the wall built by Constable Anne de Montmorency,[70] six horsemen had caught the sound of the horns and the baying of the dogs, and had stopped on the side of the road, stroking the necks of their panting horses and appearing to confer with one another.

Seeing their brand-new clothes, the shining harness of their mounts, the glossy cloaks fashionably hanging from their shoulders on to their horses' rumps and the array of weapons that could be glimpsed through artistically arranged gaps in their clothing, one might have been surprised at finding these gentlemen all alone, so handsome and so spruce, at a time when all the nobility of the region was gathered in the château of Chantilly.

However, their brilliance was eclipsed by the magnificence of their leader – or the man who seemed to be their leader: feathers in his hat, gilded baldric, fine boots with golden spurs and a long sword with openwork chiselling – this, together with a spendid sky-blue mantle, Spanish fashion, was the man's accoutrement.

'By God!' he exclaimed, after a moment of deep reflection, during which the six horsemen had looked at one another in some confusion. 'How do we get into the park: through the main gate or the side ones? Let's present ourselves at the first entrance that we come to and go in. Gentlemen of our appearance will hardly be left outside when men dressed like those that we have been meeting since this morning are allowed inside.'

'I tell you again, Cauvignac,' replied one of the five riders to whom the chief had been speaking. 'These poorly dressed people who, despite looking and behaving like bumpkins, are now inside the park, had an advantage over us, which is that they knew the password. We do not have that advantage and cannot get in.'

'You think not, Ferguzon?' said the man who had spoken first, with a certain deference for his lieutenant's opinion; readers will recognize him as the adventurer they met in the first pages of this story.

'Don't I believe! I'm sure of it. Do you think those people are hunting for hunting's sake? *Tatare!* It's obvious: they're conspiring.'

'Ferguzon is right,' said a third man. 'They are conspiring, and we shall not get inside.'

'Even so, a deer hunt is not bad sport when you happen to get the chance.'

'Especially when you are tired of hunting men, isn't that so, Barabbas?' said Cauvignac. 'Well, let it not be said that we let this opportunity pass by. We have all that is needed to make a worthy show at this entertainment. We are as bright as new crown pieces. If the Duke d'Enghien needs soldiers, where could he find more handsome ones? If he needs conspirators, where could he meet with more elegant ones? The least finely dressed among us looks like a captain.'

'And you, Cauvignac,' said Barabbas, 'you could easily pass for a duke and peer of the realm if need be.'

Ferguzon said nothing. He was thinking. 'Unfortunately,' Cauvignac continued with a laugh, 'Ferguzon does not feel like hunting today.'

'A plague on it!' said Ferguzon. 'I'm not so sick of life: hunting is a gentleman's sport that suits me at any time, so I'll not turn up my nose at it for myself or discourage anyone else from it. All I'm saying is that there are fences and gates between you and this park where the hunt is taking place.'

'There!' Cauvignac cried. 'The horns are sounding the view-halloo.'

'But this does not mean,' Ferguzon went on, 'that we shall not hunt.'

'And how are we to hunt, donkey-brain, if we can't get in?'

'I'm not saying that we can't get in.'

'And how do you expect us to get in, when the entrances, open to others, are closed to us, according to you?'

'Then why don't we make a hole in this little wall for ourselves alone, through which we and our horses can pass and behind which we shall certainly find no one to ask us to pay for it?'

'Hurrah!' Cauvignac exclaimed, waving his hat in the air with joy. 'I take it all back! Ferguzon, you are the resourceful one among us! And when I've overthrown the King of France and put the prince on the throne in his place, I'll get you the place of Signor Mazarino Mazarini. To work, friends, to work.'

At this, Cauvignac leapt off his horse, and, with the help of his companions (a single one of whom was enough to hold the horses of all of them), he set about demolishing the already shaky stones of the park wall. In a short time, the five workers had made a breach in the wall three or four feet wide. Then they remounted their horses and, guided by Cauvignac, hurried through it.

'Now,' he said, heading for the place from which they could hear the sound of horns. 'Now, let's be polite and well behaved, and I invite you to dine with the Duke d'Enghien.'

XV

We have said that our newly created gentlemen were well
mounted. Their horses also had the advantage of being fresh,
unlike those of the riders who had arrived that morning. So
they soon caught up with the main body of the hunt and took
their place among the rest without being challenged. Most of
the guests came from different provinces and did not know one
another, so the intruders, once inside the park, could pass as
guests themselves.

Everything would thus have gone off splendidly, if they had
only kept to their place, or even if they had been satisfied with
going ahead of the others and mingling with the whippers-in
and the officers of the hunt. But it was not to be. After a
moment, Cauvignac seemed convinced that the hunt was being
given in his honour. He seized a horn from the hands of a
whipper-in, who did not dare refuse to give it him, charged off
at the head of the huntsmen, rode in front of the master of
hounds in all directions, broke through woods and coppices,
sounding his horn in every direction, confusing the view-halloo
with the *lancer*, or breaking from cover with driving to cover,
trampling the hounds, knocking down the whippers-in, flirting
with the ladies when he rode in front of them, swearing, shouting and getting excited when he lost sight of them, and arriving
at the fallow deer just as the creature was at bay after swimming
through the great lake.

'*Hallali*, the kill!' Cauvignac shouted. 'The deer is ours!
Corbleu! We've got it!'

'Cauvignac,' said Ferguzon, who was following a horse's
length away. 'You'll have us all thrown out. For God's sake,
calm down!'

But Cauvignac did not hear, and, seeing that the animal was
standing up to the dogs, he leapt down and drew his sword,
shouting: 'The kill, the kill!'

His companions, apart from the cautious Ferguzon, were
encouraged by his example and preparing to pounce on their

prey, when the master of the hunt, thrusting Cauvignac aside with his knife, said: 'Easy, sir, easy. It's the princess who is leading the hunt, so it's for her to cut the deer's throat or to pass the honour to whoever she wishes.'

This harsh rebuke brought Cauvignac back to his senses, and while he was retreating, quite grudgingly, he was suddenly surrounded by the main body of the hunt, Cauvignac's five minutes' pause having given the riders time to catch up. They formed a wide circle around the creature, which had its back to an oak tree, surrounded and under attack from all the hounds together.

At the same moment, down a long avenue, they saw the princess arriving ahead of the Duke d'Enghien, as well as the gentlemen and ladies who had made a point of not leaving her side. She was in a very lively mood, and it was evident that she saw this warlike sport as the prelude to a real war.

On arriving in the middle of the circle, she stopped, surveyed her surroundings in a princely manner and noticed Cauvignac and his companions who were the object of anxious and suspicious looks from the whippers-in and the hunt officials.

The master came over to her with his knife drawn. This was a knife that usually belonged to the prince, with a blade of the finest steel and a hilt of silver gilt.

'Does Her Highness know this gentleman?' he asked, in a low voice, indicating Cauvignac with a glance.

'No,' she said. 'But he has got in, so he must be known to someone.'

'He is not known to anyone, Your Highness, and everyone I have asked says that they have seen him for the first time today.'

'But surely he cannot have got past the gate without the password?'

'No, surely not,' said the master. 'However, might I dare to suggest that Your Highness should be wary of him?'

'First of all, we must know who he is,' said the princess.

'We shall find out soon, Madame,' said Lenet, who had accompanied the princess, with his usual smile. 'I have dispatched a Norman, a Picard and a Breton to him, and he will be thoroughly interrogated. But for the time being Your Highness should not seem to be paying attention to him, or he will escape us.'

'You are right, Lenet, let's get back to the hunt.'

'Cauvignac,' said Ferguzon, 'I think that we are being talked about in high places. We would do well to make ourselves scarce.'

'Do you think?' said Cauvignac. 'Oh, that's too bad! I want to be in at the kill. Let whatever happens, happen.'

'It's a splendid sight, I know,' said Ferguzon. 'But we might pay for our places more dearly than at the Hôtel de Bourgogne.'[71]

'Madame,' said the master of hounds to the princess, offering her the knife. 'To whom does Your Highness wish to grant the honour of killing the beast?'

'I shall keep it for myself, Monsieur,' the princess said. 'A woman of my rank must become accustomed to handling iron and seeing blood flow.'

'Namur,' said the master of hounds to the arquebusier. 'Get ready.'

The arquebusier stepped forward and went to stand some twenty yards from the animal with his arquebus in his hand. The idea was that he could kill the deer with a shot if, driven to despair, as sometimes happens, it rushed at the princess instead of waiting for her.

The princess dismounted, took the knife and, with fixed eyes, burning cheeks and her lips half parted, she walked towards the animal, which, almost entirely swamped by the dogs, seemed to be covered by a motley carpet of a thousand colours. The creature surely did not think that death was approaching in the form of this beautiful princess from whose hand he had eaten more than ten times, so, kneeling as he was, he tried to get up, his eye weeping that large tear that accompanies the death throes of the stag, the fallow deer and the roe deer. But he did not have time: the blade of the knife, a ray of sunlight glinting from it, disappeared to the hilt in his throat and the blood spurted out as far as the princess's face. The fallow deer raised its head, gave a howl of pain and, casting a last, reproachful look at its beautiful mistress, fell and died.

At the same moment, all the horns sounded the *morte* and a thousand cries of 'Long live the princess!' rang out, while the young prince, shifting on his saddle, clapped his hands in joy.

The princess took the knife out of the animal's throat, looking around the whole company with the eyes of an amazon, gave the bloody weapon back to the master of hounds and remounted.

Lenet came over to her.

'Would the princess like me to tell her what she was thinking of as she cut the poor creature's throat?' he asked with his usual smile.

'Yes, Lenet, I'd love to know.'

'She was thinking of Monsieur de Mazarin and wishing that he had been in the place of the deer.'

'Yes!' the princess cried. 'That's right. And I should have slit his throat without pity, I swear. But you really are a sorcerer, Lenet.' She turned towards the rest of the hunting party. 'Now that the hunt is over, gentlemen,' she said, 'please follow me. It is already too late to hunt another deer, and supper awaits us.'

Cauvignac replied to this invitation with the most gracious gesture.

'What are you doing, Captain?' asked Ferguzon.

'Why, I'm accepting. Can't you see that the princess is inviting us to sup with her, as I promised you she would?'

'Cauvignac, believe me or not, but in your place I should get back to the hole in the wall,' said his lieutenant.

'Ferguzon, my friend, your natural perspicacity has forsaken you. Did you not observe the orders given by that gentleman dressed in black, who has the hypocritical manner of a fox when he laughs and that of a badger when he doesn't? Ferguzon, the breach in the wall is guarded, and going towards the breach means revealing the fact that we wish to leave by the same means as we entered.'

'So what will become of us?'

'Don't worry, I'll take care of everything.'

At this reassurance, the six adventurers took their place among the crowd of gentlemen and made their way with them towards the château.

Cauvignac was not wrong: they were kept in sight. Lenet came riding along on their right, with the master of the hounds on his right and the steward of the house of Condé on his left.

'Are you sure that no one knows those riders?' he asked.

'No one. We've questioned more than fifty gentlemen, always with the same response: they are entirely unknown to everyone.'

The Norman, the Picard and the Breton came back to join Lenet without being able to tell him more. But the Norman had found a breach in the park wall and, being an intelligent man, had a guard put on it.

'In that case,' said Lenet, 'we shall adopt the most efficient method. A handful of spies must not force us to send away a hundred fine gentlemen to no purpose. Make sure, Steward, that no one can leave the courtyard or the gallery where the cavalry will come in. You, Captain, once the door of the gallery is closed, station a picket of twelve men with their muskets loaded in case of emergencies. Now, go. I shall keep sight of them.'

As it happened, Lenet did not have much trouble in carrying out the task that he had set himself. Cauvignac and his companions did not show the slightest desire to run away. Cauvignac took the lead, rakishly twirling his moustache. He was followed by Ferguzon, who was reassured by his promise, knowing his chief well enough to be sure that he would not have gone into this burrow unless it had a second exit. As for Barabbas and his three other companions, they followed their lieutenant and their captain, without thinking of anything except the excellent supper that awaited them. In brief, they were very materialistic fellows who were perfectly happy to leave the intellectual part of their social relations to their two leaders, in whom they had total confidence.

Everything happened as the counsellor had predicted and was carried out according to his orders. The princess sat in the great reception hall, under a canopy that served her as a throne. Near to her was her son, dressed as we described earlier.

Everyone exchanged glances. They had been promised a supper and it was clear that they were about to be given a speech.

The princess got up and began. Her discourse was rousing.*
This time, Claire-Clémence de Maillé knew no bounds and
came openly out against Mazarin. For their part, the audience,
electrified by the memory of the insult done to the whole nobility of France in the person of the princes and perhaps still more
by the hope of gaining positions at court in the event of success,
interrupted the princess's speech two or three times, loudly
swearing faithfully to serve the cause of the illustrious house of
Condé and to help to raise it from the humble position to which
Mazarin had tried to reduce it.

'So, gentlemen,' said the princess, winding up her speech,
'what the orphan here asks of your generous hearts is the
support of your valour and the gift of your devotion. You are
our friends – or, at least, that is how you have appeared to us.
What can you do for us?'

One of the nobles bowed respectfully to the princess.

'I am Gérard de Montalent,' he said. 'I am bringing with me
four gentlemen, my friends. Between us we have five good
swords and two thousand pistoles which we put at the service
of the prince. Here are our credentials, signed by the Duke de
La Rochefoucauld.'

The princess returned his bow, took the letter of credence
from the hands of the donor and passed it to Lenet. Then she
gestured to the gentlemen to move over to her right.

No sooner had they done so than another nobleman got up.

'I am Claude Raoul de Lessac, Count de Clermont,' he said.
'I am here with six gentlemen, my friends. We each have a
thousand pistoles, which we ask to be allowed to add to Your
Highness's funds. We are armed and equipped and will be
content with a simple daily allowance. Here are our credentials
signed by the Duke de Bouillon.'

'To my right, gentlemen,' said the princess, taking the letter
from Monsieur de Bouillon and looking at it as she had done

---

* Dumas's note: Those who like reading speeches can find this one in full in
the *Memoirs* of Pierre Lenet. We, for our part share the opinion of Henri IV,
who claimed that being forced to listen to long speeches was what had turned
his hair grey.

the first one, and then, like the first, passing it to Lenet. 'And accept my gratitude.'

The noblemen obeyed.

'I am Louis Ferdinand de Lorges, Count de Duras,' said a third man. 'I have come without friends or money, rich and strong only in my sword, with which I cut a path through the enemy when I was besieged in Bellegarde. Here are my credentials from the Viscount de Turenne.'

'Come here, Monsieur,' said the princess, taking the credentials in one hand and offering him the other to kiss. 'Come and stay beside me; I am going to make you one of my brigadiers.'

Their example was followed by all the noblemen, each coming with a letter of credence either from Monsieur de La Rochefoucauld, or Monsieur de Bouillon, or Monsieur de Turenne. Each of them handed over the letter and went to the princess's right. When her right-hand side was full, she pointed them to the left.

In this way, the body of the hall was gradually emptied. Soon, only Cauvignac and his henchmen formed a solitary group, towards which everyone was directing a look of anger and menace, while murmuring mistrustfully.

Lenet turned towards the door. It was completely shut. He knew that behind it was a captain with twelve well-armed men. So, turning back towards the strangers, he said: 'And you, gentlemen, who are you? Would you do us the honour of naming yourselves and showing your credentials?'

The opening of this scene had cast a shadow of anxiety over the face of Ferguzon, who, intelligent as he was, felt very uneasy about its outcome, and this unease had quietly communicated itself to his companions, who, like Lenet, were glancing towards the door. But their chief, magnificently robed in his cloak, had remained quite impassive and at Lenet's invitation, took two steps forward and saluted the princess with an infinite amount of flowery self-importance.

'Madame,' he said, 'I am Roland de Cauvignac and I am bringing to serve Your Highness my five gentlemen, who belong to the first families of Guyenne, but who wish to remain incognito.'

'But you surely did not come to Chantilly without being recommended by someone, gentlemen?' said the princess, concerned at the dreadful uproar that would result from the arrest of these six suspects. 'Where are your credentials?'

Cauvignac bowed, like a man accepting the correctness of the request, felt inside his doublet and took out a piece of paper, folded into four, which he passed over to Lenet with the most profound salutation.

Lenet opened it and read. A most joyful expression spread over his features, which had been contracted by a quite natural sense of apprehension.

While Lenet was reading, Cauvignac surveyed the assembly with a look of triumph.

'Madame,' Lenet said softly, bending to speak in the princess's ear. 'Look at this. It is most fortunate. A letter of attestation from Monsieur d'Epernon!'

'Monsieur,' the princess said to Cauvignac, with a gracious smile, 'thank you! Three times thank you – for my husband, for myself and for my son!'

The whole company was struck dumb with surprise.

'Monsieur,' Lenet said, 'this paper is so precious that I am sure you do not mean to hand it over to us without conditions. This evening, after supper, we shall speak, if you will, and you must tell me how we can do you service.'

Lenet folded the letter of attestation into his pocket, and Cauvignac had the delicacy not to ask for it back.

'Well!' he said to his companions. 'Didn't I tell you that I was inviting you to sup with the Duke d'Enghien?'

'Now, let us dine,' said the princess.

The double door at the side of the hall opened at these words, and they saw a splendid supper laid out in the great gallery of the château.

The supper was a thunderous occasion. The prince's health was proposed more than ten times and always drunk by the guests, kneeling, with swords in hand, hurling curses against Mazarin loud enough to bring the walls down.

Everyone did justice to the good food of Chantilly. Even Ferguzon, the prudent Ferguzon, allowed himself to be seduced by the wines of Burgundy, which he was encountering for the first time. Ferguzon was a Gascon, and he had until then only been in a position to appreciate the wines of his own region, which he considered excellent – but which, if one is to believe the Duke de Saint-Simon,[72] were not of great renown.

This was not the case with Cauvignac. Cauvignac, much though he could appreciate the virtues of Moulin-à-Vent, Nuits and Chambertin, consumed them only in moderation. He had not forgotten the crafty smile that Lenet had given him and considered that he would need all his faculties if he were to strike a deal with the sly counsellor that he would not later regret, so he aroused the amazement of Ferguzon, Barabbas and his three other companions, who, not realizing the causes of this temperance, were simple enough to believe that their chief must be repenting of past sins.

Towards the end of the meal, as the toasts started to become more frequent, the princess made herself scarce, taking the Duke d'Enghien with her and leaving her guests entirely free to continue the feast as far into the night as it suited them. Everything had happened as she had wished, and she wrote a detailed account of the scene in the hall and the meal in the gallery, only leaving out one thing, which was Lenet's remark to her, whispered as she was getting up from the table: 'Your Highness will not forget that we are leaving at ten o'clock.'

It was nearly nine. The princess began to get ready.

Meanwhile, a look passed between Lenet and Cauvignac. Lenet got up, and Cauvignac did the same. Lenet left through a little door in a corner of the gallery, and Cauvignac, seeing what was required, followed.

Lenet led him into his study, the adventurer walking behind, with a confident, carefree air. Even so, as he walked, his hand was idly toying with the handle of a long dagger at his waist, and his eyes, bright and quick, were glancing through half-opened doors and shifting tapestries.

He was not precisely afraid of being tricked, but he made a point of always being prepared for perfidy.

Once inside the study, only half lit by one lamp, but which a glance confirmed was empty, Lenet motioned him to a seat.

Cauvignac sat down on one side of the table, where the lamp was burning, Lenet on the other.

'Monsieur,' Lenet said, intending to gain this gentleman's confidence from the start, 'here, first and foremost, is your letter. It *is* yours, I suppose?'

'It is, Monsieur,' Cauvignac replied, 'the possession of whoever has it, since as you can see, there is no name on it except that of the Duke d'Epernon.'

'When I asked if it was really yours, I was asking if you possessed it with the consent of Monsieur d'Epernon.'

'I have it from his own hand, Monsieur.'

'So it was not taken or extorted by violence? I don't mean by you, but by someone else from whom you might have received it. Perhaps you only have it second-hand?'

'As I told you, it was given to me by the duke, quite freely and in exchange for a paper that I passed over to him.'

'Did you put yourself under any obligation to the duke to make a particular use of this paper rather than any other?'

'I made no commitment to the Duke d'Epernon.'

'So the person who owns this can use it quite safely?'

'He can.'

'So why do you not use it yourself?'

'Because if I keep this letter of attestation, I can only obtain one thing from it, while if I hand it over, I can obtain two.'

'And what are those two things?'

'Money, first of all.'

'We have none.'

'I shall be reasonable.'

'And the second thing?'

'A commission in the princes' army.'

'The princes have no army.'

'But they will have one.'

'Would you not prefer to have a licence to raise a company?'

'I was going to suggest that arrangement.'

'So all that remains is the money?'

'Yes, that's all.'

'How much would you like?'

'Ten thousand livres. I told you I should be reasonable.'

'Ten thousand livres!'

'Yes, I need an advance to arm and equip my men.'

'Indeed, it's not too much.'

'So you agree?'

'It's a deal.'

Lenet took out a licence that was already signed, filled in the names that the young man gave him, stamped it with the seal of the princess and gave it to the holder. Then, opening a sort of cashbox with a secret lock, in which he kept the funds of the rebel army, he withdrew the ten thousand livres in gold, which he set out in piles of twenty louis each.

Cauvignac counted them scrupulously one after another, then at the last one he nodded to Lenet that the letter of attestation was his.

Lenet took it and shut it up in the box, thinking no doubt that such a precious document could not be too closely guarded.

Just as Lenet was putting back the key of the cashbox in his pocket, a valet came in in a state of great excitement and said that he was needed for an affair of importance. So Lenet and Cauvignac went out of the study, Lenet to follow the servant, and Cauvignac to go back to the gallery.

Meanwhile, the princess was making her preparations for leaving, which consisted in changing her grand dress for an amazon's clothes, suitable both for riding in a carriage and riding on horseback. She also went through her papers, in order to burn those that were not needed and to take the important ones with her, and finally collected together her diamonds, which she had taken out of their settings so that they would occupy less space and be easier to use if she needed them.

As for the Duke d'Enghien, he would have to leave in the clothes that he had worn for the hunt, since there had been no time to make him any other knee-breeches. His groom Vialas was to remain constantly beside the coach door, riding the white horse, which was a pure thoroughbred, ready to take the duke on his own saddle if need be and gallop off with him. At first they had been afraid that he would fall asleep and had brought Pierrot to play with him, but this proved unnecessary: his pride at seeing himself dressed as a man kept him awake.

The coaches, secretly harnessed and prepared as though to take the Viscountess de Cambes back to Paris, had been led out under a dark alleyway of chestnut trees, where they could not be seen. There they stayed, with their doors open and coachmen seated ready, a mere twenty yards from the main entrance. They were waiting only for the signal, which was to be a fanfare of horns. The princess, looking at the clock which showed five minutes to ten, was already getting up and going over to the Duke d'Enghien to take his hand, when suddenly the door burst open and Lenet, rather than entering, materialized in the room.

The princess, seeing his pale face and anxious look, found herself sharing his pallor and his anxiety.

'My God!' she said, going over to him. 'What's wrong with you? What's happened?'

'What's happened,' said Lenet in a voice overcome with emotion, 'is that a gentleman has just arrived and is asking to speak to you on behalf of the king.'

'Great heavens!' the princess exclaimed. 'We're lost. My dear Lenet, what can we do?'

'Just one thing.'

'Which is?'

'Get the Duke d'Enghien undressed at once and put his clothes on Pierrot.'

'But I don't want my clothes taken off and given to Pierrot!' the young prince cried, ready to burst into tears at the very idea, while Pierrot, overjoyed, was not sure he could believe his ears.

'You must, Monseigneur,' Lenet said in that powerful voice that people find on serious occasions and which can impress even a child. 'Or else you and your mother will be taken to the same prison as the prince, your father.'

The Duke d'Enghien said nothing, while Pierrot, on the contrary, unable to control his feelings, gave way to an unspeakable outburst of joy and pride. The two of them were taken to a low room next to the chapel, where the metamorphosis was to take place.

'Fortunately, the dowager is here, or else Mazarin would have beaten us,' said Lenet.

'Why is that?'

'Because the messenger had to start by visiting the dowager, and he is in her antechamber at this moment.'

'But this messenger from the king is only a spy, I suppose, an agent who has been sent here by the court?'

'As Your Highness says.'

'Then his orders must be to keep watch on us.'

'Yes, but what does that matter, if it is not you whom he is watching?'

'I don't understand, Lenet.'

Lenet smiled. 'But I do understand, Madame, and I shall take charge of everything. Have Pierrot dressed as the prince and the prince as a gardener, and I will make sure that Pierrot learns what to say.'

'Oh, goodness, no! Let my son leave alone!'

'Madame, your son will leave with his mother.'

'Impossible!'

'Why? If we have found a false Duke d'Enghien, we can just as well find a false Princess de Condé.'[73]

'Ah, now! Brilliant! I do understand, my dear Lenet, my good Lenet. But who will stand in for me?' she asked uneasily.

'Have no fear, Madame,' replied the imperturbable counsellor. 'The Princess de Condé, whom I shall use and whom I intend to be kept under surveillance by Mazarin's spy, has just hastily got undressed and is at this moment getting into your bed.'

The following are the events that Lenet had just described to the princess.

While the noblemen were continuing to drink toasts to the princes and to curse Mazarin in the gallery, while Lenet was in his study dealing with Cauvignac over the letter of attestation, and while the princess was making her final preparations for departure, a horseman had arrived at the main gate of the château, followed by his lackey, and rung the bell.

The concierge opened it, but behind the concierge, the new arrival found the halberdier whom we have already met.

'Where have you come from?' he asked.

'From Mantes,' the horseman replied.

So far, so good.

'Where are you going?' asked the halberdier.

'To see the Dowager Princess, then the Princess de Condé and finally the Duke d'Enghien.'

'No entry!' said the halberdier, barring the way with his halberd.

'By order of the king!' the horseman replied, taking a piece of paper from his pocket.

At these formidable words, the halberd was lowered, the sentry called out, an officer of the house ran up, and His Majesty's messenger, after showing his credentials, was immediately introduced into the family apartments.

Fortunately, Chantilly was large and the apartments of the Dowager Princess were a long way from the gallery, where the final scenes of the rowdy celebration (the first part of which we described) were being played out.

If the messenger had asked first of all to see the princess and her son, everything would truly have been lost. But etiquette demanded that he should first go and greet the princess's mother, so the first valet showed him into a large room adjoining Her Highness's bedroom.

'Excuse us, Monsieur,' he said. 'But Her Highness suddenly felt indisposed the day before yesterday and has just been bled, for the third time, less than two hours ago. I shall announce your arrival to her, and in a minute I shall have the honour to introduce you.'

The gentleman nodded his assent and remained alone, not noticing that, through the locks of the doors, three curious pairs of eyes were watching his appearance and trying to recognize him.

The first pair belonged to Pierre Lenet, the next to Vialas, the prince's groom, and the third to La Roussière, master of the hunt. In the event of either one of these men recognizing the new arrival, he would have gone in and, under the pretext of keeping him company, would have engaged him in conversation and gained time.

But none of them was able to recognize the person whom they were so interested in persuading. He was a handsome

young man in the uniform of the infantry. With a listlessness
that one might easily have interpreted as lack of enthusiasm for
the mission with which he was charged, he was looking at
the family portraits and the furnishings of the room, pausing
particularly in front of the portrait of the dowager, to whom
he was about to be introduced, a portrait that had been made
at the height of her youth and beauty.

Faithful to his promise, the valet returned after just a few
moments to fetch the gentleman and take him to see the
Dowager Princess.

Charlotte de Montmorency had sat up in bed. Her doctor,
Bourdelot, had just left her side and met the officer in the
doorway, where he greeted him in a very ceremonious manner,
which the officer returned in kind.

When the princess heard the visitor's steps and the words he
exchanged with the doctor, she quickly made a sign on the side
of the *ruelle*,[74] and then the heavily fringed tapestry hanging
around the bed (except on the side which the dowager had left
open to receive her visitor) moved imperceptibly for two or
three seconds.

The young Princess de Condé was, in fact, inside the
dowager's *ruelle*, having entered there by a secret door in the
panelling, and with her was Lenet, impatient to know, from
the start of the interview, what the king's messenger could have
to do with the princesses at Chantilly.

The officer took three steps into the room and bowed with a
respect that was not only demanded by etiquette.

The dowager's large black eyes were wide open, with the
proud look of a queen who is about to lose her temper: her
silence was heavy with impending storms. Her hand, its dull
whiteness made even whiter by the triple bleeding she had
undergone, indicated to the messenger that he should hand over
the dispatch he was carrying.

The captain reached out his hand towards that of the
Dowager Princess and respectfully placed in it the letter from
Anne of Austria. Then he waited for the princess to read the
four lines that it contained.

'Very well,' said the dowager, folding the paper again with

an imperturbability that was too great not to be affected. 'I understand the queen's intention, much though it is wrapped round with polite words: I am your prisoner.'

'Madame!' the officer exclaimed, with embarrassment.

'A prisoner who will be easy to guard, Monsieur,' the Dowager Princess went on. 'Because I am in no state to run very far. And, as you may have seen as you came in, I have a strict warder: my doctor, Monsieur Bourdelot.'

As she said this, the dowager looked more closely at the messenger, whose appearance seemed pleasant enough for her to moderate somewhat the bitter welcome that the bearer of such an order deserved.

'I knew that Monsieur de Mazarin was capable of many unworthy acts of violence,' she continued. 'But I had not believed him so timid yet as to fear a sick old woman, a poor widow and a child – since I assume that the order that you carry also concerns my daughter, the princess, and my grandson, the duke.'

'Madame,' the young man said. 'I should be desperately sorry were Your Highness to judge me according to the mission that I have the misfortune to be obliged to carry out. I arrived in Mantes with a message for the queen. The postscript to this message recommended the messenger to Her Majesty, so the queen had the kindness to ask me to remain with her, since she would in all probability have need of my services. Two days after that, she sent me here. But even as I accepted the mission that Her Majesty deigned to accord me, whatever it was – as my duty required me to do – I might dare to say that I did not ask for this one and should even have refused it, if one could refuse a monarch.'

As he said these words, the officer bowed a second time as respectfully as the first.

'I am reassured by your explanation, and I hope, now that you have given it to me, that I shall be able to be ill in peace. However, let's have no false modesty, Monsieur: tell me the truth at once. Shall I have someone to watch me even in my room, as my poor son did in Vincennes? Shall I have permission to write and will my letters be inspected or not? If, contrary to all appearances, this illness should ever allow me to get up again, will my walks be limited?'

'Madame,' the officer replied. 'Here are the instructions that the queen did me the honour to give me herself: "Please assure my cousin, de Condé," Her Majesty told me, "that I shall do everything for the princes that the safety of the state allows me to do. I beg her by this present letter to receive one of my officers, who can serve as intermediary between her and me for any messages that she sends. This officer," the queen added, "will be you." Those, Madame,' the young man continued, still with the same signs of respect, 'were Her Majesty's own words.'

The princess had listened to this with the close attention that one gives to a diplomatic dispatch, to discover the meaning that is often hidden behind a word placed here rather than there, or a comma put in such and such a place.

Then after a moment's reflection, the Dowager Princess, no doubt seeing in this message all that she had originally feared to see in it – that is, espionage, plain and simple – pursed her lips and said: 'You will stay in Chantilly, Monsieur, as the queen desires, and moreover you will tell us which apartment would be most pleasing to you and most convenient for carrying out your duties, and that apartment shall be yours.'

'Madame,' the young man replied, slightly raising an eyebrow. 'I have had the honour to explain to Your Highness many things that were not in the instructions. Between Your Highness's anger and the queen's will, I am dangerously placed – I, a poor officer and, above all, a bad courtier: yet it seems to me that Your Highness might be generous enough to abstain from mortifying a man who is only a passive instrument. It is unpleasant for me, Madame, to have to do what I am doing. But since the queen has ordered it, I must obey her orders to the letter. I should not have asked for this task, and I should have been happy were it to have been given to someone else; it seems to me that it is saying a lot . . .'

And the officer raised his head with a blush that brought a similar redness to the haughty forehead of the princess.

'Monsieur,' she replied. 'In whatever rank of society we are placed, as you say, we owe obedience to Her Majesty. I shall therefore follow the example that you have given me and obey as you do. But you should nonetheless understand how hard it is for me not to be able to receive a worthy gentleman like yourself without being free to offer him, as I should wish, the honours of the house. From now on, you are the master here. Continue.'

The officer bowed deeply and replied: 'Madame, God forbid that I should ever forget the distance that separates me from Your Highness and the respect that I owe to your house. Your Highness will continue to command in her home, and I shall be the first among her servants.'

With these words, the young man retired without awkwardness, without servility and without arrogance, leaving the dowager prey to an anger that was all the more violent since she could not take it out on an officer who was so discreet and so respectful.

So Mazarin was the subject of conversation that evening, a conversation that would have struck the minister down from the depth of the *ruelle*, if curses had the power to kill like projectiles.

The gentleman went back to the antechamber, to the lackey who had announced him.

'Now, Monsieur,' the man said, coming over to the messenger. 'The Princess de Condé, with whom you have requested an audience on behalf of the queen, agrees to receive you. Please follow me.'

The officer understood this form of speech that saved the face of the princesses and seemed as grateful for the favour that was being done him as if the favour had not been imposed by an order from above. So, going through the apartments on the heels of the valet, he reached the door of the princess's bedchamber.

At this point, the valet turned round.

'The princess went to bed after the hunt,' he said, 'and since she is tired, she will receive you lying down. Whom shall I announce to Her Highness?'

'Announce the Baron de Canolles, on behalf of Her Majesty the Queen Regent,' the young man replied.

At this name, which the supposed princess heard from her bed, she made a start of surprise that, had it been seen, would have seriously compromised her identity. Quickly pulling down her lace cap over her eyes with her right hand, while the left one brought the richly embroidered quilt up to her chin, she said, in a trembling voice: 'Show him in.'

The officer came in.

BOOK II
MADAME DE CONDÉ

I

Canolles was shown into a huge room lined with dark hangings, lit only by a night light set on a chest of drawers between the two windows. By the little light that came from it, however, one could make out a large painting above the lamp showing a woman, full-length, holding a child by the hand. At the angles of the four corners sparkled the three golden fleurs-de-lys: all that was needed to make the three fleurs-de-lys of France was to remove the heart-shaped bend from them. Finally, in the depths of a huge alcove, where the weak, shimmering light barely penetrated, could be seen under the heavy curtains of a bed, the woman on whom the name of the Baron de Canolles had produced such a striking effect.

The young man addressed the usual polite greetings to her: that is to say, he took the three regulation steps towards the bed, bowed, and took a further three steps. After that the two maids who had doubtless helped Madame de Condé into her bed retired, and after the valet had shut the door behind him, Canolles was alone with the princess.

It was not Canolles's place to open the conversation, so he waited for her to say something to him. But since the princess, too, apparently wished to preserve an obstinate silence, the young officer decided that it was better to ignore convention rather than to remain any longer in such an awkward situation. However, he had no doubt in his mind that the storm, still contained by this contemptuous silence, would burst at the first words, and that he would have to confront a second outburst of anger from a princess who was still more formidable than the first, being younger and more interesting.

But the young man was emboldened by the extreme nature of the offence that was being committed against him, and he bowed for the third time, as fitted the circumstances, that is in a stiff, formal manner, indicating the bad temper that was rising inside his Gascon brain.

'Madame,' he said, 'I have had the honour to request an audience of Your Highness on behalf of Her Majesty the reigning Queen, and Your Highness has deigned to grant me one. Now could Your Highness stretch her goodness to the very limit and indicate by a word or a sign that she has been gracious enough to notice my presence and is ready to hear me?'

A movement of the curtains and under the blankets told Canolles that he was about to have a reply. And a voice could be heard, so full of emotion that it was almost stifled.

'Speak, Monsieur,' said the voice. 'I am listening.'

Canolles adopted a rhetorical tone and began:

'Her Majesty the Queen,' he said, 'has sent me to you, Madame, to assure Your Highness of her wish to maintain good friendly relations with her.'

There was a visible movement behind the curtains of the four-poster, and the princess interrupted the speech.

'Monsieur,' she said, in an unsteady voice, 'speak to me no more of the friendship between Her Majesty the Queen and the house of Condé. There are proofs to the contrary in the dungeons at Vincennes.'

'Huh!' Canolles thought. 'It appears that they have been rehearsing and will all repeat the same thing.'

Meanwhile, a new movement that the messenger did not observe, because of the awkwardness of the situation, was taking place in the bed. The princess went on: 'So, what precisely do you want, Monsieur?'

'I, myself, do not want anything, Madame,' Canolles said, standing upright. 'It is Her Majesty the Queen who desired that I should enter this château, that, unworthy though I am of the honour, I should keep company with Your Highness, and that I should strive with all my strength to restore harmony between the two princes of the blood, who are divided without cause at such a painful moment.'

'Without cause!' the princess exclaimed. 'You are claiming that the breach between us is without cause!'

'Excuse me, Madame,' Canolles went on. 'I am claiming nothing. I am not a judge, only an interpreter.'

'And until this fine harmony is restored, the queen will have me spied upon, under the pretext . . .'

'So!' Canolles exclaimed in exasperation. 'Now I'm a spy! You have said the word! I thank Your Highness for her frankness.'

In the despair that had started to overtake him, Canolles made one of those fine movements that painters so eagerly seek to portray in their scenes of actors and life immobilized in their living pictures.

'So, that's it, it's decided, I'm a spy!' Canolles went on. 'Well, then, Madame, please treat me as such wretches are treated, forget that I am the envoy of a queen and that this queen takes responsibility for all my actions and that I am no more than a mote of dust obedient to her breath. Have me driven out by your lackeys and killed by your men; put me in front of those to whom I can respond with a stick or a sword, but please do not so cruelly insult an officer who is obeying his duty both as a soldier and as a subject – you, Madame, who are so elevated in birth, merit and misfortune!'

These words straight from the heart, with the agony of a groan and the stridency of a reproach, were bound to produce an effect, and so they did. As she listened, the princess sat up, leaning on her elbow, with eyes shining and trembling hands, to make a gesture full of anguish towards the messenger.

'Heaven forbid,' she said, 'that I should ever intend to insult such a fine gentleman as yourself. No, Monsieur de Canolles, no, I do not suspect your loyalty. I take back my words which are wounding, I admit, and I never wished to wound you. No, no, you are a noble officer, Baron, and I acknowledge that fully.'

The princess, in speaking these words, doubtless carried away by the generous feeling that drew them from her heart, had involuntarily moved forward outside the shadow of the canopy formed by the thick curtains. Her white forehead had been visible under her cap, and seeing her blonde hair falling in braids, her lips of burning red and her soft, moist eyes, Canolles shuddered because a kind of vision had just passed before him, and he thought that he could once again smell a scent, the very memory of which intoxicated him. It seemed to him as though one of those golden gates through which the happiest dreams pass had opened to release a swarm of delightful thoughts and restore to him the joys of love. He looked more directly and more clearly at the princess's bed, and, in the space of a second, in the brief light of a flash of lightning that lit up all the past, he recognized, in the princess in the bed before him, the Viscount de Cambes.

In the event, he had been so agitated for the past few minutes that the false princess could have attributed it to the unfortunate remark that he said caused him so much pain, and since the movement that she made, as we said, lasted only a moment and she had been careful to withdraw almost immediately once more into the shadows, cover her eyes and quickly hide even the white hand, so slender that it might give away her identity, she tried – not without emotion, but at least without anxiety – to resume the conversation where she had left it off.

'You were saying, Monsieur?' the young woman asked.

But Canolles was dazzled, fascinated . . . Visions passed back and forth in front of his eyes, his mind was in a whirl, and he was losing his memory, plus his common sense: he was even going to lose respect and question her. A single instinct, perhaps the same that God puts into the heart of those in love, which women call shyness, but which is only avarice, warned Canolles to keep up the pretence and wait; not to lose his dream and not, by an incautious or over-hasty word, to compromise the happiness of his whole life.

He did not add a further gesture or word to the minimum that he ought to say or do. Good heavens! What would happen to him if this great princess suddenly recognized him and if she should conceive a loathing for him here, in her château at Chantilly, as she had conceived a mistrust of him in the inn of Master Biscarros? What if she were to return to the accusation that she had now set aside and imagine that, thanks to an official title and a royal order, he intended to resume a pursuit that was excusable towards the Viscount or Viscountess de Cambes, but insolent and almost criminal when its object was a princess of the blood?

And yet, he suddenly thought, is it possible that a princess of that name and rank could have travelled alone, with only one servant?

As always happens in such circumstances, when a shaken and troubled mind is seeking to steady itself on something, Canolles was distraught. He looked around him and his eyes rested on the portrait of the woman holding her son's hand. At the sight of it, a sudden realization came to him, and, despite himself, he took a step closer to the painting.

The false princess herself could not repress a little gasp, and when, hearing it, Canolles turned round he saw that her face, that had been veiled, was now entirely masked.

'Ah, ha!' Canolles thought to himself. 'What is the meaning of this? Either it was the princess that I met on the Bordeaux road, or I am the victim of a deception and she is not the person in that bed. In any case, we shall see.'

'Madame,' he said, bruquely, 'I am not sure now how to interpret your silence, and I have recognized . . .'

'What have you recognized?' exclaimed the lady in the bed sharply.

'I have recognized,' Canolles continued, 'that I have the misfortune to have inspired the same feeling in you as I did in the Dowager Princess.'

'Ah!' said the voice, with a sigh of relief that its owner could not suppress.

Canolles's remark was perhaps not especially logical or even relevant to the matter in hand, but it had achieved the desired effect. He had noticed the startled movement that interrupted it and the happy one that greeted his last words.

'However,' he went on, 'I am nonetheless obliged to tell Your Highness, however unpleasant this may be, that I must stay in the château and accompany Your Highness wherever she chooses to go.'

'What!' the princess exclaimed. 'I am not to be allowed even to be alone in my room? Oh, Monsieur, this is more than an indignity!'

'I told Your Highness that such were my instructions, but Your Highness has no need to worry,' Canolles added, staring hard at the lady in the bed and emphasizing every word. 'Your Highness must know better than anyone that I am ready to accede to a woman's demands.'

'I should?' the princess exclaimed, in a voice that still expressed more uneasiness than astonishment. 'In truth, Monsieur, I don't know what you mean; I can't think to what situation you refer.'

'Madame,' the officer continued, with a bow. 'I believe that the valet who let me in told Your Highness my name. I am the Baron de Canolles.'

'Well?' said the princess, in quite a firm voice. 'What has that to do with me?'

'I thought I had already had the honour to be of service to Your Highness.'

'To me? In what way, I beg you?' the voice continued, at a pitch that reminded Canolles of an intonation, at once very irritated and very fearful, that was lodged in his memory. He decided that he had gone far enough; in any case, he was more or less certain of what he wanted to know.

'By not carrying out my instructions to the letter,' he continued, in a tone of the deepest respect.

The princess seemed to be reassured.

'I don't want to put you in the wrong, Monsieur,' she said. 'Carry out your instructions, whatever they may be.'

'Fortunately, Madame,' said Canolles, 'I still do not know how to persecute a woman and still less how to offend a princess. I therefore have the honour to repeat to Your Highness what I already told the Dowager Princess, namely that I am her very humble servant. Please, give me your word that you will not leave the château unless I accompany you, and I shall relieve you of my presence – which, as I well understand, must be abhorrent to Your Highness.'

'But in that case,' the princess said, urgently, 'you will not be carrying out your orders?'

'I shall do what my conscience tells me to do.'

'Monsieur de Canolles,' said the voice. 'I swear to you that I shall not leave Chantilly without informing you.'

'In that case, Madame,' said Canolles, with a deep bow, 'forgive me for having been the involuntary cause of your anger a moment ago. Your Highness will not see me again unless she calls for me.'

'Thank you, Baron,' said the voice, with an expression of joy that seemed to echo beneath the canopy. 'Thank you, you may leave. I shall have the pleasure of seeing you again tomorrow.'

This time, there was no mistaking it: the baron recognized the voice, the eyes and the indescribably voluptuous smile of that delightful creature who had, so to speak, slipped through his fingers on the evening when the unknown rider had arrived bringing the order from the Duke d'Epernon. There were those intangible emanations that perfume the air breathed by the loved one, that warm vapour which comes from the body whose contours the entranced soul imagines it is embracing ... through a supreme effort of the imagination; that deceiving elf that feeds on the ideal as matter feeds on the actual.

A last glance at the portrait, ill-lit though it was, showed the baron, whose eyes were starting to become accustomed to this half light, the aquiline nose of the Maillé family, the black hair and deep-set eyes of the princess, while, before him, the woman who had just played the first act of the very demanding role that she had undertaken had eyes set level with her face, a straight nose with flared nostrils, a mouth wrinkled at the corners by the habit of smiling and the rounded cheeks that dispel any notion of tedious meditation.

Canolles knew all that he needed to know, so he bowed once more with the same respect as if he still believed that he was dealing with the princess and retired to his quarters.

II

Canolles had no definite plan: so, on returning to his room, he started to walk quickly back and forth (as people are inclined to do when they are undecided), without noticing that Castorin, who had been waiting for him, had got up and was following him, completely covered by the dressing gown that he was holding out in front of him.

Castorin bumped into a piece of furniture, and Canolles turned round.

'Well?' he said. 'What are you doing there with that garment?'

'I'm waiting for you to take off your jacket, Monsieur.'

'I see no reason to take off my jacket. Put the dressing gown on a chair and wait.'

'What! Monsieur is not going to take off his jacket?' Castorin, a naturally capricious valet, appeared more cantankerous than ever that evening. 'So. Is Monsieur not going straight to bed?'

'No.'

'And when does Monsieur intend to go to bed then?'

'What does it matter to you?'

'A great deal, since I'm very tired.'

'Oh, really?' said Canolles, stopping and looking directly at Castorin. 'You're very tired, are you?'

The baron could clearly read on his groom's face the impertinent expression worn by servants who are dying to get themselves dismissed.

'Very tired,' said Castorin.

Canolles shrugged his shoulders.

'Go outside,' he said. 'Stay in the antechamber. When I need you, I'll ring.'

'I must warn you, Monsieur, that if you wait too long, I shall no longer be in the antechamber.'

'And where will you be, may I ask?'

'In my bed. It seems to me that after travelling two hundred leagues, one should take some rest.'

'Monsieur Castorin,' said Canolles, 'you are a weakling.'

'If the baron feels that a weakling is not worthy of serving him, he has only to say the word, and I shall relieve him of my service,' Castorin replied, assuming his most majestic air.

Canolles was not feeling patient at that moment, and if Castorin could have merely glimpsed the shadow of the storm that was brewing in his master's mind, it is certain that, however keen he was to acquire his freedom, he would have waited until another time before making the proposal that he had just suggested. The baron marched directly up to his groom, and taking one button on his jerkin between his thumb and index finger (a gesture that has since become associated with a greater man[1] than poor Canolles ever was), he said: 'Repeat.'

'I repeat,' Castorin replied with the same impertinence, 'that if the baron is not satisfied with me, I shall relieve him of my services.'

Canolles let go of Castorin and with a serious manner went over to get his cane. Castorin realized what was about to happen.

'Monsieur!' he cried. 'Beware of what you are about to do. I am no simple lackey. I am in the service of the princess.'

'Ah, ha!' said Canolles, lowering the cane that he had already raised. 'Ah, ha, so you are in the service of the princess.'

'Yes, Monsieur, for the past quarter of an hour,' said Castorin, straightening up.

'And who hired you to serve her?'

'Monsieur Pompée, her steward.'

'Monsieur Pompée!'

'Yes.'

'Why didn't you tell me this at once?' Canolles exclaimed. 'Yes, yes, my dear Castorin, you were right to leave my service, and here are two pistoles to make up for the blows that I was just about to give you.'

'But . . .' said Castorin, not daring to take the money. 'But what does this mean. Is the baron making fun of me?'

'Not at all. On the contrary – go and be a groom in the service of the princess, my friend. When is your service supposed to begin?'

'As soon as the baron releases me.'

'Very well, I shall release you from tomorrow morning.'

'And between now and tomorrow morning?'

'Until then you are still my groom, and you must obey me.'

'Happily! What are the baron's orders?' asked Castorin, making up his mind to take the two pistoles.

'Since you wish to sleep, I order you to undress and get into bed.'

'What! What does the baron mean? I don't understand.'

'You don't need to understand, just to obey. Get undressed, I'll help you.'

'What! Monsieur wants to help me?'

'Of course. Since you are going to play the role of the Baron de Canolles, I shall have to play that of Castorin.'

And, without waiting for his groom's permission, the baron took off his jerkin and put it on himself, removed his hat and put it on his own head and, double-locking the door behind him before Castorin had recovered from his surprise, hurried downstairs.

Canolles was at last starting to penetrate this mystery, though part of what had happened was still shrouded in obscurity. For the past two hours, it seemed to him that nothing he had seen or heard was quite natural. The attitude of everyone at Chantilly was stilted: everyone that he met seemed to him to be playing a part, yet the details merged into a general theme that suggested to the investigator on his mission from the queen that he would have to be twice as watchful if he did not wish to be the victim of some great ruse.

The association of Pompée with the Viscount de Cambes was very enlightening.

Whatever doubts Canolles still retained were finally dispelled, when, as soon as he emerged from the courtyard, despite the profound darkness of the night, he saw four men approaching and preparing to go in by the very door through which he had just emerged. The four men were led by the same man-servant who had taken him to see the princesses. Another man, wrapped in a cloak, followed behind.

As they reached the door, the little group stopped, waiting for the orders of the man in the cloak.

'You know where he is staying,' he said, in an imperious voice, speaking to the servant. 'You know him, since you are the one who guided him. So keep watch on him: make sure he cannot leave. Put your men in the stairway, in the corridor, wherever you want, it doesn't matter, just as long as he is kept under guard himself, without knowing it, instead of him guarding Their Highnesses.'

Canolles made himself more insubstantial than a dream in the darkest corner, and from there, without being seen, he saw the five guards assigned to him disappear through the archway, while the man in the cloak, after making sure that they were carrying out his order, went back the way that he had come.

'This still does not prove anything very precise,' Canolles thought, watching him go. 'Because mere irritation might be making them return the favour. Now, as long as that devil Castorin doesn't decide to shout, cry out or do anything silly! I was wrong not to gag him. Too bad! It's too late now. Off we go, let's start our rounds.'

At that, Canolles cast an enquiring glance around him, crossed the courtyard and arrived at the wing of the building behind which the stables were situated.

All the life of the château seemed to have taken refuge here. There were the sounds of horses neighing and people hurrying by. The saddle room was echoing with the clink of bit and harness. Carriages were being wheeled out of the coachhouses, and voices, muffled by apprehension, but audible nonetheless if one listened carefully, exchanged comments.

Canolles stayed for a moment and listened. There could be no doubt about it: they were preparing for departure.

He crossed the space between one wing and the other, went through an arch and arrived in front of the château.

There he stopped. The windows on the ground floor were too brightly illuminated for him not to guess that a large number of torches were lit inside, and as these torches were going backwards and forwards, casting huge shadows and vast rays of light across the lawns, Canolles realized that the place in which there was all this activity was also the centre of the enterprise.

At first, he hesitated to uncover the secret that they were

trying to hide from him. But he soon thought that his title, as the queen's emissary, and the responsibility that this mission laid on him, excused many things, even to the most scrupulous conscience.

So, advancing cautiously and keeping close to the wall, the bottom of which was all the darker, the more the windows, set six or seven feet from the ground, were brightly lit, he climbed on to a stone post and from there to a ledge in the wall, and, steadying himself with one hand in an iron ring and with the other on the edge of the casement window, he stared through the corner of the glass with the closest and most piercing look that ever surveyed the headquarters of a conspiracy.

Here is what he saw. Near a woman who was standing up and fixing the last pin for holding her travelling hat on her head, a few chambermaids were completing the dressing of a child in a hunting costume. The child's back was turned towards Canolles, who could only make out his blond hair. But the lady, her face fully lit by the two six-branched candlesticks that two valets were holding like caryatids on either side of her, offered Canolles the exact original of the portrait that he had seen earlier in the half light of the princess's apartment, which had the long face, stern mouth and imperiously curved nose of the woman whose living image Canolles now had before him. Everything in her spoke of power: her bold gestures, her fiery eyes and the sudden movements of her head. Everything in those around her spoke of deference: their bows, their haste to bring whatever she demanded and their readiness to reply to their sovereign's voice or to study her looks.

Several officers of the house, among whom he recognized the valet, were piling jewels, or money, or that arsenal of women that is known as her 'finery', some into suitcases, some into boxes, some into trunks. Meanwhile, the little prince was playing and running around among the busy servants; but, by some peculiar chance, Canolles did not manage to see his face.

'I guessed as much,' he murmured. 'I'm being tricked and these people are preparing to leave. Yes, but I can with a single gesture change this scene of deception to one of mourning: I have only to run out on to the terrace and blow three times on this silver whistle, and in five minutes, in answer to its shrill note, two hundred men will have burst into the castle, arrested the princesses and garrotted all these officers with their sly smiles. Yes,' he went on (except that now it was his heart and not his lips that spoke), 'yes, but what about her ... She, who is sleeping there, or pretending to sleep. I should lose her irretrievably: she would hate me, and this time her hatred would be well deserved. More than that: she would despise me, saying that I carried out my mission as a spy to the end. Yet, since she obeys the princess, why should I not obey the queen?'

At that moment, as though fate wanted to shake this newly recovered resolve, a door opened in the room where the princess's preparations were underway, and two people – a man of fifty and a young woman of twenty – hurried joyfully through it. Canolles was riveted by what he saw. He had just recognized the fine hair, fresh lips and intelligent expression of the Viscount de Cambes, who, still smiling, came to plant a respectful kiss on the hand of Claire-Clémence de Maillé, Princess de Condé. But this time the viscount was wearing the clothes of her true sex and had been transformed into the most charming viscountess on earth.

Canolles would have given ten years of his life to hear their conversation, but it was no good him pressing his head to the window, as only an unintelligible hum reached his ears. He saw the princess make a farewell gesture to the young woman and kiss her forehead, while giving her some piece of advice that got a laugh from everyone around, before she went back to the ceremonial apartments with some under-officers, who were wearing the uniforms of superior officers. He even saw the worthy Pompée, swelling with pride in his orange coat with silver trimmings, puffing out his chest and, like Don Japhet of Armenia,[2] leaning on the hilt of an enormous rapier as he accompanied his mistress, who was lifting up the skirts of her long satin dress. Then on the left, through the opposite door, the princess's escort began to retire, the princess herself leading the procession, with the air of a queen rather than a fugitive. Behind her came the equerry, Vialas, carrying the little Duke d'Enghien wrapped in a cloak, Lenet, bearing an embossed casket and some bundles of papers, and finally the captain of the château, bringing up the rear of the procession, accompanied by two officers with bared swords.

All this crowd of people was leaving through a secret corridor. Canolles immediately jumped down from his observation post and ran to the archway, where, in the meantime, the lights had been put out. There he saw the whole procession silently making for the stables: departure was imminent.

At that moment, the notion of the duties imposed by the mission which the queen had entrusted him with rose up in Canolles's mind. This woman leaving – this meant that it was the hounds of civil war, fully armed, that he was letting out once more to ravage the entrails of France. Of course, being a man, he was ashamed of being a spy and standing guard over a woman, but the Longueville lady who had set light to all four corners of Paris was a woman, too.

Canolles rushed to the terrace overlooking the park and put the silver whistle to his lips.

This was the end of all the preparations: Madame de Condé would not leave Chantilly, or, if she did, she would not have to travel a hundred yards before being surrounded, her and her escort, by a force three times its size. In this way, Canolles could accomplish his mission without the slightest risk. At a single blow he would destroy the fortune and the future of the house of Condé, and, at the same time, on the ruins of that house, he would build his fortune and lay the foundations of his future as the Vitrys and the Luynes had once done, and more recently the Guitauts and the Miossens,[3] in circumstances perhaps still more threatening to the safety of the monarchy.

Then Canolles looked up at the apartment where, behind red velvet curtains, the light of the night light burning for the false princess shone soft and melancholy, and he thought he could see her beloved shadow against the great white blinds.

All sensible resolutions and selfish plans were scattered by this ray of soft light, just as the first light of day dispels the dreams and phantasms of night.

'Monsieur de Mazarin,' he thought, with a surge of passion, 'is rich enough to do without all these princes and princesses who are escaping from him here, but I am not rich enough to lose the treasure that I now hold, over which I shall watch as closely and as jealously as a dragon. For the moment she is alone, in my power, depending on me. I can enter her apartment at any time of the day or night. She will not run away without telling me: I have her sacred word on that. So what do I care if the queen is deceived and Monsieur de Mazarin is angry! I was told to watch the Princess de Condé, and I am doing so. They only had to give me a description of her, or send a more able spy than I am to look after her.'

Canolles put the whistle back in his pocket and listened to the bolts grating, the distant thunder of the coaches on the bridge in the park and the vanishing sound of a cavalcade growing ever more distant. Then when all had gone from sight and hearing, without considering that he had just hazarded his life for the love of a woman, that is to say for the mirage of happiness, he slipped into the second empty courtyard and cautiously went up his staircase, which, like the doorway, was plunged into the most profound darkness.

But despite his caution, when he reached the corridor Canolles could not help bumping into someone, who appeared to be listening at his door and gave a muffled cry of terror.

'Who are you? Who are you?' the person asked in a frightened voice.

'Why, for goodness' sake!' said Canolles. 'And who are you, gliding around this corridor like a spy?'

'I am Pompée!'

'The princess's steward?'

'Yes, yes, that's right.'

'Why, that's perfect,' said the baron. 'I'm Castorin.'

'Castorin – the Baron de Canolles's valet?'

'The very same.'

'Oh, my dear Castorin,' said Pompée. 'I'm sure I gave you a dreadful fright.'

'Me?'

'Yes, you know . . . When you haven't been a soldier . . . But can I help you, my good friend?' Pompée went on, recovering his self-important air.

'Yes, you can.'

'Tell me how.'

'You can announce at once to the princess that my master wishes to speak to her.'

'At this hour?'

'Exactly.'

'Impossible!'

'You think so?'

'I'm sure of it.'

'So she will not receive my master?'

'No.'

'The king's orders, Monsieur Pompée. Go and tell her that.'

'The king's orders!' Pompée exclaimed. 'I'm going.'

And Pompée dashed down the stairs, driven at once by respect and fear, two greyhounds that would make a tortoise run.

Canolles continued on his way, returning home to find Castorin snoring, while royally stretched out in a large armchair. He put his officer's clothes back on and awaited the events that he himself had put in motion.

'My word!' he thought. 'I may not be doing much on behalf of Monsieur de Mazarin, but it strikes me that I'm not doing too badly for myself.'

He waited in vain for Pompée to come back, and, after ten minutes, seeing that he was not coming, or anyone else in his place, he decided to make the introductions himself. So he woke up Castorin, whose wrath had been somewhat appeased by an hour's sleep, commanded him sternly to be ready for any eventuality, and set out towards the princess's rooms.

At her door, the baron found a footman in a very bad temper because the bell had just summoned him at the moment when his shift was ending, and when he thought, like Master Castorin, that he would at last be able to start a restorative sleep after his tiring day.

'What do you want, Monsieur?' the footman asked, when he saw Canolles.

'I want to pay my respects to the Princess de Condé.'

'At this hour, Monsieur?'

'What do you mean, at this hour?'

'Why, it seems to me that it is very late.'

'How dare you say that, fellow?'

'But, Monsieur . . .' the lackey stammered.

'I am no longer requesting. I wish,' said Canolles, in the haughtiest of voices.

'You wish! Only the princess gives orders here.'

'The king gives orders everywhere. By order of the king!'

The footman shuddered and bowed his head.

'Forgive me, Monsieur,' he said, trembling. 'I am just a poor servant. I cannot take the responsibility of opening the princess's door to you myself. Let me go and wake up a chamberlain.'

'Do the chamberlains usually go to bed at eleven o'clock in the Château de Chantilly?'

'We have been hunting all day,' the footman stammered.

'That's right,' Canolles said to himself. 'They do need time to dress someone up as a chamberlain.'

Then, aloud, he said: 'Very well, go on, I'll wait.'

The footman left at the double to spread the alarm through the château, where Pompée, scared by his own dreadful encounter, had just caused indescribable panic.

Canolles was left alone, listening and watching.

He could hear people running around rooms and along corridors. He saw, by the light of fading lamps, men armed with muskets, taking up positions on the stairs. Finally, he was aware of a general and threatening murmur replacing the amazed silence that had reigned throughout the château a moment earlier.

Canolles picked up his whistle and went over to a window, through which he could see, as a dark, cloudy mass against the night sky, the crests of the tall trees beneath which he had stationed the two hundred men he had brought with him.

'No,' he thought. 'That would lead us directly into battle and that's not what I need. Better to wait. The worst that can happen if I wait is for me to be killed, while if I move too soon, I might lose her.'

He had just thought this to himself, when a door opened and a new figure appeared.

'The princess cannot be seen,' the man said, so quickly that he did not even have time to greet the baron. 'She is in bed and has forbidden anyone at all to enter her room.'

'Who are you?' said Canolles, looking the strange figure up and down. 'And who made you insolent enough to speak to a gentleman with your hat on?'

With the end of his cane, he knocked off the other man's hat.

'Monsieur!' said the man, proudly taking a step backwards.

'I asked you who you are,' said Canolles.

'I am, as you can see . . .' said the man. 'As you can see by my uniform, captain of Her Highness's guard.'

Canolles smiled. He had had time to size up the man in front of him and realized that he was dealing with some cellarer with a belly as round as his bottles, some ruddy Vatel[4] squeezed into an officer's jerkin, which either lack of time or too much belly had prevented him from fully lacing up.

'Very good, Captain of the Guard,' said Canolles. 'Pick up your hat and answer me.'

The captain carried out the first of these requests like a man who has studied that fine axiom of military discipline: to learn how to command, one must know how to obey.

'Captain of the Guard!' said Canolles. 'Dammit! That's a fine rank.'

'Yes, Monsieur. Rather fine. So what?' said the man, standing up.

'Don't puff yourself up too much, Captain,' said Canolles. 'Or else you'll break your last lace and end up with your breeches round your ankles, which would be most unbecoming.'

'So, tell me, Monsieur, who are you yourself?' the alleged captain asked, in a question of his own.

'I shall copy the example of good manners that you have shown me, Monsieur, and answer your question as you have mine. I am a captain in Navailles, and I am here in the name of the king as an ambassador who may assume the character of a peaceful envoy or a violent one. I shall resort to whichever of these is appropriate, according to whether His Majesty's orders are obeyed or not.'

'Violent, Monsieur?' the false captain exclaimed. 'You may be violent?'

'Very violent, I warn you.'

'Even in the presence of Her Highness?'

'Why not? Her Highness is only the first among His Majesty's subjects.'

'Do not attempt to use force, Monsieur. I have fifty men at arms who are ready to avenge Her Highness's honour.'

Canolles did not want to mention that these fifty men were as many lackeys and skivvies, worthy of serving under such a commander, and that, as far as the princess's honour was concerned, it was at that moment hastening with her along the roads to Bordeaux. He contented himself by responding with the composure that is more intimidating than a threat, usual among brave men, accustomed to danger: 'If you have fifty men at arms, Captain, I have two hundred soldiers who are the advance force of a royal army. Do you intend to rebel openly against His Majesty?'

'No, Monsieur, no!' the fat man quickly replied, much humiliated. 'Heaven forfend! But I beg you to bear witness that I only gave in to force.'

'That is the least I can do for a colleague.'

'In that case, I shall take you to the Dowager Princess, who is not yet asleep.'

Canolles did not need to think to realize the terrible danger presented by this trap, but he soon escaped from it thanks to the absolute authority invested in him.

'I have no orders to see the Dowager Princess, but Her Highness, the young princess.'

The captain of the guard bowed his head again, got his legs moving in a backward direction, dragged his long sword across the wooden floor and majestically proceeded once more through the door between two sentries who had been trembling throughout the scene: the announced arrival of two hundred men had nearly driven them to abandon their post, so little were they inclined to become faithful martyrs in the sack of Chantilly.

Ten minutes later, the captain, followed by two guards,

returned and with endless ceremonial fetched Canolles to take him to the princess, into whose room he was ushered without any further delay.

Canolles recognized the apartment, the furniture, the bed and even the scent of the room. But he looked in vain for two things: the portrait of the real princess, which he had noticed on his first visit and which had given him the first hint of the trick that they were trying to play on him, and the face of the false princess, for whom he had just made such a great sacrifice. The portrait had been taken away, and, as a somewhat late precaution, no doubt consequent on the first one, the face of the person in the bed was turned towards the canopy, in a show of royal impertinence.

Two women were standing near her, by the canopy.

The baron would willingly have overlooked this lack of consideration, but since he was afraid that some new substitution might allow Madame de Cambes to escape as the princess had done, his hair rose in terror on his head, and he decided immediately to make sure of the identity of the person in the bed by calling on the supreme power accorded to him by his mission.

'Madame,' he said, giving a deep bow. 'I beg Your Highness's forgiveness for presenting myself to her in this manner, especially after I gave my word that I would wait for your orders, but I have just heard a great deal of noise in the château and . . .'

The person in the bed shuddered, but did not answer. Canolles looked for some sign that might reassure him that the woman before him was indeed the one he was looking for, but in the midst of the clouds of lace and the soft thickness of the eiderdowns and curtains, it was impossible to distinguish anything except the shape of a person lying down.

'And I owe it to myself,' Canolles went on, 'to ensure that this bed still contains the same person with whom I had the honour to speak for half an hour.'

This time, it was not a simple shudder, but a real start of terror. Canolles observed the movement and was alarmed by it.

'If she has deceived me,' he thought, 'and if, despite the solemn promise that she gave, she has fled, I shall leave this château, mount my horse, take the head of my two hundred men and catch up with the fugitives, even if I have to set fire to thirty villages to light my way.'

He waited for a moment longer, but the person in the bed did not reply or turn round. It was evident that she wished to gain time.

'Madame,' Canolles said finally, with an impatience that he no longer had the strength to disguise, 'I beg Your Highness to remember that I am the king's envoy, and it is in the king's name that I demand the honour of looking at Your Highness's face.'

'This inquisition is unbearable,' said a trembling voice which sent a shudder through the young officer, for he recognized a tone that no other voice could imitate. 'If, as you say, it is the king who is forcing you to behave in this way, this is because the king, who is only a child, has not yet learned the duties of a gentleman. To force a woman to show her face is to subject her to the same insult as if one tore off her mask.'

'Madame, there is a phrase before which ladies bow when it comes from kings, and kings when it comes from fate: it must be.'

'Very well, since it must be,' said the young woman. 'And since I am alone and defenceless against the orders of the king and the demands of his messenger, I obey. Look at me, Monsieur.'

At this, a brusque movement thrust aside the rampart of pillows, blankets and lace behind which the beautiful prisoner was besieged, and through this improvised breach in the walls, blushing with modesty rather than indignation, appeared the blonde hair and delightful face announced by the voice. With the swift glance of a man accustomed to take in situations that were, if not similar, at least equivalent, Canolles was reassured to find that it was not anger that kept those eyes lowered beneath their golden lashes and caused that white hand to tremble against the pearly neck as it held back the restless waves of hair and the perfumed cambric of the sheets.

The false princess held the pose for an instant, wishing it to seem threatening, though it expressed only annoyance, while

Canolles looked at her, delightedly breathing in her scent and restraining with both hands the beating of his joyful heart.

'Well, Monsieur,' said the beautiful victim after a few seconds. 'Am I humiliated enough? Have you examined me at your leisure? Your triumph is complete, is it not? So, now be a generous victor and leave me!'

'I should like to do so, Madame, but I must fulfil my instructions to the end. So far I have only accomplished the part of my mission that concerns Your Highness. But it is not enough to have seen you; I must now see the Duke d'Enghien.'

At these words, spoken in the tone of a man who knows that he has the right to command and who wishes to be obeyed, there was a fearful silence. The false princess rose up, leaning on her hand, and turned on Canolles one of those looks that only she seemed capable of giving, so much was contained in it. It said: Have you recognized me? Do you know who I really am? And if you do, spare me, forgive me, you are the stronger; have pity on me!

Canolles understood everything that was implied by the look, but hardened his heart against its seductive eloquence and replied to the look in words: 'Impossible, Madame. My order is clear.'

'Then let everything be done as you wish, Monsieur, since you make no concession to my situation or my rank. Go! These ladies will conduct you to my son, the prince.'

'Could not these ladies, instead of conducting me to the prince, bring him to you, Madame?' Canolles said. 'That, it seems to me, would be infinitely preferable.'

'Why, Monsieur?' asked the false princess, clearly more worried by this latest request than she had been by any other.

'Because, while they are away, I shall inform Your Highness of a part of my mission that I can only share with her alone.'

'With me alone?'

'With you alone,' Canolles replied, giving a deeper bow than any he had offered her so far.

This time, the princess's face, which had successively expressed dignity, then supplication, and supplication followed by anxiety, now stared at Canolles with the intensity of terror.

'What is it about this tête-à-tête that you apparently find so terrifying, Madame?' Canolles asked. 'Are you not a princess and I a gentleman?'

'You are right, Monsieur, and I am wrong to be afraid. Yes, although this is the first time that I have the pleasure of seeing you, I have heard of your decency and honesty. Go and fetch the Duke d'Enghien, ladies, and come back here with him.'

The two women left the canopy of the bed, went across to the door and turned round once more to confirm that this order was indeed correct; then, on a sign confirming their mistress's words, went out.

Canolles watched them until they had closed the door behind them. Then he turned eyes shining with joy back on the princess.

'Come now,' she said, sitting up and folding her arms. 'Come now, Monsieur de Canolles, why are you persecuting me?'

As she said this, she looked at the young officer, not with the haughty look of a princess that she had tried on him, unsuccessfully, but on the contrary with such a touching and meaningful expression that all the charming details of their first interview, all the intoxicating events of the journey and, finally, all the memories of his burgeoning love welled up, wrapping the baron's heart in a kind of balmy mist.

'Madame,' he said, taking a step towards the bed. 'The person against whom I am proceeding in the name of the law is Madame de Condé, and not you, who are not the princess.'

The woman to whom these words were addressed gave a little cry, went very pale and put a hand to her heart, exclaiming: 'What do you mean, Monsieur? So who do you think I am?'

'Oh, as far as that is concerned,' Canolles replied, 'I should be at some pains to describe it, because I should almost swear that you are the most charming viscount, were it not that you are the most adorable viscountess.'

'Monsieur!' said the false princess, hoping that a reminder of her dignity would have some effect on Canolles. 'I can only understand one thing out of everything that you are saying to me, which is that you are lacking in respect for me. You are insulting me!'

'One is not lacking in respect for God, Madame, because one

adores him,' Canolles replied. 'One does not insult the angels by falling on one's knees before them.'

At that, he leant forward as though to kneel.

'Monsieur,' the viscountess said hastily, stopping him. 'The Princess de Condé cannot tolerate . . .'

'The Princess de Condé is at this moment hurrying along on a fine horse, side by side with Monsieur Vialas, her groom, Monsieur Lenet, her counsellor, with her gentlemen, her captains . . . in short, with her whole household, on the Bordeaux road, and she has nothing to do with what is at present occurring between the Baron de Canolles and the Viscount, or Viscountess de Cambes.'

'But what are you telling me, Monsieur? Are you mad?'

'No, Madame, I am saying only what I have seen and telling you only what I have heard.'

'Well, then, if you have seen and heard what you say, your mission must be over.'

'Do you think so? Am I then to go back to Paris and admit to the queen that, rather than cause displeasure to a woman whom I love – I am not naming anyone, Madame, so don't arm your eyes with anger – I disobeyed her orders, allowed her enemy to flee, closed my eyes to what I was seeing, and in the end betrayed – yes, betrayed – the cause of my king.'

The viscountess seemed touched and looked at the baron with something like compassion.

'Don't you have the best excuse of all,' she said, 'the excuse of impossibility? Could you alone have arrested the princess's large escort? Were you required to fight fifty men on your own?'

'I was not on my own, Madame,' Canolles said, shaking his head. 'I have and I still have, in the wood, fifty yards away from us, two hundred soldiers, whom I can assemble and call to me with a single blast of the whistle. It would have been easy for me to stop the princess, and it was she, in fact, who could not have resisted. Then even had my escort been weaker than hers, I could still have fought, I could still have died fighting. It would have been as easy for me,' the young man went on, bending further and further towards her, 'as it would be sweet for me to touch this hand, if I dared to do it.'

The hand at which the baron was staring with such burning eyes, the fine, white, rounded hand, this intelligent hand had fallen outside the bed and was throbbing at every word the young man spoke. The viscountess herself, blinded by the electricity of love, the effect of which she had already felt in the little inn at Jaulnay, did not recall that she should remove the hand that had offered Canolles such a nice point of comparison. So she left it there, and the young man, slipping to his knees, pressed his mouth with voluptuous timidity on the hand, which, as soon as his lips touched it, was withdrawn as though it had been burnt by a red-hot iron.

'Thank you, Monsieur de Canolles,' the young woman said. 'Thank you from the bottom of my heart for what you have done for me. Believe me, I shall never forget it. But now double the value of the service you have done for me by understanding my position and leaving me. Must we not part, now that your task is over?'

This 'we', spoken with such a sweet intonation that it seemed to contain a hint of regret, caused the most secret chords in Canolles's heart to ache: a feeling of pain, indeed, is almost always to be found somewhere in the profoundest joy.

'I shall obey, Madame,' he said. 'But I might just point out – not in any refusal to obey, but to spare you any possible regret – that by obeying you, I shall be destroying myself. As soon as I admit my fault and do not appear to have been taken in by your deceit, I become the victim of my leniency . . . I shall be declared a traitor, imprisoned . . . and perhaps executed. Quite simple: I am a traitor.'

Claire gave a cry and this time took Canolles's hand herself, though she let it go at once, with a charming show of embarrassment.

'So what are *we* going to do?'

The young man's heart swelled: this happy *we* was definitely becoming Madame de Cambes's favourite expression.

'Destroy you! You who are so good and so generous,' she went on. 'I, destroy you – never! Oh, how can I save you? Tell me! Tell me!'

'You must allow me, Madame, to play my part to the end.

As I say, I must appear to be deceived by you, and I must report to Monsieur de Mazarin what I can see, not what I know.'

'Yes, but if he knew that it was for me that you were doing all this, if he were to learn that we have already met and that you have already seen me, I am the one who would be lost. Think of that!'

'Madame,' Canolles replied, with a perfect affectation of melancholy, 'I do not think, judging by your cold behaviour and the dignity which it costs you so little to sustain in my presence, that you would blurt out a secret that, in any case, in your heart at least, does not exist.'

Claire remained silent, but a glance, a hint of a smile, that the beautiful prisoner involuntarily let slip, gave such an answer to Canolles that it made him the happiest of men.

'So, shall I stay?' he asked, with an indescribable smile.

'Since you must!' the viscountess replied.

'In that case, I shall write to Monsieur de Mazarin.'

'Yes, off you go.'

'What do you mean?'

'I am telling you to go off and write to him.'

'No, no, I must write to him here, from your room. The letter must be dated from the foot of your bed.'

'But that is not decent.'

'Here are my instructions, Madame, read them for yourself.'

And Canolles handed a sheet of paper to the viscountess, who read:

'"The Baron de Canolles will keep watch on the princess and the Duke d'Enghien, her son."'

'Keep watch,' said Canolles.

'Keep watch: yes, that's what it says.'

Claire realized how much a man in love, as Canolles was, could take advantage of such instructions, but she also realized the service that she was rendering to the princess by carrying on with the deception.

'Very well, write,' she said, with resignation.

Canolles looked at her, and she, also with a look, indicated a box containing everything that he needed to write. The young man opened it, took out paper, a quill and some ink, put them on a table, drew the table over as close as he could to the bed, asked permission to sit down (as though Claire was still the princess – a permission that was granted) and wrote the following dispatch to Mazarin:

Monseigneur,
   I arrived at the Château of Chantilly at nine o'clock this evening. You can see that I have been prompt, because I only left Your Eminence at half past six.
   I found the two princesses in bed: the dowager quite seriously ill and the young princess tired after a long hunt, in which she had taken part during the day.
   Following Your Eminence's instructions, I presented myself to Their Highnesses who immediately dismissed all their guests. I am keeping watch at this moment over the princess and her son.

'And her son,' Canolles repeated, turning to the viscountess. 'Damn! It seems to me that I am lying, and I should much prefer not to do that.'

'Don't worry,' Claire replied, with a laugh. 'If you have not yet seen my son, you will do so.'

'And her son,' Canolles repeated, also laughing.

And, continuing his letter from where he had left off, he wrote: 'It is in the princess's own room and sitting at her bedside that I have the honour to address this letter to Your Eminence.'

He signed it, and, after respectfully asking Claire's permission, he pulled a bell. A valet came in.

'Call my footman,' said Canolles, 'and when he is in the antechamber, let me know.'

Five minutes later, the baron was informed that Castorin was at his post.

'Here,' Canolles told him, 'take this letter to the officer commanding my two hundred men and tell him to send it post-haste to Paris.'

'But, Baron,' said Castorin, who found this order one of the most disagreeable to carry out in the middle of the night, 'I thought I told you that Monsieur Pompée had enrolled me in the service of the princess.'

'And it is in the princess's name that I am giving you this order. Your Highness,' said Canolles, turning round, 'would you confirm what I am saying? Your Highness knows how important it is for this letter to be delivered as soon as possible.'

'Go!' said the false princess, in a tone and with a gesture that were full of authority.

Castorin gave a deep bow and left.

'Now,' Claire said, reaching towards Canolles with two little hands, clasped together in supplication. 'You will leave, won't you?'

'Excuse me,' said Canolles. 'What about your son?'

'That's right,' Claire said smiling. 'You'll see him.'

And indeed, no sooner had Madame de Cambes said these words than there was a scratch on her door – as was the custom in those days; it was Cardinal Richelieu, who, no doubt because of his love of cats, had made this manner of knocking fashionable. So, for the long period in which he was in favour, they scratched on Monsieur de Richelieu's door, and then on Monsieur de Chavigny's, who was certainly entitled to the succession, if only by reason of being the natural heir;[5] and finally on Monsieur de Mazarin's. They could certainly, therefore, scratch on the door of the princess.

'Someone's coming,' said Madame de Cambes.

'Very well, I'll resume my official character, then.'

Canolles put the table back, drew back the chair, put his hat on and stood respectfully four paces away from the princess's bed.

'Come in,' said the viscountess.

At that, the most ceremonious procession one could imagine came into the room. It consisted of the maids, officers, chamberlains and all the household servants of the princess.

'Madame,' said the first footman. 'The Duke d'Enghien has been woken up. He can now receive His Majesty's messenger.'

A glance from Canolles to Madame de Cambes said as clearly as he could have in words: 'Is that what we agreed?'

This look, bearing with it all the supplication of a heart in distress, was perfectly understood, and, no doubt out of gratitude for what Canolles had done – and then perhaps a little because she wished to exercise that mischievous streak that lurks eternally in the depths of even the best woman's heart – she said: 'Bring the Duke d'Enghien here. Monsieur will see my son in my presence.'

They hurried to obey, and a moment later the young prince was led into the room.

We have mentioned already that, while he was following the princess's final preparations for her departure, the baron had watched the prince playing and running around, but without seeing his face; Canolles had only noticed his clothes, which were a simple hunting outfit. It occurred to him, therefore, that it was not in his honour that the boy had been dressed in the splendid costume in which he now appeared in front of him. His earlier idea, namely that the prince had left with his mother, thus became almost a certainty. For a while, he examined the heir to the illustrious Prince de Condé in silence, and, while not at all detracting from the respect with which his whole person was imbued, a smile of barely perceptible irony fluttered on his lips.

'I am only too happy,' he said, 'at being allowed the honour of presenting my respects to Monseigneur the Duke d'Enghien.'

The child was staring with his large eyes at Madame de Cambes, who signalled to him to bow, and since it appeared to her that Canolles was following all the details of this scene with rather too cynical a look, she said, with a mischievous intent that made Canolles shudder (already guessing from the movement of the viscountess's lips that he was to be the victim of some feminine wile): 'My son, the officer before you is Monsieur de Canolles who has been sent here by His Majesty. Give Monsieur de Canolles your hand to kiss.'

At that order, Pierrot, appropriately dressed by Lenet – who, as he had promised the princess, had taken charge of instructing the child – offered a hand that there had been neither the time or the means to transform into that of a gentleman, and Canolles, amid the stifled laughter of those around, was obliged to imprint a kiss on this hand that even a person less expert in the subject than himself would easily have recognized as not belonging to a member of the aristocracy.

'Ah, Madame de Cambes,' Canolles muttered to himself, 'you will pay for that kiss!'

He bowed respectfully to Pierrot, in gratitude for the honour he had done him. Then, realizing that after this ordeal, the last item on the programme, it was impossible for him to remain any longer in the bedroom of a lady, he turned to the bed and said: 'My mission this evening is accomplished, and I have only to ask your permission to retire.'

'Go then, Monsieur,' said Claire. 'You can see that we are very peaceful here. You can rest easy.'

'Before that I have one great favour to demand of you, Madame.'

'What is that?' Madame de Cambes asked uneasily, understanding from the tone of the baron's voice that he was preparing a revenge.

'To grant me the same favour as I have just received from the prince, your son.'

This time, the viscountess was trapped. She could hardly refuse an officer of the king the formal courtesy that he had requested in front of everyone; so Madame de Cambes held out a trembling hand towards Canolles.

He advanced towards the bed as though towards the throne of a queen, took the proffered hand in the tips of his fingers, went down on one knee and planted a long kiss on the fine, white, shivering skin, a kiss that everyone attributed to respect and only the viscountess interpreted as an ardent embrace of love.

'You promised, you even swore to me,' Canolles whispered as he got up, 'not to leave the château without telling me. I am counting on your promise and on your word.'

'You may count on it, Monsieur,' said Madame de Cambes, falling back against her pillow, nearly fainting.

Canolles, trembling at the emotion in the tone, tried to find confirmation in the lovely prisoner's eyes of the hope that her voice had given him. But the viscountess's eyes were tightly sealed.

Canolles told himself that locked boxes are the ones that contain the most precious treasures and withdrew with joy in his heart.

To describe how our baron spent that night; to describe how his sleeping and waking moments were only one long dream, in the course of which he went over and over in his mind all the details of the fabulous adventure that had given him possession of the most precious treasure that ever any miser could have nursed within the recesses of his heart; to describe the plans that he made in order to subject the future to the designs of his love and the whims of his fancy; to describe the reasons that he gave to persuade himself that he was acting properly, would be impossible, madness being a tiresome matter for any mind except that of a madman.

Canolles went to sleep late – if you can call 'sleep' the feverish delirium that followed wakefulness, yet the morning sun had barely lit the tops of the poplar trees and had not yet reached as far as the surface of the fine lakes, in which the large-leaved water lilies sleep, whose flowers only open in sunlight, before Canolles was already leaping from his bed. Dressing quickly, he went down into the garden. His first visit was to the wing inhabited by the princess, his first look was at the window of her apartments. Either the prisoner had not gone to bed, or else she was already awake, because a light too strong to be merely that of a night light was throwing a red glow on the damask curtains, which were fully drawn. Canolles stopped and looked, the sight no doubt immediately suggesting all kinds of senseless conjectures to his mind, and, without continuing his walk any further than the pedestal of a statue which hid him reasonably well, all alone with his fancy, he entered into that eternal dialogue of a loving heart discovering the object of its love amid the poetic emanations of the natural world.

The baron had been at his post for around half an hour and was watching these curtains (which anyone else would have passed heedlessly by) with inexpressible happiness, when he saw a window open in the gallery, and in it almost immediately appeared the sturdy figure of Master Pompée. Everything that concerned the viscountess was of exceptional interest to Canolles, so he turned away from the compelling windows and thought that he could see Pompée trying to communicate with him in sign language. At first, Canolles could not believe that the gestures were meant for him and looked round about him, but Pompée, noticing the baron's uncertainty, accompanied the gestures with a whistle, which might have been considered somewhat inappropriate on the part of a groom trying to attract the attention of one of His Majesty's envoys, if the whistle had not been justified by a sort of white spot, almost invisible to any eyes except those of a man in love, who immediately recognizes in this white spot a sheet of rolled-up paper. 'A letter!' Canolles thought. 'She has written to me. What does this mean?'

He walked over, anxiously, although his first reaction was one of great joy, but in the great joys of those in love there is a certain element of apprehension, which is perhaps their greatest charm: to be assured of one's love is to be no longer happy.

As Canolles approached, Pompée dared to show more and more of the letter. Eventually, Pompée was holding out his arm and Canolles his hat. As we can see, the two men understood one another perfectly. Pompée dropped the letter, and Canolles caught it very skilfully. Then he immediately slipped into an arbour, where he could read it at his leisure, and Pompée, fearing no doubt that he might catch cold, closed the window.

However, one does not read the first letter from the woman one loves just like that, especially when this unexpected letter has no reason to come and bother you except to upset your tranquillity. What, indeed, could the viscountess have to tell him, if nothing had changed in the plans they had drawn up between them the evening before? So the letter could only contain some bad news.

Canolles was so convinced of that that he did not even bring the paper up to his lips, as lovers are accustomed to do in such circumstances. On the contrary, he turned it round and round with growing alarm. However, since it had to be opened at some time or another, he summoned up all his courage, broke the seal and read:

Monsieur,
    I hope that you will agree with me that to stay any longer in our present situation is quite impossible. You must suffer from

appearing to all the members of the household like an unpleasant warder, while I, for my part, may fear, if I greet you more warmly than the princess would do in my place, that it will be discovered that we are putting on a double act, the outcome of which will be the certain loss of my reputation.

Canolles wiped his brow. His premonition had not been wrong. With daylight, which so surely chases away ghosts, all his gilded dreams had disappeared. He shook his head, sighed and read on.

Pretend to discover the trick that we have used. There is a very simple means to achieve this discovery, which I shall supply to you myself if you promise to do as I ask. As you see, I am not concealing from you how much I depend on you. If you do as I ask, I will have someone give you a portrait of me with my name and my coat of arms under the painting. You will say that you have found this portrait in one of your night rounds and that, thanks to it, you have discovered that I am not the princess.

Do I need to tell you that, as a souvenir of the gratitude that I shall keep in the depths of my heart if you leave this morning, I permit you to keep this miniature – assuming that you attach some value to it?

Leave us then, without seeing me again, if possible, and you will take with you all my gratitude, while I, for my part, will carry your memory as that of one of the noblest and most loyal knights that I have ever known.

Canolles reread the letter and remained petrified. Whatever favour is contained in a letter of dismissal, whatever honey is poured over a refusal or a farewell, such a farewell, refusal and dismissal are still a cruel disappointment for the heart. No doubt, the portrait was a sweet gift, but the reason behind the gift deprived it of much of its value.

In any case, what use is the portrait when the original is there, when one has it beneath one's hand and the means to retain it?

Yes, but Canolles, who had not shrunk from the idea of

facing the wrath of the queen and Mazarin, trembled at that of a raised eyebrow from Madame de Cambes.

How this woman had tricked him, though, firstly on the road, then in Chantilly, taking the place of the princess, then yesterday, offering him a hope, only to take it away the day after! But out of all these deceptions, the last was the cruellest. On the road, she had not known him and was merely getting rid of an awkward companion, nothing more. By taking the place of Madame de Condé, she was obeying an order, playing a role demanded by a sovereign: she could not have acted otherwise. But this time, now that she knew him, after having appeared to appreciate his devotion and after having twice spoken that word, *we*, that had resonated in the very fibres of the young man's heart, now to retreat, to disavow her kindness, to repudiate her gratitude and finally to write such a letter, was in Canolles's eyes more than cruel, it was almost to scoff at him.

So he felt vexed, angrily full of painful vexation, without noticing that behind the curtains, where all the lights had gone out as though daylight had made them unnecessary, a woman, well hidden by the damask and sheltered by the panelling, was watching his dumb show of despair and perhaps enjoying it.

'Yes, yes,' he thought, accompanying his thoughts with gestures appropriate to the feelings that were uppermost in is mind, 'yes, this is a very straightforward, very definite dismissal, a great event crowned by a banal outcome, a poetic hope changed into a cruel disappointment. But I shall not accept this ridicule that is being heaped on me. I prefer her hatred to this pretended gratitude that she promises me. Oh, yes! Can I rely on her promise now? I might as well rely on the constancy of the wind or the calmness of the sea. Oh, Madame, Madame,' Canolles went on, turning towards the window. 'Let me just have a similar opportunity and you will not escape from me a third time.'

Canolles went back up to his room, intending to get dressed and enter the viscountess's apartments, if need be by force. But as he came into the room and glanced at the time, he noticed that it was barely seven o'clock.

No one in the château was up yet. Canolles slumped down on a chair, closing his eyes in order to think more clearly and, if that were possible, to drive away the ghosts dancing around him; he opened his eyes only to consult his watch every five minutes or so.

The clock rang eight. The château was beginning to wake up, gradually filling with movement and noise. Canolles waited another half an hour, though with great difficulty. Finally, he could bear it no longer and went down, to find Pompée proudly sniffing the air in the great court, surrounded by servants, to whom he was describing his campaigns in Picardy under the late king.

'Are you Her Highness's steward?' Canolles asked, as though seeing poor Pompée for the first time.

'Yes, Monsieur,' Pompée said, with astonishment.

'Be so good as to tell Her Highness that I wish to have the honour to present my respects.'

'But, Monsieur, Her Highness . . .'

'. . . has got up.'

'And yet . . .'

'I thought that Monsieur's departure . . .'

'My departure will depend on the interview that I am about to have with Her Highness.'

'I say that because I have no order from my mistress.'

'And I say that,' said Canolles, 'because I have orders from the king.'

At these words, Canolles imperiously patted the pocket of his jerkin, a gesture that he considered the most satisfying of all that he had used since the previous day.

And yet, even as he carried out this coup d'état, our negotiator felt his courage slipping away. Indeed, since the previous day, his importance had considerably diminished. The princess had left almost twelve hours earlier. She must surely have been travelling all night, so she would be twenty or twenty-five leagues from Chantilly. However much Canolles urged his men to make haste, there was now no means of catching her up, and even if he did so, taking with him a hundred or so of his men, who was to be sure that the fugitive's own escort had not by

now increased to three or four hundred supporters? As he
mentioned the day before, Canolles still had the option of
getting himself killed; but, did he have the right to get the men
accompanying him killed with him and so to make them pay
the bloody price for his amorous whims? If he had been mistaken the day before about her feelings towards him and if her
anxiety was only a game, then Madame de Cambes could
openly make fun of him; in that case, it would be a matter of
hisses from the servants, hisses from the soldiers hidden in the
forest, disgrace from Mazarin, anger from the queen and, above
all of these, the ruin of his burgeoning love, because no woman
has ever loved a man, whom she has, for a single instant,
considered subjecting to ridicule.

As he was turning these ideas over and over in his head,
Pompée returned, with his tail between his legs, saying that the
princess was expecting him.

This time, there was no question of ceremonial. The viscountess was waiting in a little salon next to her bedchamber, dressed
and standing. On her charming face were traces of sleeplessness
that she and her maids had tried in vain to disguise: in particular, a slight, but dark shadow around her eyes showed that
those eyes had not shut, or hardly so.

'As you see, Monsieur,' she said, without giving him a chance
to speak first, 'I am giving in to your wishes, but in the hope,
I must confess, that this interview will be the last and that you
will in your turn give in to mine.'

'Forgive me, Madame,' said Canolles. 'But from our talk
yesterday evening, I had hoped for less inflexibility in your
demands, and I assumed that in exchange for what I have done
for you – and for you alone, since I do not know Madame de
Condé, you understand – you would have been good enough
to allow me to stay longer in Chantilly.'

'Yes, Monsieur, I must confess,' said the viscountess, 'in the
first moment . . . the confusion that was an evident consequence
of the situation in which I found myself . . . the interests of the
princess, who wanted me to gain time for her, may have induced
me to utter some words that were not wholly consistent with
my true thoughts . . . But through this long night I have been

thinking, and any longer stay in this château by either you or myself has become impossible.'

'Impossible, Madame!' said Canolles. 'Are you forgetting that anything is possible to him who speaks in the name of the king?'

'Monsieur de Canolles, I hope that before all else you are a man of honour and that you will not take advantage of the situation in which my devotion to Her Highness has placed me.'

'Madame,' Canolles replied, 'before all else I am mad – as you have seen, for heaven's sake! Only a madman would have done what I have done. So, take pity on my madness, Madame, and do not send me away, I beg of you.'

'In that case, Monsieur, I am the one who will cede the place to you. I am the one, who, despite yourself, will bring you back to your duty. We shall see if you can stop me by force and if you would expose both of us to the embarrassment of a public scandal. No, no, Monsieur,' the viscountess continued, in an urgent tone that Canolles was hearing for the first time. 'No, consider that you cannot remain for ever at Chantilly: you will recall that you are expected somewhere else.'

When she said this, it was like a lightning flash bursting in front of Canolles's eyes, recalling the scene in the inn at Biscarros and Madame de Cambes's discovery of the young man's liaison with Nanon. Everything was now clear to him.

Her insomnia had not been caused by present anxieties but by memories from the past. This morning's resolve to avoid Canolles was not the result of any design, but an expression of jealousy.

There was a moment's silence between these two people as they stood facing one another, but during this silence each of them was listening to their own thoughts speaking with the beating of the hearts in their breasts.

'Jealous!' Canolles thought. 'Jealous! Ah, now I understand everything. Yes, yes, she wants to be sure that I love her enough to sacrifice everything for our love! It's a test!'

For her part, Madame de Cambes was thinking: 'I'm simply an amusement for Monsieur de Canolles. He met me on his way, no doubt at the moment when he was forced to leave

Guyenne, and he followed me as the traveller follows a will-o'-the-wisp, but his heart has remained in that little house surrounded by trees where he was going on the evening when I met him. It is therefore impossible for me to keep beside me a man who loves another, and with whom, if I should see him any longer, I might myself be weak enough to fall in love. Oh, were I to be so feeble as to love the agent of her persecutors, that would not only mean betraying my honour, but still more betraying the interests of the princess.'

So she cried out at once, in response to her own thought: 'No, Monsieur, no! You must leave. Leave or I shall go myself.'

'You are forgetting, Madame,' said Canolles, 'that I have your word that you will not leave without informing me of the fact.'

'Well, then, Monsieur: I am informing you that I shall be leaving Chantilly at once.'

'And do you think I shall permit that?' asked Canolles.

'What!' the viscountess exclaimed. 'Would you keep me here by force?'

'Madame, I do not know what I shall do. What I do know is that it is impossible for me to leave you.'

'So I am your prisoner?'

'You are a woman whom I have already lost on two occasions, and whom I do not wish to lose a third time.'

'So! Violence!'

'Yes, Madame, violence,' Canolles replied. 'If that is the only way to keep you.'

'Why! What happiness – keeping a woman who is languishing in agony, begging for her freedom . . . a woman who does not love you, who hates you!'

Canolles shuddered and tried quickly to unravel what was in the words and in the thought.

He realized that the time had come to hazard everything.

'Madame,' he said. 'The words that you have just spoken with such truth in your voice that no one could doubt their meaning, have settled all my doubts. You, moaning! You, a slave! And would I hold prisoner a woman who did not love me . . . who hated me? No, Madame, no, have no fear, it will not be so. I had thought, because of the happiness that I felt in seeing you, that you would be able to bear my presence. I had hoped that, after I had lost my reputation, the peace of my conscience, my future, perhaps even my honour, that you would compensate me for this sacrifice by the gift of a few hours, which I shall doubtless never have again. All that was possible, if you had loved me ... or even if I had been a matter of indifference for you, because you are kind and would have done out of pity, what another might have done for love. But it is not indifference that confronts me, but hatred, and in that case, it is a different matter, you are right. Just forgive me, Madame, for not having realized that one could be hated, when one loves so completely. It is your place to remain queen, mistress and free in this château as everywhere else. My place is to leave here, and I do so. In ten minutes' time you will have regained all your freedom. Farewell, Madame, farewell for ever.'

Canolles, in a state of dismay, that, though feigned at the beginning, had become real and painful by the end of this speech, bowed to Madame de Cambes, turned on his heels and, searching for the door, but not finding it, repeated 'Farewell, farewell', in such a voice of such deep feeling that, coming from the heart, it went to the heart. True love, like a storm, has its own voice.

Madame de Cambes was not expecting such obedience from Canolles: she had gathered her forces for a struggle, not for a victory, and she in her turn was affected by such resignation allied to such love. As the young man was already taking two steps towards the door, feeling his way in front of him with a kind of sob, he suddenly felt a hand on his shoulder, exercising the most significant pressure: he was not merely being touched, he was being stopped.

He turned round.

She was still standing in front of him. Her arm, gracefully extended, was still touching his shoulder, and the expression of dignity that had been a moment before imprinted on her face had melted into a delightful smile.

'Well, now, Monsieur!' she said. 'This is how you obey the queen! You would leave when you have her order to stay here, traitor that you are!'

Canolles gave a cry, fell to his knees and pressed his burning brow on the two hands that she was holding out to him.

'Oh, I could die of happiness!' he exclaimed.

'Alas, do not rejoice too soon,' said the viscountess. 'If I have stopped you, it is so that we should not part in this way, so that you should not go away with the idea that I can be ungrateful, so that you can voluntarily release me from the promise that I gave you, and so that you should at least see in me a friend, since the opposing factions to which we belong prevent me from ever being more than that for you.'

'Oh, my God!' cried Canolles. 'I was wrong again. You do not love me.'

'Let us not speak of feelings, Baron, but of the risks that we are both running if we remain here. Come, now: let's go – or let me go. We must.'

'What are you saying to me, Madame?'

'The truth. Leave me here, go back to Paris. Tell Mazarin and the queen what has happened to you. I shall help you as much as it is in my power to do so, but leave, leave!'

'Must I repeat it to you?' said Canolles. 'To leave you is to die!'

'No, no, you will not die, because you will keep the hope that in happier times we may meet again.'

'Chance has put me in your way, Madame – or, rather, has put you in mine – twice already. Chance will grow weary, and if I leave you, I shall not find you again.'

'Well, then, I am the one who will seek you out.'

'Madame, ask me to die for you; death is a moment of pain, nothing more. But do not ask me to leave you again. My heart breaks at the very idea. Just think: I have hardly seen you or spoken to you.'

'So, if I allow you to stay for today, and you can see me and speak to me all day, then will you be satisfied, tell me?'

'I promise nothing.'

'Then neither do I. However, I did agree one thing with you, which was to tell you when I was leaving. Well, I am telling you: I leave in an hour.'

'So must I do whatever you want? Must I obey you in everything? Must I renounce myself in order to follow your will blindly? Well, if that is what you wish, be contented. You have in front of you no more than a slave ready to obey. Order me, Madame, order me!'

Claire held out a hand to the baron and in her softest and most soothing voice said: 'A new treaty, in exchange for my word. If I do not leave between now and nine o'clock this evening, will you leave here at nine?'

'I swear.'

'Come on, then. The sky is blue and promises a delightful day. There is dew on the lawns, perfume in the air, balm in the woods. Hey! Pompée!'

The worthy steward, who had no doubt received an order to wait by the door, immediately came in.

'My hacking horses,' said Madame de Cambes, with her princely air. 'I am going this morning to the ponds and coming back through the farm, where I shall have lunch. You will accompany me, Baron,' she went on. 'This is one of the duties ascribed to you, since Her Majesty the queen ordered you not to lose me from sight.'

A stifling cloud of joy swept over the young man and encircled him like one of those vapours that used in antiquity to carry the gods up to heaven. He let himself be led, without opposition and almost without willpower. He was panting, intoxicated, mad. Soon, in the midst of a charming wood, under mysterious alleys of trees whose branches fell down on to his bare forehead, he recovered a sense of the material world. He was on foot, silent, his heart enveloped by a joy almost as intense as pain, walking along, his hand in that of Madame de Cambes, who was as pale, as silent and no doubt as happy as he was.

Pompée followed behind them, close enough to see everything, but far enough away to hear nothing.

III

The end of this intoxicating day arrived as inevitably as the end of a dream. The hours had passed like seconds for the fortunate baron, but it still seemed to him that he was gathering enough memories in this single day for three ordinary lifetimes. Each avenue in the park had been enriched by a word or a memory of the viscountess: a look, a gesture, a finger against the lips . . . everything had a meaning. As they got into the boat, she had squeezed his hand; when they disembarked again, she had supported herself on his arm; while she was walking beside the park wall, she had felt tired and sat down. And at each of these dazzling events, which had passed like a flash before the eyes of the young man, the landscape, lit by some fantastic light, had stayed in his memory, not only as a whole, but in its smallest details.

For the whole day, Canolles did not leave the viscountess's side: as they took lunch, she invited him to dinner, and as they dined, to supper.

In the midst of all the formalities that the false princess had to go through to receive the king's envoy, Canolles perceived the considerate attentions of a woman in love. He forgot the servants, etiquette, society; he even forgot his promise to retire, and thought that he was settled for a happy eternity in this earthly paradise, where he would be Adam and Madame de Cambes would be Eve.

But when night came and supper was finished, as all the other events of the day had passed, that is to say in unspeakable joy; when at dessert a lady-in-waiting had brought on Monsieur Pierrot, still disguised as the Duke d'Enghien, and he had taken advantage of the situation to eat like four princes of the blood together, and when the clock began to strike and Madame de Cambes had looked up and assured herself that it was about to strike ten times, she said with a sigh: 'Now it is time.'

'What time?' Canolles asked, trying to smile and hoping to ward off a great misfortune with a small quip.

'Time to keep your word.'

'Oh, Madame,' Canolles answered sadly, 'do you never forget?'

'I might perhaps have forgotten as you did,' said Madame de Cambes, 'except that this has reminded me.'

Out of her pocket, she took a letter, which she had received just as they sat down at the table.

'Who is it from, this letter?' Canolles asked.

'From the princess. She demands that I join her.'

'At least, you have this pretext! Thank you for having tried to spare my feelings.'

'Make no mistake, Monsieur de Canolles,' the viscountess replied with a sadness that she did not try to disguise. 'Even if I had not received this letter, at the appointed time I should have reminded you of your departure, as I have just done. Do you think that the people around us can go for much longer without noticing the understanding between us? Admit it: our behaviour is not that of a persecuted princess and her persecutor. But now, if this separation is as painful to you as you pretend, let me tell you, Baron, that it is up to you if you wish to ensure that we are not parted.'

'Tell me!' Canolles exclaimed. 'Tell me!'

'Can't you guess?'

'Yes, indeed, Madame! I can, and perfectly well. You are suggesting that I should join you in following the princess?'

'She herself speaks to me of it in this letter,' Madame de Cambes said excitedly.

'I am grateful that the idea does not come from you, and thank you, too, for your hesitation in broaching the subject. Not that my conscience rebels against serving one party or the other – no, I have no principles. Who does, in this war, apart from those directly involved? If the sword is drawn, let the blow strike me from this side or from that: it doesn't matter. I do not know the court, or the princes. My fortune makes me independent, and I have no ambition, so I expect nothing from either faction. I am an officer, nothing more.'

'So will you agree to follow me?'

'No.'

'Why not, if things are as you tell me?'

'Because you would think less of me for it.'

'Is that the only thing that is stopping you?'

'I swear that it is.'

'Well, have no fear on that score . . .'

'You don't believe that yourself,' Canolles said, smiling and holding up a finger. 'A turncoat is always a traitor: the first word is gentler, but both mean the same thing.'

'Yes, you're right,' said Madame de Cambes. 'I shall not mention it again. If you had been in an ordinary position, I should have tried to win you over to the princes' cause, but since you are the king's envoy, with a confidential mission from Her Majesty the Queen Regent and the prime minister, and honoured with the favour of the Duke d'Epernon, who, despite my original suspicions, is protecting you in a very special way . . .' (Canolles blushed.) 'I shall be as tactful as I can, but listen, Baron: we are not separating for ever, you may be sure of that. My intuition tells me that we shall see one another again.'

'Where?' said Canolles.

'That I don't know, but we shall certainly meet again.'

Canolles sadly shook his head.

'I'm not counting on it, Madame,' he said. 'There is a war between us, and that is too much when there is not love at the same time.'

'So does this day mean nothing to you?' said the viscountess, in the most seductive voice.

'It is the only one, since I came into this world, in which I am quite sure that I have lived.'

'So, you see how ungrateful you are.'

'Give me another day like this one.'

'I cannot. I have to leave this evening.'

'I was not asking you for tomorrow, or the day after. I am asking for a day, in the future. Take as long as you wish, choose whatever place you wish, but let me live with one certainty: I should suffer too much if all I had was hope.'

'Where are you going after you leave me?'

'To Paris, to report on my mission.'

'And then?'

'Quite possibly the Bastille too.'

'But supposing that you do not go there?'

'I shall return to Libourne, where my regiment must be.'

'And I to Bordeaux, where I shall find the princess. Do you know a very quiet little village on the road between Bordeaux and Libourne?'

'I know one, which is almost as dear to my memory as Chantilly.'

'Jaulnay?' the viscountess asked, with a smile.

'Jaulnay,' Canolles repeated.

'Well, it takes four days to go to Jaulnay. Today is Tuesday. I shall be there on Sunday for the whole day.'

'Thank you, thank you!' Canolles exclaimed, pressing his lips to a hand that Madame de Cambes did not have the strength to take away from him. Then, after a moment, she said: 'Now, we have to put on our little act.'

'Ah, yes! As you say, Madame, the little act that should cover me with ridicule in the eyes of all France. But I cannot complain. I am the one who wanted it to be like this, and I am the one who chose, not the role that I play, but who devised the ending that concludes it.' Madame de Cambes lowered her eyes. 'Now, tell me what I have to do,' said Canolles, impassively. 'I await your orders, ready for anything.'

Claire was so moved that Canolles could see her velvet dress rising with the fast, uneven movements in her breast.

'I know that you are making an enormous sacrifice for me; but, in heaven's name, do believe me: I shall be eternally grateful. Yes, for my sake you will be risking the shame of the court; yes, you will be severely judged. I beg you, Monsieur, to despise all this if it gives you any pleasure to think that you have made me happy.'

'I shall try, Madame.'

'Believe me, Baron,' Madame de Cambes went on. 'This cold pain that I sense is eating away in you arouses dreadful remorse in me. Others might perhaps reward you more fully than I have done; but, Monsieur, a reward that was granted so easily would not be a worthy recompense for what you have done.'

As she said these words, Claire lowered her eyes with a sigh of modesty and suffering.

'Is that all you have to say to me?' asked Canolles.

'Here,' said the viscountess, taking a miniature portrait out of her bosom and handing it to Canolles. 'Here, take this portrait and, whenever this unfortunate business causes you any pain, look at it and tell yourself that you are suffering for her whose image you see here, and that each of your sufferings is earned with her regret.'

'Is that all?'

'With esteem.'

'Is that all?'

'With sympathy.'

'Oh, Madame, one word more!' Canolles exclaimed. 'What would it cost you to make me entirely happy?'

Claire made a quick movement towards the young man, held out her hand and opened her mouth to add: 'With love.'

But as her mouth opened, so did the door, and the pretend captain of the guard appeared together with Pompée.

'I shall finish at Jaulnay.'

'Your sentence or your thought?'

'Both: one always expresses the other.'

'Madame,' said the captain of the guard. 'Your Highness's horses are harnessed to the coach.'

'Look surprised,' Claire whispered to Canolles.

The baron gave a smile of pity that was addressed to himself.

'Where is Your Highness going?'

'I am leaving.'

'But has Your Highness forgotten that I have been commanded by Her Majesty not to let you out of my sight?'

'Monsieur, your mission is over.'

'What does that mean?'

'It means that I am not Her Highness, the Princess de Condé, but merely the Viscountess de Cambes, her first lady-in-waiting. The princess left yesterday evening, and I am going to join her.'

Canolles stayed motionless. He was visibly loath to go on playing this farce for an audience of servants. So Madame de Cambes, to encourage him, cast him a gentle look, which fortified him a little.

'So the king has been deceived,' he said. 'And where is the Duke d'Enghien?'

'I ordered Pierrot to go back to his flowerbeds,' said a low voice at the door of the room. It belonged to the Dowager Princess, who was standing on the threshold, supported by two ladies-in-waiting.

'Go back to Paris, to Mantes, to Saint-Germain, or go back to the court, because your mission here is at an end. You will tell the king that those who are persecuted have to turn to trickery, which cancels the use of force. Nonetheless, you are free to remain in Chantilly and watch over me. I have not left and shall not leave the château, because I do not intend to do so. And with that, Baron, I bid you farewell.'

Canolles, blushing with shame, could hardly find the strength to bow, while looking at the viscountess and muttering, reproachfully: 'Oh, Madame, Madame!'

The viscountess understood the look and the words.

'Will Your Highness permit me,' she said, turning to the dowager, 'to play the part of the princess for a moment longer. I wish to thank the Baron de Canolles, in the name of the illustrious hosts who have left this castle, for the respect that he has shown and the tact that he brought to carrying out such a difficult mission. I dare believe, Madame, that Your Highness is of the same opinion and to hope that she will consequently join her thanks to mine.'

The dowager, touched by these forceful words – and her profound wisdom perhaps revealing to her one of the faces of this new secret grafted on to the old one – said the following, in a voice that was not devoid of feeling: 'Everything that you have done against us, Monsieur, is forgotten, and for all that you have done for my family, there is gratitude.'

Canolles knelt before the princess who gave him the hand to kiss that had so often been kissed by Henri IV.

This was the finale of the scene and the inexorable dismissal: nothing was left for Canolles but to leave, as Madame de Cambes was about to do. He therefore went back to his rooms

and hastily wrote Mazarin the most discouraging letter that
he could manage. The purpose of this report was to spare
himself the rebuff of the first, astonished reaction. Then walking through the ranks of the servants at the château, rather
afraid that he would be insulted by them, he went down to the
courtyard where his horse was ready and waiting.

Just as he was about to put his foot in the stirrup, an imperious voice spoke these words: 'Pay your respects to the envoy of
His Majesty, our king and master.'

At this, every head bowed to Canolles who, after having
himself bowed towards the window where the princess was
standing, spurred his horse and went on his way, with his head
held high.

Castorin, disappointed in the fine dream that the false
steward Pompée had encouraged in him, followed his master
with his head hanging.

IV

It is now time to return to one of the most important figures in
this story, who, mounted on a good horse, is riding down
the highway between Paris and Bordeaux, surrounded by five
companions, whose eyes grow wider at every tinkle from a sack
full of gold coins that Lieutenant Ferguzon has hanging from
the tree of his saddle. This music rejoices and refreshes the
troop just as the sound of drums and pipes revives a soldier on
the march.

'No matter, no matter,' one of the men was saying. 'Ten
thousand livres is a fine sum.'

'What you might say is that it would be a magnificent sum,'
Ferguzon said, 'if it owed nothing to anyone; but this money
owes a company of soldiers to the princess. *Nimium satis est*,
as they used to say in olden times, which means: "Only too
much is enough." And, my dear Barabbas, we don't have that
mighty *enough* that makes up *too much*.'

'It's an expensive business, looking respectable,' said

Cauvignac. 'All the money from the royal collector of taxes went in jerkins and embroidery. We are as magnificent as lords and have even allowed ourselves the luxury of purses – true, there's nothing in them . . . Ah, what we do for appearance's sake!'

'Talk for us, Captain, not for yourself,' retorted Barabbas, 'you've got the purse and ten thousand livres with it.'

'My friend,' said Cauvignac. 'Didn't you hear, or did you fail to grasp what Ferguzon just said about our obligations towards the princess? I am not one of those who promise one thing and do another. Monsieur Lenet counted out ten thousand livres for me to muster a company, and I shall raise one, or the devil take me. Now he will give me a further forty thousand on the day when the company is assembled. So if he fails to pay those forty thousand, we shall see . . .'

'With ten thousand livres!' four ironic voices cried simultaneously – because Ferguzon, who was full of confidence in his chief's abilities, seemed to be the only one in the troop convinced that Cauvignac would achieve the promised goal. 'You're going to muster a company, with ten thousand livres?'

'Yes,' said Cauvignac. 'With a little bit added on.'

'And who's going to add something on?' asked a voice.

'Not me,' said Ferguzon.

'So who?' asked Barabbas.

'Heavens, the first comer! There, look, I can see a man on the road over there. Watch and see . . .'

'I understand,' said Ferguzon.

'Is that all?' asked Cauvignac.

'And I admire.'

'Yes,' one of the other horsemen said, riding up to Cauvignac. 'Yes, I can see that you are keen to fulfil your obligations, Captain, but we might well lose by being too respectable. Today, we are necessary, but if tomorrow the company has been mustered, they will put their trusty officers to command it and send us packing, after we've been to the trouble to assemble it.'

'You are a fool, in four letters, my dear Carrotel, and it's not the first time I've told you so,' retorted Cauvignac. 'The feeble argument that you have just put forward will deprive you of the rank that I intended to award you in the company – because it's obvious that we will be the six officers in this nucleus of an army. I should have appointed you sub-lieutenant straight-away, Carrotel, but now you will be merely a sergeant. Thanks to the pathetic speech you have just heard, Barrabas, you, who kept quiet, will take the officer's rank until such time as – Ferguzon having been hanged – you become lieutenant by right of seniority. But let's not forget my first soldier, whom I can see over there.'

'Do you know anything about this man, Captain?' Ferguzon asked.

'Nothing at all.'

'He must be a bourgeois, because he has a black coat.'

'Are you sure?'

'Huh! Look, the wind's blowing it up. Can you see?'

'If he has a black coat, he is a rich bourgeois. So much the better. We are recruiting men to serve the princes, so it is important that the company should be of high quality. If it was for that lily-livered Mazarin, anything would do, but for the princes, *peste*! Ferguzon, I have a notion that my company will do me honour, as Falstaff says.'

The whole troop spurred its horses on to catch up the bourgeois, who was riding along peacefully in the middle of the road.

When the worthy man, mounted on a good mule, saw the fine horsemen galloping towards him, he moved respectfully to the side of the road and saluted Cauvignac.

'He's polite,' said Cauvignac. 'That's good, at least. But he doesn't know how to give a military salute yet. We'll teach him.'

Cauvignac returned the salute and drew up alongside him.

'Monsieur,' he enquired, 'could you tell us if you love the king?'

'Indeed, I do!' said the bourgeois.

'Admirable!' said Cauvignac, rolling his eyes in delight. 'And the queen?'

'The queen? I have the utmost veneration for her.'

'Excellent! What about Monsieur de Mazarin?'

'Monsieur de Mazarin is a great man, whom I admire.'

'Perfect. So,' Cauvignac went on, 'we have the pleasure of meeting a good servant of His Majesty?'

'I pride myself on it, Monsieur!'

'And one ready to demonstrate his attachment?'

'On any occasion.'

'How fortunate that is! Such encounters only happen on the highway.'

'What do you mean?' the bourgeois asked, starting to look at Cauvignac with some anxiety.

'I mean, Monsieur, that you must follow us.'

The bourgeois leapt in his saddle with surprise and alarm.

'Follow you! Where, Monsieur?'

'I don't quite know where we are going.'

'But I only travel in the company of men whom I know.'

'Quite right. You're a cautious man. So, I'm going to tell you who we are.'

The man made a gesture indicating that he thought he knew this already, but Cauvignac appeared not to notice and went on: 'I am Roland de Cauvignac, captain of a company of men, which is, it must be said, absent, but worthily represented by Louis-Gabriel Ferguzon, my lieutenant, by Georges-Guillaume Barabbas, my sub-lieutenant, by Zépharin Carrotel, my sergeant, and by these two gentlemen, one of whom is my quartermaster and the other my billeting sergeant. Now you know us, Monsieur,' Cauvignac went on, in the most affable manner, 'and I do hope you no longer feel any antipathy towards us.'

'But, Monsieur, I have already served His Majesty in the town guard, and I pay my taxes, duties, tolls and so on regularly,' the man replied.

'So, Monsieur,' Cauvignac continued, 'it is not in His Majesty's service that I am enrolling you, but in that of the princes, whose unworthy representative you see before you.'

'In the service of the princes! Enemies of the king!' the bourgeois exclaimed, ever more amazed. 'But why, then, did you ask if I loved His Majesty?'

'Because if you had not loved the king, if you had accused the queen, and if you had cursed Monsieur de Mazarin, I should have been very careful not to bother you in whatever you are doing. You should have been sacred to me, like a brother.'

'But, Monsieur, I'm not a slave, I'm not a serf.'

'No, you're a soldier, that is to say absolutely free to become a captain, as I am, or a marshal of France, like Monsieur de Turenne.'[6]

'I have often been in court in my life.'

'Oh, dear, that's a pity, a real pity: it's such a bad habit getting involved in trials. I've never done it myself, perhaps because I studied to be a lawyer.'

'But in the course of doing so I learned the laws of the kingdom.'

'There are plenty of them. You know, Monsieur, that from the *Pandects* of Justinian[7] down to the bill of Parliament, which states, on the subject of the death of the Marshal d'Ancre, that no foreigner can ever be a minister in France,[8] there are 18,772 laws, not to mention other regulations, but then there are some specially favoured beings who have an astonishing memory: Pico della Mirandola[9] spoke twelve languages by the age of eighteen. And what benefit have you gained from knowing these laws, Monsieur?'

'The benefit of knowing that one does not press-gang people on the highway without authorization.'

'I have that, Monsieur. Here it is.'

'From the princess?'

'From Her Highness's own self.'

And Cauvignac respectfully raised his hat.

'So are there two kings in France?' the bourgeois exclaimed.

'Yes, Monsieur, and that is why I have the honour to require you to prefer mine, and that I consider it a duty to enrol you in my service.'

'I shall appeal to the parliament of Bordeaux.'

'That is indeed a third king and you will probably have the opportunity to serve it as well. Ours is a broad church. And so, forward, Monsieur!'

'But this is impossible: I'm expected on business.'

'Where?'

'In Orléans.'

'By whom?'

'My attorney.'

'Why?'

'On financial business.'

'Your first business is the service of the state.'

'Can't it do without me?'

'We were counting on you, and we shall most surely miss you. However, if as you say, you were going to Orleans on financial business . . .'

'Yes, on financial business.'

'How much finance was involved?'

'Four thousand livres.'

'Which you were to receive?'

'No, which I was to pay.'

'To your attorney?'

'Just so, Monsieur.'

'For a case he had won?'

'No, for one he lost.'

'That's something to think about. Four thousand livres!'

'Four thousand livres.'

'That is the very amount that you would pay, should the princes agree to replace your services by those of a mercenary . . .'

'Surely not! I could get a replacement for a hundred écus!'

'A replacement of your calibre, one who rides his mule with feet outside like you, one who knows 18,772 laws! Come now, Monsieur, for an ordinary fellow, yes, a hundred écus would surely be enough, but if we were to be content with ordinary fellows, it would hardly be worthwhile competing with the king. What we need are men of quality, of your rank and your height. For goodness' sake, you shouldn't undervalue yourself: I think you're worth at least four thousand livres!'

'I can see what's coming,' said the bourgeois. 'This is a highway robbery.'

'You are insulting us, Monsieur,' said Cauvignac, 'and we should skin you alive in atonement for this insult, were it not that we are keen to preserve the good name of the princes' armies. No, Monsieur, give me your four thousand livres, but at least don't imagine that this is extortion; it is a necessity.'

'So who will pay my attorney?'

'We shall.'

'You?'

'Us.'

'But will you bring me a receipt?'

'Duly made out.'

'Signed by him?'

'Signed by him.'

'Well, that's a different matter.'

'As you see. So, do you accept?'

'I must, since I have no alternative.'

'Now, give us the address of the attorney and a few essential details of the case.'

'I told you that it was a judgement resulting from a lost suit.'

'Against whom?'

'Against a certain Biscarros, who was pleading as the heir of his wife, an Orléanist.'[10]

'Careful!' said Ferguzon.

Cauvignac gave him a wink that meant: Don't worry, I'm keeping an eye open.

'Biscarros,' he repeated. 'Isn't he an innkeeper from somewhere near Libourne?'

'Just so. He lives between that town and Saint-André-de-Cubzac.'

'At the hostelry of the Golden Calf?'

'The very same. Do you know him?'

'A little.'

'The wretch! Having me ordered to pay back money . . .'

'That you didn't owe him?'

'Well, yes . . . but which I hoped never to pay.'

'I understand, it's hard.'

'So I give you my word that I should rather see this money in your hands than in his.'

'In that case, I think you will get what you want.'

'But my receipt?'

'Come with us and you can have it, duly signed.'

'How will you manage that?'

'That's my business.'

They continued their ride towards Orléans, where they arrived two hours later. The bourgeois led the gang of crimps to the inn nearest to his attorney. It was a frightful low dive, at the sign of the Dove of the Ark.

'Now,' said the bourgeois, 'how do we go about this? I should very much prefer not to hand over my four thousand livres until I have a receipt.'

'Don't worry about it. Do you know your attorney's writing?'

'Very well.'

'So when we bring back the receipt, you won't make any trouble about handing over the money to us?'

'None at all. But without the money, my attorney won't give you a receipt. I know him.'

'I'll make him an advance.'

At which, taking four thousand livres out of his satchel, two thousand of it in louis and the rest in demi-pistoles, he put up the piles of coins in rows in front of the astonished bourgeois's eyes.

'Now,' he said, 'what is your attorney's name?'

'Maître Rabodin.'

'Well, then, take a quill and write.'

The bourgeois obeyed.

'Maître Rabodin, I am sending you herewith the four thousand livres in damages, which I was ordered by the court to pay to Master Biscarros, whom I strongly suspect of wishing to make some criminal use of the money. Please be so kind as to give your receipt duly made out to the bearer of this.'

'And then?' asked the bourgeois.

'And then, date and sign.'

The bourgeois did so.

'Now, take this letter and this money,' Cauvignac said to Ferguzon. 'Disguise yourself as a miller and go round to the attorney.'

'And what shall I do at the attorney's?'

'Give him the money and take his receipt.'

'Is that all?'

'That's all.'

'I don't understand.'

'So much the better: your task will be carried out all the more efficiently.'

Ferguzon had immense confidence in his captain, and so, without reply, he went to the door.

'Get them to send up some wine, and the best,' said Cauvignac. 'This gentleman must be thirsty.'

Ferguzon nodded obediently and went out. Half an hour later he returned and found Cauvignac sitting at table with the bourgeois, both of them paying their respects to that famous little Orléans wine that so much pleased Henri VI's Gascon palette.

'Well?' Cauvignac asked.

'Well! Here's the receipt.'

'It this right?' Cauvignac asked, passing the piece of stamped paper across to the bourgeois.

'That's it.'

'And the receipt is all in order?'

'Perfectly.'

'So you won't object to giving me your money for this receipt?'

'Not at all.'

'Very well, do so.'

The bourgeois counted out the four thousand livres. Cauvignac put them in his satchel where they replaced the missing four thousand.

'And with that, I am released?' said the bourgeois.

'Good heavens, yes, unless you absolutely insist on serving . . .'

'No, not personally, but . . .'

'But what? Come now,' said Cauvignac, 'I have a presentiment that we shall not leave one another without doing business again.'

'Quite possibly,' said the bourgeois, who was entirely reassured by the possession of his receipt. 'I have a nephew . . .'

'Ha, ha!'

'A stubborn, rowdy lad.'

'And you'd like to get rid of him?'

'Not exactly, but I think he'd make an excellent soldier.'

'Send him to me, I'll make a hero of him.'

'You'll take him on?'

'With pleasure.'

'There's my godson, too, a fine boy who wants to take holy orders, for whom I have to pay a large boarding fee.'

'So you'd rather he took military orders? Very well, send me the godson and the nephew. It will cost you five hundred livres for the pair, that's all.'

'Five hundred livres! I don't understand.'

'Of course. You pay on entry.'

'So why did you make me pay for not entering?'

'That was a special case. Your nephew and your godson will each pay two hundred and fifty livres, and you'll never hear of them again.'

'Damn it! That's an attractive proposition. Will they be all right?'

'What I mean is that once they have enjoyed serving under me, they will not change their position for that of the Emperor of China. Ask these gentlemen how I feed them. Go on, Barabbas; answer, Carrotel.'

'The truth,' Barabbas said, 'is that we live like lords.'

'And how are they dressed: just look . . .'

Carrotel pirouetted on the spot to show off all sides of his splendid attire.

'It's a fact,' said the bourgeois. 'There's nothing to be said where dress is concerned.'

'So? You'll send us the two young men?'

'I'd very much like to. Will you be here long?'

'No, we're leaving tomorrow morning; but, so that they can catch up, we'll go at walking pace. Give us the five hundred livres and the deal is done.'

'I only have two hundred and fifty.'

'Give them the other two hundred and fifty livres: this will even give you a reason to send them to me. Otherwise, you see, if you had no pretext, they might suspect something.'

'But they may tell me that only one of them is the only messenger needed.'

'Tell them that the roads are unsafe and give each one twenty-five livres, an advance on their pay as an inducement.'

The bourgeois opened his eyes wide in astonishment.

'You have to admit,' he said. 'Only a soldier can find a way round every difficulty.'

After counting out the two hundred and fifty livres to Cauvignac, he left, delighted at having found an opportunity, for only five hundred livres, to set up a nephew and a godson who cost him more than two hundred pistoles a year.

V

'Now, Master Barabbas,' said Cauvignac, 'do you have some clothes in your bag that are slightly less elegant than the ones you have on, ones which would make you look like a clerk with the Revenue?'[11]

'I have the tax collector's, you know, the one we –'

'Good, very good. And no doubt you have his written authority?'

'Lieutenant Ferguzon told me not to lose it, so I have kept it carefully.'

'Lieutenant Ferguzon is the most prudent man I know. Dress up as the collector and take the authority.'

Barabbas went out and returned ten minutes later completely transformed. He found Cauvignac dressed entirely in black and looking for all the world like a man of law.

The two of them hurried towards the attorney's house. Maître Rabodin lived on the third floor, at the back of an apartment entirely composed of an antechamber, an office and a study. There were surely other rooms, but since they were not open to clients, we shall not speak of them.

Cauvignac crossed the antechamber, left Barabbas in the office, threw an appreciative glance as he went by at the two clerks who were pretending to scribble away while playing noughts and crosses and entered the *sanctum sanctorum*.

Maître Rabodin was sitting behind a desk so loaded with

files that the respectable attorney seemed actually to be buried in duplicates and court rulings. He was a tall, dry, yellow man wearing a black coat, which clung tightly to his limbs as the skin of an eel clings to its body. Hearing Cauvignac's footsteps, he raised his long torso from where it was bent over and lifted his head, which was now raised above the rampart surrounding him.

For a moment, Cauvignac thought he had rediscovered the basilisk (that animal which modern scientists consider to be fabulous), so strongly were the attorney's eyes shining with the dark glow of avarice and cupidity.

'Monsieur,' Cauvignac said, 'I apologize for introducing myself without being announced, but,' he added, with his most charming smile, 'that is the privilege of my office.'

'A privilege of your office?' said Maître Rabodin. 'And what office is that, may I ask?'

'I am His Majesty's exempt.'[12]

'His Majesty's exempt?'

'I have that honour.'

'Excuse me, I don't understand.'

'You will. I believe you know Monsieur Biscarros . . . ?'

'I do, indeed. He's my client.'

'What do you think of him, I wonder?'

'What do I think of him?'

'Yes.'

'Why, I think . . . I think . . . I think he's a very fine man.'

'Well, Monsieur, you are wrong.'

'I'm wrong? How's that?'

'Your fine man is a rebel.'

'What! A rebel!'

'Yes, Monsieur, a rebel who is taking advantage of the isolated situation of his inn to make it a hotbed of conspiracy.'

'Really!'

'He has sworn to poison the king, the queen and Monsieur de Mazarin, should they stop at his inn.'

'Really!'

'And I have just arrested him and had him brought to the prison at Libourne, charged with the crime of *lèse-majesté*.'[13]

'Monsieur, you take my breath away!' said Maître Rabodin, slumping back in his chair.

'There is more,' continued the fake exempt. 'There is the fact that you are compromised in this affair.'

'Me, Monsieur!' the attorney exclaimed, his colour going from orangey-yellow to apple-green. 'Me? Compromised? How is that?'

'You are in possession of a sum that this scoundrel Biscarros intended for the payment of a rebel army.'

'It is true, Monsieur, that I did receive, on his behalf . . .'

'The sum of four thousand livres. He was subjected to the torture of the boot and at the eighth wedge,[14] the wretch admitted that this sum must be with you.'

'It is, indeed, but it has only been here a moment.'

'Too bad, Monsieur, too bad.'

'Why is it too bad?'

'Because I shall be obliged to take you into custody.'

'Take me in?'

'Of course. The charge sheet names you as an accomplice.'

The attorney's face changed in colour from apple-green to bottle-green.

'Now, if you had not received the money,' Cauvignac went on, 'it would be a different matter. But you admit to having received it: it's evidence, you see.'

'Monsieur, suppose I were to give it up, to hand it over to you at once, to say that I have no connection with the wretched Biscarros, to deny . . .'

'Grave suspicions would still hang over you . . . though I must say that the immediate return of the money . . .'

'At once, Monsieur!' Maître Rabodin cried. 'The money is still there, in the bag in which it was handed to me. I checked the amount, that's all.'

'Was it correct?'

'Count it yourself, Monsieur, count it yourself.'

'No, I shall not, if you don't mind. I do not have authority to touch His Majesty's money, but I do have with me the tax collector of Libourne, who was seconded to me to collect the various sums of money that the wretch, Biscarros, distributed around in this way, so that he could later collect them.'

'He did indeed request me, when I received these four thousand livres, to send them to him without delay.'

'You see! He must already know that the princess has fled Chantilly and is heading towards Bordeaux. He was gathering all his forces to make himself head of her faction.'

'Scoundrel!'

'And you suspected nothing?'

'Nothing, Monsieur, nothing.'

'No one warned you?'

'No one.'

'But what are you telling me?' Cauvignac asked, pointing towards the bourgeois's letter, which had remained wide open on Maître Rabodin's desk, among a host of other papers. 'What are you saying, while you yourself are showing me proof to the contrary?'

'What proof?'

'Just read that!'

Rabodin read in a trembling voice: 'Maître Rabodin, I am sending you herewith the four thousand livres in damages, which I was ordered by the court to pay to Master Biscarros, whom I strongly suspect of wishing to make some criminal use of the money.'

'"Criminal use"!' Cauvignac repeated. 'You see: your client's dreadful reputation had already reached this far.'

'I am overwhelmed, Monsieur,' said the attorney.

'I cannot conceal from you that my orders are strict.'

'I swear to you, Monsieur, that I am innocent.'

'Well, now! Biscarros said the same, until they subjected him to torture. It was not until the fifth wedge that he changed his tune.'

'I'm telling you, Monsieur: I'm ready to hand the money over to you. Here it is, take it.'

'Let's do things properly,' said Cauvignac. 'I've already advised you that I do not have the authority to touch the king's money.' So, going towards the door, he said: 'Come here, Tax Collector. Each man to his own duty.'

Barabbas approached.

'This gentleman has confessed everything,' said Cauvignac.

'What! Have I confessed something?' cried the attorney.

'Yes. You've confessed that you were in communication with Biscarros.'

'But, Monsieur, I only ever received two letters from him, and I only wrote one.'

'This gentleman confesses that he was in possession of funds belonging to the accused.'

'Here they are! All I have ever received for him are these four thousand livres which I am ready to hand over to you.'

'Tax Collector,' said Cauvignac, 'show your letter of authority, take the money and return a receipt in the name of His Majesty.'

Barabbas handed the letter of authority to the attorney, who pushed it away, not wishing to insult him by reading it.

'Now you must come with me,' said Cauvignac, while Barabbas, to avoid any mistakes, was counting the money.

'Come with you?'

'Of course. Didn't I tell you that you are a suspect?'

'But, Monsieur, I swear that His Majesty has no more faithful servant than I.'

'It's not enough to say so, we must have proof.'

'I'll give you proof.'

'What?'

'All my past life.'

'Not enough. I need a guarantee for the future.'

'Tell me what I can do, and I'll do it.'

'There might be one way to prove your loyalty in an undeniable way.'

'What is that?'

'There is at this moment here in Orléans a captain, who is a friend of mine, and who is raising a company of troops for the king.'

'So?'

'Well, you could enlist in this company.'

'I, Monsieur? An attorney . . .'

'The king has dire need of attorneys, because his affairs are highly involved.'

'I should do it willingly, but what about my practice?'

'Let your clerks manage it.'

'Impossible! What about the signatures?'

'Excuse me, gentlemen, if I interrupt,' said Barabbas.

'What!' said the attorney. 'Speak, Monsieur, speak!'

'It appears to me that if this gentleman, who would not make much of a soldier, were to offer . . .'

'You're right,' said the attorney. 'Not much of a soldier . . .'

'If the gentleman were to offer your friend . . . or rather the king . . .'

'What? What can I offer the king?'

'His two clerks . . .'

'Certainly!' the attorney exclaimed. 'Certainly and with the greatest pleasure. Let your friend take them both, he can have them: they're two delightful lads.'

'One looked like a child to me.'

'Fifteen years old, Monsieur! Fifteen! And a wizard on the drums. Come here, Fricotin.'

Cauvignac gestured in a way that showed he wanted young Fricotin to be left where he was.

'And the other?'

'Eighteen, Monsieur. Five feet six inches, a candidate as beadle at Saint-Sauveur,[15] and so already used to handling a pikestaff. Come here, Chalumeau.'

'But with a frightful squint, as far as I can see,' said Cauvignac, gesturing again as before.

'So much the better: you can put him on sentry duty, and, since he squints outwards, he can watch to left and right, while the others can only see straight ahead.'

'That's an advantage, I admit. But you see the king is in difficulties just now: when a case is argued with cannon, it's even more expensive than one argued with words, so the king cannot afford to equip these two fellows. It's as much as he can do to take on their training and their pay.'

'If that's all that's needed to prove my loyalty to the king,' said Rabodin, 'well, I'll make a sacrifice.'

Cauvignac and Barabbas exchanged glances.

'What do you think, Tax Collector?' asked Cauvignac.

'I think the gentleman seems to be in good faith.'

'In that case, we must be considerate towards him. Give him a receipt for five hundred livres.'

'Five hundred livres!'

'A receipt acknowledging the fitting out of two young soldiers, which Maître Rabodin is donating to His Majesty as a token of his ardent support.'

'Then shall I, at least, in return for this sacrifice, be left in peace?'

'I believe so.'

'I shall not be troubled?'

'I hope not.'

'And suppose that, contrary to all justice, I were to be prosecuted?'

'You could appeal to me as a witness. But will your two clerks agree?'

'They'll be delighted.'

'Are you sure?'

'Yes, though one should not tell them . . .'

'. . . how they are to be honoured?'

'It would be wiser.'

'So what shall we do?'

'Very simple. I'll send them to your friend. What's his name?'

'Captain Cauvignac.'

'I'll send them to your friend, Captain Cauvignac, on some pretext or other. It would be better that the meeting should take place outside Orléans, to avoid any scandal.'

'Yes, and to avoid the people of the town trying to beat you with whips as Camillus[16] did the schoolmaster in antiquity . . .'

'So, I'll send them outside the town.'

'On the main road from Orléans to Tours, for example.'

'At the first inn.'

'Yes. They'll find Captain Cauvignac at the table, he'll offer them a glass of wine, they'll accept, he'll propose a toast to the king's health, they'll drink enthusiastically and there they are – soldiers.'

'Exactly. Now you can call them.'

The two young men were called in. Fricotin was a little rascal of barely four feet in height, quick, sharp and stocky, while Chalumeau was a gangling ninny of five feet six inches, thin as a beanpole and red as a carrot.

'Gentlemen,' Cauvignac told them, 'Maître Rabodin, your attorney, is giving you a confidential mission. You must come tomorrow morning to the first inn on the road from Orléans to Tours to collect a sheaf of papers relating to a case that Captain Cauvignac is bringing against Monsieur de La Rochefoucauld. Maître Rabodin will reward each of you with a gratuity of twenty-five livres for this mission.'

Fricotin, who was easily duped, leapt three feet in the air. Chalumeau, of a more suspicious nature, looked at Cauvignac and the attorney with a doubtful expression that made him squint three times as much as usual.

'Wait a moment,' Maître Rabodin quickly interjected. 'I didn't agree to fifty livres.'

'For which sum,' continued the fake exempt, 'Maître Rabodin will be reimbursed in the fee for the trial between Captain Cauvignac and the Duke de La Rochefoucauld.'

Maître Rabodin bowed his head. He was trapped: this was the door through which he had to pass to avoid the doors of prison.

'Very well,' the attorney said, 'I agree, but I hope that you will give me a receipt accordingly.'

'Here,' said the tax collector. 'See how I've anticipated your wish.'

And he handed him a sheet of paper with the following message: 'Received from Maître Rabodin, most loyal subject of His Majesty, as a voluntary offering, the sum of five hundred livres to assist His Majesty in his war against the princes.'

'If you insist,' said Barabbas, 'I shall put the two clerks on the receipt.'

'No, no,' said the attorney, hurriedly, 'it's perfectly fine as it is.'

'By the way,' said Cauvignac. 'Tell Fricotin to take his drum and Chalumeau his pikestaff. They will be that much equipped already.'

'But what reason can I possibly give them for suggesting that?'

'Why, tell them it's so that they can amuse themselves on the way.'

At this, the fake exempt and the fake tax collector withdrew, leaving Maître Rabodin quite stunned by the danger he had been in and only too happy to have got off so lightly.

VI

The next day, everything happened as Cauvignac had intended: the nephew and the godson arrived first, both riding on the same horse, followed by Fricotin and Chalumeau, the former with his drum, the latter with his pikestaff. There was some objection on both their parts when it was explained to them that they had the honour to be enlisted in the service of the princes, but these objections were overruled by Cauvignac's threats, Ferguzon's promises and the logic of Barrabas.

The horse belonging to the nephew and the godson was seconded to carry equipment, and, since Cauvignac was commissioned to raise an infantry regiment, the two new recruits could not argue with that.

They set off again. Cauvignac's march was like a triumph. The wily mercenary had found the means to get the most stubborn advocates of peace to go to war with him. He had made some embrace the king's cause, others the princes'. Some thought they were serving Parliament, and some others the King of England, who was talking of a raid into Scotland to recover his crown.[17] At first, there had in fact been some divergence in insignia and discord in demands which Lieutenant Ferguzon, persuasive though he was, had been hard put to reduce to a condition of passive obedience. However, with the help of constant mystification – which Cauvignac said was essential to the success of the operation – they marched on, soldiers and officers, without knowing what they were to do. Four days after leaving Chantilly, Cauvignac had collected twenty-five men, and this, as we can see, was quite a fine little company. A lot of rivers that make a big fuss as they flow into the sea start from less impressive origins.

Cauvignac was looking for a centre. He reached a little village lying between Châtellerault and Poitiers, and thought that this was what he had been looking for. It was the village of Jaulnay. Cauvignac recognized it from having come here one evening to bring an order to Canolles, and he set up his headquarters in the inn, where he recalled having supped quite decently on that occasion. In any case, there was no choice: as we have said, this inn was the only one in Jaulnay.

In this situation, straddling the main road from Paris to Bordeaux, Cauvignac had behind him the troops of the Duke de La Rochefoucauld, who was besieging Saumur, and in front of him those of the king, which were concentrated in Guyenne. Offering a hand to each one and being careful not to show one flag or the other prematurely, he was concerned only to muster a core force of a hundred men and use them to his advantage. And recruitment was proceeding well: Cauvignac had almost half the number he needed.

One day when Cauvignac, having spent his whole morning man-hunting, was on the lookout as usual at the door of the inn, chatting with his lieutenant and sub-lieutenant, he saw a young woman on horseback appear at the far end of the street, followed by a groom, also on horseback, and two mules laden with baggage.

The easy manner in which the fair amazon was handling her mount and the stiff, proud bearing of the groom who was with her, rang a bell in Cauvignac's memory. He put a hand on Ferguzon's arm – the lieutenant was in low spirits that day and had been brooding in a rather melancholy way – and said, pointing to the rider: 'There's the fiftieth soldier in Cauvignac's regiment, or I'm a goner!'

'Who? That lady?'

'Just so.'

'Great! We've already got a nephew who should be a lawyer, a godson who was to be a churchman, the attorney's two clerks, two pharmacists, a doctor, three bakers and two goose-minders. I should have thought that was enough dud soldiers, without adding a woman – because one day we'll have to fight.'

'Yes, but our exchequer is still only twenty-five thousand livres' (it will be seen that the exchequer, like the troop, had expanded), 'and if we could reach a round figure, say, thirty thousand livres, I think that would not be such a bad thing.'

'Well, if that's how you see it, I can't argue. I totally agree.'

'Hush! You'll see.'

Cauvignac went up to the young lady, who had stopped by one of the windows of the inn and was questioning the inn-keeper's wife about rooms.

'Your servant, my good sir,' he said, shrewdly, gallantly putting a hand to his hat.

'Good sir! Me?' the lady said, smiling.

'You, indeed, my fine viscount.'

She blushed.

'I don't know what you're talking about, Monsieur,' she replied.

'Oh, yes, you do. And to prove it your cheeks are already covered in red.'

'You are most surely mistaken, Monsieur.'

'No, no, not at all, I know perfectly well what I'm saying.'

'Come, now, enough of this joke.'

'I am not joking, *Monsieur*, and if you want proof, I can give it to you. I had the honour of meeting you, three weeks ago, in the proper clothing of your sex, one evening on the banks of the Dordogne, followed by your loyal groom, Pompée. Do you still have Pompée? Ah, there he is, dear Monsieur Pompée! Will you also tell me that I don't know him?'

The young woman and the groom exchanged an astonished look.

'Yes, yes,' Cauvignac went on, 'you may well be surprised, my dear viscount. But do you dare tell me that it was not you I met, there, as you well know, on the road to Saint-André-de-Cubzac, a quarter of a league from the inn of Master Biscarros?'

'I don't deny the meeting, Monsieur.'

'There! You see!'

'Except that it was on that occasion that I was in disguise.'

'Not at all. It's today that you're disguised. In any case, I understand that a description of the Viscount de Cambes has been circulated throughout Guyenne, so you consider it politic, in order to ward off suspicion, to temporarily adopt this dress – which, in fact, to be fair, suits you perfectly, my good sir.'

'Monsieur,' the viscountess said, trying in vain to conceal her disquiet. 'If you did not slip a few sensible words into your conversation, I should honestly think you mad.'

'I shall not pay you the same compliment, and I consider it most reasonable to disguise oneself when one is conspiring.'

The young woman looked at Cauvignac with increasing unease.

'It does indeed seem to me,' she said, 'that I have seen you somewhere, but I cannot recall where.'

'The first time, as I told you, was on the banks of the Dordogne.'

'And the second?'

'The second was in Chantilly.'

'On the day of the hunt?'

'Precisely.'

'Then I have nothing to fear: you are one of ours.'

'Why is that?'

'Because you were with the princess.'

'Let me tell you that that is not a reason.'

'But I think . . .'

'There were a lot of people for you to be sure that everyone there was a friend.'

'Take care, Monsieur, or you will give me an odd idea of you.'

'Think what you like. I'm not sensitive.'

'But what do you want, anyway?'

'To do you the honours of this inn, if you wish.'

'I am grateful to you, Monsieur, but I have no need of you. I am expecting someone.'

'Very well, dismount, and while you are waiting for someone, well, we can talk . . .'

'What should I do, Madame?' asked Pompée.

'Dismount, ask for a room and order dinner,' said Cauvignac.

'But, Monsieur,' said the viscountess. 'I think it's for me to give the orders.'

'That depends, Viscount, seeing that I am in command in Jaulnay and have fifty men at my disposal. Pompée, do as I say.'

Pompée bowed his head and went into the inn.

'So does this mean that you are arresting me?' the young woman asked.

'Perhaps.'

'What? Perhaps?'

'Yes, it depends on the conversation that we are about to have. But please dismount, Viscount ... there. Now take my arm. The servants at the inn will lead your horse to the stable.'

'I obey because, as you said, you are the stronger. I have no means to resist, but I warn you of one thing, which is that the person I am waiting for will come, and he is an officer of the king.'

'Well, now, Viscount, you may do me the honour of introducing us, because I should be delighted to make his acquaintance.'

The viscountess realized that no resistance was possible and went ahead, motioning to him that he was free to follow her.

Cauvignac accompanied her to the door of the room that Pompée had had prepared for her and was about to enter behind her, when Ferguzon, hurrying upstairs, came over and whispered: 'Captain, there's a carriage with three horses, a young man, masked, in the carriage and two lackeys at the doors.'

'Good,' said Cauvignac. 'It's probably the gentleman we were expecting.'

'Oh, are we expecting a gentleman?'

'Yes, and I shall go down to meet him. You stay in the corridor, don't take your eyes off the door. Let everyone go in, but no one come out.'

'As you say, Captain.'

A chaise had just drawn up at the door of the inn, brought

there by four men of Cauvignac's company, who had met it a quarter of a league outside the town and escorted it from there on.

A young man, dressed in blue velvet and wrapped in a great fur coat, was lying rather than sitting inside the chaise. As soon as the four men had surrounded his coach, he asked them a large number of questions, but seeing that, however pressing the questions might be, he was not to get any reply to them, he seemed to have resigned himself to wait, only occasionally raising his head enough to see whether some leader or other might not be approaching, from whom he could demand an explanation of the unusual behaviour of these men towards him.

In any case, it was impossible to make an accurate assessment of the effect of this event on the young traveller, since his face was half covered by one of those black satin masks called a 'wolf', which were so popular at the time. However, what this mask did allow one to see, namely the upper part of the forehead and the lower part of the face, suggested youth, beauty and wit. The teeth were small and white, and the eyes, through the mask, were shining.

Two tall lackeys, pale and trembling, despite the fact that they had muskets on their knees, rode on their horses on either side of the carriage and seemed nailed to the two doors. The scene could have been one of highwaymen arresting travellers, were it not for the broad daylight, the inn, the laughing face of Cauvignac and the self-possession of the two supposed robbers.

At the sight of Cauvignac – who, as we said, was appearing in the doorway, alerted by Ferguzon – the young man under arrest gave a little gasp of surprise and brought his hand quickly up to his face, as if to ensure that his mask was still on. Assuring himself of this seemed to make him calmer.

Brief though the movement was, it had not escaped Cauvignac. He looked at the traveller in the way that a man does when he is used to reading signs on even the most dissimulating face, then, despite himself, shuddered with astonishment almost as great as that which had been shown by the man in blue. However, he collected himself, and, putting his hat in his hand with a particular flourish, said: 'Fair lady, welcome!'

The traveller's eyes shone with astonishment through the openings in his mask.

'And where are you going like that?' Cauvignac went on.

'Where am I going?' the traveller said, ignoring Cauvignac's greeting and simply answering the question. 'Where am I going? You must know better than I do, since I am no longer free to continue on my way. I am going where you lead me.'

'Might I point out, dear lady,' said Cauvignac, with increasing politeness, 'that this is not a reply. Your arrest is only temporary. When we have spoken for a while about our mutual affairs, with open heart and face, you can resume your journey without hindrance.'

'Excuse me,' said the young traveller, 'but before we go any further, let's put one thing right. You are pretending to take me for a woman, when in reality you can very well see from my clothes that I am a man.'

'You know the Latin proverb: *ne nimium crede colori* – "The wise man does not judge by appearances." And I lay claim to being a wise man, which means that, beneath this deceptive costume, I recognized . . .'

'What did you recognize?' the traveller asked, impatiently.

'Why! Just what I told you: a woman.'

'But if I am a woman, then why arrest me?'

'My goodness, because in our day, women are more dangerous than men – so our war might, properly, be called the women's war. The queen and Madame de Condé are the two belligerent powers. They have taken as their lieutenants general: Mademoiselle de Chevreuse, Madame de Montbazon, Madame de Longueville . . . and you. Mademoiselle de Chevreuse is the general of the coadjutor, Madame de Montbazon is the general of Monsieur de Beaufort, Madame de Longueville is the general of Monsieur de La Rochefoucauld, and, as for you, you look to me like nothing so much as the general of the Duke d'Epernon.'

'You are mad, Monsieur,' the young traveller said, shrugging his shoulders.

'I shall not believe you, fair lady, any more than I believed a handsome young man, a short time ago, who paid me the same compliment.'

'And I suppose you told her that she was a man.'

'Just so. I recognized my little gentleman because I had seen him on a particular evening at the start of May prowling around Master Biscarros's inn, so I was not taken in by his skirts, his hairstyle and his high-pitched little voice – any more than I was fooled by your blue jerkin, your grey hat and your laced boots. And I said to myself: "My dear young friend, take whatever name you wish, put on whatever dress you like, assume whatever voice pleases you, you are nonetheless Viscount de Cambes."'

'The Viscount de Cambes!' the young traveller exclaimed.

'Ah, the name means something to you, apparently. Do you know him, by any chance?'

'A very young man, almost a child.'

'Seventeen or eighteen, at the most.'

'Very fair-haired?'

'Very.'

'With large blue eyes?'

'Very large, very blue.'

'Is he here?'

'He is.'

'And you say that he is . . .'

'Disguised as a woman, the naughty boy, just as you are disguised as a man, naughty girl.'

'What is he doing here?' the young rider exclaimed, with a violence and anxiety that were becoming increasingly visible as Cauvignac, on the contrary, became more measured in his gestures and sparing of words.

'However,' Cauvignac replied, weighing each word, 'he claims to have a rendez-vous with one of his friends.'

'One of his friends?'

'Yes.'

'A gentleman?'

'Probably.'

'A baron?'

'Perhaps.'

'Whose name . . .'

Cauvignac's brow furrowed under the effect of a complicated idea that had for the first time entered his mind and which, as it did so, had visibly caused a revolution in his brain: 'Ah, ha!' he murmured. 'That would be a fine catch!'

'Whose name . . . ?' the young traveller repeated.

'Wait a second,' Cauvignac said. 'Wait, now . . . It was a name ending in *olles*.'

'Baron de Canolles!' exclaimed the young traveller, whose lips went deathly pale, making the black mask stand out against the whiteness of the skin in the most sinister manner.

'That's it, Canolles,' said Cauvignac, watching the effect of this revelation on the visible part of the young man's face and throughout his body. 'Monsieur de Canolles: you were right. So you know Monsieur de Canolles, too! Well, I never! Do you know everyone?'

'That's enough!' stammered the young man, shaking in every limb and apparently about to faint. 'Where is this lady?'

'In that room: look, the third one along from here, with yellow curtains.'

'I want to see her!' cried the traveller.

'Oh, oh!' said Cauvignac. 'Was I wrong? Could you be the Monsieur de Canolles whom she is expecting? Or might Monsieur de Canolles not be the fine horseman who is just trotting up, followed by a lackey who looks to me like an accomplished nincompoop?'

The young traveller plunged so hard towards the front window of the carriage that he hit his forehead on it.

'That's him! That's him!' he cried, not even noticing that a few drops of blood were oozing from a slight wound. 'Oh, misery! He is coming, he will meet her, I am lost!'

'Ah, you see: you are a woman!'

'They had an assignation,' the young man went on, wringing his hands. 'Oh, I shall have my revenge!'

Cauvignac was about to try another pleasantry, but the young man gave him an imperious gesture with one hand, while with the other, he tore off his mask. It was then that the pale face of

Nanon could be seen appearing, fully armed with menace, before the calm eyes of Cauvignac.

VII

'Hello, Little Sister,' said Cauvignac to Nanon, offering the young woman his hand with the most unshakeable sangfroid.

'Hello! So you recognized me, did you?'

'As soon as I saw you. It was not enough to hide your face, you should also have covered that charming little beauty spot and those pearly teeth. Do at least put on a mask for the whole face when you want to disguise yourself, my sweet impostor – but you don't bother . . . "*et fugit ad salices*" . . .'[18]

'Enough,' said Nanon, imperiously. 'Let's talk seriously.'

'I ask nothing better: it is only by means of serious talk that one does good business.'

'So, you are telling me that the Viscountess de Cambes is here?'

'Herself.'

'And that Monsieur de Canolles is arriving at the inn at this moment?'

'Not yet. He is dismounting and throwing the reins to his grooms. Ah! He's been seen from this side, too. The window with the yellow curtains is opening, and the head of the viscountess is peering out. There! She's given a cry of joy. Monsieur de Canolles is hurrying into the house. Hide, Little Sister, or everything is lost!'

Nanon leapt back, convulsively grasping the hand of Cauvignac, who was giving her a look of paternal sympathy.

'And I was going to meet him in Paris!' Nanon exclaimed. 'I was risking everything to see him again!'

'What sacrifices, Little Sister! And for an ungrateful wretch, too! Honestly, you could distribute your generosity better.'

'What will they say, now that they are together again? What will they do?'

'Really, my dear Nanon, that's a very embarrassing question,' said Cauvignac. 'Why, I suppose that they are going to love one another a great deal.'

'No, no! It cannot be!' cried Nanon, furiously biting her nails, which were as polished as ivory.

'On the contrary, I think it will,' Cauvignac replied. 'Ferguzon, who had orders not to allow anyone to leave, was not told to prevent anyone coming in. In all probability, at this moment, the viscountess and the Baron de Canolles are exchanging all kinds of nothings, each sweeter than the next. Goodness, my dear Nanon, you are too late.'

'You think so?' the young woman retorted with an indefinable expression of profound irony and venomous subtlety. 'You think so? Well, come up beside me, you poor diplomat!'

Cauvignac did as she said.

'Here, Bertrand,' she went on, speaking to one of the musket-bearers. 'Tell the coachman to turn round, without making a fuss about it, and wait under that clump of trees that we saw on the right as we came into the village.' Then, turning back to Cauvignac: 'Won't that be a good place to talk?'

'Excellent, but let me take a few precautions of my own.'

'Go on.'

Cauvignac signalled to four of his men who had been strolling around outside the inn, humming and buzzing like hornets in the sun, and told them to follow him.

'You do well to bring these men,' said Nanon. 'And if you take my word, you'll take six rather than four. We'll be able to make work for them.'

'Good!' said Cauvignac. 'Work is what I need.'

'Then you won't be disappointed,' the young woman replied.

The chaise, doing an about-turn, took away Nanon, blushing with the ardour of her thoughts, and Cauvignac who, though apparently calm and cold, was nonetheless preparing to give his full attention to the opportunities that his sister had in store for him.

While this was happening, Canolles, drawn by the shout of joy that Madame de Cambes had given when she saw him, had rushed into the inn and straight to the viscountess's apartment, taking no notice of Ferguzon, whom he had met standing in the corridor, but who, having no orders about Canolles, made no attempt to stop him.

'Oh, Monsieur!' exclaimed Madame de Cambes when she saw him. 'Hurry to me, because I have been waiting impatiently for you.'

'Those words would have made me the happiest man in the world, Madame, except that your pale face and anxious expression tell me that it was not for my own sake alone that you were waiting for me.'

'You are right,' Claire answered, with her most charming smile. 'I want to put myself under a further obligation to you.'

'What is it?'

'To save me from some unknown danger that is threatening me.'

'Danger!'

'Yes. Wait . . .' Claire went to the door and shot the bolt. 'I have been recognized,' she said, when she came back.

'By whom?'

'By a man whose name I do not know, but whose face and voice are familiar to me. I think I heard his voice on the evening when in this same room you received the order to leave at once for Mantes, and I think I saw his face at the hunt in Chantilly on the day when I took the place of Madame de Condé.'

'And what do you think this man is?'

'An agent of the Duke d'Epernon, and consequently an enemy.'

'The devil he is!' said Canolles. 'And you say he recognized you?'

'I'm certain of it. He called me by name, though insisting that I was a man. Everywhere around here there are officers of the royal faction. I am known to belong to the princes' party, so perhaps they meant to bother me. But now you are here, I am not afraid of anything. You are an officer yourself. You belong to the same party as they do, so you will serve as my protector.'

'Alas!' Canolles replied. 'I'm very much afraid that I can offer you no other defence and protection than that of my sword.'

'Why?'

'From now on, Madame, I am no longer in the service of the king.'

'Is that true?' Claire cried, overwhelmed with joy.

'I promised myself that I would send my resignation dated from the place where I met you, if I did. I have met you, and my resignation will be dated from Jaulnay.'

'Free, free! You are free! You can embrace the party of justice and loyalty, you can serve the cause of the princes, that is to say of all the nobility. Oh, I knew that you were too worthy a man not to do so.'

Claire gave Canolles a hand which he kissed with rapture.

'How did it happen? What brought you to it? Tell me all the details.'

'It won't be a long story. I wrote in advance to Monsieur de Mazarin to inform him of what had happened. When I reached Mantes, I received the order to go and see him. He called me brainless; I called him weak in the head. He laughed; I lost my temper. He raised his voice; I told him to go to the devil. I went back to my lodging, where I waited for him to throw me into the Bastille. He was waiting for sober reflection to make me leave Mantes. After a day, the sober reflection came – and that, too, I owe to you, because I remembered what you promised and thought that you might be waiting for me, if only for a second. So, filling my lungs with the open air and free of all responsibilities and duties, with no party, no commitment and almost no preference, I recalled only one thing, Madame, which is that I loved you and that now I could tell you so boldly and openly.'

'So you have lost your rank for my sake, you have shamed yourself for my sake, you have ruined yourself for my sake! Dear Monsieur de Canolles, how could I ever repay you what I owe, how could I ever prove my gratitude?'

With a smile and a tear that returned him a hundred times more than he had lost, Madame de Cambes made Canolles fall at her feet.

'Oh, Madame,' he said. 'On the contrary, from this moment I am rich and happy, because I shall follow you and never leave you again, so I shall be happy in seeing you and rich with your love.'

'So nothing will stop you?'

'Nothing.'

'You will belong to me entirely and, while keeping your heart, I can offer your arm to fight for the princess?'

'You may.'

'You have sent your resignation?'

'Not yet. I wanted to see you first. But as I said, now that I have seen you, I shall write it here, this moment. I was leaving myself the happiness of being able to obey you.'

'Then write! Do it at once! If you don't write, you will be considered as a traitor. And before you make any definite move, you must wait for your resignation to be accepted.'

'Don't worry, my dear little diplomat. They will grant it to me, and willingly. My clumsy handling of affairs in Chantilly will mean that they have few regrets. Didn't they say that I was "brainless"?' Canolles went on, with a laugh.

'Yes, but we shall make up to you for the low opinion that they have of you. Your affairs in Chantilly will seem more successful in Bordeaux than in Paris, believe me. But write, Baron, write, so that we can leave! I have to tell you that staying in this inn does not make me feel at all secure.'

'Are you talking about the past and making yourself so afraid with your memories?' said Canolles, casting a loving look around him and pausing on the little alcove with two beds that had already attracted his attention more than once.

'No, I'm talking about the present, and you are no longer the cause of my anxieties. It is not you that I am afraid of now.'

'What are you afraid of, then? What do you have to fear?'

'God knows!'

At that moment, as though to justify the viscountess in her fears, three knocks sounded on the door. They were delivered with grave solemnity.

Canolles and the viscountess fell silent and exchanged an anxious look.

'Open!' said a voice. 'In the name of the king!'

Suddenly, the fragile door burst open. Canolles tried to grab his sword, but in no time a man had leapt between his sword and him.

'What does this mean?' the baron asked.

'You are the Baron de Canolles, I believe?'

'Certainly.'

'A captain in the regiment of Navailles?'

'Yes.'

'Sent on a mission from the Duke d'Epernon?'

Canolles nodded.

'In that case, in the name of the king and of Her Majesty the Queen Regent, I arrest you.'

'Where's your warrant?'

'Here.'

'But, Monsieur,' said Canolles, handing back the paper after glancing quickly at it, 'I have a feeling that I know you.'

'Indeed you do! Was it not in this same village where I am arresting you today that I brought you the order from the Duke d'Epernon to leave for the court? Your fortune was in that order, my fine fellow. You failed in it, and so much the worse for you.'

The colour drained from Claire's face and she fell weeping into a chair. She, too, had recognized the indiscreet enquirer.

'Monsieur de Mazarin is taking his revenge,' Canolles murmured.

'Come, Monsieur, let's go,' said Cauvignac.

Claire was motionless. Canolles seemed hesitant and almost mad. His misfortune was so great, so dire and so unexpected that he was crushed beneath its weight: he bent his head and resigned himself to his fate. Indeed, at that time, the words 'In the name of the king!' still retained some magic power, and no one tried to resist.

'Where are you taking me, Monsieur?' he asked. 'Or are you even forbidden from giving me the consolation of knowing where I am going?'

'No, Monsieur, I shall tell you: we are taking you to the fortress on the Ile Saint-Georges.'

'Adieu, Madame,' said Canolles, bowing respectfully before Madame de Cambes. 'Adieu.'

'Well, well,' Cauvignac said to himself. 'Things are not so

advanced as I would have thought. I'll tell Nanon: she'll be pleased.' Then, going to the doorway, he shouted: 'Four men to escort the captain! And four other men ahead.'

'And me,' cried Madame de Cambes, reaching out her arms towards the prisoner. 'And me – where are you taking me? Because if the baron is guilty, I am even more so than he is!'

'You, Madame, can go,' Cauvignac replied. 'You are free.'

And he left with the baron.

Madame de Cambes got up, revived by a glimmer of hope, and prepared everything for her departure, before these good intentions were replaced by contrary orders. 'I am free,' she said. 'So I can keep watch over him. Let's go.'

Hurrying to the window, she saw the cavalcade taking Canolles away, exchanged a last wave with him and, calling Pompée – who, hoping for a stay of two or three days, had settled down in the best room he could find – she gave him orders to prepare everything for their departure.

VIII

The journey was even sadder for Canolles than he had expected. The horse, that gives even the most closely guarded prisoner a false sense of freedom, had been replaced by a carriage, a ghastly leather four-wheeler, the shape and shuddering of which still survive in Touraine. Moreover, Canolles's knees were locked in those of a man with a nose like an eagle's beak, whose hand was resting in a sort of proprietorial manner on the butt of an iron pistol. Sometimes at night (because he slept during the day), Canolles hoped to catch this new watchdog off guard, but beside the eagle's beak shone two great owl's eyes, round, blazing and entirely suited to seeing in the dark, so that, whichever way he turned, Canolles could still see these two round eyes shining in his direction.

While he was sleeping, one of the eyes also slept, but only one: nature had given the man the ability to sleep with only one eye shut.

Canolles spent two days and two nights in sombre reflections: the fortress of the Ile Saint-Georges, though a fairly innocent fortress in reality, assumed terrifying proportions in the eyes of the prisoner, as fear and remorse gradually sank deeper and deeper into his heart.

Remorse, because he realized that his mission to the princess was a confidential one, which he had sacrificed to his love, and the outcome of the sin that he had committed because of this was terrible. In Chantilly, Madame de Condé was only a fugitive, but in Bordeaux, Madame de Condé was a seditious princess. And, as well as remorse, he felt fear, because he knew from her reputation how savage could be the revenge of an enraged Anne of Austria.

Another less precise feeling of remorse was perhaps even more profound than the first. Somewhere there was a beautiful, intelligent young woman who had used her influence only to advance his career and her credit only to protect him, a woman who, through her love for him, had twenty times risked her position, her future and her fortune ... This woman was not only the most charming mistress, but also the most devoted friend. He had left her suddenly, cruelly, with no excuse and no justification, at a time when she was thinking of him, and instead of taking revenge, she had followed him with still more generosity; her name, instead of sounding to him in the accents of reproach, had sung in his ears with the soothing sweetness of an almost royal favour. It is true that the favour had arrived at a bad moment, a moment when, indeed, Canolles would have preferred a disservice, but was that Nanon's fault? All that Nanon had seen in this mission for His Majesty was an increase in fortune and position for the man who was constantly in her thoughts.

So all those who have loved two women at once – and here I must beg forgiveness of my female readers: this phenomenon is incomprehensible for them, for they have only ever had one love, while it is commonplace among us men – so, I say, all those who have loved two women at once will understand how, as Canolles sank deeper into his reflections, Nanon regained the influence over his mind that he thought she had lost. The rough edges of character, which hurt as they rub together in intimacy and cause momentary feelings of irritation, are smoothed out with distance, while, by contrast, certain sweeter memories regain their former intensity in solitude. Finally (and it's sad to say), ethereal love, which promised only favours, evaporates in isolation, while in the same situation material love, on the contrary, appears to memory armed with all its earthly pleasures, which also have their value. Lovely and lost, generous and deceived: this is how Canolles now saw Nanon.

It was because Canolles was searching his soul candidly and not with the bad faith of those accused persons who are forced to make a general confession. What had Nanon done for him to abandon her? What had Madame de Cambes done for him to pursue her? What was there, then, so desirable and magnificently amorous in the little rider at the inn of the Golden Calf? Was Madame de Cambes so far superior to Nanon? Is blonde hair so much better than dark hair for a man to become unfaithful and ungrateful towards his mistress, and a traitor and disloyal towards his king, by simply exchanging these dark locks for those fair ones? And yet – oh, how wretchedly is mankind designed! – Canolles presented himself with all these arguments (eminently reasonable, as one can see), and yet was not persuaded.

The heart is full of such mysteries, which are the joy of lovers and the despair of philosophers.

This did not prevent Canolles from being angry with himself and thoroughly upbraiding himself.

'I shall be punished,' he thought, feeling that punishment eradicates sin. 'I shall be punished, so much the better! There will be some fine captain there, a rough type, very rude and brutal, who in his capacity as jailer-in-chief, will read me an order from Monsieur de Mazarin, then point me to a dungeon and send me to rot fifteen feet below the ground with rats and toads, while I could have lived in broad daylight and blossomed in the sun, in the arms of a woman who loved me, and whom I loved . . . and, by Jove, whom I may still love.

'Away with you, cursed little viscount! Why did you serve as covering for such a delightful viscountess?

'Yes, but is there in the world any viscountess who is worth what this will cost me? The prison governor and the dungeon fifteen feet below ground are not all. If they think I am a traitor, they will not leave things only half explained: they will want to argue about that stay in Chantilly, which I could never pay at too high a price, I agree, if it had been more fruitful for me, but which, when you add it up, brought me three kisses on the hand altogether. What a three-times fool I am, having had the power and the ability to misuse it, for not taking advantage of it! Brainless fool, as Monsieur de Mazarin said, who became a traitor and did not get the reward of his treachery! And who is going to pay me now?'

Canolles shrugged his shoulders, the gesture scornfully replying to the question in his thoughts.

The man with the round eyes, sharp-sighted as he was, could not understand a word of this dumbshow and was looking at him with amazement.

'If they question me,' Canolles went on, 'I shall not reply. For what should I have to answer? That I did not like Monsieur de Mazarin? Then I ought not to have served him. That I did love Madame de Cambes? There's a fine reason to give a queen and a prime minister! So I shall not answer. But judges are easily offended: when they ask a question, they want an answer. There are some savage places in these provincial jails: they will break those little knees that I was so proud of and send me back all twisted to my rats and toads. I'll be all knock-kneed, like the Prince de Conti, for the rest of my life, which is very ugly, even if His Majesty's pardon is extended to me, which it won't be.'

Apart from that governor, those rats and toads and those savage places, there were certain scaffolds where rebels were beheaded, gallows where traitors were hanged and parade grounds where deserters were shot. But, you will understand, such considerations were nothing for a handsome lad like Canolles, compared with knock-knees.

So he resolved to clear up the matter and to ask his travelling companion about it.

The round eyes, aquiline nose and sullen appearance of

the man were only moderate inducements to the prisoner to open a conversation. Yet since any face, however impassive, must have some moments when it relaxes a little, Canolles took advantage of a second when a grimace which resembled a smile passed across the features of the subordinate exempt, who was keeping such good watch over him.

'Monsieur,' he said.

'Monsieur,' replied the exempt.

'Excuse me if I am interrupting your reflections.'

'No apology needed, Monsieur. I never reflect.'

'The devil you don't! You must have a happy constitution, Monsieur.'

'I'm not complaining.'

'Well, that's not the case with me, because I would very much like to complain.'

'Of what, Monsieur?'

'Of the fact that I have been carried off like this, just when I least expected it, and taken I know not where.'

'That you do, Monsieur. They told you.'

'Quite right. We're going to the Ile Saint-Georges, aren't we?'

'Just so.'

'Do you think I'll be there a long time?'

'I don't know, Monsieur, but from the way you were described to me, I should think so.'

'Ah! And is it a very ugly spot, this Ile Saint-Georges?'

'Don't you know the fortress?'

'Inside, no. I've never been there.'

'Well, it's not beautiful. And apart from the governor's rooms, which have just been done up and which are very pleasant, apparently, the rest of the lodgings are pretty grim.'

'Very well. Do you think I'll be interrogated?'

'That's fairly usual.'

'And if I don't reply?'

'If you don't reply?'

'Yes.'

'Why, in that case, as you know, you will be put to the question.'

'Ordinary?'

'Ordinary or extraordinary, according to the charge. What are you accused of, Monsieur?'

'I'm afraid I've been accused of a crime against the state.'

'Ah, in that case you qualify for the extraordinary question . . . Ten pots.'

'What? Ten pots?'

'Yes.'

'What are you saying?'

'I'm saying that you'll have ten kettles.'

'So the water torture is the one practised on the Ile Saint-Georges?'

'Why, Monsieur, on the Garonne, you see . . .'

'Quite so: the stuff is to hand. And how many buckets make ten kettles?'

'Three buckets . . . three and a half . . .'

'I'll swell up a bit, then.'

'A bit. But if you take the precaution of getting on the right side of the jailer . . .'

'What then?'

'You'll be better off.'

'And just what is the service that the jailer can do me, if I may ask?'

'He can give you oil to drink.'

'Oil is a specific in the case?'

'A sovereign remedy, Monsieur.'

'Do you think?'

'I'm speaking from experience. I've imbibed . . .'

'You've imbibed?'

'I beg your pardon. I meant to say: I've revived . . . The habit of talking with Gascons means that I sometimes pronounce "b" as "v", and vice versa.'

'So you were saying,' said Canolles, unable to repress a smile, despite the serious topic under discussion. 'You were saying that you've "revived" . . .'

'Yes, Monsieur. I've revived a man after drinking ten kettles with the greatest of ease, thanks to the oil which had correctly prepared the tubes. It's true, he did swell up, as usual, but with a good fire we got him unswollen without too much damage.

This is the main feature of the second part of the operation. Remember these two words: heat without burning.'

'I understand,' said Canolles. 'Could it be that you were an executioner by any chance?'

'No, Monsieur,' the man replied, politely and modestly.

'An assistant, perhaps?'

'No, Monsieur. An onlooker, merely an interested amateur.'

'Oh, really? And your name?'

'Barabbas.'[19]

'A fine name, an old name, well reputed from the scriptures.'

'In the Easter service, Monsieur.'

'That's what I meant, but out of habit I used the other expression.'

'You prefer the scriptures? Are you a Huguenot, then?'

'Yes, but a very ignorant one. Would you believe that I know barely three thousand verses of psalms?'

'That's certainly not a lot.'

'I can remember music better. We have been much hanged and burned in my family.'[20]

'I hope that the gentleman is not destined for the same fate.'

'No, they're much more tolerant nowadays. I'll just be submerged.'

Barabbas began to laugh.

Canolles's heart leapt with joy: he had won over his guard. And indeed, if this temporary jailer should become a permanent one, he had every chance of getting some oil, so he decided to resume the conversation where he had left off.

'Monsieur Barabbas,' he said, 'are we to be separated soon, or will you do me the honour of remaining in my company?'

'When we get to the Ile Saint-Georges, I shall most regretfully have to leave you. I must return to our company.'

'Very well. Do you belong to a company of archers?'

'No, Monsieur, to a company of soldiers.'

'One raised by the prime minister?'

'No, Monsieur, by Captain Cauvignac. The same who had the honour to arrest you.'

'And you serve the king?'

'I think so.'

'What on earth do you mean? Aren't you sure?'

'One can be sure of nothing in this world.'

'So, if you are in doubt, you should do one thing to be certain.'

'What's that?'

'Let me go.'

'Impossible, Monsieur.'

'But I should reward you handsomely for obliging me.'

'What with?'

'Why, with money, of course!'

'But the gentleman has none.'

'What do you mean? I have none?'

'Just so.'

Canolles felt in his pockets.

'You're right,' he said. 'My purse has vanished. So who took my purse?'

'I did, Monsieur,' Barabbas replied, with a respectful bow.

'Why did you do that?'

'So that Monsieur could not bribe me.'

Canolles looked at the worthy warder with amazement and admiration. And since the argument seemed to him unanswerable, he did not answer it.

Consequently, the travellers having once more lapsed into silence, the journey drew towards its end in the same melancholy mode in which it had started.

IX

Dawn was starting to break when the carriage arrived at the village nearest to the island towards which they were headed. Canolles, feeling it draw to a halt, put his head through the little hole – an opening designed to provide air for free men and quite convenient for denying it to prisoners.

A pretty little village, made up of a hundred houses clustered around a church, on the slope of a hill and overlooked by a castle, appeared bathed in the clear air of morning and gilded by the rays of sunlight, which were driving sheets of mist before them like floating gauze.

At that moment, the carriage was climbing a hill and the coachman had got down from his seat to walk along beside it.

'My friend,' Canolles asked. 'Do you come from around here?'

'Yes, Monsieur, I am from Libourne.'

'In that case, you must know this village. What is that white house? And these delightful cottages?'

'That is the manor of Cambes and this village one of those on the estate.'

Canolles shuddered and his colour faded in an instant from the deepest purple to an almost livid pallor.

'Monsieur,' said Barabbas, whose eagle eye missed nothing. 'Did you by any chance hurt yourself on that little window?'

'No . . . thank you.' Then, continuing to question the peasant, he asked: 'And whose is that mansion?'

'It belongs to the Viscountess de Cambes.'

'A young widow?'

'Very beautiful and very rich.'

'And consequently much in demand.'

'Of course. A beautiful woman, a beautiful dowry: you don't lack suitors when you have that.'

'A good reputation?'

'Yes, but a fanatical supporter of the princes.'

'I believe I have heard so.'

'A demon, Monsieur, a real demon!'

'An angel!' Canolles murmured to himself: every time that he thought of Claire, he did so with transports of adoration. 'An angel!' Then, aloud, he added: 'Does she live here sometimes?'

'Very rarely, Monsieur, but for a long time she did. Her husband left her there, and all the time she was in residence it was a blessing for all hereabouts. Now, so they say, she is with the princes.'

The carriage, having gone up, was ready to go down. The driver made a sign, asking permission to go back on his seat. Canolles, afraid of arousing suspicion if he continued to question him, put his head back inside the carriage, and the heavy vehicle set off again at a slow trot, its fastest speed.

After a quarter of an hour, during which Canolles, still under the watchful eye of Barabbas, had been sunk in the darkest thoughts, the carriage came to a halt.

'Are we stopping here for lunch?' asked Canolles.

'We're stopping altogether, Monsieur. We've arrived. This is the Ile Saint-Georges. We have only the river to cross.'

'Right,' murmured Canolles. 'So near and yet so far!'

'They are coming for you, Monsieur,' said Barabbas. 'Please get ready to descend.'

Canolles's second warder, who was sitting on the seat beside the coachman, got down and unlocked the door, to which he had the key.

Canolles looked back at the little white castle, which he had kept in sight, on the fortress that was to become his home. First of all, on the other side of quite a swiftly flowing river, he noticed a ferry and beside it a guard post with eight men and a sergeant. Behind that rose the walls of the citadel.

'So!' thought Canolles. 'I was expected. Precautions have been taken.'

'Are those my new guards?' he asked Barabbas aloud.

'I should like to give Monsieur a pertinent reply,' said Barabbas. 'But the truth is I don't know.'

At that moment, after giving a signal that was repeated by the sentry mounting guard at the gate of the fort, the eight soldiers and the sergeant got into the ferry, crossed the Garonne and stepped ashore just as Canolles was getting down from the carriage.

The sergeant, seeing an officer, came over and gave a military salute.

'Do I have the honour to address the Baron de Canolles, captain of the regiment of Navailles?' he asked.

'I am he,' said Canolles, astonished by the man's politeness.

The sergeant at once turned round to his men, ordered them to present arms and indicated the boat to Canolles with the end of his pike. Canolles got in between his two warders. The eight soldiers and the sergeant followed them, and the boat moved away from the shore, while Canolles cast a final glance towards Cambes as it vanished behind some higher ground.

Almost the whole island was covered in escarps and counterscarps, glacis and bastions, and all these military fortifications were overlooked by a little fort in quite good condition. The entrance to this was through an arched door, in front of which the sentry was marching backwards and forwards.

'Who goes there?' he shouted.

The little troop halted, the sergeant stepped forward and said a few words to the sentry, who shouted: 'Present arms!'

At once, some twenty men who made up the garrison came out of the guardroom and hurried at the double to line up in front of the door.

'This way, Monsieur,' the sergeant told Canolles.

The drum beat a salute.

'What does all this mean?' the young man wondered. He went forward towards the fort, not understanding anything of what was going on, because all these preparations looked more like the military honours paid to a superior than precautions taken against a prisoner.

This was not all. Canolles had not noticed that at the very moment when he got down from the carriage, a window had opened in the governor's lodging, and an officer closely supervised the movements of the boat and the welcome given to the prisoner and his two guards. As soon as this officer saw that Canolles had set foot on the island, he came to meet him.

'Ah, ha!' Canolles said when he saw him. 'Here's the commander of the fort who has come to meet his tenant.'

'Just so,' said Barabbas. 'It seems, Monsieur, that you will not languish like some people who are left for whole weeks in a waiting room. You'll be sent directly to a cell.'

'So much the better,' said Canolles.

Meanwhile, the officer was walking across to them. Canolles adopted the proud and dignified attitude of a persecuted man.

When he was a few yards away from Canolles, the officer doffed his cap and asked: 'Do I have the honour to address Baron de Canolles?'

'Monsieur,' the prisoner replied. 'To tell the truth, I am embarrassed by your politeness. Yes, I am Baron de Canolles.

Now I beg you to treat me with the courtesy due from one officer to another and to house me the least poorly that you can.'

'The lodging is quite special, Monsieur,' the officer replied. 'But, as though in anticipation of your wishes, every possible improvement has been made to it.'

'And whom should I thank for these unusual arrangements?' Canolles asked with a smile.

'The king, Monsieur, who does everything that he does well.'

'Of course, of course. Heaven forbid that I should slander His Majesty, especially on this occasion. However, I should be gratified if I could have some information.'

'If you so order, Monsieur, I am at your disposal, but may I take the liberty of pointing out that the garrison is waiting to receive you?'

'Damnation!' murmured Canolles. 'A whole garrison to accept one prisoner when he is being locked up: this is a lot of fuss, I must say.' Then, aloud, he continued: 'I am the one taking your orders, Monsieur, ready to follow you wherever you would like to lead me.'

'So, please let me go ahead and do you the honours.'

Canolles followed him, silently congratulating himself on having fallen into the hands of such a polite man.

'I think you'll get away with the ordinary question,' Barabbas whispered, coming over to him. 'Four kettles only.'

'So much the better,' said Canolles. 'I'll only swell up half as much.'

On arriving in the courtyard of the fortress, Canolles found part of the garrison presenting arms, and, at this, the officer who was leading him drew his sword and bowed.

'My goodness, what a to-do!' Canolles thought.

At the same moment, the drum sounded under a nearby archway, and Canolles turned round to see a second line of soldiers emerging and drawing up behind the first.

At this, the officer presented Canolles with two keys.

'What's this?' the baron asked. 'What are you doing?'

'We are carrying out the usual ceremony under the strictest rules of protocol.'

'But who do you think I am?' Canolles asked in complete amazement.

'Why, the person who you are, I imagine: the Baron de Canolles.'

'And he is?'

'Governor of the Ile Saint-Georges.'

Canolles almost fell to the ground in astonishment.

'I shall have the honour,' the officer continued, 'shortly to hand the governor the supplies that I received this morning, together with a letter announcing your arrival today.'

Canolles looked at Barabbas, whose two round eyes were staring at him with an expression of stupefaction that is impossible to describe.

'So,' Canolles stammered, 'I am Governor of the Ile Saint-Georges?'

'Yes, Monsieur,' the officer replied. 'And we are most delighted with His Majesty's choice.'

'You're sure there is no mistake?'

'Please be so good as to follow me into your apartments,' said the officer. 'You will find your authority there.'

Canolles, dazed by these events, so contrary to what he had been expecting, marched forward without a word, following the officer who led the way, amid the sound of the drums which had resumed their beat, between the ranks of soldiers presenting arms and all the inhabitants of the fortress who made the air ring with their cheers as he responded with waves to right and left, pale and shivering, and giving Barabbas a terrified look.

Finally, they arrived in quite an elegant drawing room, from the windows of which he immediately noticed that you could see the Château de Cambes. Here he read his authority, drawn up in the proper manner, signed by the queen and countersigned by the Duke d'Epernon.

At the sight of this, Canolles's legs gave way entirely, and he slumped down, in a stupor, on to a chair.

However, after all the fanfares, the musket firing and the noisy demonstration of military honours, and in particular after the first surprise that these exhibitions had produced in him, Canolles wanted to know what he should truly believe about the position that the queen had entrusted to him and looked up, having for some time before that kept his eyes fixed on the floor.

This is when he saw in front of him, no less amazed than he was, his former jailer, now his most humble servant.

'Ah, it's you, Barabbas,' he said.

'It is indeed, Governor.'

'Would you explain to me what has taken place, which I am finding it very difficult not to imagine is all a dream?'

'I must explain to you, Monsieur, that when I spoke to you of the extraordinary question, that is of the ten kettles, I thought, by Barabbas, that I was sweetening the medicine for you.'

'So you were convinced, then?'

'Yes, that I was bringing you here to be broken on the wheel, Monsieur.'

'Thank you,' said Canolles, shuddering in spite of himself. 'Now, do you have any definite opinions about what is happening to me?'

'Yes, Monsieur.'

'Then please be good enough to inform me.'

'Here you are: the queen must have realized how difficult the mission was with which she had entrusted you. Once she had got over the first rush of anger, she felt sorry, and since, all things considered, you are not a detestable person, Her Gracious Majesty must have rewarded you because she had punished you too severely before.'

'Unacceptable,' Canolles replied.

'Unacceptable, you think?'

'Improbable, at least.'

'Improbable?'

'Yes.'

'In that case, Governor, there is nothing more for me except to present you with my most humble salutations. You can be as happy as a king on the Ile Saint-Georges: excellent wine, the game from the surrounding plains and the fish that the ships of Bordeaux and the women of Saint-Georges bring in with every tide. Oh, Monsieur, what a miracle it is!'

'Very well, I shall try to follow your advice. Take this order that I have signed and go to the paymaster, who will give you ten pistoles. I should willingly give them to you myself, but since you prudently took my money . . .'

'And I did the right thing, Monsieur!' Barabbas exclaimed. 'Because, after all, if you'd corrupted me, you would have escaped, and if you had escaped, you would quite naturally have lost the high office to which you have now come, and I should never have got over it.'

'Very powerfully argued, Master Barabbas. I've noticed already that logic is your strongest point. Meanwhile, take this paper as a testimony to your eloquence. The ancients, as you may know, represented eloquence with golden chains emerging from her lips.'

'Monsieur,' said Barabbas, 'suppose I dared suggest to you that I think it pointless to go and see the paymaster.'

'What! Are you refusing?' Canolles exclaimed, in amazement.

'No, no, heaven forbid! Thank goodness, I do not suffer from such false pride. But I can see on your mantelpiece a small chest with certain cords emerging from it, which look to me like purse strings.'

'You are well versed in strings, Monsieur Barabbas,' said Canolles, surprised, because there was indeed on the mantelpiece a box of old-fashioned faience, encrusted with silver and Renaissance enamel work. 'We shall see if your prediction is correct.'

Canolles opened the lid of the box and did indeed find inside it a purse, and in the purse a thousand pistoles with this little note attached:

'For the private treasury of the Governor of the Ile Saint-Georges.'

'*Corbleu!*' Canolles exclaimed, with a blush. 'The queen knows how to do things.'

And the memory of Buckingham[21] came unbidden to his mind. Perhaps the queen had seen the victorious face of the handsome captain behind some tapestry; perhaps she was protecting him with peculiarly tender care; or perhaps . . . You will recall that Canolles was a Gascon.

Unfortunately, the queen was twenty years older than she had been at the time of Buckingham.

However that was, and regardless of where it came from, Canolles reached into the purse and extracted ten pistoles, which he gave to Barabbas, who then left the room, with the most reiterative and respectful bows.

X

Once Barabbas had left, Canolles called the officer and asked him to guide him in a review of his new domain. The officer at once put himself at Canolles's disposal.

At the door, he found a kind of command post, consisting of the other main figures in the fortress. Talking to them, chatting with them and getting them to explain all the features of the place, he visited the fortifications: the bastions, the glacis, the demilunes, the blockhouses, as well as the cellars and the attics. Finally, at eleven o'clock in the morning, he returned after visiting everywhere. His escort dispersed and he remained with the first officer whom he had originally met.

'Now,' the officer said, approaching him mysteriously. 'All that remains for the governor to see is one apartment and one person.'

'I beg your pardon?' said Canolles.

'That person's apartment is here,' said the officer, pointing towards a door which Canolles had not yet opened.

'Ah, it's there?' said Canolles.

'Yes.'

'And the person, too?'

'Yes.'

'Very well. But, excuse me, I am tired after travelling night and day, and my head this morning is not quite clear, so would you be so good as to explain yourself a little more clearly?'

'Very well, Governor,' the officer went on, with his most canny smile. 'The apartment . . .'

'. . . of the person . . .' Canolles continued.

'... who is waiting for you, is there. Now do you understand?'

Canolles started, as though emerging from the land of con-
jecture into the real world.

'Yes, yes, fine,' he said. 'Can I go in?'

'Of course, you are expected.'

'Off we go then,' said Canolles.

His heart beating fit to burst in his chest, bemused, feeling
his fears and desires mingle to the point of madness, Canolles
pushed open a second door and saw, behind a tapestry, the
laughing and effervescent face of Nanon, who gave a loud
cry as though to scare him and ran over, throwing both arms
around his neck.

Canolles stayed motionless, his arms hanging at his side,
staring blankly.

'You!' he stammered.

'Me!' she said, laughing even more loudly and showering
him with kisses.

The memory of the wrongs he had done her flashed into
Canolles's mind, and, guessing at once the new favour that this
loyal friend had done him, he was overwhelmed with feelings
of remorse and gratitude.

'So it is you who saved me,' he said. 'While I was destroying
myself like an idiot! You are watching over me, you are my
guardian angel.'

'Don't call me your angel,' said Nanon, 'because I'm a devil.
However, I do only appear at the right moment, you must
admit.'

'You are right, my dear friend, because I truly believe that
you have saved me from the scaffold.'

'I think so, too. Really, Baron! You who are so far-sighted
and sharp-witted, how did you manage to be taken in by those
snooty little princesses?'

Canolles blushed to the whites of his eyes, but Nanon had
decided not to notice his embarrassment.

'Honestly,' he said, 'I don't know. I don't understand it
myself.'

'Oh, it's because they're up to all the tricks! You men! You try to make war on women! What did they tell me? Instead of the young princess, they showed you a lady-in-waiting, a chambermaid, a scullery maid . . . or what was it?'

Canolles felt a fever rising from his trembling fingers to his overheated brain.

'I thought I was seeing the princess,' he said. 'I didn't know her.'

'And who was she?'

'A lady-in-waiting, I believe.'

'Oh, you poor boy! It's that traitor Mazarin's fault. After all, when you give someone such a difficult mission as that, you should supply a portrait. If you had merely seen the princess's portrait, you would certainly have recognized her. But let's not bother with that any longer. Do you know that frightful Mazarin, on the grounds that you betrayed the king, wanted to have you thrown to the toads?'

'I guessed as much.'

'And I said: "Let's have him thrown to the Nanons." Did I do the right thing, then?'

Canolles, preoccupied as he was with the memory of the viscountess, and even though he carried the viscountess's portrait next to his heart, could not withstand this supreme goodness, this spirit radiating from the loveliest eyes in the world. He lowered his head and put his lips to the lovely hand extended to him.

'And you came here to wait for me?'

'I was going to join you in Paris to accompany you here. I was bringing your authority. It seemed a long time that we had been apart, and only Monsieur d'Epernon returned with all his weight into my monotonous existence. I heard about your disappointment. By the way, I was forgetting to tell you: you are my brother, you know.'

'That's what I thought I understood from your letter.'

'We must have been betrayed. The letter that I wrote you fell into the wrong hands. The duke arrived in a fury. I named you, confessed that you were my brother, poor Canolles, and now we are protected by the most legitimate of bonds. You are almost married, my poor friend.'

Canolles allowed himself to be carried away by the woman's incredible energy. After kissing her white hands, he kissed her dark eyes . . . The shade of Madame de Cambes had to take its leave, mournfully covering its head.

'This means,' said Nanon, 'that everything has been covered and settled. I have made Monsieur d'Epernon your protector, or rather your friend, and I have turned aside the wrath of Mazarin. Finally, I have chosen Saint-Georges as our refuge, because, as you know, dear friend, I am still a target for hatred. Only you, in the whole world, love me a little, my dear Canolles. Come now, tell me that you do!'

The ravishing siren, putting both arms around Canolles's neck, stared deep into the young man's eyes with a burning look that seemed to be reaching for his thoughts in the depth of his heart.

And in this same heart where Nanon was trying to read, Canolles felt that he could not remain indifferent to such devotion. A secret premonition told him that there was something more than love in Nanon, that there was generosity – and that not only did she know how to love, but also to forgive.

The young man nodded in reply to her question, because he did not dare tell her aloud that he loved her, even though so many memories were pleading in her favour.

'So, I chose the Ile Saint-Georges,' she went on, 'to put my money, my jewels and myself in safe keeping. And who else could better defend my life, I asked myself, than the man who loves me? Who other than my master can guard my treasures for me? Everything is in your hands, dear friend, my life and my wealth. Will you keep good watch over all of them? Will you be a loyal friend and a faithful warden?'

At that moment, a trumpet sounded in the courtyard and found an echo in Canolles's heart. He had before him love, more eloquent than it had ever been, and at the same time, a hundred yards from him, war, threatening, war that inflames and intoxicates.

'Oh, yes, Nanon!' he exclaimed. 'Your person and your possessions are safe with me, and I swear to die to protect you from the slightest danger.'

'Thank you, my noble knight,' she said. 'I am as certain of your courage as I am of your generous spirit. Alas,' she added, with a smile, 'I wish I could be as sure of your love.'

'Oh, be sure . . .' Canolles murmured.

'Very well,' said Nanon. 'Love is not proved by promises, but by actions. We shall judge your love, Monsieur, by what you do.'

At that, putting the loveliest arms in the world round Canolles's neck, she rested her head on the young man's beating chest.

'Now,' she thought to herself, 'he must forget. And he will forget . . .'

XI

The same day as that on which Canolles was arrested in Jaulnay in front of Madame de Cambes, she herself left with Pompée to join the princess, who was within sight of Coutras.

The worthy steward's first consideration was to prove to his mistress that if Cauvignac's band did not demand any ransom or commit any violence against the beautiful traveller, she owed this good fortune to his own resolute manner and military experience. It is true that Madame de Cambes, who was less easy to persuade than Pompée had originally hoped, pointed out to him that for almost an hour he had disappeared entirely, but Pompée explained that during this time he had been hiding in a corridor, where, with the help of a ladder, he had prepared a secure escape route for the viscountess. However, he had had to ward off two frenetic soldiers who tried to get the ladder away from him, and had done so, as one might imagine, with his usual invincible courage.

This conversation naturally led Pompée to a word in praise of the soldiers of his own time, savage in fighting the enemy, as they had proved at the siege of Montauban and the Battle of Corbie,[22] but mild and well-mannered towards their compatriots – all of them qualities, it had to be said, which, nowadays, soldiers did not pride themselves on.

The fact is that, without realizing it, Pompée had just avoided an immense danger: that of being press-ganged. As he was accustomed to walk along with shining eyes, his chest puffed out in a warlike manner and with the bearing of a Nimrod, he attracted Cauvignac's attention from the start. But subsequent events had changed the captain's mind. After all, he had received two hundred pistoles from Nanon to look after the Baron de Canolles; then there was the philosophical reflection that jealousy is the most magnificent of passions and one that you should make the most of when you come across it. So the dear brother had left Pompée alone and allowed Madame de Cambes to continue on her way to Bordeaux – actually, in Nanon's view, Bordeaux was still very close to Canolles. She would have preferred the viscountess to be in Peru, or India, or Greenland.

On the other hand, when Nanon considered that from now on she had her dear Canolles to herself between four solid walls, and that excellent fortifications, very hard for the king's men to breach, would also be keeping Madame de Cambes a prisoner, she felt herself swell with those infinite joys that only children and lovers can know on this earth.

We have seen how her dream was realized and how Canolles and Nanon met again on the Ile Saint-Georges.

So, Madame de Cambes, on her side, was travelling along, sad and anxious. Pompée was far from reassuring her, despite his boasting, and when, on the evening of the day that she left Jaulnay, she saw quite a large troop of horsemen approaching down a side road, she felt an acute sense of fear.

The riders were those same gentlemen who were returning from the famous burial of the Duke de La Rochefoucauld, an occasion that under the pretext of paying appropriate respects to his father had served the Prince de Marsillac[23] as an excuse to bring together all the nobility from France and Picardy who hated Mazarin even more than they were devoted to the princes. But one odd thing struck Madame de Cambes – and, even more, Pompée – which was that among the horsemen, some had their arms in slings, others had legs hanging limply in the stirrups, wrapped round with splints, and several had bloody bandages around their foreheads. As a result, one had to look very closely at them to recognize, in these gentlemen who were so unkindly fitted out, the spruce and sprightly sportsmen who had hunted the deer in the park at Chantilly.

But fear has sharp eyes: under the bloody wrappings, Pompée and Madame de Cambes recognized a few faces that they knew.

'Curses!' said Pompée. 'There's a burial that went down a few very weird roads. Most of these gentlemen must have fallen off their horses: look how knocked about they are.'

'That is just what I was looking at,' said Madame de Cambes.

'It reminds me of the return from Corbie,' said Pompée, proudly. 'Except that, on that occasion, I was not among the brave men who were returning, but among those who were brought back.'

'But weren't these gentlemen under the command of some officer?' asked Claire, feeling somewhat anxious about an undertaking that appeared to have had such a bad outcome. 'Don't they have a leader? Has he been killed, if we can't see him? Look!'

'Madame,' Pompée replied, sitting up proudly in his saddle. 'Nothing is easier than to recognize a leader among the people whom he commands. In general, in a troop, the officer goes in the centre, with his under-officers, while in battle he goes behind or on the flank. Look in the different places I have indicated, and you can judge for yourself.'

'I can't see anything. But I think we are being followed: look behind us.'

'Hum, hum!' said Pompée, coughing, but without turning round in case he did, indeed, see someone. 'No, Madame, there's no one. But wait for the leader. Might it be that red plume? No ... Or that gilded sword? No ... The pied horse, next to Monsieur de Turenne's? No ... That's odd. There is no danger, so the leader could very well show himself. It's not like Corbie here.'

'You're wrong, Master Pompée,' said a strident, mocking voice from behind the poor steward's back, almost making him fall over backwards. 'You're wrong: it's worse than Corbie.'

Claire swiftly turned round and saw, a couple of yards away

from her, a horseman of modest height and dressed in an affectedly simple way, who was looking at her with bright little eyes, sunk like those of a fox. With his thick black hair, his slender, shifting lips, his bilious pallor and his woeful brow, the man aroused a feeling of melancholy in daylight, but after dark, he could well have inspired terror.

'Prince de Marsillac!' Claire exclaimed, quite overcome. 'Oh, Monsieur! Welcome!'

'Say, rather: Duke de La Rochefoucauld, Madame, because now that my father the duke is dead, I have inherited this name as the one against which the actions of my life will be recorded, for good or ill.'

'You are returning?' said Claire, hesitantly.

'We are returning defeated, Madame.'

'Defeated! Heavens above! You!'

'I say that we are returning defeated, Madame, because I am not boastful by nature, and because I tell myself the truth as I tell it to others; otherwise, I might claim that we are returning as victors. But in reality, we were defeated, since our plan for Saumur failed. I arrived too late; we have lost this important place, which Jarzay had just ceded. From now on, assuming that the princess has Bordeaux, as she was promised that she would, the whole war is going to be concentrated in Guyenne.'

'But, Monsieur,' Claire asked. 'If, as I understand it, the capitulation of Saumur took place without a blow being struck, what is the meaning of this spectacle, and why are all these gentlemen wounded in this way?'

'Because we met some soldiers of the king,' said the Duke de La Rochefoucauld with a kind of pride that he could not hide, despite his mastery over his emotions.

'And you fought?' Madame de Cambes asked urgently.

'Why, yes, Madame.'

'And so,' she murmured, 'the first French blood has already been spilled by Frenchmen. And it is you, Duke, who set the example.'

'It was I, Madame.'

'You, who are so calm and cold and wise!'

'When an unjust cause is defended against me, sometimes

in my passionate advocacy of reason, I become quite un-reasonable.'

'At least you are not wounded?'

'No, this time I was luckier than at Les Lignes or Paris. I even thought then that I had received enough from civil war not to have any further account with it, but I was wrong. What can we do? Men always make their plans without considering passion, the only true architect of our lives, which rebuilds its edifice, except when it destroys it entirely.'

Madame de Cambes smiled: she recalled that Monsieur de La Rochefoucauld had said that, for the lovely eyes of Madame de Longueville, he had made war against kings and would make war against the gods.

The smile was not lost on the duke, who, not allowing the viscountess time to follow the smile with the thought that had inspired it, went on: 'But you, Madame, let me compliment you, because you are a model of daring.'

'How is that?'

'Why, travelling alone like this, with a single servant, like a Clorinda or a Bradamante![24] Oh, by the way, I learned of the charming part you played in Chantilly. They assure me that you admirably deceived a poor devil of a royal officer ... An easy victory, I suppose?' the duke added, with that smile and that look, which, in him, meant so much.

'What do you mean?' Claire asked, with concern.

'I say "easy", because he was not competing with you on equal terms. However, one thing did strike me in the account I was given of this adventure.'

And the duke stared even more closely at the viscountess with his small, piercing eyes.

Madame de Cambes had no possibility of retreat, so she prepared to defend herself as strenuously as she could.

'Tell me, Duke,' she said, 'what was the thing that struck you?'

'It was your extreme skill, Madame, in playing this little comedy. Indeed, if I am to believe what one tells me, the officer had already seen your groom and yourself.'

These last words, although spoken with all the reserve of a

tactful man, nonetheless made a profound impression on Madame de Cambes.

'You are saying that he had already seen me, Monsieur?'

'One moment, Madame. Let's be clear: I am not the one who is saying it, but that still undefined character whom we call "one", to the power of whose words kings are subject as are the meanest of their subjects.'

'And where was I seen?'

'*One* says that it was on the road from Libourne to Chantilly, in a village called Jaulnay; however, the interview was not long, the gentleman having received an order from Monsieur d'Epernon to leave at once for Mantes.'

'But if the gentleman had seen me, Duke, how was it that he did not recognize me?'

'Ah! The famous *one* whom I mentioned just now – and who has a reply for everything – says that the interview took place in the dark.'

The viscountess was quivering with emotion. 'This time, Duke,' she said, 'I really don't know what you are implying.'

'In that case,' the duke replied, with affected geniality, 'I must have been misinformed, and then, after all, what is a momentary encounter? It's true, Madame,' he added, ingratiatingly, 'that your figure and your face are such as to leave a deep impression even after a brief meeting.'

'But it's not possible anyway,' said the viscountess, 'since, as you said yourself, the interview took place in darkness.'

'Quite right and very acute of you, Madame. So I was wrong – unless, of course, the young man had already noticed you before that interview, in which case, though, the adventure at Jaulnay would not be an encounter exactly . . .'

'What would it be, then?' Claire asked. 'Beware of what you are saying, Duke.'

'And so, as you see, I am leaving the matter. Our dear French language is so impoverished that I am looking in vain for a word to express my thought. It would be . . . an *appuntamento*, as the Italians say, or an *assignation*, as the English put it.'

'But unless I am mistaken, Duke,' said Claire, 'those two words are translated into French as *rendez-vous*.'

'Well, now, listen to me: I'm being ridiculous in two languages, and I have met someone who happens to know both of
them! Forgive me, Madame: it seems that Italian and English
really are as impoverished as French.'

Claire pressed her left hand to her heart, so that she could
breathe more easily: she was suffocating. Something occurred
to her that she had always suspected, which was that Monsieur
de La Rochefoucauld had, at least in thought and in desire,
been unfaithful to Madame de Longueville with her and that if
he was speaking in that way he was driven by a feeling of
jealousy. Indeed, two years earlier, the Prince de Marsillac had
courted Claire as assiduously as was possible for this cunning
man, with the constant doubts and endless timidity that made
him the most implacable of enemies when he was not the most
grateful of friends. So the viscountess preferred not to quarrel
openly with a man who combined public affairs with the most
private considerations in this way.

'Do you know, Duke,' she said, 'that you are a precious asset,
above all in our present circumstances, when Mazarin, despite the pride he has in his spies, has less effective intelligence
than yours?'

'If I knew nothing, Madame,' the Duke de La Rochefoucauld
replied, 'I should be only too like that dear minister, and then
I should have no reason to make war on him. Consequently,
I try to keep informed of almost everything.'

'Even the secrets of your allies – should they have any?'

'You have just said something that could be taken very badly
were one to interpret it as "a woman's secret". So were that
journey and that meeting a secret, then?'

'Let us be quite clear, Duke, because you are only half
right. The meeting was an accident. The journey was a secret,
and even a women's secret, because it was indeed known only
to me and the princess.'

The duke smiled. This good defence sharpened his perspicacity.

'And to Lenet,' he said. 'And to Richon and Madame de
Tourville, and even to a certain Viscount de Cambes, who is
unknown to me and whose name I heard mentioned for the

first time on this occasion ... It's true that, since he is your brother, you will say that this means that the secret did not go outside the family.'

Claire began to laugh, to avoid irritating the duke, whose eyebrow she could already see starting to twitch.

'Do you know one thing?' she asked.

'No, but tell me, and if it is a secret, I promise you, Madame, that I shall be as discreet as you and tell only my general staff.'

'Well, do so, I ask nothing better, even though I risk making an enemy of a great princess whose hatred it is not a good idea to incur.'

The duke blushed imperceptibly.

'So what is this secret?' he asked.

'In this journey that they got me to undertake, do you know who was the companion that the princess intended for me?'

'No.'

'It was you.'

'Ah, yes, I remember the princess getting someone to ask me if I could serve as escort to a person who was returning from Libourne to Paris.'

'And you refused.'

'I was unavoidably detained in Poitou.'

'Yes, you had to receive some dispatches from Madame de Longueville.'

La Rochefoucauld looked keenly at the viscountess, as if raking the depths of her heart, before the trace of her words had vanished and, coming closer to her, said: 'Are you reproaching me for that?'

'Not at all, Duke, your heart is so well placed in that respect that you are entitled to compliments rather than reproaches.'

'Ah!' he sighed, in spite of himself. 'Would to heaven that I had made the journey with you.'

'Why is that?'

'Because I should not have gone to Saumur,' he said, in a tone of voice that implied he had another reply ready, but either did not dare or did not wish to make it.

Claire thought: 'Richon must be the one who told him everything.'

'But in any event,' the duke continued, 'I am not complaining about my private misfortune since it was to the general good.'

'What are you saying, Duke? I don't understand.'

'I mean that if I had been with you, you would not have met this officer, who, as it turned out – so well does heaven protect our cause – was the same that Mazarin sent to Chantilly.'

'Oh, Duke! Don't joke about that unfortunate officer,' said Claire, her voice choking with the memory of a recent event.

'Why not? Is he some sacred figure?'

'Yes, he is now, because great misfortunes consecrate noble hearts as much as great good fortune. That officer may now be dead, having paid with his life for his mistake or his loyalty.'

'Dead for love?' asked the duke.

'Please be serious, Monsieur. You know very well that if I were to give my heart to anyone, it would not be to a chance acquaintance on the highway. I am telling you that the unfortunate man was arrested this very day on the order of Monsieur de Mazarin.'

'Arrested!' said the duke. 'How do you know? Another encounter?'

'Why, yes, as it happens. I was passing through Jaulnay. Do you know Jaulnay?'

'Very well. I took a sword wound in the shoulder there . . . So, you were passing through Jaulnay, and then, is that not the same village that the story tells us of?'

'Let's forget the story, Duke,' Claire said, blushing. 'I was passing through Jaulnay, as I said, when I saw a troop of armed men arresting a man and taking him away. He was that man.'

'He was! Oh, beware, Madame, you said "he".'

'He, the officer. My word, Duke, how deep you are. Please, enough of your wit, and if you do not feel pity for that unfortunate . . .'

'Pity! I!' exclaimed the duke. 'Why, Madame, do I have time to feel pity, especially for those I do not know?'

Claire looked askance at La Rochefoucauld's pale face and his thin lips bent into a cold smile, and she shuddered involuntarily.

'I should like to have the honour of escorting you further,

Madame,' he went on. 'But I must put a garrison in Montraud, so please forgive me if I leave you. Twenty gentlemen who are more fortunate than I will protect you until you meet up with the princess, to whom I beg you to present my respects.'

'You are not coming to Bordeaux?' Claire asked.

'No, for the time being I have to go to Turenne to meet Monsieur de Bouillon. We are vying to refuse politely the role of general in this war. I have a strong opponent, but I would like to overcome him and remain a lieutenant.'

With this, the duke ceremonially saluted the viscountess and headed off slowly along the road taken by his troop of cavalry.

Claire looked after him, murmuring: 'His pity! I mentioned his pity! He said it himself: he hasn't time to feel pity!'

At this moment she saw a group of horsemen break off towards her, and the rest of the troop disappear into the nearby wood.

Behind them, meditatively, his reins resting on his horse's neck, rode the man with the deceptive eyes and white hands, who would later, at the start of his memoirs, write the following observation – rather a strange one for a moral philosopher: 'I think that one must be content with showing compassion, but beware of feeling it. It is a passion that is good for naught in a well-made soul, one that only serves to weaken the heart. It should be left to the common people, who, never acting from reason, need passion to accomplish anything.'[25]

Two days later, Madame de Cambes had rejoined the princess.

XII

Madame de Cambes had many times instinctively considered what might come of attracting the hatred of someone like Monsieur de La Rochefoucauld, but since she was young, beautiful, rich and well in favour, she did not realize that this hatred, assuming that it should occur, could ever have a fateful influence on her life.

However, when Madame de Cambes knew for certain that he had been enough concerned about her to have learned what he knew, she decided to make the first move with the princess.

'Madame,' she said, in reply to the compliments that the princess was paying her, 'don't be too quick to congratulate me on the skill that I am supposed to have shown on that occasion, because some people are suggesting that the officer that we fooled, in reality knew the truth about the real and the pretend Princess de Condé.'

However, since this assumption denied the princess the share of the credit that she claimed for her part in carrying out the ruse, she was naturally unwilling to believe this.

'Yes, yes, my dear Claire,' she replied. 'Yes, I understand. Now that our gentleman sees that we have tricked him, he is trying to claim that he was humouring us. Unfortunately, he is taking this line a bit late – after waiting to be disgraced for his mistake! But, incidentally, you told me that you met Monsieur de La Rochefoucauld on your way?'

'Yes, Madame.'

'What news did he give you?'

'He told me he was going to Turenne to consult Monsieur de Bouillon.'

'Yes, there is a conflict between them, I know. Although each pretends to refuse the honour, it is about which one will be the general-in-chief of our army. And then, when we make peace, the more fearsome the rebel has been, the higher the price he will be able to demand to rejoin us. But Madame de Tourville has given me a plan to make them agree.'

The viscountess smiled at the mention of this name: 'Ah! Is Your Highness reconciled with her counsellor?'

'Needs must. She met us at Montrond, bearing her roll of paper with such solemnity that Lenet and I were dying with laughter.'

'"Although Your Highness attaches no importance to these reflections," she said, "which are the fruit of industrious burning of the midnight oil, I am bringing my tribute to the general cause."'

'Was that really what she said?'

'Word for word.'

'And Your Highness replied?'

'I didn't. I referred her to Lenet, who said: "Madame, we have never doubted your zeal, still less your wisdom; they are so precious to us that the princess and I every day regretted not having them . . ." Finally, he said such a host of fine things to her that she was captivated, and eventually she gave him her plan.'

'Which is?'

'To appoint neither Monsieur de Bouillon nor Monsieur de La Rochefoucauld general-in-chief, but Monsieur de Turenne.'

'Upon my word,' Claire said, 'it seems to me that the counsellor gave you good counsel this time. What does Monsieur Lenet say?'

'I say that the viscountess is right and that she adds a further good voice to our deliberations,' Lenet replied, coming in at that moment with a roll of paper that he was holding as gravely as Madame de Tourville might have done. 'Unfortunately, Monsieur de Turenne cannot leave the army in the north, and our plan requires him to march on Paris when Mazarin and the queen march on Bordeaux.'

'Observe, my dear, that Lenet is the man of impossibilities. So it is not Monsieur de Bouillon, or Monsieur de La Rochefoucauld, or Monsieur de Turenne who is our general-in-chief. Our general-in-chief is Lenet! What does Your Excellency have there? Is it a proclamation?'

'Yes, Madame.'

'Madame de Tourville's, of course.'

'Precisely, Madame. Apart from a few necessary alterations to the wording – the chancellery style, you understand . . .'

'Fine, fine!' said the princess, laughing. 'We are not concerned with every letter. As long as the spirit is there, that's all we need.'

'It is, Madame.'

'And where will Monsieur de Bouillon sign?'

'On the same line as Monsieur de La Rochefoucauld.'

'That doesn't tell me where Monsieur de La Rochefoucauld will sign, though.'

'Monsieur de La Rochefoucauld will sign underneath the Duke d'Enghien.'

'The Duke d'Enghien should not sign such an act. A child! Think of it, Lenet.'

'I have done so, Madame. When the king dies, the dauphin succeeds him, if only for a day. Why should the same not be true of the house of Condé as it is for the house of France?'

'But what will Monsieur de La Rochefoucauld say? And Monsieur de Bouillon?'

'The first has spoken, Madame, and left after he spoke; the second will know about the matter when it is done and so will say what he likes, it is of no consequence to us.'

'And is this the cause of the coldness that the duke showed towards you, Claire?'

'Leave him cold, Madame,' said Lenet. 'He will warm up at the first cannon that the Marshal de La Meilleraie fires against us. These gentlemen wish to make war, so let them make it!'

'Beware of upsetting them too much, Lenet,' said the princess. 'They are all we have.'

'And they have only your name. Let them try to fight on their own behalf, and you'll see how long they last. Tit for tat.'

Madame de Tourville had come in a few seconds earlier, and the radiant, beaming smile on her face had given way to a hint of anxiety, which was increased by the last words of her rival, the counsellor.

She hurried forward.

'Could it be that the plan that I suggested to Your Highness was unfortunate enough not to receive the approval of Monsieur Lenet?'

'On the contrary, Madame,' said Lenet, bowing. 'I have kept the greater part of your report. However, instead of the proclamation being signed by the Duke de Bouillon or the Duke de La Rochefoucauld, it will be signed by the Duke d'Enghien. The names of the other gentlemen will come after that of the prince.'

'You will compromise the young prince, Monsieur.'

'It is only right that he should be compromised, Madame, since he is the one for whom we are fighting.'

'But the people of Bordeaux like the Duke de Bouillon, they adore Monsieur de La Rochefoucauld, but they don't even know the Duke d'Enghien.'

'There you are wrong,' Lenet replied, as usual taking a piece of paper from his pocket, the capacity of which always astonished the princess. 'Here is a letter from the president of the parliament of Bordeaux, in which he begs me to have proclamations signed by the young duke.'

'Huh! Scoff at parliaments, Lenet,' the princess exclaimed. 'There's no point in escaping from the power of the queen and Monsieur de Mazarin if we are to fall under that of the parliaments.'

'Does Your Highness wish to enter Bordeaux?' asked Lenet.

'Of course.'

'Then that is the *sine qua non*. They won't fire a shot for anyone except the Duke d'Enghien.'

Madame de Tourville bit her lip.

'So,' the princess continued, 'you have made us flee Chantilly and cover a hundred and fifty leagues only to be insulted by the people of Bordeaux?'

'What you consider an insult, Madame, is in fact an honour. What could be more flattering, indeed, for the Princess de Condé to see that she is the one being welcomed and not the others?'

'So the Bordelais will not receive the two dukes?'

'They will only receive Your Highness.'

'What can I do alone?'

'Why, go in anyway, and as you do so, leave the gate open, and the others will come in after you.'

'We cannot do without them.'

'That is my opinion, and in a fortnight it will be the opinion of the parliament. Bordeaux is repulsing your army, but in a fortnight it will call on you for its defence. Then you will have the credit of having twice done what the townsfolk asked, and at that moment, have no fear, they will die for you, from the first to the last.'

'So is Bordeaux threatened?' asked Madame de Tourville.

'Very much so,' said Lenet. 'This is why it is urgent for us to take up our position there. While we are not there, the city can, without compromising its honour, refuse to open its gates to us. But once we are inside, Bordeaux cannot chase us away without dishonouring itself.'

'And who is threatening Bordeaux, may I ask?'

'The king, the queen, Mazarin . . . The royal army is gathering strength and our enemies are taking up their positions. The Ile Saint-Georges, which is only three leagues from the city, has just received reinforcements, additional munitions and a new governor. The Bordelais will try to take the island, and, naturally, they will be beaten, because they will be facing the king's best troops. Once they have been well and truly thrashed, as it is only proper that they should be when city folk try to ape soldiers, then they will cry out loud for the dukes of Bouillon and La Rochefoucauld. And then, Madame, you, holding both these dukes in the palm of your hand, can make your own conditions to the parliament . . .'

'But would it not be better to try to win over this new governor before the people of Bordeaux have suffered a defeat that might discourage them?'

'If you are in Bordeaux when the defeat takes place, you have nothing to fear . . . As for winning over the governor, that's impossible.'

'Impossible? Why?'

'Because this governor is a personal enemy of Your Highness.'

'A personal enemy?'

'Yes.'

'And where does this enmity come from?'

'From the fact that he will never forgive Your Highness the trick that was played on him in Chantilly . . . Ah, Monsieur de Mazarin is not the fool that you persist in thinking that he is, ladies – even though I keep telling you the opposite. The proof is that he has put, in the Ile Saint-Georges, that is, in the key position in the country . . . Guess whom?'

'I've already told you that I have absolutely no idea who it might be.'

'Very well: it's the officer that you laughed so much at – and who, by some unbelievable mistake, let Your Highness escape from Chantilly.'

'Monsieur de Canolles!' Claire exclaimed.

'Yes.'

'Monsieur de Canolles is Governor of the Ile Saint-Georges?'

'The very same.'

'Impossible! I saw him being arrested in front of me, before my eyes . . .'

'Correct. But he must have powerful protection, and his disgrace has changed into favour.'

'And you thought he was already dead, my poor Claire!' said the princess, laughing.

'Are you quite sure, Monsieur?' Claire asked, in astonishment.

Lenet, as usual, put his hand in the famous pocket and took out a piece of paper.

'Here is a letter from Richon,' he said, 'which gives me all the details of the new governor's inauguration and expresses his regret that Your Highness did not place Richon himself in the Ile Saint-Georges.'

'The princess put Monsieur Richon in the Ile Saint-Georges!' said Madame de Tourville, with a triumphant laugh. 'Do we make the appointments of His Majesty's governors?'

'We do have one at our disposal, Madame,' Lenet retorted, 'and that is enough.'

'Which is that?'

Madame de Tourville shuddered as she saw Lenet put his hand into his pocket.

'The Duke d'Epernon's letter of attestation!' the princess exclaimed. 'That's right. I had forgotten.'

'Huh! What's that?' Madame de Tourville said contemptuously. 'A bit of paper, that's all!'

'This bit of paper,' Lenet said, 'is the nomination that we need to counterbalance the one that has just been made. It is the counterweight to the Ile Saint-Georges, in short, our salvation. It is another place on the Dordogne, as the Ile Saint-Georges is on the Garonne.'

'And are you sure that it is the same Monsieur de Canolles who was arrested in Jaulnay who is now Governor of the Ile Saint-Georges?' asked Claire, who had not listened to anything that had been said in the previous five minutes, still pondering the news that Lenet had given them, confirmed by Richon.

'I am sure of it, Madame.'

'Monsieur de Mazarin has an odd way of taking his governors to their posts.'

'Yes,' said the princess. 'And there must be something behind it.'

'There is,' said Lenet. 'There is Mademoiselle Nanon de Lartigues.'

'Nanon de Lartigues!' cried the viscountess, a dreadful memory gnawing at her heart.

'That slut!' said the princess contemptuously.

'Yes, Madame,' Lenet replied. 'That slut whom Your Highness refused to see when she begged the honour of being presented to you, and whom the queen, less strict than you are about the laws of etiquette, did receive. The result of which was that Nanon replied to your chamberlain that the Princess de Condé might indeed be a greater lady than Anne of Austria, but that Anne of Austria has decidedly more prudence than the Princess de Condé.'

'Your memory fails you, Lenet, or else you are trying to spare me,' the princess exclaimed. 'The insolent hussy did not only say "more prudence", she also said "more wit".'

'Possibly,' said Lenet with a smile. 'I was going into the antechamber at that moment and did not hear the end of the sentence.'

'But I was listening at the door,' said the princess, 'and I heard all of it.'

'Well, then,' said Lenet, 'you understand that this is a woman who will make war on you without remorse. The queen would send you soldiers to fight, Nanon will send you enemies who must be destroyed.'

'Perhaps, had you been in Her Highness's place,' Madame de Tourville said sourly to Lenet, 'you would have received her with reverence?'

'No, Madame,' said Lenet. 'I should have received her with a laugh, and I should have bought her.'

'Very well, then, we must buy her. There is still time.'

'There may still be time, but I think that now she will probably be too expensive for us.'

'So what is her price?' the princess asked.

'Five hundred thousand livres, before the war.'

'And now?'

'A million.'

'For that money I could buy Monsieur de Mazarin!'

'That might well be so,' said Lenet. 'Things that have already been sold and resold fall in price.'

Madame de Tourville was still in favour of violence: 'If we can't buy her, we must capture her!'

'You would be doing a real service to Her Highness if you could do that. But it will be a difficult task, since we have no idea where she is. In any case, let's not bother about that, but first of all enter Bordeaux and then take the Ile Saint-Georges.'

'No, no!' Claire exclaimed. 'No, let's first of all go into the Ile Saint-Georges!'

This exclamation, straight from the viscountess's heart, made both women turn towards her, while Lenet examined Claire as closely as Monsieur de La Rochefoucauld might do, though with added benevolence.

'You're mad,' said the princess. 'You heard Lenet say that the place is impregnable.'

'Perhaps,' said Claire, 'but I believe we will take it.'

'Do you have a plan?' asked Madame de Tourville, with the anxious look of a woman who fears that there may be a rival on the horizon.

'I may do,' said Claire.

'But if the Ile Saint-Georges costs as much as Lenet says,' the princess laughed, 'we may not be rich enough.'

'We shan't buy it,' said Claire, 'but we shall have it even so.'

'By force, then,' said Madame de Tourville. 'My dear, you're coming back to my plan.'

'That's right,' said the princess. 'We'll send Richon to besiege Saint-Georges. He comes from round there, he knows the place, and if any man can capture the fortress, which you claim is so impregnable, he's the one.'

'Before you do that,' said Claire, 'let me try something. If I fail, you can still do it in your own way.'

'What!' the princess exclaimed in astonishment. 'You will go to the Ile Saint-Georges?'

'I shall.'

'Alone?'

'With Pompée.'

'Are you afraid of nothing?'

'I shall go as a negotiator, if Your Highness will be so good as to appoint me.'

'Now that's something new!' Madame de Tourville cried. 'I really do think that you can't just invent a diplomat like that and that you have to make a long study of the art, that Monsieur de Tourville, one of the finest diplomats of his time, as he would also have been one of the greatest soldiers, claimed was the hardest art of all to master.'

'However inadequate I may be, Madame,' said Claire, 'I shall try nonetheless, if the princess will allow me to!'

'The princess will most certainly allow you,' said Lenet, glancing at Madame de Condé. 'I am even sure that if anyone in the world can succeed in this negotiation, you are that person . . .'

'And what will Madame do that no one else can?'

'Quite simple; she'll haggle over Monsieur de Canolles, which a man could not attempt without being thrown from the window.'

'A man, perhaps,' Madame de Tourville went on, 'but a woman . . .'

'If a woman is to go to the Ile Saint-Georges,' said Lenet, 'it might as well – or even, it had better – be Madame rather than anyone else, since she was the first to have the idea.'

At that moment, a messenger came in, bringing a letter from the parliament of Bordeaux.

'Ah, this must be the answer to my request,' said the princess.

The two women came over, driven by feelings of curiosity and interest, while Lenet stayed in his place, with his usual calm, no doubt knowing already what was in the letter. The princess read it eagerly.

'They are asking for me, calling for me, waiting for me!' she cried.

'Ah!' said Madame de Tourville triumphantly.

'What about the dukes, Madame?' asked Lenet. 'What about the army?'

'They don't mention those.'

'Then we are stripped bare,' said Madame de Tourville.

'No,' said the princess. 'Thanks to the Duke d'Epernon's letter of attestation, I shall have Vayres, which controls the Dordogne.'

'And I shall have Saint-Georges,' said Claire, 'which is the key to the Garonne.'

'And I,' said Lenet, 'shall have the dukes and the army, provided you give me time.'

BOOK III
VISCOUNTESS DE CAMBES

I

Two days later they arrived in sight of Bordeaux; they had to decide how they would enter the town. The dukes with their army were now only at a distance of around ten leagues, so they could try either to enter peacefully or by force. The essential thing was to decide whether it was better to rule in Bordeaux or to obey the parliament. The princess called a meeting of her council, which consisted of Madame de Tourville, Claire, her ladies-in-waiting and Lenet. Madame de Tourville, knowing her opponent, had strongly argued that he should not attend this council meeting, since the war was a war of women in which they only used men for fighting. But the princess insisted that Lenet had been imposed on her by her husband, the prince, so she could not keep him out of the council chamber, where, in any case, his presence would be quite unimportant, since they had agreed in advance that, while he could speak as much as he wished, no one would listen to him.

Madame de Tourville's caution was not pointless; she had spent the two days of marching that had just ended in turning the princess's head towards ideas of war (to which she was already only too inclined), and she was afraid that Lenet might again destroy all the scaffolding of her laboriously constructed edifice.

When the council had gathered, Madame de Tourville explained her plan, which was secretly to fetch the dukes and their army; to obtain, either by force or by persuasion, a certain number of boats, and to enter Bordeaux down the river, amid cries of: 'Join us, people of Bordeaux! Long live Condé! No to Mazarin!'

So the princess's entry would become a veritable triumph, and Madame de Tourville, by a roundabout way, returned to her famous plan of taking Bordeaux by force and so making the queen afraid of an army whose first outing would be such a brilliant show of strength.

Lenet nodded in approval of everything, interrupting Madame de Tourville with admiring exclamations, then, when she had finished describing her plan, he said: 'That's magnificent, Madame! Now, would you kindly sum it up for us.'

'That's easy and can be done in two words,' said the good woman in triumph, becoming excited by her own telling. 'Amid a hail of shot, to the sound of bells and the popular cries of fury or of adoration, weak women will be seen courageously pursuing their generous mission. A child will be seen in the arms of his mother begging the parliament for its protection. This touching spectacle will not fail to move the fiercest souls. And so we shall win: partly by force, partly by the justice of our cause – which is, I think, the aim of Her Highness the princess.'

The summary was even more of a success than the speech: the princess applauded. Claire, increasingly pricked by the desire to be appointed negotiator on the Ile Saint-Georges, applauded. The captain of the guards, whose role in life was to seek for great feats of swordsmanship, applauded. And, finally, Lenet did more than applaud: he took Madame de Tourville's hand and exclaimed, pressing it with more respect than feeling: 'Did I not know, Madame, how great is your prudence and how profoundly you understand the great civic and military question that concerns us – whether by instinct or through study, I do not know or care – I should surely be persuaded at this hour and bow before the most useful counsellor that Her Highness could ever find . . .'

'Isn't that right, Lenet?' said the princess. 'Isn't this a fine thing! That was my opinion, too. Come now, Vialas, quickly, let us give the Duke d'Enghien the little sword that I had made for him and dress him in his helmet and armour.'

'Yes, do that, Vialas. But just one word, first, if you please,

Madame,' said Lenet, while Madame de Tourville, at first puffed up with pride, was starting to deflate, being as she was well acquainted with Lenet's sly designs where she was concerned.

'Yes?' said the princess. 'Come on, what more is there?'

'Nothing, Madame, certainly not, because never was anything presented to us more in harmony with the character of a princess like yourself, and such an opinion could only possibly come from your family.'

These words produced a new puffing up of Madame de Tourville and brought a smile to the lips of the princess, who was starting to raise an eyebrow.

'But, Madame,' Lenet went on, his eyes following the effect of this terrible *but* on the face of his arch-enemy, 'while adopting this plan, the only suitable one, I shall not even say without repugnance, but with enthusiasm, I should like to suggest a slight modification to it.'

Madame de Tourville swung round, stiff, dry and ready to defend herself. The princess's eyebrow rose again.

Lenet bowed and made a gesture showing that he was asking for permission to go on.

'The sound of bells, the adoring cries of the people,' he said, 'fill me in advance with a joy greater than I can express. But I am not as happy as I should like to be with the hail of shots that Madame mentioned.'

Madame de Tourville pulled herself up, adopting a martial pose. Lenet bowed even deeper and continued, lowering his voice by half a tone: 'Certainly, it would be fine to see a woman and her child calm in the midst of this tempest that ordinarily frightens even men. But I would be afraid that one of those musket balls, striking blindly as brutal and unintelligent things are liable to do, might serve the cause of Monsieur de Mazarin against us and spoil our plan which is otherwise so magnificent. My opinion, as Madame de Tourville said with such eloquence, is that people should see the young prince and his noble mother opening a way to the Parliament, but by supplication, not by force of arms. In the end, I think it would be finer to soften the fiercest minds in this way than by other means to defeat the strongest hearts. Finally, I think that one of these two courses offers infinitely better chances of success than the other, and that the princess's aim, above all, is to enter Bordeaux. And I might say that nothing is less certain than that she will do so if we engage in battle.'

'You see,' Madame de Tourville sourly, 'this gentleman, as usual, is going to demolish my plan point by point and quietly suggest one of his own devising in its place.'

'I! The most devoted of your admirers!' Lenet exclaimed, while the princess was reassuring Madame de Tourville with a smile and a glance. 'No, no, a thousand times no! But I have learned that an officer of His Majesty's, called Monsieur Dalvimar, has entered the town coming from Blaye, and that his mission is to rouse the aldermen and the people against Her Highness. And I may add that if Monsieur de Mazarin can end the war in one fell swoop, he will do so. This is why I fear the hail of shots that Madame de Tourville mentioned just now – and among those shots, perhaps even more the intelligent musket balls than the brutal and unreasoning ones.'

This last remark by Lenet seemed to have given the princess pause for thought.

'You always know everything, don't you, Monsieur Lenet,' replied Madame de Tourville, in a voice trembling with anger.

'A good, hot skirmish would have been a fine thing, even so,' said the captain of the guard, drawing himself up and lunging forward as he might have done in a fencing school – an old soldier who believed in force and who would have gained a great deal of stature in the event of a battle.

Lenet trod on his foot while giving him the most friendly smile.

'Yes, Captain,' he said. 'But you do agree that the Duke d'Enghien is necessary to our cause and that if he were to be killed or captured, the real general-in-chief of the princes' army would be captured or killed?'

The captain of the guard, who knew that this high-sounding title of general-in-chief, apparently bestowed on a seven-year-old prince, in reality made him the first brigadier in the army, realized that he had done something foolish and gave up his proposal, giving whole-hearted support to Lenet.

Meanwhile, Madame de Tourville had gone over to the princess and said something to her in a whisper. Lenet saw that there would be a fresh battle to fight. And, so indeed, turning back to him, Her Highness said in an irritated voice: 'Nonetheless, it is strange to put so much relentless fury into undoing something that was so well put together.'

'Your Highness is wrong,' said Lenet. 'Never have I put relentless fury into the advice that I have had the honour to give Your Highness, and if I unmake, it is only in order to remake. If, despite the reasons that I have had the honour to put before you, Your Highness still wishes to have yourself killed together with your son, then you are the mistress, and we shall be killed at your side. This is a simple matter, and the first valet in your household or the least bumpkin in the town would do the same. But if we wish to succeed, despite Mazarin, despite the queen, despite the parliaments, despite Mademoiselle Nanon de Lartigues, and, finally, despite all the disadvantages that inevitably attach to the weakness of our position, this, I believe, is what we must do . . .'

'Monsieur!' Madame de Tourville cried, seizing on Lenet's last sentence. 'Monsieur, there is no weakness where you have the name of Condé on the one hand, and two thousand soldiers of Rocroi, Nordlingen and Lens[1] on the other. And if, despite that, there is weakness, then we are lost in any event, and it will not be your plan, however splendid that might be, that will save us.'

'I have read,' Lenet replied calmly, savouring in advance the effect that he was about to produce on the princess, who was listening closely, despite herself. 'I have read, Madame, that the widow of one of the most illustrious Romans under Tiberius, the generous Agrippina, whose husband Germanicus had been unjustly taken from her, a princess who could have raised at will an army seething at the memory of the dead general, preferred to enter Brindisi alone, to cross Puglia alone, dressed in widow's weeds and holding a child by each hand, and so march along, pale, her eyes red with tears, her head bowed, while the children sobbed and looked imploringly ... And that, seeing this, all those present, of whom there were more than two million between Brindisi and Rome, burst into tears, overflowed with curses and shouted out threats, and that this woman's cause was won not only in Rome but throughout Italy;[2] not only for her contemporaries, but for posterity, because she found not a hint of resistance to her tears and sighs, while if she had offered lances, she would have seen pikes against them, and swords against swords. I think that there is much resemblance between Your Highness and Agrippina, as there is between the prince and Germanicus – and, finally, between Piso, the minister who was a persecutor and a poisoner, and Monsieur de Mazarin. Well, since the resemblance is identical and the situation comparable, I suggest that we should follow the same course, because in my view it is impossible that what succeeded so well in one age should not succeed in another ...'

A smile of approval spread across the princess's face and assured Lenet that his speech had succeeded. Madame de Tourville took refuge in a corner of the room, pulling a veil across her face like an antique statue. Madame de Cambes, who had found a friend in Lenet, returned the support that he had given her by nodding her head, the captain wept like a military tribune, and the little Duke d'Enghien cried: 'Mummy, will you hold my hand and dress me in mourning?'

'Yes, Son,' the princess replied. 'Lenet, you know that I have always intended to present myself to the people of Bordeaux dressed in black ...'

'All the more so,' said Madame de Cambes, 'since black is so becoming to Your Highness.'

'Hush, dear girl!' said the princess. 'Madame de Tourville will proclaim it loudly enough without you even having to whisper it.'

The programme for the entry into Bordeaux was thus drawn up as Lenet had suggested. The ladies of the escort were ordered to get ready, and the young prince was dressed in a coat of white baize decked with black and silver braid, and a hat covered with black and white feathers.

As for the princess, she dressed in black with no jewellery, affecting the greatest possible simplicity so as to resemble Agrippina, on whom she had decided to model herself on all points.

Lenet, the director of the event, rushed around everywhere to ensure a brilliant success. The house where he lived, in a little town two leagues from Bordeaux, was constantly full of supporters of the princess, who, before getting her to enter Bordeaux, wanted to find out what kind of entry would be most acceptable to her. Lenet, like a modern theatrical director, advised them on flowers, cheers and bells; then, wanting to give some recognition to the warlike Madame de Tourville, suggested a few cannon shots.

On the following day, 31 May, at the invitation of the parliament of Bordeaux, the princess set out. In fact, a certain Lavie, advocate general to the parliament and a fanatical supporter of Mazarin, had ordered the gates to be closed two days earlier to stop the princess from being welcomed in if she should present herself; however, at the same time, the supporters of the Condés had acted, and that same morning, excited by them, the crowd had assembled to cries of: 'Long live the princess! Long live the Duke d'Enghien!', before breaking down the gates with axes, so that in the end nothing stood in the way of the famous entry into Bordeaux, which thus took on the appearance of a veritable triumph. In addition to which, observers could see the two events as reflecting the two leaders whose supporters divided the town, since Lavie received advice directly from the Duke d'Epernon, and the populace had its leaders advised by Lenet.

Hardly had the princess got through the gate than the scene, which had long been prepared, took place on a massive scale. A military salute was given by the ships that were in the harbour, and the town's cannon replied. Flowers fell from the windows or covered the way in garlands, so that the streets were carpeted with them and the air perfumed.[3] Cries of welcome were chanted by thirty thousand enthusiasts of all ages and both sexes, whose support grew with the interest inspired by the princess and her son, and the hatred that they felt for Mazarin.

Moreover, the little Duke d'Enghien was the most accomplished actor on the whole of this stage. The princess had decided not to lead him by the hand for fear of tiring him or having him smothered by roses, so he was carried by one of his equerries, with the result that his hands were free to blow kisses to right and left, and to doff his plumed hat gracefully.

The people of Bordeaux are easily intoxicated: the women were moved to frenzied adoration of this lovely child who wept so charmingly, and old magistrates were touched by the little orator's words when he told them: 'Gentlemen, be a father to me, since the cardinal has taken mine away.'

The supporters of the minister tried in vain to put up some opposition: fists, stones and even halberds advised them to be cautious. They had to leave the field to the victors.

Meanwhile, Madame de Cambes, pale and serious, walking behind the princess, attracted her own share of attention. She did not consider such glory without it occurring to her painfully that today's success might make them forget yesterday's resolution. So while she was on the road, jostled by admirers, trampled by the crowd, inundated with flowers and respectful caresses and trembling at the idea of being carried in triumph (as some were now threatening to do with the princess, the Duke d'Enghien and their attendants), seeing Lenet, who, noticing her difficulty, offered her his hand to get into his carriage, she said, replying to his own thoughts: 'Ah, you are a happy man, Monsieur Lenet: you make your opinions prevail in everything, and your advice is always followed. It is true,' she added, 'that it is good advice and to our benefit . . .'

'It seems to me,' Lenet said, 'that you have nothing to complain about, Madame, and that the one piece of advice that you gave was approved.'

'How do you mean?'

'Isn't it agreed that you should try to win us the Ile Saint-Georges?'

'Yes, but when shall I be allowed to start my campaign?'

'As soon as tomorrow, if you promise me that you will fail.'

'Have no fear: I am only worried that I might meet your expectations in that respect.'

'So much the better.'

'I don't quite understand . . .'

'We need the Ile Saint-Georges to resist if we are to obtain our two dukes and their army from the people of Bordeaux. The dukes and the army, which, I must say, even though my opinion on this point comes close to that of Madame de Tourville, appear to me to be entirely necessary to us in our present circumstances.'

'Certainly,' Claire replied. 'But, although I do not have Madame de Tourville's understanding of the arts of war, it seems to me that one does not attack a place without first requiring it to yield.'

'That is quite right.'

'So we shall be sending an emissary to the Ile Saint-Georges?'

'Undoubtedly.'

'Well, I ask that I may be that emissary.'

Lenet's eyes widened in surprise.

'You!' he said. 'You? But have all our ladies become amazons, then?'

'Allow me this whim, my dear Lenet.'

'You are right. The worst thing that can happen, after all, is for you to capture Saint-Georges.'

'So is it agreed?'

'Yes.'

'But promise me one thing.'

'What is that?'

'That no one shall know the name or the nature of the emissary whom you have chosen, unless that emissary is successful.'

'Agreed,' said Lenet, offering Madame de Cambes his hand.

'When shall I leave?'

'When you like.'

'Tomorrow.'

'Very well, tomorrow.'

'Good. Now the princess and her son are about to go up on the terrace of President de Lalasne, I shall leave my share of the triumph to Madame de Tourville. Please make my excuses to Her Highness, saying that I am indisposed. Have me taken to the lodging that has been prepared for me. I am going to make my preparations and reflect on my mission, which gives me some anxiety, since it is the first of its kind that I have undertaken, and they say that everything in this world depends on the beginning.'

'*Peste!*' said Lenet. 'I am not surprised any longer that Monsieur de La Rochefoucauld was on the point of being unfaithful to Madame de Longueville over you: you are her equal in some respects and much better in others.'

'That may be,' said Claire. 'I do not entirely dismiss the compliment, but if you should have any influence with Monsieur de La Rochefoucauld, my dear Lenet, strengthen him in his first love, because the second frightens me!'

'Well, well, we shall do our best,' said Lenet with a smile. 'This evening I shall give you your instructions.'

'So do you agree that I should take Saint-Georges for you?'

'So be it, if that is what you want.'

'And the two dukes and the army?'

'I have another way up my sleeve to make them come here.'

And, after giving the coachman the address of the place where Madame de Cambes was to stay, he took his leave of her with a smile and went to join the princess.

II

The day after the entry of the princess to Bordeaux, there was a great dinner on the Ile Saint-Georges, Canolles having invited the chief officers of the garrison and other governors in the province.

At two in the afternoon, the time set for the start of the meal, Canolles thus found himself amid some dozen gentlemen, most of whom he was meeting for the first time, and who, in describing the previous day's great event, were making fun of the ladies who accompanied the princess, saying that they did not look very much like people about to engage in a military campaign and to whom the most serious interests of the kingdom have been entrusted.

Canolles, radiant, splendidly attired in his gilded coat, fuelled the merriment by example. Dinner was about to be served.

'Gentlemen,' he said, 'I beg you accept my apologies, but one guest is still missing.'

'Who is that?' the young people asked, looking at one another.

'The Governor of Vayres, to whom I wrote, though I do not know him – and who, precisely because I do not know him, has the right to some consideration. So I would ask you to let me give him another half hour's grace.'

'The Governor of Vayres!' said an old officer, no doubt accustomed to military punctuality, who had sighed at the idea of this delay. 'The Governor of Vayres! But wait: I think that is the Marquis de Bernay. But he does not manage the fort himself. He has a lieutenant.'

'In that case,' said Canolles, 'he will not come, or else his lieutenant will come in his stead. As for the marquis, he is no doubt at court, the abode of favours.'

'But, Baron,' said one of those in the room, 'I don't think it is necessary to be at court to get on: there's one commander I know who should have no complaints. Why! In three months: captain, lieutenant-colonel and Governor of the Ile Saint-Georges. Not a bad career, you must admit.'

'I do,' said Canolles, blushing. 'And since I don't know what I should thank for these favours, I just have to accept that there is some good genie in my house, since it is prospering so well.'

'We know who the governor's good genie is,' said the lieutenant who had made Canolles's introduction into the fortress, with a bow. 'It's his own merit.'

'I don't deny the merit, far from it,' replied another officer. 'I'm the first to recognize it. But I should add to that merit the recommendation of a certain lady, the most intelligent, benevolent and adorable woman in France – after the queen, of course.'

'Enough of beating about the bush,' said Canolles, smiling at this new speaker. 'If you have any secrets of your own, keep them for yourself. If they belong to your friends, keep them for them.'

'I must confess,' said an officer, 'that when I heard speak of a delay, I thought that we should receive an apology for some magnificent costume. Now I see that I was mistaken.'

'Shall we be dining without ladies, then?' asked another.

'Why, unless I were to invite the princess and her attendants,' said Canolles, 'I really can't see whom we might have. And don't forget, gentlemen, that ours is a serious dinner: if we wish to talk business, at least we shall only be annoying ourselves.'

'Well said, Commander, though in truth, if we are not careful, the ladies will be undertaking at this moment a veritable crusade against our authority. Just consider what the cardinal said in my presence to Don Louis de Haro.'

'And what did he say?' Canolles asked.

'"You are very lucky! Spanish women are concerned only with money, with their appearance and with admirers, while women in France no longer take a lover without quizzing him on his politics, to the point where," he said despairingly, "a lovers' tryst nowadays is spent in serious consideration of affairs of state."'

'Hence,' said Canolles, 'the fact that the war in which we are engaged is called the women's war, which is nothing if not flattering for us.'

At that moment, since the half hour's delay that Canolles had requested was over, the door opened and a lackey appeared, announcing that the governor was to be served.

Canolles invited his guests to follow him, but as they were starting to do so, another announcement rang across the ante-chamber: 'The Governor of Vayres!'

'Ah!' said Canolles. 'This is most kind of him.'

He stepped forward to greet a colleague whom he did not know, but suddenly started back in surprise.

'Richon!' he exclaimed. 'Richon – Governor of Vayres!'

'Indeed so, my dear baron,' Richon replied, maintaining his usual serious air, despite his affability.

'But so much the better! A thousand times so!' said Canolles, warmly shaking him by the hand, and adding: 'Gentlemen, you do not know this gentleman, but I do, and I tell you plainly that one could not give an important post to a finer man.'

Richon surveyed his surroundings with his usual proud look, as haughty as an attentive eagle, and seeing only a slight surprise, moderated by a great deal of goodwill, in those around him, he said: 'My dear baron, now that you have given me such a fine recommendation, I beg you to introduce me to those of these gentlemen whom I do not have the honour to know.'

Richon looked towards two or three of those present to whom he was a total stranger.

There followed an exchange of those extreme civilities that gave all relationships at that time a character at once so noble and so sociable. A quarter of an hour later, Richon was a friend of all those young officers and could ask any one of them for the use of his sword or his purse. His warrant was his well-known courage, his unblemished reputation and the nobility imprinted in his look.

'By heavens, gentlemen!' said the Commander of Braunes. 'You must admit that, a man of the church though he may be, Monsieur de Mazarin does know a thing or two about soldiers and has been managing affairs well for some time. He scents the coming of war and chooses his governors: Canolles here, Richon in Vayres.'

'Are we to fight, then?' Richon asked casually.

'Are we to fight!' retorted a young man, coming in directly from the courtyard. 'Are you asking if we are to fight, Monsieur Richon?'

'Yes.'

'Well, then, I for my part would ask you what is the state of your bastions?'

'They are more or less new, Monsieur, because in the three days that I have been there, I have made more repairs than had been done over the previous three years.'

'Well, it's not long before they'll get their first taste of fire.'

'Very good,' said Richon. 'What do soldiers want? War!'

'That's fine,' said Canolles. 'The king can sleep easy, because he is holding the people of Bordeaux in check with his two rivers.'

'The fact is that the person who put me there can count on me,' said Richon.

'And how long do you say you have been in Vayres?'

'For three days. What about you, Canolles: how long in Saint-Georges?'

'A week. Were you given a welcome like mine, Richon? My entrance was splendid, and, to tell the truth, I haven't yet sufficiently thanked these gentlemen for it. I had the bells, the drums, the huzzahs and everything except the cannon – but I'm promised that very shortly, which consoles me.'

'Well, there's the difference between us,' said Richon. 'My entrance, my dear Canolles, was as simple as yours was magnificent. I had the order to introduce a hundred men into the fortress, a hundred men of the regiment of Turenne, and I did not know how I would do it, when my warrant arrived at Saint-Pierre, where I was staying, signed by Monsieur d'Epernon. I set out at once, gave my letter to the lieutenant and, with no drums or trumpets, I took over. And now, there I am.'

Canolles, who had been laughing at first, felt his heart tighten with a sinister premonition on hearing how the last words were spoken.

'And you are at home there?' he asked Richon.

'I'm arranging to be so,' Richon replied calmly.

'And how many men do you have?'

'First of all, the hundred men from the regiment of Turenne, old soldiers from Rocroi, who can be counted on, and with them a company that I am mustering in the town and training as the recruits turn up: tradespeople, young men, workers ... around two hundred men. Lastly, I am expecting a final reinforcement of a hundred or a hundred and fifty men who have been recruited by a captain of the region.'

'Captain Ramblay?' one of the guests asked.

'No, Captain Cauvignac,' Richon replied.

'Don't know him,' several of them replied.

'But I do know him,' said Canolles.

'Is he a tried and trusted royalist?'

'I can't say, one way or the other. But I have every reason to think that Captain Cauvignac is a protégé of Monsieur d'Epernon and devoted to the duke.'

'Well, that answers it: whoever is devoted to the duke is devoted to His Majesty.'

'He's someone associated with the king's advance guard,' said the old officer, who was catching up, now they were at table, with the time he had lost waiting. 'I've heard people speak of him in that way.'

'Is His Majesty on his way?' Richon asked in his usual calm manner.

'At this moment,' replied the young man from the court, 'the king must at least have reached Blois.'

'Are you sure?'

'Very much so. The army will be commanded by Marshal de La Meilleraie, who is due to meet up somewhere near here with the Duke d'Epernon.'

'At Saint-Georges, perhaps?' said Canolles.

'Or more probably in Vayres,' said Richon. 'Monsieur de La Meilleraie will be coming from Britanny, and Vayres is on his way.'

'Whoever suffers the assault of the two armies will find his ramparts have a hard time of it,' said the Governor of Braunes. 'Monsieur de la Meilleraie has thirty pieces of cannon, and Monsieur d'Epernon has twenty-five.'

'It will make a fine firework show,' said Canolles. 'It's a pity we won't see it.'

'Unless one of us declares for the princes,' said Richon.

'Yes, but Canolles, at least, is sure to see some kind of action. If he does declare for the princes, he will be fired on by Monsieur de La Meilleraie and Monsieur d'Epernon, while if he stays loyal to His Majesty, he will take the fire of the people of Bordeaux.'

'Oh, where those last are concerned,' Canolles replied, 'I don't think they are very fearsome, and I must confess I am a little ashamed at only having to deal with them. Unfortunately, I belong heart and soul to His Majesty, so I shall have to make do with a purely bourgeois war.'

'Which you shall have, don't worry,' said Richon.

'Do you know if there is a possibility of that?' Canolles asked.

'Better than that,' said Richon. 'I know it for a certainty. The council of townsfolk decided that the first thing they would do would be to take the Ile Saint-Georges.'

'Very well,' said Canolles. 'I'm expecting them.'

They had reached this point in the conversation and were just starting on the dessert, when suddenly there was a sound of drums beating at the gate of the fortress.

'What does that mean?' Canolles asked.

'Why, by heaven!' exclaimed the young officer who had given news of the court. 'It would be an odd thing if they were to attack you right now, my dear Canolles. What a delightful after-dinner treat an assault and an escalade would be!'

'By the devil, it looks very much like it to me,' said the old commander. 'Those wretched townsfolk are always bothering one during one's siesta. I was in the forward line at Charenton in the days of the War of Paris and we could never have lunch or dinner in peace.'

Canolles rang, and the orderly from the antechamber came in.

'What's going on?' Canolles asked.

'I don't know yet, Governor. Some messenger from the king or from the town, I expect.'

'Find out and bring me the news.' The soldier left at the double. 'Come, gentlemen, let's go back to our meal,' Canolles said to his guests, most of whom had got up. 'It will be time for us to leave the table when we hear the cannon.'

All the guests sat down again, laughing. Only Richon, whose face had clouded, remained uneasy, his eyes fixed on the door, waiting for the soldier to return. But, instead of the orderly, an officer arrived, with drawn sword, announcing: 'Monsieur, a negotiator has arrived.'

'A negotiator?' said Canolles. 'On whose behalf?'

'From the princes . . .'

'Coming from where?'

'From Bordeaux.'

'From Bordeaux!' all the guests exclaimed, except Richon.

'Well, I never! That means war has really been declared,' said the old officer. 'If they're sending negotiators.'

Canolles thought for a moment, and in that moment his face,

which had been smiling only ten minutes before, took on all the gravity demanded by the occasion.

'Gentlemen,' he said. 'Duty above all. I am probably going to have a hard question to resolve with the emissary of the Bordelais. I do not know when I shall be able to rejoin you.'

'No, no!' cried the guests, as one man. 'Send us away, Commander: what is happening to you is a warning to all of us to go back to our respective posts. It is important therefore that we should separate at once.'

'It was not for me to suggest it, gentlemen,' said Canolles. 'But since you make the offer, I am forced to admit that it is the most prudent course, and I accept. Bring these gentlemen's horses and carriages!'

Almost at once, as quickly as though they were already on the battlefield, the guests leapt into the saddle or got into their coaches, and, followed by their escorts, set off towards their various residences.

Richon was the last to leave.

'Baron,' he said to Canolles, 'I did not want to leave you exactly as the others did, seeing that we have known one another longer than you have known them. So farewell, now, give me your hand – and good luck!'

Canolles shook Richon's hand.

'Richon,' he said, looking at him closely, 'I know you: there is something going on inside you. You will not tell me what, because it is probably not your secret to tell . . . Yet you are troubled . . . and when a man of your stamp is troubled, it is not for a trifle.'

'Isn't it because we shall be apart?' asked Richon.

'We were going to be apart when we said goodbye to each other at Biscarros's inn, yet then you were calm . . .'

Richon smiled sadly.

'Baron,' he said, 'I have a premonition that we shall not see one another again!'

Canolles shuddered: the normally firm voice of the daring partisan had such a note of profound melancholy as he said this.

'Well, if we do not see one another again, Richon,' he said, 'that will be because one of us two will be dead . . . and have died a soldier's death. In that case, the one who is stricken will at least be sure, as he dies, that he will survive in the heart of a friend! Let us embrace, Richon! You wished me good luck, and I say to you: be of good cheer!'

The two men fell into each other's arms and remained for some time with their noble hearts pressed to one another.

When they separated, Richon wiped away a tear, perhaps the only one that had ever clouded his proud eye; then, as though fearing that Canolles might have seen this tear, he rushed from the room, no doubt ashamed at having given such proof of weakness to a man whose own courage he well knew.

III

The dining room had remained empty except for Canolles and the officer who had announced the arrival of the envoy; he was standing by the door.

'What are the governor's orders?' he asked, after a moment's silence.

Canolles, who had at first been absorbed in his thoughts, shuddered at the sound of this voice, looked up and came out of his reverie.

'Where is the envoy?' he asked.

'In the arms room, Monsieur.'

'Who has he brought with him?'

'Two guards from the Bordeaux town militia.'

'And who is he?'

'A young man . . . as far as one can tell. He is wearing a broad-brimmed hat and wrapped in a large cloak.'

'And how did he announce himself?'

'As the bearer of letters from the princess and from the parliament of Bordeaux.'

'Ask him to wait for a moment,' said Canolles. 'I shall be with him soon.'

The officer left to carry out this order, and Canolles was preparing to follow him, when the door opened, and Nanon appeared, looking pale and shivering, but with her usual affectionate smile. Grasping the young man's hand, she asked: 'An envoy. What does this mean, my friend?'

'This means, dear Nanon, that the gentlemen of Bordeaux either wish to frighten me or to seduce me.'

'And what have you decided?'

'To receive him.'

'Can't you avoid it?'

'Impossible: there are some formalities that cannot be avoided.'

'Oh, my God!'

'What is it, Nanon?'

'I am afraid . . .'

'Of what?'

'Didn't you say that this emissary has come to frighten you or to seduce you?'

'Of course: an envoy is only good for one or other of those two functions . . . Are you afraid that he will frighten me?'

'Oh, no! But he might seduce you . . .'

'You are insulting me, Nanon.'

'Alas, my friend, I am telling you what I'm afraid of . . .'

'Do you doubt me so much? What do you take me for, then?'

'For the person you are, Canolles, that is to say for a generous, but tender heart.'

'Huh!' said Canolles, laughing. 'But what negotiator are they sending me? Cupid himself?'

'Perhaps.'

'Have you seen him?'

'No, I haven't seen him, but I have heard his voice. It is very soft, for an emissary's voice.'

'Nanon, you're mad! Let me carry out my duties. You made me governor . . .'

'To defend me, my friend.'

'So do you think I'm cowardly enough to betray you? Honestly, Nanon, you insult me with your lack of faith.'

'So, are you really determined to see this young man?'

'I must, and I should really resent it were you to stand any longer in the way of my carrying out this duty.'

'You are free, my friend,' said Nanon, sadly. 'Just one word more . . .'

'Say it.'

'Where will you receive him?'

'In my study.'

'Canolles, one favour . . .'

'Which is?'

'Instead of receiving him in your study, do so in your bedroom.'

'What are you thinking of?'

'Can't you see?'

'No.'

'My room opens on to your alcove . . .'

'So you will listen?'

'Behind the curtains, if you will let me.'

'Nanon!'

'Let me stay close to you, my dear. I have faith in my destiny, I'll bring you luck.'

'But, Nanon, suppose this negotiator . . .'

'Well, what?'

'. . . has come to entrust some state secret . . .'

'Can't you entrust a state secret to the woman who has entrusted her life and her fortune to you?'

'Well, then, Nanon, listen to us if you absolutely insist, but don't keep me any longer: the envoy is waiting.'

'Go on, Canolles, go on. But first, let me bless you for the favour you are doing me.'

And the young woman made to kiss her lover's hand.

'You are crazy!' said Canolles, drawing her to his breast and kissing her forehead. 'So, you will be . . .'

'Behind the curtains on your bed. From there, I can see and hear.'

'At least, don't laugh, Nanon. These are serious matters.'

'Don't worry,' she said. 'I won't laugh.'

Canolles gave orders for the messenger to be brought in and

went through to his room, a huge chamber furnished in the reign of Charles IX and austere in appearance. Two candlesticks were burning on the mantelpiece but only gave a weak light in the vast apartment. The alcove, at the far end, was entirely in the dark.

'Are you there, Nanon?' Canolles asked.

He heard a stifled, breathless 'yes'.

At that moment there was the sound of footsteps, and the sentry presented arms. The messenger came in and kept watching the person who had introduced him until he was – or thought he was – alone with Canolles. It was then that he raised his hat and tossed back his cloak – and at once a mass of blonde hair fell across those charming shoulders, while the fine, shapely form of a woman appeared beneath the gold baldric, and, from her soft, sad eyes, Canolles recognized the Viscountess de Cambes.

'I told you that I should find you, and I am keeping my word,' she said. 'Here I am!'

Canolles, with a start of amazement and anguish, clapped his hands and slumped down into a chair.

'You!' he murmured. 'You! Oh, my God! Why have you come here? What do you want?'

'I want to know, Monsieur, if you still remember me.'

Canolles gave a deep sigh and put both hands in front of his eyes to shield them from this alluring and, at the same time, disastrous apparition. Now he understood everything. Nanon's uneasiness, her pallor and her trembling ... and most of all her desire to be present at this interview. Nanon, with the eyes of jealousy, had recognized a woman behind the envoy.

'I have come to ask you,' Claire continued, 'whether you are ready to abide by the undertaking you made to me in that little room in Jaulnay, to give your resignation to the queen and join the princes.'

'Oh! Silence, silence!' Canolles cried.

Claire shuddered at the tone of alarm in the young man's trembling voice and looked around her uneasily.

'Are we not alone here?' she asked.

'We are, Madame,' said Canolles. 'But might not someone hear us through these walls?'

'I thought that the walls of the fort of Saint-Georges were more solid than that,' said Claire, with a smile.

Canolles did not answer.

'So I have come to ask you how it is,' Claire went on, 'that in the eight or ten days that you have been here, I have not heard a word about you. So much so that I should still not have known who was in command of the Ile Saint-Georges, were it not that fate, or rather rumour, had informed me that it was the man who swore to me, barely a dozen days ago, that his fall from grace was a blessing, because it would allow him to devote his sword, his courage and his life to the party to which I belong.'

Nanon could not contain a movement that made Canolles shudder and Madame de Cambes turn round.

'What's that?' she asked.

'Nothing,' Canolles replied. 'One of the usual noises in this old room, which is full of gloomy creaking sounds.'

'If it is anything else,' Claire said, putting a hand on Canolles's arm, 'don't conceal it from me, Baron, because you must realize the importance of the discussion that we are about to have, since I have come here in person to see you.'

Canolles wiped the sweat off his brow and tried to smile as he said: 'Speak, then.'

'I have come to remind you of your promise and to ask if you are prepared to keep it.'

'Alas, Madame!' Canolles replied. 'That has become impossible.'

'Why?'

'Because since that time some unexpected events have occurred, and some ties that I thought were broken have been restored. In place of the punishment I thought I deserved, the queen has seen fit to give me a reward of which I was unworthy. I am now attached to Her Majesty's party by . . . gratitude.'

A sigh: poor Nanon had no doubt been expecting another word than the one that had been spoken.

'Say "by ambition", Monsieur de Canolles, and I will understand you. You are noble, of high birth; at twenty-eight you are made lieutenant-colonel and governor of a fortress. That's fine, I admit, but it is not the natural reward for your fine qualities, and Monsieur de Mazarin is not the only one to appreciate them.'

'Madame, not another word, I pray you,' said Canolles.

'Forgive me, Monsieur,' said Claire, 'but now it is not the Viscountess de Cambes who is speaking, but the envoy of the princess who has a mission to accomplish here ... and this she must fulfil.'

'Speak, then, Madame,' Canolles replied, with a sigh that was like a groan.

'Very well! The princess, knowing the feelings that you displayed first of all in Chantilly and then in Jaulnay, and eager to discover which party you will finally support, had resolved to send you a negotiator in order to appeal to you. I took on this mission, which someone other than myself might perhaps have carried out well enough ... I took it on myself, thinking that, since I am privy to your secret thoughts on the matter, I could accomplish it better than anyone.'

'Thank you, Madame,' said Canolles, tearing at his breast with his hand, because, in the brief pauses in the dialogue, he could hear Nanon's rapid breathing.

'So this is what I am suggesting to you, Monsieur ... in the name of the princess, you understand, because if it were in my own name,' Claire continued, with her charming smile, 'I should have reversed the order of the proposals.'

'I am listening,' said Canolles in a dull voice.

'You will hand over the Ile Saint-Georges on one of the three conditions that I am about to suggest, as you wish. The first is this – and remember, I am not the one who is speaking – the sum of two hundred thousand livres.'

'Oh, Madame! Say no more,' said Canolles, trying to break off the conversation. 'The queen has entrusted me with a command, the command of the Ile Saint-Georges, which I shall defend to the death.'

'Remember the past, Monsieur,' Claire exclaimed, with sadness. 'That is not what you told me in our previous conversation, when you offered to leave everything to follow me and were already holding the quill in your hand to offer your resignation to those for whom you now wish to sacrifice your life.'

'I may have offered you that, Madame, when I was free to choose my path. But today I am no longer free . . .'

'You are no longer free!' Claire exclaimed, going pale. 'What do you imply by that, Monsieur? What do you mean?'

'I mean that I have a debt of honour.'

'Very well. Then hear my next proposal.'

'What is the use?' Canolles said. 'Have I not told you often enough that I am firmly resolved? So do not try to tempt me; it would be pointless.'

'Forgive me, Monsieur,' Claire replied, 'but I too have a duty to perform, and I must do so to the end.'

'Go on,' Canolles murmured. 'But you are truly very cruel.'

'Tender your resignation, and we shall then act more effectively on your successor than on you. In a year, or in two years, you will resume your service under the prince, with the rank of brigadier.'

Canolles sadly shook his head.

'Alas, Madame, why do you ask the impossible of me?'

'Is it to me that you are saying this?' said Claire. 'Frankly, Monsieur, I fail to understand you. Weren't you on the point of signing that very resignation? Did you not say at that time to the person who was then close to you, and whom you listened to with such joy, that you were resigning of your own free will and from the bottom of your heart? So why will you not do here, when I am asking you . . . imploring you . . . what you intended to do in Jaulnay?'

Each of these words entered like a dagger into the heart of Nanon, and Canolles felt them enter.

'What at that time was an action of no significance would today be an act of treachery, of infamous treachery!' Canolles said, in a low voice. 'Never shall I give up the Ile Saint-Georges! Never shall I tender my resignation!'

'Wait, wait,' said Claire, in her softest voice, while looking anxiously around her, because Canolles's resistance, and in particular the inhibition that he seemed to be feeling, appeared peculiar to her. 'Listen to this last proposal, the one with which I should have wished to begin, since I knew in advance that you would refuse the first two. Material benefits, as I am pleased to have guessed, are not the things that tempt a heart such as yours. What you need are other expectations than those of ambition or fortune: noble instincts require noble rewards. So listen . . .'

'In the name of heaven, Madame,' Canolles said. 'Have pity on me!' And he made as though to leave.

Claire thought that his resolve had been shaken and was convinced that what she was about to say would complete her victory, so she held him back and continued: 'If instead of base rewards we were to offer you a pure and honourable reward . . . Suppose we were to pay for your resignation – this resignation that you can tender without disgrace, since hostilities have not yet begun, this resignation that is neither a defection nor an act of perfidy, but a pure and simple choice . . . If, I say, this resignation were to be rewarded with an alliance . . . If a woman whom you have told that you love her, to whom you have sworn to love her for ever, and who, despite these professions of love, has never responded to your passion . . . suppose this woman were to tell you: "Monsieur de Canolles, I am free, I am rich, I love you, become my husband, let us leave together . . . Go wherever you wish, far from all civil strife, outside France . . ." Well, Monsieur, this time would you not accept?'

Despite Claire's blushes and despite her charming hesitations, despite the memory of the pretty little Château de Cambes which he could have seen from his window, if, during the progress of the scene which we have just described, night had not fallen, Canolles remained unwavering and firm in his resolve, because from afar he could see emerging between the Gothic curtains and pale in the shadows, the dishevelled head of Nanon, trembling with anxiety.

'Why, answer me, in heaven's name!' the viscountess went on. 'I cannot understand your silence. Was I mistaken? Are you not the Baron de Canolles? Are you not the same man who told me in Chantilly that you loved me, who repeated it to me in

Jaulnay, who swore that you loved only me in the world and
that you were prepared to sacrifice every other love to me? Say,
say something! For heaven's sake, answer me! Answer me!'

A groan was heard, this time so unambiguous and so clear
that Madame de Cambes could not doubt that a third person was present in the discussion. Her eyes, appalled, followed
the direction in which Canolles was looking, and he could not
turn away quickly enough to prevent the viscountess's eyes,
guided by his, from observing the pale, motionless head, like
that of a ghost, and the breathless figure of the woman who
was following every stage of the conversation.

In the darkness, the two women exchanged a burning look,
and both of them gave a cry.

Nanon vanished.

As for Madame de Cambes, she quickly seized her hat and her
cloak and turned towards Canolles, saying: 'Monsieur, now I
understand what you call duty and gratitude. I understand the
nature of the duty that you refuse to abandon or to betray. I
understand at last that there are feelings that cannot be seduced
by any blandishments. I leave you entirely to these feelings, to
that power, to that gratitude. Farewell, Baron, farewell!'

She made as if to leave, while Canolles did not try to restrain
her; then a painful memory held her back.

'One last thing, Monsieur,' she said. 'In the name of the
friendship that I owe you for the service that you did me, in the
name of the friendship that you owe me for the service that
I, too, have done you, and in the name of all those who love
you and whom you love – and I make no exception – do not
engage in battle. Tomorrow, or perhaps the next day, you will
be attacked in Saint-Georges: do not cause me the pain of
knowing that you are either defeated or dead.'

At these words, the young man started and came back to his
senses.

'Madame,' he said, 'I thank you on my knees for the assurance that you have given me of a friendship that is more dear
to me than I can say. Ah, let them attack me, let them attack
me, by God! I appeal to the enemy with more ardour than he
will ever devote to opposing me. I need to fight, I need danger

to raise myself in my own estimation. So let battle come, let danger come, let even death come, and it will be welcome, since I know that I shall die, rich in your friendship, strengthened by your compassion and honoured by your esteem.'

'Farewell,' said Claire, going to the door.

Canolles followed her. When they came to the middle of the dark corridor, he grasped her hand and said in a voice so low that even he could barely hear the words that he uttered: 'Claire, I love you more than I have ever loved you, but misfortune has decreed that I can only prove this love by dying far from you.'

For the moment, Madame de Cambes's only reply was an ironic little laugh. But hardly had she left the fort than a painful sob rose in her throat, and she wrung her hands, crying: 'Oh, he does not love me! Oh, God, he does not love me! And I, wretch that I am, I love him . . .'

IV

When he left Madame de Cambes, Canolles went back to his room. Nanon was standing there, pale and still, in the middle of the room. Canolles went over to her with a sad smile. As he approached, Nanon's knee bent, he held out his hand to her, and she fell at his feet.

'Forgive me, Canolles,' she said. 'Forgive me. I am the one who brought you here, I am the one who obtained this difficult and dangerous post for you. If you should be killed, I shall be the cause of your death. I am an egotist who thought only of her own happiness. Abandon me! Leave!'

Canolles gently raised her up.

'I – abandon you!' he said. 'Never, Nanon, never! You are sacred to me. I have sworn to protect and defend you, to save you – and I shall save you or die!'

'Do you say this from your heart, Canolles, unhesitatingly, with no regrets?'

'Yes,' Canolles said, smiling.

'Thank you, worthy, noble friend, thank you. You see, this

life that was so dear to me, I would sacrifice for you today
without complaint, because only today do I know what you
have done for me. You were offered money: are my treasures
not yours? You were offered love: but will there ever be, in the
world, a woman who loves you as I do? You were offered
promotion . . . Listen, they are going to attack you. Well, let us
buy soldiers, gather weapons and munitions. Let's double our
forces and defend ourselves. I shall fight for my love, you for
your honour. You will defeat them, my brave Canolles, and the
queen will say that she has no finer captain than you. Then
I shall take care of your promotion, no? And when you are
rich, laden with glory and honour, then you can abandon me
if you wish. I shall have my memories to console me.'

And as she said this, Nanon looked at Canolles, waiting for
the reply that women always expect to exaggerations, that is
something as crazy and elated as their own words. But Canolles
sadly shook his head.

'Nanon,' he said, 'you will never suffer any harm or have to
put up with any affront as long as I am living on the Ile
Saint-Georges. So be calm, because you have nothing to fear.'

'Thank you,' she replied. 'Though that is not all I am
expecting.' And she added under her breath: 'Alas, I am lost;
he no longer loves me.'

Canolles surprised the blazing look in her eyes, flashing like
lightning, and the dreadful, momentary pallor that reveals so
much inner pain. 'Let us be generous to the full,' he thought.
'Anything else would be base.'

'Come, Nanon,' he said. 'Come, my dear. Put the coat around
your shoulders and take your man's hat: the night air will do
you good. I may be attacked at any moment, so I am going to
do my night watch.'

Nanon, trembling with joy, dressed as her lover had told her
and followed him.

Canolles was a true captain. Little more than a child when
he entered the service, he had made a proper study of his
profession, which meant that he made his inspections not only
as a commander, but as an engineer. The officers who had seen
him arrive as a favourite, and who thought they were dealing

with a mere ceremonial governor, were questioned one after another by their chief on every means of attack and defence. They were thus obliged to accept that this light-hearted young man was also an experienced captain, so even the oldest among them spoke of him with respect. The only thing that they might hold against him was the softness of his voice when he gave orders, and his extreme politeness when he questioned them. They were afraid that this courtesy was a sign of weakness. However, since each of them was aware of their imminent danger, the governor's orders were carried out swiftly and punctually, in a manner that gave the leader an equal respect for his men as they had for him. A company of sappers had arrived during the day. Canolles ordered work that was started at once. Nanon tried in vain to bring him back to the fort to spare him the exhaustion of a night spent in this way, but Canolles went on with his inspection, and he it was who gently dismissed Nanon, demanding that she should return home. Then, having sent out three or four scouts whom the lieutenant had recommended as the most intelligent of those in his service, he went to lie down on a block of stone, from which he could keep an eye on the work.

But while his eyes were mechanically following the movement of the trenching tools and the pickaxes, Canolles's thoughts, far from the material things that were going on in front of him, were entirely concerned not only with the events of that day, but with all the strange adventures in which he had been the hero since the time when he first saw Madame de Cambes. But, strangely enough, his mind did not go beyond that: it seemed to him that it was only from that moment that he had started to live, that until then he had existed in another world, one of inferior instincts and incomplete sensations. From that moment on, there had been a light in his life that gave a different appearance to everything – and in this new light Nanon (poor Nanon!) was pitilessly sacrificed to another love, violent from the moment of its birth, like those passions that take over entirely the life into which they have entered.

So, after painful reflection, mingled with heavenly rapture at the idea that he was loved by Madame de Cambes, Canolles admitted that duty alone demanded that he should be a man of honour and that the love he felt for Nanon played no part in his resolve.

Poor Nanon! Canolles described his feeling for her as one of friendship. And friendship in love is very close to indifference.

Nanon was also awake. She could not bring herself to go to bed. Standing at a window, wrapped in a black mantle so that she would not be seen, she was not watching the sad, veiled moon drifting through the clouds, or the tall poplars swaying gracefully in the night wind, or the majestic river Garonne, which seems much more like a rebellious vassal rising up to make war on its master than a faithful serf bringing its tribute to the ocean . . . It was not any of these that she was following, but the slow, painful case building up against her in the mind of her lover: in his dark outline on the stone, in his motionless shadow crouching in front of a lantern, she saw the living spectre of her past happiness. She who had once been so energetic, so proud and so adept, had now lost all skill, all pride, all energy. It was as though her senses, fired by the awareness of her misfortune, were doubly perceptive and subtle. She felt the love germinating in the depths of her lover's heart – as God, leaning across the great dome of the sky, can feel a shoot of grass germinating in the bowels of the earth.

Daybreak came, and only then did Canolles return to his room. Nanon had already gone back to hers, so he was unaware that she had stayed awake all night. He dressed carefully, assembled the garrison once more, inspected the various batteries in daylight, particularly those overlooking the left bank of the Garonne, had the little gate closed with chains, set up kinds of barges laden with muskets and blunderbusses, reviewed his men, encouraged them again with his vivid and generous words, and was consequently only able to return to his quarters around ten o'clock.

Nanon was waiting with a smile on her lips. This was no longer the proud and imperious Nanon whose whims made even Monsieur d'Epernon shudder; this was a shy mistress, a fearful slave who did not even demand to be loved, but merely asked to be allowed to love him.

The day passed uneventfully, except for the ins and outs of the inner drama that was being played out in the souls of each of these young people. The scouts that Canolles had sent out returned one after another. None of them brought any positive news, apart from reporting a great deal of activity in Bordeaux: it was clear that something was being prepared there.

As it happened, Madame de Cambes, when she returned to the town, while concealing all the details of the interview in the most secret recesses of her heart, reported the outcome to Lenet. The people of Bordeaux clamoured for the Ile Saint-Georges to be captured. They came along en masse to take part in the expedition. The leaders agreed for it to go ahead, while pointing to the absence of any soldiers to lead it and trained men to support it. Lenet took advantage of this to slip in the name of the two dukes and to offer their army. This proposal was received enthusiastically, and even people who on the previous day had voted for the gates to be shut against them called for them loudly.

Lenet hurried to bring this good news to the princess, who immediately summoned her council. Claire excused herself on the ground of tiredness from taking any decision against Canolles and went to her room where she could weep at her leisure. From the room, she could hear the cries and threats of the people; all these cries and threats were directed against Canolles.

Soon the drum sounded, the companies assembled, the magistrates had the people armed; the people demanded pikes and muskets. The cannon was taken out of the arsenal, gunpowder distributed and two hundred boats were made ready to sail up the Garonne with the help of the night tide, while three thousand men, marching along the left bank, would attack on land.

The fleet was to be commanded by d'Espagnet, counsellor to the parliament of Bordeaux, a brave and wise man; the land army was to be commanded by Monsieur de La Rochefoucauld, who had just entered the town with some two thousand followers. The Duke de Bouillon was not due to come until the following day, with a further thousand. So Monsieur de La

Rochefoucauld pressed ahead vigorously with the attack in order to complete it before his colleague arrived.

V

While Canolles was doing his tour of inspection around the ramparts, on the day after the one when Madame de Cambes had appeared in the guise of a negotiator on the Ile Saint-Georges, he was informed that a messenger with a letter was asking to speak to him.

The messenger was immediately shown in and gave his dispatch to Canolles. It was clearly not an official communication: a small letter, longer than it was broad, written in a fine and slightly quavering hand on polished and scented paper, tinted blue.

Merely at the sight of the paper, Canolles felt his heart involuntarily beating faster.

'Who gave you this letter?' he asked.

'A man of fifty-five to sixty years old.'

'With a moustache and a small beard, *à la royale*, going grey?'

'Yes.'

'Stooping?'

'Yes.'

'Yet of military bearing?'

'That's right.'

Canolles gave the man a louis and gestured to him to leave at once. Then he walked away, his heart thumping, and hid behind a turret so that he could read the letter that he had just received at his leisure.

It contained the following three lines: 'You are going to be attacked. If you are no longer worthy of me, at least show that you are worthy of yourself.'

The letter was not signed, but Canolles recognized Madame de Cambes's handwriting, as he had recognized Pompée. He looked to make sure that no one was watching, then blushing like a boy in his first love affair, he put the paper to his lips, kissed it ardently and put it next to his heart.

Then he went up on to the roof of the bastion, from where he could see the course of the Garonne for nearly a league as well as the full extent of the surrounding plain. There was nothing to be seen either on the river or in the countryside.

'This is how I shall spend the morning,' he murmured. 'They won't be coming in full daylight. They must have rested on their way and will start the attack this evening.'

Canolles heard a slight noise behind him and turned round. It was his lieutenant.

'Well, Monsieur de Vibrac,' Canolles said. 'What are they saying?'

'They are saying that the flag of the princes will be flying over the Ile Saint-Georges tomorrow.'

'Who is saying that?'

'Two of our scouts who have just come back and who saw the preparations that the townsfolk are making against us.'

'So what was your answer to those who said that the flag of the princes will be flying over the Ile Saint-Georges tomorrow?'

'I replied that that was all the same to me, since I should not be seeing it.'

'In that case, you have stolen my reply, Monsieur,' said Canolles.

'Bravo, Commander! That's all we ask. The soldiers will fight like lions when they learn of your reply.'

'Let them fight like men, that's all I ask. And what are they saying about the type of attack?'

'Why, General, that they have a surprise in store for us,' said Vibrac with a laugh.

'Damn! What a surprise that is!' said Canolles. 'You're the second person to tell me so. Who is leading the assault?'

'Monsieur de La Rochefoucauld for the army, d'Espagnet, the parliamentary counsellor, for the water landing.'

'Very well,' said Canolles. 'Then I'll give him some advice.'

'Whom?'

'The adviser to the parliament of Bordeaux.'

'What would that be?'

'To reinforce his urban militia with some good, well-disciplined soldiers who can teach those bourgeois how to withstand heavy fire.'

'He did not wait for your advice, Commander, because before becoming a man of law he was, I believe, something of a man of war, and for this expedition he joined forces with the regiment of Navailles.'

'What! The regiment of Navailles?'

'Yes.'

'My old regiment?'

'The same. It appears that it has gone over lock, stock and barrel to the princes.'

'And who is commanding it?'

'Baron de Ravailly.'

'Really?'

'Do you know him?'

'Yes ... a charming lad, as brave as his sword. So, in that case it will be hotter than I thought. We'll have a jolly time of it!'

'What are your orders?'

'That the sentries should be doubled tonight and the soldiers go to bed fully clothed, with their weapons loaded and within reach. Half will keep watch, while the other half rest. The half that is on watch should remain below the level of the fortifications ... Wait one moment.'

'I am waiting.'

'Have you told anyone of the messenger's report?'

'No one at all.'

'Good. Keep it secret for a while longer. Choose ten or so of your worst soldiers ... you must have some poachers and fishermen here?'

'Only too many of them.'

'Well, then. As I say, choose around ten and give them leave until tomorrow morning. They will go and cast their lines in the Garonne or set their snares on the plain. Tonight, d'Espagnet and de La Rochefoucauld will capture them and interrogate them.'

'I don't understand . . .'

'Don't you see that our attackers must think that we are entirely ignorant of their plans? Well, these men, as they do not know anything, will swear convincingly – and be believed, since they will not be pretending – that we are fast asleep.'

'Ah, very good!'

'Let the enemy approach, let him land, let him raise up his ladders.'

'So when shall we fire?'

'When I give the order. If a single shot comes from our ranks before my order is given, by my faith, I shall have the person who fired it shot.'

'Heavens!'

'Civil war is war twice over. It's important that a civil war should not be conducted like a hunting party. Let the people of Bordeaux laugh, and laugh yourselves if it pleases you. But only do so when I tell you to laugh.'

The lieutenant left and conveyed Canolles's orders to the other officers, who exchanged astonished looks. There were two men in the governor: the courteous gentleman and the implacable commander.

Canolles went back to dine with Nanon, though their supper was brought forward by two hours. Canolles had decided that he would not leave the ramparts from dusk to dawn. He found Nanon looking through a voluminous correspondence.

'You can put up a stiff defence, dear Canolles,' she said, 'because it will not be long before you are relieved. The king is coming, Monsieur de La Meilleraie is leading an army here, and Monsieur d'Epernon is on the way with fifteen thousand men.'

'But in the meantime they have a week, or perhaps ten days, Nanon,' said Canolles, smiling. 'The Ile Saint-Georges is not impregnable.'

'Oh, as long as you are in command here, I'm quite confident.'

'Yes, but precisely because I am in command here, I may be killed . . . Nanon, what would you do if that happened? Have you thought about it, at least?'

'Yes,' said Nanon, smiling in her turn.

'Well, then, keep your trunk packed and ready. A boatman will be at the appointed place, and if you should have to jump in the water, there will be four of my people who are strong swimmers, with orders not to leave you; they will take you to the other bank.'

'All these precautions are pointless, Canolles. If you are killed, I shall no longer need anything.'

A servant announced that dinner was ready. Ten times, as they were eating, Canolles got up and went to the window overlooking the river. He left the table before the end of the meal. Night was falling.

Nanon tried to follow him.

'Nanon,' he said. 'Go back to your apartment and swear to me that you will not leave it. If I knew that you were outside, in the open, in some kind of danger, I don't know what I should do. It is a question of my honour, Nanon. Don't trifle with my honour.'

Nanon offered Canolles her crimson lips, made even redder by the pallor of her cheeks. Then she went back to her room, saying: 'I obey you, Canolles! I want both friends and enemies to know the man I love. Go!'

Canolles left. He could not help admiring this creature who was obedient to all his desires and wishes. Hardly had he reached his post than night came, frightful and threatening, as it always seems to be when its dark recesses hold a murderous secret.

Canolles had taken up his place at the end of the Esplanade, from where he could see the river and both of its banks. There was no moon. A veil of dark clouds slid heavily across the sky. It was impossible to be seen, but also impossible to see.

However, at midnight he thought he made out some dark shapes moving on the far bank, and huge forms gliding along the river. But there was no noise other than the night wind moaning in the leaves on the trees.

The shapes halted, and the forms stayed put, some distance away. Canolles thought he had been mistaken, yet he doubled in vigilance. His bright eyes pierced the gloom, and his ears were pricked to catch the slightest sound.

Three o'clock sounded on the fortress clock, and the echoes of the ringing faded slowly and lugubriously into the night. Canolles began to suspect that he had been misinformed and was about to go to bed, when Lieutenant de Vibrac, who was beside him, quickly put a hand on his shoulder and, with the other, pointed towards the river.

'Yes, yes,' said Canolles. 'It's them. Come, we shall have lost nothing by waiting. Go and wake up the men who are sleeping and tell them to take up their posts behind the wall. You told them, I hope, that I would kill the first man who fired?'

'Yes.'

'Well, tell them again!'

As the first light of day appeared, you could see the long boats approaching, laden with men laughing and talking quietly, while on the plain you could see a kind of hillock that had not been there the day before. It was a battery of six cannons that Monsieur de La Rochefoucauld had set up overnight. The men in the boats had only delayed for so long, because the battery had not until then been ready to open fire.

Canolles asked if the weapons were loaded and, when told that they were, gave a signal for them to wait.

The boats were getting closer and closer, and in the first light of day, Canolles could soon make out the distinctive leather trappings and hat of the company of Navailles – which, as we know, had once been his. At the bow of one of the first boats was Baron de Ravailly, who had replaced him as commander of the company, and at the stern, the lieutenant who was his foster brother and much loved by his comrades for his merry disposition and unending stock of jokes.

'You see,' he was saying. 'They won't budge. Monsieur de La Rochefoucauld will have to wake them up with his cannon. Heavens above! How soundly they sleep in Saint-Georges! When I'm ill, this is where I'll come.'

'Canolles is too kind,' Ravailly replied. 'He thinks that a governor is like a father: he's afraid his men will catch cold if they have to do guard duty at night.'

'Quite right,' said another, 'you can't even see a sentry.'

'Hey, there!' shouted the lieutenant, stepping on to the bank. 'Wake yourselves there and give us a hand to climb up!'

At that last quip, a burst of laughter ran along the whole line of the attackers, and, while three or four boats made towards the port, the rest of the army disembarked.

'Come on, now,' said Ravailly. 'I understand. Canolles wants to appear to be surprised so as not to fall out with the court. So, gentlemen, let's return the compliment and not kill anybody. Once we are inside, spare them all, except the women, who will probably not want it in any case, by God! Now, boys, don't forget that this is a war between friends, so the first man to draw his sword, I'll run him through.'

At this order, given in a truly French spirit of merriment, the laughter resumed, and the soldiers shared their officers' hilarity.

'Very good, my friends,' said the lieutenant. 'It does us good to laugh, but we mustn't forget why we're here. To the ladders, and up we go!'

At this, Canolles got up, and, with his cane in his hand and his hat on, like a man taking a stroll in the morning air, he went over to the parapet, which only came up to his waist.

It was light enough for him to be recognized.

'Well, now, Navailles! Good morning to you,' he said, addressing the whole regiment. 'Good morning, Ravailly, good morning, Remonenq.'

'Why, it's Canolles!' the young men exclaimed. 'So you're up at last, Baron.'

'Indeed, I am. We live the life of Reilly[4] here: early to bed and late to rise. But what are you doing in these parts so early?'

'I would think you could see that,' said Ravailly. 'We come to lay siege to you, that's all.'

'And why have you come to do that?'

'To capture your fort.'

Canolles laughed.

'Come now,' said Ravailly. 'You give in, don't you?'

'First of all, I must know whom I am surrendering to. How is it that Navailles is fighting against the king?'

'My word, my dear fellow, it's because we've taken up

rebellion. When we thought about it, we decided that Mazarin was definitely a coward and not worthy to be served by gallant gentlemen, and as a result we went over to the princes. How about you?'

'Why, dear chap, I'm a raging Epernonist.'

'Huh! Leave your people there, and come with us.'

'Can't do it. Hey, you down there: leave the chains on the bridge alone. You know very well that one should look at those things, but from a distance, and it's bad luck to touch them. Ravailly, tell them not to touch the chains,' Canolles continued, frowning. 'Otherwise, I'll give the order to fire at them. And, I warn you, Ravailly, I've got some excellent marksmen.'

'Why, you're joking!' the officer replied. 'Let them capture you, you're haven't got the strength.'

'I'm not joking. Down with those ladders! Ravailly, I beg you: this is the king's house that you are attacking, so beware!'

'Saint George – the king's house?'

'Why not? Just look, and you'll see the flag on the tip of the bastion. Come, now. Put your boats back in the water, and your ladders in the boats, or I'll fire. If you want talk, come alone or with Remonenq, and then we can have breakfast as we talk. I have an excellent cook on the Ile Saint-Georges.'

Ravailly started to laugh and gave his men a look of encouragement. Meanwhile, another company was preparing to disembark.

At this, Canolles realized that the decisive moment had come. And, resuming the firm attitude and serious manner appropriate to a man bearing his heavy responsibilities, he shouted: 'Halt! Ravailly, no more joking. Not another word, a step or a gesture, or I shall give the order to fire as surely as that is the king's flag up there and as you are marching against the fleur-de-lys of France.'

As good as his word, he forcibly overturned the first ladder that was jutting above the battlements.

Five or six men who were in more of a hurry than the rest had begun to climb, and they were thrown off. They fell back, and their fall caused a huge burst of laughter from the attackers and the defenders. It was like a schoolboy game.

At that moment, a signal indicated that the attackers had broken the chains that had closed the entry to the port.

At once, Ravailly and Remonenq grasped a ladder and began in their turn to go down into the ditch, crying: 'With us, Navailles! Forward, onward and upward!'

'My poor Ravailly,' Canolles shouted. 'Stop, I beg you . . .'

But at that moment the battery, which had been silent until then, burst out in thunder and lightning, and a cannon shot threw up the earth next to Canolles.

'Very well,' Canolles cried, pointing with his cane. 'Since they insist, fire! Fire my friends, all along the line!'

At this, though not a single man could be seen, a row of muskets bent down towards the rampart, and a belt of flame wrapped around the crest of the wall, while two huge artillery pieces exploded in response to the Duke de La Rochefoucauld's cannon.

A dozen men fell, but instead of discouraging their companions, their loss spurred them on. The land battery replied to the fort battery, a shot brought down the royal flag, and another crushed one of Canolles's lieutenants, whose name was d'Elboin.

Canolles looked around him again and saw that his men had already reloaded their guns.

'General fire!' he ordered.

This command was carried out no less promptly than the previous one.

Ten minutes later, there was not a single unbroken window on the Ile Saint-Georges. The stones shuddered and burst into splinters, the cannon fire broke through the walls, cannonballs smashed on to the wide paving stones, and a thick cloud of smoke darkened the air, full of shouts, threats and groans.

Canolles saw that the chief threat to his fort came from Monsieur de La Rochefoucauld's battery.

'Vibrac,' he said, 'take care of Ravailly and make sure he does not gain an inch of ground while I am away. I am going to our battery.'

At this, he ran across to the two guns that were replying to La Rochefoucauld's fire, took command of them himself, and became loader, aimer and commander. In a moment, he had silenced three out of the six enemy guns and brought down some fifty men. The rest, who had not been expecting this fierce resistance, started to scatter and take to their heels. La Rochefoucauld, rallying them, was hit by a splinter of stone that knocked his sword out of his hand.

When he saw this, Canolles left the remainder of the task to the head of the battery and ran back to the place where the company of Navailles, together with d'Espagnet's men, was pressing its assault.

Vibrac was holding his ground, but he had just been shot in the shoulder. Canolles's return lifted the spirits of his troops, and his presence was greeted with cries of joy.

'Forgive me,' he shouted to Ravailly. 'I had to leave you for a moment, dear friend, as you see, to take care of Monsieur de La Rochefoucauld's guns. But have no fear, I'm back now!'

And as the captain of the regiment of Navailles, who was too busy to reply to this quip – which, indeed, in the midst of the frightful din made by the artillery and musketry, he might very well not have heard – was leading his men to the assault for the third time, Canolles drew a pistol from his belt and, pointing it towards his former comrade, now his enemy, pulled the trigger. The shot was aimed by a firm hand and sure eye. It broke Ravailly's arm.

'Thank you, Canolles!' he shouted, having seen where the shot came from. 'Thank you, I'll pay you back for that.'

But despite his self-control, the young captain was forced to halt, and his sword fell from his grasp. Remonenq ran across to support him in his arms.

'Would you like to have the wound dressed here, Ravailly?' Canolles cried. 'I've got a surgeon who is as good in his way as my cook.'

'Certainly not, I'm going back to Bordeaux. But expect me to return at any moment, because I shall do so, I promise. But next time I will choose my time.'

'Retreat! Retreat!' Remonenq shouted. 'We're pulling back. Farewell, Canolles. The first match is yours.'

Remonenq was right: the artillery had wreaked havoc in the

army on the ground, which had lost around a hundred men at least. As for the army on the water, it had lost almost as many. But the greatest losses of all had been in the regiment of Navailles, which, to sustain the honour of the uniform, had always insisted on marching ahead of the citizens led by d'Espagnet.

Canolles raised his empty pistol.

'Cease fire! Let them retreat in peace. We cannot afford to waste any munitions.'

Indeed, any shots they fired would have been more or less wasted. The attackers were retreating at full speed, leaving their dead, but carrying off their wounded. Canolles counted his own casualties: sixteen wounded and four dead. As for himself, he had not suffered a scratch.

'*Peste!*' he exclaimed, ten minutes later, as he accepted Nanon's joyful embraces. 'My dear friend, we did not have to wait long before I earned my governor's spurs. What a stupid shambles! I killed a hundred and fifty of them, at least, and broke the arm of one of my best friends, to prevent him getting himself killed outright.'

'Yes,' said Nanon. 'But you are safe and sound, aren't you?'

'Thank God, I am! And you no doubt brought me good fortune, Nanon. But look out for the next round. Those Bordeaux men are stubborn. And in any event, Ravailly and Remonenq promised me that they would be back.'

'So?' said Nanon. 'The same man is in command at Saint-Georges, and the same soldiers are defending it. Let them come, and the second time, they will be even better welcomed than the first. Because, between now and then, you will have time to improve your defences, won't you?'

'My dearest,' Canolles said confidentially. 'One only gets to know something by using it, and I learned just now, by experience, that this place is not impregnable. If I were called the Duke de La Rochefoucauld, I should have the Ile Saint-Georges tomorrow morning . . . By the way, d'Elboin will not be taking lunch with us.'

'Why is that?'

'Because he was cut in two by a cannonball.'

VI

The return of the attackers to Bordeaux was a pitiful sight to behold. The townspeople had left triumphantly, counting on their numbers and the skill of their generals, in short, entirely confident of the outcome of the expedition, thanks to familiarity, that additional reassurance for a man in danger – for what man among them had not in his youth roamed the woods and fields of the Ile Saint-Georges, alone or with some sweet companion? What man of Bordeaux had not plied an oar, aimed a hunting gun or cast a fishing net in the country that he was to revisit as a soldier? So for these townsfolk the defeat was doubly cruel: the countryside shamed them as well as the enemy, and they returned with heads bowed, listening with resignation to the sound of lamentation and the moans of the women who, counting the gaps in the ranks in the manner of the savages of America, were increasingly made aware of the losses suffered in the defeat.

So a great murmur filled the town with mourning and confusion. The soldiers returned home, each describing the disaster in his own way. Their leaders went to the princess, who, as we have said, was staying with the president.

Madame de Condé was waiting for the expedition to return, standing at her window. Born into a family of warriors, wife of one of the greatest generals in the world and brought up to despise the rusty armour and ridiculous plumes of the citizen militia, she could not help feeling vaguely uneasy at the thought that these townspeople, her supporters, were going out to fight an army of experienced soldiers. But three things reassured her, in spite of that: the first was that Monsieur de La Rochefoucauld was leading the expedition; the second was that the regiment of Navailles was in the vanguard; and the third was that the name of Condé was on the banners.

But, in a contrast that is not hard to understand, all that was hope for the princess was pain for Madame de Cambes – just as everything that was about to become an agony for the illustrious lady would be a triumph for the viscountess.

It was the Duke de la Rochefoucauld who presented himself to them, covered in dust and bleeding. The sleeve of his black doublet was torn, and his shirt was covered in blood.

'Is it true, what they tell me?' the princess exclaimed, hurrying forward to meet him.

'And what do they tell you, Madame?' the duke asked coldly.

'They say that you have been repulsed.'

'What they say does not go far enough, Madame. In truth, we were beaten.'

'Beaten!' the princess exclaimed, the blood draining from her cheeks. 'Beaten! It's impossible!'

'Beaten,' the viscountess murmured. 'Beaten by Monsieur de Canolles!'

'And how did this happen?' Madame de Condé asked, in a tone that betrayed the depth of her indignation.

'It happened, Madame, as all miscalculations in gaming, in love or in war: we attacked a more skilful or a stronger force than ourselves.'

'So is he such a fine, brave fellow, this Monsieur de Canolles?' asked the princess.

Madame de Cambes's heart leapt with joy.

'Why, in faith,' said La Rochefoucauld, shrugging his shoulders, 'as brave a fellow as any! It is just that he had fresh troops and solid walls, and he was on his guard, no doubt having been warned of our arrival, so he made a meal of our townsfolk. Oh, Madame, by the by, what miserable soldiers! They fled at the second volley.'

'And Navailles?' Claire exclaimed, without seeing how unwise it was to do so.

'The whole difference between Navailles and the towns-people, Madame,' said La Rochefoucauld, 'is that the towns-people fled, and Navailles retreated.'

'All that's left now is for us to lose Vayres!'

'I don't deny it,' La Rochefoucauld replied coldly.

'Beaten!' the princess said, stamping her foot. 'Beaten by nobodies, led by a person called Canolles! The name is ridiculous.'

Claire blushed to the whites of her eyes.

'You consider that a ridiculous name, Madame,' said the duke. 'But Monsieur de Mazarin thinks it sublime. And I might almost venture to say . . .' he went on, giving Claire a brief, but penetrating glance '. . . that he is not alone in that opinion. Names are like colours, Madame,' he continued, giving one of his peevish smiles. 'There's no arguing about them.'

'Do you think that Richon is a man who will let himself be beaten?'

'Why not? I was! We must wait until we have worked through our bad luck. War is a game, and one day or another we shall have our revenge.'

'This would not have happened,' said Madame de Tourville, 'if my plan had been followed.'

'That's right,' said the princess. 'No one ever wants to do what we suggest, on the grounds that we are women and understand nothing about war . . . The men do as they please and get beaten.'

'Yes, by God, Madame, but it can happen to the best of generals. Aemilius Paulus was defeated at Cannae, Pompey at Pharsalia and Attila at Châlons.[5] Only Alexander and you, Madame de Tourville, have never been defeated. What was your plan?'

'My plan, Duke,' Madame de Tourville replied in her curtest voice, 'was to conduct a regular siege. No one bothered to listen to me; they preferred an outright capture. And this is what happened.'

'Answer Madame de Tourville, please, Lenet,' said the duke. 'I don't feel that I know enough about strategy to compete.'

Lenet's lips had not yet opened, except to smile. 'Madame,' he said, 'the argument against a siege is that the people of Bordeaux are not soldiers, but townsmen; they have to take dinner at home and sleep in their marital beds. And a conventional siege excludes a number of conveniences to which our fine citizens are accustomed, so they went to besiege the Ile Saint-Georges as amateurs. Don't blame them for failing today. They will go back over the four leagues and return to the same war as often as they must.'

'Do you think they will go back?' asked the princess.

'Oh, yes, I'm sure of that, Madame,' said Lenet. 'They love their island too much to leave it to the king.'

'And will they capture it?'

'Certainly, one day or another.'

'Well, when they do,' the princess cried, 'I want to have that insolent Canolles shot, unless he surrenders unconditionally.'

Claire felt a deathly shudder run through her.

'Shot!' said La Rochefoucauld. '*Peste!* If that's how Your Highness sees war, I am sincerely relieved to be counted among the number of her friends.'

'Well, then. Let him surrender.'

'I should like to know what Your Highness would say if Richon should surrender.'

'It's not a matter of Richon, Duke. It's not a question of Richon. Now, bring me a citizen, a juror, a counsellor . . . in short, something to which I can speak, and who will assure me that this shame will cause those who made me swallow it to regret bitterly what they have done.'

'Perfect!' said Lenet. 'Why, here is Monsieur d'Espagnet who requests the honour of being introduced to Your Highness.'

'Show him in,' said the princess.

Claire's heart, throughout this conversation, had either been beating fit to burst or crushed as if in a vice. In fact, she too had been thinking that the people of Bordeaux would make Canolles pay dearly for his first triumph. But it was much worse when d'Espagnet's protestations were added to Lenet's assurances.

'Madame,' he told the princess, 'Your Highness can rest assured: instead of four thousand men, we shall send eight thousand, and instead of six cannon we shall set up a dozen, and instead of a hundred men, we shall lose two hundred, three hundred, four hundred if necessary – but we shall retake Saint-Georges.'

'Bravo!' cried the duke. 'Now you're talking! You know that I'm your man, as leader or volunteer, each and every time you make the attempt. But you should observe that, with the loss of five hundred men each time, assuming that it takes us four attempts such as the last, our army will be reduced to one-fifth of its size.'

'There are thirty thousand of us in Bordeaux able to bear arms, Duke,' said d'Espagnet. 'If need be, we can drag all the cannons in the arsenal in front of the fortress and create a bombardment that would reduce a granite mountain to rubble. I myself shall cross the river, leading the sappers, and we shall retake Saint-Georges. We have just made a solemn oath that we will do it.'

'I doubt whether you will take Saint-Georges as long as Monsieur de Canolles is alive,' Claire said, in a barely audible voice.

'Very well,' d'Espagnet replied. 'We shall kill him or have him killed. Then we shall retake Saint-Georges.'

Madame de Cambes stifled a cry of terror that was about to emerge from her breast.

'Do you want to capture Saint-Georges?'

'What! Do we want it!' the princess exclaimed. 'I should think so. That's the one thing we do want.'

'Then, leave it to me and I'll take the fort,' said Madame de Cambes.

'Pooh!' said the princess. 'You promised me that once and failed.'

'I promised Your Highness to make an attempt to win over Monsieur de Canolles. That attempt failed: I found Monsieur de Canolles to be unmovable.'

'Do you think that he will be any more flexible after his triumph?'

'No. So this time I did not tell you that I should deliver the governor to you, I said that I should deliver the fort.'

'How?'

'By bringing your soldiers inside the courtyard of the fortress.'

'Are you a witch, Madame, to undertake such a thing?' asked La Rochefoucauld.

'No, Monsieur, I am a landowner.'

'You are joking,' said the duke.

'Not at all, not at all,' said Lenet. 'I can guess at a lot of things in the four words that Madame de Cambes has just spoken.'

'That is enough for me,' said the viscountess. 'Monsieur Lenet supports me entirely. So, I repeat that Saint-Georges will be taken, if you will let me say a few words in private to Monsieur Lenet.'

'I, too, shall take Saint-Georges, Madame,' said Madame de Tourville. 'If you will let me.'

'First let Madame de Tourville tell us openly what is her plan,' said Lenet, stopping Madame de Cambes, who was trying to lead him into a corner. 'Then you will whisper yours to me.'

'Tell us, Madame,' said the princess.

'I shall leave at night with twenty boats carrying two hundred musketeers. Another troop, of the same number, is making its way cautiously along the right bank, while four or five hundred others are going up the left bank. Meanwhile, a thousand, or twelve hundred men of Bordeaux . . .'

'Careful, Madame,' said La Rochefoucauld. 'You've already mobilized a thousand or twelve hundred men.'

'And I,' said Claire, 'will take Saint George with a single company. Let me have Navailles and I guarantee it.'

'It's worth considering,' said the princess, while La Roche-foucauld, with his most contemptuous smile, looked pityingly at all these women debating matters of war that the boldest and most enterprising of men might find it difficult to resolve.

'I am listening,' said Lenet. 'Come on, Madame.' He took the viscountess into the recess by one of the windows.

Claire whispered her secret into his ear, and Lenet gave a shout of joy.

'Indeed, now,' he said, coming back to the princess. 'This one time, if you will agree to give a free hand to Madame de Cambes, Saint-Georges will be taken.'

'When?' asked the princess.

'When you wish.'

'The lady is a great captain,' said La Rochefoucauld sarcastically.

'You may judge for yourself, Duke,' Lenet replied, 'when

you enter Saint-Georges in triumph without having fired a single shot.'

'Then I shall approve her plan.'

'Well, then,' said the princess. 'If the business is as certain as you say, let everything be made ready for tomorrow morning.'

'For whatever day and time Her Highness wishes,' Madame de Cambes replied. 'I shall await your orders in my apartment.'

Saying which, she curtsied and retired to her chamber. The princess, who had passed from anger to hope in a moment, did the same, and Madame de Tourville followed her. D'Espagnet repeated his assurances, then left, leaving the duke alone with Lenet.

VII

'My dear Lenet,' said the duke. 'Since the women are taking over the war, I think it would be a good thing for the men to become involved in a little intrigue. I have heard you speak of a man called Cauvignac, whom you commissioned to raise a company, and who has been represented to me as a useful companion. I asked for him: is there any chance of seeing him?'

'He is waiting, Monseigneur,' said Lenet.

'Let him come in then.'

Lenet pulled the cord of a bell, and a servant entered.

'Bring in Captain Cauvignac,' said Lenet.

A moment later, our old acquaintance appeared in the door: and, still being a prudent man, he waited there.

'Come over, Captain,' said the duke. 'I am the Duke de La Rochefoucauld.'

'I recognize you very well, Monseigneur,' said Cauvignac.

'Ah, so much the better. You have been commissioned to levy a company?'

'I have done so.'

'How many men do you have at your disposal?'

'One hundred and fifty.'

'Are they well equipped and armed?'

'Well armed and poorly equipped. I took care of the weapons first, as being the most essential. As for the equipment, I am a very disinterested man, inspired chiefly by my love of the princes, and having received only ten thousand livres from Monsieur Lenet, money was short.'

'With ten thousand livres you enlisted a hundred and fifty soldiers?'

'Yes, my lord.'

'Wonderful.'

'I have means by which I operate, my lord, known only to myself.'

'Where are these men?'

'They are here. You'll see what a fine company it is, my lord, especially from the spiritual point of view: all are men of quality, with not a single low-born scoundrel among them.'

The Duke de La Rochefoucauld went over to the window and did indeed see a hundred and fifty individuals in the street, of all ages, sizes and states, drawn up in two ranks by Ferguzon, Barabbas, Carrotel and their other two companions, wearing their most splendid clothes. These individuals were considerably more like a troop of bandits than a company of soldiers.

As Cauvignac had said, they were dressed in rags, but well armed.

'Have you received any orders concerning your men?' asked the duke.

'I have received the order to take them to Vayres, and I am only waiting for your lordship to entrust all my company to the hands of Monsieur Richon, who is waiting for it.'

'What about you? Won't you stay in Vayres with them?'

'I make a point of never shutting myself up between four walls when I can be wandering around the countryside. I was not born to lead a patriarch's life.'

'Fine! Stay where you wish, but send your men to Vayres.'

'So they will definitely be part of the garrison of the fort?'

'Yes.'

'Under Monsieur Richon?'

'Yes.'

'But, my lord,' said Cauvignac, 'what are my men going to do, since there are already some three hundred men in the fort?'

'You are very curious.'

'Oh, it's not a matter of curiosity, my lord, it's fear.'

'What are you afraid of?'

'I'm afraid that they might be condemned to inaction and that would be unfortunate: it is wrong let a good weapon rust.'

'Do not worry, Captain, they will not get rusty. In a week they shall be fighting.'

'But then they'll be killed, I suppose?'

'Very likely, unless as well as a means for recruiting soldiers, you also have one for making them invulnerable.'

'Oh, that's not the problem! It's just that before they get killed, I'd like to be paid for them.'

'Didn't you say that you were given ten thousand livres?'

'Yes, in cash. Ask Monsieur Lenet, who is a tidy man and who, I am sure, has remembered our agreements.'

The duke turned to Lenet.

'That's true, Duke,' said the irreproachable counsellor. 'We gave Monsieur Cauvignac ten thousand in cash for his original expenses, but we also promised him a hundred écus per man over and above these ten thousand livres.'

'So we owe the Captain thirty-five thousand francs?'

'Precisely, my lord.'

'You will be given them.'

'Might we not speak in the present tense, Duke?'

'No, that's impossible.'

'Why?'

'Because you are one of our friends, and strangers must take precedence over everyone. You will understand that it is only when one is afraid of people that one has to mollify them.'[6]

'An excellent maxim!' said Cauvignac. 'However, in every deal it is customary to set a term.'

'Fine! Let's say a week,' said the duke.

'Let's say a week,' Cauvignac agreed.

'But suppose we have not paid in a week?' asked Lenet.

'Then I shall take back the charge of my company.'

'That is only fair,' said the duke.

'And I shall do as I wish with it.'

'Since it will be yours.'

'However . . .' Lenet said.

'Pooh!' said the duke. 'Since they'll be shut up in Vayres.'

'I don't like this kind of deal,' said Lenet.

'It's very commonly met with in Normandy,' said Cauvignac. 'They call it a repurchase option.'

'Do we agree, then?' asked the duke.

'Absolutely,' Cauvignac replied.

'And when will your men leave?'

'At once, if those are your orders.'

'I order it, then.'

The captain went down, said two words in Ferguzon's ear, and Cauvignac's company, together with all the onlookers who had been drawn in a crowd around it by its peculiar appearance, set off for the port where three boats were waiting to take it up the Dordogne as far as Vayres, while its leader, loyal to the principle of freedom that he had enunciated a moment earlier to the Duke de Le Rochefoucauld, watched it go with a great deal of affection.

Meanwhile, the viscountess had retired to her apartments, where she was weeping and sobbing. 'Alas!' she told herself. 'I could not entirely save his honour, but I shall at least save the appearance of it. He must not be overcome by force: I know him; if he were to be overcome by force, he would die defending himself. So he must appear to be overcome by treachery. Then, when he knows what I have done for him and above all why I have done it, even though he is defeated, he will still bless me.'

Reassured by this hope, she got up, wrote a few words that she hid in her breast and went to see the princess, who had just called for her so that the two of them could go and succour the wounded, and bring the consolation of money to the widows and orphans.

The princess gathered all those who had taken part in the expedition. In her name and that of the Duke d'Enghien, she lauded the deeds of those who had distinguished themselves in the action, talked for a long time with Ravailly – who, with his arm in a sling, swore that he was ready to fight again the next day – put a hand on the shoulder of d'Espagnet, saying that she considered him and his brave townspeople as the strongest pillar of her cause, and finally so roused their spirits that the most downcast swore that they would take their revenge and were all for returning to the Ile Saint-Georges at that very moment.

'No, not immediately,' said the princess. 'Take a day and a night of rest and the day after tomorrow you will be settled there for good.'

This assurance, given in a firm voice, was greeted with warlike cries, each of which sank deep into the viscountess's heart like a dagger threatening her lover's life.

'See what I have undertaken to do, Claire,' said the princess. 'It is for you to acquit my debt to these good people.'

'Fear not, Madame,' the viscountess replied. 'I shall keep my promise.'

That very evening, a messenger left at full speed for Saint-Georges.

VIII

The following day, as Canolles was doing his morning round, Vibrac came up to him and handed over a letter and a key that an unknown man had brought during the night and left with the lieutenant in charge, saying that no reply was expected.

Canolles trembled when he recognized Madame de Cambes's handwriting, and his hand shook as he opened the letter.

This is what he read:

In my last letter, I warned you that the fort of Saint-Georges would be attacked during the night; in this one, I am warning you that tomorrow the fort of Saint-Georges will be captured. As a man, as a soldier of the king, you run no greater risk than that of being taken prisoner, but Mademoiselle de Lartigues's situation is quite different, and the hatred felt for her is so great that I could not answer for her life were she to fall into the hands of the people of Bordeaux. Persuade her to escape. I shall tell you how.

At the head of your bed, behind a tapestry bearing the arms of the lords of Cambes, to whom the Ile Saint-Georges used to belong in former times, being a part of their lands that the late Viscount de Cambes, my husband, gave to the king, you will find a door. Here is the key. It is one of the openings to the great underground tunnel that passes under the river and leads to the Château de Cambes. Get Mademoiselle Nanon de Lartigues to flee through this tunnel, and if you love her, flee with her . . .

I will answer for her life with my honour.

Farewell. We are quits.

Viscountess de Cambes.

Canolles read and reread this letter, shuddering with terror at every line, and paling as he read. Without knowing why, he felt that a strange power was enfolding him and disposing of him. This underground passage, which linked the head of his bed to the Château de Cambes, and which ought to allow him to save Nanon, could surely have served, if the secret of it were known, to deliver Saint-Georges to the enemy?

Vibrac was reading the most recent of these emotions on the governor's face.

'Bad news, Commander?' he asked.

'Yes, it appears that we shall be attacked once again to-morrow night.'

'The stubborn devils!' said Vibrac. 'I would have thought they might consider themselves thoroughly enough trounced and that we should not hear from them again for a week, at least.'

'I don't need to instruct you to keep the closest watch.'

'Don't worry, Commander. No doubt they will try to surprise us, as they did last time?'

'I don't know, but let's be ready for anything and take the

same precautions as we did then. Finish the round on my behalf. I'm going back to my rooms. I have some orders to send out.'

Vibrac made a sign of agreement and strode off with that military nonchalance with regard to danger that is shown by men who are in a position to meet danger at every step. As for Canolles, he went back to his room, taking as much care as possible not to be seen by Nanon. And, after ensuring that he was alone, he locked the door.

At the head of his bed were the arms of the lords of Cambes on a piece of tapestry, hemmed by a kind of gold ribbon.

Canolles lifted the ribbon, which, as it came away from the tapestry, revealed the outline of a door.

The door opened with the key that the viscountess had sent him at the same time as her letter, and Canolles found himself looking at the gaping mouth of a tunnel, which led off clearly in the direction of the Château de Cambes.

For a moment, he remained silent, the sweat beading on his forehead. This mysterious passage, which might quite easily not be the only one, filled him with terror despite himself.

He lit a candle and prepared to explore it.

First of all, he went down twenty steep stairs, then continued his descent into the depths of earth by a more gentle slope.

He soon heard a dull sound that frightened him at first, since he did not know what was causing it, then, as he went further, he could distinguish above his head the rumbling of the great river flowing towards the sea.

Several cracks had appeared in the vault, through which, at different times, water must have seeped, but these gaps, having no doubt been noticed in time, had been sealed with a sort of cement that had become harder than the stones it held together.

For almost ten minutes, Canolles heard the water flowing above his head. Then the sound gradually faded and soon was no more than a murmur. Finally, the murmur too vanished and was replaced by silence; after fifty yards or so in this silence, Canolles came to a staircase similar to the one down which he had entered, closed on its last step by a massive door that ten men together could not have broken and made fireproof by a thick plate of iron.

'Now I understand,' thought Canolles. 'They will wait for Nanon at this door, and she will be safe.'

He went back, passed once more under the river, came to his staircase, returned to his room, pinned back the ribbon and went to see Nanon, deep in thought.

IX

Nanon, as usual, was surrounded by maps, letters and books. The poor woman was fighting the civil war on the royalist side in her own way. As soon as she saw Canolles, she reached out to him in delight.

'The king is coming,' she said. 'In a week, we shall be out of danger.'

'He keeps on coming,' said Canolles, smiling sadly. 'Unfortunately, he never arrives.'

'Ah, this time I'm well informed, dear Baron, and he'll be here within a week.'

'However much he hurries, Nanon, he'll still be too late for us.'

'What are you saying?'

'I'm telling you that instead of getting excited about those maps and papers, you would do better to think about ways to escape.'

'Escape? Why?'

'Because I have bad news, Nanon. They are preparing for a new assault. This time, I might go under.'

'Very well, my dear: aren't we agreed that your fate is mine, and your fortune mine?'

'No, that cannot be. I should be too weak if I had to fear for you. Did they not try to burn you in Agen? Did they not try to throw you in the river? Listen, Nanon, for my sake, don't insist on staying. If you were here, I might do something cowardly.'

'Canolles, you are frightening me.'

'I beg you, Nanon, swear to me that if I am attacked, you will do what I order.'

'Good Lord! What use would such an oath be?'

'It would give me the strength to go on living. If you do not promise to obey me blindly, I swear that I shall have myself killed at the first opportunity.'

'Whatever you want, Canolles, everything, I swear it by our love.'

'Thank God! Now I can rest easy, Nanon. Collect up your most precious jewels. Where is your gold?'

'In a tub with an iron band around it.'

'Get that ready, so that all of it can be taken with you.'

'Canolles, you know that the real treasure of my heart is not my gold or my jewels. I hope all this is not just to send me away from you?'

'You know me for a man of honour, Nanon, don't you? Well, on my honour: everything that I am doing here is from fear of the danger to you.'

'Do you truly think I am in danger?'

'I believe that the Ile Saint-Georges will be captured to-morrow.'

'How?'

'I have no idea, but I do believe it.'

'And if I agree to escape?'

'I shall do everything I can to stay alive, I swear.'

'You order, my dear, and I shall obey,' said Nanon, giving Canolles her hand and, in the warmth of his look, forgetting two large tears that were running down her cheeks.

Canolles pressed Nanon's hand and left the room. If he had stayed a moment longer, he would have picked up these two pearls with his lips, but he put a hand on the viscountess's letter and, like a talisman, it gave him the strength to leave.

The day was hard. That emphatic threat: 'Tomorrow, the Ile Saint-Georges will be captured', constantly rang in Canolles's ears. How? By what means? What made the viscountess certain enough for her to talk in that way? Would it be attacked from the water? From the ground? From what unknown direction would this invisible, yet certain misfortune strike?

Throughout the day, Canolles burned his eyes against the

sun, looking for enemies everywhere. In the evening, he wore
his eyes out peering into the depths of the wood, across the
plain and around the bends of the river. It was all in vain: he
could see nothing.

When night came, a wing of the Château de Cambes was
lit up: this was the first time that Canolles had seen any
light there since he had come to Saint-Georges. 'Ah!' he said.
'Those are Nanon's saviours at their post.' And he gave a
deep sigh.

What a strange, mysterious enigma is that of the human
heart! Canolles no longer loved Nanon, Canolles adored
Madame de Cambes, and yet at the moment of separating from
the woman whom he no longer loved, Canolles felt his heart
break . . . It was only when he was far from her or about to
leave her that he realized the true force of what he felt for this
delightful woman.

The whole garrison was up and watching on the ramparts.
Canolles, weary with looking, listened to the silence of the
night. Never had darkness been more empty of noise or seemed
more lonely. No sound disturbed a calm which was like that of
the desert.

Suddenly, it struck Canolles that it might be through the
same underground passage he had recently examined that the
enemy would enter the fortress. This was unlikely, since if it
were the case, he would not have been warned, but he resolved
to guard the tunnel nonetheless. He had a barrel of gunpowder
made ready with a fuse, chose the bravest of his sergeants,
rolled the barrel to the top step of the tunnel, lit a torch and
put it in the sergeant's hand. Two other men were stationed
close by.

'If more than six men appear in this tunnel,' he told the
sergeant, 'order them to withdraw, and, if they refuse, light the
fuse and set the barrel rolling. Since the tunnel slopes down-
wards, it will explode among them.'

The sergeant took the torch, while the two soldiers stood
motionless behind him, lit by its reddish glow, with the barrel
containing the gunpowder at their feet.

Canolles returned, feeling calm, at least where this was concerned. But when he reached his room, he found Nanon, who had seen him come down from the ramparts and return to his room, and had followed him in case there was news. She was staring in terror at this unexpected, gaping hole.

'My God!' she asked. 'What is this door?'

'The door of the tunnel through which you will escape, Nanon.'

'You promised me only to insist that I left you if there was an attack.'

'I still promise that.'

'Everything around the island seems very quiet, dear.'

'And everything seems very quiet inside too, doesn't it? Well, despite that, only twenty yards from us there is a barrel of gunpowder, a man and a torch. If the man put the torch to the barrel, a second later not a stone in the fortress would be left standing on another. That's how quiet everything is, Nanon!'

The blood drained from the young woman's face.

'You're making me shudder,' she said.

'Call your women,' said Canolles. 'Tell them to come here with your boxes. Get your valet to bring your money here. I may be wrong: perhaps nothing will happen tonight. No matter, let's be prepared.'

'Who goes there?' shouted the voice of the sergeant in the tunnel.

Another voice replied, but not in a hostile tone.

'Here,' said Canolles. 'Someone has come to fetch you.'

'We're not under attack yet, my dear. Everything is calm. Keep me beside you, they are not coming.'

As Nanon was saying this, the shout of 'Who goes there?' resounded three times in the inner courtyard, and the third time was followed by the sound of a musket shot.

Canolles ran to the window and opened it.

'To arms!' the sentry cried. 'To arms!'

In a corner of the courtyard, Canolles saw a black, moving mass: it was the enemy, streaming out of a low, arched door, which opened into a cellar that served as a wood store. No doubt, there was some unknown entrance in this cellar as there was at the head of Canolles's bed.

'There they are!' Canolles shouted. 'Hurry up! There they are!'

At the same moment, some twenty shots replied to the one that the sentry had fired. Two or three musket balls broke the window as Canolles was shutting it. He turned round to see Nanon on her knees, and the women and her manservant running into the room.

'There's not a moment to lose,' Canolles cried. 'Come! Come!'

He picked the young woman up in his arms, as though he were picking up a feather, and plunged into the tunnel, shouting to Nanon's servants to follow.

The sergeant was at his post, his torch in hand, while the two soldiers were standing by with their muskets primed, ready to fire on a group in the midst of which, pale-faced and making many protestations of friendship, was our old friend, Pompée.

'Ah, Monsieur de Canolles!' he cried. 'Tell them that we are the people you were expecting. By all that's wonderful! These are not the sort of jokes to play on one's friends.'

'Pompée,' said Canolles. 'Take care of Madame. Someone you know gave me a guarantee on her honour. And you will answer to me for her with your life.'

'Yes, yes, I promise,' said Pompée.

'Canolles, Canolles! I won't leave you!' Nanon cried, clasping him around the neck. 'Canolles, you promised to follow me.'

'I promised to defend the fortress of Saint-Georges as long as a stone remained standing, and I shall keep that promise.'

And, despite Nanon's cries, tears and entreaties, Canolles handed her over to Pompée, who, assisted by two or three servants of Madame de Cambes and some of the fugitive's own people, led her into the depths of the tunnel.

Canolles looked after this sweet, white ghost for a moment as it disappeared, still holding out its hands to him. But suddenly he recalled that he was expected elsewhere and ran to the staircase, calling out to the sergeant and the two soldiers to follow him.

Vibrac was in the room, hatless, pale and holding a sword in his hand. 'Commander!' he shouted, seeing Canolles. 'The enemy . . . the enemy!'

'I know.'

'What can we do?'

'Huh! That's a fine question! Get ourselves killed.'

Canolles rushed into the courtyard. As he went, he noticed a miner's axe and grabbed it.

The courtyard was full of the enemy: sixty soldiers of the garrison, standing together, were trying to defend the door of Canolles's apartments. From the ramparts, you could hear cries and shots, indicating that the battle was raging everywhere.

'The commander! The commander!' the soldiers cried, when they saw Canolles.

'Yes!' he replied. 'The commander, who is going to die with you! Courage! They attacked treacherously, because they could not defeat you.'

'All's fair in war,' said Ravailly's mocking voice: with his arm in a sling, he was rallying his men to capture Canolles. 'Give up, Canolles, give up. You'll be well treated.'

'Ah, it's you, Ravailly,' Canolles shouted. 'I thought I'd paid my debt of friendship to you. You're not satisfied? Well, just wait.'

And Canolles, leaping five or six paces forward, threw the axe he was holding at Ravailly with such force that it struck an officer of the townspeople who was standing next to the captain of Navailles, splitting his helmet and his gorget and killing him on the spot.

'Damn!' said Ravailly. 'That's how you reply to our courtesies. Though I ought to be used to your manners. My friends, he is rabid. Fire at him! fire!'

On this order, a powerful burst of fire came from the enemy ranks, and five or six men fell next to Canolles.

'Fire!' he cried in turn. 'Fire!'

However, barely three or four musket shots replied. Surprised at the moment when they were least expecting it, and disturbed by the dark, Canolles's men were losing heart.

Canolles saw that there was nothing to be done. 'Go back,' he told Vibrac. 'And take your men inside. We'll barricade ourselves and only surrender when they have taken us by assault.'

'Fire!' repeated two other voices – those of d'Espagnet and La Rochefoucauld. 'Remember your dead comrades who demand revenge. Fire!'

And the hail of musket balls came whistling again around Canolles, without hitting him, but once more decimating his little troop.

'Withdraw!' Vibrac said. 'Withdraw!'

'Have at them!' yelled Ravailly. 'Forward, my friends, forward!'

The enemy plunged forward. Canolles, with about ten men at the most, withstood the onslaught. He had picked up a gun from a dead soldier and was using it as a club.

His companions went inside, and he was the last to follow them, with Vibrac. Both men braced themselves against the door and managed to close it, despite the efforts of the assailants, before shutting it with a huge iron bar.

There were grilles over the windows.

'Axes, levers, cannon if necessary!' cried the voice of the Duke de La Rochefoucauld. 'We must take them all, dead or alive!'

A frightful burst of gunfire followed these words. Two or three balls got through the door, and one smashed Vibrac's thigh.

'Commander,' he said, 'I've had my day. Now see what you can do for yours. It's not my business any more.' And he slumped down beside the wall, unable to stand.

Canolles looked round. A dozen men were still able to defend themselves, among them the sergeant whom he had put in charge of the tunnel.

'The torch,' he said. 'What did you do with the torch?'

'Why, Commander, I dropped it near the barrel.'

'Is it still alight?'

'Probably.'

'Good. Take these men out through the back doors and windows. Get the best terms you can for them. The rest is up to me.'

'But, Commander . . .'

'Do as I say.'

The sergeant bowed his head and signalled to his men to follow him. They all went out through the back rooms, having understood what Canolles meant to do, and not wishing to be blown up with him.

For a moment, Canolles listened. The door was being broken in with axes, though this did not stop the gunfire which was directed aimlessly at the windows, behind which the besieged men were assumed to be hiding.

Suddenly, a great roar announced that the door had given way, and Canolles heard the crowd rushing into the castle with cries of joy. 'Very well,' he thought. 'In five minutes those cries of joy will be shouts of despair.' And he hurried into the tunnel.

But there was a young man sitting on the barrel, with the torch at his feet, his head resting in both hands. At the noise, this young man looked up, and Canolles recognized Madame de Cambes.

'Ah, here he is at last!' she exclaimed.

'Claire!' Canolles said. 'What do you want here?'

'To die with you, if you want to die.'

'I am dishonoured, lost, I must die.'

'You are saved and glorious! Saved by me!'

'Lost by you! Can you hear them? They are coming, they are here. Claire, you must escape, through this tunnel. You have five minutes. That's more than you need.'

'I am not going to escape. I'm staying here.'

'But do you know why I have come down here? Do you know what I am going to do?'

Madame de Cambes picked up the torch and took it over to the barrel of gunpowder.

'I can guess,' she said.

'Claire,' Canolles said in horror. 'Claire!'

'Tell me again that you want to die, and we shall die together.'

The viscountess's pale face showed such resolve that Canolles realized she would keep to her word. He stopped.

'But what do you want?' he asked

'I want you to give up.'

'Never!' Canolles exclaimed.

'We have not got much time,' the viscountess continued. 'Give up. I offer you life, I offer you honour, since I give you the excuse of treason.'

'Let me flee, then. I shall go and lay my sword at the king's feet and ask him for the opportunity to take my revenge.'

'You would not flee.'

'Why not?'

'Because I cannot live in this way ... because I cannot live apart from you ... because I love you.'

'I surrender, I surrender!' Canolles cried, falling at Madame de Cambes's feet and casting away the torch that she had been holding.

'Oh,' said the viscountess to herself. 'This time I have him, and no one will take him from me again.'

There is a strange phenomenon, which can nonetheless be explained, which means that love could act in such a different way on these two women.

Madame de Cambes, reserved, soft and shy, had become determined, bold and strong.

Nanon – capricious and wilful – had become shy, soft and reserved.

This is because Madame de Cambes increasingly felt herself loved by Canolles.

And because Nanon realized that every day Canolles's love for her was fading.

X

The second entry of the princes' armies into Bordeaux was very different from the first. This time, there were laurels for everyone, even for the defeated.

With tact and delicacy, Madame de Cambes had granted a fair share of them to Canolles, who, as soon as he had broken through the barrier beside his friend, Ravailly, whom he had nearly killed for the second time, was surrounded like a great captain and congratulated like a gallant soldier.

Those defeated two days earlier, especially those who had taken a few knocks in the battle, had conceived a certain measure of resentment against their conqueror, but Canolles was so good, so fine and so simple, he bore his present situation with such good humour and such dignity, he had been supported by a retinue of such eager and considerate friends, and the officers and soldiers of the regiment of Navailles praised him so highly as their captain and as Governor of the Ile Saint-Georges, that the Bordeaux men soon forgot. In any case, they had a lot else to think about.

Monsieur de Bouillon was coming the next day or the one after, and the most reliable news reported that, in a week at the latest, the king would be at Libourne.

Madame de Condé was dying to see Canolles. At her window, hidden behind the curtain, she watched him go by and found that he had an altogether triumphal appearance, which corresponded perfectly to the reputation that both friends and enemies had given him.

Madame de Tourville, differing from the opinion of the princess, claimed that he was lacking in distinction. Lenet stated that he considered him an honourable gentleman, and La Rochefoucauld merely said: 'Ah, so this is the hero!'

Canolles was given rooms in the great fortress of the town, the Château-Trompette.[7] By day, he was quite free to wander around the town, conduct his business or indulge his pleasure. At curfew, he went back indoors: all on his word of honour that he would not try to escape and not correspond with anyone outside.

Before making this last promise, Canolles had asked permission to write four lines. The permission was granted, and he had the following letter taken to Nanon.

A prisoner, but free inside Bordeaux on my word of honour that I shall not communicate with anyone outside, I am writing these few words to you, dear Nanon, to assure you of my friendship, which my silence might otherwise make you doubt. I am relying on you to defend my honour to the king and queen.
Baron de Canolles

The influence of Madame de Cambes could be felt in the conditions of his capture, which, as one can see, were very mild.

It was five or six days before Canolles had done with all the meals and celebrations that were given for him by his friends. He was constantly to be seen with Ravailly, who walked around with his left arm linked in that of Canolles's and his right arm in a sling. When the drum beat, and the people of Bordeaux left on some expedition or hurried to quell some riot or other, you were bound to see Canolles at the roadside, with Ravailly on his arm, or else alone, his hands clasped behind his back, looking on and smiling, curious and harmless.

In fact, since his arrival he had only rarely had a sight of Madame de Cambes and had barely spoken to her. It seemed to be enough for the viscountess that he was not beside Nanon, and she was happy, as she had said, to be keeping him close to her. So Canolles had written gently to complain, and she had had him invited to one or two houses in the town, with that protection, invisible to the eyes, but tangible to the heart, so to speak, of the woman who loves but does not want to reveal it.

There was more. Through Lenet, Canolles had received permission to pay court to Madame de Condé, and the handsome prisoner appeared there from time to time, buzzing and clucking around the princess's women.

Moreover, there was no man who appeared less interested in political affairs than Canolles. Seeing Madame de Cambes, exchanging a few words with her, or, if he could not manage to speak to her, eliciting an affectionate gesture, pressing her hand as she climbed into her coach . . . and, Huguenot though he was, offering her some holy water in church – these were the great matters of the prisoner's day.

At night, he thought about what had happened during the day.

However, after a while, this entertainment was not enough for him. And, since he understood the fine feelings of Madame de Cambes, who was more afraid for Canolles's honour than for her own, he tried to expand the circle of his activities. First of all, he fought duels with an officer of the garrison and two townsmen, which did occupy him for a few hours. But since he disarmed one of his adversaries and wounded the other two, this amusement was soon denied him, as there were not enough people willing to provide it.

Then he had one or two pieces of good luck. This was not surprising: apart from the fact that Canolles, as we have said, was a very handsome youth, he had become an object of extreme interest since being taken prisoner. For three full days and the whole morning of the fourth, people had spoken about his captivity, which was almost as much time as had been devoted to that of the prince.

One day when Canolles was hoping to see Madame de Cambes in church – and when Madame de Cambes, perhaps for fear of meeting him, had not come – Canolles, stationed at his post beside the column, offered holy water to a charming lady, whom he had not previously met. This was not Canolles's fault, but the viscountess's: if she had come, he would not have thought of anyone but her, seen anyone but her, or offered holy water to anyone but her.

The same day, as Canolles was wondering who this charming brunette could be, he received an invitation to spend the evening with the advocate general Lavie, the same man who had tried to prevent the entrance of the princess into Bordeaux, and who, as a supporter of the royal authority, was detested almost as much as Monsieur d'Epernon. Canolles, who felt an increasing need to distract himself, gratefully welcomed the invitation and at six o'clock went to the house of the advocate general.

To our modern partygoers, this may seem to be an odd time of day, but there were two reasons why Canolles went to see the advocate general so early. The first was that, in those days, as lunch was taken at midday, evenings began much sooner; and the second was that as Canolles regularly returned to Château-Trompette at half past nine at the latest, if he wanted to do more than simply make an appearance, he had to be among the first to arrive.

As he entered the drawing room, Canolles gave a cry of joy:

Madame Lavie was none other than the charming brunette to whom he had so gallantly offered holy water that very morning.

He was greeted in the home of the advocate general as a royalist who has proved his loyalty. Hardly had he been presented than he was overwhelmed with tributes that might have turned the head of one of the seven sages of Greece. His defence against the first attack was compared to that of Horatius Cocles, and his later defeat to the capture of Troy, brought down by the wiles of Ulysses.[8]

'My dear Monsieur de Canolles,' said the advocate general. 'I know from a reliable source that you have been much spoken of at court and that your fine defence covered you in glory. The queen has sworn that she will exchange you for another prisoner as soon as she can and that on the day when you return to serve her it will be with the rank of colonel or brigadier. Now, do you wish to be exchanged?'

'Why, Monsieur,' Canolles replied, casting a lethal glance at Madame Lavie, 'I promise you that my greatest desire is that the queen should not be in too much of a hurry: she would have to exchange me for money or for a good soldier. I would not like to occasion this expenditure, and I do not deserve such an honour. I shall wait until Her Majesty captures Bordeaux, where I am at present very content. Then she will have me for nothing.'

Madame Lavie gave Canolles a charming smile.

'My goodness!' said her husband. 'You are lukewarm about your freedom, Baron.'

'Why should I get heated about it? Do you think that it is much of a pleasure for me to return to active service and find myself liable at any moment to kill one of my friends?'

'But what kind of life do you have here?' asked the advocate general. 'A life unworthy of a man of your calibre, kept aside from every discussion and every undertaking, forced to see others serving the cause to which they belong, while you have your arms folded. Useless, set aside – that's what you are. You must find it hard.'

Canolles looked at Madame Lavie, who returned his look.

'No,' he said, 'you are wrong. I'm not at all bored. You concern yourself with politics, which is very tedious, while I make love, which is very diverting. You are one of the queen's servants, while the rest serve the princess ... And I am not attached to any sovereign: I am the slave of all women.'

This retort was much appreciated, and the lady of the house gave another smile, showing what she thought of it.

Soon they split into groups for cards. Canolles began to play. Madame Lavie joined the game with him against her husband, who lost five hundred pistoles.

On the following day, the people, I don't know why, decided to have a riot. A supporter of the princes who was more fanatical than the rest suggested that they go and throw stones through Madame Lavie's windows. When the windowpanes had been broken, another suggested setting fire to the house. They were already running to get torches, when Canolles arrived with a detachment of the regiment of Navailles, carried Madame Lavie to safety and rescued her husband from the hands of a dozen enthusiasts, who, prevented from burning him, wanted to hang him at least.

'Well, sir, you man of action!' said Canolles to the advocate general, who was white with terror. 'What do you think of my idleness now? Is it not better for me to do nothing?'

At that, he went back into Château-Trompette, as the curfew was just sounding. When he arrived, he found a letter on his table shaped in a way that made his heart beat faster and in a handwriting that made him tremble.

It was the handwriting of Madame de Cambes.

Canolles opened the letter and read: 'Tomorrow, be alone at the Carmelite church at six in the evening and go to the first confessional on the left as you enter. You will find the door open.'

'Why!' Canolles thought. 'That's an original idea!'

There was a postscript. 'Do not boast,' it said, 'of where you went yesterday and today. Bordeaux is not a royalist town: consider that and let the fate that the advocate general would have suffered without you give you pause for thought.'

'Good!' thought Canolles. 'She is jealous. So I was right, whatever she says, to go to Monsieur Lavie's yesterday and today.'

XI

Since arriving in Bordeaux, Canolles had gone through all the torments of unhappy love. He had seen the viscountess fussed over, the centre of attention and adulated, without being able to pay court to her himself, and his only consolation had been to catch the occasional glance that Claire managed to give him when the gossipmongers' heads were turned. After the scene in the tunnel and the passionate words that he and the viscountess had exchanged at that supreme moment, this state of affairs no longer seemed to him lukewarm, but like ice. However, since Canolles felt behind all this coolness that he was truly and deeply loved, he had decided to be the most unfortunate of fortunate lovers. After all, it was easy to do. Because he had given his word not to have any contacts outside the city, he had relegated Nanon to that small corner of the conscience which is reserved for remorse in affairs of the heart. And, since he had no news of the young woman and consequently spared himself the worry that always comes from conflict – that is to say, the tangible memory of the woman to whom one is being unfaithful – his remorse was not excessively unbearable.

However, occasionally, even at a moment when the happiest smile spread across the young man's face, and when his voice was exulting in witty and joyful remarks, a cloud would suddenly pass across his brow, and a sigh escape, if not from his heart, at least from his lips. The sigh was for Nanon; the cloud was the memory of past times throwing its shadow over the present.

Madame de Cambes had noticed these instants of sadness. Her eyes had penetrated to the depths of Canolles's heart, and it occurred to her that she could not afford to leave Canolles abandoned to his own devices in this way. Between an old love which was not quite extinct, and a new passion that might flare up, this excess of amorous vigour which had previously been used up in military affairs and the prospect of high office might become a threat to that pure love that she sought to inspire in him. In any case, she was only trying to gain time until the memory of all these romantic adventures might be more or less obliterated, after having aroused the curiosity of everyone in the princess's court. It could be that Madame de Cambes was wrong, and that, if she had declared her love openly, people would have been less preoccupied with it, or else for a shorter time.

The person, however, who was most attentively and most successfully following the progress of this mysterious affair was Lenet. His observant eye had for some time recognized the existence of the viscountess's passion without knowing its object. He had not, it is true, guessed the precise status of this feeling and did not know whether it was requited or not; simply that Madame de Cambes, who was sometimes trembling and uncertain, sometimes strong and determined, and almost always indifferent to the pleasures that were being enjoyed around her, seemed to him to have been truly enraptured. Suddenly the passionate interest that she had taken in the war had faded, and she was no longer anxious or strong, wavering or decisive: she was pensive, smiling without evident cause, weeping without evident cause, as if her lips and her eyes were responding to the movements of her thoughts and the contrary impulses of her mind. This change had happened over the previous six or seven days, and it was six or seven days since Canolles had been captured. There was no longer any doubt that Canolles was the object of her love.

Moreover, Lenet was quite ready to give his support to a feeling that might one day provide such a brave defender for the princess.

Monsieur de La Rochefoucauld was perhaps still further advanced than Lenet in his exploration of Madame de Cambes's heart, but his gestures, his eyes and his mouth said so exactly what he allowed them to say, and no more, that no one could have told whether he felt love or hatred for Madame de Cambes.

As for Canolles, he did not speak of him, look at him or take any more account of him than if he had not existed, while acting the warrior more than ever and posing as a hero – a pretension in which he was aided by unfailing courage and genuine military skills – to give daily more importance to his own position as the general's second-in-command. Monsieur de Bouillon, on the contrary, was cold, mysterious and scheming, as well as being admirably served in his schemes by attacks of gout that sometimes arrived so conveniently that one was inclined to doubt their reality; he continued to negotiate and to keep out of sight as much as possible, unable to get used to the immense change from Richelieu to Mazarin and constantly fearing for his head, which he almost lost on the same scaffold as Cinq-Mars, and which he was able to save only by handing over Sedan, his home town, and renouncing his status as a sovereign prince, in fact at least, if not in law.[9]

As for the town itself, it was carried away by the tide of courtly manners that swept over it on all sides. Caught between two fires, between two deaths and between two ruins, the people of Bordeaux were so unsure of the morrow that they had to do something to make this precarious existence more agreeable, as they could only count on the future second by second.

They recalled La Rochelle, which had previously been laid waste by Louis XIII, and they recalled Anne of Austria's great admiration for this feat of arms . . . Why might Bordeaux not offer this princess a second La Rochelle for her hatred and her ambition?

They forgot that the one who stood too high above the rest or whose head appeared above the parapet was dead and that Cardinal Mazarin was hardly a shadow of Cardinal Richelieu.

So everyone let himself go, and Canolles was carried away by this fever like the rest. It is true that sometimes he would doubt everything, and in such fits of scepticism he would even doubt Madame de Cambes's love, with the rest of the things of this world. In such moments, Nanon would grow larger and more tender in his heart, and more devoted, by her very absence. In such moments, had Nanon appeared before him, inconstant fellow that he was, he would have fallen at her feet.

It was amid all these confusions of ideas (of a kind that only a heart can understand that has found itself torn between two loves), that Canolles received the viscountess's letter. Of course, every other thought vanished at that moment. After reading it, he could not understand that he could ever have loved anyone but Madame de Cambes, and after rereading it, he believed that he never had loved anyone but her.

Canolles spent one of those feverish nights that both excite and relax, happiness providing a counterweight to insomnia. Although he had hardly closed his eyes throughout the night, he was up as soon as day broke.

We know how lovers spend the hours before a meeting: looking at their watches, running backwards and forwards and ignoring their dearest friends because they no longer recognize them. Canolles did all the foolish things demanded by his state.

On the dot (he was coming into the church for the twentieth time), he went to the confessional, which was open. The rays of the setting sun were shining through the dark windows, and the whole of the sacred building was lit with that mysterious light which is so pleasant to those who pray and those who love. Canolles would have given a year of his life not to lose hope at that moment.

He looked around to make sure that the church was empty, peering into each chapel, and then, when he was convinced that no one could see him, went into the confessional and closed the door behind him.

XII

A moment later, Claire herself, wrapped in a thick mantle, appeared at the door, leaving Pompée outside as sentry, then, after making sure in her turn that she ran no risk of being seen, went and knelt on one of the stools in the confessional.

'At last! It's you!' said Canolles. 'Finally, you have taken pity on me.'

'I had to, since you were destroying yourself,' Claire replied, quite disturbed at speaking a lie in this court of truth – a very innocent lie, but one nonetheless.

'So if you are good enough to come here, I have to thank a simple feeling of commiseration,' said Canolles. 'Why, surely you must admit that I am entitled to expect better than that from you!'

'Let us speak seriously,' said Claire, trying in vain to control the trembling in her voice. 'And in a manner fitting to this holy place. I repeat, you will be lost if you visit Monsieur Lavie, who is the sworn enemy of the princess. Yesterday, Madame de Condé learned of it from Monsieur de La Rochefoucauld, who knows everything, and spoke these words that struck fear into me: "If we also have to fear plotting by our prisoners, we shall have to apply severity, where previously we showed indulgence. In dangerous situations, firm decisions are needed: not only are we ready to make them, but also determined to carry them out."'

The viscountess said these words in a firmer voice: she felt that in view of the reason, God would excuse the action, and this was a sort of salve to her conscience.

'I am not a knight of Her Highness's, Madame,' Canolles replied. 'I am your knight and none other. I delivered myself to you and to you alone: you know the circumstances and the conditions.'

'I had not thought that there were any conditions made,' said Claire.

'Not in so many words, perhaps, but in the heart. Oh, Madame! After what you said to me, after the happiness that you allowed me to glimpse and after the hope that you gave me! Oh, admit honestly that you have been most unkind!'

'My friend,' Claire replied. 'Can you reproach me for taking as much care of your honour as of my own? Do you not realize – I have to admit this to you, since you would certainly guess it – do you not realize that I have suffered as much as you, perhaps more so, since I have not had the strength to bear this suffering? Listen to me, and let my words, which come from the bottom of my heart, go to the depths of yours. I told you, my friend, that I have suffered more than you, being obsessed with a fear that you cannot experience, since you know that I love no one but you. In staying here, do you have any yearning for the person who is no longer here, and, in your dreams of the future, do you have any wishes that are not connected with me?'

'Madame,' said Canolles, 'you ask me to be frank, and I am going to speak to you frankly. Yes, when you abandoned me to my painful thoughts, when you left me alone with my past, when you condemned me by your absence to spend my time in low haunts with those foppish simpletons, courting their little women, and when you avoided me with your eyes or made me pay so dearly for a word, a gesture or a look – which maybe I do not deserve . . . yes, then I regret not having died fighting and reproach myself for surrendering. I feel regret and remorse.'

'Remorse?'

'Yes, Madame, remorse, because as truly as God is on this holy altar, in front of which I am telling you that I love you, there is at this moment a woman who weeps, who moans, who would give her life for me, and yet who believes that I am either a coward or a traitor.'

'Monsieur!'

'Indeed, Madame: did she not make me everything that I am? Did she not have my word that I would save her?'

'But you did save her, surely . . .'

'Yes, from enemies who might have tormented her life, but not from the despair that is tearing her heart, if that woman knows you are the person to whom I surrendered.'

Claire bowed her head and sighed.

'Ah, you do not love me!' she said. And Canolles sighed in turn. 'I do not wish to tempt you, Monsieur,' she continued. 'I do not want to make you lose a friend of whom I am not worthy; yet, as you know, I too love you. I came here to ask for your devoted and exclusive love. I came to tell you: I am free, here is my hand. I offer it to you, because I, for my part, have no one to set against you, and I know no one who is superior to you.'

'Madame, you have transported me!' cried Canolles. 'You make me the happiest of men!'

'Ah,' she said, sadly. 'But you, Monsieur, do not love me.'

'I love you – I adore you. But words cannot express what I suffered by your silence and your reserve.'

'Oh, Lord! Do you perceive nothing, you men?' Claire replied, raising her lovely eyes to heaven. 'Do you not realize that I wanted to avoid making you play a ridiculous part: I didn't want it to be possible for anyone to believe that the surrender of Saint-Georges was arranged between us? No, I wanted you to be exchanged by the queen or ransomed by me, so that you would belong to me unreservedly. Alas, you could not wait!'

'Now, Madame, now I shall wait. An hour like this and a promise in your sweet voice telling me that you love me, and I can wait for hours, days, years . . .'

'You still love Mademoiselle de Lartigues,' Madame de Cambes said, shaking her head.

'If I were to tell you that I do not have a feeling of grateful friendship for her,' Canolles replied, 'I should be lying. Believe me and accept me with that feeling. I give you all the love that I can, and that is a lot.'

'Alas,' said Claire, 'I do not know if I should accept, because you are demonstrating that you have a generous heart, but also a very amorous one.'

'Listen,' Canolles continued. 'I should die to spare you a tear, and I am unmoved at knowing that I am making the person you mention weep. Poor woman, she has enemies indeed, and those who do not know her speak ill of her. You have only friends. Those who do not know you, respect you, and those who do know you, love you. So you may judge the difference in these two feelings: one is dictated by my conscience, the other by my heart.'

'Thank you, my dear. But perhaps you are giving way to an immediate affection produced by my presence, and you may later relent. So weigh my words. I am giving you until tomorrow to reply. If there is anything you want to tell Mademoiselle de Lartigues, if you want to see her, you are free, Canolles: I shall take you by the hand and lead you through the gates of Bordeaux myself.'

'Madame, it is pointless to wait until tomorrow,' Canolles replied. 'I tell you this with a burning heart, but a cool head. I love you, I love only you, and I shall never love anyone but you.'

'Thank you, thank you, my friend!' Claire cried, sliding back the grille and putting her hand through the opening. 'My hand is yours, my heart is yours.'

Canolles grasped the hand and covered it with kisses.

'Pompée is signalling to me that it is time to leave,' she said. 'No doubt they are going to close the church. Farewell, dear, or rather goodbye until we meet again. Tomorrow you will know what I want to do for you, that is to say for us. Tomorrow you will be happy, because I shall be happy.'

And, unable to restrain the feeling that drew her towards him, she pulled his hand towards her, kissed the ends of his fingers and lightly fled, leaving Canolles as happy as the angels whose celestial choirs seemed to be echoing in his heart.

XIII

Meanwhile, as Nanon had said, the king, the queen, the cardinal and Marshal de La Meilleraie had set out to punish a rebel town that had dared openly to take the side of the princes. They were approaching slowly, but they were approaching.

When they reached Libourne, the king received a deputation of the citizens of Bordeaux, who came to assure him of their respect and devotion. This assurance, given the state of affairs, was strange. So the queen received the ambassadors in her haughtiest Austrian manner.

'Gentlemen,' she told them, 'we are going to continue our route through Vayres, so we shall soon be able to judge for ourselves whether your respect and devotion are as sincere as you say.'

At the mention of Vayres, the envoys, no doubt informed of

some circumstance that was unknown to the queen, looked at one another with something like anxiety. Anne of Austria, who missed nothing, did not fail to notice these looks.

'Let's go at once to Vayres,' she said. 'We are assured by the Duke d'Epernon that the place is good, so we shall put the king up there.' Then she turned to her captain and the members of her entourage. 'So who is in charge in Vayres?' she asked.

'They say, Madame, that it is a new governor,' Guitaut[10] replied.

'A reliable man, I hope?' the queen said, raising an eyebrow.

'One of the Duke d'Epernon's men.'

The queen's face lit up.

'If that's the case,' she said, 'we'll march quickly.'

'Your Majesty must do as she wishes,' said the Marshal de La Meilleraie. 'But I think that we should not march faster than the army. A warlike entry into the fortress of Vayres would do wonders. It is good for the king's subjects to know His Majesty's forces: it encourages the loyal and discourages plotters.'

'I think that Marshal de La Meilleraie is right,' said Cardinal Mazarin.

'And I think he is wrong,' the queen retorted. 'We have nothing to fear from Bordeaux. The king is strong in himself and not through his troops. My household will be enough.'

Marshal de La Meilleraie bowed his head obediently.

'As Your Majesty demands,' he said. 'Your Majesty is queen.'

The queen called Guitaut, ordering him to round up the guards, the musketeers and the light horse. The king mounted a horse and rode to the front. Mazarin's niece and the ladies-in-waiting got into a carriage, and they all started out for Vayres. The army followed, and, as the distance was only six leagues, it could expect to arrive three or four hours after the king and camp on the left bank of the Dordogne.

The king was barely twelve years old, yet he was already a fine rider, handling his mount elegantly and possessing in all his person the inbred pride that would later make him the most demanding of European kings in the matter of etiquette.

Brought up under the eyes of the queen, but persecuted by the cardinal's unending miserliness that meant he lacked some basic necessities, he was waiting with furious impatience for the time when he would reach the age of majority, on the following fifth of September; and already, in advance, he would occasionally forget himself enough to let slip those royal jests that suggested what he would one day become. He had therefore been very much delighted with this campaign: it was in some sense an anticipation, a training in captaincy, an essay in monarchy. He rode along proudly, sometimes beside the door of the coach, waving to the queen and making eyes at Madame de Frontenac (with whom he was said to be in love), and sometimes at the head of his household, chatting with Marshal de La Meilleraie and old Guitaut about the campaigns of King Louis XIII and the prowess of the late cardinal.[11]

Proceeding in this way and chatting as they went, they made good time and were beginning to see the towers and galleries of the fortress of Vayres. The weather was splendid and the countryside picturesque; the sun cast its slanting rays across the river; they appeared to be taking a walk, so much did the queen pretend to be joyful and in good humour. The king was advancing between Marshal de La Meilleraie and Guitaut, keeping his eye on the fortress in which not a movement could be seen, though it was more than probable that the sentries, who were visible, had noticed for their part and reported this brilliant advance party of the king's army.

The queen's coach speeded up and took its place at the head of the procession.

'But one thing astonishes me, Marshal,' said Mazarin.

'What is that, Monseigneur?'

'It seems to me that good governors usually know what is going on around their fortresses and that when a king takes the trouble to march towards one of them, they at least owe him a deputation.'

'Pooh!' said the queen, bursting out into a raucous, strained laugh. 'Mere ceremonies! There's nothing to that: I prefer loyalty.'

Monsieur de La Meilleraie covered his face with a handker-chief to conceal either a grimace, or at least the desire that he had to make one.

'But the fact is that no one is moving,' said the young king, quite displeased by such disregard for the rules of etiquette, respect for which would later form the basis of his greatness.

'Sire,' Anne of Austria replied. 'Monsieur de La Meilleraie here and Guitaut will tell you that a governor's first duty, especially in enemy country for fear of being surprised, is to keep quiet and under cover behind his fortifications. Do you not see your flag, the flag of Henri IV and François I, flying above the fortress?'

And she pointed proudly to this meaningful emblem, which showed how right she was in her expectation.

The procession continued on its way, and as it did so came across an outwork that seemed to have been put up only a few days earlier.

'Ha!' said the marshal. 'It appears that the governor really is a professional. This outwork is well placed and the retrench-ment well designed.'

The queen looked out of the window of her coach, and the king stood up in his stirrups.

A lone sentry was marching on the demi-lune, but apart from that, the retrenchment seemed as silent and solitary as the fortress itself.

'Be that as it may,' said Mazarin. 'Though I am not a soldier, and I do not know the military duties of a governor, I do find this way of behaving towards a royal person a little odd.'

'Let's keep on,' said the marshal. 'We'll soon see.'

When the little troop was only a hundred yards from the retrenchment, the sentry, who until then had been marching up and down, halted. Then, after looking for a moment, he cried: 'Who goes there?'

'The king!' Monsieur de La Meilleraie replied.

At this single word, Anne of Austria expected to see soldiers running around, officers hurrying, bridges being lowered, doors opening and raised swords flashing.

Nothing of the kind took place.

The sentry stood to attention, set his musket to bar the way to the newcomers and merely said in a loud, firm voice: 'Halt!'

The king went pale with anger, while Anne of Austria bit her lips till they bled. Mazarin muttered an Italian swear word which was not current in France, but which he had never managed to discard. The Marshal de La Meilleraie gave just one glance at Their Majesties, but it spoke volumes.

'I like it when people take precautions in my service,' said the queen, trying to lie to herself, because despite the artificial look of confidence on her face, she was starting to feel very worried.

'I like it when they respect my person,' muttered the young king, fixing a bleak stare at the impassive sentry.

XIV

Meanwhile, the cry: 'The king! The king!' – given by the sentry more as a warning than as a mark of respect – was repeated by two or three voices and reached the main fortress. At this, a man was seen to appear on the ramparts, and the garrison formed up around him.

This man raised his baton in the air, and at once the drums started to sound the general salute. The soldiers in the fortress presented arms and the deep, solemn sound of a cannon shot rang out.

'You see,' said the queen. 'They have remembered their duty. Better late than never. Proceed!'

'Excuse me, Madame,' said Marshal de La Meilleraie. 'I don't see any sign of them opening the gates, and we cannot proceed until the gates are opened.'

'They have forgotten to open them because of their astonishment and fervour at this unexpected and august visit,' said a courtier.

'That is not the sort of thing one forgets,' the marshal retorted. Then, turning to the king and queen, he added: 'Might I be allowed to give Their Majesties a piece of advice?'

'What is that, Marshal?'

'Their Majesties should withdraw five hundred paces with Guitaut and his guards, while I go and reconnoitre the situation with the musketeers and light horse.'

The queen replied sharply: 'Proceed! And we'll see if they dare to refuse us entry.'

The young king, delighted, spurred his horse and in no time was twenty yards ahead of them. The marshal and Guitaut hurried to catch up with him.

'Halt!' said the sentry, adopting the same hostile posture as before.

'It's the king!' the pages shouted.

'Withdraw!' the sentry cried, with a threatening gesture.

At the same time, the hats and muskets of the soldiers guarding the first retrenchment appeared above the parapet.

A long murmur followed these words and this spectacle. Marshal de La Meilleraie grasped the bit of the king's horse and forced it to turn about, at the same time ordering the queen's coachman to move back. The two offended Majesties therefore retired to about a thousand paces from the first retrenchment, while their followers scattered like a flock of birds after a shot from a huntsman's gun.

At this, Marshal de La Meilleraie, now in control of the situation, left some fifty men to guard the king and queen, then collected the remainder of his troop and returned with it towards the outworks.

When he was a hundred yards from the fortifications, the sentry, who had resumed his calm, measured march, halted once again.

'Guitaut,' said the marshal. 'Take a bugler, put your handkerchief on the end of your sword and go and order this impertinent governor to surrender.'

Guitaut obeyed and, displaying the signs of peace that protect a herald in every country on earth, went forward towards the fortifications.

'Who goes there?' shouted the sentry.

'Parley!' Guitaut replied, waving his sword with the piece of cloth on it.

'Let him come,' said the man, who had already been seen on the ramparts, and who had doubtless reached this forward post by some covered way.

The gate opened, and a bridge was lowered.

'What do you want?' asked an officer waiting by the gate.

'To speak to the governor,' said Guitaut.

'I am here,' said the man, who had already been seen twice, once on the ramparts of the fortress and once on the parapet of the outworks.

Guitaut noticed that the man was very pale, but calm and polite.

'Are you the Governor of Vayres?' he asked.

'Yes, Monsieur.'

'And you are refusing to open the gate of your fortress to His Majesty the King and the Queen Regent?'

'I have that misfortune.'

'And what do you intend to gain by it?'

'The freeing of the princes, whose captivity is ruining and laying waste the kingdom.'

'His Majesty does not barter with his subjects.'

'Alas, Monsieur, we know that, which is why we are ready to die, knowing that we shall die to serve His Majesty, even though we are apparently making war on him.'

'Very well,' said Guitaut. 'That is all we needed to know.'

And, after calmly saluting the governor, who replied with a most courteous bow, he retired.

On the fort, nothing moved.

Guitaut went back to the marshal and gave him an account of his mission.

'Let fifty men go at the gallop into this village,' said the marshal, pointing towards the village of Isson, 'and immediately bring back all the ladders they can find there.'

Fifty men set off at full tilt, and as the village was not far away they reached it in no time.

'Now, gentlemen, dismount,' said the marshal. 'Half of you, armed with muskets, will cover the attack, while the rest scale the walls.'

This instruction was greeted with cries of joy. The guards,

the musketeers and the light horse quickly dismounted and loaded their weapons. Meanwhile, the fifty foragers returned with some twenty ladders.

In the fort, all was still calm. The sentry marched backwards and forwards, and the ends of muskets and tips of hats could still be seen above the parapet.

The king's household set off, commanded by the marshal himself. It was made up of around four hundred men in total, half of whom, as the marshal had ordered, were preparing to mount an assault, while the other half covered their attack.

The king, the queen and the court followed the movements of the little troop from a distance. Even the queen seemed to have lost all her confidence. In order to get a better view, she had ordered her coach to be turned sideways, so that one of its windows was looking towards the fortifications.

The attackers had hardly advanced twenty paces, when the sentry came to the edge of the rampart and cried in a resounding voice: 'Who goes there?'

'Do not answer,' said Monsieur de La Meilleraie. 'But keep on going.'

'Who goes there?' the sentry cried again, preparing his gun. 'Who goes there?' he said a third time, taking aim.

'Fire at that fellow!' said Monsieur de La Meilleraie.

At the same moment, a volley of musket shots rang out from the royalist ranks, and the sentry staggered under them, dropped his musket, which rolled into the ditch, and fell, shouting: 'To arms!'

A single cannon shot replied to the start of hostilities. The cannonball whistled through the front rank, crashed into the second and the third, knocked over four soldiers and ricocheted away, to split open the belly of a horse on the queen's coach.

A long cry of terror arose from the group guarding Their Majesties. The king was pulled back, Anne of Austria almost fainted with fury and Mazarin with fear. They cut the harness of the dead horse and the living ones who, rearing in terror, were threatening to smash the coach. Eight or ten guards harnessed themselves to it and pulled the queen to safety beyond the reach of the cannon.

Meanwhile, the governor revealed a battery of six cannon.

When Monsieur de La Meilleraie saw this battery, which threatened in a few instants to tear his three companies to pieces, he decided that it would be pointless to press home the attack and ordered a retreat.

As soon as the king's household took its first step backwards, all sign of hostility from the fortress vanished.

The marshal returned to the queen's side and invited her to choose a place in the vicinity as her headquarters, so the queen picked an isolated little house on the far side of the Dordogne, hidden by the trees, looking like a little château.

'See whose house that is,' she told Guitaut, 'and ask for hospitality for me.'

Guitaut left at once, crossed the river in the boat of the Isson ferryman and returned, saying that the house was uninhabited except by a sort of steward, who had informed him that, since the house belonged to Monsieur d'Epernon, it was entirely at Her Majesty's disposal.

'Let's go then,' said the queen. 'But where is the king?'

They called little Louis XIV, who had gone off by himself a short distance away. He turned round, and, though he tried to hide his tears, they could see that he had been crying.

'What is it, sire?' the queen asked.

'Nothing, Madame,' the child answered. 'Except that one day I shall be king, I hope, and then . . . woe betide those who have offended me!'

'What is the name of this governor?' the queen asked.

No one knew what the governor was called. So they asked the ferryman, who replied that his name was Richon.

'Very well,' said the queen. 'I shall remember that name.'

'And so shall I,' said the young king.

XV

About one hundred men of the king's household crossed the Dordogne with Their Majesties, the rest remaining with Monsieur de La Meilleraie, who, having decided to lay siege to Vayres, was waiting for the army.

Hardly had the queen settled down in the little house – which, thanks to Nanon's taste for luxury, she found infinitely more habitable than she had expected – than Guitaut arrived to say that a captain who claimed to have an important matter to discuss was asking for the honour of an audience.

'Who is this captain?' the queen asked.

'A Captain Cauvignac, Madame.'

'Does he belong to my army?'

'I believe not.'

'Find out, and if he is not part of my army, tell him that I cannot receive him.'

'I beg Your Majesty's pardon if I venture to disagree on this point,' said Mazarin. 'It seems to me that if he is not of Your Majesty's army that is a good reason to receive him.'

'Why?'

'Because if he is from Your Majesty's army, and he is asking for an audience with the queen, that means that he is a loyal subject, while, on the contrary, if he belongs to the enemy forces, he may be a traitor. And at this moment, Madame, traitors are not to be scoffed at, since they may be very useful.'

'Show him in, then,' said the queen, 'since the cardinal thinks we should.'

The captain was shown in at once and introduced himself with an ease and nonchalance that astonished the queen, used as she was to produce the opposite impression on those around her.

She looked Cauvignac up and down, but he did not flinch in the least from the royal scrutiny.

'Who are you, Monsieur?' the queen asked.

'Captain Cauvignac,' the newcomer replied.

'And in whose service are you?'

'In Your Majesty's, if she so desires.'

'If I so desire? Of course. In any event, is there another service in the kingdom? Are there two queens in France?'

'Decidedly not, Madame, there is only one queen in France, and she is the one at whose feet I have the good fortune at this moment to be paying my very humble respects. But there are two points of view – or so, at least, it seemed to me just now.'

'What do you mean?' the queen asked, raising an eyebrow.

'I mean, Madame, that I was travelling about the countryside and just happened to be on a small eminence that overlooks the whole of the surroundings, admiring the landscape – which, as Your Majesty may have observed, is enchanting – when it seemed to me that I noticed that Monsieur Richon was not receiving Your Majesty with all the respect due to her. This confirmed me in a belief that I had already formed, which was that there are in France two points of view: the royalist one and another, and that Monsieur Richon belongs to the other.'

A cloud was descending across the face of Anne of Austria.

'Huh! So you thought that, did you?'

'Yes, Madame,' Cauvignac replied, in an entirely disingenuous tone. 'I even thought I saw that a cannon loaded with a cannonball was fired from the fort and that this cannonball upset Your Majesty's coach.'

'Enough. Did you ask me for an audience, Monsieur, just to impart your idiotic observations?'

'Ah, you are rude to me,' Cauvignac thought to himself. 'In that case, you'll pay more.'

'No, Madame, I asked for an audience to tell you that you are a great queen, and that I cede to no one in my admiration for you.'

'Really!' the queen answered drily.

'And because of your greatness and my admiration, which naturally follows from it, I have decided to devote myself entirely to Your Majesty.'

'Thank you,' said the queen, ironically. Then, turning to her captain of the guard, she said: 'Here, Guitaut! Remove this chatterbox.'

'I beg your pardon, Madame,' said Cauvignac. 'I shall go willingly, without it being necessary to remove me, but if I do so, you will not have Vayres.'

And, saluting Her Majesty with delightful courtesy, Cauvignac turned on his heels.

'I think that you are wrong to send this man away, Madame,' Mazarin whispered.

'Here!' said the queen. 'Come back and tell us. After all, you are odd, and I find you entertaining.'

'Your Majesty is most kind,' Cauvignac replied, with a bow.

'So, what were you saying about getting into Vayres?'

'I was saying, Madame, that if Your Majesty is still of the same mind that I think I observed this morning, namely to enter Vayres, I shall make it my duty to bring her there.'

'How will you do that?'

'I have a hundred and fifty of my men in Vayres.'

'Your men?'

'Yes, mine.'

'So?'

'I shall deliver these hundred and fifty men to Your Majesty.'

'And then?'

'And then?'

'Yes.'

'And then it seems to me a devil of a business, if Your Majesty, having one hundred and fifty gatekeepers, cannot open a gate.'

The queen smiled. 'A funny fellow,' she thought.

Cauvignac must have guessed the compliment, because he bowed again.

'How much do you need, Monsieur?' she asked.

'Heavens, Madame! Five hundred livres per gatekeeper. Those are the wages that I give them.'

'You shall have it.'

'And for myself?'

'Oh! Are you asking for something for yourself as well?'

'I should be proud to hold a commission granted by Your Majesty.'

'What rank are you requesting?'

'I should like to be governor at Braune. I have always wanted to be a governor.'

'Agreed.'

'In that case, apart from one small formality, the deal is done.'

'And what formality is that?'

'Would Your Majesty sign this paper which I prepared in advance in the hope that my services would be pleasing to my magnanimous sovereign?'

'What paper is that?'

'Read it, Madame.'

Rounding his arm gracefully and bending his knee in the most respectful manner, Cauvignac offered the queen a sheet of paper.

She read: 'The day on which I shall enter Vayres without striking a blow, I shall pay Captain Cauvignac the sum of seventy-five thousand livres, and I shall make him Governor of Braune.'

'So,' the queen said, repressing her anger. 'Captain Cauvignac does not have faith enough in our royal word and wants something in writing.'

'In writing seems best to me, Madame, in important matters,' Cauvignac said, with a bow. 'The old Latin proverb says: "*Verba volant*", which I take to mean in the vernacular: "*Words steal*". And with all due respect, I've just been robbed.'

'Insolent fellow!' the queen shouted. 'This time, get out!'

'I'm leaving, Your Majesty,' Cauvignac said. 'But you shall not have Vayres.'

Again, the captain, repeating a manoeuvre that had already worked for him, turned on his heels and made for the door. But Anne of Austria was more annoyed with him this time and did not call him back.

Cauvignac left.

'Will someone deal with that man?' said the queen.

'Excuse me, Madame,' said Mazarin. 'But I believe that Your Majesty would be wrong to let herself be carried away by a first angry impulse.'

'Why?' asked the queen.

Guitaut made a movement to obey.

'Because I am afraid that you may need him later, and if Your Majesty molests him in any way, she will have to pay double.'

'Very well,' said the queen. 'We'll pay what we have to. But, meanwhile, keep an eye on him.'

'Ah, now that's a different matter, and I am the first to applaud that precaution.'

'Guitaut, go and see what's happened to him,' the queen said.

Guitaut left and returned after half an hour.

'Well?' asked Anne of Austria. 'What's he up to?'

'Your Majesty has nothing at all to worry about,' Guitaut replied. 'Your man is not trying to go away at all. I made enquiries: he is lodging three hundred yards from here, with an innkeeper called Biscarros.'

'And is that where he has gone?'

'Not so, Madame. He went up a hill and from there is watching Monsieur de La Meilleraie's preparations for storming the retrenchments. The sight seems to be amusing him a great deal.'

'And the rest of the army?'

'It is on its way, Madame, and taking up its battle stations as it arrives.'

'So the marshal is on the point of attacking?'

'I believe, Madame, that rather than risking an attack, it is better to give the troops a night's rest.'

'A night's rest!' Anne of Austria exclaimed. 'The royal army is to be halted a day and a night in front of this old shack! Impossible. Guitaut, go and tell the marshal to attack at once. The king wishes to sleep in Vayres tonight.'

'Madame,' said Mazarin, 'I think that the marshal's precaution . . .'

'And I think,' said Anne of Austria, 'that when the royal authority has been challenged, it cannot be avenged too quickly. Go on, Guitaut – and tell Monsieur de La Meilleraie that the queen is watching him.'

Dismissing Guitaut with a regal gesture, the queen took her son's hand and went out in her turn, climbing a staircase that lead to a terrace, without looking round to see if anyone was following them.

The terrace, its vistas and viewpoints arranged with the greatest skill, overlooked the whole of the surrounding countryside.

The queen quickly looked all around. The Libourne road ran two hundred yards behind her; on it the white inn of our friend Biscarros stood out. At her feet, the Gironde was flowing, calm, swift and majestic. To her right was the fort of Vayres, silent as a ruin, while all around the fort lay the circle of newly raised retrenchments. A few sentries were walking on the ramparts, while the bronze necks and gaping mouths of five cannon extended through the embrasures. To her left, Monsieur de La Meilleraie was setting up camp. As Guitaut said, the whole army had arrived and was gathering around him.

On a hillock, a man was standing, carefully watching every movement of the besieged and the besiegers. This was Cauvignac.

Guitaut was crossing the river by the Isson fisherman's ferry.

The queen was standing quite still on the terrace, frowning and holding the hand of little Louis XIV, who was watching this scene with some curiosity, while occasionally saying to his mother: 'Let me get up on my fine charger and join Monsieur de La Meilleraie, who is going to punish those insolent people.'

Mazarin was near the queen, his fine, ironic face having for the moment taken on the thoughtful, serious look that he wore only on great occasions, while behind the queen and the minister were the ladies-in-waiting, who, taking their cue from Anne of Austria's silence, hardly dared exchange a few words among themselves in a hurried whisper.

At first, all this suggested calm and peace, but it was the tranquillity of a mine that a single spark could transform into a destructive tempest.

All eyes were chiefly on Guitaut, because the explosion, for which they were all waiting with different feelings, would come from him.

Expectation was great on the side where the army was, because scarcely had the messenger touched the left bank of the Dordogne and been recognized than all eyes turned towards him. When Monsieur de La Meilleraie saw him, he left the group of officers among whom he was standing and walked over to meet him.

Guitaut and the marshal exchanged a few words. Although the river was quite wide at this point, and although the distance separating the royal group from the two officers was considerable, it was not so far that they could not see the astonishment on the face of the marshal. It was clear that the order he had received appeared to him untimely, so he raised a doubtful face towards the group, in the midst of whom the queen could be seen. But Anne of Austria, who understood what the marshal was thinking, gave such an imperative gesture with her head and her hand that the marshal – who had long been acquainted with his imperious sovereign – lowered his head, if not in sign of assent, at least of obedience.

At the same moment, on the marshal's order, three or four captains, who were serving him more or less in the role of a modern aide-de-camp, leapt into their saddles and galloped off in three or four different directions.

Wherever they passed, the work of pitching camp, which had just been started, was instantly interrupted, and, to a roll of drums and a blaring of trumpets, the soldiers could be seen dropping, in some cases, the straw that they were carrying, in others, the hammers with which they were driving in the tent pegs. All ran to get their weapons, which were in stacks, the grenadiers grasping their guns, the ordinary soldiers their pikes and the artillerymen their implements. There was an incredible confusion as all these men crossed one another, running in different directions; then, bit by bit, the pieces on the huge chessboard sorted themselves out, order succeeded chaos and everyone was lined up under his own regimental banner: the grenadiers in the centre, the king's household on the right flank, the artillery on the left. The trumpets and the drums fell silent.

A single drum answered from behind the fortifications, then it too stopped, and a funereal silence settled over the plain.

Then a clear, precise and determined command rang out. At the distance where she was, the queen could not hear the words, but she saw the troops form columns at the same moment. She took out her handkerchief and waved it, while the young king cried: 'Forward! Forward!' in an excited voice, stamping his foot.

The army replied with a single shout of 'Long live the king!', then the artillery set off at a gallop to station itself on the little hillock, and the columns surged forward to the sound of the drum beating the charge.

This was not a proper siege, but a simple assault. The retrenchments that Richon had hastily erected were earth ramparts, so there was no trench that needed to be opened, but only a direct attack was required. However, the shrewd commander of Vayres had taken every precaution, and it was evident that he had used exceptional skill to take advantage of all the resources of the terrain.

Richon had doubtless imposed the rule on himself that he would not fire the first shot, because this time he waited once more for the royal troops to provoke a response; however, as in the first attack, one could see again the lowering of that terrible row of muskets which had previously made such dreadful ravages in the king's household.

At the same time, the six guns of the battery rang out, and earth could be seen flying up from the parapets and the palisades above them.

The response came quickly. The artillery on the retrenchments rang out in its turn, cutting deep furrows through the ranks of the king's army. But, on an order from the commanders, these gaps in the ranks vanished, the edges of the wound that had been momentarily opened were closed, and the main column, having been briefly shaken, marched forward once more.

Now it was the turn of the musketry to crackle, while the cannon were being reloaded.

Five minutes later, the two opposing volleys answered one another in a single roar, like two storms colliding or two claps of thunder occurring simultaneously.

Then, as the weather was calm and there was no breeze to ruffle the air, the smoke gathered above the battlefield, and the two sides vanished into a cloud, broken here and there by a roaring flash of flame from the thunder of the artillery.

From time to time, there were men emerging at the rear of the royal army, painfully dragging themselves along, only to fall at different distances, leaving a trail of blood behind them.

Very soon, the number of wounded increased. The noise of the cannon and the musket fire continued, but the royal artillery was now only firing haphazardly and cautiously, because in the midst of the thick smoke it could not distinguish friend from foe.

As for the artillery in the fort, since it had only enemies in front of it, it blasted out more frightfully and more urgently than ever.

Finally, the royal artillery ceased firing altogether. It was clear that the assault had begun, and the troops were engaged in fighting hand to hand.

There was a moment's anxiety on the part of the spectators, while the smoke, no longer thickened by the fire of the cannon and the musketry, gradually rose. What they saw then was the royal army being driven back in disorder, leaving the foot of the ramparts covered with its dead. A sort of breach had been made, and a few palisades had been torn out, leaving an opening, but one that was crowded with a jumble of men, pikes and muskets. And in the midst of these men, covered with blood, yet calm and cool, as though he were merely a spectator in the tragedy where he had just played such a frightful part, stood Richon, holding in his hand an axe blunted by the blows that he had struck with it.

The man seemed to be protected by some charm: though he was always in the thick of the fighting, always in the front rank, constantly erect and uncovered, no shot had struck him or pike touched him. He was as invulnerable as he was impassive.

Three times Marshal de La Meilleraie in person led the royal troops in the assault, and three times they were driven back before the eyes of the king and queen.

Silent tears were running down the young king's pale cheeks. Anne of Austria was wringing her hands and muttering: 'Oh, that man, that man! If he should ever fall into our hands, I shall make a terrible example of him.'

Fortunately, night was falling, dark and swift, like a sort of veil over the royal shame. Marshal de La Meilleraie ordered the retreat to be sounded.

Cauvignac left his post, came down from the hillock where he had been standing and strolled across the field towards Biscarros's house with his hands in his pockets.

'Madame,' Mazarin said, pointing at him, 'there's a man who could have saved you all the blood we have just spilled for a little gold.'

'Huh!' said the queen. 'Is that the advice of an economical man like yourself, Cardinal?'

'It's true that I'm economical,' said the cardinal. 'I know the price of gold, but I know the price of blood too, and at the moment, blood is dearer than gold to us.'

'Never you fear,' said the queen. 'The blood that has been spilt will be avenged. Here, Comminges!' she added, turning to the lieutenant of her guard. 'Go and bring Monsieur de La Meilleraie to me.'

'And you, Bernouin,' the cardinal said to his valet, pointing out Cauvignac, who had just reached the door of the Golden Calf. 'Can you see that man?'

'Yes, Monseigneur.'

'Well, go and fetch him for me and bring him secretly into my room tonight.'

The day after her interview with her lover in the Carmelite church, Madame de Cambes went to see the princess, with the idea of carrying out the promise that she had made to Canolles.

The whole town was abuzz, having just heard of the king's arrival before Vayres and, at the same time, of Richon's admirable defence of the fortress, twice repulsing a royal army of twelve thousand men with a force of just five hundred. The princess was one of the first to hear the news and, in her delight, clapped her hands, saying: 'Oh, if only I had a hundred captains like Richon!'

Madame de Cambes joined in the general enthusiasm, doubly happy at being able to applaud warmly the conduct of a man whom she admired, and also at finding a timely opportunity to put in a request that might have been compromised by the report of a defeat, while on the contrary its success was more or less guaranteed by the announcement of a victory.

However, even in the midst of her joy, the princess had too much on her mind for Claire to dare risking her request. There was the matter of sending reinforcements to Richon, which, as they could easily imagine, he needed, given the fact that Monsieur d'Epernon's army would shortly be joining the royal one. The council was organizing these reinforcements, and Claire, seeing that political affairs were for the moment taking precedence over affairs of the heart, resumed her role as counsellor of state, and there was no mention of Canolles that day.

A brief, but affectionate, note advised the prisoner of this delay. This was less difficult for him to bear than one might think: the expectation of a happy event brings almost as many sweet sensations as the event itself. Canolles's heart was too full of amorous delicacy not to enjoy what he called the antechamber of happiness. Claire was asking him to wait patiently, and he did so almost with joy.

On the following day, the relief of Vayres was organized, and at eleven in the morning the soldiers left upstream. But since the wind and the current were contrary, they calculated that, however hard they tried, they would not arrive on the following day, since they had to rely solely on their oars. Captain Ravailly, leading the expedition, had the order to reconnoitre the fortress of Braune at the same time, which belonged to the queen, and which was known to be without a governor.

The princess spent the morning supervising the preparations and details of the expedition. The afternoon was to be devoted to a great council meeting with the aim of preventing the Duke d'Epernon and the Marshal de La Meilleraie from joining forces, or at least delaying it until the reinforcements that were being sent to Richon had entered the fortress. Claire had no alternative but to continue waiting until the next day, but at around four o'clock she found an opportunity to make a charming sign to Canolles as he was passing under her window – such a charming sign, so full of regret and love, that he was almost happy at being obliged to wait.

However, in the evening, to make sure that the wait would

not be extended any further, and to force herself to confide to the princess a secret that she found somewhat embarrassing, Claire asked for a private audience with Madame de Condé on the following day; as we might imagine, this audience was granted unquestioningly.

So at the appointed hour Claire came into the princess's apartments and was welcomed with the most charming smile. The princess was alone, as Claire had requested.

'Now, my girl,' the princess said, 'what is so serious that you have asked me for a private and secret audience, when you know that I am at the disposal of my friends at any hour of the day?'

'The thing is this, Madame,' the viscountess said. 'In the midst of the happiness that Your Majesty has so well deserved, I would like to ask her to cast her eyes on her loyal servant, who also requires a little happiness.'

'With great pleasure, my dear Claire, and never will the happiness that God sends equal that which I desire for you. So ask me . . . What favour would you request? If it is in my power, be sure that it is already granted.'

'A widow, free, and too free, because this freedom is more burdensome to me than slavery would be,' Claire replied, 'I should like to exchange my loneliness for a better condition.'

'In other words, you wish to marry, is that it, dear?' Madame de Condé asked, laughing.

'I think I do,' said Claire, blushing.

'Very well, so be it . . . This concerns us . . .' Claire raised a hand. 'Calm, now! We shall consider your feelings: you must have a duke and a peer, Viscountess. I will look for one among our supporters.'

'Your Highness is too considerate,' Madame de Cambes replied. 'I did not mean you to trouble yourself with that.'

'Oh, but I shall be happy to do so, because I owe you a return of happiness for the loyalty you have shown me. But you will wait until the war is over, won't you?'

'I shall wait as short a time as possible, Madame,' said the viscountess with a smile.

'You talk as though your choice was already made, as though

you had the husband that you are asking me for already
to hand.'

'That is because it is just as Your Highness says.'

'Really! So who is this happy man? Tell me, don't be afraid.'

'Oh, Madame!' Claire said. 'Forgive me ... I don't know
why, but I am trembling all over.'

The princess smiled, took Claire's hand and drew her close.

'My child!' she said. Then, looking at her with an expression
that only made the viscountess more embarrassed, added: 'Do
I know him?'

'I think that Your Highness has seen him several times.'

'I don't need to ask if he is young?'

'Twenty-eight.'

'And noble?'

'He is of good family.'

'Brave?'

'He has a reputation for courage.'

'Rich?'

'I am.'

'Yes, my dear, yes, and we have not forgotten that. You are
one of the wealthiest nobles in our dominion, and we are happy
to recall that, in this present war, Monsieur de Cambes's gold
louis and the fat écus of your farmers have more than once
come to our aid in time of need.'

'Your Highness honours me by recalling how much I am
devoted to her.'

'Very well. We shall make him a major in our army, if he is
only a captain, and a colonel if he is only a major – because
I assume he is one of us?'

'He was at Lens, Madame,' Claire replied with all the subtlety
that she had acquired in her recent study of diplomacy.

'Excellent! Now, there is only one more thing I need,' said
the princess.

'Which is?'

'The name of the fortunate gentleman who already has the
heart and will soon possess the person of the loveliest soldier
in my army.'

Claire, driven back to her last defences, was gathering all

her courage to say the name of the Baron de Canolles, when suddenly the sound of a galloping horse rang around the courtyard, followed by one of those dull murmurs that accompany important news.

The princess heard both these sounds and ran over to the window. The messenger, covered in sweat and dust, was leaping off his horse and, surrounded by four or five people who had been attracted to him by the sound of his entrance, appeared to be giving details, which, even as they emerged, were plunging his hearers into consternation. The princess could no longer contain her curiosity and, opening the window, cried out: 'Let him come up!'

The messenger looked upwards, recognized the princess and ran to the stairs. Five minutes later, he was coming into the room, though covered in mud, with ruffled hair and strangled voice, and saying: 'Forgive me, Your Highness, for appearing before you in my present state! But I am bringing the sort of news that has merely to be spoken to burst wide the door: Vayres has capitulated!'

The princess staggered backwards, Claire's arms fell in despair, and Lenet, coming in behind the messenger, went pale.

Five or six other people, who, momentarily forgetting the respect due to the princess, had invaded her room, remained dumb with astonishment.

'Monsieur Ravailly,' said Lenet (because the messenger was none other than our captain from Navailles), 'repeat what you have just said, because I can hardly believe it.'

'I said that Vayres has capitulated.'

'Capitulated!' the princess repeated. 'What about the reinforcements that you were bringing?'

'We came too late, Madame. Richon was surrendering as we arrived.'

'Richon surrendering!' the princess cried. 'The coward!'

This exclamation sent a chill through the veins of everyone present, yet no one said anything, apart from Lenet.

'Madame,' he said sternly, and with no consideration for Madame de Condé's pride. 'Don't forget that the honour of men resides in the word of princes, just as their lives are in the

hands of God. So don't call the bravest of your servants a
coward, in case tomorrow the most loyal desert you, when they
see how you treat their fellows, leaving you alone, accused
and lost . . .'

'Monsieur!' the princess exclaimed.

'Madame,' Lenet continued. 'I repeat to Your Highness that
Richon is no coward, I answer for him with my own head, and
if he capitulated it was because he could not do otherwise.'

The princess, pale with fury, was about to scold Lenet with
one of those aristocratic outbursts in which arrogance took the
place of good sense, but at the sight of all the faces turning
away from her and eyes refusing to meet hers, Lenet with his
head high and Ravailly with his head lowered, she realized
that she would indeed be lost if she continued along this
self-destructive path; so she appealed to them with her usual
argument.

'Unhappy princess that I am!' she said. 'Everything has abandoned me then – both fortune and mankind! Oh, my child, my
poor child, you will be destroyed like your father.'

The cry of the weak woman and the outburst of maternal
suffering always find an echo in people's hearts. This play-
acting, which had so often before achieved the princess's goal,
produced the desired effect once more.

Meanwhile, Lenet had been getting from Ravailly all that he
had learned about the capitulation of Vayres.

'I knew it!' he exclaimed, after a moment.

'What did you know?' the princess asked.

'That Richon was not a coward, Madame.'

'And how do you know that?'

'Because he held out for two days and two nights, and
because he would have let himself be buried in the ruins of his
fortress, riddled with bullets, if a company of recruits had not
rebelled and forced him to capitulate.'

'He should have died rather than surrender,' said the princess.

'Does one die when one wishes, Madame?' Lenet asked.
Then, turning to Ravailly, he added: 'He is a prisoner on terms,
I hope?'

'No terms at all, I fear,' Ravailly replied. 'They tell me that it was a lieutenant of the garrison who parleyed, so there may well be some treachery there, and instead of offering conditions for surrender, Richon may have been betrayed.'

'Yes, yes,' Lenet exclaimed. 'Betrayed, handed over to the enemy, that's it! I know Richon, and I know him to be incapable, I won't say of cowardice, but of weakness. Madame,' Lenet continued, turning to the princess, 'betrayed, handed over, you understand? Quickly, let's take care of him. A treaty made by a lieutenant, you say, Ravailly? Some great misfortune has befallen Richon. Quickly, Madame, write, I beg you.'

'Write!' exclaimed the princess. 'I – write? Why should I?'

'To save him, Madame.'

'Huh!' said the princess. 'When one delivers up a fortress to the enemy, one should take the necessary precautions.'

'But don't you understand that he did not deliver it to them? Didn't you hear what the captain said: that he was betrayed, perhaps sold? That it was some lieutenant and not Richon who dealt with the enemy?'

'So what do you expect them to do to him, your Richon?'

'What will they do to him? Madame, are you forgetting the trick that he used to enter Vayres? That we used a letter of attestation from Monsieur d'Epernon? That he held out against a royal army commanded by the queen and the king in person? That Richon is the first to raise the standard of rebellion? That, in short, they will make an example of him? Oh, Madame, in heaven's name, write to Monsieur de La Meilleraie, send a messenger, an envoy.'

'And what mission should we give this envoy?'

'The mission of preventing at any cost the death of a brave captain, because if you do not hurry . . . I know the queen, Madame, and your messenger may even arrive too late!'

'Too late,' said the princess. 'Don't we have hostages? Don't we have officers of the king in Chantilly, in Montrond and even here, who are our prisoners?'

Claire rose up, appalled.

'But, Madame, Madame!' she cried. 'Do what Monsieur Lenet tells you: reprisals would not give Richon back his freedom.'

'It's not a matter of freedom, but of life,' said Lenet with grim persistence.

'Very well,' said the princess. 'What they do, we do: prison for prison, the scaffold for the scaffold.'

Claire gave a cry and fell to her knees.

'But, Madame,' she said. 'Monsieur Richon is one of my friends. I came to ask a favour of you, and you promised me to grant it. Well, I am asking you to do all that you can to save Monsieur Richon.'

Claire was on her knees. The princess took the opportunity to grant to Claire's entreaties what she was refusing to Lenet's rough counsel. She went over to a table, took a pen and wrote to Monsieur de La Meilleraie to ask for Richon to be exchanged for one of the officers whom she was holding prisoner, the choice to be the queen's. When the letter was finished, she looked round to decide whom to send as messenger. At this, though still suffering from his old wound and exhausted from his recent efforts, Ravailly offered to go himself, provided he was given a fresh horse. The princess gave him permission to take whichever horse he wanted from her stables, and the captain left, spurred on by the shouts of the crowd, the encouragements of Lenet and the entreaties of Claire.

A moment later, one could hear the sounds of the assembled people to whom Ravailly had explained his mission, and who were shouting as loudly as they could: 'Long live the princess! Long live the Duke d'Enghien!'

Exhausted by these daily demonstrations, which had more the character of orders than of ovations, the princess was momentarily tempted to refuse the people what they were asking, but as usually happens in such circumstances, they persisted, and the cries soon degenerated into shouts.

'Come on,' said the princess, taking her son by the hand. 'Come on! Slaves that we are, let's do as they wish.'

And, putting on a gracious smile, she appeared on her balcony and greeted her people – their sovereign and their slave.

XVI

At the moment when the princess and her son were appearing on the balcony amid the enthusiastic cheers of the crowd, they suddenly heard the sound of pipes and drums in the distance, together with a joyful hum.

At the same time, the noisy crowd that had gathered round the house of President de Lalasne to see Madame de Condé turned towards this new noise and, regardless of the rules of etiquette, began to move in its direction, while the noise got nearer and nearer. It was quite simple: they had already seen the princess a dozen times, a score of times, perhaps even a hundred times, while the noise promised something novel to them.

'At least they are honest,' said Lenet, smiling, where he stood behind the indignant princess. 'But what are this music and these shouts? I must confess to Your Highness that I am almost as eager to find out as those discourteous people.'

'Very well,' said the princess. 'You go too, and run about the streets with them.'

'I should indeed, immediately,' said Lenet, 'if I were sure of bringing you good news.'

'Huh! Good news!' the princess replied, looking ironically towards the magnificent sky above her head. 'I'm not expecting any of that. Our luck is not in.'

'You know, Madame, that I am seldom mistaken,' said Lenet. 'But I shall be very much so if all this noise does not announce some fortunate event.'

Indeed, the sound was drawing nearer all the time, and a crowd appeared at the end of the street, its arms raised in the air and waving handkerchiefs in such a way that even the princess was convinced that the news was good. So she listened attentively and for a moment forgot the behaviour of her courtiers. This is what she heard: 'Braune! The Governor of Braune! The governor is a prisoner!'

'Ha!' said Lenet. 'The Governor of Braune prisoner! So it's

only half bad. There we have a hostage whom we can exchange for Richon.'

'Don't we already have the Governor of Saint-Georges?' the princess retorted.

'I am happy that the plan I suggested for taking Braune was so successful,' said Madame de Tourville.

'Let's not congratulate ourselves yet on a complete victory, Madame,' said Lenet. 'Fate has a way of upsetting the plans of men and sometimes those of women too.'

'And yet, Monsieur,' snapped Madame de Tourville, drawing herself up with her usual petulance, 'if the governor has been taken, the fort must too.'

'The one is not a necessary deduction from the other; but, don't worry, if we do owe you this double success, then I shall be the first to congratulate you.'

'What I find astonishing in all this . . .' said the princess, already looking for something in the happy event (which she had been expecting) that might offend her aristocratic pride, the essential component of her character, '. . . what I find astonishing is that I am not the first to learn what is happening. It is an unpardonable breach of etiquette, like everything that the Duke de La Rochefoucauld does.'

'Why, Madame,' said Lenet. 'We are short of soldiers to fight, do you want us to take them away from their posts and make messengers of them? Alas, let's not demand too much, and when we do get good news, accept it as God sends it to us, not asking by what means He does so.'

Meanwhile, the crowd was growing as each individual group came to join the main throng, like streams flowing into a river. In the midst of this main group, consisting of perhaps a thousand people, a little cluster of soldiers could be seen, around thirty men, and in the midst of them a prisoner whom the soldiers were apparently defending from the fury of the mob.

'Death, death!' they were shouting. 'Death to the Governor of Braune!'

'Ha!' said the princess, with a triumphant smile. 'It does indeed seem that we have a prisoner, and that this prisoner is the Governor of Braune.'

'Yes,' said Lenet. 'But, look, Madame. It appears that the prisoner is in mortal danger. Can you hear the threats? Can you see those angry gestures? They are going to break through the cordon of soldiers and tear him limb from limb. Oh, the tigers! They can scent flesh and want to drink blood.'

'Let them!' said the princess, with that ferocity peculiar to women when their worst passions are aroused. 'Let them drink his blood: it is the blood of an enemy.'

'But, Madame,' said Lenet, 'that enemy is safeguarded by the honour of the house of Condé, think of that. And, in any case, how do you know that at this moment Richon, our brave Richon, is not running the same risk as that poor wretch? Oh, no! They're breaking through the cordon. If they touch him, he is lost. Twenty men!' Lenet shouted, turning round. 'Twenty men of goodwill to help to drive that mob back. If a hair of that prisoner's falls from his head, you will answer with your own! Go . . .'

Twenty musketeers from the city guard, taken from the best families in the town, plunged like a torrent down the stairs, drove their way through the crowd with the butts of their muskets and joined the escort. It was none too soon: some claws, longer and sharper than the rest, had already torn shreds of material from the prisoner's blue coat.

'In faith, I thank you, gentlemen,' said the prisoner. 'You've just saved me from being devoured by those cannibals. I'm most obliged to you. My word! If they eat men like that, when the royal army attacks your town, they'll have it for dinner!'

At this he started to laugh, shrugging his shoulders.

'Ah! He's a fine fellow!' the crowd yelled, when it saw the prisoner's (somewhat affected) calm, and they repeated this joke, which flattered their self-esteem. 'He's a real fine fellow! He's not afraid. Long live the Governor of Braune!'

'Indeed so!' cried the prisoner. 'Long live the Governor of Braune! I'd be quite pleased myself if he lived.'

From then on, the people's anger changed to admiration, and that admiration was immediately expressed in forceful terms. A warm ovation succeeded the imminent martyrdom of the Governor of Braune – that is, of our friend, Cauvignac. Because, as our readers have already guessed, it was Cauvignac who, under the pompous title of Governor of Braune, found himself making such a sad entrance into the capital of Guyenne.

However, protected by his guards and subsequently by his own presence of mind, the prisoner of war was brought into the house of President de Lalasne, and, while half his escort kept guard at the door, the other half led him to see the princess.

Cauvignac marched into the apartments of Madame de Condé calmly and with his head high, but it must be said that under this heroic exterior, his heart was beating fast. He was recognized instantly, despite the state in which the mob's enthusiasm had left his fine blue coat, his gold braid and the feather in his cap.

'Monsieur Cauvignac!' Lenet exclaimed.

'Monsieur Cauvignac, Governor of Braune!' the princess added. 'Ah, Monsieur, this has a scent of treason about it!'

'What did Your Highness say?' Cauvignac replied, realizing that now was the time, if ever, to call on all his self-control and, even more, his wits. 'I believe that Your Majesty mentioned the word "treason".'

'Yes, Monsieur: treason. In what capacity do you appear before me?'

'In the capacity of Governor of Braune, Madame.'

'Exactly: treason. Who signed the order appointing you?'

'Monsieur de Mazarin.'

'Treason, double treason, as I said! You are Governor of Braune, and it was your company that betrayed Vayres: the appointment was your reward.'

On hearing these words, an expression of the most profound astonishment appeared on Cauvignac's face. He looked round as if searching for the person to whom this peculiar remark might have been addressed; then, convinced by his investigation that the object of the princess's accusation could be none other than himself, he let his hands fall beside him in a gesture full of discouragement.

'My company betrayed Vayres!' he said. 'Is it Your Highness that reproaches me with such a thing?'

'Yes, Monsieur, I do. Pretend that you do not know it, feign astonishment . . . yes, you are a fine actor, it appears. But I shall not be fooled by your play-acting or your words, however well they are suited to one another.'

'I am not pretending anything, Madame,' Cauvignac replied. 'How can Your Highness expect me to know what happened in Vayres, when I have never been there?'

'Subterfuge, Monsieur, subterfuge!'

'I have no answer to such words, Madame, except to say that Your Highness seems discontented with me. May Your Highness forgive my forthright character and the liberty I take in defending myself, if I say that I considered that, on the contrary, I was the one who had cause to complain of her.'

'To complain of me? You, Monsieur!' the princess exclaimed, amazed by such impudence.

'Indeed, Madame,' Cauvignac replied calmly. 'On your word and that of Monsieur Lenet here present, I recruited a company of men and contracted undertakings towards them, which were still more sacred, since they were almost all verbal undertakings. And then, when I asked Your Highness for the promised money . . . a trifling sum . . . a mere thirty or forty thousand livres, not intended for my own use, note, but for the new defenders that I had recruited for the princes, Your Highness refused me! Yes, refused me! Monsieur Lenet is my witness.'

'That's true,' said Lenet. 'When Monsieur appeared, we had no money.'

'Could you not have waited a few days, Monsieur? Was your loyalty and that of your men counted by the hour?'

'I waited the amount of time that Monsieur de La Rochefoucauld himself asked me, that is to say, a week. After that week, I appeared again, and this time there was a plain refusal. Once more, Monsieur Lenet will witness to it.'

The princess turned towards her counsellor. Her lips were clenched and her eyes flashing under her frowning eyebrows.

'Unfortunately,' Lenet said, 'I have to admit that what this gentleman says is the precise truth.'

Cauvignac drew himself up triumphantly.

'Very well, Madame,' he said. 'In such circumstances, what would an intriguer have done? An intriguer would have gone to the queen to sell himself and his men to her. But I, as someone

who has a horror of intrigue, I dismissed my company, releasing
each man from his word, and then, alone, isolated – isolated in
absolute neutrality, I did what wisdom requires that we should
when in doubt, that is to say, I did nothing.'

'But what about your soldiers, Monsieur, your soldiers!' the
princess yelled furiously.

'Madame,' said Cauvignac, 'since I am neither king nor
prince, but merely a captain, and since I have neither subjects
nor vassals, I only call them *my* soldiers when I am paying
them, and since, as Monsieur Lenet says, they were not paid at
all, they were free. That is when they turned against their new
leader. What can be done about it? I admit that I have no idea.'

'But you, Monsieur, who also took the king's side, what have
you to say for yourself? You were finding your neutrality hard
to bear?'

'No, Madame, but my neutrality, innocent as it was, had
become suspect to His Majesty's supporters. One fine morning,
I was arrested at the inn of the Golden Calf on the Libourne
road and brought before the queen.'

'And you made a pact with her?'

'A man of feeling, Madame,' Cauvignac replied, 'has certain
tender spots on which a subtle ruler can attack him. My soul
was wounded. I had been dismissed from a party into which I
had flung myself blindly with all the enthusiasm and good faith
of youth. I appeared before the queen with a soldier who was
ready to kill me on either side of me. I was expecting recrimi-
nations, insults, death. After all, at least in intention, I had been
serving the cause of the princes. But, quite the opposite to what
I expected, instead of punishing me by depriving me of my
freedom and sending me to prison, or making me mount the
scaffold, this great monarch said to me: "Brave, misguided
man, I might with a word make your head fall. But as you see,
they were ungrateful to you there, but here we shall be grateful.
In the name of my patron, Saint Anne, from now on you shall
be one of us. Gentlemen," she went on, addressing my guards,
"respect this officer, because I have appreciated his merits, and
I make him your leader. And you," she continued, turning to

me, "I shall make you Governor of Braune. This is how a queen of France is avenged.'

'What could I reply?' Cauvignac asked, resuming his normal voice and manner, after imitating those of Anne of Austria in a way that was half comical and half touching. 'Nothing. I had been stricken in my dearest hopes, I had been wounded in the entirely gratuitous loyalty that I placed at Your Highness's feet, having, as I recall with joy, been able to do you some small service in Chantilly. I acted as Coriolanus did and went into the tents of the Volsci.'[12]

This speech, delivered in a dramatic voice and with sweeping gestures, had a great effect on those who heard it. Cauvignac was aware of his triumph when he saw the princess go pale with fury.

'But, in that case, Monsieur,' she asked, 'to whom are you loyal?'

'To those who appreciate the delicacy of my conduct,' he replied.

'Very well, then. You are my prisoner.'

'I have that honour, Madame. But I hope you will treat me as a gentleman. It is true that I am your prisoner, but without having fought against Your Highness. I was making my way to my governorship with my luggage when I fell upon a party of your soldiers, who arrested me. Not for a single moment did I attempt to conceal my rank or my opinions. So, I repeat, I demand to be treated not only as a gentleman, but as a superior officer.'

'You shall be, Monsieur,' the princess replied. 'You shall have the whole town as your prison, but you must swear on your honour not to attempt to leave it.'

'I shall swear on whatever Your Highness wishes.'

'Very well. Lenet, read the form of words to this gentleman and we will hear his oath.'

Lenet dictated the words of the oath which Cauvignac had to swear. Cauvignac raised his hand and solemnly swore not to leave the town until the princess had released him from the oath.

'Now go,' said the princess. 'We are relying on your loyalty as a gentleman and your honour as a soldier.'

Cauvignac did not wait to be told twice: he bowed and left, but as he was leaving, he had time to notice a gesture by the counsellor that meant: 'Madame, he is right and we are wrong: that's what happens when you skimp on the money.'

The fact is that Lenet, who appreciated all sorts of qualities, recognized the subtlety of Cauvignac's character, and, precisely because he had not been fooled in the slightest by the specious arguments that Cauvignac had offered, he was able to admire how the prisoner had worked his way out of one of the most compromising situations in which he could have found himself.

As for Cauvignac, he went down the staircase deep in thought, holding his chin in his hand and saying to himself: 'Well, then, what we must do now is to sell them for another hundred thousand livres, my hundred and fifty men, which is quite possible, since the intelligent and honest Ferguzon has obtained complete freedom for himself and for his own men ... I'll manage it, one day or another. Well I never,' Cauvignac went on, quite consoled, 'I see that by letting myself be captured I didn't get such a bad deal after all.'

XVII

Now let us take a step back and draw our readers' attention to the events that took place at Vayres, events of which they are so far only imperfectly informed.

After several assaults, which were all the more frightful since the general of the royal troops was sacrificing more men in order to take less time, the retrenchments were captured. But the brave defenders of these forward positions, after defending every inch of the territory and leaving the battlefield littered with dead, had retreated down the covered road and taken up their positions inside Vayres. And Monsieur de La Meilleraie had no illusions about the fact that, having lost five or six hundred men to capture a paltry rampart of earth with a pali-

sade on top of it, he would lose six times as many in taking a
fort that was surrounded by solid walls and defended by a man,
who, as he had already had the opportunity to learn at his
own expense, was a master of military strategy and a model of
courage.

Consequently, they had decided to open a trench and make
this a formal siege, when they saw the advance guard of the
Duke d'Epernon's army, which had just met up with the army
of Monsieur de La Meilleraie, so doubling the king's forces.
With twenty-four thousand men one can undertake what one
might shrink from doing with twelve thousand; so the assault
was fixed for the following day.

When work on the trench was interrupted, a new formation
was taken up, and, above all, at the sight of the arriving reinforcements, Richon realized that the besiegers were intending
to attack without delay. Guessing that there would be an attack
on the following morning, he called his men together to sound
out their feelings – though, given the way in which they had
helped him in the defence of the first retrenchments, he had no
reason to doubt what these were. So he was extremely surprised
when he saw the garrison's new attitude. His men were casting dark and anxious looks on the royal army, and a sullen
murmuring arose from their ranks.

Richon did not allow levity from soldiers under arms, and
especially not of that kind.

'Now, then! Who is muttering there?' he asked, turning in
the direction from which the disapproving murmurs had been
clearest.

'I am,' said one soldier, bolder than the rest.

'You!'

'Yes, me.'

'Come here and explain yourself.'

The soldier left the ranks and marched over to his chief.

'What do you need, that makes you complain like that?'

'What do I need?'

'Yes, what do you need? Do you have your ration of bread?'

'Yes, Commander.'

'Your ration of meat?'

'Yes, Commander.'

'Are your barracks uncomfortable?'

'No.'

'Are you owed any back pay?'

'No.'

'So tell me: what do you need? What do you want? What is the meaning of this murmuring?'

'The meaning is that we are fighting against our king, and that is hard for a French soldier.'

'So you wish you were serving His Majesty?'

'Yes.'

'And you'd like to go and join your king?'

'Yes,' said the soldier who, taken in by Richon's calm manner, thought it would all end with him merely being expelled from the ranks of the Condés' troops.

'Very well,' said Richon, grabbing the man by his jerkin. 'But since I've closed the gates, you'll have to take the only path left to you.'

'What's that?' cried the terrified soldier.

'This one,' said Richon, lifting him up with his Herculean arm and throwing him over the parapet.

The soldier gave a cry and fell into the moat which, fortunately for him, was full of water.

A gloomy silence followed this decisive action. Richon thought that he had quelled the rebellion, and, like a gambler risking everything, he turned back to his men.

'Now, if there are any other supporters of the king here,' he said, 'let them speak and they'll leave by the same route.'

A hundred men shouted: 'Yes! Yes! We support the king and want to leave.'

'Ah, ha!' said Richon, realizing that what was emerging was not the feeling of a few, but a general rebellion. 'That's another matter. I thought I was faced with just one mutineer, but I see I am dealing with five hundred cowards.'

It was a mistake for Richon to accuse them all at once. Only a hundred men had spoken, while the rest had remained silent, but the rest, now that they were included in this accusation of cowardice, also began to murmur.

'Come now,' said Richon, 'Don't all talk at once. Let one officer, if there is one who is ready to betray his oath, be the spokesman for you all. I promise you that he will be able to speak with impunity.'

At this, Ferguzon stepped forward and said, saluting his commander with exquisite courtesy: 'Commander, you have heard the wishes of the garrison: you are fighting against His Majesty, our king, and the majority of us were not warned that we were being enrolled to make war on such an enemy. One of our gallant fellows here, whose feelings have been outraged in this manner, could very well in the midst of the battle have made a mistake in the direction towards which he was pointing his musket and put a shot through your head. But we are true soldiers and not cowards, as you wrongly described us. So this is the opinion of my comrades and myself, which we respectfully put before you: give us back to the king, or we shall do so of our own accord.'

This speech was greeted with a general cheer, showing that the lieutenant's opinion was, if not that of the whole garrison, at least shared by the majority. Richon realized that he was lost.

'I cannot defend myself alone,' he said. 'And I do not wish to surrender. Since my soldiers have abandoned me, let somebody negotiate for me as he and they think best, but that somebody will not be me. As long as the few brave men who have remained loyal to me are given safe conduct, that is all I want. So, who will be your negotiator?'

'I shall do it, Commander, if you agree and if my comrades honour me with their trust.'

'Yes, yes! Lieutenant Ferguzon! Lieutenant Ferguzon!' shouted five hundred voices, among which could be heard those of Barabbas and Carrotel.

'It will be you, then, Monsieur,' said Richon. 'You are free to come and go in and out of Vayres as you wish.'

'Do you have any particular instructions to give me, Commander?' said Ferguzon.

'Freedom for my men.'

'And for yourself?'

'Nothing.'

Such self-denial would have changed the minds of men who had been misled, but these men had not only been misled, they had been sold.

'Yes, yes! Freedom for us!' they cried.

'Have no fear, Commander,' said Ferguzon. 'I shall not forget you in the surrender.'

Richon smiled sadly, shrugged his shoulders, returned to his quarters and locked the door.

Ferguzon immediately went over to the royalists. But Monsieur de La Meilleraie was not willing to do anything without authorization from the queen, and she had left Nanon's little house, because, as she said herself, she did not want to watch the disgrace of the army. She had retired to the town hall in Libourne.

Marshal de La Meilleraie put two soldiers to guard Ferguzon, mounted a horse and rode to Libourne. He went to find Mazarin, expecting that he would be announcing a great piece of news, but as soon as he began to speak, the minister stopped him with his usual smile.

'We know all that, Marshal,' he said. 'The matter was settled yesterday evening. Negotiate with Lieutenant Ferguzon, but only give a verbal assurance as far as Richon is concerned.'

'What! A verbal assurance?' the marshal said. 'But when I give my word, it's the same as putting something in writing, I hope.'

'Calm down, Marshal. I have received special indulgences from His Holiness the Pope which allow me to relieve people from their oaths.'

'That may be,' the marshal said. 'But those indulgences do not apply to marshals of France.'

Mazarin smiled and signalled to the marshal that he could return to the camp.

The marshal went back, grumbling, gave Ferguzon a written safe conduct for himself and his men, and gave his word where Richon was concerned.

Ferguzon returned to the fort, which he and his fellow soldiers abandoned an hour before dawn, after letting Richon know of the marshal's verbal assurance. Two hours later, when

Richon could already see from his window the reinforcements arriving for him with Ravailly, men came into his room and arrested him in the name of the queen.

To begin with, the brave commander's face wore an expression of deep satisfaction. While he was free, Madame de Condé could suspect him of treason, but if he was caught, his captivity answered for his honour. This was why, instead of leaving with the rest, he had stayed behind in the fort.

However, they were not satisfied merely with taking his sword, as he had at first expected, but after he had been disarmed, four men waiting for him by the door jumped on him and tied his hands behind his back.

Richon resisted this humiliating treatment with the calm and resignation of a martyr. He was one of those steadfast souls who were the ancestors of the popular heroes of the eighteenth and nineteenth centuries.[13]

He was brought to Libourne and taken before the queen, who looked him up and down with an arrogant stare; then before the king, who crushed him with a fierce glare; and finally before Monsieur Mazarin, who said: 'You played for high stakes, Monsieur Richon.'

'And I lost, didn't I, Monseigneur? Now it remains to see what the stakes were.'

'Your head, I'm afraid,' said Mazarin.

'Inform Monsieur d'Epernon that the king wishes to see him,' said Anne of Austria. 'As for this man, he can await his sentence here.'

Monsieur d'Epernon had arrived an hour earlier, but being an old man in love, his first call had been on Nanon. In the depths of Guyenne, he had learned of Canolles's spirited defence of the Ile Saint-Georges, and, still full of confidence in his mistress, he complimented her on her dear brother's conduct, quite innocently adding that this brother's appearance had not led him to expect such nobility and valour.

Nanon was too preoccupied to be amused by the continued success of her deception. Not only her own happiness was at risk, but also her lover's freedom. She loved Canolles so desperately that she could not believe that he could have betrayed her, even though the idea had often come into her head. She had interpreted his efforts to get her away from the fort as nothing more than anxiety about her safety. She thought that he was being kept prisoner by force and wept for him, longing only for the moment when, thanks to Monsieur d'Epernon, she would be able to set him free.

So she had done all she could to speed up his return, by writing ten letters to the duke.

Now, finally, he had arrived and Nanon had begged him on behalf of her pretended brother whom she was anxious to deliver as soon as possible from the hands of his enemies; or, rather, from those of Madame de Cambes – because she thought that in reality Canolles was in danger of nothing more serious than to fall ever more deeply in love with the viscountess.

But for Nanon, this danger was crucial, so she begged the Duke d'Epernon for her brother's freedom, with clasped hands.

'It's perfect,' said the duke. 'I have just learned that the Governor of Vayres has let himself be captured. Very well, we'll exchange him for this brave Canolles.'

'Oh, my dear duke,' said Nanon. 'It's a gift from heaven.'

'So do you love this brother of yours very much?'

'More than my life.'

'How odd that you never mentioned him to me, until that famous day when I was stupid enough . . .'

'So, Duke?' Nanon interrupted him.

'So I'll send the Governor of Vayres to Madame de Condé, and she'll send us back Canolles. It happens every day in wartime. It's a simple exchange of prisoners.'

'Yes, but would not Madame de Condé judge Canolles to be worth more than a simple officer?'

'Very well, in that case, instead of one officer, we'll send her two, we'll send her three . . . We'll arrange everything as you please, you see, my sweet? And when our brave commander of the Ile Saint-Georges comes back to Libourne, we'll greet him with a triumph.'

Nanon was beside herself with joy. There was nothing she wanted more than to have Canolles back again. What Monsieur

d'Epernon would say when he realized who this Canolles was
... well, she scarcely bothered about that. Once Canolles had
been saved, she would announce that he was her lover: she
would say so aloud, in front of everybody!

This is where things stood when the queen's messenger arrived.

'You see,' said the duke. 'It's working out perfectly, my dear
Nanon. I shall go to Her Majesty and fetch the request for the
exchange.'

'So my brother could be here ...'

'Tomorrow, perhaps.'

'Go on, then!' Nanon exclaimed. 'Don't lose a moment!
Oh, tomorrow, tomorrow!' she added, raising both arms to the
heavens with a lovely, prayerful expression. 'Tomorrow, God
willing!'

'Ah, what a soul!' murmured the duke as he went out.

When he came into the queen's chamber, Anne of Austria,
red with fury, was biting her thick lips (lips that were much
admired by her courtiers, precisely because they were the defect
of her face). So Monsieur d'Epernon, a gallant, used to receiving
the smiles of women, was welcomed like one of the rebellious
men of Bordeaux.

He stared at the queen in astonishment. She had not responded to his greeting and was frowning and looking him up
and down from the height of her royal majesty.

'Ah, it's you, Duke!' she said, after a moment's silence. 'Come
and let me compliment you on the way you make appointments.'

'What have I done, Madame?' the duke asked, in surprise.
'What has happened?'

'What has happened is that you made Governor of Vayres a
man who fired his cannon at the king, that's what.'

'I, Madame!' the duke exclaimed. 'Your Majesty must surely
be mistaken! It was not I that appointed the Governor of Vayres
... at least, not as far as I know.'

D'Epernon hesitated, because his conscience told him that he
did not always make appointments by himself.

'Now that's something new!' she replied. 'Monsieur Richon
was not appointed by you – *perhaps*.'

She put a deeply malicious stress on this last word.

The duke, who knew Nanon's talent for fitting the right man to a job, was quickly reassured.

'I do not recall having appointed Monsieur Richon,' he said. 'But if I did so, then Monsieur Richon must be a loyal servant of the king.'

'That's rich!' said the queen. 'You think Monsieur Richon is a loyal servant of the king! Good heavens! Some servant – who in three days has killed five hundred of our men!'

'Madame,' the duke said anxiously, 'if that is the case, I must admit that I was wrong. But before I am condemned, let me find proof that I really was the one who appointed him. I shall go and look for it.'

The queen made as though to stop him, then changed her mind.

'Go, then,' she said. 'And when you bring me your proof, I shall show you mine.'

Monsieur d'Epernon ran out and hurried to Nanon's.

'Well?' she said. 'Have you got the request for exchange?'

'Oh, that's the question,' the duke replied. 'The queen is furious.'

'What is making Her Majesty furious?'

'The fact that either you or I appointed Monsieur Richon Governor of Vayres, and this governor, who fought like a lion, apparently, has just killed five hundred of our men.'

'Richon!' Nanon repeated. 'I don't know him.'

'Devil take me if I do, either.'

'In that case, tell the queen outright that she is mistaken.'

'But are you sure that you are not the one who is mistaken?'

'Wait, I don't want to have any reason to reproach myself. I'll tell you.' And she went to her bureau, looked up her business register at the letter 'R' and found no sign of any commission to Richon.

'You can return to your queen,' she said, coming back, 'and tell her confidently that she is wrong.'

Monsieur d'Epernon went from Nanon's house to the town hall in a single bound.

'Madame,' he said, proudly marching into the queen's chambers. 'I am innocent of the crime that is alleged against me. The appointment of Monsieur Richon was made by Your Majesty's ministers.'

'So my ministers sign themselves "d'Epernon", do they?' the queen asked, sourly.

'What do you mean?'

'Just this: that is the signature at the bottom of Monsieur Richon's commission.'

'Impossible, Madame,' the duke replied, in the faltering tones of a man who is starting to doubt his own reason.

The queen shrugged her shoulders.

'Impossible?' she said. 'Well, read it.' And she took a commission that had been lying face down on the table with her hand on it.

Monsieur d'Epernon took the paper, read it keenly, examining every fold, every word and every letter, and was left perturbed: a frightful thought entered his head . . .

'Could I see this Richon?' he asked.

'Nothing could be simpler,' the queen answered. 'I have had him waiting in the room next door just to give you that satisfaction.' Then, turning to the guards, who were awaiting her orders by the door, she said: 'Bring the wretch in.'

The guards left, and a moment later Richon was led in with his hands tied and his hat on. The duke walked across to the prisoner and stared at him with a look that the other bore with his accustomed dignity. Since he was wearing his hat, one of the guards knocked it off with a blow from the back of his hand.

The Governor of Vayres did not flinch at this insult.

'Put a cloak over his shoulders, and a mask on his face, and give me a lighted candle,' said the duke.

To begin with, they carried out the first two requests. The queen looked at these unusual preparations with astonishment. The duke walked round the masked figure of Richon, minutely examining him and trying to bring back all his memories, but still doubtful.

'Bring me the candle I asked for,' he said. 'That will resolve all my doubts.'

A candle was brought. The duke put the commission close to

the light, and, in the warmth of the flame, a double cross, written above the signature with invisible ink, appeared on the paper.

At the sight of this, the duke's face lit up and he exclaimed: 'Madame, this commission is signed by me, that's true, but I did not sign it for Monsieur Richon or anyone else: it was extorted from me by this man in a kind of ambush. But before handing over this blank paper with my signature, I made a sort of mark that Your Majesty can see. It is overwhelming evidence against the guilty man. Look.'

The queen eagerly seized the paper and looked, while the duke pointed to the sign.

'I don't understand a word of the accusation you have just made against me,' Richon said simply.

'What!' cried the duke. 'Weren't you the masked man to whom I gave this paper on the Dordogne?'

'I have never spoken to Your Lordship before today,' Richon replied coldly. 'And I have never been masked on the Dordogne.'

'If it was not you, then it was a man sent by you who came in your stead.'

'There would be no point my hiding the truth,' said Richon, calm as ever. 'The commission that you have there, Duke, was given to me by the Princess de Condé, from the hands of the Duke de La Rochefoucauld in person. It was filled in with my name and forenames by Monsieur Lenet, whose writing you may recognize. How did the princess obtain this paper? How did it come into the hands of Monsieur de La Rochefoucauld? Where did Monsieur Lenet add my name and forenames to it? I know nothing of these things: they do not concern me or matter to me.'

'Huh! That's what you think!' said the duke in a jocular tone. And, going over to the queen, he whispered to her a fairly long story that the queen followed attentively. It was the story of Cauvignac's denunciation of Nanon and the meeting on the Dordogne. But, being a woman, the queen perfectly understood the duke's feelings of jealousy.

Then, when he had finished, she said:

'This is an infamous act to add to high treason. That's all. A man who did not hesitate to fire on his king might very easily sell a woman's secret.'

'What on earth are they talking about?' Richon thought to himself, frowning, because without being able to hear enough of the conversation to follow it, he caught enough to realize that his honour was at stake. In any case, the queen and the duke, with their flashing eyes, promised no good to him, and brave as he was, the Commander of Vayres could not help being anxious at this double threat – though it would have been impossible to make out what was going on in his mind from his face, armed with its usual contemptuous impassivity.

'He must be tried,' said the queen. 'Call a council of war. You can preside over it, Duke. Choose your fellow assessors, and let's be quick about it.'

'Madame,' said Richon, 'there's no need for a council or a judgement. I am a prisoner on Marshal de La Meilleraie's word, a voluntary prisoner, and the proof of that is that I could have left Vayres with my soldiers, or I could have fled before or after they left the fort, but I did not do so.'

'I know nothing about these matters,' the queen said, getting up to go into another room. 'If you have a good case, you can put it to your judges. This will be very suitable for you to hold the court here, won't it, Duke?'

'Yes, Madame,' he said, and, at the same moment, he chose twelve officers in the antechamber and set up the tribunal.

Richon was starting to understand. The ad hoc judges took their places, and the official reporter asked him for his name, forenames and rank.

Richon answered the three questions.

'You are acused of high treason in that you did fire cannon against the soldiers of the king,' said the reporter. 'Do you admit your guilt?'

'To deny it would be to deny what is evident. Yes, Monsieur, I did fire against the soldiers of the king.'

'By what right?'

'By right of war. By virtue of the same right invoked in similar circumstances by Monsieur de Conti, Monsieur de Beaufort, Monsieur d'Elbeuf and many others.'

'That right does not exist, Monsieur, since it would amount to no less than rebellion.'

'Nonetheless, it was by virtue of that right that my lieutenant capitulated. I appeal to that capitulation.'

'Capitulation!' d'Epernon exclaimed, ironically, sensing that the queen was listening: her unseen presence dictated this insulting tone. 'Capitulation! You – negotiate with a marshal of France!'

'Why not?' Richon asked. 'Since this marshal was negotiating with me?'

'Well, then, show me this capitalaulation, and we'll see what it's worth.'

'It was a verbal agreement.'

'Show us your witness, then.'

'I can only produce one witness.'

'Which is?'

'The marshal himself.'

'Call the marshal,' said the duke.

'No point,' said the queen, opening the door behind which she had been listening. 'The marshal left two hours ago. He is marching on Bordeaux with our vanguard.' And she shut the door.

Her appearance sent a chill through every heart, because it obliged the judges to condemn Richon.

The prisoner gave a bitter smile.

'Very well!' he said. 'So much for the honour that Monsieur de La Meilleraie attaches to his word! You are right, sir,' he said, turning to the Duke d'Epernon. 'I was wrong to negotiate with a marshal of France.'

From then on, Richon lapsed into silence and contempt, and refused to answer any question that was put to him. This greatly simplified the proceedings, and the remaining formalities lasted barely an hour. Not very much was written down and still less spoken. The prosecutor called for death, and the judges voted unanimously for the death penalty.

Richon listened to this sentence as though he were a simple onlooker and, still impassive and silent, was handed over to the provost of the army while the court was still sitting.

As for the Duke d'Epernon, he went to see the queen, finding her in excellent spirits; she invited him to dinner. The duke, who had thought himself in disgrace, accepted and went to see Nanon to tell her of his good fortune in still being in the queen's good graces.

He found her sitting on a chaise longue beside a window overlooking the main square in Libourne.

'So? Have you found anything out?' she asked.

'My dearest, I have found everything out,' he replied.

'Pooh!' she said anxiously.

'Why, yes! You remember the accusation I was foolish enough to believe, the accusation about your feelings for your brother?'

'So?'

'And you remember the signed authorization that I was asked to deliver?'

'Yes, why?'

'The accuser is in our hands, my dear, caught in the lines of his authorization like a fox in a trap.'

'Really?' said Nanon, terrified, knowing that the accuser was Cauvignac, and, though she had no deep affection for her real brother, she did not want any harm to come to him either; in any case, in trying to get himself out of a spot, this brother might say a mass of things that Nanon would much prefer to remain secret.

'The very same, my dear,' d'Epernon continued. 'What do you say to that? The scoundrel, using my signature, had on his own authority appointed himself Governor of Vayres. But Vayres has been taken, and the guilty man is in our hands.'

All these details seemed so consistent with the industrious scheming of Cauvignac that Nanon felt her terror increase.

'And . . . this man,' she asked, 'what have you done with him?'

'Goodness me,' said the duke. 'You can see for yourself what we've done with him. Yes, indeed,' he said, standing up. 'It's perfect. Open the curtain, or rather, open the window itself. He's an enemy of the king, and you can see him hang.'

'Hang!' Nanon cried. 'What are you saying, Duke? Hang the man with the authorization?'

'Yes, dearest. Look: can you see in the covered market, that beam, the rope hanging from it and the crowd hurrying? There,

there: look at the soldiers bringing the man, there on the left? There! That's the king at his window.'

Nanon's heart rose to her mouth, though a glance had told her that the man who was being brought out was not Cauvignac.

'Come, come,' said the duke. 'This fellow Richon will be hanged high and short. That will teach him to slander women.'

'But the poor man's not guilty,' Nanon exclaimed, grasping the duke's hand, and gathering all her strength. 'He may be a brave soldier and a gentleman . . . You may be about to kill an innocent man!'

'No, not at all, my dear, you're quite wrong. He's a forger and a slanderer. In any case, were he nothing more than the Governor of Vayres, he would be guilty of high treason and were that his only crime, it seems to me that it would be quite enough.'

'But didn't he have Monsieur de La Meilleraie's word?'

'He said so, but I don't believe it.'

'How was it that the marshal did not enlighten the tribunal on such an important point?'

'He left two hours before the accused came before his judges.'

'Oh, my God! Monsieur! Something tells me that this man is innocent,' Nanon cried. 'His death will bring misfortune to us all. Oh, Monsieur, in heaven's name, you who are so powerful, you who say that you will refuse me nothing, grant me that man's life!'

'Impossible, my dear. The queen herself condemned him, and where she is, no other power exists.'

Nanon gave a sigh that sounded like a groan.

At that moment, Richon arrived under the roof of the market. He was led, still as calm and silent, to the beam with the rope hanging from it. A ladder had been set up already, and was waiting. Richon climbed the ladder with a firm step, his noble head showing above the heads of the crowd, on whom he cast a look full of cold contempt. Then the prevost put the rope around his neck and the town crier announced in a loud voice that the king's justice would punish Étienne Richon, forger, traitor and peasant.

'We have reached a time,' said Richon, 'when it is better to be a villain as I am than to be a marshal of France.'

Hardly had he spoken these words than the ladder was

knocked away, and his body swung trembling from the fatal beam.

The crowd dispersed with a general feeling of horror, without a single cry of 'Long live the king!' being heard, even though everyone could see the king and queen at their window. Nanon, hiding her head in both hands, had fled to the furthest corner of the room.

'Well, Nanon,' said the duke. 'Whatever you think, I believe that this execution will set a good example, and I am curious to see what they will do when they see in Bordeaux what we think of their governors.'

At the idea of what they might do, Nanon opened her mouth to speak, but could only let out a dreadful cry, raising both hands to heaven, as though to beg that Richon's death might not be avenged. Then, as though all her life's springs had broken inside her, she fell full length on the floor.

'Why, why!' the duke exclaimed. 'What's wrong, Nanon? Can you really be in such a state, just for having seen a low-born traitor hanged? Come, my dear, get up and pull yourself together ... But, for heaven's sake, she's fainted! And those people of Agen who say she has no feeling! Here, someone! Bring some smelling salts! Some cold water!'

Seeing that no one came when he called, the duke ran out himself to fetch what he had asked his servants in vain to bring him. They were no doubt unable to hear him, being still taken up with the free spectacle with which they had just been provided by the generosity of the Crown.

XVIII

At the same moment as the terrible drama that we have just described was taking place in Libourne, Madame de Cambes, sitting beside an oak table with corkscrew legs, and with Pompée in front of her writing out a sort of inventory of all her goods, was composing the following letter to Canolles:

A further delay, my friend. Just as I was about to speak your name to the princess and ask for her blessing on our union, news arrived of the capture of Vayres, which froze the words on my lips. But I know how you must be suffering, and I do not have the strength both to bear your pain and my own. The successes and misfortunes of this fateful war may carry us too far, unless we decide to take matters into our own hands ... Tomorrow, my friend, tomorrow at seven in the evening, I shall be your wife.

Here is the plan that I beg you to follow. It is crucial that you should stick to it in every detail.

You will spend the time after dinner at Madame de Lalasne's; since I presented you to her, she, like her sister, has held you in high esteem. People will be playing cards. Do the same, but do not make any engagement for supper. More: when evening comes, send away your friends, if you have any with you. Then, when you are on your own, you will see a messenger come in – I am not sure who it will be – who will call you by name, as if you were required for some business. Whoever it is, go out confidently with him, because he will come on my behalf, and his mission will be to take you to the chapel where I shall be waiting.

I should like it to take place in the Carmelite church, which already has such sweet memories for me, but I dare not hope for that yet. But it will be so, if they agree to close the church for us.

Until then, do with my letter what you do with my hand, when I forget to take it away from you. Today I am saying: until tomorrow. Tomorrow I shall be saying: for ever!

Canolles was in one of his misanthropic moods when he got this letter: the whole of the previous day and all the morning of that one he had not even had a glimpse of Madame de Cambes, although in the space of twenty-four hours he had passed perhaps ten times by her window. So the young man, being in love, had reacted as he usually did, accusing the viscountess of frivolity, doubting her love. Despite himself he returned to his memories of Nanon – so kind, so devoted, so warm – almost glorying in this love, which apparently was to Claire a matter for shame, and, poor heart, he sighed, caught as he was between this satisfied love that would not be snuffed out and that yearning love that could not be satisfied. The viscountess's letter decided everything in her favour.

Canolles read and reread it. As Claire had anticipated, he kissed it twenty times, as he would have kissed her hand. When he thought about it, taking everything into account, Canolles could not deny that his love for the viscountess had been the most serious affair of his life. With other women, his feelings had always assumed a different aspect and, above all, a different course. Canolles had played his role as a ladykiller, had posed as victor and had almost reserved to himself the right to be inconstant. With Madame de Cambes, on the contrary, he was the one who felt subjected to a superior force, against which he did not even try to react, because he felt that today's slavery was sweeter than yesterday's power. In the moments of discouragement, when he doubted the reality of Claire's sentiments – those moments when the stricken heart turns in on itself and probes its wounds with thought – he would admit, without even blushing at a weakness that a year earlier he would have considered unworthy of a great mind, that the loss of Madame de Cambes would be an unbearable calamity for him.

But loving her, being loved by her, possessing her in heart, soul and body; possessing her in all the independence of his future (since the viscountess did not even demand of him the sacrifice of his opinions to the princess's side, and asked only for his love) . . . The happiest future, the richest officer of the king – because, after all, why forget wealth? Wealth does no harm . . . remaining in His Majesty's service if His Majesty rewarded his loyalty suitably, or leaving it, if, as kings are inclined to be, His Majesty was ungrateful . . . Was this not, in truth, the greatest, most magnificent happiness (if one can call it such), that in his sweetest dreams he could ever have hoped for?

And Nanon?

Oh, Nanon, Nanon: she was the dull, aching sense of remorse that always lies in the depths of every noble soul. Only in vulgar hearts does the pain that they cause leave no echo. Nanon, poor Nanon! What would she do, what would she say, what would she become, when she learned the dreadful news that her lover was another woman's husband? Alas, she would not be avenged,

even though she had in her hands all the means of vengeance –
and this was the idea that caused Canolles the most acute pain.
Why, if only Nanon would try to take her revenge, or even do so
in some way, the faithless lover could see her merely as an enemy
and would at least be relieved of his remorse.

However, Nanon had not replied to the letter in which he
had told her not to write to him again . . . How could she have
followed his instructions so scrupulously? Surely, if Nanon had
wanted, she could have found the means to get ten letters to him
– which meant that Nanon had not tried to correspond with
him. Oh, if only it could be that Nanon no longer loved him!

Yet Canolles's brow furrowed at the mere possibility that
Nanon no longer loved him. How sad it is, indeed, to find the
egotism of pride even in the noblest of hearts.

Fortunately, Canolles had one means of forgetting everything, which was to read and reread Madame de Cambes's letter.
He did so, and the remedy worked. In this way, our hero in love
managed to blind himself to all that was not his own happiness.
And, first of all obeying his mistress, who ordered him to go to
Madame de Lalasne, he made himself look good, which was not
hard for a man of his youth, elegance and good taste, then set
out for Madame de Lalasne's just as the clock struck two.

Canolles was so engrossed in happiness that, as he walked
beside the river, he did not see his friend Ravailly, who was signalling frantically to him from a boat travelling along as fast as
oars could drive it. Lovers, in their moments of happiness, walk
with such a light step that they seem not to touch the ground, so
Canolles was already far away when Ravailly came to shore.

Hardly had he disembarked than he gave a few brief orders to
the oarsmen and headed quickly towards Madame de Condé's.

The princess was at table, when she heard a noise in the
anteroom. She asked what the commotion was and was told
that the Baron de Ravailly, whom she had sent to Monsieur de
La Meilleraie, had just that moment returned.

'I think that it would be a good thing for Your Highness to
receive him without delay,' said Lenet. 'Whatever the news he
brings, it must be important.'

The princess gave the order, and Ravailly came in, but he

was so pale and his face so distraught that the mere sight of him told Madame de Condé that she was looking at a messenger bearing bad news.

'What is it, Captain?' she asked. 'What has happened now?'

'Madame, excuse me for appearing in this way before Your Highness, but I thought that the news I am bringing could not wait.'

'Speak. Have you seen the marshal?'

'The marshal refused to receive me, Madame.'

'The marshal refused to receive my envoy!'

'Oh, Madame, that is not all . . .'

'So what else is there? Tell me, I'm listening.'

'Poor Richon!'

'Yes, I know, he is a prisoner – since I sent you to discuss his ransom.'

'Quickly though I went, I was too late.'

'What do you mean: too late?' cried Lenet. 'Has something happened to him?'

'He is dead.'

'Dead!' the princess repeated.

'He was tried as a traitor, condemned and executed.'

'Condemned! Executed! Oh, do you hear that, Madame?' Lenet said, in consternation. 'I told you!'

'And who condemned him? Who dared?'

'A tribunal under the Duke d'Epernon; or, rather, the queen herself. So they were not satisfied with merely putting him to death, they wanted his death to be a shameful one.'

'What, Richon!'

'He was hanged, Madame! Hanged, like a wretch, like a thief, like a murderer! I saw his body in the market at Libourne.'

The princess rose from her seat as though propelled by an invisible spring. Lenet gave an anguished cry. Madame de Cambes, who had got up, slumped back in her chair, putting her hand to her heart, like someone who has received a deep wound. She had fainted.

'Take the viscountess away,' said the Duke de La Rochefoucauld. 'We have no time just now to bother with swooning women.'

Two women servants removed her.

'This is a brutal declaration of war,' the duke said impassively.

'It's outrageous!' said the princess.

'It's savage!' said Lenet.

'It's impolitic,' said the duke.

'And I hope we shall be avenged,' the princess exclaimed. 'And cruelly!'

'I have a plan!' cried Madame de Tourville, who had been silent up to now. 'Reprisals, Your Highness, reprisals!'

'One moment, Madame,' said Lenet. 'My goodness, how you go at it! This matter is serious enough for us to give it some thought.'

'No, Monsieur, on the contrary: at once!' Madame de Tourville retorted. 'The faster the king struck, the faster we must hasten to reply, striking the same blow.'

'Well, Madame,' said Lenet. 'I must say, you're talking about shedding blood, as though you were the queen of France. At least wait until Her Highness asks for your opinion before you give it.'

'The lady is right,' said the captain of the guard. 'Reprisals: that's the law of war.'

'Come, come,' said the Duke de La Rochefoucauld, calm and impassive. 'Let's not waste time in words. The news will travel around the town, and in an hour we shall no longer be in control of events, or of people's feelings, or of the people themselves. Your Highness's first consideration must be to take such a firm attitude that you are considered unshakeable.'

'Very well,' said the princess, 'I shall leave that task up to you, Duke, and rely entirely on you to avenge my honour and your feelings – because, before he entered my service, as you told me, Richon was in yours, and you led me to think that he was one of your friends rather than one of your servants.'

'Have no fear, Madame,' the duke replied, bowing. 'I shall remember what I owe to you, to myself and to that poor corpse.'

He went over to the captain of the guard and whispered to him for a long time, while the princess left, accompanied by Madame de Tourville and followed by Lenet, beating his brow with grief.

The viscountess was at the door. Her first thought on coming to herself had been to go back to Madame de Condé. She met her on the way, but wearing such a stern look that she did not dare question her directly.

'My God, my God! What is to be done?' she asked timidly, clasping her hands in supplication.

'We are going to have revenge,' said Madame de Tourville imperiously.

'Revenge! But how?' Claire asked.

'If you have any sway with the princess,' said Lenet, 'use it, so that there is not some frightful murder committed in the name of reprisals.'

And he too went past, leaving Claire in a state of terror.

Indeed, by one of those extraordinary intuitions that make one believe in an ability to see into the future, the young woman's mind had suddenly and painfully been filled with the memory of Canolles. It was as though she could hear a sad voice in her heart speaking to her of this absent friend. Returning home in furious haste, she began to get dressed for their meeting, when she realized that the meeting was not to take place for three or four hours.

Meanwhile Canolles had presented himself at Madame de Lalasne's, as the viscountess had instructed him. It was the birthday of her husband, the president, and they were giving him a kind of party. As these were the finest days of the year, all the guests were in the garden, where a game of quoits had been set up on a wide lawn. Canolles, whose skill was exceptional and his manner elegant, had taken up several challenges and, thanks to his dexterity, constantly ensured victory.

The ladies were laughing at the awkwardness of Canolles's rivals and admiring his skill. There were prolonged cheers at every point he won, handkerchiefs were waved in the air, and it would have taken little for the bouquets of flowers to fly from the ladies' hands and fall at his feet.

This triumph was not enough to turn Canolles's mind from the idea that obsessed it, but it helped him to be patient. However anxious one is to reach one's goal, one can excuse delays on the route when these are caused by ovations.

However, as the expected time approached, the young man's

eyes strayed increasingly towards the gate through which the guests were arriving or leaving – and through which, naturally, the promised envoy would appear.

Suddenly, just as Canolles was congratulating himself on having in all probability only a very short time to wait, a strange murmur spread through the happy crowd. He noticed that groups were forming here and there, and talking in subdued voices, looking at him with strange curiosity and, at the same time, with what seemed like a measure of pain. At first he attributed the interest to his physique and his skills, and congratulated himself on this attention, being far from suspecting its true cause.

He began, however, as we said, to notice that there was something uncomfortable in the attention directed at him. Smiling, he went over to one of the groups. The people in it tried to smile, but their faces were visibly embarrassed, and those who were not speaking to Canolles drifted away.

Canolles turned around and saw that bit by bit everyone was vanishing. It was as though some fatal piece of news which had stricken everyone with terror had suddenly spread through the gathering. Behind him, President de Lalasne was walking, with one hand on his chin, the other on his chest, and with an air of dejection. His wife, who had her sister on her arm, took advantage of a moment when she could not be seen and made a step towards Canolles. Without speaking to anyone in particular, she said, in a tone of voice that caused the young man deep anxiety: 'If I were a prisoner of war, even one on parole, in case my captors did not respect the parole that I had been given, I should leap on a good horse and ride to the river where I would give ten louis, twenty louis, a hundred if need be, to a boatman, and I would leave . . .'

Canolles looked at the two women with astonishment, and both of them simultaneously made a sign of terror that he could not understand. He stepped forward, trying to get them to explain the words that had just been spoken, but they slipped away like ghosts, one putting a finger to her mouth, telling him to keep quiet, while the other raised an arm in a sign that he should flee.

At that moment, the name of Canolles rang out at the gate.

He shuddered throughout his body. It must be the messenger of Madame de Cambes speaking his name. He ran to the gate.

'Is the Baron de Canolles here?' asked a loud voice.

'Yes,' Canolles cried, forgetting everything, the better to recall Claire's promise. 'Yes, here I am.'

'You are Monsieur de Canolles?' asked a kind of sergeant, stepping through the gate, behind which he had stayed until then.

'Yes, Monsieur.'

'Governor of the Ile Saint-Georges?'

'Yes.'

'Former captain in the regiment of Navailles?'

'Yes.'

The sergeant turned and motioned to four soldiers, who were hidden by a carriage and immediately came forward. The carriage, too, advanced to the point where its running board was beside the gate. The sergeant asked Canolles to get inside.

The young man looked around him. He was entirely alone. He could, however, make out Madame de Lalasne and her sister in the distance, among the trees, like two shades, leaning on one another, and apparently looking at him with compassion.

'Well I never!' he thought, not understanding what was going on. 'Madame de Cambes has chosen an unusual escort here. But let's not be fussy about the choice of conveyance,' he added, smiling at the idea.

'We are waiting for you, Monsieur,' said the sergeant.

'I beg your pardon, gentlemen, I'm coming,' said Canolles, and got into the carriage.

The sergeant and two soldiers followed. One of the two remaining soldiers took up a position beside the coachman and the other behind him. Then the heavy vehicle set off as fast as two strong horses could pull it.

All this was peculiar and starting to make Canolles wonder, so he turned to the sergeant and said: 'Now that we're alone, Monsieur, could you tell me where you are taking me?'

'To prison, first of all, Commander,' replied the man to whom the question had been addressed.

Canolles looked at him in amazement.

'What! To prison?' he said. 'Weren't you sent by a woman?'

'We were.'

'Was that woman not the Viscountess de Cambes?'

'No, Monsieur, the woman was the Princess de Condé.'

'The Princess de Condé!' Canolles exclaimed.

'Poor young man,' said a woman going past outside, and she crossed herself.

Canolles felt a shudder run through his veins.

Further on, a man who was running along with a pike in his hand stopped on seeing the carriage and the soldiers. Canolles leant out, and the man must have recognized him, because he shook his fist at him with a furious, threatening look.

'Why, they're mad in this town of yours!' Canolles said, still trying to smile. 'Have I become in one hour an object of pity or hatred, for some people to sympathize with me and others to threaten?'

'Ah, Monsieur,' the sergeant replied, 'those who feel sorry for you are not wrong, and those who threaten you may well be right.'

'If only I could understand something, at least,' said Canolles.

'You soon will, Monsieur,' the sergeant replied.

They reached the door of the prison, and Canolles was taken down in the midst of a crowd that was starting to gather. But, instead of taking him to his usual room, they made him go down to a dungeon full of guards.

'Come, now, I must at least know what's up,' said Canolles to himself. And, taking two louis out of his pocket, he went over to a soldier and put them in his hand.

The soldier was hesitant about taking them.

'Go on, my friend,' said Canolles. 'The question I am going to ask will not compromise you at all.'

'Then ask away, Commander,' the soldier replied, after first putting the two louis in his pocket.

'Well, I'd like to know the cause of my sudden arrest.'

'It would seem that you're not aware of the death of poor Monsieur Richon,' said the soldier.

'Richon dead!' Canolles exclaimed, with a cry of profound grief (as we know, they were close friends). 'Was he killed, for heaven's sake?'

'No, Commander, he was hanged.'

'Hanged!' Canolles muttered, going pale and clasping both hands, as he looked round at his ominous surroundings and the fierce looks of his guards. 'Hanged! By God, that might mean an indefinite delay to my wedding!'

XIX

Madame de Cambes had completed her toilet, dressing in a manner that was both simple and charming. She threw a kind of cape across her shoulders and signalled to Pompée to go ahead of her. It was almost night, and, thinking that she was less likely to be noticed on foot than in a carriage, she had given orders for her coach to wait for her only when she was leaving the Carmelite church, near a chapel in which she had obtained permission for them to be married. Pompée came down the stairs, and the viscountess followed. This task of pathfinding reminded the old soldier of the famous patrol that he had undertaken on the eve of the Battle of Corbie.

At the bottom of the stairs and as the viscountess was walking past the drawing room, in which there was a great commotion, she met Madame de Tourville, who was pulling the Duke de La Rochefoucauld towards the princess's private chamber, talking to him as they went.

'Oh, Madame,' she said. 'One word, I beg you. What has been decided?'

'My plan has been adopted!' Madame de Tourville exclaimed in triumph.

'What was your plan, Madame. I do not know it.'

'Reprisals, my dear! Reprisals!'

'Forgive me, but I am unfortunately not so well acquainted as you with the terms of war. What do you understand by "reprisals"?'

'Nothing could be simpler, my child.'

'Please explain.'

'They hanged an officer of the princes' army, didn't they?'

'Yes. But what then?'

'Well, let's look for an officer of the king's army in Bordeaux and hang him.'

'Great heaven!' Claire cried, in horror. 'What are you suggesting?'

'Tell me, Duke,' the dowager went on, apparently without noticing the viscountess's state. 'Haven't we already arrested the governor who was in command at Saint-Georges?'

'Yes, Madame,' the duke replied.

'Monsieur de Canolles has been arrested!' Claire exclaimed.

'Yes, Madame,' the duke said coldly. 'Monsieur de Canolles has been arrested or shortly will be. The order was given in my presence, and I saw the departure of the men charged with carrying it out.'

'But did they know where he would be?' Claire asked, grasping at a last straw.

'He was in the private house of our host, Monsieur de Lalasne, where I am told he was even enjoying great success at quoits.'

Claire gave a cry, and Madame de Tourville turned round in astonishment, while the duke looked at the young woman with a barely perceptible smile.

'Monsieur de Canolles has been arrested!' the viscountess continued. 'But what has he done, for goodness' sake? What connection is there between him and the dreadful event that is upsetting all of us?'

'What connection? Every connection, dear. Isn't he a governor, like Richon?'

Claire tried to speak, but her heart was so crushed that the words froze on her lips. However, grasping the duke's arm and giving him a terrified look, she managed to murmur:

'Oh, but surely it's a ruse, isn't it, Duke? A show, that's all. They can't do anything – as I understand it – they can't do anything to a prisoner on parole.'

'Richon was a prisoner on parole too, Madame.'

'Duke, I beg you . . .'

'Spare your entreaties, Madame, they are useless. I can do nothing in the matter: the council alone will decide.'

Claire let go of Monsieur de La Rochefoucauld's arm and

hurried to Madame de Condé's private chamber. Lenet, pale and agitated, was striding up and down, while Madame de Condé was talking to the Duke de Bouillon. Madame de Cambes slipped in beside the princess, light and pale as a ghost.

'Oh, Madame,' she said. 'In heaven's name, I beg you: just a word . . .'

'Oh, it's you, dear girl,' the princess replied. 'I have no time at the moment, but I shall be all yours after the council meeting.'

'But, Madame, I must talk to you before the council meeting.'

The princess was about to relent, when a door opened in front of the one through which the viscountess had entered, and the Duke de La Rochefoucauld appeared.

'The council is assembled, Madame,' he said. 'It is impatiently waiting for Your Highness.'

'You see, my dear,' Madame de Condé said. 'I really can't listen to you at the moment. But come into the council with us, and when it is over we shall leave together and talk.'

There was no way for Claire to insist. Dazzled, fascinated by the horrifying speed with which events were proceeding, the poor woman was starting to feel dizzy. She looked around wildly, her mind seeing and understanding nothing in the eyes and gestures that she saw, and without the strength to rouse herself from this frightful dream.

The princess went towards the salon. Claire followed her like an automaton, without noticing that Lenet had clasped in his hands the ice-cold one that she had hanging at her side, like the hand of a corpse.

They entered the council chamber. It was around eight o'clock in the evening.

The council chamber was a huge room, already dark in itself, but made darker still by vast tapestries. A sort of dais had been raised between the two doors opposite the windows, through which came the last light of the dying day. On the dais were two high chairs, one for Madame de Condé, the other for the Duke d'Enghien. On either side of these chairs was a line of stools for the women who formed Her Highness's private council. All the other judges were to sit on benches lined up for that purpose.

The Duke de Bouillon stood behind the princess's chair and the Duke de La Rochefoucauld behind that of the little prince.

Lenet had taken his seat opposite the clerk, with Claire beside him, standing, trembling and confused.

Six officers of the royal army, six officials of the municipality and six aldermen of the town were shown in. They sat on the benches.

The only lighting for this improvised assembly was provided by two candelabra, each with three candles. These were placed on a table in front of the princess, casting their light on the central group, while the remainder of those in the room faded progressively into the gloom, according to how near or far they were from this feeble source of light.

Soldiers of the princess's army were on guard at the doors, pikestaffs in hand. Outside, you could hear the braying of the crowd. The clerk called the roll, and everyone rose in turn to answer his name.

Then the reporter outlined the case. He described the capture of Vayres, the way in which Monsieur de La Meilleraie's word had been dishonoured, and the shameful death meted out to Richon.

At that moment an officer, who had been given an order in advance and posted there for that very purpose, opened a window, and a gust, as it were, of voices entered, shouting: 'Revenge for brave Richon! Death to the Mazarins!' (which was their name for the royalists).

'Can you hear that?' said Monsieur de La Rochefoucauld. 'That is what the great voice of the people is demanding. And in two hours either the people will have shown its contempt for our authority and taken the law into its own hands, or it will no longer be the moment for reprisals. So let's reach a verdict, gentlemen, without further delay.'

The princess stood up.

'Why judge?' she cried. 'What is the good of a verdict? You've just heard the verdict: the people of Bordeaux delivered it.'

'Yes, indeed,' said Madame de Tourville. 'Nothing could be simpler than this situation: an eye for an eye, that's what it is.

This kind of thing should be done on the spur of the moment, strictly between one provost and another.'

Lenet could not bear to hear any more. Leaping from his place, he went to the centre of the circle.

'Not another word, I beg you, Madame,' he exclaimed. 'Such a view would be fatal, were it to prevail. You are forgetting that even the monarchy, by punishing Richon in its own way, that is to say in an infamous manner, did at least show some respect for judicial formalities, and had the punishment, whether fair or not, confirmed by judges. Do you think you have the right to do what the king himself did not?'

'Huh!' said Madame de Tourville. 'I only have to give an opinion for Monsieur Lenet to be of the opposite one. Unfortunately, on this occasion my opinion is shared by Her Highness . . .'

'Yes, unfortunately,' said Lenet.

'Monsieur!' said the princess.

'Madame,' said Lenet, 'do at least keep up appearances. You'll still be free to condemn, won't you?'

'Monsieur Lenet is right,' said the Duke de La Rochefoucauld, composing himself. 'The death of a man is too serious a matter, especially in these circumstances, for us to leave the responsibility for it on a single head, even a princely one . . .' And leaning over to whisper in the princess's ear, so that only the group closest to her could hear, he added: 'Ask everyone for their opinion and only retain that of the people whom you trust most to take part in the trial. In that way, we shall not have to fear that our revenge will escape us.'

'One moment, please,' Monsieur de Bouillon interrupted, leaning on his cane and raising his gouty leg. 'You have spoken of taking the responsibility away from the princess, and I do not myself shirk it, but I should like others to share it. I ask nothing better than to continue to be a rebel, but in company with the princess on one side of me and the people on the other. Damn it, I don't want to be isolated! I lost my command of Sedan to that kind of farce. At that time, I had a town and a head. Cardinal Richelieu took my town, and now I have only a head, so I don't want Cardinal Mazarin to take that from me. So I am asking for the leading citizens of Bordeaux as the panel of judges.'

'Their signatures beside ours,' muttered the princess. 'Pooh!'

'The mortice supports the beam, Madame,' the Duke de Bouillon replied. The Cinq-Mars conspiracy[14] had left him cautious for the rest of his life.

'Is that your opinion, gentlemen?'

'Yes,' said the Duke de La Rochefoucauld.

'And you, Lenet?'

'Fortunately, Madame,' said Lenet, 'I am not a prince, nor a duke, nor an officer, nor a judge, so I have the right to abstain, and I do so.'

At this, the princess got up, inviting the meeting that she had called to respond forcefully to the provocation of the royalist side. She had barely finished her speech, when the window opened once more, and for the second time those in the court-room heard the thousand voices of the people crying as one: 'Long live the princess! Revenge for Richon! Death to the Epernonists and Mazarins!'

Madame de Cambes grasped Lenet's arm.

'Monsieur Lenet,' she said. 'I'm dying!'

'The Viscountess de Cambes asks Her Highness's permission to withdraw,' he said.

'No, no! I don't!' said Claire. 'I want . . .'

'This is not the place for you, Madame,' Lenet interrupted. 'You can do nothing for him. I shall keep you informed of everything, and we will try to save him.'

'The viscountess can retire,' said the princess. 'Any ladies here who do not wish to take part in this session are free to follow her. We only want men here.'

Not one of the ladies made a move. It is one of the eternal ambitions of that half of the human race which is destined to seduce, that it aspires to exercise the rights of the half that is destined to command. As the princess said, these ladies saw this as an opportunity to become men for a while. It was too fortu-nate an occasion for them not to take advantage of it.

Madame de Cambes went out, supported by Lenet. On the stairs, she found Pompée, whom she had sent for news.

'Well?' she asked.

'Well,' he said. 'He has been arrested.'

'Monsieur Lenet,' Claire said. 'I no longer have confidence except in you or hope except in God.' And she retired to her room, in a state of desperation.

'What questions shall I ask of the man who is to appear before us?' the princess was asking, as Lenet resumed his place near the clerk. 'And which is the fated one?'

'Nothing could be simpler, Madame,' the duke answered. 'We have perhaps three hundred prisoners, among whom there are ten or twelve officers. Let us just ask them their names and ranks in the royal army. The first who is acknowledged to be a governor like Richon, well, that's the one designated by fate.'

'There's no sense in wasting time interrogating ten or twelve different officers, gentlemen,' said the princess. 'You have the register, Clerk, so look at it and tell me the names of those prisoners who were of equal rank to Richon.'

'Only two, Madame,' the clerk replied. 'The Governor of the Ile Saint-Georges and the Governor of Braune.'

'That's right! We've got two!' said the princess. 'Fate, as you can see, is kind to us. Have they been arrested, Labussière?'

'Indeed, they have, Madame,' said the captain of the guard. 'Both of them are waiting in the fortress for your order to appear.'

'Well, let them be brought before the tribunal.'

'Which shall we bring?' asked Labussière.'

'Bring them both,' the princess replied. 'But we shall start with the last to arrive, namely the Governor of the Ile Saint-Georges.'

XX

This order was followed by horrified silence, broken only by the sound of footsteps as the captain of the guards marched away and by the constantly renewed murmur of the crowd, which was about to push the princes' rebellion down a dreadful road, and one still more dangerous than the one along which they had proceeded up to now. A single action would, in a sense, cast the princess and her counsellors, the army and the city outside the law; it would implicate a whole population in the interests and above all in the passions of a few; it would do on a small scale what the Paris Commune did on 2 September[15] (but the Paris Commune, as we know, acted on a grand scale).

Not a breath could be heard in the room. All eyes were fixed on the door through which the prisoner would come. The princess, to suit her role as presiding judge, pretended to be looking through some registers. Monsieur de La Rochefoucauld had adopted a pensive look, and Monsieur de Bouillon was chatting with Madame de Tourville about his gout, which gave him a lot of pain.

Lenet went over to the princess to make one final attempt, not because he had any hope of dissuading her, but because he was one of those conscientious people who feel under an obligation to carry out their duty.

'Think, Madame,' he said. 'You are risking the future of your family on a single throw of the dice.'

'There is no merit in it,' the princess replied drily. 'I'm bound to win.'

Lenet turned to La Rochefoucauld. 'Duke,' he said, 'with your superior intelligence, you are above human passions: you advise moderation, surely?'

'I am just now debating the matter with my reason,'[16] the duke replied, hypocritically.

'Debate it rather with your conscience,' Lenet retorted. 'That would be better!'

At that moment, there was a dull noise: it was the iron gate shutting. The sound echoed in every heart, because it heralded the arrival of one of the two prisoners. Very soon, footsteps reverberated up the stairway, halberds clashed on the stone floor, the door opened, and Canolles appeared.

Never had he been so elegant, never had he been so handsome. His face, full of serenity, still had the bright flush of joy and ignorance. He walked forward easily and without affectation, as though he were in the house of the lawyer Lavie or President Lalasne, and bowed respectfully to the princess and the dukes.

The princess herself seemed amazed by this perfect composure and spent a moment looking at the young man.

At last, she broke the silence.

'Come here, Monsieur,' she said. Canolles obeyed and bowed again. 'Who are you?'

'I am Baron Louis de Canolles, Madame.'

'And what rank do you hold in the royal army?'

'I am a lieutenant-colonel.'

'Were you not Governor of the Ile Saint-Georges?'

'I had that honour.'

'Have you told us the truth?'

'In every respect, Madame.'

'Clerk, have you written down the questions and answers?'

The clerk bowed and nodded.

'Then sign, Monsieur,' said the princess.

Canolles took the pen like a man who does not understand why he is being asked to do something, but obeys out of deference for the rank of the person making the request; then he signed, smiling.

'Very well, Monsieur,' said the princess. 'You may go now.'

Canolles bowed once more to his noble judges and left with the same ease and grace, without the slightest sign of curiosity or surprise.

Hardly had he gone through the door and the door been closed behind him, than the princess got up.

'Well, gentlemen,' she said.

'Well, Madame, let's vote on it,' said the Duke de La Rochefoucauld.

'Let's vote,' the Duke de Bouillon repeated. Then, turning to the town councillors, he went on: 'Would these gentlemen like to give their opinion?'

'After you, my lord,' one of the townsfolk replied.

'No, before you!' cried a thundering voice, so forcefully that it astonished everyone.

'What does that mean?' the princess asked, trying to recognize the face of the man who had spoken.

'What it means,' said a man, rising to his feet, so that there should be no further doubt about his identity, 'is that I, André

Lavie, advocate of the king and parliamentary counsellor, demand in the name of the king, and above all in the name of humanity, privilege and safety for the prisoners who are being kept in Bordeaux on parole. Consequently, I conclude . . .'

'Ah, now, Lawyer,' said the princess superciliously, 'don't let's have any flowery lawyers' language in front of me, I beg you, because I don't understand it. What we have here is a matter of feeling, not a mean and pettifogging trial, and I suppose that all the members of this tribunal will accept that.'

'Yes, yes!' cried the townsfolk and the officers in chorus. 'Let's vote, let's vote!'

'I said, and I repeat that I am demanding privilege and safety for the prisoners who are held on parole,' Lavie continued, not at all put out by the princess's intervention. 'This is not flowery lawyers' language, but the language of people's rights.'

'And I would add,' said Lenet, 'that Richon was heard before being so cruelly treated, so it is only fair that we should also hear the accused.'

'And I . . .' said d'Espagnet, the leading townsman who had attacked Saint-Georges with the Duke de La Rochefoucauld. 'I declare that if we show clemency, the town will be up in arms.'

A murmur from outside seemed to be replying in confirmation of this assertion.

'Hurry up,' said the princess. 'What is our sentence on the accused man?'

'The accused men, Madame,' said some voices. 'There are two of them.'

'Is one not enough for you?' Lenet asked, smiling with contempt at the savagery of these obsequious brutes.

'Which one then? Which?' the same voices repeated.

'The fattest, you cannibals!' Lavie cried. 'Why! You complain of injustice and sacrilege, yet you want to respond to one killing by two murders! It's a fine meeting of soldiers and philosophers, this, when they both turn out to be cut-throats.'

The blazing eyes of most of the judges seemed ready to strike down the brave advocate. Madame de Condé had got up, and leaning forward with her hands on the table, looked round the room, as though trying to convince herself that the words she had heard had really been spoken and that there was a man in the world bold enough to say such things to her face.

Lavie realized that his presence was not helpful and that his method of defending the accused would not save them, but have the opposite result; so he decided to leave, not like a retreating soldier, but as a judge who declines to participate in the proceedings.

'In the name of God,' he said, 'I protest at what you are trying to do, and in the name of the king, I forbid it.'

Knocking over his chair in a gesture of imperious rage, he left the room, with resolute steps and head held high, like a man firm in the accomplishment of a duty and careless of what might result from it.

'Insolent fellow,' the princess muttered.

'Fine, fine, leave him,' said a few voices. 'His turn will come.'

'Let's put it to a vote,' said almost all the judges.

'But why vote,' said Lenet, 'until you have heard both the accused? One might seem more guilty than the other. You may exact a revenge on one that you would rather share with both.'

At that moment, they heard the gate open for the second time.

'Very well, then,' said the princess. 'We'll vote on both at once.'

The court, which had already risen noisily to its feet, sat down again. Once again, the sound of footsteps was heard and the crash of halberds, the door opened, and Cauvignac appeared.

The new arrival presented a marked contrast with Canolles. His clothing, only partly restored after the attacks of the crowd, still showed the evidence of their attentions, despite his efforts to cover it. His eyes looked sharply around the sheriffs, the officers, the dukes and the princess, taking in the whole court with one turning glance. Then, like a wily fox, he moved forward, as it were feeling his way at each step, ears pricked, pale and clearly anxious.

'Your Highness has done me the honour of having me brought before her?' he said, without waiting to be questioned.

'Yes, Monsieur,' the princess replied. 'I wished you to clarify for us certain points about which we are concerned and that relate to you.'

'In that case,' Cauvignac replied, bowing, 'I am here, Madame, ready to respond to the favour that Your Highness has done me.' And he bowed in the most gracious manner he could, though this was evidently neither natural or easy.

'It will not take long,' said the princess, 'particularly if you answer our questions in as straightforward a way as we shall put them.'

'I should point out to Your Highness that since questions are always prepared in advance and the answers never,' said Cauvignac, 'it is harder to answer than to ask.'

'Ah, but our questions shall be so clear and precise,' said the princess, 'that you will have no need to ponder your answers. What is your name?'

'Just as I said, Madame! There is a difficult question right at the start.'

'Why is that?'

'Because it often happens that a person has two names, the one he received from his parents and the one that he gave himself. In my case, I felt the need to give up my first name and take another, less well-known one. So which of these names are you demanding from me?'

'The one under which you presented yourself in Chantilly, the one under which you agreed to raise a company for me, the one under which you did raise such a company and finally the one under which you sold yourself to Monsieur Mazarin.'

'Excuse me, Your Highness,' Cauvignac said, 'but I think I already had the honour of answering all these questions quite satisfactorily in the audience that Your Highness was kind enough to grant me this morning.'

'And now I am only asking you one question,' said the princess, starting to lose patience. 'Just your name.'

'And that is precisely the difficulty for me.'

'Write down: Baron de Cauvignac,' said the princess.

The accused did not demur, so the clerk wrote it down.

'Now,' said the princess, 'what is your rank? I hope you won't have any trouble answering that one.'

'On the contrary, Madame, that happens to be a question that I consider one of the hardest. If you mean my rank in society, I am a bachelor of letters, with a degree in law and a doctorate in theology – and I am answering, as you see, without hesitation.'

'No, Monsieur, we are speaking of your military rank.'

'Now that's a question that I am quite unable to answer to Your Highness.'

'Why?'

'Because I have never been sure myself exactly what I was.'

'Try to make up your mind, would you, Monsieur, because I should like to know.'

'Well, first of all I made myself a lieutenant, on my own private authority, but since I had no power to sign a commission for myself, and since I have never had more than six men under my command for the whole time that I have had this title, I rather think that I do not have the right to avail myself of it.'

'But I,' said the princess, 'I myself made you a captain, so that is what you are.'

'Ah, now, that's just what makes me doubly perplexed and causes my conscience to rebel. I have since become convinced that any military rank in the state must emanate from the king's authority if it is to have any value. And while, undeniably, Your Highness did have the desire to make a captain of me, I believe that you did not have the right to do so. And in that case I am no more a captain than I was a lieutenant.'

'Agreed, Monsieur. But let's suppose that you were not a lieutenant on your own authority or a captain on mine, seeing that neither you nor I had the power to sign a commission, at least you were Governor of Braune. And since this time it is the king who signed your papers, you cannot deny the value of the commission.'

'Madame,' Cauvignac replied, 'of the three, that is the one that is most questionable.'

'Why on earth?' the princess cried.

'Because I was appointed, I agree, but I did not take up my position. And what constitutes the rank? Not the ownership of the title, but carrying out the functions attributed to it. I did not fulfil any of the functions of the role to which I had been appointed, or set foot in my jurisdiction, or start to carry out my office, so I was no more Governor of Braune than I was captain before being governor or lieutenant before being captain.'

'And yet, you were found on the road to Braune, Monsieur.'

'Certainly, but a hundred yards from the point at which I was arrested, the road forks: one path leads to Braune, while the other goes to Isson. Who says that I might not have been going to Isson rather than Braune?'

'Very well,' the princess said. 'The court will consider your defence. Clerk, write: "Governor of Braune".'

'I have done so, Madame,' he replied.

'Good. Now, Monsieur,' the princess told Cauvignac, 'sign your deposition.'

'It would give me the greatest pleasure, Madame,' said Cauvignac. 'I should have been delighted to do something to please Your Highness, but while I was struggling this morning against the Bordeaux mob – a situation from which Your Highness graciously relieved me through the intervention of her musketeers – I had the misfortune to injure my right wrist, and I have never been able to write with the left hand.'

'Note the prisoner's refusal,' the princess said.

'Incapacity, clerk, write "incapacity",' Cauvignac said. 'Heaven forbid that I should refuse anything to such a great princess as Your Highness, were it in my power.'

Bowing in the most respectful manner, Cauvignac left, together with his two guards.

'I think you are right, Monsieur Lenet,' said the Duke de La Rochefoucauld. 'We made a mistake in not getting that man on our side.'

Lenet had too much on his mind to reply. His normal perspicacity had let him down on this occasion; he had been hoping that Cauvignac would attract the full anger of the court, but the mercenary, with his endless evasions, had amused his judges, rather than annoying them. His cross-examination had merely erased the effect produced by that of Canolles: the nobility, honesty and loyalty of the first prisoner had, so to speak, vanished beneath the wiles of the second: Cauvignac had wiped out Canolles.

So, when it was put to the vote, the result was unanimously in favour of death.

The princess had the votes counted and, rising to her feet, solemnly pronounced the verdict of the court.

Then each of them in turn signed the record of the proceedings. The first was the Duke d'Enghien, a poor child who did not know what he was doing, and whose first official signature was to cost a man's life. After him, the princess, then the dukes, the ladies of the council, the officers and the sheriffs – meaning that everyone had a share in the reprisals, and all would have to be punished: nobility and bourgeoisie, army and parliament. And, as we know, when everyone in general has to be punished, no one is.

Then, when everyone had signed, the princess – finally having her revenge, and one that satisfied her pride – went herself to open the window that had already been opened twice and gave way to her overwhelming need for popular acclaim, shouting aloud: 'People of Bordeaux! Richon will be avenged, and worthily so – count on us!'

A shout of 'Hurrah' like a clap of thunder greeted this announcement, and the people scattered through the streets, joyfully anticipating the spectacle promised by the princess's words.

But Madame de Condé had hardly returned to the room with Lenet, who was following sadly behind, still hoping to make her change her mind, than the door opened, and Madame de Cambes, pale and distraught, threw herself at the princess's knees.

'Madame, Madame, in heaven's name, listen to me! I beg you, do not push me aside!'

'What is it, child?' the princess asked. 'Why are you weeping?'

'I am weeping, Madame, because I have been told that the sentence was death and that you confirmed it. But, Madame, you cannot kill Monsieur de Canolles.'

'Why not, dear? After all, they killed Richon.'

'But this was the same Monsieur de Canolles who saved Your Highness in Chantilly.'

'Should I be grateful to him for being taken in by our trick?'

'Ah, Madame, that's just where you're wrong. Monsieur de Canolles was not taken in for a moment by the substitution. He recognized me at first glance.'

'You, Claire!'

'Yes, Madame. We came part of the way together. Monsieur de Canolles knew me and . . . in short . . . Monsieur de Canolles was in love with me. And in those circumstances . . . well, Madame! He may have been wrong, but you should not reproach him for it. In those circumstances, he sacrificed his duty to his love.'

'So the man with whom you are in love . . .'

'Yes,' the viscountess replied.

'The one you came to ask my permission to marry . . .'

'Yes.'

'It was . . .'

'It was Monsieur de Canolles himself,' said the viscountess. 'Monsieur de Canolles who surrendered to me on Saint-Georges and who, were it not for me, would have blown himself up together with your soldiers . . . Monsieur de Canolles, in fact, who could have fled, but gave me his sword, so as not to be separated from me. You will see then, that if he dies, I must do so as well, because I shall have killed him!'

'My dear child,' the princess said, quite moved. 'You must see that what you are asking is impossible. Richon is dead and must be avenged. A sentence was passed and must be carried out. Even if my own husband were to ask me what you are asking, I should refuse it.'

'Oh, wretch that I am!' Madame de Cambes cried, falling to the ground and bursting into tears. 'I have killed the one I love.'

At this, Lenet, who had not yet spoken, came over to the princess.

'Madame,' he said. 'Will you not be satisfied with one victim? Do you need two heads to pay for Monsieur Richon's one?'

'So, Mr High Principles, what you mean is that you are asking for the life of one man and the death of another, is that it? Tell me, is that quite fair?'

'Very much so, Madame: it is fair, first of all, that when two men are to die, only one should do so, if possible, assuming that any mouth has the right to blow out the flame that God's hand has lit. And then it is fair, if a choice has to be made, that the upright man should be saved rather than the schemer. Only a Jew would set free Barabbas and crucify Jesus . . .'[17]

'Monsieur Lenet, oh, Monsieur Lenet,' Claire exclaimed. 'Speak for me, I beg you, because you are a man and may be listened to. And you, Madame,' she continued, turning towards the princess, 'only remember that my whole life has been devoted to serving your family.'

'And mine too,' said Lenet. 'And yet, I have never asked Your Highness for anything in exchange for thirty years' loyalty. But on this occasion, if Your Highness shows no pity, I shall ask for just one favour for those thirty years.'

'What is that?'

'To give me leave, Madame, so that I might go and throw myself at the feet of the king, to whom I shall devote the rest of the life that I have had the honour to give to your house.'

'Now, then!' said the princess, overwhelmed by these united prayers. 'Don't threaten me, old friend, don't cry, my sweet Claire . . . in short, both of you, rest assured: only one will die, since that is what you want. Just as long as no one comes and begs me to pardon the one who is destined to perish.'

Claire clasped the princess's hand and covered it with kisses.

'Oh, thank you, Madame, thank you!' she said. 'From this moment onwards, my life and his belong to you.'

'In doing this,' said Lenet, 'you are both fair and merciful, something that up to now has been the privilege of God alone.'

'Now can I see him, Madame?' Claire begged impatiently. 'Can I see him? Can I free him?'

'For the moment, anything like that is impossible,' said the princess. 'It would be the end of us. We'll leave the prisoners in prison and bring them out at the same time, one for freedom, the other for death.'

'But can I not at least see him, reassure him and console him?'

'Reassure him! My dear friend,' the princess replied, 'I don't think you have any right to do so: the decision would be revealed, and there would be comments on the favour he was being done. Impossible. Be content with knowing that he is saved. I shall announce my decision to the two dukes.'

'In that case, I am resigned,' said Claire. 'Thank you, Madame, thank you!'

And Madame de Cambes hurried away to weep freely and to thank God from the depths of her heart, which was overflowing with joy and gratitude.

XXI

The two prisoners of war occupied two cells in the same fortress. These cells adjoined one another and were situated on the ground floor (though the ground floor in prisons is really the third floor, since prisons do not start like homes at ground level, but usually have two storeys of dungeons underneath).

Each door in the prison was guarded by a detachment of men picked from the princess's guards. But the crowd, seeing the preparations that would satisfy its desire for vengeance, had gradually drifted away from the prison area, to which it had come when it was told that Canolles and Cauvignac had been brought there. So the guards, who had been positioned there (more to protect the prisoners from the fury of the mob than from fear that they might escape) had left their posts and were content merely to double the ordinary number of sentries.

Indeed, the people, having nothing more to see where they were, had gravitated towards the place where executions were held, that is to say, the Esplanade.[18] The words shouted from the heights of the council chamber into the crowd had spread instantly through the town, each person commenting on them in his or her own way. What they most clearly implied, however, was that there would be some dreadful scene that night, or at the latest on the following day, and this was an added pleasure for the mob, not knowing exactly what to expect from the spectacle, because this gave it the appeal of surprise.

So workers, tradesmen, women and children ran to the ramparts, and, as it was a dark night and the moon was not due to rise until around midnight, many came with torches in their hands. In addition to that, almost all windows were open, and many people had also put burning links or lanterns on the window sills, as on feast days. Yet from the murmurs of the crowd, the fearful glances of onlookers and the succession of patrols on foot or on horseback, you could see that the event that was being so ominously prepared was no ordinary one.

From time to time, furious shouts arose from different groups, which formed or broke up with the kind of rapidity only associated with certain occurrences. The shouts were the same as those which, two or three times, had reached inside the courtroom: 'Death to the prisoners! Revenge for Richon!'

The shouts, the lights and the sound of horses' hooves had disturbed Madame de Cambes in her prayers. She went to the window and with horror observed all these men and women, who, with their wild looks and savage cries, resembled some ravenous beasts let loose in a Roman circus, roaring for the human victims that they were to devour. She wondered how it was possible that so many creatures, to whom the prisoners had never done any harm, should be so furious in demanding the death of two of their fellow men: and she could find no answer to her question, being a poor woman, who was acquainted only with those human passions that soften the heart.

From her window, Madame de Cambes saw the tips of the high, dark towers of the fortress rising above the houses and gardens. Canolles was there, and it was there particularly that she looked. However, she could not help glancing down into the street from time to time, and it was then that she saw the threatening faces and heard the cries for vengeance which sent deathly shivers through her veins.

'They may forbid me to see him,' she thought, 'but I must! Those shouts may have reached his ears, he may think that I have forgotten him, he may be accusing me and cursing me. Every moment that goes by in which I do not try to reassure him seems like a betrayal! I cannot stay here and do nothing, when he may be calling to me for help. Oh, I must see him! But how, dear God? Who will take me to the prison? What power will open its doors to me? The princess refused me a pass, and, seeing how much she has already granted me, she has the right to do so. There are guards, there are enemies around the fortress and a whole mob of people bellowing, scenting blood and unwilling to have its prey snatched from it. They will think that I want to carry him off, to save him. Oh! I would save him, if he were not already in safety under the protection of Her Highness's word ... They wouldn't believe me, if I were to tell them that I just want to see him; they would refuse ... And if I did try something like that against the princess's will, might I not be in danger of losing the favour she has done me? Might I not risk her going back on her word? And yet ... leaving him in anguish and torment through the long hours of the night – oh! I feel that is impossible for him, and above all for me! Let me pray to God, who may inspire me.'

So once again Madame de Cambes knelt in front of her crucifix and began to pray with a fervour that would have moved the princess herself, if the princess could have heard her.

'I shan't go, I shan't go,' she said, 'because I know that it is impossible for me to go. Perhaps he will be accusing me throughout the night ... But tomorrow, tomorrow – isn't it true, God? Tomorrow will absolve me in his eyes.'

At the same time, the noise, the mounting exaltation of the crowd and the sinister flashes of light that momentarily lit up her otherwise darkened room, caused her such horror that she blocked her ears with her hands and pressed her closed eyes against the cushion of her prayer stool.

The door opened, and, without her hearing him, a man entered, stopped a moment on the threshold and looked at her with affectionate sympathy. Then, seeing her shoulders heaving with such painful sobs, he sighed and went across to touch her arm.

Claire started up.

'Monsieur Lenet!' she said. 'Monsieur Lenet! You have not forsaken me!'

'No,' he said. 'It occurred to me that you might not yet be fully reassured, and I ventured to come and ask if there was anything I could do for you.'

'Oh, my dear Monsieur Lenet,' she exclaimed. 'How good you are! And how grateful I am!'

'It seems I was right,' said Lenet. 'God knows, one is seldom wrong in thinking that someone is in pain,' he added with a melancholy smile.

'Yes, yes,' said Claire. 'That's true: I am in pain!'

'But surely you got all that you wanted, and I must confess more than I hoped myself?'

'Yes, of course, but . . .'

'But I understand: you are frightened at seeing the joy of this mob thirsting for blood, and you mourn the fate of the other wretch who will die in your lover's stead, is that it?'

Claire got up and stayed motionless for an instant, pale and staring at Lenet; then she brought an icy hand to her forehead, covered in sweat.

'Oh, forgive me – or, rather, curse me!' she said. 'Selfish as I am, I didn't even think of that. No, Lenet, no: I admit in all the humility of my heart that these fears, these tears and these prayers are for the one who is to live, for I am so taken up in my love that I forgot the one who is to die!'

Lenet smiled sadly.

'Yes,' he said. 'That must be so, because it is human nature. Perhaps the selfishness of the individual is the salvation of the many. Each of us makes a circle around him with his sword. Come, come, Madame, confess everything,' he continued. 'Admit frankly that you cannot wait for the wretch to meet his fate, because his death ensures the life of your fiancé.'

'Oh, Lenet, I promise you, I hadn't yet thought of that. Please don't ask my mind to consider it, because I love him so much that I don't know what I might be able to wish for in the madness of my love.'

'Poor child!' Lenet said, in a voice of profound pity. 'Why didn't you say all of this earlier?'

'Good Lord! You are frightening me. Is it too late then? Is he not yet completely safe?'

'He is,' Lenet replied, 'since the princess has given her word, but . . .'

'But what?'

'But, alas, is one ever sure of anything in this world? And you, even thinking as I do that he is safe, are weeping instead of rejoicing . . .'

'I am weeping because I cannot visit him, my friend,' Claire replied. 'Just think: he must be hearing those dreadful sounds and thinking that danger is close. Imagine: he might be accusing me of coldness, of forgetting him, or of betraying him. Oh, Lenet, Lenet, what torture it is! If only the princess knew how I am suffering, she would have pity on me.'

'So you must see him, then, viscountess.'

'See him? I can't! You know that I asked Her Highness for permission and that it was refused.'

'I do, and I entirely approve of the decision. Yet . . .'

'Yet you are encouraging me to disobey,' Claire exclaimed in surprise, staring at Lenet, who lowered his eyes, embarrassed by her look.

'My dear viscountess, I am old,' he said, 'and for that very reason I am mistrustful – not on this occasion, because the princess's word is sacred: she said that only one of the prisoners will die. But in the course of a long life I have become accustomed to see fate turn against those who feel most favoured by it, so it is my principle always to grasp whatever opportunity offers itself. Go and see your fiancé, Viscountess, see him, I urge you.'

'Now, Lenet,' Claire exclaimed, 'you really are frightening me.'

'I do not intend to. Or would you like me to advise you not to see him? No, surely not! And you would no doubt scold me even more if I came to tell you the opposite of what I just have.'

'Yes, I admit that. But you are talking of seeing him: that was my one single desire, that is what I was praying to God when you arrived. But can it be done?'

'Is anything impossible for the woman who captured Saint-Georges?' Lenet said, with a smile.

'Alas, I have been struggling for two hours to devise a way to get into the fortress, but so far in vain.'

'And if I were to offer you such a way, what would you give me?'

'What would I give you? Oh, I know, I would give you my hand on the day I go to the altar with him.'

'Thank you, child,' said Lenet. 'You are right: I do indeed love you like a father. Thank you.'

'So how?' said Claire. 'How?'

'Here's how. I asked the princess for a pass, so that I could talk to the prisoners, because if there was any way to save Captain Cauvignac, I should have liked to bring him over to our side. But now the pass is useless, since you have just condemned him to death through your entreaties on behalf of Monsieur de Canolles.'

Claire gave an involuntary shudder.

'So take this paper,' Lenet went on. 'As you see, there is no name.'

Claire took the pass and read: 'The jailer of the fortress will let the bearer of this present converse with whichever of the two prisoners of war he wishes to speak to, for half an hour. Claire-Clémence de Maillé.'

'You have a man's clothes,' said Lenet. 'Put them on. You have the pass. Use it.'

'That poor officer!' Claire murmured, unable to rid her mind of the idea of Cauvignac being executed in place of Canolles.

'He is subject to the general law,' said Lenet. 'Being weak, he is devoured by the strong; having no protector, he is paying for those who have. I shall be sorry: he is a clever lad.'

Meanwhile, Claire was turning the paper round in her hands.

'Do you know,' she said, 'that you are tempting me most cruelly with this piece of paper? Do you know that once I have my poor friend in my arms, I shall be liable to take him to the ends of the earth?'

'I would advise you to do so, Madame, if that were possible. But this pass is not a letter of attestation, and you can use it only for the purpose it has.'

'That's true,' said Claire. 'And yet I have been granted Monsieur de Canolles: he is mine! No one can take him away from me!'

'And no one wants to. Come now, Madame, waste no time; put on your disguise and leave. This pass gives you half an hour. I know that half an hour is not much, but a lifetime will follow it. You are young, and your life will be long. I pray God it will also be happy!'

Claire grasped Lenet's hand, pulled him to her and kissed his forehead as she would have kissed the dearest of fathers.

'Go, now,' Lenet said, gently pushing her away. 'Lose no time. 'The man who truly loves is never resigned.'

Then, watching her as she went into another room, where Pompée came to her call and was waiting to dress her in men's clothes, he muttered: 'Alas! Who knows?'

XXII

The shouts, screams, threats and turmoil of the crowd had certainly not gone unnoticed by Canolles. Through the bars of his cell window, he was able to enjoy the lively, bustling spectacle unfolding before his eyes; it was the same, in fact, from one end of the angry town to the other.

'By God!' he told himself. 'This is a pretty pickle. Richon's death . . . Poor Richon, he was a fine fellow. His death will mean a much harder captivity for us: I won't be allowed to run around the town as I used to; there'll be no more meetings and no marriage, unless Claire is happy with a prison chapel. She will be. One is just as properly married in one chapel as in another. But it's not a good omen. Why on earth did we not get the news tomorrow instead of today?' Then, going over to the window and leaning over to look, he went on: 'What a close watch! Two sentries! And to think that I'll be shut up here for a week, perhaps a fortnight, until something happens to make them forget about this. Fortunately, the way things are, events are coming thick and fast, and the people of Bordeaux are not serious-minded. But in the meantime, it won't stop me having some very unpleasant moments. Poor Claire! She must be desperate. Fortunately, she knows that I have been arrested. Ah, yes! She knows, so she knows that it was not my fault. Goodness! Where the devil are all those people off to? It seems as though they are heading towards the Esplanade – but there's no parade or execution there at this time. They're all going in the same direction. You really would think that they knew I was here, like a bear in a cage . . .'

Canolles took a few steps around the cell, with his arms folded. The walls of a real prison had momentarily brought him round to philosophical ideas that he usually worried very little about.

'Stupid business, war!' he muttered. 'There's poor Richon, with whom I was having dinner hardly a month ago, dead. He would have died at his guns, brave man that he was, as I ought to have done myself – as I should have done, had anyone but the viscountess besieged me. This women's war is certainly the most to be feared of all wars. At least, I didn't contribute at all to the death of my friend. Thank God, I didn't draw my sword against my brother, and that's a consolation. Why, I owe that to my good female angel, as well! When it comes down to it, I owe her a lot.'

At that moment, an officer came in, interrupting Canolles's soliloquy.

'Do you need some supper, Monsieur?' he said. 'If so, give me your order. The jailer has instructed me to let you have whatever dishes you like.'

'Well now,' Canolles thought. 'It seems that they intend at least to treat me decently for as long as I am here. For a moment, I feared the contrary, seeing the princess's tight lips and the unpleasant faces on all those judges of hers.'

'I am waiting,' said the officer, with a bow.

'So you are – forgive me. The extreme politeness of your enquiry gave me pause . . . Back to business: yes, Monsieur, I should like supper, since I am very hungry, but I am a man of simple tastes, and a soldier's meal will suit me.'

'Now,' the officer said, approaching him with interest. 'Do you have any commission to be carried out, in town? You're not expecting anything? You say that you are a soldier; so am I, and you can treat me as a comrade.'

Canolles looked at the officer with astonishment.

'No, Monsieur,' he said. 'No, I don't have any commission

in town. I'm not expecting anyone, except one person whom I cannot name. As for treating you as a comrade, thank you for the offer. Here's my hand on it, and if later I need anything, I shall remember it.'

This time, it was the officer's turn to look surprised.

'Very well,' he said. 'Dinner will be served at once.' And he left.

A short time afterwards, two soldiers came in carrying a ready prepared supper. It was of better quality than Canolles had requested. He sat down at the table and ate heartily.

The soldiers, in their turn, looked at him with astonishment. Canolles mistook this for envy, and, as the wine was an excellent one from Guyenne, he said: 'Friends, ask for two glasses.'

One of the soldiers went out and came back with the two glasses. Canolles filled them, then poured a few drops of wine into his own.

'Your health, friends!' he said.

The two soldiers took the glasses and clinked them mechanically against his, before drinking without returning the toast.

'They are not very polite,' Canolles thought. 'But they drink well. You can't have everything.' And he went on with his meal, finishing it triumphantly.

When he was done, he got up, and the soldiers removed the table. The officer returned.

'Well, I must say, Monsieur,' Canolles told him. 'You should have dined with me: it was an excellent supper.'

'I could not have the honour, Monsieur, because I have just had dinner myself, a moment ago ... And I have come back ...'

'To keep me company?' said Canolles. 'If that's the case, I'm most grateful, because it's extremely kind of you.'

'No, Monsieur, I have a less pleasant task. I've come to tell you that there is no minister in the prison and that the chaplain is Catholic. Knowing that you are Protestant, I thought this difference in faith might perhaps upset you.'

'Upset me? Why?' Canolles asked naively.

'But . . . in your devotions,' said the officer, embarrassed.

'My devotions! Fine!' said Canolles. 'I'll think about that tomorrow. I only make my devotions in the morning, you know.'

The officer looked at Canolles with an amazement that gradually changed to profound commiseration. He saluted and went out.

'Well I never!' said Canolles. 'Everyone's going mad. Since poor Richon died, everyone I meet seems to be half-witted or raging. God's teeth! Am I never to see a slightly reasonable face?'

He had hardly finished saying this, when the cell door opened, and, before he could take in who it was, someone had rushed into his embrace, and, placing his arms around her, was drenching his face with tears.

'Come now!' the prisoner said, struggling free of the embrace. 'Another madman! I really must be in Bedlam!'

However, the movement that he made in starting back knocked the stranger's hat off, and the lovely blonde hair of Madame de Cambes fell around her shoulders.

'You!' said Canolles, running over to take her in his arms. 'Here! Oh, forgive me for not having recognized you or, rather, for not having sensed your presence . . .'

'Quiet!' she said, quickly picking up her hat and replacing it on her head. 'Quiet! If anyone knew that it was me, my happiness might be taken from me. At least, I can see you once more. Oh, God! How happy I am!'

Claire, feeling her chest crushed, burst into violent sobs.

'*Once more!*' said Canolles. 'You say you are allowed to see me *once more*? And you say it with tears. What! Were you not supposed to see me again?' he asked, laughing.

'Please don't laugh, my dearest,' said Claire. 'It hurts me when you laugh. I beg you, don't laugh. It was so hard for me to get to see you . . . If only you knew . . . And I nearly didn't come. Were it not for that fine man, Lenet . . . But let's talk about you, my poor love. Good heavens! You are here! Is it really you? Can I really hold you against my heart?'

'Yes, yes, it's me, it's really me,' said Canolles, smiling.

'Oh, please,' said Claire, 'there's no point in putting on that happy look. I know everything. They did not know that I was in love with you, so they hid nothing from me.'

'And what do you know?' asked Canolles.

'Weren't you expecting me?' asked the viscountess. 'Weren't you worried by my silence? Aren't you already blaming me?'

'Why? I was worried and unhappy, of course, but I didn't blame you. I realized that some circumstances beyond your control were keeping us apart, and my greatest unhappiness, in all this, is that our wedding had to be put off for a week, or perhaps a fortnight . . .'

It was Claire's turn to look at Canolles with the same amazement as the officer had shown a short time earlier.

'What!' she said. 'Are you serious? Are you really not more alarmed than that?'

'Alarmed?' said Canolles. 'Alarmed at what? Can it be,' he said, laughing, 'that I am in some danger that I am not aware of?'

'Oh, the poor man!' she cried. 'He knew nothing!'

Then, doubtless afraid that she might accidentally reveal the whole truth to the person who was so cruelly threatened by it, she made a tremendous effort and halted the words that were rising from her heart to her lips.

'No, I'm not aware of anything,' Canolles said gravely. 'But you will tell me everything, won't you? I am a man. Speak to me, Claire, speak . . .'

'You know that Richon is dead?' she asked.

'Yes, I know.'

'And do you know how he died?'

'No, but I can guess . . . He was killed at his post, surely, on the breach at Vayres?'

Claire was silent for a moment, then, as solemn as the bronze bell tolling for the dead, she said: 'He was hanged in the market at Libourne.'

Canolles started back.

'Hanged!' he cried. 'Richon! A soldier!' Then, suddenly going pale and passing a trembling hand across his forehead, he went on: 'Ah, now I understand everything. I understand my arrest,

my interrogation, the words of the officer, the silence of the
soldiers . . . I understand what you have done and why you
wept at seeing me so unconcerned . . . And finally I understand
the crowd, the shouts, the threats . . . Richon, assassinated!
And he is to be avenged on me.'

'No, no, my love! My dear heart!' Claire said, bursting with
joy, grasping both of Canolles's hands and looking deep into
his eyes. 'No, you are not the one to be sacrificed, my dear
prisoner! You were right: you had indeed been chosen, yes, and
condemned. You were going to die, yes, you came very close to
death, my lovely fiancé! But don't worry, you can talk of happiness and the future. The woman who is going to devote her
whole life to you has saved yours. So be happy, but be quiet,
because you might wake up your unfortunate companion,
the one on whom the storm will fall, the one who is to die in
your place.'

'Oh, don't say that, don't say that, my dearest! You chill me
with horror,' Canolles said, barely recovered from the terrible
blow he had just received, despite Claire's warm caresses. 'I
who was so calm and so confident, so naively happy, I was in
mortal danger! And when? At what time? Heavens above! At
the moment when I was to become your husband. I swear, it
would have been a double killing.'

'They are calling it reprisals,' said Claire.

'Yes, that's true, they are right.'

'Come, come, now you're gloomy and thoughtful again.'

'Oh, I'm not afraid of death,' Canolles said. 'But of death
separated from you.'

'If you had died, my beloved, I should have died too. But
instead of feeling sad like this, rejoice with me. Come, now:
tonight, perhaps within the hour, you will leave prison. I shall
come to fetch you myself or wait for you at the gate. Then,
without losing a moment, a second, we shall flee . . . oh! at
once. I don't want to wait. I'm afraid of this accursed town.
Today, I managed to reach you again, but who knows what
unexpected misfortune might take you away from me again
tomorrow?'

'My dear, beloved Claire,' Canolles said, 'do you know that

you are giving me too much happiness all at once ... Oh, yes, truly, too much happiness ... I shall die from it.'

'Very well, then, recover your merry, carefree mood.'

'Then you must recover yours.'

'Look, I'm laughing.'

'And that sigh?'

'That sigh, my friend, is for the unfortunate man who is giving his life for our happiness.'

'Yes, yes ... you're right! Why couldn't you take me away at once? Come, my good angel, open your wings and carry me off!'

'Patience, my dear husband, patience! Tomorrow, I shall take you away. Where? I don't know. To the paradise of our love. Meanwhile, I am here.'

Canolles took her in his arms and pressed her to him. She threw her arms around the young man's neck and abandoned herself, trembling, against a heart that, stifled by so many various emotions, could hardly beat.

Suddenly, and for the second time, a painful sob rose from her breast to her lips, and, happy as she was, Claire bathed Canolles's face in tears.

'Now, now!' he said. 'Is this your merriment, poor angel?'

'It is the remains of my sorrow.'

At that moment, the door opened, and the officer who had come earlier announced that the half hour allowed on the pass had expired.

'Farewell!' Canolles murmured. 'Or hide me in a fold of your cloak and carry me off!'

'Hush, my poor friend,' she said. 'You are breaking my heart. Can't you see that I am dying to do that? Be patient for yourself and still more for me. In a few hours we shall be together, never to separate again.'

'I shall be patient,' Canolles said joyfully, completely re-assured by this promise. 'But we must part. Come, be brave. We must say the word: farewell. Farewell, Claire, farewell!'

'Farewell,' she said, trying to smile. 'Fare–'

But she could not finish the cruel word. For the third time, her voice was drowned in sobs.

'Farewell, farewell!' said Canolles, clasping the viscountess once more and covering her brow with ardent kisses. 'Farewell!'

'*Diable!*' the officer thought. 'I'm glad that I know the poor boy no longer has much to fear, because otherwise this scene would break my heart.'

He led Claire to the door and returned.

'Now, Monsieur,' he said to Canolles, who had slumped down on a chair, still overcome with emotion. 'Now, it's not enough to be happy, one must also show compassion. Your neighbour, your unfortunate companion, the one who is to die, is alone with no one to protect or console him. He is asking to see you. I took it upon myself to grant this request, but it still needs your consent.'

'I do consent, indeed I do,' said Canolles. 'Certainly. The poor wretch. I am waiting for him with open arms. I don't know him, but what does that matter?'

'Nonetheless, he seems to know you.'

'Does he know the fate that awaits him?'

'No, I think not. So you will understand that we must keep him in ignorance.'

'Oh, don't worry.'

'So, listen. Eleven is going to strike, and I'll go back to the guardroom. After eleven, the warders reign alone inside the prison. Yours has been warned, and he knows that your neighbour will be in your cell. He will come to fetch him, when he has to take him back to his own. If the prisoner knows nothing, tell him nothing: but if he does realize something, let him know that we soldiers, for our part, all pity him from the depth of our hearts, because after all, dying is nothing, but to be hanged is to die twice.'

'So is it certain that he will die?'

'In the same way as Richon. It will be a complete reprisal. But we are chatting here, and no doubt he is anxiously awaiting your reply.'

'Go and bring him, Monsieur, and believe me when I say that I am grateful for both of us.'

The officer went out, opened the door of the adjoining cell and Cauvignac, a little pale, but with a firm step and head high, came into Canolles's cell as Canolles stepped forward to greet him.

The officer made a final sign of farewell to Canolles, looked pityingly at Cauvignac and left, taking his soldiers with him. It was some time before their heavy steps had ceased to echo through the vaults.

The warder soon made his rounds. They heard his keys clanking in the corridor.

Cauvignac was not downcast, because he was a man with an unshakeable confidence in himself and an inexhaustible belief in the future. And yet a deep feeling of grief had insinuated itself beneath his calm appearance and almost jolly expression and, like a serpent, was biting his heart. This sceptical mind which had always doubted everything was now dubious about doubt itself.

Since Richon's death, Cauvignac had not eaten or slept. Accustomed to jest about the misfortunes of others, because he accepted his own with a laugh, our philosopher had not even thought to smile at an event which had come to this dreadful conclusion; moreover, despite himself, he sensed the impassive hand of Providence in all the mysterious threads that made him responsible for Richon's death, so that he was starting, if not to believe in rewards for good acts, at least in punishment for evil ones.

So he turned to resignation and thought; but, resigned as he was, as we have said, he neither ate nor slept.

And such was the unusual nature of this soul, which while being individual was not egotistic, the thing that struck him even more than his own death, which he anticipated, was the death of this companion, whom he knew to be only a couple of yards away from him and awaiting either the fatal decree or execution without decree. All this reminded him again of Richon, his vengeful ghost, and the double catastrophe that was the outcome of what at first had seemed to him merely a delightful jest.

His first thought had been to escape, because even though he was a prisoner on parole, since by putting him in prison they had failed to fulfil their agreement with him, he thought that he need have no remorse in disregarding his own promises. But, despite his perspicacity and ingenuity, he had had to accept that escape was impossible. It was then that he became all the more convinced that he was caught in the meshes of some inexorable fate. Henceforth all he wanted was one thing: to speak for a few moments with his companion, whose name had caused him such sad surprise, and to be reconciled in himself with the whole of that human race, against which he had so cruelly offended.

We are not saying that all his thoughts were of remorse. No . . . Cauvignac was far too philosophical to feel that; but, at the least, what he did feel was something much like remorse, namely a violent regret at having done ill to no end. With time and circumstances that might keep Cauvignac in this state of mind, the feeling might have had the same outcome as remorse, but time was what they did not have.

As he came into Canolles's cell, Cauvignac first waited, with his customary caution, until the officer who had shown him in had left. Then, seeing that the door was properly shut and the little Judas window[19] hermetically sealed, he went over to Canolles (who, as we have said, had made a few steps towards him) and they shook hands.

Despite the gravity of the situation, Cauvignac could not avoid smiling when he recognized the handsome, elegant young man, with the adventurous spirit and joyful temperament, whom he had already twice surprised in very different circumstances from those in which they now found themselves: once having sent him to Nantes and the other time having brought him to Saint-Georges. Moreover, he recalled the momentary appropriation of his name and the resulting trick played on the duke. And, gloomy though the prison was, this memory was such a happy one that for a second the past took precedence over the present.

Canolles, for his part, recognized Cauvignac at first sight, having already been in contact with him in the two circumstances that we have mentioned, and since on those occasions Cauvignac had been a messenger of good news for him, his distress over the fate awaiting the poor man increased, all the more since he knew that it was his own salvation that had doomed Cauvignac. Such a thought, in a soul as delicate as that of Canolles, caused far greater feelings of remorse than a real crime would have caused to his companion.

So he greeted him in the most kindly way.

'Well, Baron,' Cauvignac said. 'What do you think about the situation we are in? It seems to me quite precarious.'

'Yes, we are prisoners, and God knows when we'll get out of here,' Canolles replied, putting a good face on it in an attempt at least to ease his companion's pain with hope.

'When we get out!' Cauvignac replied. 'May God, whom you mentioned, be so good in his mercy to make it as late as possible! But I don't think he's inclined to give us much grace. Out of my cell, I saw, as you may have from yours, a raging mob running towards a certain place which must be the Esplanade, unless I am much mistaken. You know the Esplanade, dear Baron, and what it is used for?'

'Oh, come! I think you're exaggerating our plight. Yes, the crowd was running towards the Esplanade, but no doubt to witness the handing out of some military punishment, surely. It would be outrageous to make us pay for Richon's death, because both of us are innocent of it.'

Cauvignac shuddered and stared at Canolles with an expression of gloom that gradually faded to one of pity. 'Well, well,' he said to himself. 'Here's another one who doesn't know the danger he's in. I shall have to set him straight on it, because there's no point in deluding him so that the blow will be even harder to bear later, while at least, when you've had time to prepare yourself, the drop seems a little gentler.'

So, after a new moment of silence and thought, he took Canolles's hands and continued to stare hard at him with a look that Canolles found quite upsetting, saying: 'Monsieur, my dear Monsieur, let's ask for a bottle or two of that good Braune wine that you know of, if you will. Alas, I should have drunk it at leisure had I been a governor for longer, and I can admit to you that it is even probable that my liking for that excellent wine was what made me ask for the government of that place in particular. God is punishing my greed.'

'Very well,' said Canolles.

'Yes, and I'll tell you all about it as we drink – and if the news is bad, then at least the wine will be good. One will help to swallow the other.'

So Canolles knocked at the door, but there was no answer. He knocked again, and after a while a child who was playing in the corridor came over to the prisoner.

'What do you want?' the child asked.

'Wine,' said Canolles. 'Tell your papa to bring two bottles.'

The child went off and reappeared a moment later.

'Papa is busy at the moment talking to a gentleman,' he said. 'He will come presently.'

'Excuse me,' Cauvignac said. 'Might I ask a question of my own?'

'Yes.'

'My good friend,' he said in his most ingratiating voice, 'who is the gentleman your papa is talking to?'

'A tall gentleman.'

'What a delightful child,' said Cauvignac. 'Wait, we'll learn something from him. And how is the gentleman dressed?'

'All in black.'

'The devil he is! Do you hear that? All in black. And what's the name of this tall gentleman, all in black? Do you happen to know that, my young friend?'

'He's called Monsieur Lavie.'

'Ah!' said Cauvignac. 'The king's advocate. I don't think we have much harm to fear from him. So let's take advantage of the fact that they're talking to have a chat ourselves.' And, slipping a coin under the door, he went on: 'Here, my little friend, this is to buy marbles. It's a good thing to make friends wherever you are,' he added, getting up.

The child took the coin with delight and thanked the two prisoners.

'So, you were saying, Monsieur . . .' said Canolles.

'Ah . . . yes,' Cauvignac replied. 'I was saying that you appear to be much mistaken as to the fate that awaits us when we leave this prison. You are talking about the Esplanade, military discipline, whipping for some strangers. Now, I should be

inclined to think that something more than that is coming and
that we are the ones concerned.'

'Come, come!' said Canolles.

'Ah, Monsieur, you see things in a less sombre light than I,
perhaps because you do not have quite the same reason to fear
them as I do. But don't congratulate yourself too much on your
situation; it's not too wonderful, either. But yours is nothing to
mine, and mine, I have to tell you, because this is what I believe,
is a horrible mess. Do you know who I am?'

'That's a strange question! As far as I know, you're Captain
Cauvignac, Governor of Braune.'

'Yes, for the time being, but I have not always had this name
or held that title. I've often changed my name and tried out
different ranks: for example, one day I called myself Baron de
Canolles, just like you.' Canolles stared at Cauvignac, who
went on: 'Yes, yes, I understand: you're wondering if I'm mad,
aren't you? Well, have no fear, I am in full possession of my
mental faculties and have never been so reasonable in my life.'

'Explain yourself, then,' said Canolles.

'Nothing could be easier. The Duke d'Epernon . . . You know
the duke, I believe?'

'By name. I've never seen him.'

'You are fortunate. As I say, Monsieur d'Epernon once discovered me in the house of a woman, where I knew you were
also welcome, and I took the liberty of borrowing your name.'

'Monsieur, what do you mean?'

'Now, now, don't get worked up. You won't be so self-
centred as to feel jealous about one woman just as you are
going to marry another! And even if you were – as you could
well be, man being a rotten sort of beast – you'll forgive me
shortly. We're too close now to quarrel.'

'I don't understand a word you are saying.'

'I'm saying that I have the right to be treated as a brother, or
at least a brother-in-law.'

'You're talking in riddles, and I still don't understand.'

'Well, one word, and you will. My true name is Roland de
Lartigues, and Nanon is my sister.'

Canolles switched from suspicion to a sudden rush of feeling.

'Why, you're Nanon's brother!' he exclaimed. 'Oh, you poor man!'

'Yes, poor man indeed,' said Cauvignac. 'You said it, you put your finger right on it, because among a host of other unpleasantnesses that will arise from my little trial here, I also have the disadvantage of being called Roland de Lartigues and being Nanon's brother. You know that my dear sister is not the sweetest-smelling flower in the nostrils of these gentlemen of Bordeaux. If they find out that I am Nanon's brother, I shall be three times lost – and we have here one La Rochefoucauld and one Lenet who know everything.'

What Cauvignac was saying brought back old memories to Canolles, who said: 'Now I understand why poor Nanon once called me her brother in a letter. Dearest girl!'

'Yes, indeed, she's a good woman and I am very sorry that I have not always followed her advice to the letter; but, of course, if we could foresee the future, we should have no need of God.'

'And how is she?' asked Canolles.

'Who can tell! Poor woman, she is certainly in despair, not over me, since she does not know I have been arrested, but about you, since she may have learned your fate.'

'Don't worry,' said Canolles. 'Lenet won't say that you are Nanon's brother, and Monsieur de La Rochefoucauld has no reason to hold anything against you. No one will know anything about this.'

'While no one may know about this, there is something else they will know, for example, that I am the one who gave a particular letter of attestation . . . and that this letter of attestation . . . Ah, well! Let's not think about it, if we can. What a shame that no wine is coming.' He turned to the door. 'There's nothing like wine to help you forget.'

'Now, now, courage!' said Canolles.

'*Pardieu!* Do you think I'm a coward? You'll see, at the crucial moment when we go for a walk on the Esplanade. There's just one thing bothering me: will they shoot us, behead us or hang us?'

'Hang us!' Canolles cried. 'Good God! We're gentlemen. They wouldn't commit such an outrage against the nobility!'

'Just see if they're not capable of picking holes in my family tree . . . And then . . .'

'Then what?'

'Will you or I be the first to go?'

'But for heaven's sake, my dear friend, don't think about such things. Nothing could be less certain than this death that you are worried about in advance. No one is judged, condemned and executed like that in one night.'

'Listen,' said Cauvignac, 'I was there when they tried poor Richon, God rest his soul! Well, the trial, sentence and hanging all took at the very most three or four hours. Let's slow things down a bit, because Anne of Austria is Queen of France, while Madame de Condé is only a princess of the blood, and that gives us four or five hours. And, as it's three hours since we were arrested, and two hours since we appeared in front of our judges, that gives us, by my calculation, one or two hours left to live. It's not long.'

'In any case, they will at least wait until daylight to execute us.'

'Ah, that's not at all certain. An execution by torchlight is a very fine thing. True, it costs more, but since the princess has a great need for the people of Bordeaux just now, she might decide to bear the extra expense.'

'Hush!' said Canolles. 'I can hear footsteps.'

'Damn it!' said Cauvignac, going a little pale.

'They must be bringing up the wine.'

'Oh, yes!' said Cauvignac, staring very closely at the door. 'There is that. If the jailer comes in with two bottles, that's good; but otherwise . . .'

The door opened, and the jailer came in with two bottles.

Cauvignac and Canolles exchanged a meaningful look, but the jailer took no notice. He seemed in such a hurry, time was so short, and it was so dark in the dungeon . . .

He closed the door and came inside. Then, going over to the prisoners and taking a sheet of paper out of his pocket, he said: 'Which of you two is the Baron de Canolles?'

'Damn!' they both said together, exchanging another look.

However, Canolles hesitated to reply and so did Cauvignac: the first had had the name for too long to think that the question

was addressed to him, while the other had had it long enough
to fear that it would catch up with him.

Canolles realized that some reply had to be made.

'That's me,' he said.

The jailer came over to him.

'You're the governor of a fortress?'

'Yes.'

'But I'm also the governor of a fortress and I've been called
Canolles as well,' said Cauvignac. 'Let's be quite clear about
this and make no mistakes. What happened to poor Richon
was bad enough, without me causing the death of another man.'

'So you are called Canolles now?' asked the jailer.

'Yes,' said Canolles.

'And you were called Canolles earlier?' the jailer asked
Cauvignac.

'Yes,' he replied. 'Earlier. Just for one day. And I'm starting
to think it was not such a good idea.'

'And both of you are governors of fortresses?'

'Yes,' Canolles and Cauvignac replied simultaneously.

'Now, one last question that will make everything clear . . .'
The two prisoners listened in the deepest silence. 'Which of the
two of you,' said the jailer, 'is the brother of Madame Nanon
de Lartigues?'

At this Cauvignac made a face that would have been comic
at any less solemn moment.

'Didn't I tell you?' he interjected, turning to Canolles. 'Didn't
I tell you, my dear friend, that this was the weak point where
they would attack?' Then, turning to the jailer, he asked: 'And
if I told you that I am the one who is Madame Nanon de
Lartigues's brother, what would you say to me, friend?'

'I should tell you to follow me at once.'

'Damn it!' said Cauvignac.

'But she has also called me her brother,' said Canolles, trying
to draw off some of the lightning that was clearly gathering
above his unfortunate companion's head.

'One moment, now,' Cauvignac said, stepping in front of the
jailer and taking Canolles to one side. 'One moment, my good
fellow. It's not right that you should be Nanon's brother in

these circumstances. I have made others pay for me often enough before this, and it's only fair that I should pay now.'

'What do you mean?' Canolles asked.

'Oh, I haven't got time. In any case, you can see that our jailer is starting to stamp his foot with impatience. It's all right, friend, it's all right, calm down, I'm coming with you. Farewell, my dear friend,' he went on. 'At least I'm assured of one thing: I'm going first. I pray God that you don't follow me too closely. All that remains to be seen is the form of death. The devil! As long as it's not the rope! Hey, I'm coming, I'm coming, by God! You're in an awful hurry, my good fellow. So, my dear brother, my dear brother-in-law, my dear companion, my dear friend . . . A last farewell, and goodnight!'

Cauvignac took a step nearer Canolles and held out his hand. Canolles took the hand in his and pressed it affectionately. As he was doing so, Cauvignac was looking at him with a peculiar expression.

'What do you want?' asked Canolles. 'Do you have a request for me?'

'Yes.'

'Well, go on then.'

'Do you pray sometimes?' Cauvignac asked.

'Yes,' Canolles replied.

'Well, when you pray, say a word for me.' And turning to the jailer, who seemed increasingly impatient, he said: 'I am the brother of Nanon de Lartigues. Come, friend . . .'

The jailer did not wait to be asked twice and quickly led out Cauvignac, who gave a last wave to Canolles at the door of the cell.

Then that door closed, and their footsteps faded along the corridor. Everything returned to a silence that seemed to the remaining prisoner like the silence of death.

Canolles remained deeply sunk in a feeling of sadness that was close to terror. This manner of taking away a man, at night, silently, with no ceremony, with no guards, was more frightening than the preparations for an execution in the full light of day. Yet all Canolles's fear was for his companion: his confidence in Madame de Cambes was so great that, since seeing her, despite the dreadful news that she had brought, he had no further fear for himself.

So the only thing really on his mind at that moment was the fate of the companion who had just been taken away from him. And then he recalled Cauvignac's last request. He went down on his knees and prayed. A short while after, feeling consoled and strengthened, he got up, expecting only one thing: the arrival of the help promised by Madame de Cambes, or her own arrival.

Meanwhile, Cauvignac was following the jailer down the dark corridor, saying nothing and thinking as seriously as he could.

At the end of the corridor, the jailer shut the door as carefully as he had that on Canolles's cell, and, after listening to some vague sounds coming up from the floor below, he turned sharply back to Cauvignac and said: 'Come on! Off we go, good sir.'

'I am ready,' said Cauvignac, quite loftily.

'Don't shout so loudly,' said the jailer. 'And walk faster.' He led them down a passage leading to the underground dungeons.

'Ho, ho!' thought Cauvignac. 'Are they going to cut my throat in a dark corner, or throw me into some dungeon? I have heard that they sometimes just displayed the four limbs on the public square, as Cesare Borgia did for Don Ramiro d'Orco.[20] Now, this jailer is all alone, with the keys on his belt. Those keys must open some door or other. He's small, I'm large; he's weak, and I'm strong. He is in front and I am behind. I could easily strangle him, if I want. Do I want?'

Cauvignac, who had answered himself in the affirmative, was already reaching out with his two bony hands to do as he intended, when the jailer suddenly turned round in a fright.

'Hush!' he said. 'Did you hear something?'

'There is definitely something I can't explain in all this,' Cauvignac continued, still thinking to himself. 'If all these precautions don't reassure me, they should alarm me very much.' So he stopped and said: 'And where are you taking me then?'

'Can't you see?' said the jailer. 'To the cellars.'

'Huh! Are they going to bury me alive?'

The jailer shrugged his shoulders, led the way through a labyrinth of corridors and, reaching a low, damp, arched door, behind which there was a strange noise, he opened it.

'The river!' Cauvignac exclaimed, terrified at the sight of water flowing past, as dark as that of the Styx.

'Yes, of course. The river. Can you swim?'

'Yes . . . well, no . . . yes . . . I mean . . . Why do you ask?'

'Because if you can't swim, we'll be forced to wait for the boat, which is moored over there, which means a delay of a quarter of an hour, not to mention the fact that someone might see the signal that I would have to make and so might catch us.'

'Catch us!' Cauvignac said. 'My good fellow, are we escaping then?'

'Good heavens, of course we are!'

'Where to?'

'Wherever we want.'

'So am I free?'

'As free as air.'

'Good Lord!' Cauvignac cried. And, without adding a word to this eloquent exclamation or looking to right or left, or wondering whether his companion was following him, he ran to the river and dived into it faster than a hunted otter. The jailer followed suit, and both of them, after a quarter of an hour's silent struggle against the current, came in sight of the boat. At this, the jailer whistled three times as he swam, and the boatmen, hearing the agreed signal, came to meet them, quickly hauled them into the boat and, without a word, plied the oars strongly so that in less than five minutes they were putting both men off on the further bank.

'Whew!' said Cauvignac, who had not spoken a word since he had so resolutely thrown himself into the water. 'Whew! I'm saved, then. Dear jailer of my heart, God will reward you.'

'And while I wait for His reward,' said the jailer, 'I have received some forty thousand livres which will help me to be patient.'

'Forty thousand livres!' Cauvignac exclaimed in astonishment. 'Who the devil can have paid out forty thousand livres for me?'

BOOK IV
THE ABBEY OF PESSAC

I

A word of explanation is required, after which we will pick up the thread of our story.

In any case, it is time to return to Nanon de Lartigues, who, at the sight of poor Richon expiring in the marketplace at Libourne, had cried out and fallen to the ground in a faint.

And yet Nanon, as you must already have seen, was not a woman of fragile temperament. Despite the delicacy of her body and her slender frame, she had borne many disappointments, supported tiredness and braved many dangers. This exceptionally steadfast soul, at once loving and energetic, knew how to bend to circumstances and then return with redoubled strength at every opportunity that fate allowed.

The Duke d'Epernon, who knew her (or, rather, thought that he knew her), was therefore astonished to see her so completely overwhelmed by the spectacle of physical suffering. She, who had almost been burned alive in the fire of her house in Agen without a single cry, because she did not want to give satisfaction to her enemies, who were gasping for this torment that one of them, driven to greater exasperation than the rest, had prepared for the favourite of the hated governor. Yet Nanon, who had seen two of her women perish in the chaos, murdered in mistake for her and in her place, had not blinked an eyelid.

Nanon's faint lasted for nearly two hours and ended in terrible nervous attacks, in which she was unable to speak, only to emit inarticulate cries. It was so bad that the queen herself, after sending many messages to the patient, came to see her in person, while Monsieur Mazarin, who had recently arrived, insisted on going to her bedside to administer some medicine, since he had great pretensions to skill in this area: medicine for the body under threat, theology for the soul in peril.

But Nanon did not regain consciousness until well into the night. Even then, it took her some time to collect her thoughts, but finally, taking her head in both hands, she cried in piteous tones: 'I'm lost! They've killed him for me.'

Fortunately, these words were odd enough for those around to attribute them to delirium, which they did. However, they did remember them, and when that morning the Duke d'Epernon returned from a mission that had kept him away from Libourne since the previous day, on enquiring about Nanon's indisposition, he learned what she had said on coming to her senses. The duke knew all the ebullience of this ardent soul and realized that there was more here than just delirium, so he hurried to see Nanon and took advantage of the first moment alone with her that her other visitors allowed.

'Dear friend,' he said, 'I have been told what you suffered at the death of Richon, whom they were foolish enough to hang right outside your window.'

'Oh, yes!' Nanon exclaimed. 'It's appalling! It's outrageous!'

'Next time, don't worry,' said the duke. 'Now that I know how it affects you, I'll have rebels hanged on the Place du Cours, not in the marketplace. But whom did you mean, when you said that they had killed him for you? I assume it could not be Richon, since Richon has never been anything to you, not even a mere acquaintance.'

'Oh, Duke, is that you?' Nanon said, rising on to her elbow and taking his arm.

'Yes, it's me and I am very pleased that you recognize me: it proves that you're better. But whom were you talking about?'

'About him, Duke, about him!' Nanon said, still slightly delirious. 'You are the one who has killed him! Oh, the wretch!'

'Dear heart, you are alarming me! What are you saying?'

'I'm saying that you've killed him. Don't you understand, Duke?'

'No, my dear,' Monsieur d'Epernon replied, trying to get Nanon to speak by picking up the ideas suggested by her delirium. 'How can I have killed him, since I don't know who he is?'

'Don't you know that he is a prisoner of war, that he was a captain, and a governor, that he had the same position and the same rank as that poor Richon, and that the people of Bordeaux will avenge on him the murder of the man you have just had killed? Because though you put on a show of justice, it is a true murder, Duke!'

The duke, unnerved by this exclamation, the fire of those blazing eyes and the force of her feverish gesture, stepped back, turned pale and struck his brow.

'Why, that's right, that's right!' he exclaimed. 'Poor Canolles! I forgot about him!'

'My brother, my poor brother!' Nanon cried in her turn, happy at being able to express her feelings, and giving her lover the status under which Monsieur d'Epernon knew him.

'By Jove, you're right,' said the duke. 'I'm the one who's out of his mind. How could I have forgotten our poor friend? But there's no time to lose, though by now they will only just have learned the news in Bordeaux. The time to get together, to judge him . . . Even then, they will hesitate.'

'Did the queen hesitate?' said Nanon.

'The queen is the queen: she has the power of life and death. They are rebels.'

'Alas,' said Nanon. 'All the more reason for them to have no scruples. But, tell me, what can you do?'

'I don't know yet, but trust in me.'

Nanon tried to get up: 'Even if I have to go to Bordeaux myself and offer myself in his place, he shall not die.'

'Calm down, my dearest, it's my business now. I caused the trouble, and I shall make it right, by my faith as a gentleman. The queen still has some friends in the town, so don't worry.'

The duke made this promise from the depths of his heart. Nanon could read the certainty, sincerity and, above all, determination in his eyes. She felt such a surge of joy that she grasped the duke's hands and, kissing them with her burning lips, she said: 'Oh, my lord! If you succeed in this, I shall love you so much!'

The duke was moved to tears. This was the first time that Nanon had spoken to him with such ardour and made him such a promise.

He left the room, again assuring Nanon that she had nothing to fear. Then, calling one of his servants, whom he knew to be intelligent and loyal, he instructed him to go to Bordeaux, to get inside the town even if this meant scaling the ramparts and to give the lawyer Lavie the following message, written entirely in his own hand:

> Prevent anything unpleasant from happening to Monsieur de Canolles, captain and fortress commander in the service of His Majesty.
>
> If this officer is arrested, as we suppose he will be, free him by any possible means, buy the warders at whatever price they demand, a million if necessary, and give them the offer of management of a royal château on the word of the Duke d'Epernon.
>
> If corruption fails, try force. Stick at nothing: violence, arson and murder will be accepted.
>
> Description: tall, brown eyes, hooked nose. In case of doubt, ask: 'Are you Nanon's brother?'
>
> *With all haste*. There is not a moment to lose.

The messenger left. Three hours later, he was in Bordeaux. He went into a farmhouse, exchanged his clothes for a peasant's smock and got inside the town, leading a cart full of flour.

Lavie received the letter a quarter of an hour after the decision of the council of war. He got into the fortress, spoke to the head jailer, offered him twenty thousand livres, which he refused, then thirty thousand, which he also refused, and finally forty thousand, which he accepted.

We already know how, misled by the question that the Duke d'Epernon thought should avoid any misunderstanding ('Are you the brother of Nanon?'), Cauvignac, who, in perhaps the only generous impulse of his whole life, had replied 'yes', so

taking Canolles's place, and found himself, much to his astonishment, a free man.

Cauvignac was taken on a swift horse to the village of Saint-
Loubès, which belonged to the Epernonists. There they found
a messenger from the duke, who had come to meet the fugitive
on the duke's own horse, a priceless Spanish mare.

'Have you saved him?' he shouted to the head of the group
escorting Cauvignac.

'Yes,' said the man. 'We're bringing him with us.'

This is all that the messenger needed to hear. He turned his
horse round and sped swift as a meteor towards Libourne. An
hour and a half later, the exhausted horse collapsed at the
town gate and sent its rider tumbling by the feet of Monsieur
d'Epernon, who was gasping with impatience as he waited for
the answer: 'Yes!' The messenger, almost dead, just managed
to say the word 'Yes', which had cost so much, and the duke,
without wasting a moment, hurried to Nanon's house. She was
still lying on her bed, staring blankly at the servants blocking
the door.

'Yes!' the duke cried. 'Yes! He is safe, dear heart, he is coming
behind me, and you will see him.'

Nanon leapt up in bed with joy, these few words having
removed the weight that had been suffocating her. She raised
both hands to heaven, and then, bathed in the tears that this
unexpected happiness had brought to eyes parched by despair,
she cried in an indescribable voice: 'Oh, my God, my God!
Thank you!'

Then, looking down from heaven to earth, she saw the duke
beside her, so pleased with her happiness that you might have
thought that he had as much of an interest in the welfare of
the prisoner as she had. It was only then a disturbing thought
entered her mind: 'How is the duke to be rewarded for his
kindness and consideration, when he sees a stranger in place of
my brother and the betrayal of an almost adulterous love
instead of the pure emotion of fraternal affection?'

Nanon's reply to herself was brief and to the point: 'So what?
No matter!' thought this heart, sublime in both its self-sacrifice
and its devotion. 'I shall not deceive him any longer, I shall tell

him everything. He will reject me, he will curse me, and then I shall throw myself at his feet to thank him for all that he has done for me in the past three years. After that, poor, humiliated, but happy, I shall leave here rich in my love and rejoicing in the new life that awaits us.'

It was in the midst of this daydream of self-denial, in which ambition was sacrificed to love, that the crowd of servants parted, and a man ran into the room where Nanon was lying, shouting: 'Sister! Sister!'

Nanon sat up, opened her eyes wide in horror, went whiter than the embroidered sheet behind her head, and for the second time fell back swooning and muttering: 'Cauvignac! My God, Cauvignac!'

'Cauvignac,' the duke repeated, looking around him in astonishment, clearly looking for the person answering to this name. 'Cauvignac? Who's called Cauvignac here?'

Cauvignac resisted any temptation to reply: he was still not safe enough to risk being honest – something that, in any case, was not his custom even in the normal circumstances of life. He realized that, if he did reply, it would be disastrous for his sister and that a disaster for her also spelled his own ruin. So, inventive though he was, he was at a loss, leaving it up to Nanon to reply, while reserving the right to correct what she said.

'And Monsieur de Canolles?' she shouted, in tones of furious reproach, her eyes flashing in Cauvignac's direction.

The duke frowned and started to bite his moustache. Everyone else, apart from Finette, who was very pale, and Cauvignac, who was doing his best not to lose colour, had no idea what this unexpected anger meant and exchanged astonished glances.

'Poor Sister!' Cauvignac whispered to the duke. 'She was so frightened for me that she is delirious and unable to recognize me.'

'Talk to me, wretch!' Nanon shouted. 'Talk to me! Where is Monsieur de Canolles? What has happened to him? Answer me!'

Cauvignac took a desperate decision: he had to risk everything and rely on his effrontery to pull him through, because resorting to a confession, revealing to the Duke d'Epernon the double character that he had assumed of this false Canolles and that true Cauvignac who had raised troops against the queen, then sold these very same soldiers to her, was the shortest way to join Richon on the gallows. So he went over to the duke with tears in his eyes and said: 'Oh, Monsieur! It's not delirium, but madness, and grief, as you can see, which have addled her brains to the point where she can no longer recognize those closest to her. You will understand that if anyone can return her to her lost wits, I am the person. So I beg you have all these servants leave, except Finette, who will be there to care for her if need be. Because, like me, you would be distressed at seeing indifferent strangers laugh at the plight of my poor sister.'

The duke might not have accepted this explanation – credulous as he was, Cauvignac was starting to arouse suspicions in him – were it not that a messenger from the queen had arrived to say that she was expecting him in the palace where Monsieur de Mazarin had called an extraordinary meeting of the council.

While the queen's envoy was delivering his message, Cauvignac leant over Nanon and quickly told her: 'In heaven's name, calm down, Sister. If we can only exchange a few words in private, everything will be all right.'

Nanon fell back on to her bed, if not calm, at least in control of herself, because, however small the dose in which it is administered, hope is a balm that soothes the suffering heart.

As for the duke, deciding to play the parts of Orgon and Géronte[1] to the end, he returned to Nanon and kissed her hand.

'Come now, dear friend,' he said. 'The crisis is over, I hope. Collect yourself. I'm leaving you with this brother whom you love so much, because the queen is asking for me. Believe me when I tell you that it would take nothing less than an order from Her Majesty to make me leave you in such circumstances.'

Nanon felt that she was about to collapse. She did not have the strength to reply, but stared at Cauvignac and pressed his hand as though saying: 'You haven't deceived me, have you, Brother? I really can hope?'

Cauvignac replied to this pressure of her hand with an equal pressure of his own and, turning back to the duke, said: 'Yes, Duke, at least the worst of the crisis is past, and my sister will understand that she has a faithful friend and a devoted heart beside her, ready to do anything to restore her to freedom and happiness.'

Nanon could not bear it any longer. She burst into tears, strong-minded and self-controlled though she was. She had suffered so much that she was no more than an ordinary woman, which is to say, weak and needing to cry. The Duke d'Epernon left, shaking his head and giving a look that meant he entrusted Nanon to Cauvignac. Hardly had he gone than Nanon cried, 'Oh, how that man made me suffer! If he had stayed an instant longer, I think I should have died.'

Cauvignac motioned to her to keep quiet. Then he went and put his ear to the door to make sure that the duke was really leaving.

'What do I care!' said Nanon. 'Let him listen or not! You whispered two words to reassure me. Tell me . . . What do you think? What are your hopes?'

'Sister,' Cauvignac replied, putting on a serious air that was not at all usual with him. 'I shan't say that I am certain of success, but I repeat what I have already told you, which is that I shall do everything I can.'

'Succeed in what?' Nanon asked. 'Do we really understand one another this time or is there some dreadful misunderstanding between us again?'

'Succeed in saving poor Canolles.'

Nanon looked at him with terrible intensity.

'He's finished, isn't he?'

'Alas,' said Cauvignac, 'if you're asking for my honest opinion, I must admit that things don't look good.'

'How calmly he says it!' Nanon exclaimed. 'You do realize, don't you, wretch, what that man means to me?'

'I know that he's a man whom you prefer to your own brother, since you would rather save his life than mine, and when you saw me you greeted me with a curse.' Nanon made an impatient gesture. 'Why, you're quite right,' Cauvignac went on. 'I'm not saying this to you as a reproach, but as a simple observation. Because, I can say with my hand on my heart that if we were still, both of us, in the dungeon at the Château-

Trompette, and I knew what I do now, I should say to Monsieur de Canolles: "Nanon has called you her brother, and you are the one who is being asked for, not I." And he would have come in my place, and I have died in his.'

'Then he is to die!' Nanon exclaimed with an outpouring of grief which proves that in the most rational minds the idea of death is never a certainty, but always a dread, since asserting it has such a violent effect. 'Then he is to die!'

'All I can tell you, Sister,' said Cauvignac, 'is this, which must serve as the basis for our actions. It is nine in the evening. A lot may have happened in the two hours during which I have been escaping. Don't despair, for goodness' sake, because it could well be that absolutely nothing has happened. And I have an idea.'

'Tell me, quickly.'

'A league from Bordeaux I have a hundred men and my lieutenant.'

'Can he be trusted?'

'It's Ferguzon.'

'So?'

'So, Sister, whatever Monsieur de Bouillon says, whatever Monsieur de La Rochefoucauld does, and whatever the princess thinks – and she thinks herself a better captain than those two generals – I think that with a hundred men, by sacrificing half of them, I could reach Monsieur de Canolles.'

'No, you're wrong, Brother. You won't manage it! You won't manage it!'

'By heaven, I will, or die in the attempt.'

'Alas, your death would convince me of your goodwill, but not save him. He is lost!'

'And I tell you he isn't, even if I have to take his place!' Cauvignac exclaimed, even surprising himself with this outburst of near selflessness.

'Take his place?'

'Yes, indeed I would, because no one has any reason to hate that good man, Canolles, and everyone loves him, or almost, while people detest me.'

'You? Why do they detest you?'

'Why, quite simply because I have the honour to be linked to you by the closest of blood ties. Excuse me, dear Sister, but what I have just said is extremely flattering for a good royalist.'

'One moment,' Nanon said slowly, putting a finger to her lips.

'What?'

'You're saying that the people of Bordeaux hate me?'

'I might even say that they loathe you.'

'Really?' Nanon said with a smile that was half thoughtful and half happy.

'I didn't think that I was telling you something that you wanted to hear.'

'You're wrong,' said Nanon. 'I did, it's very gratifying, or at least it makes good sense. Yes, you're right,' she continued, talking to herself rather than to her brother. 'It is not Canolles that they hate, or you, for that matter. Wait a moment . . .'

She got up, wound a long silk cloak about her lithe and ardent form, sat down at the table and hastily wrote some lines that Cauvignac guessed must be quite important, to judge by her flushed face and the heaving of her breast.

'Take this,' she said, sealing the letter. 'Hurry alone, with no servants or escort, to Bordeaux. There is a mare in the stable that can cover the distance in an hour. Get there as fast as humanly possible, and take this letter to the princess. Canolles will be saved.'

Cauvignac looked at his sister with astonishment, but knowing the sharp intelligence of her strong mind, he did not waste time in discussion. He ran to the stable, leapt on the horse she had mentioned and within half an hour was already more than halfway to Bordeaux. As for Nanon, as soon as she had seen him start on his way through her window, she knelt down and, despite her unbelief, said a short prayer. Then she placed her gold, jewels and diamonds in a chest, called for a carriage and got Finette to dress her in her finest clothes.

II

Night was falling over Bordeaux, and, apart from the district around the Esplanade towards which everyone was hurrying, the town seemed to be deserted. There was no sound apart from the footsteps of nightwatchmen in the streets far from this particular place, and no human voice, except that of a few old women returning home and shutting their doors in terror.

But near the Esplanade, far away in the evening mist, one could hear a dull, continuous rumble like the roar of an ebbing tide.

The princess had just finished her correspondence and informed the Duke de La Rochefoucauld that she could receive him. At her feet, crouching on a rug and studying her face and mood with the most acute anxiety, was Madame de Cambes, who seemed to be waiting for a chance to speak; however, this disciplined patience and studied modesty were contradicted by the wringing of her hands as they twisted and tore her handkerchief.

'Seventy-seven signatures!' the princess exclaimed. 'You see, Claire, it's not all fun playing at being queen.'

'Yes, Madame,' said the viscountess. 'Because by taking the queen's place you have assumed her finest privilege, which is that of granting mercy.'

'And of punishing, Claire,' the Princess de Condé replied, arrogantly. 'Because one of these seventy-seven signatures is placed under a death sentence.'

'And the seventy-eighth will be under a letter of pardon, won't it, Madame?' Claire added in a beseeching tone.

'What are you saying, child?'

'I'm saying that I think it is time for me to go and free my prisoner. Wouldn't you like me to spare him the frightful sight of his companion being led off to die? Madame, since you are granting a pardon, let it be a full and total one.'

'Why, indeed! You are right, child. In the midst of all these grave concerns, I had forgotten my promise. You did well to remind me of it.'

'And so . . .' said Claire, joyfully.

'And so, do as you wish.'

'Then one more signature, Madame,' Claire said with a smile that would have softened the hardest heart, a smile that no painting could convey, because it is a smile that belongs only to a woman in love, in other words to life in its most divine essence.

She put a paper on the table in front of the princess, and showed her place where her hand should write.

Madame de Condé wrote: 'Order to the Governor of the Château-Trompette to allow Madame the Viscountess de Cambes access to Monsieur the Baron de Canolles, to whom we are granting full and total freedom.'

'Will that do?' the princess asked.

'Oh, yes, Madame!' cried Madame de Cambes.

'And I must sign it?'

'Yes, indeed.'

'Well, then dear,' said Madame de Condé, with her most charming smile, 'I must do all that you wish.'

And she signed.

Claire fell on the paper like an eagle on its prey. She hardly took the time to thank Her Highness, before pressing the paper to her heart and rushing out of the room.

On the stairs, she met the Duke de La Rochefoucauld, whose perambulations through the town were always followed by quite a large body of captains and admiring citizens. Claire gave him a happy little wave. De La Rochefoucauld, surprised by this, stopped for a moment on the landing, and before going in the Madame de Condé's room, continued to look at Claire until she reached the bottom of the staircase. Then, coming in to Her Highness's room, he said: 'Everything is ready, Madame.'

'Where?'

'There.'

The Duchess racked her brains.

'On the Esplanade,' the duke explained.

'Very good,' said the princess, pretending to be quite calm, because she felt that he was looking at her, and, though her feminine nature told her to shudder, she thought more of her dignity as the leader of her faction and that told her not to weaken. 'Very well, if everything is ready, go on, Duke.'

The duke paused.

'Do you think it proper that I should be present?' the princess asked, her voice trembling slightly – something that, despite her strength of will, she could not entirely suppress.

'As you wish, Madame,' replied the duke, who might very well have been engaged at that moment in one of his studies of human nature.

'We shall see, then. You know that I have pardoned many condemned persons.'

'Yes, Madame.'

'And what do you say about that?'

'I say that everything Your Highness does is well done.'

'Yes,' the princess went on. 'I prefer that. It would be more worthy of us to show the Epernonists that we are not afraid of taking reprisals, to deal on equal terms with His Majesty, to show that we are confident in our own strength and so return ill for ill without anger or excess.'

'Most politic.'

'Isn't it, Duke?' said the princess, trying to perceive Monsieur de La Rochefoucauld's real intentions behind his measured tones.

'However,' the duke went on, 'it is still your view that one of the two men should compensate for the death of Richon, because if that death is left unrevenged, it will be thought that Your Highness has little regard for the brave men who devote themselves to your service.'

'Oh, yes, definitely, one of the two will die, on my word. Don't worry.'

'Might I know which of the two Your Highness has seen fit to pardon?'

'Monsieur de Canolles.'

'Ah!'

This 'Ah!' was said in a peculiar manner.

'Do you have something in particular against that gentleman, Duke?' the princess asked.

'Madame! Do I ever have anything for or against someone?

I put men into two categories: obstacles and supports. The first must be overthrown and the second encouraged . . . as long as they support us. That is my policy; I might almost say my morality.'

'What trouble is he stirring up here?' Lenet thought to himself. 'What is he up to? He seems to hate that poor Canolles.'

'Very well, then,' said the duke. 'If Your Highness has no further orders for me . . .'

'No, Duke.'

'I shall take leave of Your Highness.'

'So it's to be this evening . . .'

'In a quarter of an hour.'

Lenet prepared to follow the duke.

'Are you going to watch it, Lenet?' asked the princess.

'Oh, no, Madame,' he said. 'I don't like these shocks, as you know. I shall be content to go halfway, as far as the prison, and see the moving scene of poor Canolles being freed by the woman he loves.'

The duke pulled a face of philosophical scepticism, Lenet shrugged his shoulders and the funerary procession left the palace for the prison.

Madame de Cambes had only taken five minutes to cover the same distance. When she arrived, she showed the order to the sentry at the drawbridge, then to the guardian at the gate, then called for the governor.

The governor examined the order with that dull eye that governors have, when they never get excited over death sentences or pardons. He recognized Madame de Condé's seal and signature, bowed to the messenger and, turning towards the gate, said: 'Call the lieutenant.'

Then he motioned to Madame de Cambes to sit down. But she was so anxious that she had to move about to combat her impatience, and she remained standing. The governor felt he should say something.

'Do you know Monsieur de Canolles?' he asked, in the tone of voice he might have used to enquire about the weather.

'Oh, yes, Monsieur!' the viscountess replied.

'Is he your brother, perhaps, Madame?'

'No, Monsieur.'

'A friend?'

'He is . . . my fiancé,' said Madame de Cambes, hoping that this confession would encourage the governor to make a little more haste to release the prisoner.

'Ah!' said the governor, with no change in his tone of voice. 'I offer you my compliments, Madame.' And, having no more questions, he lapsed back into immobility and silence.

The lieutenant came in.

'Monsieur d'Outremont,' the governor said. 'Call for the turnkey-in-chief and have Monsieur de Canolles set free. Here is the order for his release.'

The lieutenant bowed and took the paper.

'Would you like to wait here?' the governor asked.

'Might I be permitted to follow this gentleman?'

'You may, Madame.'

'Then I shall. You understand, I should like to be the first to tell him that he is safe.'

'Very well, Madame, and please accept the assurance of my respects.'

Madame de Cambes quickly curtsied to the governor and followed the lieutenant. This was the same young man who had already spoken to Canolles and Cauvignac, and his sympathy made him hasten all the more. In a moment he and Madame de Cambes were in the courtyard.

'The chief turnkey!' the lieutenant shouted. Then, turning to Madame de Cambes, he added: 'Have no fear, Madame. He will be here in a moment.'

The second turnkey came.

'The turnkey-in-chief has vanished, lieutenant,' he said. 'We have called for him in vain.'

'Oh, Monsieur!' said Madame de Cambes. 'Is this going to cause some further delay?'

'No, Madame. The order is clear. Don't worry.'

Madame de Cambes thanked him with one of those looks that one only sees on the faces of women and angels.

'Do you have the spare keys for all the cells?' Monsieur d'Outremont asked.

'Yes, Lieutenant,' said the turnkey.

'Then open the cell of Monsieur de Canolles.'

'Monsieur de Canolles in number two?'

'Exactly, number two. Quickly, open it.'

'In any case,' said the turnkey, 'I think they're both together. We'll choose the right one.'

Jailers in every day and age have always been facetious. But Madame de Cambes was too happy to mind the crude joke. On the contrary, she was smiling: if necessary, she would kiss the man to make him hurry up, so that she could see Canolles a second earlier.

Finally, the door opened. Canolles, who had heard footsteps in the corridor and recognized the viscountess's voice, threw himself into her arms, while she, sublimely unaffected by modesty, forgetting that he was neither her husband nor her lover, hugged him with all her strength. The danger that he had been in and the eternal separation that had loomed before them like an abyss purified everything.

'Well, my friend!' she said, glowing with joy and pride. 'You see that I have kept my word. I have obtained a pardon for you, as I promised. Now I have come to fetch you and take you away.'

Even as she spoke, she was pulling Canolles towards the corridor.

'Monsieur,' the lieutenant told him. 'You may devote all your life to this lady, because you certainly owe it to her.'

Canolles did not answer, but his eyes looked tenderly at the liberating angel, while his hand was clasping that of the woman.

'Don't be in such a hurry,' the lieutenant said, smiling. 'It's over, you're free, so take time opening your wings.'

But Madame de Cambes, taking no notice of these reassuring words, continued to pull Canolles down the corridor. He did not resist, exchanging signs with the lieutenant. They arrived at the staircase, and the two lovers went down it as though they really had the wings that the lieutenant had just mentioned. Finally, they reached the courtyard. One last door and the atmosphere of the prison would no longer weigh on their poor hearts . . .

Finally, the last door opened. But on the far side of it

was a group of gentlemen, guards and archers blocking the drawbridge. It was Monsieur de La Rochefoucauld and his supporters.

Without knowing why, Madame de Cambes shuddered. Misfortunes had always happened to her whenever she met that man.

As for Canolles, if he felt any emotion, it stayed in the depths of his heart and did not appear on his face.

The duke greeted Madame de Cambes and Canolles and even paused to pay them some compliments. Then he gave a signal to the gentlemen and guards behind him, and their ranks parted.

Suddenly, a voice could be heard coming from the corridor of the prison and these words rang around the yard: 'Hey! Cell number one is empty! The other prisoner has not been in his room for five minutes. I've been looking for him, and I can't find him.'

These words sent a long shudder through everyone who heard them. The Duke de La Rochefoucauld started and was unable to restrain an instinctive movement, holding out his hand towards Canolles as though to stop him.

Claire saw it and went pale.

'Come on, come on,' she told the young man. 'Let's hurry.'

'Excuse me, Madame,' said the duke, 'but I must ask you to be a little patient. Let's clear up this mistake, if you please. I can assure you, it will only take a minute.'

And, at another signal from the duke, the ranks that had parted, reclosed.

Canolles looked at Claire, the duke and the staircase from which the voices were coming, and the blood drained from his face too.

'But, Monsieur,' said Claire, 'what is the point of my waiting? The Princess de Condé has signed the warrant for Monsieur de Canolles's release. Here is the order which mentions him by name. Look at it.'

'Certainly, Madame, I do not intend to deny the validity of that warrant. And it will be as valid a minute from now as it is at present. So be patient, I have just sent someone, who must surely be back soon.'

'But what has that to do with us?' Claire asked. 'What does Monsieur de Canolles have to do with prisoner number one?'

'We have just looked in vain, Duke,' said the captain of the guards, whom Monsieur de La Rochefoucauld had sent to look. 'The other prisoner cannot be found, and the turnkey-in-chief has also disappeared, while the turnkey's child, who was questioned, says that his father and the prisoner left through the secret door opening on the river.'

'Ah, ha!' the duke said. 'Do you know anything about this, Monsieur de Canolles? An escape!'

At that, Canolles understood everything and guessed everything. He realized that it was Nanon taking care of him. He realized that he was the one whom the jailer had come to look for and the one who was described as the brother of Mademoiselle de Lartigues; he realized that unwittingly Cauvignac had taken his place and found freedom when he expected to meet death. All these ideas were milling around at once in his head. He clasped his head in both hands, paled and staggered, only recovering his composure when he saw the viscountess trembling and gasping for breath at his side. Not one of these involuntary signs of terror had escaped the duke.

'Close the gates!' he shouted. 'Monsieur de Canolles, please be so good as to stay here. You understand, we must clarify all this.'

'But, Duke,' the young woman cried, 'I hope you are not presuming to countermand an order from the princess!'

'No, Madame,' the duke said. 'But I think it is important for her to be informed of what is going on. I will not say to you: "I'll go and inform her myself", because you might think that I intend to influence our august mistress. What I shall say to you is: "You go, Madame", because you are better able than anyone to beg Madame de Condé's clemency.'

Lenet made a barely perceptible signal to Claire.

'I'm not leaving him!' the Viscountess de Cambes cried, grasping the young man's arm in a convulsive grip.

'And I shall hurry to Her Highness,' said Lenet. 'Come with me, Captain – and you, Duke.'

'I shall go with you. The captain can stay here and continue his search while we are away. Perhaps they will find the other prisoner.'

As though to emphasize the final part of his sentence, the Duke de La Rochefoucauld whispered a few words in the captain's ear and went out with Lenet. At the same moment, the two young people were hustled back into the courtyard by the crowd of horsemen accompanying Monsieur de La Rochefoucauld, and the door closed behind them.

In the previous ten minutes, the scene had taken on such a dark and solemn character that all those present were pale and silent, looking at one another and at Canolles and Claire to see which of them was suffering the most. Canolles realized that all the strength had to come from him: he was serious, but affectionate towards his friend, who, white as a sheet, red-eyed and weak-kneed, was hanging on to his arm, clasping him, drawing him towards her, smiling at him with a look of appalling tenderness, then shuddering as she looked round in terror at all those men, searching in vain for one friendly face among them . . .

The captain who had received his orders from the Duke de La Rochefoucauld was speaking quietly to his officers. Canolles, eagle-eyed and straining his ears for the least word that might change doubt into certainty, heard the captain say the following, despite his efforts to keep his voice as low as possible: 'We must find some means of getting that poor woman away from here.'

At this, Canolles tried to loosen the affectionate grasp on his arm. Claire saw what he was doing and clung to him with all her might.

'But you must have another look,' she cried. 'Perhaps the search was not properly conducted, and the man will be found. Let's all look, all of us: he cannot have escaped. Why would Monsieur de Canolles not have escaped with him, if he did? Come, Captain, I beg you, order a search.'

'They have searched, Madame,' the captain said, 'and they are still searching now. The jailer knows that it's a death sentence for him if he doesn't produce his prisoner, so he has every reason, as you must realize, to search as hard as he can.'

'My God!' Claire murmured. 'And Monsieur Lenet is not back yet.'

'Patience, dear friend, patience,' said Canolles, in the soft tone that one uses when speaking to a child. 'Monsieur Lenet has only just left; he has hardly had time to reach the princess. Give him the opportunity to explain the situation and then come back with the answer.'

Even as he said this, he was gently pressing the viscountess's hand. Then, seeing the fixed stare and impatience of the officer who was in command in place of the Duke de La Roche-foucauld, he said:

'Do you want to talk to me, Captain?'

'Yes, indeed I do, Monsieur,' he answered, tormented by the viscountess's scrutiny.

'I beg you, Monsieur,' Madame de Cambes exclaimed, 'take us to the princess. What difference can it make to you? You might as well go with us to see her as stay here in this uncertainty. She will see him, Monsieur, she will see me, I will speak to her, and she will repeat her promise to me.'

'Why, that's an excellent idea, Madame,' he said, seizing on this suggestion. 'Go yourself, you have every chance of success.'

'What do you think, Baron?' she asked. 'Do you think it would be good? You would not wish to deceive me: what should I do?'

'Go, Madame,' said Canolles, making a superhuman effort to repress his feelings.

The viscountess let go of his arm and tried to walk a few steps, then went back to her lover.

'No, no!' she said. 'I won't leave him.' Then, hearing the door open, she cried: 'Oh, thank God! Monsieur Lenet and the duke are coming back.'

Behind the Duke de La Rochefoucauld, who reappeared with his face expressionless, came Lenet, looking very upset and with his hands trembling. Canolles had only to exchange one glance with the poor counsellor to realize that there was no further hope and that he really was doomed.

'Well?' said the young woman, launching herself so violently towards Lenet that she dragged Canolles with her.

'Well,' said Lenet, 'the princess is embarrassed . . .'

'Embarrassed!' Claire exclaimed. 'What does that mean?'

'It means that she is asking for you,' the duke replied. 'She wants to talk to you.'

'Is this true, Monsieur Lenet?' Claire asked, not caring that she was insultingly ignoring the duke.

'Yes, Madame,' Lenet stammered.

'What about him?' she asked.

'Him?'

'Monsieur de Canolles.'

'Well, Monsieur de Canolles will go back to his prison, and you will bring him the princess's reply,' said the duke.

'Will you stay with him, Monsieur Lenet?' Claire asked.

'Madame . . .'

'Will you stay with him?'

'I shall not leave his side.'

'Do you swear that you will not leave him?'

'Dear God!' Lenet thought, looking at the young man waiting for his sentence and the young woman who was to bring it to him. 'Dear God, since one of these two is condemned, at least give me the strength to save the other!'

'Will you not swear, Monsieur Lenet?'

'I swear,' the counsellor replied, making an effort to put a hand on his breaking heart.

'Thank you, Monsieur,' Canolles whispered. 'I understand.' Then turning back to the viscountess, he said: 'Go, Madame, you can see that I am in no danger with Monsieur Lenet and the duke beside me.'

'Don't let her go without kissing her,' said Lenet.

A cold sweat broke out on Canolles's forehead, and he felt as though a mist had drifted in front of his eyes. He stopped Claire from leaving, and, pretending to have a few words to say to her privately, he clasped her to him and bent down to whisper in her ear: 'Entreat without demeaning yourself. I want to live for you, but you must want me to live with honour.'

'I shall beg her in such a way as to save you,' she replied. 'Aren't you my husband before God?'

Canolles, letting her go, managed to touch her neck with his lips, but so cautiously that she did not even feel it, and the poor woman, senseless with grief, left without returning his last kiss. However, as she was leaving the courtyard, she turned round, but ranks of soldiers had formed between her and the prisoner, blocking her view.

'My friend, where are you?' she cried. 'I can't see you. A word, one more word, so that I can go away with the sound of your voice in my ears!'

'Go on, Claire,' Canolles said. 'I am waiting for you.'

'Go on, Madame,' said a considerate officer. 'The sooner you leave, the sooner you will be back.'

'Monsieur Lenet, dear Monsieur Lenet,' Claire's voice cried in the distance. 'I am counting on you, you must answer to me for him!'

The gate closed behind her.

'At last,' said the philosopher duke. 'It was not easy, but we are back in the real world.'

III

As soon as the viscountess had left, her voice had faded in the distance and the gate had closed behind her, the group of officers moved in around Canolles, and two men appeared, as though from nowhere, two men of sinister appearance, who came over to the duke and humbly asked him for his orders.

In reply, the duke merely indicated the prisoner. Then, going over to Canolles and saluting him with his usual icy politeness, he said: 'Monsieur, you will no doubt have realized that the departure of your companion in misfortune has meant that the fate intended for him has reverted to you.'

'Yes, Monsieur,' Canolles replied. 'Or at least I guessed as much. But what I do know for certain is that the princess specifically granted me a pardon. I have seen and you, no doubt, saw just now the warrant for my release in the hands of the Viscountess de Cambes.'

'True,' said the duke. 'But the princess was not able to foresee the present circumstance.'

'So is the princess withdrawing her signature?' Canolles asked.

'Yes.'

'A princess of the blood is going back on her word!'

The duke remained impassive. Canolles looked around.

'Has the moment arrived?' he asked.

'Yes, Monsieur.'

'I thought that we were waiting for the Viscountess de Cambes to return. She was promised that nothing would be done in her absence. So is everyone going back on their word today?'

The prisoner looked reproachfully not at the duke, but at Lenet.

'Alas, Monsieur!' Lenet said, with tears in his eyes. 'Forgive us. The princess emphatically refused to pardon you, even though I begged her. The duke will witness it and God too. But there had to be a reprisal for the death of poor Richon, and she was adamant. No, Baron, judge for yourself: instead of allowing this dreadful situation in which you find yourself to weigh both on you and on the viscountess, I dared – forgive me, because I feel that I have great need of your forgiveness – I dared to let it weigh on you alone, on you as a soldier and as a gentleman.'

'So, I shall not see her again!' Canolles stammered, his voice choked with emotion. 'When you told me to kiss her, it was for the last time!'

A sob stronger than stoicism, or reason, or pride, shook Lenet's breast, and he stepped back to weep bitterly. Canolles looked with penetrating eyes at all the men around him, but saw only men hardened by Richon's cruel death, looking to see how he behaved, and thinking that if Richon had not flinched, *he* would, and, beside these, weak men, who were straining to hide their feelings, and to swallow their tears and their sighs.

'How dreadful!' the young man thought in one of those moments of superhuman lucidity that reveal to the soul the infinite horizons of all that is called life, that is to say a few short instants of happiness dotted like islands in an ocean of tears and suffering. 'How dreadful! Here was a woman I loved, and who, for the first time, had just told me that she loved me. A long, sweet future ahead! The realization of my dearest wish! And now, in a moment, in a second, death has taken the place of all that . . .'

His heart ached, and he felt a stinging in his eyes as though he were about to weep, but he remembered, as Lenet had said, that he was a man and a soldier. 'Pride!' he thought. 'The only real courage, help me now! Am I to weep over something as futile as life? How they would laugh if they could say: "When he heard he was to die, Canolles wept!" What did I do on the day when they besieged me in Saint-Georges and the people of Bordeaux tried to kill me, as they will today? I fought, I joked, I laughed . . . Well, by heaven, which hears me and may be as mistaken as I am, and by the devil, who at this moment is struggling with my good angel, I shall do today what I did then, and, though I am not fighting any more, at least I shall keep joking and laugh on.'

At once his face became calm, as though all emotion had drained from his heart. He put a hand through his fine black hair and walked over to the Duke de La Rochefoucauld and Lenet with a firm step and with a smile on his lips.

'As you know, gentlemen,' he said, 'in this world, which is so full of various odd and unexpected occurrences, one must get used to everything. I was wrong not to ask you for the moment that it took me to get used to death. If it was too long, I offer you my apologies for having kept you waiting.'

A feeling of profound astonishment swept through the groups of men around him, and the prisoner himself felt that this astonishment was changing to admiration. That feeling, so flattering to himself, gave him greater strength.

'When you are ready, gentlemen,' he said. 'I am the one who is waiting.'

The duke, struck dumb with amazement for a moment, recovered his usual sang-froid and gave a signal. At that the gates reopened, and the procession prepared to set out.

'One moment!' Lenet said, to gain time. 'One moment, Duke. We are taking Monsieur de Canolles out to die, aren't we?'

The duke started with surprise, and Canolles looked at Lenet with astonishment.

'Why, yes,' said the duke.

'Well,' said Lenet, 'if that's the case, this worthy man cannot do without a confessor.'

'Excuse me, Monsieur, excuse me,' said Canolles. 'On the contrary, I can very well do without one.'

'How is that?' Lenet asked, making signals that the prisoner deliberately ignored.

'Because I'm a Huguenot,'[2] said Canolles. 'And a convinced one, I warn you. So, if you want to do me one last favour, let me die as I am.'

Even as he said this, he made a gesture of gratitude to Lenet, which showed that he had quite understood the other man's intention.

'Then there is nothing further to detain us, let's go,' said the duke.

'Let him confess! Let him confess!' a few angry voices shouted.

Canolles stood on tiptoe, looked around calmly and, speaking to the duke, said in a confident and stern voice:

'Are we going to behave like cowards, Monsieur? It seems to me that if anyone here has the right to do as he pleases, it is I, the hero of the event. So I refuse to have a confessor, but demand the scaffold and as soon as possible. I, too, am tired of waiting.'

'Silence, there!' the duke shouted, turning to the soldiers. Then, when they had been hushed by the power of his voice and look, he turned to Canolles and said: 'Monsieur, it shall be as you please.'

'Thank you. Then, let's go, and quickly. Agreed?'

Lenet took Canolles's arm.

'On the contrary, go slowly,' he said. 'Who knows? A reprieve, a second thought, an accident ... something might happen. Go slowly, I beg you, in the name of the woman who loves you, and who will weep so much if we go quickly.'

'Oh, don't talk to me of her,' Canolles replied. 'I beg you. All my courage is dashed against the thought that I shall be for ever separated from her. But what am I saying? On the contrary, Monsieur Lenet, talk to me of her, tell me again that she loves me, that she will always love me and that she will weep for me.'

'Now, now, my dear, unfortunate child,' said Lenet. 'Don't weaken. Consider that people are watching us who don't know what we are talking about.'

Canolles proudly lifted his head, and his fine hair, in a gesture that was full of style, fell in black ringlets across his neck. They had reached the street, where many torches were lighting the way, so that people could see his calm, smiling face. He heard some women weep, and others saying: 'Poor baron! So young and so handsome!'

They went silently on their way. Then, suddenly, he said: 'Oh, Monsieur Lenet! I truly would like to see her one more time.'

'Do you want me to go and fetch her?' said Lenet, who could no longer decide for himself.

'Yes, yes,' murmured Canolles.

'Very well, I shall run. But you will kill her.'

'So much the better,' said the egotist inside the young man's heart. 'If you kill her, no one else will ever possess her.' But then, overcoming this final weakness, Canolles put out a hand to restrain Lenet and said: 'No, no. You promised her that you would stay with me. So stay.'

'What's he saying?' the duke asked the captain of the guard.

Canolles heard the question.

'I am saying, Duke,' he replied, 'that I did not think it was so far from the prison to the Esplanade.'

'Alas, don't complain, you poor young man,' Lenet added. 'We are there.'

Even as he said this, the torches lighting the procession and the advance guard of the escort disappeared round a bend in the road.

Lenet pressed the young man's hand, and, wanting to make one further attempt before they reached the place of execution, he went over to the duke and said in a quiet voice: 'Once more,

I beg you: pardon him! You will lose our cause by executing Monsieur de Canolles.'

'Not at all,' the duke retorted. 'We are proving that we consider it to be a just one, since we are not afraid to take reprisals.'

'Reprisals are exchanged between equals, Duke. And whatever you care to say, the queen will always be the queen and we her subjects.'

'Let us not argue about such matters in front of Monsieur de Canolles,' said the duke, in a louder voice. 'You can see that it is not appropriate.'

'Don't talk about mercy to his lordship,' said Canolles. 'You can see he is in the middle of carrying out his *coup d'état*, so let's not bother him with such trivial matters . . .'

The duke did not reply, but his clenched lips and ironic glance showed that the shot had found its mark. Meanwhile, they had carried on walking, and Canolles was now at the entrance to the Esplanade. In the distance, that is to say at the far end of the square, they could see the packed crowd and a wide circle formed by the shining muzzles of the muskets. In the centre, was something black and shapeless which Canolles did not trouble to make out through the dark; he thought that it was an ordinary scaffold. But suddenly, the torches, reaching the middle of the square, lit up this sombre object that had previously been unrecognizable and showed the dreadful outline of a gibbet.

'A gibbet!' Canolles cried, stopping and pointing at the device. 'Is that not a gibbet that I can see there, Duke?'

'Yes, indeed, you are not mistaken,' the duke replied coldly.

The young man's face reddened with indignation. He pushed aside the two soldiers who were marching at his sides and in a single stride was confronting Monsieur de La Rochefoucauld.

'Have you forgotten, Monsieur, that I am a gentleman?' he shouted. 'Everyone knows, even the executioner, that a gentleman has the right to be beheaded!'

'There are some circumstances . . .'

'Monsieur,' Canolles interrupted him. 'I am not speaking to you in my name, but in that of all the nobility, in which you yourself hold such a high rank: you have been a prince, and you are now a duke. It would be a dishonour – not for me, who am innocent, but for all of you, such as you are, were one of your peers to die on a gibbet.'

'The king had Richon hanged, Monsieur!'

'Richon was a brave soldier, as noble in heart as anyone in the world, but he was not noble by birth. I am.'

'You forget,' the duke said, 'that we are dealing with an affair of reprisal. Even if you were a prince of the blood, you would be hanged.'

Canolles, without thinking, felt for his sword and, not finding it at his side, was forced back into the full realization of his situation. His anger evaporated, and he saw that his superiority lay in his weakness.

'Woe betide those who use reprisals, philosopher,' he said. 'And more still those who, in doing so, pay no heed to humanity. I am not asking for mercy, but for justice. There are those who love me, Monsieur – and I stress that word, because you, I know, are not aware that it is possible to love.[3] Well, in the heart of those people you will for ever impress, beside the memory of my death, the ignoble image of the gibbet. A sword thrust, I beg you, or a musket ball. Give me your dagger so that I can strike myself, and afterwards you can hang my corpse if you wish.'

'Richon was hanged alive, Monsieur,' the duke replied coldly.

'Very well. Now listen to me: one day, a frightful misfortune will strike you, and you will see that this misfortune is a punishment from God. As for me, I am dying in the certainty that my death is your doing.'

Canolles, shivering, pale, but exultant and full of courage, walked over to the scaffold and paused, proud and disdainful before the mob, with his foot on the first step of the ladder.

'And now,' he said, 'executioners – do your work!'

'There's only one!' the crowd shouted in surprise. 'The other! Where is the other? We were promised two!'

'Ah, that's a consolation,' Canolles said with a smile. 'This fine mob is not even content with what you are doing for it. Did you hear them, Duke?'

'Death! Death! Revenge for Richon!' shouted ten thousand voices.

'Perhaps,' thought Canolles, 'if I were to annoy them, they would be quite capable of tearing me limb from limb, and then I should not be hanged, which would infuriate the duke.'

'Cowards!' he shouted. 'I can see some among you who were in the attack on the fort of Saint-Georges: I saw you running away. Now you are taking revenge on me for beating you.'

There was an answering roar.

'Cowards! Rebels! Wretches!' he went on.

A thousand knives flashed, and stones started to fall at the foot of the scaffold.

'At last,' Canolles thought. Then, aloud, he said: 'The king hanged Richon, and good riddance! When he captures Bordeaux he'll hang plenty more of you.'

At these words, the crowd charged like a flood across the Esplanade, knocked over the guards, broke down the palisades and rushed, roaring, towards the prisoner.

Meanwhile, at a signal from the duke, one of the executioners had lifted Canolles up by his armpits, while the other threw a cord around his neck.

Canolles felt the rope and yelled more insults. If he was to be killed in time, he had not a minute to lose. At that final moment, he looked around and saw only blazing eyes and threatening weapons.

One man alone, a soldier on horseback, was brandishing his musket.

'Cauvignac! It's Cauvignac!' Canolles shouted, grasping the ladder with both hands; his arms had not been tied.

Cauvignac waved his gun at the man whom he had been unable to save and took aim.

'Yes, yes!' he cried, nodding his head.

And now let us describe how Cauvignac came to be there.

IV

We saw Cauvignac leaving Libourne and we know why he did so.

When he caught up with his soldiers, under Ferguzon's command, he paused for a moment, not to catch his breath, but to carry out the plan that his inventive mind had been able to conceive in half an hour's speedy march.

First of all, he told himself, with every justification, that if he were to present himself before the princess after what had happened, the princess, who was hanging Canolles when she had nothing against him, would certainly hang Cauvignac, against whom she did have cause for reproach, so his mission, though successful in that Canolles might, perhaps, be saved, would be a failure to the extent that he himself would be hanged. So he hurriedly changed clothes with one of his men, got Barabbas, who was less familiar to the princess than he was, to put on his finest clothes and, taking him along, once more set off at a gallop down the Bordeaux road. Meanwhile, there was one thing bothering him, namely the content of the letter that he was carrying, which his sister had written with such confidence, and which, according to her, he had only to hand over to the princess for Canolles to be saved. And this unease increased to the point where he quite simply decided to read the letter, telling himself that a good negotiator can only succeed in his mission if he is fully informed of the matter concerned. Apart from which, it must be said, Canolles did not have every confidence in his sister: it was possible that Nanon, even though she was his sister – and even precisely because she was his sister – might well hold a grudge against her brother, firstly for the affair at Jaulnay, and then afterwards for his unexpected escape from the Château-Trompette, and might be helping fate to put everything back in its place (which was something of a family tradition).

So Cauvignac easily opened the document, which was only closed by a simple wax seal, and experienced a strange and quite painful sensation as he read the letter.

This is what Nanon had written:

Princess,

A victim is necessary to compensate for the unfortunate Richon. Do not take an innocent man, take the one who is really guilty. I do not wish Monsieur de Canolles to die, because killing him would be to avenge an assassination with a murder. When you read this letter, I shall have only a league to cover to reach Bordeaux with all that I possess. You can hand me over to the people who hate me – since they have twice tried to cut my throat – and keep my wealth for yourself: it amounts to two million. Madame, on bended knee I beg you this favour. I am partly to blame for this war. When I am dead, peace will return to the province and Your Highness will triumph. Give us a quarter of an hour's grace. Do not release Canolles until you have me; but then, by your soul, you will release him, won't you?
And I shall be your respectful and grateful,
Nanon de Lartigues

After reading this, Cauvignac was amazed to find that his heart was full and his eyes were damp. He remained motionless and dumbfounded as though unable to believe what he had just read. Then suddenly he cried: 'So it is true that there are in this world hearts that are generous for the pleasure of being so!⁴ Very well, by heaven! They will see that I am as capable as another of being generous when I have to.'

Since he was at the gate of the town, he handed the letter to Barabbas, with the following instructions: 'Whatever they say to you, answer only: "On the king's business!" And put this letter into the hands of Madame de Condé herself.'

While Barabbas was hurrying towards the palace where the princess was staying, Cauvignac for his part set off for the Château-Trompette.

Barabbas found nothing to stand in his way. The streets were deserted, and the town appeared to be empty, everyone in it having made for the Esplanade.

At the door of the palace, the sentries tried to stop him from passing, but, following Cauvignac's advice, he waved his letter, shouting: 'On the king's business! On the king's business!'

The sentries assumed he was a messenger from the court and raised their pikes, letting Barabbas get into the palace, as he had previously got into the town. Because, as the reader will recall, this was not the first time that Monsieur Cauvignac's worthy lieutenant had the honour to visit Madame de Condé. So he leapt down from his horse and, knowing his way, hastily ran to the staircase, rushing past some busy servants, and reached the princess's chambers. There he stopped, confronted by a woman whom he recognized as the princess, with another woman kneeling at her feet.

'Oh, Madame! Mercy, in heaven's name!' this other woman was saying.

'Claire,' the princess replied, 'hush, be reasonable. Consider that we have put aside our nature as women together with our women's clothing. We are the representatives of the prince and reason of state must dictate.'

'There is no reason of state for me,' Claire cried. 'There are no longer any political factions or opinions. There is nothing except him in this world that he is about to leave, and when he has left it, there will be nothing for me but death!'

'Claire, child, I have told you that it is impossible,' the princess replied. 'They killed Richon, and if we do not reply in kind, we shall be dishonoured.'

'Oh, Madame, no one is ever dishonoured by showing mercy; no one is ever dishonoured by making use of a privilege that is reserved for the king of heaven and the kings of the earth. One word, Madame, just one! The poor wretch is waiting!'

'But Claire, you are mad! I've told you it's impossible . . .'

'And I told him that he was safe! I showed him his pardon signed with your own hand. I told him that I would return with confirmation of that pardon.'

'I granted it on condition that the other man would pay for him. Why was the other one allowed to leave?'

'He had nothing to do with that escape, I swear! In any case, the other man may not be saved. They might find him . . .'

'Ah, yes! Beware!' thought Barabbas, who arrived at that moment.

'They are going to lead him away, Madame. Time is running out. They will be tired of waiting.'

'You are right, Claire,' said the princess. 'Because I gave the order that everything should be over by eleven o'clock, and eleven o'clock is just striking. It must all be over.'

The viscountess gave a cry and got up. As she did so, she came face to face with Barabbas.

'Who are you?' she cried. 'What do you want? Have you already come to report his death?'

'No, Madame,' said Barabbas, assuming his most affable manner. 'On the contrary, I have come to save him.'

'How?' the viscountess cried. 'Tell us quickly!'

'By giving this letter to the princess.'

Madame de Cambes reached out, snatched the letter from the messenger's hands and said, giving it to the princess: 'I don't know what is in this letter, but in heaven's name, read it!'

The princess opened the letter and read it aloud, while Madame de Cambes, her face growing paler at every line, devoured every word as it fell from the princess's lips.

'From Nanon!' said the princess. 'Nanon is there! She is surrendering! Where is Lenet? Where is the duke? Get someone, get someone here.'

'I am here,' said Barabbas, 'and ready to run wherever Your Highness pleases.'

'Then run to the Esplanade, to the place of execution and tell them to suspend it . . . But, no, they won't believe you!'

The princess, grabbing a pen, wrote the words: 'Suspend execution' at the bottom of the letter. Then she gave it, unsealed, to Barabbas, who dashed out of the room.

'She loves him more than I do,' thought the viscountess. 'Wretch that I am, she is the one to whom he will owe his life.' And, at this idea, she dropped senseless into a chair, after managing to remain standing through all the shocks of that dreadful day.

Barabbas, meanwhile, did not lose a second. He flew down

the stairs, as though he had wings, then leapt on his horse and galloped at full tilt towards the Esplanade.

While he was going to the palace, Cauvignac for his part had been hurrying directly to the Château-Trompette. There, under cover of darkness and made unrecognizable by a broad felt hat pulled right down over his eyes, he asked questions and learned every detail of his own escape and how Canolles was to pay for him. Instinctively, without planning what he was going to do, he raced towards the Esplanade, spurring his horse on furiously, pushing the crowd aside, dashing, overturning and crushing everything in his path. When he reached the execution place, he saw the gibbet and gave a cry that was drowned by the shouts of the mob, which Canolles was exciting and provoking, in the hope that it would tear him apart.

It was at this moment that Canolles saw Cauvignac, guessed his intent and nodded to show him that he was welcome.

Cauvignac stood up in his stirrups, looked around in case he could see Barabbas or a messenger from the princess and listened for the word 'Pardon!' But he could see and hear nothing except Canolles, whom the executioner was about to knock off the ladder and swing into the void – and who, with one hand, was showing him his heart.

This is when Cauvignac raised his musket towards the young man, put it to his cheek, aimed and fired.

'Thank you,' said Canolles, opening his arms. 'At least I am dying a soldier's death.'

The shot had pierced his chest.

The executioner pushed the body, which hung from the rope of shame, but it was no more than a corpse.

The shot had acted like a signal. A thousand other musket shots rang out at once, and a voice cried: 'Stop! Stop! Cut the rope!'

But it was lost in the screams of the mob. In any case, the rope was cut by a shot, while the guard resisted in vain before being swept aside by the flood of people. The gallows was torn down, smashed, obliterated. The executioners fled, and the crowd, spreading like a shadow, seized the body, pulled it away, tore it apart and dragged it in shreds around the town.

This mob, made idiotic by hatred, thought that it was adding to the baron's punishment, while in reality it was saving him from the infamy that he had so greatly feared.

While all this was going on, Barabbas had made his way to the duke, and, though he could see for himself that he was too late, he gave him the message that he had brought.

In the midst of all the firing, the duke had merely moved a little way to the side – for he was cold and calm in courage as in everything else that he did. He opened the letter[5] and read it.

'That's a shame,' he said, turning to his officers. 'What this Nanon suggests might have been more advantageous, but what is done, is done.' Then, after a moment's reflection, he added: 'In fact, since she is on the far side of the river, waiting for our reply, we may still be able to do something about it.'

And, without bothering about the messenger, he spurred his horse and returned with his escort to the princess.

At that same moment, the storm, which had been threatening for some time, burst over Bordeaux and rain, together with lightning, fell on the Place de l'Esplanade, as though to wash away the innocent blood.

V

While all this was going on in Bordeaux, while the mob was dragging the body of the unfortunate Canolles through the streets, while the Duke de La Rochefoucauld was returning to flatter the princess's pride by telling her that in doing evil she was as powerful as a queen, and while Cauvignac, along with Barabbas, was making for the gates of the town, considering that there was no sense in prolonging their stay, a carriage drawn by four breathless horses, streaming with foam, was stopping on the banks of the Garonne opposite Bordeaux, between the villages of Belcroix and La Bastide.

The clocks had just struck eleven.

A courier, following on horseback, jumped down hurriedly as soon as he saw the coach standing motionless and opened the door. A woman quickly got down, looking up at the sky, which was coloured by a blood-red light, and listening to the distant shouts and noises.

'Are you sure there was no one following us?' she asked her maid, who was climbing down after her.

'No, Madame,' the girl replied. 'The two grooms who stayed behind at Madame's orders have just caught up with the coach and saw nothing.'

'And you? Can't you hear anything from the direction of the town?'

'I think I can make out some distant shouts.'

'Can you see anything?'

'Something that looks like the glow of a fire.'

'Those are torches.'

'Yes, Madame, because they are waving about and running like will-o'-the-wisps. Do you hear that, Madame? The noise is getting louder, and one can almost hear what they are shouting.'

'My God!' the young woman stammered, falling to her knees on the damp ground. 'My God, my God!'

That was her only prayer. There was a single word in her mind, and her mouth could only utter one word: the name of Him alone who could accomplish a miracle for her.

The maid had not been mistaken. The flames of the torches were waving, and the cries seemed to be getting closer. They could hear a gunshot, followed by fifty more, then a great roar. Then the torches went out, and the shouts faded. The rain began to fall, and a storm was rumbling in the sky. But what did that matter to the young woman? It was not thunder that she feared.

She kept staring at the place where she had heard a great noise. She could no longer see or hear anything. In the flashes of lightning, it seemed to her that the square was empty.

'I can't bear to wait any longer,' she exclaimed. 'To Bordeaux! Take me to Bordeaux!'

Suddenly, they heard the sound of horses coming towards them.

'Ah!' she cried, 'They are coming at last! Here they are. Farewell, Finette, you can leave. I have to go on alone. Let her mount behind you, Lombard, and leave behind everything I brought with me in the coach.'

'But what are you going to do, Madame?' the maid asked in alarm.

'Farewell, Finette, farewell!'

'But why are you saying farewell, Madame? Where are you going?'

'To Bordeaux.'

'But don't do that, Madame, for heaven's sake! They will kill you.'

'So? Why do you think I want to go there?'

'Oh, Madame! Lombard, help me! Help me, stop Madame . . .'

'Hush, Finette. You go. I have remembered you, don't worry. I don't want you to come to any harm. Do as I say . . . They are coming . . . Here they are!'

A rider was indeed coming up, followed at a short distance by another. His horse could be heard roaring, rather than breathing.

'Sister, Sister!' he shouted. 'I have got here in time!'

'Cauvignac!' Nanon cried. 'Well, is it agreed? Are they waiting? Let's go.'

But instead of replying, Cauvignac leapt off his horse and grasped Nanon in his arms. She let him embrace her, with the inertness of a ghost and the rigidity of the insane. Cauvignac placed her in the carriage, told Finette and Lombard to get in beside her, closed the door and got back on his horse. Poor Nanon, who had come back to her senses, was shouting and struggling in vain.

'Don't let her go,' said Cauvignac. 'Don't let her go for anything in the world. You, Barabbas, keep an eye on the other door, and, Coachman, if you slow to less than a gallop, I'll blow your brains out.'

These orders came so fast there was a moment's hesitation. The carriage took some time to get started, the servants were shivering and the horses unwilling to leave.

'By all the devils, won't you hurry up!' Cauvignac bellowed. 'They're coming, they're coming!'

In the distance, one could start to make out the sound of horses' hooves echoing, like the rolling of thunder as it approaches, swift and threatening.

Fear is contagious. Hearing Cauvignac's voice, the coachman realized that some great danger was approaching, and he seized his horses' reins.

'Where are we going?' he stammered.

'To Bordeaux, to Bordeaux!' Nanon shouted, from inside the carriage.

'To Libourne, damnation take it!' yelled Cauvignac.

'Monsieur, the horses will drop before they have done two leagues.'

'I'm not asking them to do as much as that,' Cauvignac said, whipping them with the blade of his sword. 'As long as they reach Ferguzon's camp, that's all I ask.'

The heavy machine shuddered, set off and advanced with fearful speed. The men and the horses, sweating, panting and bloody, drove one another forward, the first with shouts, the second with neighs.

Nanon tried to fight, to struggle, to leap out of the carriage. But she had exhausted all her strength. She slipped back, powerless, neither hearing nor seeing. Trying to distinguish Cauvignac in the tangled mass of fleeting shadows, she felt dizzy and closed her eyes. She gave a cry and sank, cold and lifeless, into the arms of her chambermaid.

Cauvignac had ridden on ahead of the carriage, overtaking the horses. His own mount struck a trail of sparks from the cobbles.

'Here, Ferguzon! Here!' he cried, and heard what sounded like a cheer in the distance. 'Hell,' Cauvignac shouted. 'You're playing against me, but I think that you'll lose again today. Ferguzon, help me! Ferguzon!'

Two or three shots rang out behind them, but ahead there was a general volley of fire. The carriage stopped. Two of the horses had dropped from exhaustion, and a third had been struck by a musket ball.

Ferguzon and his men fell upon the troops of the Duke de La Rochefoucauld. As they were three times as many, the men from Bordeaux were unable to fight back and turned about. Victors and vanquished, pursuers and pursued, like a cloud carried on the wind, vanished into the night.

Cauvignac was left alone with the servants and Finette beside Nanon's unconscious form.

Fortunately, they were only a hundred yards from the village of Carbonblanc. Cauvignac took Nanon in his arms as far as the first house on the outskirts, and there, after giving orders for the carriage to be brought, he put his sister on a bed, and, taking something from his breast which Finette could not make out, he slipped it into the poor woman's clenched fist.

The next day, waking from what she took to be a frightful dream, Nanon put that same hand to her face and something silky and sweet-smelling caressed her pale lips. It was a lock of Canolles's hair that Cauvignac had saved, at the risk of his life, from the tigers of Bordeaux.

VI

For eight days and nights Madame de Cambes remained delirious on the bed, where she had been brought, swooning, after she learned the dreadful news.

Her maids attended to her, but it was Pompée who kept guard at the door: only this old servant, kneeling beside the bed of his unfortunate mistress, could light a spark of understanding in her.

Many people came to visit, but the faithful retainer, keeping as strictly to his duty as an old soldier, bravely refused entry to anyone, firstly out of his own belief that any visit would be unwelcome to his mistress, then on the orders of the doctor, who was afraid of the effects of any strong emotion on Madame de Cambes.

Every morning, Lenet presented himself at the poor young woman's door, but he was no more allowed entry than anyone else. The princess herself arrived one day with a large retinue after visiting the mother of poor Richon, who was living in a suburb of the town. Madame de Condé's aim, apart from the concern that she felt for the viscountess, was to demonstrate her total impartiality.

So she arrived, intending to play the queen, but Pompée respectfully informed her that he had clear and formal instructions, and that all men, even dukes and generals, and that all women, even princesses, were subject to these orders – and Madame de Condé more than anyone, since after what had happened, her visit might cause a frightful relapse in the patient.

The princess, who was answering a call of duty (or thought she was) was only too happy to leave and did so, with her train, without needing to be asked twice.

On the ninth day, Claire regained her senses. It was observed that throughout her delirium, which had lasted eight times twenty-four hours, she had not ceased to weep. Although normally fever dries up tears, hers had, as it were, left a furrow beneath her eyelid, which was circled with red and pale blue, like that of the sublime Virgin by Rubens.[6]

On the ninth day, as we said, at the moment when it was least expected, when they were starting to despair of her reason, she recovered it suddenly and as if by enchantment. Her tears ceased, and her eyes looked all round her, pausing with a sad smile for the women, who had served her so well, and for Pompée, who had guarded her so faithfully. For a few hours, she remained silent, leaning on her elbow and following, dry-eyed, the same thought that constantly returned with increased force to her reawakened mind.

Then, suddenly, without considering whether she was strong enough, she said: 'Dress me.'

The women came over to her, amazed, and tried to make some suggestions. Pompée came into the room and clasped his hands as though begging her. But the viscountess simply repeated, softly but firmly: 'I asked you to dress me, so do it.'

The maids began to obey. Pompée bowed and backed out of the room.

Alas, the plump pink cheeks were now as pale and thin as those of a dying woman. Her hand, still lovely and elegant, had a transparency and dull pallor like ivory, as it lay on her breast, whiter than the linen she was wearing. Under her skin ran those violet veins which are a symptom of exhaustion after much suffering. The clothes that she had taken off, as it were, the day before, and which outlined her elegant figure, now fell around her in long, broad folds. They dressed her, as she had asked, but it was a long business, because she was so weak that on three occasions she nearly fainted. Then, when she was dressed, she went over to a window. But starting back, as though the sight of the sky and the town had terrified her, she went and sat at a table, asked for a pen and ink and wrote to the princess, asking her to grant the favour of an audience. Ten minutes after the letter had been sent to the princess by Pompée, they heard the sound of a carriage drawing up in front of the house, and almost immediately afterwards Madame de Tourville was announced.

'Is it really you who wrote to the princess to ask for an audience?' she asked the viscountess.

'Yes, Madame,' said Claire. 'Will she refuse?'

'Oh, no, quite the opposite, dear child. I have hurried here to tell you on her behalf that you do not need an audience, that you can see Her Highness at any hour of the day or night.'

'Thank you, Madame,' said the viscountess. 'I shall take advantage of the offer.'

'What!' Madame de Tourville exclaimed. 'Are you going out in your present state?'

'Have no fear, Madame,' the viscountess replied. 'I am feeling perfectly well.'

'And when are you coming?'

'In a moment.'

'I shall inform Her Highness.'

Madame de Tourville left as she had entered, after making an eleborate curtsey to the viscountess. The news of the unexpected visit, as one may imagine, produced a considerable stir in this little court: the viscountess's situation had inspired a lively and universal interest, because not everyone by any means approved of the princess's behaviour in recent events. So curiosity was at its height: officers, ladies-in-waiting and courtiers filled Madame de Condé's rooms, unable to believe in the coming visit, because only the day before Claire's state had been reported to be almost desperate.

Suddenly, they announced the Viscountess de Cambes, and Claire appeared.

At the sight of this face, as pale as wax, as cold and fixed as marble, with what seemed like only a single glimmer in her hollow, dark-ringed eyes – the last reflection of the tears she had shed – a murmur of sympathy rose around the princess.

Claire seemed unaware of it.

Lenet came to meet her, very moved, and shyly offered her his hand. But Claire, without giving him hers in return, saluted Madame de Condé with dignity and nobility, then walked towards her along the whole length of the hall, with firm steps, though she was so pale that at every step one might have thought she was about to fall.

The princess, herself very pale and anxious, watched Claire approach with something like terror, and she did not have the strength to disguise this feeling.

'Madame,' the viscountess said in a solemn voice, 'I asked Your Highness for this audience, which she has been good enough to grant me, in order to enquire in the presence of everyone, whether, in the time that I have had the honour to serve you, you have been satisfied with my loyalty and my devotion.'

The princess put a handkerchief to her lips and replied, stammering: 'Of course I am, dear Viscountess. I have always had occasion to praise you, and I have more than once expressed my gratitude to you.'

'This acknowledgement is precious to me, Madame,' the viscountess replied, 'because it allows me to beg Your Highness to let me go.'

'What, Claire!' the princess exclaimed. 'Are you leaving me?'

Claire bowed respectfully, but said nothing.

On every face there were signs of shame, remorse or grief. A funereal silence hovered around the room.

'But why are you leaving?' the princess asked.

'I have only a short time to live, Madame,' the viscountess

replied. 'And I should like to use this short time in working towards my salvation.'

'Claire, dear Claire,' the princess said. 'Please consider . . .'

'Madame,' the viscountess interrupted. 'I have two favours to ask of you. May I hope that you will grant them?'

'Oh, speak, speak,' said Madame de Condé. 'I should be so happy to do something for you.'

'You can do something, Madame.'

'So what are the favours?

'The first is to give me the place of abbess at Sainte-Radegonde, which has been vacant since the death of Madame de Montivy.'

'You, an abbess, my child! You can't be thinking of it.'

'And the second, Madame,' Claire said, with a slight trembling in her voice, 'is that I may be permitted to have buried in my estate at Cambes the body of my fiancé, Baron Raoul de Canolles, who was murdered by the inhabitants of Bordeaux.'

The princess turned away, grasping her heart with a trembling hand. The Duke de La Rochefoucauld went pale and lost his composure. Lenet opened the door of the room and ran out.

'Your Highness does not reply,' said Claire. 'Do you refuse? Perhaps I have asked too much.'

Madame de Condé had only the strength to give a nod of assent, before falling back, fainting, into her chair.

Claire turned round with the stiffness of a statue and, as the crowd parted to let her through, marched upright and impassive past the rows of bending foreheads. It was only when she had left the room that they realized that no one had thought to assist Madame de Condé.

Five minutes later a carriage slowly drove out of the courtyard. It was the viscountess leaving Bordeaux.

'What has Your Highness decided?' Madame de Tourville asked Madame de Condé, when she came round.

'That the two wishes expressed by the Viscountess de Cambes just now should be carried out and that she should be asked to forgive us.'

THE ABBESS OF
SAINTE-RADEGONDE
DE PESSAC

A month had passed since the events just described.

One Sunday evening, after vespers, the Abbess of the Convent of Sainte-Radegonde de Pessac was the last to return from the church which stood at the far end of the convent garden. From time to time, she would turn her eyes, red with tears, towards a dark clump of limes and fir trees, with an expression of such regret that one might have thought her heart had stayed at that spot and she could not move away from it.

In front of her, in single file along the path to the house, a long line of nuns, silent and veiled, looked like a procession of ghosts returning to their tombs, with another ghost behind them, turning away and still yearning for earth.

Gradually, one by one, the nuns vanished beneath the dark vaults of the cloister. The mother superior watched them until the last one had gone, then slumped down with an indescribable look of despair on the capital of a gothic column, half buried in the grass.

'Oh, my God, my God!' she said, putting a hand to her heart. 'You are my witness that I cannot bear this life. I had no notion of it. It was solitude and obscurity that I sought in the cloister, not all these eyes staring at me.'

She got up and took a step towards the little cluster of firs.

'After all,' she said, 'what do I care for this world, since I have renounced it? The world has done me nothing but harm; society has been cruel towards me. So why should I worry about what the world thinks? I have taken refuge with God and belong only to Him. But perhaps God has forbidden this love which still lives in my heart and devours it. Well, then! Let Him tear it from my soul, or tear my soul from my body.'

Hardly had the poor unfortunate woman spoken these words than, looking down at the habit that she was wearing, she felt a rush of horror at a blasphemy that was so inappropriate to someone in her holy dress. She wiped the tears from her eyelids with her thin, white hand and, raising her eyes to heaven, offered up her eternal suffering in a single look.

At that moment, she heard a voice in her ear. The abbess turned round. It was the sister who received visitors to the convent.

'Madame,' she said, 'there is a woman in the parlour who would like to be allowed to speak to you.'

'What is her name?'

'She will say that only to you.'

'To what rank in life does she appear to belong?'

'A distinguished one.'

'Society, again,' murmured the abbess.

'What shall I tell her?' the sister asked.

'That I am expecting her.'

'Where, Madame?'

'Bring her here. I shall receive her in this garden, sitting on this bench. I need air. I feel stifled when I am not in the open.'

The sister left and a short time later returned, followed by a woman whose clothes, luxurious even in their sober simplicity, marked her out as a woman of distinction. She was short in stature, and, though her quick walk might have lacked some nobility, it had an inexpressible charm. Under her arm, she carried a little ivory box, its flat whiteness standing out against the black satin of her dress with its jade ornaments.

'Madame, this is the mother superior,' said the nun.

The abbess lowered her veil and turned towards the stranger, who lowered her eyes. The abbess, seeing that she was pale and shivering with emotion, gave her a look that was full of kindness and said: 'You asked to speak to me, Sister. I am ready to hear you.'

'Madame,' said the stranger. 'I was so happy that in my pride I might have thought that even God himself could not destroy my happiness. Now, God has blown it away. I need to weep, I need to repent. I have come to ask you for shelter, so that my sobs may be stifled by the thick walls of your convent; so that my tears, which have carved deep furrows down my cheeks, may no longer make me a laughing stock; and so that God, who may perhaps expect me to be joyful and full of fun, may find me in a sacred refuge, praying at the foot of His altar.'

'I can see that your soul is deeply wounded, because I too know what it means to suffer,' the young abbess replied. 'And in its pain your soul does not know how to distinguish between reality and what it desires. If you need silence, if you need mortification, if you need penitence, Sister, come in here and suffer with us. But if you are looking for a place, where one can ease one's heart in unrestrained sobbing and where you can cry out freely in your despair and where no one stares at you, poor victim as you are, then, Madame, oh, Madame . . .' she said, shaking her head, 'go away, shut yourself up in your room. People will see you much less than you will be seen here and the tapestries in your private chapel will absorb your sobs far better than the bare boards of our cells. As for God, unless He has been forced by some too dreadful sins to turn away from you, then He will see you wherever you are.'

The stranger looked up and stared in astonishment at the young abbess who was saying this to her.

'Madame,' she said, 'should not all those who suffer come to the Lord, and is not your house a holy station on the way to heaven?'

'There is only one way of going to God, Sister,' replied the nun, carried away by her own despair. 'What do you regret? Why do you weep? What do you desire? Society has mistreated you, friendship has let you down, you have been short of money and a transitory pain has led you to believe in pain eternal . . . is that not so? You are suffering now, and you feel that you will always suffer, as when one sees an open wound and thinks that it will never close. But you are wrong. Any wound that is not mortal will heal. So, suffer, then, and let your suffering take its course. You will be cured, and then, if you are chained to us here, another suffering will begin, this time a truly eternal one, implacable and unimagined. You will see the world, to which you cannot return, through a gate of brass, and you will curse the day on which the barrier of this holy hostelry, that you consider to be a station on the road to heaven, was shut behind you. What I am telling you may not be in the rules of my order, I have not been an abbess long enough to know them fully, but it is according to my heart. This is what I see at every moment, not in myself, thank God, but around me.'

'Oh, no, no!' the stranger cried. 'The world is finished for me, and I have lost whatever made me love it. No, fear not, Madame, I shall never have any regret. Oh, I am certain of it! Never!'

'So is your burden more heavy than I thought? Have you lost a reality, not an illusion? Have you been separated for ever from a husband, a child . . . or a friend? In that case I do truly pity you, Madame, because your heart has been pierced through and through, and your ill is incurable. So come to us, Madame, and the Lord will console you. He will replace the relatives or the friends that you have lost with us, who form one great family, a flock with Him as our shepherd. And . . .' the nun added, in a quiet voice, 'if He does not console you, which is possible, well, you will have this last consolation of weeping with me, because I came here, as you have, in search of consolation and have not yet found it.'

'Alas!' the stranger exclaimed. 'Are these the sort of words that I should be hearing? Is this how you support a person in misfortune?'

'Madame,' the mother superior said, holding a hand out to the young woman, as though to push aside the reproach that she had just made. 'Do not speak of misfortune to me. I do not know who you are or what has happened to you, but you do not know what unhappiness is.'

'Oh, you do not know me, Madame,' said the stranger, in a voice of such grief that the mother superior shuddered to hear it. 'Because if you did know me, you would not speak to me in that way. In any case, you are not the judge of the extent of my suffering, because to be able to do so, you should have to have suffered as I do. Meanwhile, welcome me, take me in, open the door of the house of God to me, and from my tears, my cries and my daily sufferings, you will see whether or not I am truly unhappy.'

'Yes,' the mother superior said. 'I can tell from your voice and from your words that you have lost the man whom you loved, is that not so?'

The stranger gave a sob and wrung her hands.

'Oh, yes!' she said.

'Very well, since that is what you wish,' the abbess went on, 'come into the convent. But I warn you, should you be suffering as much as I am, this is what you will have in these cloisters: two pitiless, everlasting walls, which, instead of raising up our thoughts, as they should, to heaven, constantly drag them down to the earth that you will have left behind. Nothing is extinguished, when the blood goes round, the pulse quickens and the heart loves. Isolated though we are and hidden though we think ourselves to be, the dead call us from the depths of their tombs. Why are you leaving the tomb of your dead?'

'Because everything that I have loved in this world is here,' the stranger replied, in a choking voice, falling to her knees in front of the mother superior, who was looking at her in amazement. 'Now you know my secret, Sister; now you can appreciate my pain, Mother. I beg you on my knees – you can see my tears – to accept the sacrifice that I am making to God or rather to grant the favour that I ask. He is buried in the church at Pessac. Let me weep on his tomb, which is here.'

'Who is here? What tomb? Who do you mean? What are you saying?' the mother superior cried, shrinking back from this kneeling woman and looking at her almost in terror.

'When I was happy,' the penitent went on in such a quiet voice that it was covered by the sound of the wind blowing through the trees. 'And I was very happy . . . I was called Nanon de Lartigues. Do you now recognize me and know what I am asking of you?'

The abbess leapt up as though driven by a spring, and, for a moment, with her eyes looking towards heaven and her hands clasped, she remained silent and pale.

'Oh, Madame,' she said finally, in a voice that appeared calm, but behind which one could hear a last tremor of emotion. 'Madame, you don't know me either, if you ask me for permission to come here and weep on a tomb. Don't you know that I sacrificed my freedom, my happiness in this world and all the tears in my heart for the sad joy that you come here asking to share? You are Nanon de Lartigues. I, when I had my name, was called the Viscountess de Cambes.'

Nanon gave a cry, went over to the mother superior and, lifting up the hood covering the nun's dulled eyes, recognized her rival.

'It is her!' Nanon murmured. 'She who was so beautiful when she came to Saint-Georges. Oh, poor woman!'

She took a step back, keeping her eyes fixed on the viscountess and shaking her head.

'Ah!' the viscountess exclaimed, carried away by that satisfaction of pride that comes from knowing that we can suffer more deeply than others. 'Ah! You have just said a kind word, and it does me good. Yes, I have suffered cruelly, and if I am so cruelly changed, it is because I have wept so much – so I am unhappier than you, since you are still beautiful.'

And, as if searching for Canolles, the viscountess raised heavenwards eyes that were shining with the first ray of joy that had lit them in the previous month.

Nanon, still kneeling, hid her face in her hands and burst into tears.

'Alas, Madame,' she said. 'I did not know whom I was addressing, because for the past month I have been unaware of anything that was happening: what kept me beautiful is no doubt that I was mad. Now I am here. I do not wish to make you jealous even unto death, I am merely asking to enter this convent as the humblest of your nuns. You can do what you like with me: you will have the discipline, the dungeon and the *in pace*[1] to use against me if I disobey. But at least from time to time,' she added in a trembling voice, 'you will let me see the resting place of the man whom we have loved so much, won't you?'

And she fell, gasping and exhausted, on the grass.

The viscountess did not reply. Leaning back against the trunk of a sycamore that she had turned to for support, she too seemed ready to expire.

'Oh, Madame, Madame!' cried Nanon. 'You are not answering! You refuse! Well, there is one single treasure remaining to me. It may be that you have nothing of him, yourself . . . But I do have something. Grant my wish, and this treasure is yours.'

Taking a large locket hanging round her neck on a golden chain, which had been hidden in her bosom, she offered it to Madame de Cambes. The locket stayed open in the hand of Nanon de Lartigues.

Claire gave a cry and pounced on the relic, kissing those cold, dry hairs with such savage emotion that it seemed as though her soul had risen to her lips to join her in the kiss.

'Well,' said Nanon, still kneeling and gasping at her feet. 'Do you think that you have ever suffered as I do at this moment?'

'You have triumphed, Madame,' said the Viscountess de Cambes, lifting her up and clasping her in her arms. 'Come, come, Sister, for now I love you more than the whole world, because you have shared this treasure with me.'

Leaning towards Nanon as she raised her gently from the ground, the viscountess let her lips brush the cheek of the woman who had been her rival . . .

'You will be my sister and my friend,' she said. 'Yes, we shall live and die together, speaking about him and praying for him. Come, you are right, he sleeps near here in our church. This was the only favour that I was able to obtain from the woman to whom I had dedicated my life. May God forgive her!'

At these words, Claire took Nanon de Lartigues by the hand and, step by step, so lightly that they were hardly brushing against the grass, they arrived under the mass of limes and firs that hid the church.

The viscountess led Nanon to a chapel, in the midst of which, four inches off the ground, was a simple stone, on which was carved a cross.

Without saying a single word, Madame de Cambes merely pointed at this stone.

Nanon knelt down and kissed the marble. Madame de Cambes leant on the altar, kissing the lock of hair. One of them was trying to get used to the idea of death, the other to dream one last time of life.

A quarter of an hour later, the two women returned to the house. Except to speak to God, neither of them had broken their mournful silence with a single word.

'Madame,' the viscountess said, 'from now on you have your cell in this convent. Would you like it to be next door to mine? In that way we shall be less far apart . . .'

'I thank you most humbly for your offer, Madame,' said Nanon de Lartigues, 'and accept with gratitude. But before I leave the world for ever, let me say a last farewell to my brother, who is waiting for me at the gate and who is also overcome with sorrow.'

'Alas!' said Madame de Cambes, recalling despite herself that Cauvignac had been saved at the expense of his fellow captive's life. 'Go, then, Sister.'

Nanon went out.

BROTHER AND SISTER

Nanon was right. Cauvignac was waiting for her, sitting on a rock, two yards from his horse and looking sadly at it, while the animal itself was cropping the dry grass as far as its reins allowed, raising its head from time to time and looking intelligently at its master.

In front of the adventurer ran the dusty road, disappearing a league ahead into the elm trees on a small hill, which seemed to leave the convent and extend to eternity. You could say – and, little though he was inclined to philosophic notions, our adventurer himself might have thought – that over there was the world, whose noise humbly petered out against this iron grille surmounted by a cross.

Indeed, Cauvignac had attained such a degree of sensitivity that one might believe him to have such thoughts. But he had already thought too long about such sentimental matters for a man of his character; so he recalled his masculine dignity and started regretting having been so weak. 'What!' he exclaimed. 'I, who am so superior to those people of the court in wits, shall I not be their equal in feeling – or at least the lack of it! Damn it! Richon is dead, that's true. Canolles is dead, that's also true. But I'm alive, and I have to say it seems to me that that is the main thing.

'In fact, it's precisely because I'm alive that I think, and when I think, I remember, and when I remember, I'm sad. Poor Richon – what a brave captain he was! And poor Canolles – what a fine gentleman! Hanged, both of them, by all the devils – and through my fault, that of Roland Cauvignac. Ah, that's sad! It chokes me.

'Not to mention that my sister, who has not always had reason to be pleased with me, now has no further reason to keep on the right side of me, since Canolles is dead, and she has been stupid enough to fall out with Monsieur d'Epernon – not to mention that she must have a mortal grudge against me, and as soon as she has a moment will take advantage of it to disinherit me while she is alive.

'That is definitely the real misfortune, not those cursed memories that plague me. Canolles, Richon, Richon, Canolles . . . So? Haven't I seen hundreds of men die? What of it? On my word, there are times when I even regret not having been hanged with them, at least I should have died in good company, while now who knows who'll be with me when I go . . .'

At that moment, the convent bell struck seven. This sound brought Cauvignac back to himself. He remembered that his sister had told him to wait until seven, that the ringing told him Nanon was going to reappear and that he had to play his part in consoling her to the end.

The door did, indeed, open, and Nanon reappeared. She crossed the little courtyard, where Cauvignac might have waited for her, had he wished, because strangers had the right to come into this courtyard: while not entirely profane, it was not yet altogether sacred.

But he had not wanted to go so far, saying that the neighbourhood of monastic buildings, especially convents of women, gave him bad thoughts; so, as we said, he stayed on the road, outside the iron gate.

At the sound of footsteps on the gravel, Cauvignac turned round, and, seeing Nanon, who was still separated from him by the gate, he said, with a great sigh: 'Ah . . . here you are, Little Sister. When I see one of these frightful gates close on some poor woman, I always feel as though I were watching a tombstone closing over a corpse: I don't expect to see one without her nun's habit, or the other without its shroud.'

Nanon smiled sadly.

'Good!' Cauvignac said. 'That's something: you're not weeping, at least.'

'That's true,' said Nanon. 'I can't weep any more.'

'But you can still smile, I'm glad to see. We can go now, can't we? I don't know why, but this place gives me all kinds of ideas.'

'Salutary ones?'

'Salutary? Do you think so? Well, let's not argue about it, though I'm delighted you consider my thoughts in that way. I hope you've made a good stock of them for yourself and that you won't need to come back for a long time.'

Nanon did not reply. She was thinking.

'Among those salutary thoughts,' said Cauvignac, venturing a question, 'I hope you have put in some about forgetting trespasses against us.'

'I may not have found forgetfulness, but forgiveness at least.'

'I should prefer forgetfulness, but no matter. One should not be too fussy, when one is in the wrong. So do you forgive me my trespasses against you, Sister?'

'They are forgiven,' said Nanon.

'Oh! I'm delighted,' said Cauvignac. 'So you will see me in future without disgust?'

'Not only without disgust, but even with pleasure.'

'With pleasure?'

'Yes, my friend.'

'Your friend! Now, Nanon, there's a name that I like, because you are not obliged to give it to me, while you are obliged to call me "Brother". So you will endure my presence beside you.'

'I'm not saying that,' said Nanon. 'Some things are impossible, Roland, and we must bear that in mind.'

'I see,' said Cauvignac, with an even deeper sigh than before. 'An exile! You're sending me away, aren't you? I shall never see you again. Very well, though it pains me not to see you – on my honour it does, Nanon – I know that I deserve it, and I have brought it on myself. In any event, what can I do in France, since peace has been concluded, Guyenne is pacified, and the queen and Madame de Condé are on the way to becoming the best friends in the world? I am not foolish enough to imagine that I am in favour with either one of these two princesses. So the best thing for me to do, is to exile myself, as you say. Therefore, Little Sister, say farewell to this eternal wanderer!

There is a war in Africa. Monsieur de Beaufort is off to fight the infidel, so I can go with him. To tell you the truth, it's not as though I don't think the infidels are a thousand times more in the right than the faithful, but what of it? That's a matter for kings, not for us. You can get killed over there, which is all that matters to me. I'll go: you'll hate me less when I'm dead.'

Nanon, who had listened to this flow of words with bowed head, looked up at Cauvignac, wide-eyed.

'Is that so?' she asked.

'What?'

'What you're thinking of doing, Brother?'

Cauvignac had allowed himself to be carried away by his speech like a man who, devoid of any real feeling, is used to heating himself up with the chatter of his own words. Nanon's question brought him back to earth, and he found himself wondering how to come down from his flight of fancy to something more practical and everyday.

'Why, yes, Little Sister, I swear,' he said. 'By what? I don't know. Come, I'll swear by Cauvignac that I'm really sad and miserable since the death of Richon and more still since . . . In fact, do you know, there, on that rock just now, I was arguing over and over with myself to harden my heart – which up to now I had never heard speak to me and which now is not content with merely beating, but talks, shouts and weeps. Tell me, Nanon, is this what they call remorse?'

This cry was so natural and so full of pain, despite its mocking tone, that Nanon recognized it as coming from the depths of his heart.

'Yes,' she said. 'It is remorse, and you are a better man than I thought.'

'Very well,' said Cauvignac, 'since it is remorse, it's the campaign in Gigery[1] then. Just give me a little something for my travel and equipment, would you, Little Sister? And may I carry all your sorrows away with my own!'

'You shall not go, my friend,' said Nanon. 'And from now on, you shall live in all the prosperity that good fortune can bring. For the past ten years, you have been struggling against misfortune – I don't mean the dangers that you have incurred, because they are those of any soldier. This time, though, you have won life, when another has lost it. So it was God's will that you should live, and my wish, in accordance with His will, is that from today onwards you should enjoy happiness.'

'Come now, Little Sister. What are you saying?' Cauvignac replied. 'What do you mean by that?'

'I mean that you will go to my house in Libourne before it is pillaged, and there you will find, in the secret cupboard behind my Venetian mirror . . .'

'The secret cupboard?'

'Yes, you know it, surely?' Nanon said, with a weak smile. 'Wasn't that where you took two hundred pistoles from last month?'

'Nanon, be fair and admit that I could have taken more, had I wished, because the cupboard was full of gold, but I took only the precise sum that I needed.'

'That's true,' said Nanon. 'And if that is enough to excuse you in your own eyes, I willingly acknowledge it.' Cauvignac blushed and lowered his eyes. 'Why, good Lord!' Nanon went on. 'Forget it. You know very well that I forgive you.'

'How do I know that?' asked Cauvignac.

'Here's the proof: you will go to Libourne and open the cupboard. In it you will find all of my fortune that I have been able to realize: twenty thousand gold écus.'

'What shall I do with it?'

'Take it.'

'Who do you want to have these twenty thousand écus?'

'You, Brother. That's all I was able to make, because as you well know, as I asked nothing for myself and have left Monsieur d'Epernon, my houses and my lands were seized.'

'What are you saying, Sister?' Cauvignac exclaimed, in alarm. 'What are you thinking of?'

'I'm thinking, Roland, that as I said to you, you will take these twenty thousand écus for yourself.'

'For myself? And what about you?'

'I don't need the money.'

'Yes, I see, you have some other money, so much the better. But it's a huge sum, Little Sister. Just think: it's too much for me, at least, all at once.'

'I don't have any other money, I'm just keeping my jewels. I should like to give those to you as well, but they're my dowry to enter this convent.'

Cauvignac started back in surprise.

'Enter the convent?' he cried. 'You, Sister? You want to enter a convent?'

'Yes, my friend.'

'Oh, in heaven's name, don't do that, Little Sister! A convent! You don't know how tedious it is. I can tell you, because I was in a seminary. A convent! Nanon, don't do it, it will kill you!'

'I hope so,' said Nanon.

'Sister, I don't want your money at that price, do you understand? By God! It would burn my fingers.'

'Roland,' Nanon said. 'I'm not going in here in order to make you rich, but to make myself happy.'

'It's mad,' said Cauvignac. 'I'm your brother, Nanon, I won't stand for it.'

'My heart is here already, Roland, what would my body do anywhere else?'

'It's too frightful to contemplate,' said Cauvignac. 'Sister! My dear Nanon, for pity's sake!'

'Not another word, Roland, do you hear me? The money is yours, make good use of it, because your poor Nanon will no longer be there to give you any more, whether she wants to or not.'

'But what good have I done for you to be so kind to me, my poor sister?'

'The only good I ever wanted or expected, the greatest of all, what you brought back from Bordeaux the day he died, the day when I could not die . . .'

'Oh, yes,' said Cauvignac. 'I remember: the lock of hair . . .'

The adventurer hung his head. He felt an odd sensation in his eyes and put a hand to them.

'Another man would weep,' he said. 'I don't know how, but in truth I am suffering as much, if not more.'

'Farewell, Brother,' Nanon said, holding out a hand to the young man.

'No, no, no!' Cauvignac said. 'I shall never willingly say farewell to you. Is it fear that is making you go into this convent? Well, then, we can leave Guyenne and travel about the world together. I, too, have an arrow in my heart that I shall take everywhere with me: the pain of it makes me feel your pain. You can talk to me about him, and I shall tell you about Richon. You will weep, and maybe I shall come to weep with you, and it will do me good. Would you like us to retire to a desert? I shall serve you, respectfully, because you are a true saint. Do you want me to become a monk? No, that I couldn't do, I admit. But don't go into the convent, don't tell me farewell.'

'Farewell, Brother.'

'Do you want to stay in Guyenne, despite the people of Bordeaux and Gascony, in spite of everyone? I no longer have my company of men, but I still have Ferguzon, Barabbas and Carrotel. The four of us could do a lot. We'll look after you – the queen won't be so well protected. And if anyone gets to you or touches a hair on your head, you can say: "The four of them must be dead." *Requiescant in pace*.'

'Farewell,' she said.

Cauvignac was about to reply with some new entreaty, when they heard the sound of a coach coming down the road. A courier was riding ahead of it, wearing the queen's livery.

'What's that?' Cauvignac asked, turning to look back down the road, but without letting go of his sister's hand, which he was holding through the bars of the gate.

The coach, in the manner of the time with its huge coats of arms and open panels, was drawn by six horses and contained eight passengers with a whole army of servants and pages.

Behind it came guards and courtiers on horseback.

'Give way, give way!' cried the courier, cracking his whip at

Cauvignac's horse, which, in actual fact, was standing with quite self-effacing modesty at the side of the road.

The horse reared up in terror.

'Hey, there, friend!' said Cauvignac, letting go of his sister's hand. 'I'd thank to you watch what you're doing.'

'Make way for the queen!' said the courier, continuing on his way.

'The queen! The devil it is!' said Cauvignac. 'We'd better not make things any worse in that direction.' And he pressed himself as close as he could to the wall, holding his horse by its reins.

At that moment, a trace on the coach broke, and the coachman, with a sharp tug, forced the six horses to a halt.

'What's the matter?' asked a voice with a marked Italian accent. 'Why are you stopping?'

'A trace has broken, Monseigneur,' said the coachman.

'Open, open,' said the same voice.

Two lackeys ran forward and opened the door, but before the running board could be lowered, the man with the Italian accent was already standing on the ground.

'Ah! Signor Mazarini,' said Cauvignac. 'He didn't wait to be invited to get out first, I think.'

After him came the queen.

After the queen, Monsieur de La Rochefoucauld.

Cauvignac rubbed his eyes.

After Monsieur de La Rochefoucauld, Monsieur d'Epernon.

'And why did that brother-in-law not get hanged rather than the other?' Cauvignac said.

After Monsieur d'Epernon, Monsieur de La Meilleraie.

After Monsieur de La Meilleraie, the Duke de Bouillon.

Then two ladies-in-waiting.

'I knew that they were not fighting any longer,' said Cauvignac. 'But I didn't realize that they were so well in with one another.'

'Gentlemen,' said the queen, 'instead of waiting here for the trace to be mended, as it's fine, and the evening air is cool, would you like to walk a little?'

'As Your Majesty wishes,' said Monsieur de La Rochefoucauld, with a bow.

'Come here beside me, Duke, and you can tell me some of your fine maxims. You must have written a fair number of them since we last saw one another.'

'Give me your arm, Duke,' said Mazarin to Monsieur de Bouillon. 'I know that you suffer from gout.'

Monsieur d'Epernon and Monsieur de La Meilleraie took up the rear, chatting with the two ladies-in-waiting. All of them were laughing and chatting in the warm rays of the setting sun like a group of friends who had gathered for a party.

'Is it still far from here to Bourcy?' the queen asked. 'You can tell me that, Monsieur de La Rochefoucauld, since you've studied the lie of the land.'

'Three leagues, Madame. We'll be there surely by nine o'clock.'

'That's good. And tomorrow you will start at the crack of dawn to tell our dear cousin, Madame de Condé, that we shall be delighted to see her.'

'Your Majesty,' said the Duke d'Epernon, 'do you see that fine horseman turning his head towards the wall and the lovely lady who vanished when we were getting out of the coach?'

'Yes,' the queen said. 'I saw all that. It appears that they enjoy life at the Convent of Sainte-Radegonde de Pessac.'

At that moment, the coach, which had been repaired, arrived at a trot to join the illustrious pedestrians, who were already twenty paces or so past the convent when it caught up with them.

'Come,' said the queen. 'Let's not tire ourselves, gentlemen. You know that the king is offering us violins this evening.'

They got back into the coach with roars of laughter, then were soon lost in the sound of the carriage wheels.

Cauvignac, pondering deeply on the frightful contrast between this joy passing noisily along the road and the silent grief enclosed in the convent walls, watched them leave. Then, when they were out of sight, he said: 'No matter. I'm happy to know one thing which is that, bad as I am, there are some worse than me. And, by Our Lady, I'm going to try to ensure that there is no one equal to me. I am rich now, it will be easy.'

At that, he remounted his horse with a sigh, cast a final

look at the convent, headed at a gallop towards Libourne and
vanished at the opposite bend in the road to the one round
which the carriage had disappeared, with its load of those
illustrious persons who have played the leading roles in this
story.

We may perhaps meet them again one day, because the
alleged peace that was so badly cemented by the blood of
Richon and Canolles was to prove only a truce, and the
women's war was not over yet . . .

Appendix

*The hanging of Richon, and, in reprisal, that of Canolles, is an histori-
cal event, recounted in histories of the Fronde, though these differ in
certain details, both from each other and from the account given by
Dumas. The following are extracts from five works that Dumas might
have used as the source for* The Women's War: *the first from Petitot's
introduction to his collection of historical documents; the second from
Lenet's memoirs; the third from the memoirs of the Cardinal de Retz
(who, as the coadjutor to the Archbishop of Paris, is mentioned in the
novel); the fourth from the memoirs of the Duke de La Rochefoucauld,
who (like Lenet) plays a leading role in the story; and the fifth from
Sainte-Aulaire's history of the Fronde, published in 1841.*

Note: I have retained the variant spellings of names in these sources.

*Claude-Bernard Petitot, Collection des mémoires relatifs à l'histoire
de France (Paris: Foucault, 1824), pp. 178–9.*

Richon, a distinguished citizen of Bordeaux, was commander of the
Château of Vair on the Dordogne, and was besieged by the Marshal
de La Meilleraye. Betrayed by his garrison, which Mazarin had won
over, he was delivered to the marshal, who announced his intention
of making a major example of a rebel who had been captured bearing
arms. The Princess de Condé, warned of the danger that Richon was
in, at once sent an envoy to La Meilleraye with orders to remind him
that she had prisoners in her own power and to tell him that she would
resort to reprisals. This threat made no impression on the marshal
who ordered Richon to be hanged.

The news of this execution, instead of spreading panic in Bordeaux,
caused the most intense indignation. The Duke de Bouillon, who
was more incensed than the rest, persuaded the princess's council to
determine to kill one of the prisoners, and the chosen victim was one
of the most distinguished, the Marquis de Canoles (*sic*), who had

been captured some time earlier on the Ile Saint-Georges. All the preparations were made for the execution without the unfortunate man having the slightest suspicion of it; and, to make more people complicit in the crime, they had the order confirmed by the thirty-six captains of the town. The princess, whose tears and entreaties had done nothing to assuage the fury of her supporters, begged them at least to delay the execution until the next day, hoping that the condemned man might escape his fate. Her appeals were in vain: they went to arrest Canoles that evening, just as he was merrily disporting himself with some ladies. He was dragged to the port and attached to a gallows. Hardly had he recovered from his first terror, than he asked for a confessor, but this last consolation was inhumanely denied him. 'He's a supporter of Mazarin,' they said. 'He must be damned to hell.'

Memoirs of Pierre Lenet, in *Nouvelle collection des mémoires pour servir à l'histoire de France* (Paris: Michaud and Poujoulat, 1838), vol. II, pp. 330–32.

We learned of the taking of Vaire, and that Richon, having no news of the help that he had been led to expect and there being a large breach in his fort, sent a captain of the Fronsac regiment to capitulate; and this captain betrayed him, having been either won over or intimidated by the Marshal de La Meilleraye, who promised him his life . . .

On the fifth, hearing of the taking of Vaire and Richon, the princess, seeing that there was a danger that he might be killed for having defended a castle against a royal army, sent a messenger to the Marshal de La Meilleraye to say that, if he was treated as a prisoner of war, the same treatment would be accorded to the prisoners that she held in Montrond, Turenne and Bordeaux . . .

The Marquis de Lusignan brought the messenger from Limoges to my house who told me that he had seen Richon hanged in the market in Libourne . . .

The princess, after dinner, called together her council . . . Finally, it was decided unanimously . . . to hang Canot (*sic*), a captain in the old regiment of Navailles, who had been captured a long time before in the Ile Saint-Georges, when it was taken by our men . . .

There were serious consequences from this sentence, which was a truly military one. I explained them, giving my opinion, and, to make it more solemn and more universally agreed, I suggested calling the council before carrying it out . . . One after another, they expressed such strong feelings against Cardinal Mazarin (though we found out later that only the obstinacy of Marshal de La Meilleraye had been responsible) that I have never in my life seen or heard anything like it, and all unanimously called for the death of this public victim, inventing new tortures for him to endure. So the order was given that this sentence, which was passed without being written down, or the prisoner being heard, or any kind of trial, should be carried out at once. The princess wanted to delay it to the next day, but the people's anger was so strong that she could not persuade them ... Though it was late, the execution was carried out on the port of Bordeaux, near the suburb of Les Chartreux, and all that the princess could do was to prevent the prisoners of war from suffering the same fate, so frightful is the anger of the people when it is excited by those in authority, as it was here. In this case, it was extreme. The captain was a Huguenot, but it was not possible to persuade them to allow the poor man a priest who might try to convert him before he died. They said that he was a supporter of Mazarin, so he had to be damned to hell, and if the citizens had not been armed, he would have been torn to pieces by the mob which followed as they took him to the gallows.

Cardinal de Retz, *Mémoires* (Paris: Pléiade, 1956), p. 355.

The deputies of the parliament of Bordeaux went to the court at Libourne. They were imperiously commanded to open their gates so as to receive the king with all his troops. They replied that it was one of their privileges to protect the person of a king when he was in their town. Marshal de La Meilleraye advanced between the Dordogne and the Garonne. He captured the Château of Vayre, where Richon had three hundred men, for the people of Bordeaux, and the cardinal had him hanged in Libourne, a hundred yards from the king's residence there. In reprisal, Monsieur de Bouillon had them hang Canolle (*sic*), an officer in Monsieur de La Meilleraye's army. He then attacked the Ile Saint-Georges, which was lightly defended by La Mothe de Las and where the Chevalier de La Valette was mortally wounded.

Duke de La Rochefoucauld, *Maximes et mémoires* (Paris: Rivages, 2001), pp. 242–3.

After that, the troops of Marshal de La Meilleraye and those of the Duke d'Epernon pressed Bordeaux more closely. They even recaptured the Ile Saint-Georges, which is in the Garonne, four leagues above the town, where some fortifications had started to be built. It was defended for three or four days with some vigour, because at each high tide a fresh regiment was sent there from Bordeaux which relieved the guard. General de La Valette was wounded there and died a few days later.

But finally the boats that had brought some troops, which were due to take back those being relieved, were sunk by a battery that Marshal de La Meilleraye had set up on the bank of the river, and both the soldiers and their officers were so afraid that they all surrendered and were taken prisoners of war. So the people of Bordeaux lost the island, which was important to them, and at the same time twelve hundred men of their best infantry. This rout and the arrival of the king at Libourne, who at once attacked the Château de Vaire, two leagues from Bordeaux, threw the town into great consternation. The parliament and the people saw themselves on the brink of being besieged by the king, and they were lacking everything necessary to defend themselves. No help came to them from Spain, and fear had finally induced the parliament to assemble to debate whether deputies should be sent to ask for peace on whatever conditions it might please the king to grant them, when it was learned that Vaire had been captured and that the governor, called Richon, having surrendered on terms, had been hanged. This severity, by which the cardinal thought he would cause terror and division in Bordeaux, had quite the contrary effect; for, the news having come at a time when minds were, as I said, worried and uncertain, the Duke de Bouillon and the Duke de La Rochefoucauld were able to take such advantage of the situation that they put their affairs in a better state than they had been so far by having hanged at the same time a man called Canoles (sic), who had commanded in the Ile Saint-Georges the first time that the people of Bordeaux had captured it, when he had surrendered to them on terms. But, so that the parliament and the people should share with the generals responsibility for an action that was both necessary and daring, they had Canoles judged by a council of war presided over by the princess and the Duke d'Enghien, which was made up not only of the officers commanding the troops, but also of two deputies of the parliament, who were always present, and thirty-six captains of the town. The poor gentleman, whose only crime was his bad luck, was condemned with a single voice, and the people were so incensed that they hardly gave him time to be executed before tearing his body into shreds. This action astonished the court and gave renewed vigour to the people of Bordeaux.

Louis de Beaupoil, Comte de Sainte-Aulaire, *Histoire de la Fronde*, new edition (Paris: Ducrocq, 1841), vol. II, Chapter XIII, p. 40.

This was the state of affairs when a letter from the king, dated from Poitiers, announced his immediate arrival. His Majesty ordered parliament to send deputies to Libourne to receive orders and threatened severe punishment in the event of resistance. Far from being intimidated, the parliament replied with a proclamation stating that 'Cardinal Mazarin would not be welcomed in the town; that His Majesty was very humbly entreated to enter without troops and to entrust the protection of his person to his loyal subjects, the people of the city of Bordeaux' . . .

Cardinal Mazarin, having no remaining hope of reaching an agreement, wished to mark the king's arrival with some exploit that would spread fear of his might and attacked Vayres, the château of the President de Gourgues, which was fortified in the manner of the time and which defended the approaches to Bordeaux. A brave commoner called Richon, a native of Guîtres, a small town nearby, rushed to the fort with three hundred militiamen. He courageously withstood several attacks and drove back the assailants, but a soldier of the garrison, who had been bribed with money, showed the troops a secret gate. The Marquis de Biron broke into the fort, and Richon, overwhelmed by superior numbers, was forced to surrender, taken to Libourne and immediately ordered to be hanged.

The court was outraged by such severity: Mademoiselle de Montpensier and the Marquis de Biron strongly entreated that the prisoner should be spared, but Mazarin remained inflexible: 'Richon, who was not even a gentleman, had dared to defend a château against a royal army and it was important to shock the townsfolk with an exemplary punishment.' The unfortunate man was even refused the mercy of being beheaded, as he strongly begged, and he was strung up on a gallows that had been set up in the market place at Libourne, where his body remained exposed to view.

·When the townsfolk of Bordeaux learned of Richon's execution, they wanted in their fury to murder every royalist that the chances of war had delivered into their hands. Even the magistrates judged that this was a case when the cruel principle of reprisal should be applied, and the Chevalier de Canolles, Commander of the Ile Saint-Georges, was the designated victim. He was generally liked for his easy and sociable manner. The archers sent to arrest him found him enjoying a meal with friends. He was not at all alarmed, and when his warrant was read out to him, he could still not imagine that he was to be killed. The Princess de Condé was very concerned about his fate, being always both compassionate and fearless. She once again assembled the council of war, asked for all the captains of the Bordeaux militia to attend and tried to convince them that they were risking a great deal by following the barbarous example that the enemy had just given them.

All these entreaties were useless and the princess could not even manage to obtain a stay of execution that she had demanded in the hope of allowing the prisoner to escape. The execution took place on the port of Bordeaux and Canolles's body had to remain hanging from a gibbet facing the road to Libourne for as long as that of Richon was displayed in the market of that town.

Notes

BOOK I
NANON DE LARTIGUES

1. *one quarter of a league away*: A league is about four kilometres (2.5 miles); so the river was about a kilometre away.

2. *You can earn a crown*: In fact, an écu, a silver coin worth three livres (the livre was the basic unit of currency, originally worth one pound of silver). The value of the livre in seventeenth-century France still varied from one province to another. This is one reason why it is more or less impossible to give modern equivalents for the money of the period (even assuming that Dumas himself had any accurate notion of what the coins represented in terms of wages and purchasing power two centuries before his own time). See also notes 18 and 29, Book I.

3. *letter of attestation*: The term that Dumas uses is *blanc seing*, which is a blank document, already signed but not filled in.

4. *Duke d'Epernon*: Bernard de Nogaret de La Valette, Duke d'Epernon (1592–1661), was governor of the province of Guyenne.

5. *Guyenne*: A former province of south-west France, which in medieval times, with Gascony, formed the duchy of Aquitaine. After Bordeaux had been recaptured from the English in 1453, it became the capital of the province of Guyenne (or Guienne).

6. *the horribly tight-fisted government of Monsieur de Mazarin ... a lot of trouble in the capital*: Cardinal Jules Mazarin (Giulio Mazarini, 1602–61), a papal envoy, was naturalized as a French subject in 1634 and succeeded Cardinal Richelieu as prime minister in 1642. The object of much suspicion (like Queen Anne of Austria) because of his foreign origin, he was a strong supporter of the young king, and one of those who helped to found the absolute power of Louis XIV. He thus became one of the main

targets of the Frondeurs, who also reacted against his taxation policies (see Introduction).

7. *coadjutor*: Jean-François-Paul de Gondi, Cardinal de Retz (1613–79), was coadjutor (or assistant) to the Archbishop of Paris, a post of considerable power. He joined the Frondeurs against Mazarin, which led to his eventual disgrace and the retirement during which he wrote the most celebrated memoirs of the period, an important source for our knowledge of the Fronde (see Appendix).

8. *Monsieur de Beaufort*: François de Vendôme, Duke de Beaufort (1616–69), was implicated in the conspiracy of Cinq-Mars (see note 107) and a leading member of the Fronde against Mazarin. The Duchess de Montbazon was his mistress.

9. *Madame de Longueville*: The Duke de La Rochefoucauld's mistress.

10. *Orléans*: Gaston, Duke d'Orléans (1608–60), son of Henri IV and Marie de' Médicis, was a lifelong conspirator, involved in the Cinq-Mars conspiracy (see note 9, Book III) and subsequently in the conflict of the princes against Mazarin in the Fronde. He was exiled in 1652.

11. *the Parliament*: The Paris *parlement* was established in the mid-fourteenth century as a higher court or court of appeal, and from the following century provincial *parlements* were set up in a number of major towns, including one in Bordeaux, in 1462, which features in Dumas's novel. With time, all the *parlements* acquired a range of judicial and administrative functions, but the one in Paris became the focus of opposition to Mazarin during the Fronde. In this translation, 'Parliament' refers to the Paris *parlement*, while the Bordeaux *parlement* is consistently referred to as the 'parliament of Bordeaux'. The Paris Parliament was a body of much greater power and significance than the parliament of Bordeaux.

12. *Monsieur de Condé . . . fighting for France*: The Prince de Condé was one of the most famous and successful French generals of the time, particularly after his victory at Rocroi (1643) against the Spaniards. Eight years earlier, France had entered the Thirty Years' War against Spain. However, shortly before the battle, in May 1643, Louis XIII died, a fact that the young Condé kept from his troops, in order to avoid demoralizing them. It was his skill in tackling a much larger Spanish force that eventually won the day.

13. *the princes' cause*: The so-called princes' Fronde was occasioned

by the arrest in 1651 of the Prince de Condé (see Introduction).

14. *broken on the wheel*: The punishment for aristocrats, who were spared the indignity of hanging.

15. *I could open the way . . . a successor to the Governor of Guyenne and stop the civil war*: D'Epernon's unpopularity as Governor of Guyenne was one of the causes of the Fronde and of the strength of the anti-government forces in Bordeaux (see Introduction).

16. *At this maxim . . . Boileau would put in verse*: The poet Nicholas Boileau-Despréaux (1636–1711), one of the dominant cultural figures of his age and an important arbiter of classical literary taste, wrote in his mock-heroic poem *Le Lutrin* (1674–83): '. . . remember this: A dinner once reheated never tasted good' (Book I, ll. 103–4).

17. *paletot*: The long, loose jacket worn by a musketeer.

18. *the thousand louis*: The gold louis was worth between 10 and 24 livres (see note 2, Book I).

19. *Gaston d'Orléans*: Gaston d'Orléans (1608–60), brother of King Louis XIII, was leader of the Orléanist faction in the Fronde (each of the main protagonists in opposition to Mazarin having his own supporters). (See also note 10, Book I.)

20. *Oedipus*: Oedipus, King of Thebes, gained a reputation for wisdom after solving the riddle set by the Sphinx, which had asked what animal walks on four legs in the morning, on two legs in the afternoon, and on three in the evening. The answer that Oedipus gave was: man, who walks on all fours as a baby, on two legs as an adult and with a stick in the evening of his life.

21. *The Duke d'Epernon*: See notes 4 and 5, Book I.

22. *parliament of Bordeaux*: The *parlements* were local courts and provincial administrative bodies. See note 11, Book I.

23. *the princess*: The Princess de Condé, wife of Louis II de Bourbon, Prince de Condé, a soldier, who was imprisoned because of his opposition to Mazarin (see Introduction). During her husband's imprisonment, the princess was the figurehead of the Frondeurs.

24. *my young Nestor*: Nestor was the oldest and wisest of the Greeks at the time of the Trojan War (see Homer's *Iliad*).

25. *Agen*: A town in south-west France, on the Garonne.

26. *that inseparable friend of Henri IV*: Jean-Louis de Nogaret, Duke d'Epernon (1554–1642), a governor of Provence who was, as Dumas says, a close friend of King Henri IV, the king who was assassinated for religious reasons by Ravaillac in 1610 and succeeded by his son, who reigned as Louis XIII until 1643.

27. *Catherine de' Médicis*: Wife of Henri II, Catherine de' Médicis (1519–89) was mother of Marguerite de Valois, who married Henri de Navarre, the future King Henri IV. After his divorce from Marguerite, Henri married another member of the Florentine Medici family in 1600, Marie de' Médicis (1573–1642), who became regent after his death.

28. *Mazarin*: See note 6, Book I.

29. *five hundred pistoles*: A pistole was a gold coin worth about the same amount as a louis (see note 2, Book I).

30. *the princes of Condé, Conti and Longueville*: The three children of Henri de Bourbon, cousin of King Henri IV of France, were: Louis, Prince de Condé, his brother, Armand, Prince de Conti, and their sister, Anne-Geneviève, who married Henri II d'Orléans, Duke de Longueville. All three men – Louis, Armand and their brother-in-law, Henri – were imprisoned in 1650 because of their opposition to Mazarin (see Introduction).

31. *Cyrano de Bergerac*: Though he was immortalized in the nineteenth-century play by Edmond de Rostand as a frustrated lover with a large nose, Cyrano de Bergerac (1619–55) was in fact a remarkable writer, the author of essays, plays and a fantasy about a journey to the moon called *L'Autre Monde* (not published until 1657, after his death), which was a satire on the society, politics and religion of his time. He started as an opponent of Mazarin, then rallied to the royalist cause against the Frondeurs.

32. *Monsieur de La Rochefoucauld*: François, Duke de La Rochefoucauld (1613–80), who played a prominent part in the Fronde, was an ally of the Prince de Condé. He writes about the events which form the background to the novel in his memoirs, but he is best remembered for his maxims, written during his retirement after the failure of the Fronde (*Maximes*, 1665), which express his disillusionment in brief, witty and often cynical comments on human nature. Dumas makes him one of the key figures in this novel (see Introduction and Appendix).

33. *Under the other cardinal*: Cardinal Richelieu (1585–1642), the powerful prime minister of Louis XIII, whose death, shortly before that of the king, helped to cause a power vacuum in the country (see Introduction).

34. *the Battle of Corbie*: The Battle of Corbie (1636), in Picardy, took place during the campaign by Louis XIII's first minister, Cardinal Richelieu, against the royal family of Austria.

35. *Collioure*: Wine from Collioure, in what is now the southern French region of Languedoc-Roussillon.

36. *Perhaps too, as a Huguenot ... by drinking water and eating roots*: 'Huguenot' is a general term for the members of various Protestant faiths. The country had been divided by religious wars during the previous century, with a number of noble families adopting the reformed faiths. The St Bartholemew's Day massacres in August 1572, instigated by Catherine de' Médicis and her son, King Charles IX, were the most violent attempt to repress the Huguenots. During the reign of Henri IV, however, they were guaranteed certain rights by the Edict of Nantes (1598).

37. *Ganymede*: In Greek mythology, a beautiful Trojan youth whom Zeus took to Olympus and made the cupbearer of the gods.

38. *Igne tantum perituri ... who was afraid of drowning*: It has not been possible to trace the source of this obscure song, which Canolles cites for Richon's benefit. However, the Latin verse implies that there was a prediction that the Prince de Condé would die by fire, so, during a crossing of the Rhine he was reassuring his companions that since they were with him, neither he, nor therefore they, would be drowned.

39. *a martingale for trente-et-quarante*: A card game, a bit like pontoon, involving two rows of cards, in which the points must not be less than thirty-one or more than forty. A 'martingale' is a system for winning by progressively increasing one's stake.

40. *Vayres*: A small town with a castle that used to belong to King Henri IV, on the Dordogne river, north-west of Bordeaux.

41. *the Crispins and the Mascarilles of his day*: Typical names of servants in comedies by the dramatist Molière (Jean-Baptiste Pocquelin, 1622–73) and his contemporaries.

42. *Rabelaisian*: François Rabelais (?1494–1553) is famous for the bawdy humour of his stories *Pantagruel* (1532) and *Gargantua* (1534–5).

43. *Céladon*: the shepherd who is the hero of the pastoral novel, *L'Astrée* (1607–27), by Honoré d'Urfé (1567–1625). The reference is obliquely quite apt. Céladon is sent away by Astrée because she thinks that he has been unfaithful to her; he later returns in the disguise of a girl.

44. *I'll discount it*: Bills of exchange (which, like promissory notes, were documents requesting a third party to pay a certain sum at a given date in the future) could be 'discounted' (that is bought or sold before the date when they fell due, with a deduction for interest).

45. *Greek like Homer, Latin like Cicero and theology like Jan Hus*: Cauvignac implies that the Greek poet, Homer (c.800 BC), the

Roman orator, Cicero (106–43 BC) and the Czechoslovakian religious reformer, Jan Hus (*c.*1372–1415) were experts in their fields, as he is himself.

46. *Pico della Mirandolas, Erasmuses and Descartes*: Famous philosophers. Count Giovanni Pico della Mirandola (1453–94), was an Italian Platonist philosopher, Desiderius Erasmus (1466–1536) was a Dutch humanist and René Descartes (1596–1650) was the French thinker who gave his name to Cartesian philosophy.

47. *the Trappist order*: The Cistercian Order of the Strict Observance was in fact founded in 1664 by Armand-Jean de Rancé at the monastery of La Trappe. The Trappists are famous for their vow of silence.

48. *Dunois, Duguesclin, a Bayard . . . fearless, blameless knight*: The three names are those of famous knights. Jean, Comte de Dunois, the Bastard of Orleans (1403–68), was one of the companions of Joan of Arc at the end of the Hundred Years' War; Bertrand du Guesclin (1320–80) was a Breton knight in the early part of the Hundred Years' War; and Pierre Terrail, Seigneur de Bayard (1473–1524) served most of his life in the French army, fighting in Italy and Spain. It was the last of the three who earned the nickname '*chevalier sans peur et sans reproche*' – the fearless and blameless (or untainted) knight.

49. *I would not . . . Sforza . . . ask what is meant by fear*: The condottieri were mercenaries employed by the Italian city states, the most famous of whom was Muzio Attendolo, nicknamed 'Sforza' (1369–1424).

50. *as Plautus says . . . foreign to me*: Cauvignac is confusing the two best-known Roman comic dramatists: Titus Maccius Plautus (*c.*254–184 BC) and Publius Terentius Afer (Terence, *c.*185–159 BC). It was, in fact, the latter who wrote the line that Cauvignac quotes, in his *Heauton Timoroumenos* ('The Self Tormentor', *c.*163 BC).

51. *the Abbé de Gondi*: See note 7, Book I and Appendix.

52. *wheel*: The type of gun used by Pompée was an arquebus of the wheel-lock type, in which when the trigger mechanism was released it spun a wheel against a flint, letting off sparks. These then ignited the gunpowder in the pan and discharged the shot.

53. *Don Quixote*: The hero of Miguel de Cervantes Saavedra's (1547–1616) novel *Don Quixote* (1605) attacked some windmills, under the impression that they were armed knights.

54. *Baron des Adrets*: François de Beamont, Baron des Adrets (1513–

87) was a leader of the Huguenots during the wars of religion, who is said to have impressed even his own side by his ruthlessness and cruelty.

55. *Horatius pretended to flee*: Lempriere's *Classical Dictionary* (1828) tells the story as follows: 'Horatii . . . three brave Romans, born at the same birth, who fought against the Curiatii, about 667 years before Christ. This celebrated fight was fought between the hostile camps of the people of Alba and Rome, and on their success depended the victory. In the first attack, two of the Horatii were killed, and the only surviving one, by joining artifice to valour, obtained an honourable trophy: by pretending to fly from the field of battle, he easily separated his antagonists, and, in attacking them one by one, he was enabled to conquer them all.'

56. *the viscount's Barb*: A north African breed of horse.

57. *but like Virgil's Orpheus . . . he embraced only air*: In Greek myth, when Orpheus's wife Eurydice died, he was allowed to visit her in the Underworld and so charmed Pluto with his singing that the king of the Underworld permitted him to take her back to earth, provided she walked behind him and he did not look round while they were leaving his domain. Unfortunately, Orpheus was unable to resist the temptation, and her shade vanished again into the Underworld. Virgil describes the scene in the *Georgics*, Book IV (ll. 485–503), in a passage that is probably the one to which Dumas refers.

58. *Monsieur de la Calprenède's Cléopâtre . . . Mademoiselle de Scudéry's Grand Cyrus*: These were three popular romances of the day. Gauthier de Costes, Seigneur de la Calprenède (*c*.1610–63) wrote *Cléopâtre* in 1648. Madeleine de Scudéry (1608–1701) was one of the most prolific novelists of her time; *Artamène, ou Le Grand Cyrus* (1649–53) was probably her most popular work. For Honoré d'Urfé, see note 43, Book I.

59. *the Great Condé*: Louis II de Bourbon, Prince de Condé (1621–86), uncle of Louis XIV. Led the French Army against the Spaniards at Rocroi in 1643 and Lens in the Netherlands in 1648, and against the forces of the Holy Roman Empire at Nordlingen in Germany in 1645. Later on, he opposed the king during the Fronde, at the time this novel is set (see Introduction).

60. *facchino italiano*: An Italian porter or general servant. *Modi di facchino* means 'coarse manners'.

61. *Anne of Austria*: Anne of Austria (1601–66), widow of Louis XIII and Queen Regent during the minority of her son, Louis

XIV, is a central figure in Dumas's *The Three Musketeers* (1844) and its sequels. (See Introduction.)

62. *The princess, a Themistocles in a mobcap, has her Miltiades in skirts*: Miltiades (c. 550–489 BC) led the Greek army to victory at the Battle of Marathon, but was later disgraced and died in prison. Themistocles (c. 514–449 BC) was his successor as general of the Athenian armies. So the Princess de Condé is Themistocles, her mother-in-law, Miltiades.

63. *the laurels of Madame de Longueville . . . prevent her from sleeping*: Anne-Geneviève de Bourbon, Duchess of Longueville (1619–79) was the sister of the Prince de Condé and reputed to be the most beautiful woman of her day. She was a leading figure in the Fronde and appears in several of Dumas's other novels about this period.

64. *Monsieur de Saint-Aignan*: François-Honorat de Beauvilliers, Duke de Saint-Aignan (1607–87) was a soldier and counsellor of the king, who also distinguished himself as a patron of literature and the arts, and a member of the French Academy.

65. *Monsieur Pierre Lenet*: Pierre Lenet (?–1671), procurator-general and counsellor of state, came from a family that had long been in the service of the princes of Condé. He was generally admired for his intellect. However, the rest of his character, as it appears in the novel, is the invention of Dumas. Lenet's memoirs (published in *Nouvelle collection des mémoires pour servir à l'histoire de France* (Paris: Michaud and Poujoulat 1838, vol. II)), were certainly one of Dumas's sources for the history of the period, since he mentions them in the novel.

66. *Duke de La Rochefoucauld*: Rochefoucauld (see note 32, Book I) was Prince de Marsillac until the death of his father in 1650.

67. *Fama nocet*: 'Fame is harmful.' This Latin tag, sometimes used as a heraldic device, may be taken from the remark by the historian Publius Cornelius Tacitus (AD c. 55–120) that a good reputation may be as dangerous as a bad one (in *Agricola*, 5).

68. *Have you forgotten . . . the Grand Prior de Vendôme, Marshal d'Ornano and Puy-Laurent . . . worth its weight in arsenic*: These were victims of Richelieu, who imprisoned them in the Château de Vincennes. The fact that they all died in the same dungeon explains the remark about that particular jail being 'worth its weight in arsenic' – a particularly deadly place of incarceration.

69. *like Achilles, she had retired to her tent*: After the Greeks plundered the city of Lyrnessus, in Cilicia, Agamemnon deprived the warrior Achilles of the girl, Briseis, a captive who had been

Achilles's share of the booty, so he refused to fight, only coming back to the field after the death of his friend Patroclus (see Homer, *The Iliad*, Books I and II).

70. *constable Anne de Montmorency*: Anne, Duke of Montmorency (1473–1567), was constable (or chief military officer) of France under King François I. He played a leading role in the sixteenth-century wars of religion.

71. *Hôtel de Bourgogne*: The main theatre of Paris, on the right bank of the Seine.

72. *the Duke de Saint-Simon*: Louis de Rouvroy, Duke de Saint-Simon (1675–1755), was the author of celebrated memoirs of the court of Louis XIV.

73. *false Duke d'Enghien ... false Princess de Condé*: The story of the Princess de Condé's escape from Chantilly is told in Claude-Bernard Petitot's *Collection des mémoires relatifs à l'histoire de France* (Paris: Foucault, 1824), vol. XXXV, pp. 166–8. For the purposes of the story, Dumas has changed several details. The officer sent by the queen and Mazarin to prevent the princess's escape was called Du Vouldy. The Dowager Princess did, indeed, pretend to be ill. An Englishwoman called Gerber was substituted for the princess, and the Duke d'Enghien, whose place was taken by a boy of his own age, was disguised as a girl.

74. *ruelle*: Literally a 'small street': the part of the bedchamber used by ladies for receiving guests.

BOOK II

MADAME DE CONDÉ

1. *a gesture that has since become associated with a greater man*: Napoleon Bonaparte (1769–1821), Emperor of France.

2. *Don Japhet of Armenia*: The Quixotic hero of the play *Don Japhet of Armenia* (1651–2) by Paul Scarron (1610–60).

3. *Guitauts and Miossens*: Soldiers who had done service to the royal family and been rewarded for it. Guitaut appears as a character in Dumas's play, *The Youth of Louis XIV*, the Captain of the Guards, who, on Anne of Austria's orders, arrested the three princes, Condé, Conti and Longueville. He is also mentioned in the memoirs of the Duke de La Rochefoucauld (*Maximes et mémoires* (Paris: Rivages, 2001)), who says that he was appointed Governor of Saumur as a reward.

4. *some ruddy Vatel*: François Vatel, a celebrated chef of the house

of Condé, who, according to Madame de Sévigné's letters, committed suicide after the fish failed to arrive in time for a dinner that he was serving for King Louis XIV.

5. *the natural heir*: Léon Bouthillier, Count de Chavigny et Buzancais (1608–52) became one of King Louis XIII's chief ministers after the death of Cardinal Richelieu in 1642 and was rumoured to be Richelieu's son (a fact that Dumas mentions in his novel *Twenty Years After* (1845)).

6. *Monsieur de Turenne*: Henri de La Tour d'Auvergne, Viscount de Turenne (1611–75) and younger brother of the Duke de Bouillon, distinguished himself in the Thirty Years' War and was made a marshal of France in 1643. However, like his brother, he was implicated in the conspiracy of Cinq-Mars (see note 9, Book III).

7. *the Pandects of Justinian*: Justinian (*c.*482–565 AD) became emperor of Byzantium in 527 and was famous for his books of laws, including the *Pandects* (533).

8. *the bill of Parliament . . . no foreigner can ever be a minister in France*: Among those who came from Italy to the French court with Marie de' Médicis (see note 27, Book I) was Concino Concini, later marquis, and Marshal d'Ancre. He exercised an important influence over the queen during the minority of Louis XIII and attracted great hostility from the nobles, particularly the Condé family. He was assassinated in 1617.

9. *Pico della Mirandola*: See note 46, Book I.

10. *Against a certain Biscarros . . . the heir of his wife, an Orléanist*: That is to say, a supporter of Gaston d'Orléans against Mazarin (see note 10, Book I).

11. *the Revenue*: The French text refers to two kinds of taxes under the Old Regime (the one which existed before the French Revolution of 1789): the *aides*, which were a form of purchase tax, and the *gabelle*, a tax on salt. Taxation was a particular cause of popular unrest under the monarchy.

12. *I am His Majesty's exempt*: An exempt was an officer of the police.

13. *the crime of lèse-majesté*: Treason.

14. *He was subjected to the torture of the boot . . . the eighth wedge*: The torture of the boot (or *brodequin*) was one of the most severe, almost always resulting in permanent injury. It took various forms, all based on the principle of encasing the victim's feet and legs in a device that could be tightened to crush the bones. In some cases, the tightening was done by hammering

wedges into the boot; eight was considered to be the maximum.

15. *as beadle at Saint-Sauveur*: The beadle, like the Swiss guards at the Vatican, would have carried a pike.

16. *Camillus*: Marcus Furius Camillus (446–365 BC), Roman general and political leader. According to the historian Livy, when Camillus was besieging Falerii, a schoolmaster of the town offered to betray the sons of some of its leading citizens to him; Camillus responded to this treacherous act by getting the young men to beat the schoolmaster back inside the gates.

17. *Some thought they were serving Parliament . . . some others the King of England . . . to recover his crown*: Charles Stuart, son of King Charles I, went into exile in France in 1649 after his father's execution and did, indeed, lead an expedition into Scotland in 1650 in an attempt to recover the throne. He was defeated by Cromwell.

18. *et fugit ad salices*: A quotation from Virgil, *Eclogues* (Book III, l. 65): 'and runs away to the willow trees'. The whole passage reads: 'Galatea throws me an apple and runs away to the willow trees, hoping that I have seen her.' Cauvignac is implying that Nanon wants someone to see through her disguise.

19. *Barabbas*: Barabbas shares his name with the thief who was released in place of Christ (Matthew 27:16).

20. *A fine name, an old name, well reputed from the scriptures . . . much hanged and burned in my family*: As a Protestant, Canolles would know the Bible and base his faith on it, while the Catholic Barabbas would take his knowledge of religion from what he heard in church (including his own name in the Easter service). Another mark of Canolles's Protestantism is his knowledge of the Psalms. He goes on to refer delicately to the religious persecution of Huguenots in the previous century.

21. *the memory of Buckingham*: Anne of Austria's affair with the Duke of Buckingham is a central theme in the plot of Dumas's *The Three Musketeers*.

22. *siege of Montauban and the Battle of Corbie*: Louis XIII besieged Montauban in 1620 during the religious war against the Huguenots. For the Battle of Corbie, see note 34, Book I.

23. *the Prince de Marsillac*: The new Duke de La Rochefoucauld. In his memoirs, he describes how he used his father's funeral as an opportunity to assemble an army of the nobility who supported the princes. See François de La Rochefoucauld, *Maximes et mémoires* (Paris: Rivages, 2001), pp. 230–41 and note 3, Book II.

24. *like a Clorinda or a Bradamante*: Heroines, respectively, of
    Torquato Tasso's *Gerusalemme Liberata* ('Jerusalem Delivered',
    1581) and Ludvico Ariosto's *Orlando Furioso* (1516).

25. *I think that one must be content . . . to accomplish anything*: The
    quotation is not, in fact, from La Rochefoucauld's memoirs, but
    from the self-portrait ('Portrait of the Duke de La Rochefoucauld
    written by himself') which is included as a preface to his memoirs
    in *Nouvelle collection des mémoires pour servir à l'histoire de
    France* (Paris, 1838, vol. V, p. 378), which is Dumas's probable
    source. He abridges and misquotes slightly. In full, the passage
    reads: 'However, there is nothing that I would not do to ease the
    suffering of an afflicted person, and this even includes showing
    him a lot of compassion in his woes; for unfortunate people are
    so silly that this has the greatest possible benefit for them. But I
    also believe that one should be content with showing it and be
    most wary of feeling it: this is a passion that is good for naught
    in a well-made soul, one that only serves to weaken the heart. It
    should be left to the common people, who, never acting from
    reason, need passion to accomplish anything.' The passage, illus-
    trating La Rochefoucauld's belief that the superior being should
    act from reason alone, is taken by Dumas to show his lack of
    human feeling and moral sense.

BOOK III
VISCOUNTESS DE CAMBES

1. *Rocroi, Nordlingen and Lens*: The Prince de Condé distinguished
   himself in the war against Spain and the Hapsburgs at Rocroi
   (1643), Nordlingen (1645) and Lens (1648).

2. *I have read, Madame . . . but throughout Italy*: The story of
   Agrippina the Elder (14 BC–AD 33), wife of Germanicus, is told
   by the historian Publius Cornelius Tacitus (AD *c*.55–*c*.117) in his
   Annals (Books II and III).

3. *Hardly had the princess got through the gate . . . and the air
   perfumed*: La Rochefoucauld (*Maximes et mémoires*, p. 237)
   describes the scene as follows: 'As soon as it was known in
   Bordeaux that she and the Duke d'Enghien were to arrive at
   Lormont near the town, public signs of celebration were
   observed. A very great number of people came out to meet them,
   their way was covered with flowers and the boat which was
   bringing them was followed by all those that were on the river.

The vessels in the port saluted them with all their artillery and so they entered Bordeaux . . .'

4.   *the life of Reilly*: In fact, the reference is to a certain Roi d'Yvetot, who had a proverbially easy time of it, 'rising late and going to bed early', in the song by the popular poet Pierre-Jean de Béranger (1780–1857). Of course, there is an anachronism in Canolles referring to this (which is why I feel justified in translating it by the similarly anachronistic 'life of Reilly').

5.   *Aemilius Paulus was defeated at Cannae . . . Attila at Châlons*: Aemilius Paulus and Terentius Varro were the two Roman consuls who in 216 BC led a much stronger army against Hannibal and suffered Rome's greatest military defeat at Cannae. Gnaeus Pompeius Magnus (or Pompey, 106–48 BC), was a member, with Julius Caesar and Crassus, of the first triumvirate; later he opposed Caesar and was defeated by him at Pharsalia in 48 BC. Attila (AD *c.*406–53), King of the Huns, ravaged the Eastern Roman Empire during 445–50; after making peace with Theodosius, he invaded the Western Empire and was defeated at Châlons by Aëtius in 451.

6.   *You will understand that it is only . . . to mollify them*: This is not one of La Rochefoucauld's maxims, but very much in the spirit of maxim 42: 'We promise according to our hopes and keep our promises according to our fears' (*Maximes et mémoires*).

7.   *Château-Trompette*: The fortress in Bordeaux, which was used as a prison. Built at the end of the Hundred Years' War, it was destroyed during the Fronde after the events described in Dumas's novel, then rebuilt by Louis XIV and finally destroyed in 1819.

8.   *Hardly had he been presented . . . seven sages of Greece . . . Horatius Cocles . . . wiles of Ulysses*: As usual, Dumas likes to include a few references to classical history and myth. The seven sages were in fact rather more in number, since there is disagreement in Greek sources on which wise men were distinguished enough to qualify for inclusion in their number. Horatius Cocles was a legendary Roman hero who defended the bridge across the Tiber against the Etruscans. Ulysses (Odysseus) was the fictional Greek hero who is sometimes credited with having had the idea of using the Wooden Horse as a means to get inside the besieged town of Troy; his wanderings after the war are the subject of Homer's epic *The Odyssey*.

9.   *Monsieur de Bouillon . . . the same scaffold as Cinq-Mars . . . if not in law*: Henri Coeffier Ruzé d' Effiat, Marquis de Cinq-Mars,

was leader of a group of noblemen in a plot against Richelieu, the subject of a novel (*Cinq-Mars*, 1826) by Alfred de Vigny and an opera of the same name by Charles Gounod (1818–93), which was first performed in 1877. Cinq-Mars was executed in 1642. Among the main supporters of his conspiracy was Frédéric Maurice de La Tour d'Auvergne, Duke de Bouillon (1605–52). Bouillon came from the Protestant family that ruled the independent principality of Sedan. When Bouillon was arrested after the Cinq-Mars conspiracy, his wife threatened to allow the Spanish Army to occupy Sedan, a strategic point on the border between France and Belgium. Bouillon was pardoned, but obliged to hand over Sedan to the French government.

10. *Guitaut*: See note 3, Book II.

11. *He rode along proudly ... the campaigns of King Louis XIII and the prowess of the late cardinal*: I.e. Richelieu (see note 33, Book I).

12. *I acted as Coriolanus ... the tents of the Volsci*: After being unjustly treated by his own people and banished from Rome in the fifth century BC, the general Gaius Martius Coriolanus joined the army of the Volsci, one of Rome's enemies. The Greek biographer Plutarch (AD *c.*46–*c.*120), wrote an account of Coriolanus's life in his *Parallel Lives* (AD 75), which provided the material for the play *Coriolanus* (1607) by William Shakespeare (1564–1616).

13. *He was one of those steadfast souls ... the popular heroes of the eighteenth and nineteenth centuries*: Dumas is thinking particularly of those who took part in the Revolution and the Napoleonic wars.

14. *I lost my command of Sedan ... The Cinq-Mars conspiracy*: See note 9, Book III.

15. *it would do on a small scale what the Paris Commune did on 2 September*: Not, of course, the more famous Commune of 1871, but the revolutionary Commune set up in 1789, which, from 2–7 September 1792, under Robespierre, initiated a bloody repression of counter-revolutionaries, during which some 1,200 political prisoners were taken from their prisons and massacred, after at best a summary trial.

16. *I am just now debating the matter with my reason*: Dumas recalls La Rochefoucauld's 'heartless' remark about compassion, which he quoted earlier (Book II, chapter XI). See also note 25, Book II.

17. *Only a Jew would set free Barabbas and crucify Jesus*: Christians

long blamed the Jewish people for the death of Jesus because, when Pilate offered them a choice between the robber Barabbas and Jesus, the Jewish leaders chose to spare Barabbas and have Jesus crucified (see John 18:40, Mark 15:7, Luke 23:19, Matthew 27:16–26 and Acts 3:14). Dumas and his contemporaries would not have felt it was unjust or reprehensible to attribute the guilt for this to the Jewish people as a whole. See also note 20, Book II.

18. *Esplanade*: The Esplanade des Quinconces in Bordeaux is a huge open space overlooking the river Garonne.

19. *the little Judas window*: A Judas window is a small peephole in a door, so called because it can betray the secrets of those who are being spied on through it.

20. *I have heard that they sometimes ... as Cesare Borgia did for Don Ramiro d'Orco*: Cesare Borgia appointed Don Ramiro Governor of Romagna, where Don Ramiro distinguished himself by his cruelty and suppressed all dissent in the region. But, once the province was pacified, Cesare decided that such energetic measures were no longer expedient and that he might have made himself unpopular as a result of Don Ramiro's actions, so he had him put to death and cut into pieces, which were then exhibited in the market square in Cesena (see Niccolò Machiavelli's (1469–1527) *The Prince*, Chapter VII).

BOOK IV

THE ABBEY OF PESSAC

1. *As for the duke ... Orgon and Géronte*: Orgon and Géronte are foolish and easily deluded old men in two comedies by Molière: *Tartuffe* (1664) and *Les Fourberies de Scapin* (1671).

2. *Because I'm a Huguenot*: As a Protestant, Canolles would not need the last rites from a priest.

3. *There are those who love me ... that it is possible to love*: One of La Rochefoucauld's maxims says that love is like the apparition of spirits – much spoken of, but seldom seen.

4. *So it is true ... hearts that are generous for the pleasure of being so*: Another of Rochefoucauld's maxims is that generosity is the studious exercise of disinterestedness, the better to achieve some greater interest. Cauvignac, though superficially as cynical as the duke, proves in the end to be a sort of anti-Rochefoucauld – a cynic with heart.

5. *He opened the letter*: The original text says: 'unsealed the letter',
    Dumas presumably having forgotten his earlier statement that
    the princess left the letter unsealed.
6. *Although normally fever dries up tears . . . like that of the sublime
    Virgin by Rubens*: Peter Paul Rubens (1577–1640) painted sev-
    eral pictures of the Virgin Mary. The one referred to here could
    be the *Virgin in Adoration Before the Christ Child* in the Louvre.

THE ABBESS OF SAINTE-RADEGONDE
DE PESSAC

1. *the discipline, the dungeon and the in pace*: The discipline was a
    knotted cord which those in a religious order used for whipping
    themselves, the *in pace* a form of solitary confinement. As we
    can see from the whole of this chapter, Dumas was not an admirer
    of the monastic system. Compare Victor Hugo's *Les Misérables*
    (1862), Chapter 2.

BROTHER AND SISTER

1. *Gigery*: On the Barbary Coast, on the Mediterranean shores of
    North Africa, the target of a French expedition in 1664.